MIDNIGHT FAE ACADEMY

Elemental Fae Academy
Book One
Book Two
Book Three
Elemental Fae Queen

Midnight Fae Academy
Ella's Masquerade
Book One
Book Two
Book Three
Book Four

Fortune Fae Academy
Book One
Book Two
Book Three
Book Four
Book Five

Hell Fae
Hell Fae Captive
Hell Fae Warden
Hell Fae Commander
Hell Fae Prince
Hell Fae King

Nightmare Fae
Their Lethal Pet
Their Blood Queen
Their Pixie Mate

Standalone Fae World Novels
Candela
Winter Fae Queen

BITTEN BY THE FAE

Midnight Fae Academy Books 1-4

USA Today
Bestselling Author

Lexi C. Foss

This is a work of fiction. Names, characters, places, and incidents are either the product of the author's imagination or are used fictitiously, and any resemblance to actual persons, living or dead, business establishments, events, or locales is entirely coincidental.

Midnight Fae Academy: The Complete Series

Editing by: Outthink Editing, LLC

Proofreading by: Jean Bachen & Katie Schmahl

Cover Design: Ljiljana Romanovic - Moonchild

Cover Page: Atlantis Cover Design

Interior Illustrations by Arnild Aldepolla

Published by: Ninja Newt Publishing, LLC

Digital Edition

ISBN: 978-1-68530-342-6

Print Edition:

ISBN: 978-1-68530-341-9

 Created with Vellum

USA TODAY BESTSELLING AUTHOR
LEXI C. FOSS
MIDNIGHT FAE ACADEMY
THE COMPLETE SERIES

A forbidden bite led to my capture and recruitment.

There are no flowers here.
No life.
Only death.

I'm an Earth Fae who doesn't belong here.
They can play their little mind games all they want, but I'm going to find a
way back to my elemental world. Even if it kills me.

Except Headmaster Zephyrus is one step ahead of my every move.
Prince Kolstov won't stop cornering me.
And Shadow—the reason I'm in this damn mess to begin with—haunts my
dreams.

My affinity for the earth is dying and being replaced by something more
sinister. Something powerful. Something deadly.

The Midnight Fae believe this is my fate.
They claim that I was "recruited" for a purpose.
To battle a rising presence.
Or to die trying.

I don't owe them a damn thing. But if I have to pass their trials to find my way
home, then so be it. I survived a plague and far worse in the Elemental Fae
realm. An ominous energy? Please. What a joke.

Give it your best shot.
I'm waiting.
And don't you dare bite me.
Or I'll make you regret it.

Author's Note: This is a dark paranormal reverse harem series with bully
romance (enemies-to-lovers) elements. Despite Aflora's opinions on the matter,
there will definitely be biting. Shadow, a.k.a. Shade, guarantees it. This book
ends on a cliffhanger.

CHAPTER ONE

AFLORA

Glacier was late.

Again.

This whole long-distance relationship thing where we met in the Human Realm for dates was just not working for me. The damn Water Fae never showed up on time.

Instead, he left me sitting in this coffee shop in the middle of Orlando with a mouse-shaped mug of inky liquid. How humans stomached this stuff was beyond me. One sip and I wanted to puke.

But I came here to make him happy. Because I hadn't seen him in over a month due to summer solstice break.

Things would be fine when we went back to the Academy in a few weeks. Maybe. Except we would always have this elemental problem hanging over our heads, what with me being the heiress to the Earth Fae throne and him being a regular old Water Fae.

I blew on my steaming liquid, more to mask my frustrated sigh than to cool the liquid. Because yeah, I wasn't going to drink this. I had some spritemead in my fridge back home, just waiting to be cracked open.

Another glance at the clock had me shaking my head.

"This is ridiculous," I muttered to myself. I should not have to wait over an hour for a boy to arrive. Especially one who proclaimed to adore me.

"It is," a feminine voice replied as a puffy, blue-dotted, edible thing appeared beside my mug. "Have a muffin. On the house."

I frowned at the *muffin* before glancing up at the woman who had delivered it.

My eyebrows lifted in surprise. "A Fortune Fae," I said, glancing around to make sure no one heard my admission, before noting her vibrant green apron. "A Fortune Fae working in a human coffee shop?" It came out as a question because what kind of fae chose to reside in this realm? Particularly one of her heritage. "That must be a daunting job, what with people touching you all day."

I took an entire course last year about Fortune Fae. While they loved to deal cards—to tell the future—they hated to be touched. It inspired visions, typically unwanted ones. And I imagined humans would have the same impact.

She tossed her long dark hair—similar to my own—over her shoulder and laughed. At least she didn't tinkle like some fae preferred. That grew old quickly.

No, this fae wasn't afraid to express humor.

A trait that endeared her to me immediately.

"Who are you?" I wondered out loud.

Her smile reached her blue eyes. "Gina," she replied, taking the seat across from me. "I thought you could use some company since your date is a no-show. Oh, but it's not through any fault of his own, I assure you. Fortunately, or perhaps unfortunately, it'll be the least of your concerns very soon." She blinked, her blue irises turning clear for half a second before returning to normal.

A vision, I realized. A notorious habit of her kind, as was the cryptic commentary.

I sighed. "I expected as much. I don't think his parents care for our relationship." I picked at the wrapping around the *muffin,* trying to figure out why a human would eat such a thing. It resembled fabric. "I'm Aflora, by the way."

"I know," she replied, her expression lighting up. "Sole heir to the Earth Fae throne. It's a pleasure to make your acquaintance, Your Highness."

The teasing quality of her voice had me snorting. "Yeah, somehow I doubt you mean that." I narrowed my gaze. "Which tells me you're here for another reason entirely."

"Oh, I am," she agreed. "However, our paths crossing is just a coincidence of happenstance. I only became aware of your destiny recently when I sensed the balance disturbance. It's going to be an interesting year for you, Aflora. Assuming you take the path left. Hmm, but if you go right, I suspect it'll catch you eventually anyway. You're in his thoughts now, after all."

"Uh-huh." This chick was proving all my textbooks right about Fortune Fae and their penchant for talking in riddles. "Well, that sounds fun."

"It will be." She smiled again, only to falter as her gaze flickered once more. "*Shit.*" She glanced at the clock and pushed away from the table. "I'd offer some advice for the road ahead, but I've gotta run. My future keeps finding me despite my deviations from the trail." She gave me a little finger wave and darted out of the cafe, still wearing her apron.

I gaped after her, as did several of the patrons around me.

From what I could tell, she was the only one on duty.

And this is why hiring a fae is a bad idea, I thought at the owner. *We're not the most reliable sort in your world.*

Case in point, my late date.

With a sigh, I pushed my coffee and muffin aside, done waiting. At least I'd understood that part of Gina's prophecy—*Glacier isn't coming.*

Fine. I preferred my spritemead over a date with a boy anyway.

Gathering my purse, I left my mouse-mug and the papery dough cake on the table and headed out into the early afternoon sunshine.

Orlando at least had the weather right. Muggy, hot, and oh-so bright. I smiled as I wandered toward the portal, absorbing the elements along the way. The tropical plants here wouldn't survive easily in my home world, but maybe I could manufacture a greenhouse to accommodate them.

I paused to touch a particularly beautiful tree with large green leaves sprouting from the top. *Mmm, this would be easy to—*

Pain shot up my side as something hard rammed into me, sending me several steps forward. "Sorry!" a human shouted as he pedaled by on a two-wheeled contraption.

A bicycle, my memory supplied, recalling a course on mortal transportation.

I glowered after him, ready to give him a piece of my mind, when a hand brushed my arm. "Are you all right?" a deep, masculine voice asked, the accent decidedly smooth.

"Oh, I, yes. Thanks." I glanced up into a pair of ice-blue eyes, the color and perfection of the irises stunning me into silence.

"Are you sure?" he pressed, his fingers trailing up my arm and leaving a trail of goose bumps in their wake. His lips kicked upward, revealing a pair of dimples that didn't seem to match his ruggedly square jaw or the dark brown stubble dotting his chin.

A proper five o'clock shadow, I mused. Then blinked. *Wait, why do I care about such a thing?*

"Careful, beautiful," he cautioned, his arm sliding around my waist. "You're swaying."

"I am?" I whispered, my throat going dry as his intoxicating scent surrounded me. *Mmm, a dark spice tinted with an earthy aroma.* I leaned into him, pressing my side into his hard torso.

Melting.

Falling.

Ensnared by his masculinity and grace.

That's not right, I thought, frowning. *I don't even know this guy.*

I attempted to step away, only my feet refused my mental command.

What's happening to—

"You're bleeding," he murmured, his hold tightening as his opposite hand drifted across my arm.

I glanced down to see the trickle of red oozing from my skin.

And blinked.

"How?" I asked, trying to shake myself out of this daze, to force my legs to work. But I felt spellbound, lost to the stranger's touch, as if being pulled into a dream.

A part of me recognized the magic, felt the dark tendrils of it seeping into my pores. With it brought memories of the time I nearly died, how I'd fought to cling to the source of my existence in a futile effort to save everyone but myself.

"The bike," the stranger beside me said softly, drawing me from the nightmarish image threatening to capture my mind. "He clipped you as he took the corner. Clumsy fool."

"Oh." I swallowed. "I'm... okay."

Minus the daydreamy state I'd lost my senses to.

The world shifted as he moved us into the doorway of a building, one I recognized as my destination. *Odd.* I could have sworn that was a block away.

Who is this guy? Why is he holding me?

His arm loosened, giving me a chance to flee, but I found my back pressed up to a wall instead, my vision lost to a haze of momentary darkness.

Something's wrong. A thought that had tried to appear moments ago, only to disappear beneath this strange magnetism. Whatever spell he'd cast over me had my mind short-circuiting, my body bending beneath his command.

Must... stop... this...

"He warned me you would be beautiful, Aflora," the voice whispered, his face far too close to my neck. "But I didn't expect you to be such a delicate little flower."

My lips curled down at the phrase. "Wh-what?" I stuttered, my breath seeming to escape me as he kissed my throat. *What are you doing?* I wanted to demand, but my mouth rejected the words, choosing to moan instead. *How do you know my name?*

This can't...

Oh...

His mouth touched my skin, causing my knees to buckle.

Holy Elements...

This was bad. I felt the illicitness of it crawling inside me, igniting my instincts, only to be tampered down by a seductive, dusky cloud.

Dark magic, I recognized, my heart skipping a beat. It swam all around us, infiltrating my ability to reason. To think. To *run.*

"Stop," I managed to say, my demand lost to the raspy quality of my tone.

He chuckled against my neck, his tongue darting out to tease my racing pulse. "I wish I could, delicate flower. But I've been given a task. *You.*"

My fingers curled into fists, my limbs locking up as I fought to break the spell he'd woven over my form.

Which only earned me another chuckle from the powerful Midnight Fae before me. "Mmm, yes. More of that, please." He nipped the tender skin behind my ear, his amusement palpable. "I was beginning to wonder if perhaps I'd found the wrong fae, what with your easy acquiescence and all."

Easy acquiescence.

I'd show him *easy acquiescence.*

Just as soon as I could find my will to freaking move.

But his magic swathed me in a sea of black, cutting off my access to the element I relied upon for survival, and sank harsh claws into my soul.

I gritted my teeth, furious that I'd allowed him to trap me so effortlessly. That bike had momentarily stunned me, allowing this Midnight Fae jackass to hook me in his dark web.

Fortunately, it wasn't my first date with his kind of magic.

Closing my eyes, I ignored the inky strands floating around me and focused on finding the core of my strength.

Earth.

It was dangerous to access the source of my element, but my royal bloodline enabled me to seek it out, to see the original World Tree. Its massive roots resembled a tangle of life reaching out to every living Earth Fae, the thickest band connecting to me—the last Earth Fae heir.

I crawled along it, absorbing its strength and readying my attack.

The Midnight Fae wouldn't know what—

His canines sank into my flesh, eliciting a scream from my throat. Dread, darkness, and desire flooded my senses at once. A denial parted my lips. My soul screaming at the wrongness of his bite. While my body melted into him in a stark betrayal of my mind.

A tear slid from my eye, the pleasure from his embrace cutting deep into my spirit while my mind recognized the absolute horror of what this meant.

Midnight Fae were not meant to consort with other fae in any capacity. And that included tasting the blood of an elemental or any other fae.

This defied every rule I'd ever learned, and not just because of his teeth in my neck, but because of the very visceral need his touch elicited from within me.

"Stop," I demanded, but the moan underlying the word belittled my intention.

He captured my hip with one hand, his chest a solid wall of muscle at my front. How could my assailant feel so good? Every part of him seemed to line up perfectly against me, including the impressive erection digging into my lower belly.

Wrong, I reminded myself. *But feels so good.*

I wanted to crumple into a pile of agony and ecstasy at the same time. But with every pull, I felt my connection to the elements faltering, the life energy I adored slipping from my grasp.

To give in to him, to lose myself in this way... *No.* I couldn't. I had to fight. My fae brethren would understand. They'd prosecute him for this. Because it wasn't my fault. They had to know that.

I hope.

However, if I didn't at least make my displeasure known, they'd assume me to be complicit in this crime. And then we'd both be punished.

My limbs began to cool as my blood flowed in the wrong direction— toward his mouth. There wasn't much time. I had to make my stand now, while the feed distracted him.

Closing my eyes, I allowed myself to go limp, feigning submission. *Come to me,* I called to the source of my elemental power. *Fill me with the vitality I need.*

This would be easier in the elemental world, the Human Realm far away from the core of my energy. But it heeded my call, recognizing my royal bloodline and filling me with enough strength to rock the foundation of the ground below.

It knocked the stranger's footing out from under him, causing him to lose his grip for just a moment.

I sprang out of his hold, grabbed the nearby rocks of the walls, and commanded them to pelt him.

Only, he deflected them with a flick of his wrist, his icy gaze glowing with his dark essence. "You're going to regret that, princess."

"I think I'm going to regret a lot of things," I countered, calling on a heftier brick to fly in his direction.

He shoved it aside before whirling into a gray cloud.

My lips parted, shocked by his disappearing act.

Which was exactly what he wanted—a distraction.

Shadowy ropes tied around my torso, yanking me backward into the nearby portal. "Oh Fae, no," I said, trying futilely to break the smoky bands, but they just reattached every time I sliced through one.

And then the doors closed.

I dove toward the buttons, but he was faster, his hand appearing to key in a foreign code that definitely didn't match the destination I had in mind.

"Oh dear," he murmured, materializing beside me. "It seems I need to confess to committing a crime. I hope you don't mind Midnight Fae, darling. Because you're about to meet a whole council of them."

CHAPTER TWO

AFLORA

I'd never been a particularly violent person, but I really wanted to kill the smirking lunatic sitting across from me. He'd wrapped my wrists in some sort of impenetrable smoke before shoving me into a chair in what appeared to be a reception area of sorts.

Only there wasn't a receptionist.

And the room was anything but welcoming.

Snakelike vines climbed the walls, their beady red eyes glowing intently at the ends. I seemed to be the object of their focus, their rattling tails hissing to an ominous beat that unsettled my insides.

Every time I moved, they slithered faster. Just as they did now. The crazy Midnight Fae across from me tsked out a warning, suggesting I not irritate the guardian serpents, causing my jaw to clench. Not only wouldn't he tell me his name, but he also refused to explain why he'd bitten me.

I shuddered, the sensation of his fangs in my neck still very tangible and real. He'd left behind some sort of inky bond that I could feel more than see.

I smacked at it again, then flinched as the wall hissed louder in response.

"What are they?" I demanded.

"Magicked vines," my captor drawled. "Protects the royal grounds from intruders. Which, if I'm understanding their writhing correctly, they believe you're a threat. So I would stay put, princess, or they might just bite."

"Like you?" I snapped.

His lips curled. "Hmm, no, my bite inspires pleasure." His icy blue eyes glanced at the snake closest to my head. "Their bite, not so much."

I opened my mouth to offer a retort, when the ebony doors at the end of the hall swung open and a dark-haired male dressed in long, flowing robes stomped toward us. "What is the meaning of this, Shadow?"

Shadow? I eyed my companion. *Really?*

I supposed he did have a penchant for disappearing into thick clouds of smoke.

"What would you like me to say?" Shadow asked, his arms sprawled out across the back of the couch in the epitome of lazy nonchalance. "The Earth Fae Royal and I got a little carried away, my fangs slipped, and wouldn't you know? Her blood reacted to my bite."

My lips parted at his horrible recollection of what happened. "Carried away? Fangs slipped?" I repeated, jumping to my feet, only to be snatched back by the vines slithering across the wall.

I screamed, the smoke around my wrists tightening as a snake wrapped itself around my neck and squeezed to silence the sound.

The newcomer sighed and produced a wand. "*Release,*" he hissed, waving the violet stick through the air.

A sizzle of energy kissed my skin, the darkness of it in direct contrast to my earth essence inside. I shivered, the wrongness leaving me unnerved even as the snakes and my smoky bonds disappeared.

My knees buckled on instinct, sending me crashing into something hard and masculine.

Shadow.

His chest met my nose, his arms wrapping around me as he caught me before I could hit the ground.

I nearly growled, but my modesty took precedence first.

After fixing my blouse and skirt, I shoved him away. "Don't touch me."

"That's not what you said an hour ago, princess."

A growl unlike any I'd ever released before burst from my mouth as I launched myself at him, desiring to do the utmost damage. Only, he caught me up in his arms again, chuckling the entire time.

"See what I mean, Father? She's a wildcat who can't keep her hands off me."

Father?

I shook my head. *Who cares?* "I'm going to kill you!"

"Try" was Shadow's arrogant reply.

Gah! I wanted to scream, to call on a tree to pound this dick into the ground, but my powers refused me here, my access to the source cut off through some means of dark magic. Otherwise, I would have used it to escape as soon as we arrived.

"You bit her," Shadow's father said.

A genius, he clearly was, because I still had the marks on my neck from the attack. And if I had my arms free, I'd have pointed to it for reference, just in case he needed to see it up close. But Shadow had me locked up against him, my breasts smashed to his chest as he held me captive in his far-too-muscular hold.

Shadow smiled down at me. "As I said, one thing led to another and—"

"Do you have any idea what you've done?" his father demanded, cutting off his jackass of a son.

"Well, I thought it'd just be a taste, but yeah, I'm pretty aware of the mate-bond snapping into place. Why else would I have voluntarily stepped into this dreadful place if not to report the mistake?"

Mate-bond? "What mate-bond?" I wrestled in his arms once more, but he held me with the ease of a much stronger fae.

This was why I needed to take more physical defense classes. I'd grown used to relying on my element, which apparently didn't work in this dark realm.

"Our mate-bond," Shadow murmured. "We're connected now, princess. Forever."

"Stop calling me that."

"It's what you are, right? An Earth Fae Princess?" He cocked his head to the side. "Or are you a queen as the only Earth Fae heir?"

"*Enough*," his father inserted, his cloak billowing around him with power. Blue eyes—the same color as his son's—narrowed at Shadow. "You realize you could be excommunicated for this."

Shadow shrugged. "Saves me from another year at the Academy."

A low, angry sound rumbled from his father's chest. "And what about the girl? Interspecies mating is illegal. They might demand her death, or worse, *your* death."

Wait, how's his death worse than mine? "I don't even want to be here," I said, furious. "And you can't kill me. I'm the sole heir to earth. If I die, the element dies with me." Not exactly true. Someone, maybe Sol, would probably take over my access to the source. But hopefully, they didn't know that.

His father didn't even look at me, his smoldering gaze on his son. "Take her to the dungeon and lock yourselves inside. You know the way. I'll come for you if and when the Council needs a comment."

"Excuse me, but I'd like to give a *comment* right now," I demanded. "Your son bit me against my will, then kidnapped me and brought me into this realm. I shouldn't be here. Nor can you keep me here. The Elemental Fae Council will not stand for this."

Well, they might.

Being bitten by a Midnight Fae definitely broke several of the interspecies laws governing fae relations. But it was against my will. Queen Claire would side with me. She knew me well enough to know I would never do something like this.

"I'm the sole Earth Fae heir," I added. "My people rely on my connection to the source to thrive. Every moment you keep me here is—"

"Enough," Shadow's father bit out, his expression resembling stone. "The Midnight Fae Council operates very differently from your own. If you have something of importance to say, your intended will deliver the information on your behalf, as females are not permitted within the Council Chamber."

My eyebrows hit my hairline. What kind of backward-thinking realm had I been swept off to? *Nope, better question...* "Who the hell is my intended?"

Shadow chuckled. "Me, darling."

"*What?*" I sputtered. "He assaulted me and you want to let him speak on my behalf?" Un-freakin'-believable. "This is utter wallopberries."

"Utter what?" Shadow asked.

"Let go of me," I replied instead. He didn't deserve an answer to that query or any other.

"Can't do that, princess. I've been ordered to take you downstairs. Council rules." He gave an unapologetic shrug that had me itching to punch him.

"Now, Shadow," his father said, the command in his tone sending a shiver down my spine.

What in the pixie dust have I gotten myself into?

Shadow lifted me off the ground as if I weighed nothing at all—which, compared to him, I probably did. He had at least a foot on me, the bastard.

"Put me down."

"And you questioned my nickname," he muttered in reply. "Issuing demands left and right just like a goddamn princess."

"Because you insist on manhandling me," I snapped, wishing more than ever that I could access my gifts. I'd wrap a vine of my own around his neck and see what he thought of it. Then I'd take a tree root and smash his skull.

The beautiful image behind my eyes dispersed as he kicked open an iron door and began descending the steps.

Every part of me iced over at the very real threat of going underground.

"Shadow," I whispered. "Please."

He frowned at me. "Please what? It's not like I'm going to hurt you. Yet, anyway." He shook his head. "Seriously, I expected a little more fire, princess. Instead, you're as weak as a youngling."

My jaw clenched even as my heart began to pound.

Each step brought us deeper underground. My lungs began to seize from my inability to pull in a breath.

Elemental Fae didn't belong here.

Elemental Fae required sunshine.

Elemental Fae *died* underground.

It took weeks, sometimes months, but just the very threat of being taken somewhere so dark and murky had panic freezing every limb.

Shadow said something, but I couldn't hear him over the harsh beating in my ears.

My back hit a soft cushion that I barely felt.

Stone and vines and unspeakable things danced through my vision. A dark cloud. New voices.

Fight, some part of me urged. *This is all in your mind.*

Yeah, pretty sure the gargoyle statue glowering down at me was pretty damn real.

Oh, I'd read about those. They shot lasers from their eyes. Good. Fun. Why was one in my cell?

Shadow appeared to be talking to it.

Right, because they were likely old friends.

Except they seemed to be arguing.

Maybe I'd get to watch the stone creature flay my "intended" alive. Mmm,

I'd enjoy that very much. Warmth began to stir inside me at the thought, my initial terror subsiding beneath a much more violent wave.

As long as he didn't keep me down here for long, I'd be fine.

Which meant I needed to pull myself together and find a way out. Not an easy feat considering he'd locked the door.

What kind of idiot willingly puts himself in a dungeon?

"A smart one," Shadow replied.

My brow furrowed. "Did I ask that out loud?"

"No, but you practically shouted it at me." He winced and collapsed onto a pile of pillows on the obsidian floor.

"That doesn't make any sense."

He tapped his head. "Use your mind, princess."

Yeah, because you're so great at using yours, I thought sourly.

He snorted as if he heard that.

Then I realized what he meant.

"Ohhhhh, no. You are so not in my head." I'd have a colossal headache otherwise.

"No, I'm in your blood, Princess Flower," he replied, sounding exasperated. "Seriously, do you not study the mating of other cultures where you're from? Because I had to take an entire semester on your weak kind last year, and while it's proving to be useful now, it bored me near to death."

"We are not weak," I countered. "And for your information, yes, I took one class on fae politics. You want to talk about boring, *that* course takes the lily cookie."

"Lily cookie?" he repeated, arching a brow. "What the fuck is a lily cookie?"

"I thought you studied my kind, Shadow. Perhaps you missed that chapter in your book."

He snorted. "Whatever." He stretched out his long legs, crossing them at the ankles as he relaxed further into his makeshift bed. "We're going to be here a while, princess. Best get some rest before the Council delivers their verdict."

Sleep. Yeah, that was going to happen.

Even with him giving me the bed—a gesture I refused to evaluate—I would never be able to sleep down here. Not with him lurking so close. Or that stone gargoyle hanging out in the corner.

I met the creature's red eyes and flinched.

As a product of the earth, I should be able to command him.

But the source refused my call just as it had since I arrived in this hell.

"What if I have to use the restroom?" I asked, looking for a way to leave this cell.

Shadow pointed at a bucket in the corner. "Enjoy."

I gasped. "That's unacceptable."

"What's unacceptable is you still talking. I said it's time to sleep."

"Yeah, because I take orders from you. Oh, wait…" I rolled my eyes and stood up, pacing across the rocks in my heels.

Why had I dressed up for Glacier, again? Because I wanted to impress him. And he stood me up.

Which meant he wouldn't be looking for me later, and when he tried to call to apologize, he'd just assume I was ignoring him.

Pixie sticks.

Maybe Sol would feel my missing energy.

Yes. Yes, he would. He'd alert his mate, Claire, and they'd search for me. But would they know to look here?

I blew a raspberry with my lips.

"Wow, do not make that sound again," Shadow said, giving a theatric shudder. "Talk about an irritating noise."

"Similar to your voice," I replied sweetly. "Maybe we are *intended* to be together."

He smirked. "You have no idea, baby."

"Seriously, cut it out with the nicknames."

He blew me a kiss. "You love it, princess."

That's it. I took advantage of his prone position, jumping on him and straddling him, and sent my fist directly into his too-perfect nose.

A sensation of victory warmed my veins at the sight of his blood, only to have it washed out of me by a cold wave as I suddenly found myself beneath him on the floor.

"Not a smart move, darling," he murmured, my wrists locked over my head beneath one of his hands.

How the heck did he do that?

"Magic," he breathed, replying yet again to the thought in my head.

"Stop that."

"Make me," he countered, dropping his head to my neck.

"Shadow."

"Aflora." His hips settled into mine, his lips caressing the bite mark on my skin.

"What are you doing?"

"Enjoying myself," he said softly, his tongue tracing my throat. "You remind me of the sun. Warm, yet brutal."

I squirmed beneath him, which only caused him to lie more heavily upon me. "Don't you dare bite me again, Shadow."

"Mmm, but it was so fun the first time." His incisors skimmed my pulse. "And you moaned so beautifully."

"Because you enchanted me!"

"Only partly," he replied, not sounding the least bit contrite and far too intrigued. "I didn't expect to enjoy it," he added in a whisper. "But I did."

"Shadow," I warned.

He sighed. "Relax, pet."

"How can I relax with you on top of me?"

"You started it," he returned, nipping my chin on his way back up. "You tried to break my nose with a poor excuse for a punch."

"Poor excuse for a…?" My eyes widened. "You're such a dick!"

"Tell me how you really feel, darling," he taunted, cocking his head to the side. "I'm listening."

"I want to kill you."

"Yes, and…?"

"Gah, would you just get off me, please?"

"Please?" he repeated, snorting. "My, but you are a polite little girl, aren't you?"

"I am not little."

"You act like an innocent child."

My blood boiled at the unveiled insult. "You know nothing about me."

"Likewise."

"Pixie dust, you are impossible. Get. Off. Me."

"Pixie dust?" He actually appeared confused. "Wait, is that your version of a curse?" When I didn't reply, he started to laugh. "Oh, sweet girl, the things I'm going to teach you."

"Not if I kill you," I muttered.

A pair of dimples flashed as he studied me intently. "I truly hope you try. Punishing females is a favorite pastime of mine."

"As is raping them, apparently," I tossed back.

His eyebrows shot up at that accusation. "Rape? I've barely touched you."

"You bit me against my will!"

"You were quite willing, Aflora. Trust me."

"Because you freakin' cast a spell over me or whatever it is you did."

"Freakin'?" He shook his head and tsked. "*Fucking*, darling. The word you're looking for is *fucking*."

"Dear gods, just get off me already!"

"No." He had the audacity to bend and brush a kiss over my lips. I immediately tried to bite him, which earned me an amused sound. "You need to rest. There'll be trials ahead."

Yeah, whatever that meant. "I need to go home," I corrected.

"You are home, Aflora. You just haven't realized it yet." With that proclamation, he began to hum the most beautiful melody.

"What are you doing?"

He didn't reply, his strange song continuing and surrounding me in an odd sea of bliss.

Another spell, my mind recognized.

But my lips refused to issue a retort, my kidnapper captivating me with his song.

Stop, I pleaded in my mind. *Please stop.*

"I'm only trying to calm you," he whispered in response.

I shook my head, trying to clear it and force him out. *This is wrong. Everything you've done is so wrong!*

A deep sigh.

The hint of mint on his breath as he pressed his forehead to mine. "I know," he agreed. "Trust me, I know."

What?

Only, he didn't elaborate.

Instead, he hummed even louder, causing my eyes to roll back in my head.

Soon darkness took over, lulling me into a restless sleep filled with nightmarish images that depicted my new reality. Including the cruelly handsome fae who held me tight, his lips whisper-soft against my ear as he said, "I'm sorry, Aflora."

That was when I knew I truly dreamed.

Because from what I knew of Shadow, he wasn't the kind of male who ever apologized.

CHAPTER THREE

KOLS

"Any idea what this is about?" Tray asked as we stepped into the portal.

I entered the Council Chamber code and shook my head. "No idea, but Dad said it's urgent."

"Clearly," my twin replied, adjusting his tie. We wore matching suits, but that was where our similarities ended. He represented the darkness of our kind in his hair and eyes, similar to our mother. My features, however, favored the golds and bronze tones of our father's lineage. "You think it's related to Aswad?"

I lifted a shoulder. "Could be anything, but probably." Whatever this was, I just wanted to get it over with so I could enjoy my final week of freedom before the Academy started up again.

Only six hundred and nineteen days to go, I thought, rolling my neck to loosen my stiff muscles. Then fate would take over, and I'd officially have to step in line with Emelyn Jyn at my side. *Can't fucking wait,* I thought, fighting an internal groan.

Royal politics came with certain privileges. Arranged marriage was not one of them.

The doors opened to reveal the obsidian interior of Council Headquarters.

I glanced sideways. "Ready?"

"Am I ever?" Tray countered.

With a snort, I led the way inside. Several Councilmen nodded at us as we moved into the room toward our father at the head of the table. He always left the two chairs to his right available for us, and we took them as expected.

Emelyn's father, Lima, sat in the position of Second Elite Blood on my dad's other side. In less than two years' time, he would serve beneath me in the same capacity unless I chose to replace him.

The stoic male gave me a nod of acknowledgment, as he always did. He expected my betrothal to his daughter to be enough to maintain a partnership. Little did he realize I loathed Emelyn. Being related to the female devil incarnate did not win him any points in my book. But I returned the gesture. I was kind like that.

Then I nodded at the other Councilmen in the room who had arrived with their Seconds. My father and Aswad were the only members with heirs of age and status to attend, yet Shade seemed to be playing hooky again. He couldn't make it any clearer that he had no interest in taking over the Death Magic mantle from his father. *Prat.*

Silence fell as Tadmir entered, his white hair flowing down his back. "Apologies." The Malefic Councilman dropped into his chair beside Raz, his second-in-command. "I wasn't in the realm when the notice arrived."

My father dipped his chin in acceptance of the apology, then focused on the male sitting at the opposite head of the rectangular-shaped table. "Well, get on with it, then. Why are we here, Councilman Aswad?"

Those two final words dripped with disdain, thickening the air with unveiled animosity.

My twin stiffened beside me, just like half the damn board.

The Elite Bloods and Death Bloods had been at odds for centuries, never seeing eye to eye with how the Midnight Fae Council ran itself. Unfortunately for Aswad and his dark line of necromancers, my family had no intention of stepping down. I accepted the ascension rites on my eighteenth birthday, hence the inky black vines writhing across my skin. They fueled my veins with more power every day, waiting to unleash on my twenty-fifth year.

Ergo, the ticking time clock on my life.

And the dwindling minutes on my priceless freedom.

"Well?" my father prompted, his patience clearly at an end.

The Death Blood actually appeared paler than usual as he cleared his throat. "Shadow has taken a mate not of the Council's choosing."

I could've heard a pin drop after that announcement.

My eyebrows actually hit my hairline.

What?!

"And there's more," the Death Blood Councilman continued. "She is not a Midnight Fae but an Elemental Fae."

Phoenix fires, I thought, my jaw on the fucking ground. Of all the things for this meeting to be about, I never in a million years would have guessed that.

Tray seemed just as startled beside me.

Meanwhile, the rest of the Council went up in literal flames as magic lashed across the obsidian stone table.

Aswad deflected the incoming blow with his wand, sending Tadmir's burst into the high ceiling above, where my father trapped it beneath a web of energy that sizzled across my skin. "*Stop,*" he demanded, his single word laying down the law without fail.

Malik of Elite Blood had led the Midnight Fae Council for over a thousand years.

Ignoring him earned the harshest of penalties.

I knew firsthand what he could do, had sat through countless trials where he stripped other Midnight Fae of their lives for infractions far less potent than the one Shade had just committed.

The bastard had been promised to Tadmir's oldest daughter, Cordelia.

To take another mate against the Council's wishes not only broke the laws of our kind but it also issued a massive insult against the Malefic bloodline.

"Excommunication," Tadmir hissed.

"How bonded?" Svart asked instead, his Warrior Blood energy swarming him in an inky cloak of impenetrable magic. His kind excelled at defensive arts. The complete opposite to the Malefic Blood, who favored offensive talents.

"First level," Aswad said, taking his seat with a sigh. "And we don't even know if it'll hold. She's not a Midnight Fae."

"Which doesn't make the infraction any better," Lima muttered. My betrothed's father was clearly not amused, his black irises narrowing at the Death Blood across from him. "What did he have to say for himself?"

"Nothing of importance," Aswad replied.

"Meaning he's not even apologetic," my father translated.

I nearly snorted. Shadow, a.k.a. Shade, was never apologetic about anything. The arrogant dick fancied himself untouchable, even on Academy grounds. His taking a mate against Council wishes didn't surprise me in the slightest.

But I couldn't pretend it didn't leave me a little jealous. I'd considered similar acts more than once throughout my twenty-four years.

Anything to avoid marrying Emelyn Jyn. Just thinking of her gave me hives.

"That's what I thought," my father said when Aswad didn't voice a comment to the contrary. "Then his punishment is easy—kill the partially bonded mate and force him to uphold the binding contract with Tadmir's Malefic bloodline. Shadow will suffer an eternity of an unfulfilled connection yet produce the requisite heirs." He spread out his hands. "Now, that wasn't so hard. This emergency meeting is—"

"She's the last Earth Fae Royal," Aswad interjected. "To kill her would be perceived as an act of war against the Elemental Fae. It would also sever them from the earth source."

Tray whistled low beside me, his reaction one I rivaled in my thoughts with an added, *Oh, fuck.*

"Aflora?" I asked, unable to remain quiet.

All eyes turned to me with questions in them.

Yeah, I knew of the Earth Fae Royal. I'd never met her, but I saw her at the Water King's coronation a few months ago. I explained that to the Council and added, "One of Queen Claire's mates is an Earth Fae. I doubt he'll take lightly to us exterminating the sole Earth Fae heir."

A note of respect glimmered in Aswad's gaze as he considered me, but it disappeared before my father turned to face him.

Was he surprised that I knew the politics of other realms? I'd been training for my father's position since the day I spoke my first word. Understanding all the fae, regardless of the type, was critical to my future. So yeah, I knew pretty much everything about the Elemental Fae. It also helped that two of the kings of that realm were acquaintances of mine.

"This complicates matters," my father muttered.

"Yes," Aswad agreed. "It does."

Silence befell the room while Tadmir stewed in his chair, his fury palpable.

Councilman Svart and Councilman Chern looked on in contemplative silence.

Lima stroked the dark hair dusting his chin, considering.

I shared a glance with Tray, who seemed as perplexed as everyone else.

"Do we even know if the bond will hold?" I wondered out loud. "Elemental Fae mate differently than we do. What if the mating bond fades?"

Everyone looked at me again, and this time my father's expression held a hint of pride. I'd begun speaking up more often lately, taking charge where I could, just to prove my worth. And each move I made seemed to appease him more and more.

"Has anything like this ever occurred in our history?" I asked him.

"No, because it's forbidden to mix fae lines," he replied.

Right, which meant Aflora and Shade could never physically mate to produce an heir—the various Fae Councils would require the immediate death of their child. Abominations were not tolerated. Intermingling between species created beings of too much power, and too much power led to insanity.

Case in point, the most recent incident in the Elemental Fae realm where a hybrid Midnight-Elemental Fae tried to absorb too much power, costing several fae their lives.

"So we don't know what will even happen to their bond, or to her." Midnight Fae were supposed to bite humans, not other fae. Rumors suggested our powers would mix if we drank from another fae, which was why the Council forbade the act. "As I said, it could fade."

"Or it might morph her into an abomination," Chern spoke up, his Sangré bloodline known for their infinite wisdom. "But I agree with the future king that we won't know until the transition has taken its course."

"Which could take months," Tadmir put in sourly.

"How old is she?" my father asked. "Twenty-two? Twenty-three?"

"She just turned twenty-two," Aswad replied. "I had my assistant pull all the information she could while I waited for the meeting to begin." He waved his wand through the air, causing papers to appear before all the Councilmen. "This would be her final year at Elemental Fae Academy, marking her as a third year at our own, but given her impressive test scores, she could probably join the fourth-year class."

Tray and I shared a look.

He couldn't be suggesting—

"You want her to attend Midnight Fae Academy?" My father sounded as dubious as I felt. "Have you lost your damn mind?"

"Actually, it's an interesting suggestion," Chern interjected in that thoughtful way of his, his gray irises surrounding his pupils blinking in and out of focus.

His calm demeanor always appealed to me. I leaned forward, curious to hear what other wisdom he would bestow upon us.

"The Elemental Fae will be just as concerned by their potential mating as we are," he continued. "However, extermination in this situation is impossible with her being the lone Royal Earth Fae. Sending her back could potentially upset the balance. Keeping her here, well, we have wards in place to monitor her."

"And Shadow?" Tadmir interjected, his white hair flickering with blue flames at the ends. "Does he just return to the Academy as if nothing has happened?"

"I daresay he also requires monitoring," Chern replied. "He's initiated the mating with a powerful Earth Fae. That may impact his powers as well."

Silence met his reply.

If what he predicted was true, then Shade's life might be in jeopardy. All Fae Councils took the balance very seriously. Any disturbance to it typically resulted in death.

"What do you recommend?" my father asked, his focus on the Sangré Councilman. "Your line is known for strategy and analytics. How do you see this playing out?"

Chern considered for a long moment, his thumb and forefinger stroking his silver goatee. It was the only sign of hair on him, his familial line preferring to tattoo their bald heads with vibrant colors. The more intricate the design, the more intelligent the Sangré Blood was considered to be. In Chern's case, he wore the most complex pattern of all as the leader of his line.

"Mating the Earth Fae will awaken her access to dark magic, and the Elemental Fae Council doesn't have the means to control her. We do. The Academy professors can train her on the various lines while we supervise her growth and work on a contingency plan for her strengthening powers. It's an appropriate interim solution while we work with the Elementals on a complete solution. They will be just as keen on finding a resolution as we are."

He tapped his fingers on the table, his focus shifting to Aswad.

"As for Shadow, he will require the same monitoring. I suggest we observe the damage he's caused before assigning his punishment."

Meaning Shade would temporarily get away with breaking some of our oldest customs. Not to mention the slight against Tadmir's familial line. The Malefic Councilman's expression confirmed how he felt about the suggestion. Disapproval radiated from him in waves, but he smartly kept quiet.

Shade would be punished in due time.

Just as soon as we assessed the damage.

It made sense, but I wanted to know *how* this would work. "Who is going to observe Aflora's growth?" I wondered out loud.

Then the implication struck me across the face.

Chern's knowing glimmer as he met my gaze confirmed it.

"Me," I said. "I'll be the one monitoring her."

"You are the most capable, yes," Chern agreed. "Your connection to the source will grant you the insight into power fluctuations. You're also the only one with the ability to shut her down, should the need arise."

The only one with the means to kill her, I translated. Being the future king came with harsh responsibilities. This was one of them.

I nodded to confirm my understanding and acceptance of the burden.

My father considered me for a long moment, then nodded as well. "If this is the path we choose, then I move for this to be considered one of his ascension trials."

Murmurs of agreement echoed around the table.

I had seven that would need to be completed before I could fully ascend.

Three were already done.

This would be item number four.

Babysitting an Earth Fae Royal.

Well, there were worse burdens. I'd seen Aflora before. She was certainly pretty to look at. I wouldn't mind having a reason to watch her. Maybe she would make my final year more intriguing.

Or harder.

That remained to be seen.

I just hoped she stayed in line because if she became a threat, I'd exterminate her without blinking an eye.

It was my duty, after all.

My future.

And I intended to fulfill it appropriately.

CHAPTER FOUR

T$alk about a wicked dream$, I thought, stretching against something warm and solid.

I frowned.

Did I fall asleep at Glacier's place again? I wondered.

Wait…

My eyes sprang open to find an icy gaze watching me intently.

I attempted to scramble backward, but a set of iron bars held me captive while my front was entirely caged in by a lounging predator in jeans and a shirt. "Shadow," I whispered, recalling the reality I'd hoped was a really bad dream.

"Shade," he replied.

"What?"

"It's my name, darling flower. As we're betrothed now, I imagine you should use my preferred appellation."

Appellation? I repeated to myself. *Seriously?* His vocabulary matched the pompous arching of his dark brow.

"Are you ready to leave yet?" he asked. "Because we're well into the midnight hours and I have things I want to do today."

"What?"

He sighed. "Is that your chosen word of the day? Because I'm already bored. What a dull mate you'll turn out to be at this rate." He rolled along the concrete floor, popping easily to his feet and holding out a hand. "Jacket, please. You've been drooling all over it for the last hour."

I nearly repeated my "chosen word of the day" because I felt like needling him, but the realization that I was snuggling into his coat captured my attention. Black leather surrounded my entire upper body, the soft part of it under my head.

How…? I glanced up at him. Had he given me this while I slept?

His expression told me not to bother asking, that he would probably insult me if I tried. So I shoved away from the makeshift bed on the ground and stood. If he wanted his precious jacket back, he could pick it up himself.

He did.

After putting it around his shoulders in a quick shift of his strong arms, he rolled his neck. "Prince Kolstov is waiting for us upstairs." With that, he opened the door and left.

I glanced at the stone gargoyle, waiting for him to react. When he didn't, I tentatively followed and practically had to run to catch up to Shade on the stairs. It seemed he wasn't wasting any time.

"Does this mean I'm free to go home?" I asked as we reached the top floor.

"No."

He didn't elaborate.

Just pushed through the door and led me back to the obsidian reception area we'd originally waited in.

A male in a suit with a long black cloak stood waiting for us in the center of the room. His golden irises smoldered with power as he glowered at Shade. "You took your fucking time."

"My mother taught me never to interrupt a woman in the middle of a beauty nap," my captor drawled. "Besides, I enjoyed watching her sleep. She is quite fetching." He winked at me, causing me to glare at him almost as harshly as the other man was.

"You're a willow stump," I told Shade, folding my arms. "I hope I never have to see you again."

"A willow stump," he repeated, considering. "Most women refer to my cock as more of a tree trunk than a stump, but we can elaborate on the nuances of my girth later. Prince Kolstov is in charge of you for now." He gave a little bow, backing away. "Do enjoy your time together, and I'll see you both next week."

He disappeared into a swarm of shadows before either of us could reply.

"Next week?" I repeated. "No, no. I don't want to see him again. I'm going home."

"Afraid not, sweetheart," Prince Kolstov replied. "You're going to Midnight Fae Academy. With me."

What?! "Like hell I am." I made to move around him, but he stepped into my way, my head barely clearing his shoulder.

Glowering up at him, I took in his familiar features. Strong cheekbones. Chiseled jaw. Neatly trimmed facial hair that appeared to be darker than the bronze locks on his head. Well, not exactly bronze. More like brown with streaks of red that seemed to flare beneath the lighting. Handsome, really.

No, downright hot.

But that didn't mean—

Wait…

"I know you," I said, my eyes widening. "You were at Cyrus's coronation."

I'd asked Claire who the handsome foreign fae was after catching a glimpse of him in the crowd. If I remembered right, he knew Cyrus and Exos. Which meant he could get a message to the Elemental Fae Council for me.

"Yes, I was," he confirmed.

My shoulders instantly relaxed. "Oh, good. Then this is all just a misunderstanding. You know I can't stay here."

"What I know is, you can't *leave* here," he corrected. "Not until we see how Shade's bite affects you."

"You mean the bite that was against my will? The one he forced on me before taking me captive?"

A muscle in his jaw ticked, the only indication my words meant something to him. "Regardless of how it happened, you're here now and we can't change the past. All we can do is prepare for the future. So, if you'll follow me, I'll take you to Midnight Fae Academy and your new accommodations."

He turned as if he expected me to magically agree to his command.

I placed my hands on my hips. "Yeah, no. I refuse."

Kolstov glanced at me over his shoulder, those golden irises flaring with power. "Refusal isn't an option." He turned a little and produced a wand from his cloak. "I'm trying to do this the kind way, Aflora. If you prefer the harder route, then we can dance. But I assure you, you'll lose."

I narrowed my eyes. "Queen Claire will not approve of this treatment."

"Queen Claire has no jurisdiction here or over me." He faced me once more. "Which road are we taking, sweetheart? Because my patience is already at wits' end due to Shade taking his fucking time downstairs."

Given that my powers still didn't work here, my options were limited. Either I tested the extent of what that wand in his hand could do or I pretended to play along.

Maybe my powers will regenerate outside these walls, I thought, considering him and his casual stance. *Worth a shot because staying here isn't going to fix anything.*

"All right. Fine. Take me to the Academy."

Amusement sparked in his gaze. "Dancing it is," he mused and put his wand away. His response suggested he expected me to act out despite my words. He was probably right. "Come along, pet."

I glowered at his back after he turned, not appreciating the "endearment" one bit.

Pet, I thought at him. *Yeah, I'm a pet all right. With teeth.*

He led me into an elevator of sorts, then keyed a code in plain sight, suggesting he didn't mind me knowing it. Or maybe he was just that stupid. I memorized the alphanumeric mix, just in case.

The walls shifted around us, crickets sounding in the distance. I focused on the shifting scenery, searching for anything familiar, when we suddenly materialized outside a set of iron gates that were nearly three times my height.

Kolstov murmured a foreign command that caused the doors to open, then gestured for me to cross the creepy threshold. Two stone gargoyles stood watch, their red gazes analyzing my every move.

I swallowed.

They're technically made of earth, so if I just—

"Even think of harming me, and they will cut you down," Kolstov warned. "And while they may be beings of your element, they're not yours to command, but mine."

I considered testing that theory, but the writhing snake-vines slithering along the iron posts had me retracting the idea. On top of that, I still couldn't feel my element. Closing my eyes, I searched the fractured connection, frowning when I found frayed ends flickering with lost power.

A hiss from the gate had me jumping backward.

Kolstov tsked. "Careful with your thoughts, sweetheart. They'll be on you in a second, and you can bet your ass I'll let them bite a few times before I call them off. Just to teach you a lesson."

Meaning he could control these vile creatures.

"Prince Kolstov," I mused out loud. "You're next in line for the Midnight Fae throne." Hence his ability to tame the beasts. I'd read enough about international fae politics to know the important names throughout the realms. It was why I'd been surprised by his presence at Cyrus's coronation.

And maybe I'd been a little interested because of his looks.

Not so into those traits now.

"Just as you're Princess Aflora, the sole Earth Royal," he returned, pressing his palm to my lower back to give me a nudge. "On you go."

I stumbled forward, my heels not made for the pebbled pathway. "If you know who I am, you know how wrong this is. The Earth Fae need me and my access to the source."

"Yes. We're working on that." Another push to the base of my spine compelled me to walk alongside him. "Your bindings are temporary until Councilman Chern can develop a better harness for your natural gifts."

Bindings? That explained why I still couldn't access my element. "It's dangerous to keep me severed from the source. I'm the conduit that allows the Earth Fae to thrive."

"We're aware," he said, directing me to the left.

Gothic architecture met my vision. The entire campus resembled a castle of horror set against a moonlit landscape. Large trees void of any life or leaves decorated the ground with black branches, their roots thicker than both Kolstov and I combined. Bats dangled from the limbs, along with other foreign winged animals of varying sizes.

A phoenix landed on top of one of the obsidian towers in the distance, its fiery wings fluttering in the breeze.

"Given your royal status, you will be housed with the Elite Bloods. Specifically, in my family's wing. Our suite has four bedrooms, a living area, a kitchen, a study room, and several bathrooms. I think you'll find it to be up to your standards."

"Elite Bloods?" I repeated, swallowing. *I have to live with this guy?*

He stopped to gape down at me. "You haven't studied the Midnight Fae lines?"

"N-no."

His expression told me that was not an appropriate response. "You're *the* Earth Fae Royal, and you know nothing about our political structure. How is that possible? I can tell you everything of importance regarding the Elemental Fae Council."

"Interspecies politics is on my course agenda this year."

"*Was,*" he corrected. "Your new schedule will be assigned this week. I'll see what I can do about having Midnight Fae politics added to it." He shook his head and continued walking. "Absolutely ridiculous."

"Oh, I'm sorry. I wasn't expecting to be kidnapped and forced into attending school in this realm. My bad for not taking a course about vampires."

He halted once more, turning slowly. "Careful, sweetheart. That tone could earn you a lot of hurt on these grounds, especially when in reference to our existence and what we are—Midnight Fae."

"Bloodsuckers. Yeah, I'm aware."

Kolstov stepped forward, invading my personal bubble. "You know all about that, don't you, love? What with Shade having already snacked upon your neck?" He hummed, the sound low and menacing. "Call me a bloodsucker again and I'll give you a thorough demonstration of what a *Midnight Fae* can do."

"As you said, I already 'know all about that.'"

"Oh, sweetheart, no. A bite is nothing compared to the power I can unleash upon you." He reached up to tuck a strand of my hair behind my ear, then cupped my cheek to allow me to feel the energy throbbing beneath his skin. "I could destroy you in seconds, baby."

"Only because you've handicapped me," I seethed. "Take off my bindings and let's see what happens."

His resulting smile oozed condescension. "As entertaining as it would be to put you in your place, I have other plans tonight that are far more important than indulging a little Earth Fae." His palm landed on my ass this time, pushing me forward.

I elbowed him in the ribs. "Do not touch me there. In fact, do not touch me at all."

He smirked and produced his wand. "Fine." With a flick of his wrist, he created a strand of magic that wound around my waist. He gave it a little tug and I jolted forward.

"Oh, come on!" I snapped. "I can walk on my own without all the theatrics."

"I know, but this is more fun." Another yank had me nearly falling on my face, but his magic righted me before I could fully trip.

A growl caught in my throat. "Stop."

He chuckled. "Make me. Oh, right…"

I ground my teeth so hard my jaw popped.

As soon as this rope disintegrated, I would introduce my fist to his arrogant jaw.

We walked the rest of the way in silence, my fury boiling hotter with every step. At least there wasn't anyone around to witness this humiliation. I nearly asked why the Academy was empty but decided against speaking again. He didn't deserve my words, my questions, or my compliance.

Instead, I studied the campus around me, searching for escape points.

There had to be a portal somewhere, because the gargoyle-guarded entrance was out of the question.

Of course, I had no way of knowing if my codes would whisk me home or to another part of this realm or to nowhere at all.

Trial and error, I decided. I just needed an exit.

"These are the Elite Blood quarters," Kolstov announced, his amusement seeming to have faded into a serious tone. He escorted me up the marble stairs to a set of grand doors. "To enter, you need to know the right spell. It also requires a wand." He glanced at me. "I'll ask Zeph to get you set up with one this week before classes begin."

Zeph? And they intended to give me a wand? *Does that mean they expect me to learn dark magic?* The questions all lined up behind my lips, but my teeth held them at bay.

This monster had already proven to be unhelpful. Why bother opening up to him now?

He arched a brow. "Silent treatment?"

"I'm cooperating," I bit back at him.

His lips twitched. "Indeed you are." With a muttered word, the magical lasso around my waist disappeared, and I launched myself at him. My palm connected with his cheek while my opposite hand formed a fist that he caught deftly before spinning me around and trapping me in his arms.

"I'm adding warrior training to your curriculum," he said, his lips at my ear. "Your form is atrocious."

"Sprinkle dust!" I shouted at him, squirming against his too-hard body.

"Sprinkle dust?" he repeated, his humor palpable. "Who taught you how to curse? A dessert pixie?"

Gah! "Release me."

"No." He held me captive with one arm and pulled out his wand with his free hand. "Listen and learn, as I won't be repeating myself." Hypnotic words fell from his lips, the language foreign to me. *"Al'damu almalakia."*

The tip of his charcoal-colored wand created an infinity pattern, causing the doors to creak and open beneath his command.

He kissed my temple, his arm releasing me. "After you, gorgeous."

I practically sprinted through the threshold, just to escape him, but my face burned from where his mouth had brushed my skin. As though he'd branded me with his power via that simple act alone.

He fixed his cloak and hid his magical tool once more, then snapped his fingers.

Flames sprang to life all around us, lighting the interior of a grand hallway with a master staircase to the left. He gestured toward them. "Two flights. We're on the top floor."

Not wanting to give him a chance to touch me with his hands or his power, I darted up the steps to the third floor and waited for him to join me.

"Someone's eager," he teased when he reached the top.

I didn't deign to offer him a reply, just waited for further instruction.

He nodded with his chin toward the end of the hall. "Three forty-seven is our suite."

Our suite. I shivered with the statement. *This is temporary. I'm not staying here.*

Only, the entire hallway was lined with more of those rattling monstrosities, all of which were watching my every move as though waiting for me to step one toe out of line.

I never did like snakes.

And these appeared to be far more deadly than the reptiles of my realm.

They wriggled along, gliding over the wooden panels I thought might be doors except for the fact that they were all missing knobs. Including our own at the end of the hall. However, there was a knocker with a tiny gargoyle lounging upon it, his blood-red eyes narrowing at me.

I paused so suddenly that Kolstov ran into my back, his hands finding my hips in the process. It aligned us perfectly, sending a shudder down my spine.

No. I'm not attracted to this jerk. Do not get any ideas.

"Sir Kristoff, this is Aflora. Scan her as appropriate, then allow us both entry. She will be staying in the suite for the foreseeable future, so you are to grant her access as you do the others on our list."

The red eyes flared to life, little black pupils moving over me in lazy regard as the gargoyle's lips curled to the side.

"Hmm," the being hummed in a low, masculine tone that sent a chill down my spine. He pushed out of the door, his little hands holding on to the ledge of the knocker while his bottom half remained inside the wood. Almost as if he were hanging out a window. "Something's not right with this one. Not right at all."

Right back at you, I thought, mortified by his lifelike form that had been made of rock just seconds ago. *Talking-goblin stone thing.*

"Perhaps, but you bow to my commands. Now scan her and allow her entry." Kolstov's tone brooked no argument.

"Yes, yes," the thing hissed. "As you wish, Master."

A blinding light beamed from the gargoyle's eyes. I would have jumped backward if Kolstov wasn't still holding me. The damn stroke of the creature's gaze burned over me, leaving an inky sensation in its wake as if it had marked me with its magic.

"You may enter." The eyes rolled back into a red gleam, the knocker turning to marble once more.

Kolstov used his hands on my hips to walk me forward *through* the door. As in, it didn't open. We moved through the wood. A shimmer of energy passed over my skin along the way, causing all the hair along my arms to rise.

This isn't natural.

"Welcome home," Kolstov said as an elegant living area appeared before us. "I hope you like it, because I suspect you'll be staying for the year."

CHAPTER FIVE

KOLS

"A year?" The gorgeous Earth Fae spun in my arms. "That's a cruel joke, right? Tell me you're kidding."

"I thought most females fancied the truth over lies, but if it's a lie you prefer, I'll happily give you one."

She shoved away from me, her petite form proving to be stronger than one would expect. I could subdue her in less than a second but opted to give her the space she required. It was the least I could do considering her circumstances.

While, outwardly, I might have appeared unapologetic, inwardly, I felt for the poor girl.

"You mean the bite that was against my will? The one he forced on me before taking me captive?"

Her admission was on repeat inside my mind. I hadn't expected her to say that. Most women fell at Shade's feet, all of them adoring his bad-boy persona. Yet it appeared this one hadn't been a willing subject in his attentions at all. Unless she'd lied to me, but I doubted it. She'd glowered at Shade with a similar contempt as the glare in her gaze now.

Not the look of a woman smitten over her betrothed.

Nor one that seemed to care for me all that much.

Well, I deserved that. I hadn't exactly been kind to her.

"Are you hungry?" I asked her, walking through the living room and to the open area of the kitchen toward the back. Windows lined the walls, overlooking the courtyard out back. Flickers of lights drew my attention to the fire gnats buzzing about the forest below. I'd have to warn Aflora to stay away from those. Dangerous little buggers.

Aflora didn't reply to me, her feet apparently glued to the runner in the foyer. She glanced up at the cathedral ceilings, took in the skylights showcasing a star-filled night, and then looked at the ample seating room. Three couches, two recliners, and a massive movie screen. Perfect for entertaining, which Tray and I did often during the school year.

Well, I did.

Tray tended to hide in his room with Ella.

Pulling open the refrigerator, I found it empty. *Idiot.* We hadn't been here all summer, and I just learned two hours ago that I needed to bring Aflora here.

Using my wand, I muttered a few incantations to create tea mugs. That would have to do until I could arrange for an Academy food delivery.

Or Zeph could handle it.

I set the mugs on the black bar counter that hung over into the living area, and slid my phone from my pocket.

Where are you? I typed, hitting Send.

Packing, was the immediate reply. *Your Highness,* came a second later.

I rolled my eyes. *Don't be a dick.*

Just doing my job, Zeph replied.

Of being a dick?

I'll be there soon. Surely you can find something to do with her until I get there. She's a female fae, right? You like those.

I snorted. *Who set your boxers on fire?*

You did.

My eyebrows shot up. *Not in a few months, if I recall right.*

Fuck off, Kolstov.

Not what you said to me the last time we met up, I sent back.

No reply.

Not that I expected one.

With a smirk, I slid the phone back into my pocket and looked up to find Aflora watching me from the other side of the bar.

"Girlfriend?" she guessed.

"I don't do girlfriends," I replied, leaning over to rest my elbows on the counter. "So don't get any ideas."

She scoffed. "Don't worry. You're not my type."

Liar, I thought. I recognized the attraction in her eyes earlier, and I could taste the lust in the air when I had her in my arms. She might not want to admit it, but the Earth Fae Royal definitely found me appealing. And the feeling was very mutual.

"I conjured you some tea," I said, nodding to the mugs. "Once Zeph arrives, we'll figure out how to find food."

She didn't touch the mug or reply, instead choosing to gaze out the windows. As I hadn't turned on any of the lights, she could see everything with clarity, including the gnats glowing below. But it was the Academy beyond that she seemed to be studying—the endless sea of gothic architecture.

"It's several blocks wide," I said. "The living quarters are spread throughout. In case you were curious, Shade resides on the opposite side of campus, which is about a fifteen-minute walk."

"I wasn't curious."

Maybe not, but I caught the glimmer of approval in her expression.

Yeah, she definitely doesn't like him.

"Zeph will give you a proper tour tomorrow, and once you have your schedule, I'll help you map out your courses." I picked up the mug closest to me and took a sip of the warm, minty liquid.

Perfection.

If she chose not to touch hers, then I'd help myself to it next.

After another swallow, I dove into an explanation of her future. "You'll have four days of classes, then two days off, then three days on again, followed by three days off. The cycle repeats after that. So twelve days total. There will be a longer break in the middle of the year for the Solstice, but otherwise, the schedule keeps."

"And what will I be learning?"

"You'll have a mixture of dark arts courses, physical training, and likely a political course." Because apparently she knew nothing about the five Midnight Fae bloodlines. Well, technically six. But only five were still in existence today.

"I'm an Elemental Fae, not a Midnight Fae."

"An Elemental Fae who was bitten by a Midnight Fae, thereby introducing you to the dark arts. It's in your blood now." Or that was what Chern had hypothesized. Given what I'd observed so far, he was likely very wrong. Without her access to the elements, Aflora seemed as harmless as a human.

Hopefully, she remained that way. Then this could all blow over. She'd return to her realm, Shade would be punished for his transgressions, and all would be right with the world again.

I met her wide gaze as I took another pull from my drink and noted her ashen cheeks. My brow furrowed. "What?"

"I... It's..." She swallowed. "His bite infected my blood?" Her small hand went to her throat as she took a step backward, her expression falling. "A... abomin... I'm a..." She collapsed onto the sofa, and her head fell to her hands.

I frowned at her. "You hadn't pieced that together already?"

No reply.

Only a hitch of her shoulders as she fought off what sounded like a sob.

Fuck.

Crying women were not my thing. I didn't know how to handle them or how to calm them. Did I walk over there and pat her head? Offer condolences? Lie to her about the inevitable?

I palmed the back of my neck. "I, uh, I'm sor—"

"I'm going to kill him!" Aflora snapped. Her tear-filled eyes captured my gaze, her cheeks red with emotion.

But it wasn't sadness or self-pity.

Aflora was *livid*.

And those weren't tears.

No. Her bright blue irises were aflame with power.

Oh, shit…

"Where is he?" she demanded, jumping to her feet. "Where is that willow stump who did this to me? If I'm going down, he's going down with me." She stomped into the kitchen, energy swarming around her in a hypnotic wave that called to my royal blood.

Ideal mate, a part of me recognized. *She's an ideal mate.*

"Tell me where he is!" she shouted in my face.

Okay. This wasn't going to work.

I set my mug down and crowded her against the bar by placing my hands on the marble on either side of her hips. "Calm down."

"Calm down?" she repeated with a semi-hysterical snort. "Are you kidding me? That pixie stick made me an abomination!"

My lips twitched at her adorable curse.

Which was apparently the wrong reaction because more of that delicious red fury coated her cheeks.

"Are you *laughing* at me? Do you find humor in him essentially raping me with his fangs and turning my world upside down?" She jabbed a finger at my chest. "You're no better than he is, and here I thought you might have a little moral high ground as a fellow royal. Apparently not."

I caught her wrist before she could stab me again and brought the offending digit up to my mouth for a reprimanding bite. Not sharp enough to break the skin—*that* was exactly what got her into this mess—but enough to assert my dominance. "I took humor with your nickname designation. *Pixie stick* has a nice ring to it. I think I'll borrow it for Shade going forward."

Some of her ire cooled, but that liquid fire in her gaze continued to burn. She reminded me of a furious Valkyrie with her waves of blue-black hair, creamy skin, and glowing eyes. All she needed were some wings.

Clearing my throat, I released her hand and reaffixed my grip to the counter beside her. "The past is already done. What you need to focus on is moving forward. Shade won't be here for another week. If it's any consolation, I imagine his father has some punishments in mind for him in the interim."

She nibbled her lower lip, drawing my focus to her alluring mouth.

Aflora really was a beautiful fae. A queen with regal bone structure and a gorgeously formed figure. *Fantastic tits*, I thought, taking in her skewed blouse. *Long, athletic legs*. If she were human, I'd seduce her in a heartbeat. Bend her over this counter, tuck up that little skirt, and fuck her raw.

Alas, her Elemental Fae blood made that problematic.

Still, it could be done.

"You're looking at me like I'm food," she whispered, her fingers curling into fists at her sides. "Please don't bite me."

"Mmm." I leaned into her, my mouth skimming the shell of her ear and eliciting a shiver from her in response. "Don't worry, sweetheart. When I bite you, I won't break the skin." I brushed my lips against her temple for the second time tonight, then forced myself to pull away. "Let's get your quarters sorted. It'll provide us both a much-needed distraction."

Because if I wasn't careful, I'd devise a different way to pass the time while we waited for Zeph. Which would only prove the Guardian right about my proclivities and earn me a world of chastisement.

And Zephyrus was the last one I wanted a lecture from right now.

I led Aflora through the living area again. She had fallen silent once more, her hands twisting in front of her. As horrifying as this had to be for her, she appeared to be handling it well. Which told me she had an escape plan in mind. It was what I would do in her position. Unfortunately, she didn't stand a chance.

Something told me the only way for that point to be driven home was to allow her to try and fail.

Allowing the starlight from the windows above to guide us, I turned into a hallway lined with doors. Stopping at the first one, I opened it to reveal a large space filled with more seating, pillows, books, and an array of bottles filled with potions. "This is the loft area where Ella and Tray lounge the most. They like to study here."

"Ella and Tray?" Aflora repeated in a low murmur.

Right. She hadn't studied Midnight Fae politics yet. Annoyance simmered in my blood, but I held it back and offered her a brief explanation.

"Trayton Nacht, also known as Tray, is my twin brother. Isabella Cinder, a Halfling, is his chosen mate." I shut the door. "You'll meet them next week."

"Oh" was all she said.

I gestured to another threshold. "Tray and Ella's room." Then I pointed across the hall. "That's a guest area and option number one for you." Several more steps brought us to another door. I motioned to it, saying, "Option number two." And finally, at the end of the hallway, I said, "This is my room."

I twisted the knob because I needed to find her some temporary clothes. Making them with my wand would likely result in something too scandalous for her to actually wear. While appealing, I couldn't risk the temptation. "I'll grab you something to wear, if you want to stay here." I pointed to the spot just inside the door, then ventured into my Academy sanctuary in search of my walk-in closet, which existed on the other side of my spacious bathroom. The familiar, warm brown tones caused my lips to curl, the scent of mint and spice still lingering from my last visit.

Mine, I thought. *At least for another year.*

Sifting through my wardrobe of Academy-sanctioned outfits, suits, and casual items, I found a plain black shirt and a pair of flannel pajama bottoms. Then I grabbed some boxers just in case the pants didn't fit.

Aflora stood in the entry, stiff as a board.

"Never been in a man's room before?" I teased.

Her lips curled down. "I'm not an innocent, Kolstov. I have a boyfriend. It's *your* bedroom I don't want to enter."

Amusement touched my chest. "Keep telling yourself that, sweetheart. Maybe you'll convince us both."

She snorted. "Are all Midnight Fae as arrogant as you and Shadow?"

"I prefer *sexy* and *confident,* at least in the description of myself," I said, winking at her. "Now which will it be, option one or option two?"

Her blue eyes rolled. "As if I care."

"Well, option one is across the hall from Ella and Tray, so you'll probably hear them fucking on occasion. Option two is between both our rooms, which means you'll get to hear me entertaining as well as Tray and Ella fucking. Therefore, perhaps you'd prefer the second option so you can think of me when you're alone at night? Picture yourself between my sheets instead of whomever I've chosen to indulge that evening?"

Aflora's full lips parted on a gasp. "What a crude thing to say."

"Better get used to it," I replied, crowding her against the wall. "This is my territory, and I won't be changing my habits just to suit your *prudish* ways."

Her nostrils flared. "I'm *not* a prude."

"Prove it," I dared, walking a dangerous line.

A muscle ticked in her cheek as she clenched her teeth. "I don't need to prove anything to you," she finally said after a beat, turning on her heel. To my utter shock, she marched off to option two as if to make her point. "I'll sleep here."

She opened the door.

And proceeded to slam it behind her.

The shift of her lock echoed in the hallway.

"Well, she has spirit," a deep voice drawled from the opening of the corridor.

My heart skipped a beat as my one weakness stepped beneath one of the skylights, his striking features glistening beneath the stars.

"Hello, Zephyrus," I greeted, my confidence seeping from my veins.

"Prince Kolstov," he returned, formal and direct. "I'll take the other guest room. Then you and I are going to have a long talk."

Two hits in one sentence.

Not only was he denying a night in my bed—which we both knew I'd be more than happy to accommodate—but he also wanted to have a discussion.

Discussions with Guardian Zephyrus never went in my favor.

I should have volunteered myself for the role of introducing Aflora to the Academy rather than allow my father to delegate the task to Zeph. The selfish part of me had rejoiced, while the practical side knew better.

Unfortunately, my selfish half had won.

And now I would pay the price for it.

CHAPTER SIX

AFLORA

Finally, something normal.

No snakes or gargoyles or fiery bugs or anything unseemly. Just a standard bedroom equipped with a double bed, a dresser, a small attached bath, and a closet.

Easy.

Elegantly furnished.

And boasting a window overlooking the Academy grounds. The entire property reminded me of a human cathedral with all the stained-glass windows and obsidian stone. Most of the buildings appeared to be the same height as this one, with random spires interspersed between. Framed by the stars and moonlight, it really did have a vampiric appeal.

Appropriate, considering the Midnight Fae's penchant for blood.

I touched my neck and walked into the bathroom in search of a mirror. Apart from my untamed hair, I still looked the same. The mark on my throat resembled more of a hickey than a bite. At least my fae healing abilities still worked. Unlike my access to the source.

Grasping the cold marble sink, I leaned in to study every crevice of my face.

What binding power did they put on me? I wondered. *And how do I break it?*

I ran my hands over my blouse and skirt, down my legs, and to my shoes, searching for anything that felt wrong or foreign. Nothing.

I stripped out of my clothes, just in case.

Still nothing.

Grabbing the sink, I scowled at my reflection. It had to be some sort of magical net that I couldn't sense. So how did I defeat it?

Padding into the bedroom on bare feet, I went to the window to search for a tree or any kind of life outside. If I could find a piece of earth and latch onto it, I might be able to call to my source and break through—

A knock interrupted my concentration, and the door opened a second later.

I spun around with a glower, irritated by the interruption.

"Aflora, Zeph is…" Kolstov trailed off, his eyes wandering over me.

I frowned at him. *What is his prob…? Oh. Oh!* My arm flew up to cover my breasts, my opposite hand falling to my lower half. "Get out!"

His palms rose in surrender as he took a step backward.

Then he bent and tossed something inside. "Clothes to, uh, wear." He seemed to shake himself before closing the door.

I scowled at the wood. *Pompous, intrusive wad of—*

Wait.

How did he open that door? I'd locked it.

Marching over, I found it distinctly unlatched.

Not okay.

Plucking the shirt off the floor, I pulled it over my head before donning the boxer shorts—an item I really hoped was clean—then threw open the door and stomped outside.

Only to freeze with one foot in the hallway.

The scene at the end of the corridor held me captive, my jaw hitting the floor.

A male had Kolstov pinned up against the wall with a palm around his throat, the other on his hip. They were locked in some sort of heated stare. And from the looks of it, the newcomer with the sharp cheekbones was definitely winning.

"Let. Go." Kolstov's command was a rasp against the air. He had the other man's lapels clenched tightly in his fists, his golden irises swirling with fire.

"You first," the male replied, his voice rich and dark and holding an edge of domination that had my knees wobbling.

Well now, who is this guy? Zeph?

He appeared slightly older. Definitely stronger. Same height as Kolstov, but with an aura of superiority that I found surprising. Who could be more powerful than a Midnight Fae Prince? Maybe the king, but this guy wasn't him. Too young for that. And he looked nothing like Kolstov, either.

"*Fuck you, Zephyrus,*" Kolstov hissed.

"That's Headmaster Zephyrus to you, *Prince Kolstov.*"

My eyebrows lifted.

Wow, so these two clearly had some sort of history. I couldn't tell if they wanted to kill each other or rip each other's clothes off.

I sort of wanted to watch just to see how it all turned out.

But I also wanted to know how Kolstov unlocked my door.

I opened my mouth to ask, when flames erupted between the two men, causing me to jump backward. There weren't any wands present, no words spoken, just fire dancing in the air as if summoned from one of their minds.

It quickly became obvious *who* created it when Zephyrus tossed Kolstov to the ground while muttering, "Foul play."

"Just using my gifts to my advantage like my mentor taught me," Kolstov tossed back at him, his hand on his throat.

Zephyrus snorted. "If that were true, you'd have relied on your physical strength and not your Elite Blood." He brushed the flames from his sleeves with a flick of his wrist, the energy dissipating into a gray cloud, leaving his blazer untouched.

Kolstov rolled his neck and shook the flickers from his own clothes, creating a tendril of steam that disappeared with the others.

The smoke cleared, leaving them both unharmed without a shred of evidence on them. Almost as if I'd imagined the whole thing.

Huh. That's interesting.

Cold green eyes met mine, narrowing. "Is this my project?"

"Yes," Kolstov replied. "Aflora, meet Zeph. Zeph, this is Aflora."

Zephyrus's gaze passed over me in clear disinterest. "How fun." His sarcasm wasn't lost on me. "I'm Headmaster Zephyrus, your new Guardian. Try to leave this suite without me and you'll regret it." With that proclamation, he turned on his heel and headed toward the living area, leaving me alone with Kolstov.

"Charming," I grumbled.

Kolstov palmed the back of his neck and blew out a breath, shaking his head. Then he followed the *headmaster* out of the corridor.

Great. A game of Chase the Pixie.

I supposed if I wanted any answers—not to mention *food*—I had to join them.

Huffing, I stomped down the hallway in their direction and found them standing off again in the living area. Only without touching this time. Tension poured off them in waves. Neither of them speaking.

I cleared my throat. "So, uh, my lock is broken."

No reply.

"Kolstov. You can't just barge into my room without—"

"Your room?" he questioned, breaking his staring contest with the headmaster to glance my way. "This is *my* suite. The locks don't apply to me."

My jaw tightened. "They do in my *guest* room."

He snorted. "No, sweetheart. They don't."

Fire licked through my veins at his declaration.

First, Shadow bit me against my will.

Then, the Council forced me to attend Midnight Fae Academy for reasons no one bothered clarifying.

And now, Prince Kolstov claimed I would have no privacy here in his quarters—a place I didn't even want to stay.

Not. Acceptable.

"Kolstov has a problem with being locked out," Zephyrus put in, completely oblivious to the turmoil brewing beneath my skin. "Don't worry. You'll get used to it."

"Are you going to be an ass to me all year?" Kolstov demanded, his focus on the headmaster.

"Likely," Zephyrus replied.

The thumping in my ears drowned out the continuation of his statement, my focus on the little tendril of power peeking at me from beneath the thick, inky waves inside me.

Oh, hello, I thought at it. *Come here.*

Closing my eyes, I followed the flare of light through the dark web in my mind.

This is where they've trapped me, I realized, the map clearing behind my eyes. *They've cast a binding spell over me.*

It must have happened while I was asleep.

Did Shade do it? Kolstov? Another fae?

It didn't matter.

What I needed to do was unravel it.

Zephyrus and Kolstov continued to bicker in the living area, neither of them seeming to remember my presence. Normally, I would consider that rude. In this case, their impudence worked in my favor.

Energy swirled inside me as I navigated each thread, carefully plucking them apart with my invisible scissors, longing to free that spark at the bottom.

The design wasn't too intricate, suggesting it'd been done in a hurry. The fact that I could suddenly see the binds implied Shade had indeed contaminated my blood and that perhaps my power was growing in darkness as a result. Or maybe I just hadn't looked in the right place.

Regardless, I could see it now.

And I seemed to be able to undo it.

Kolstov raised his voice.

Zephyrus remained calm.

The two of them were engaged in some argument about Kolstov throwing Zephyrus to the wolves three months ago. I only half listened, my attention on the growing light inside me.

There you are, I breathed, smiling at the earth source. *Come to me now. Help me.*

Power hummed through my being, revitalizing me in the strength of my core essence.

Yes, yes.

I felt alive.

Exuberant.

Whole.

I sighed, the plant life around the Academy prickling at my instincts. The trees weren't dead at all, just a different species. *A burning thwomp*, the roots told me, giving me a proper name to work from.

Nice to meet you, I murmured, rolling my neck and memorizing the heart of the species in my mind. *You'll do very well.*

With a twirl of power, I began to reconstruct the base of the charred tree, rooting it in the guest room.

Kolstov didn't want to give me a lock? Then I'd make one.

And I'd rip his suite apart in the process.

"Do you feel that?" Zephyrus asked, interrupting whatever Kolstov had just been saying.

Must work faster, I thought, directing my nurturing waves from the gap in the web to the new creation.

"What are you doing?" Kolstov demanded.

I ignored him.

His palm was suddenly on my neck, his hard body pressed along mine. "Aflora."

I didn't open my eyes.

I just continued to unweave and weave, unweave and weave. *Grow, little tree. Grow.*

The earthy force pulsed inside me, breaking through the final binds and flourishing to life. I sighed in content, my powers finally free.

Flowery scents perfumed the air, vines of my own making climbing over the walls to protect me from the snakes outside. Because I could feel them slithering in agitation, their intent to break down the threshold palpable.

Oh, but the gargoyle held them at bay.

Why?

Ah, because I'm part of this suite now. It protects everyone inside. The knowledge slammed into my mind from an unknown source, but I felt the veracity of it deep inside my bones.

"Aflora!" Kolstov yelled.

My lips curled, power rippling through me in energizing waves. *What was it he said to me earlier? Oh, right.* "I'm ready to dance now, Midnight Prince," I told him, shoving him away with a pulse of energy that put him on his ass.

He coughed, then cursed as roots grew from the ground, trapping him.

I smiled. "Those burning thwomps sure are sturdy." The one in my guest room was almost complete, the branches reaching the ceiling above. Content with the design, I told it to grow outward. I'd left the door open, giving it the opportunity to inch thick black roots down the hallway toward us.

An explosion sent me sideways into the wall, my focus temporarily disrupted as Kolstov launched to his feet. He'd lost his cape and jacket, his shirtsleeves rolled to his elbows. It all happened so quickly that I didn't know how or when he'd made the wardrobe change, but I caught the writhing lines twisting along his skin.

The dark source, I realized.

It thrived inside him.

And he was about to use it against me.

I ducked the oncoming blow, a shield of petals building along my skin in an instant.

"This is ridiculous, Aflora," Kolstov snapped. "Stop."

I tripped him with one of the roots, then stirred a myriad of pollen mites into the air around him, eliciting a sneeze.

Zephyrus stood off to the side, completely unfazed. As he didn't seem to want to join the battle, I left him alone—for now—and concentrated on my fellow Royal Fae.

Zings of electricity shot from his fingertips, all aimed my way. I deflected them with flowers, frowning as he turned the gorgeous creations into ash.

"No respect," I muttered, stirring an array of blossom motes to blind his vision. My tree from the bedroom had finally reached me, grounding me in life as I directed the thick black ropes toward my attacker.

If I could incapacitate him and Zephyrus, I could find a portal and escape. Maybe.

I honestly hadn't thought that far ahead. I just wanted out of this damn suite.

The snakes, however, would prove to be a problem.

Hence the petal shield.

A root wrapped around Kolstov's ankle, tightening, only to be engulfed in red and yellow flames.

I screamed as the fiery embers reached my heart, my tree crying out in pain. "Stop!"

"You first," Kolstov ground out, his destructive essence screeching across the floor and destroying my creation with horrifying ease.

I fell to my knees, agonized over the destruction of life, his vile powers eating at the goodness of mine.

Hatred unlike any I'd ever experienced bloomed inside me, all directed at this monster of a royal. Energy blazed from his golden eyes, overtaking mine in murderous lashes that obliterated my vines and all traces of the earth I'd brought into his suite.

Including my beloved tree.

He hadn't stopped at the roots, taking the entire thwomp and incinerating it into ash in a matter of seconds.

My chest ached at the loss.

So wrong.

How could you?

Why?

The thwomps outside wept with me, their branches rattling angrily in protest.

"That was fascinating," Zephyrus murmured.

"That's not the word I'd use for it," Kolstov retorted, his booted feet appearing in my vision. "What the actual fuck, Aflora?"

I glowered up at him. "You're a monster." My voice was hoarse, the black magic coating my earth source leaving me breathless.

He scoffed at that. "You just unleashed a *monster* into my suite, nearly killing all of us in the process. Have you lost your fucking mind?"

"It wasn't going to kill us," I returned, livid. "*You* are the murderer here."

His eyebrows lifted. "Really?" He bent down, grabbed me by the neck, and hauled me to my feet. "Let's see about that." He dragged me through the living area to the back windows. "Watch."

"No."

When I tried to struggle, he wrapped his arms around me from behind, capturing me with my back to his chest. His lips were at my ear. "Fucking watch or I'll drag you back to the Council and throw you in the dungeon for the week."

I bristled at the threat and considered conjuring more pollen dust to suffocate him with, but our heads were too close together. I'd probably end up inhaling the potent mix, too.

An outburst in the distance caught my eye, causing me to gasp. "What was that?"

"Keep watching."

I had no idea *what* he wanted me to see. It was pitch-black outside, which seemed to be their version of the day. From what I recalled, Midnight Fae held opposite hours to Elemental Fae, choosing to sleep when the sun rose and to work during the night. Not a schedule I wanted to—

An inferno billowed into the sky, followed by two more from different positions on the Academy grounds.

Narrowing my gaze, I focused on the source and gasped when I *felt* the burning thwomp closest to our building expel its burning embers into the sky.

Oh.

That was why they possessed charcoaled stems and didn't have leaves.

They literally *burned*.

"Now imagine what would have happened had your little creation gone through its hourly process inside my suite?" Kolstov released me, taking a step back.

I swallowed and pinched my lips to the side. "Well, how was I supposed to know that?" I asked, facing him.

Zephyrus stood off to the side, arms crossed, his chiseled features devoid of emotion.

"How about you not play with things you don't understand?" Kolstov suggested. "That's why you're here—*to learn*."

"No, I'm being held here because a Midnight Fae bit me against my will and you think his powers are going to mix with mine. Well, I feel fine now that I'm grounded again in my earth essence. So how about you let me leave and we call it a night?"

"You feel *fine*," he repeated, his skepticism evident. "Yeah. Because it's perfectly normal for an Earth Fae to be able to unravel a dark arts spell. One my father put on you, by the way. And it was a binding spell that other Midnight Fae wouldn't be able to dismantle in a week, let alone minutes. So yeah, I think it's safe to say Chern's suspicions about your future are already coming true."

My mouth worked without sound, his words effectively freezing me in place.

Was he right? I hadn't noticed the web before, but once it came to me, I worked through it rather quickly. And I'd wondered if the reason I could suddenly see it meant something about my growing power. It seemed it did.

Which meant… "I really am morphing into an abomination." Something I already acknowledged once, but now… now I had proof.

"It would seem so, yes," Kolstov agreed. "But it might—"

"How is this possible?" I asked, cutting him off. "All that willow stump did was bite me. We didn't exchange powers. If anything, he should be inheriting mine, not the other way around."

"A bite creates the mating bond in our world," Kolstov replied, irritation lacing his tone. "Something you should know about Midnight Fae culture. Except, that's right, you haven't studied us at all. What a fantastic royal you are turning out to be."

His barb failed to penetrate my already whirling emotions because we were beyond my studies and what I knew. What I cared about now was the future and how to use it to my advantage.

"Elemental Fae don't bond through blood. We bond with the source. So it's one-sided. I don't even feel him, and if we were truly mated, I would." *Or I hope that's the case,* I added to myself.

"It's still forming," Kolstov gritted out. "Midnight Fae mating is initiated with the first bite, sealed with the second, and promised for eternity with the third. Shade only initiated it, which means your powers and blood are mingling now, forming a new life together. Hence, you suddenly have access to dark magic. What we don't know is how deep it will go."

"Which is why the Council decided to keep her here," Zephyrus interjected. "To observe her progress. And you're the one charged with managing her."

A muscle ticked in Kolstov's jaw. "Is this the part where you call me a babysitter?"

"No. *Executioner* seems like a better term." Zephyrus pushed off the wall, his eyes narrowing. "You are the one who will have to kill her if she proves to be an abomination, yes?"

My heart stopped.

No.

Except the look on Kolstov's face said, *Yes.*

I started shaking my head in denial, refusing to believe that could possibly be a recourse, yet all the while knowing it had to be an option. Because abominations couldn't exist. Too much power led to insanity.

And I'd witnessed firsthand what happened when someone achieved too much power.

A shiver traversed my spine at the memory of Elana trying to destroy all of Earth Fae kind with her dark magic. She'd tried to suck our souls from our bodies, to absorb our abilities.

My connection to the earth source nearly fractured because of her.

I'll never be like that, I thought to myself.

But what if that was my fate? What if this connection Shade had forced upon me drove me insane?

I'd nearly unleashed a burning thwomp on this suite. What else could I do?

It didn't matter that I hadn't known. I should have known. Should have dug deeper into the being's core to determine its purpose before picking it for my plight.

My knees buckled and I hit the ground, my eyes on the floor.

How had everything gone so horribly wrong? What could I do to stop it? Learn dark magic? Control it? Would that even help?

"We're going to need a new binding spell," Kolstov muttered. "A more powerful one."

I remained silent because he was right.

Returning to the Elemental Fae realm was impossible in my current state. Bringing dark magic there would upset the balance.

I had no choice but to remain here while my future revealed itself.

All because a Midnight Fae took advantage of me in the Human Realm.

My eyes narrowed.

Kolstov might have pissed me off with his high-handedness, but it was Shade who earned my ultimate wrath.

That male would pay when I saw him again. I'd wrap him up in vines and squeeze until his gorgeous head popped off. Then I'd burn him for good measure.

"He warned me you would be beautiful, Aflora," he'd said.

He who? I pondered now. *And why did you do this to me?*

Death and I were already well acquainted, as I'd been placed at the lethal doorstep a few times before. Once as a child. And again just last year. Yet my life had won both times before.

I wasn't one to just give up and accept fate. I fought it every step of the way. And this wouldn't be any different.

A new task list brewed in my thoughts, providing me with renewed purpose.

Play along.

Learn how to control the darkness.

Behave.

Demand answers.

Kill Shade.

Yes. Yes, this would work.

And then, when I finished, I'd escape.

CHAPTER SEVEN

AFLORA

I pushed the bloody sauce across my plate with a frown. The giant hunk of brown crap sitting in the middle didn't appeal to me, nor did the strange, long white worms surrounding it.

When Kolstov claimed to be heading out to pick up some food, I thought he meant *edible* food. This was not edible. Yet Zephyrus and Kolstov seemed pretty satisfied with it, their plates already half-empty.

My lips twisted. *I can't eat this.*

Fortunately, they hadn't cut off my elemental power yet, which meant I could grow—

"It's spaghetti," Kolstov said, interrupting my thoughts. "Fresh from Italy. Why aren't you eating it?"

"Human food." My nose scrunched. "Why are you eating human food?"

Kolstov shared a look with Zephyrus. "I told you. She knows nothing about Midnight Fae."

I ground my teeth together, tired of this rhetoric.

But he wasn't done.

"When did you start learning about other fae realms, Zeph?"

The headmaster finished swallowing before saying, "As a child."

"Me, too. I remember Dorthia quizzing me about the Fae Royal names when I was, like, six or seven." Kolstov pinned me with a gaze. "Midnight Fae frequently enter the Human Realm because we need their blood to survive. As a result, our palates have evolved with theirs, making mortal food very common in this kingdom. Consider that your introductory lesson. Now open your mouth and eat what I've given you."

I considered his words and decided to go for an honest response. "Six or seven years old," I repeated, tasting the words. "Hmm. When I was around that age, my parents left me with a single mother and her two children, stating they would return. Except they didn't. Their links with the source disappeared, leaving me as the sole heir. Then, a little while after that, a psychotic fae tried to kill me and absorb my earth magic."

I paused for effect.

"So yeah," I drawled. "I've been a little busy trying to survive for the last fourteen or so years. Forgive me for not adding fae politics to my *pampered* agenda." I shoved away from the table, done with him and his pompous criticisms.

None of this was my fault.

And I was very tired of his condescending attitude.

He caught my wrist as I rounded the small dining table, his golden irises flaring. "You need to eat."

"I don't drink blood, but thank you anyway."

His brow furrowed. "I wasn't offering my neck."

I rolled my eyes. "No, just the bloody worm soup. I'm good. I'll make myself something from the earth." Assuming I could conjure up an edible plant in this realm. All the plant sources I felt around me were far from friendly.

Case in point, the burning thwomp.

Definitely not going to try to eat that.

"It's spaghetti," Kolstov repeated, tugging me back toward my chair with his too-strong arms. "Noodles, not worms. Tomato sauce, not blood. And a meatball." He finished his explanation with a shove that had me landing square in my seat again. "Take a bite. Aside from the heavy garlic, I think you'll like it."

"A meatball?" I repeated, my stomach churning. "Like, from an animal?"

"Probably a mix of pig and cow, yeah."

I gagged. *"You're eating an animal?!"*

He shared another of those looks with Zephyrus, then reached across the table to pluck the giant ball of crap off my plate and tossed it onto his own. "Now you just have noodles and tomato sauce. Bon appétit."

Zephyrus snorted, sliced a knife through the glob on Kolstov's plate, and took half the meat pile for himself.

I shuddered. *So gross.*

Elemental Fae didn't eat Human Realm animals. Their diets weren't adequate enough for our tastes. I preferred a nice slab of medium-rare orc, or even a grizzly pink potpie.

My stomach growled at the thought.

Zephyrus's gaze narrowed, those sharp green eyes seeming to peer right through me.

He patted his shirt, producing a wand from a pocket I couldn't see, then waved it around with a few muttered words. A plate appeared a moment later with a shroom loaf on top of a bed of purple leaves. He swapped it for my dish without a word and dumped the bloody worms onto his own plate.

Kolstov smirked.

Zephyrus remained silent.

And I eyed the magical creation with strong skepticism. "What did you put in it?"

"Take a bite and find out, princess," he replied with a wink.

I huffed. *Well, it's better than what they're eating*, I decided, taking my knife and fork to cut a sliver from the magically produced food.

Zephyrus ignored me, his focus on his own plate. Meanwhile, Kolstov's brow furrowed as I brought the browned fluff to my lips and took a bite.

"What is it?" he asked, sounding appalled.

"Shroom loaf," Zephyrus informed him. "Popular in their realm."

"How the hell do you know that?" he demanded.

"You're not the only one who took cultural courses, *Your Highness*." Zephyrus gave him a look that resulted in a scowl from the Midnight Prince.

Such a strange dynamic.

Zephyrus struck me as older, not because of his title, but because of the experience underlining his features. Definitely not of Academy age, yet not too much older.

Headmaster.

Something told me that term didn't mean the same in this world as it meant in others.

He wasn't in charge of the Academy because he didn't have the right air of authority for that. Too laid-back in his treatment of Kolstov. Not proper enough in my presence either.

But he could definitely pass for a professor.

"Do you teach?" I asked him while cutting off a large bite. It wasn't the most amazing shroom loaf of my experience, but I liked the smoky flavor. It provided an exotic touch, as if Zephyrus had singed the ends himself with his Midnight Fae energy.

"That is what a headmaster does, yes." He tapped his fork on the plate, staring at his food, and sighed. "Do you know anything about how Midnight Fae Academy is run? How our Houses of Magic work? The bloodlines that drive our course studies?"

My cheeks heated. "As I told Prince Kolstov, I haven't taken a course on your political structure yet. It was on my calendar for this year, in addition to devoting my time to helping my fellow Earth Fae rebuild. Which I apparently won't be doing now."

Over half of my kind had perished in the last few decades due to a wicked abomination sucking the energy from our souls in an attempt to gain access to additional elemental sources. It left the Earth Fae in shambles. Something I expected to help nurture and fix over the next fifty or so years.

Then Shade bit me and turned my plans to dust.

"I'm aware of what happened in the Elemental Fae kingdom," Kolstov murmured. "I supplied textbooks to Exos and Cyrus for——"

"Master Kolstov," a gravelly voice interrupted as the gargoyle swooped in over our heads.

My eyes widened at the breadth of his stone wings. For such a tiny body, I expected a few inches at most. But no, the width was as long as my arm.

Wow, where does he hide those while in the door?

"Yes, Sir Kristoff?" Kolstov prompted, arching a brow.

"A Sangré Blood is at the door for you, sir," the gargoyle replied, bowing low before whirling around to return to the foyer.

"Ah, Chern must have sent us a party gift." He dabbed his lips with a napkin, then excused himself. "Be back in a few minutes."

"Party gift?" I repeated, glancing at Zephyrus. "And what's a *Sangré Blood?*"

"One of the Midnight Fae bloodlines." He sipped from a glass of red liquid that was either wine or fresh from a human's veins. I didn't ask. Considering my glass contained water, I suspected it was the latter. "There are five active houses of our kind: Death, Elite, Sangré, Warrior, and Malefic. I'm a Warrior Blood. Kolstov is an Elite Blood. Shade, your betrothed, is a Death Blood."

"*Betrothed,*" I muttered, hating that word. "Soon-to-be-dead betrothed."

If Zephyrus heard me, he didn't acknowledge my comment. "Each line has an affinity for different types of dark magic. It's similar to your elemental assignments, except ours is defined in the blood more than in our souls. As your bond with Shade settles, you'll likely join his line. But your Royal Fae essence may contradict it."

"That's why the Council wants her to take courses under all the houses," Kolstov said as he returned. Rather than reclaim his seat, he moved to stand behind mine. "Lift your hair for me, gorgeous."

The request sent a chill down my spine, my hands locking around my knife and fork. "Why?"

He combed his fingers through my dark strands and bent to press his lips to my ear. "Because I need access to your throat."

I jolted, the silverware crashing against my plate as I covered the pulse points beneath my neck. If he thought to bite me, then he had another think coming. "No!"

His hands landed on my shoulders before I could even jump out of my chair. "Chill, Aflora. I just want to put a necklace on you."

"A necklace?" I repeated, trying to glance back at him. His hold kept me in place.

"It's necessary."

"That doesn't tell me—"

"The Council needs to temper your elemental abilities to ensure the safety of the students," Zephyrus explained in a bored tone. "The choker will keep you under control." He glanced up at Kolstov. "Now, was that so difficult an explanation?"

Temper my abilities?

Leather wrapped around my neck before I could voice the question out loud, Kolstov already moving my hair out of the way.

I tried to shift out of his grip, to stop him from sealing the brace around my throat, but it snapped into place with a zing that pierced my soul.

My hands flew up to tug at the choker, to find the clasp and unfasten it. Only, it was solid all the way around, sealed by magic.

"Remove it," I demanded, my spirit whimpering inside at having been cut off from my source yet again. "Remove it now."

Kolstov settled into the chair at the head of the table, his sigh long and loud. "It's necessary, Aflora. We can't risk you disturbing the balance or creating another burning thwomp where you shouldn't." He looked pointedly at the ashes still littering his living room floor. "This will also help us observe your dark-magic growth. Zeph is going to take you shopping tomorrow for a wand and other essentials."

"Yes, because apparently it's my job to play babysitter," the headmaster retorted. "If the Council is so concerned for her safety, perhaps forcing her to attend the Academy wasn't the brightest move."

Tears stung my eyes.

Protection was the least of my concerns considering they'd just wrapped a shackle around my neck to control my abilities.

It suffocated my ability to think, to continue listening to their maddening conversation. All I wanted—no, *needed*—was to rip this offending collar from my throat.

But it wouldn't budge no matter which way I pulled or yanked.

"Why are you even still here?" Zephyrus's harsh tone drew me from my turmoil, lifting my focus back to the two bickering males.

Kolstov's cheeks were a dark shade of red, his lips flattened. "To help with the transition."

"Bullshit. Your father sent me to handle it so you could go enjoy your final week of debauchery before classes begin again. If you're not planning to do that, then I'll go back to my life and you can manage her *transition*."

Kolstov slammed his fist onto the table. "I didn't ask for you to be here."

"Well, you didn't suggest otherwise either, did you?"

Silence.

"Yeah, that's what I thought. Just like the headmaster position. You claim to have balls, Prince Kolstov. And while I know they exist, they sure do seem to shrivel up into nothing where your father's edicts are concerned." With that crude statement, Zephyrus shoved himself away from the table so hard his chair toppled onto the ground.

He didn't bother righting it.

Just turned on his heel to leave.

"Ten hours, Aflora," he tossed over his shoulder. "Be ready to go."

Kolstov watched him go with burning gold irises. When the door slammed in the distance—presumably to the guest room—the Midnight Prince snapped his fingers.

An apparition appeared beside him, the ghostly female boasting a maternal glow as she stared down at him.

"Clean it up," he demanded as he stood.

"Of course, sir," the apparition breathed, her words ghosting through the air and leaving a chill in their wake.

Rather than follow Zephyrus, he headed toward the front entry, exiting through the threshold without a single word or glance back.

The dishes rose above the table, vanishing before my eyes.

I caught the contents of my dish just before the plate disappeared into the strange vacuum.

Then the translucent female form turned to air with everything else, leaving me alone and cold in the living area with a random shroom loaf clutched to my chest.

Silence.

Stillness.

Nothing.

Not even a breath—because I'd stopped inhaling and exhaling.

How had everything gone so wrong in one day? I stared down at the food in my hands.

Tomorrow would hopefully provide new opportunities.

Or possibly be a whole lot worse.

Yeah, probably that.

CHAPTER EIGHT

"I have a supply list," Zephyrus said as we left Kolstov's suite the following evening. The Midnight Prince was nowhere in sight, and I suspected I wouldn't be seeing him again until next week.

Assuming I'm still here. I sighed, shaking my head. *Who am I kidding? Of course I'll be here.*

The Earth Fae relied on me to uphold the connection to the earth source, which meant blocking any and all dangers. Including myself. And I couldn't deny that the potential binding of my abilities to Shade jeopardized my ability to lead.

What if he can access my elemental gifts? I wondered, following Zephyrus down the stairs. "Does my collar keep Shade from tapping into my earth source?" I asked out loud. "Or is he wearing one, too?" The thought of that actually had my lips twitching. *Oh, I really hope they collared him…*

Zephyrus paused to glare at me. "Were you over there daydreaming while I've been speaking?"

I grimaced. He *had* been talking. And, uh, yeah, I'd not heard a word of it after his supply list comment.

The look he gave me confirmed that the answer was written across my face and he didn't approve. His hand wrapped around my throat, his opposite palm going to my hip, as he pushed me up against the wall. My feet awkwardly found purchase on one stair, holding me upright while he captured my gaze with a lethal stare.

"When I speak, you listen. Understand?"

I swallowed. He stood over a foot taller than me, just like Kolstov. And Zephyrus also possessed the muscles of a man who had spent most of his life hardening his exterior.

Warrior Blood, I recalled from our earlier conversation. While I didn't know the complete definition, I could garner the importance of that distinction. Along with his comments about being a Guardian.

My Guardian.

This was not a male to piss off, and yet… "Do you manhandle all your students in this manner?" I asked him, tilting my head to the side.

His chest crowded mine, and his thighs—*holy crap, those thighs!*—pressed me harder into the wall. "I don't know. I haven't started my new job yet. Ask me again next week."

"You're a new professor?"

"Headmaster," he corrected. "And yes, it's a recently assigned post." His tone held a note of bitterness to it.

"What was your previous post?"

"Why are you so chatty today?" His grip tightened around my neck. "I think I preferred your moping from last night."

"I was not moping," I gritted out, my eyes narrowing. "Let me go."

"Make me."

"This is not proper behavior for a professor."

"Headmaster," he corrected again. "And I haven't technically started yet. Right now, I'm just your Guardian. Which means you'll do whatever I tell you to do, whenever I tell you to do it."

"And you make that point by strangling me?"

His lips curled into a cruel smile. "Trust me, this is nothing compared to what I can do."

I believed him. Yet, for whatever reason, I didn't fear him. His callous exterior presented an ominous front, his cold green eyes just as harsh as the rest of him, but my instincts told me to push back.

"I might be weaker with this cuff around my neck, but I'm still a Royal Fae. That said, I apologize for *daydreaming.* I was thinking about how my bloodline is tied to Shade and wondered if that means he can access my gifts, too. If he can tap into the earth source, I have much larger problems than buying books or school uniforms." Which I guessed was part of his *list.*

A glimmer of respect brightened his emerald orbs. He released me and stepped back, his cloak billowing around his ankles. The lapels were laced with green ink that sparkled beneath the firelight. I studied them, wondering what they meant, when Zephyrus turned on his heel and continued down the stairs.

"The collar around your neck should prevent him from accessing your elemental gifts. It acts as a door, and when it's clasped, that door is shut and blocks your soul from accessing the elements. Which means Shade is also locked out." He reached the bottom level and glanced up at me. "Satisfied?"

"Now you're starting to sound more like a professor," I quipped, giving him a smile. "Thank you, *Headmaster.*"

His pupils flared, heat momentarily sparking in the emerald depths. "Hmm" was all he said before turning again and leading the way outside.

Rather than lead the way toward the main gates, he took a left that directed us into the heart of the campus. Fire flickered on lampposts, gently lighting the charcoal-stoned paths. Obsidian bricks and other types of rock provided the foundation for the buildings, and gothic arches and stained glass lent the scene a palatial appeal that I had to admit was quite pretty.

Burning thwomps and other foreign plants graced the grounds, including black flowers that reminded me of roses and a series of purple-laced ivy that glowed with fiery bugs.

I bent to get a better look, only to be yanked back by Zephyrus. "Don't."

"Why?" I asked, studying the buzzing insects. "They remind me of pixies."

"Fire gnats are disgusting little jackasses who bite. Don't provoke them." Zephyrus released me. "Our wildlife isn't like yours. We coexist because we have to, not because we want to. So trust me, you do not want to touch anything in this realm. Especially not those."

I shivered at the warning, then gasped as a phoenix landed not three feet away from us. Its massive wings billowed in the flames, the eyes predatory.

"Case in point," Zephyrus muttered. "Fuck off." His words seemed to be for the bird, not for me.

The beautiful creature tilted its head, his red irises focused and intelligent. A curious little caw left its throat, causing my lips to curl. Oh, I had no doubt this being was dangerous, but I could respect its gorgeous existence. Not that I had any intention of feeding the bird or stroking it. I knew better than that.

Just as I knew not to disturb the fire gnats.

Admiring nature didn't require any sort of interference.

"You're stunning," I praised.

The phoenix preened as if it understood, his wings expanding to show off the variety of colorful flames.

Zephyrus stepped in between us, cutting off my view, and flapped his cloak in warning at the handsome being. "I won't tell you again. Fuck. Off."

A hiss of sound preceded the phoenix's departure, leaving me in awe of the way it swooped across the grounds to a nearby burning thwomp.

"Let's get something straight," Zephyrus said, facing me once more. "As your assigned Guardian, my duty is to keep you alive. To do that, I need you to obey my every word. Let's start with this: do not provoke the wildlife."

I bristled at his tone. "I wasn't provoking him."

"Don't engage with the wildlife," he amended.

"That's like telling me not to breathe."

"Then hold your fucking breath," he snapped, causing me to flinch. He cursed and turned away. "Let's go. This list is burning a literal hole in my pocket, and I want this over and done with."

"Yes, sir," I muttered.

"Better," he replied as he continued down the path past a gazebo overlaid with more of that violet ivy. I wasn't given much time to admire the architecture, his long legs leading us into a clearing filled with lava rock instead of grass. My eyebrows lifted at the bizarre textures. Then my lips parted as the ground shifted.

Not rocks.

Animals.

Zephyrus cleared his throat, his hands on his hips, as he glowered at the writhing swarm of birdlike creatures.

Oh my…

They all activated at once, their wings flickering to life and blooming with thin, sharp edges. The air around them pulsated with magic, their chattering beaks and crackling feathers grinding against the wind.

Zephyrus pressed his palm to my lower back, pushing me into the center of the flocking mass. I lifted my arms to shield my face, terrified of being cut by their jagged points. However, they resembled feathers against my skin.

I peeked through my forearms to find us being swarmed by crow-like birds. Black eyes, black beaks, black feathers. Not rocks.

"What in the…?" I trailed off as a keypad appeared.

This is a portal.

Zephyrus acted before I could catch the movements, his fingers flying over the destination code too fast for me to catch. Not that escape was much of an option for me right now, but having a backup plan couldn't hurt.

The obsidian flurry swam around us, forming a ribbon of solid ink that had me stepping closer to Zephyrus. His palm against my lower back slid to my hip in response—a protective move that didn't go unnoticed for either of us because his gaze seized mine as soon as it happened.

Intensity built between us.

Or maybe it was the aura of the transfer shifting us through space.

I couldn't say, but it escalated my heartbeat. His masculine scent invaded my pores, the minty aftershave he wore an intoxicating blanket that swathed me in his Midnight Fae essence.

All to disappear in a blink as we landed in a closet filled with cloaks.

Zephyrus released me immediately, his long fingers flying upward to unfasten the knot at his neck. He added his cape to the others, drawing my attention to the orderly fashion of the interior. Everything was color-coded by the ink etched into the trim of each formal robe.

Dark purple.

Maroon.

Forest green—Zephyrus's location.

Navy.

And solid black.

"What do they represent?" I asked softly, reaching out to stroke the soft textures.

Zephyrus caught my wrist, yanking me back. "Don't. They're charmed to only recognize their master." He seemed to consider. "Actually, no, it's a good teaching moment. Try to grab mine." He gestured to it as if I wasn't aware of where he'd just hung it up.

I narrowed my gaze. "I think I'm good, thanks."

"It won't hurt," he promised. Not that I believed him. "Just zaps a little."

"And that's all I need to know," I replied, heading for what I thought might be the door.

His arm snaked around my waist, yanking me backward. "What part of 'follow my lead' don't you get?"

"You never told me to follow you," I pointed out, glancing up at him. "And stop manhandling me."

"Stop acting impulsively," he returned, yanking me around in the other direction to face a mirror. "We're going this way. The door just leads to other portals." His grip tightened. "And don't even think about exploring them. I will hunt you down, and you will not like the consequences."

"Wow, your faith in me is charming."

He met my gaze in the mirror, one arm still wrapped like a vise around my waist. "I don't have faith in anyone but myself, Aflora. You would be wise to adopt a similar armor." With that, he shoved me through the glass—which gave way just like the entrance to Kolstov's suite at the Academy—and stepped through behind me.

Zephyrus ran his fingers through his thick mane of dark brown hair, the edges taunting his round ears. "Right. This way." He linked his fingers through mine, pulling me alongside him down a sidewalk littered with Midnight Fae.

Wow, I thought, in awe of the shops and busy atmosphere. It reminded me of strolling through the Human Realm, particularly New York City, except the buildings weren't nearly tall enough. Only four or five stories at most, but their glass exteriors were very modern.

Everyone wore business attire, allowing Zephyrus to fit in with his suit. My skirt and blouse from my date-gone-wrong barely passed the fashion test, but it beat wearing Kolstov's clothes.

"Here," Zephyrus said, pulling me toward a random building with the name *AcaWard* scrawled over the windows.

Clearly, the Midnight Fae didn't believe in doors. They just had enchanted thresholds. Because one moment the chaotic sounds of the outside world bustled around my ears, then in the next moment, we were surrounded by the warm tunes of the interior.

An endless array of outfits stretched out on racks before us. Most lined the walls in rows that climbed all the way up to the ceiling. I frowned up at them, wondering how one retrieved clothing from way up there.

Probably with a wand.

At least it proved to be an efficient use of space.

"Hello, hello," a female voice chimed. "Welcome to AcaWard. How can we help you?"

I glanced around, frowning when no one appeared. Was someone watching us on a camera and talking over a speaker system?

"Aflora needs at least seven Academy-sanctioned outfits, undergarments, and some casual wear. You are to charge the items to the Nacht account." Zephyrus slipped an envelope from his pocket with his free hand, holding it in the air. "All the details required are in here."

The note vanished, causing my eyes to widen.

"I'll return in an hour to retrieve her." He looked down at me. "We've already discussed what will happen should you try to flee. I don't recommend it."

With that, he released me and stepped backward through the glass to disappear in the throng outside.

"Wait—" I tried to follow him out, but the glass didn't give and instead smacked me in the forehead. "Ow!" I rubbed my head, irritated by my inability to leave the shop and offended by it sealing the door on me.

An array of voices erupted around me, all chattering at once.

"Hmm, yes, new clothes are needed. Indeed, indeed."

"A cloak, too."

"Don't forget a wand."

"Oh! Have you seen the new Academy skirts? I'm thinking black and red, to match the Nacht line."

"Royal, yes. Let's look at these notes. Hmm, hmm, more than seven, clearly. Too many courses."

"Shall we mix it with a touch of light blue? To match her pretty eyes?"

"Oh, is she cerulean? Haven't seen one of those in centuries."

"With hints of red, I see."

"How fascinating."

I spun around, searching for the source of the feminine tones, but found myself utterly alone in the shop.

"This way, this way," one of them said.

I felt the nudge against my backside. Then gaped as an invisible *something* grabbed my shirt to tow me forward. "Why can't I see you?" I demanded.

Tinkling laughs served as their reply.

Then they began to comment on my appearance, noting the quality of my dark hair, my clear skin, and my tiny waist.

When one of them touched my breasts, I scowled. "Show yourselves."

More tinkling.

And then they closed me in a ten-by-ten room with a mirror and three walls. No exit.

I tried walking through each barrier but found myself trapped.

Then clothes began to appear on a magical rack behind me.

"Try, try, try!" they all sang in unison.

When they started to unbutton my blouse, I whirled around and batted their figment hands away. "I will undress and dress myself, thank you."

"Oh, feisty fun," one of them murmured.

"Yes, yes. She demands privacy. We'll go."

"Try them all, love! And pick all your favorites. The note says all expenses are covered."

"Enjoy!"

They blew invisible kisses through the air, the sound caressing my cheeks in an unwelcome wave. I wiped them off with a gag, then froze as silence fell around me.

I counted to twenty before I let my shoulders fall in relief.

Finally.

At least thirty outfits waited on the rack, as well as a dozen or so shoes.

I ran my fingers along each shirt and skirt, noting the fine quality. As an Earth Fae, I always enjoyed making my own clothes from nature. But that wasn't an option here. I needed outfits that helped me assimilate to this realm. The more I blended in, the less people would notice me. And that would become important for my eventual departure.

Assuming I found a way to escape. In addition to a place to run to.

Sighing, I resigned myself to my current fate once more. Might as well pick some outfits that suited my tastes. Besides, all the expenses were covered, right?

Nacht account, Zephyrus had said. I recognized the family name as the one Kolstov belonged to. Which meant he, or maybe his father, was paying for all of this.

My lips curled.

While I'd prefer Shade foot the bill for getting me into this mess, I couldn't deny feeling a little bit of glee knowing my wardrobe spending spree would be billed directly to my primary captor.

Seven outfits?

No, surely he meant seventeen.

And a dozen or so casual ones as well.

"Ladies," I called out, glancing around and waiting.

"Yes, Miss Aflora?" one of the figments cooed.

"I'm going to need at least three times this selection," I said. "And don't forget undergarments, socks, and more shoes. Oh, and wands."

A chittering sound followed, the gleeful noise echoing in the chamber. "Oh, yes, as the madam requires!"

The room expanded around me, an entire row of clothing appearing as if waiting for my very command. A glass case followed, wands gleaming inside.

Yes, this would do.

I rubbed my hands together.

You all want me to stay here for the indefinite future? Fine. But I'll be staying in style.

I smiled at my reflection in the mirror. "Thanks for the new wardrobe, Midnight Prince," I whispered, hoping somehow that message reached his pompous ears.

Zephyrus said I had an hour?

Well, I'd take three.

"Ladies, let's get started," I mused to the magical beings. *This is going to be fun.*

CHAPTER NINE

ll right. The Midnight Fae Academy uniforms weren't bad. A lot of black, but my shirts were white.

I finished tying cloak number nine around my neck, testing the weight. All the others were too heavy, the fabric choking me worse than the leather collar around my throat. But this one was made of a light silk and fringed in dark red tones.

Smoothing my hands around it, I twirled, liking the way it feathered around my exposed legs. The Academy skirts were a bit short, hitting me midthigh. Hence, I'd requested some knee-high boots to—

"Not bad," a deep voice murmured behind me. "But I personally think you would look better in my family color, which is purple."

I spun around to find Shade lounging in a chair that didn't exist a moment ago.

"How did you…? Where did you…? What…?" I shook my head, biting my lip to keep from issuing another unfinished question at the willow stump sitting a few feet away from me.

"The collar is a nice touch. Does that make you my pet?" he asked, pushing to his feet to draw closer. "Or is Kolstov trying to claim what's mine?" His fingertips brushed the leather around my throat, sending a hum of energy across my skin and eliciting a hiss from his mouth. "Bastard."

Shade grasped the back of my neck before I could even think to react, pulling my body up against his in a move that stole my breath.

Electricity zipped down my spine from his hold and the rioting device around my throat. It didn't hurt so much as send an unpleasant sensation across my skin. "Shade…"

"How are you, love?" he asked, walking me backward into a wall. "Are they treating you all right? Apart from the collar, of course."

Some of my senses started to return as he pressed his body into mine.

He was the reason I had to wear a collar.

Because *he* had bitten me against my will.

And now he had the audacity to show up and ask me how I was doing? Like he gave a damn about my feelings?

"Oh, you!" I planted my palms against his chest and tried to shove him away. "You're the reason I'm in this mess!"

"You seem to be enjoying said mess," he returned, glancing down at my blouse and black skirt. "Playing fashionista on the royal dime. How fun."

"Because I need an outfit for the Academy I have to attend *because of you*." I attempted to push him again, but he didn't budge an inch.

Instead, he leaned into me more, his hips aligning with mine as he anchored me against the wall. "Still upset, I see." He drew his nose across my cheek, his breath fanning my face. "Allow me to make it up to you, little darling."

"Make it up to me?" I repeated, my nails digging into his blazer. "You've destroyed my life. Possibly even earned us both a death sentence. There is no living way you could make it up to me, Shadow." I was panting by the end of my statement, not because of his close proximity or the way his thigh had slid between mine, but because of the anger heating my blood. "*I hate you.*"

He chuckled and kissed the space below my ear, his palm leaving my neck to grip my hip. "Wrap your arms around me."

"No."

"Mmm." He hoisted me into the air with both hands on my waist. I grabbed his shoulders in response, gasping as he pressed his groin into the apex between my thighs. "Grip me with your legs, baby, or you'll fall."

"Put me down."

"Not a chance." He captured my mouth instead and took full advantage of my shock by slipping his tongue between my lips.

What is happening?

Why is he doing this?

And oh, no, this… can't… be… happening.

Dizziness shot through my mind.

Adrenaline fueled my limbs.

I wanted to *hurt* him.

Needed to fight.

Because this couldn't be allowed to continue!

I clamped down on his tongue, only to be rewarded with the most beautiful taste in response. I froze. Then moaned. *Oh my…* Exquisite decadence filled our mouths, distracting me from my goal and throwing me into a whirl of oblivion that I couldn't escape from. Instead, I fell headfirst into it, allowing my instincts to take over.

My legs were around his waist in a second.

My arms encircling his neck.

And his essence coated my lips, my mouth, my *throat*.

I groaned, craving another swallow more than anything else in the world.

He gave it to me with his tongue, sliding along mine, feeding me that delicious liquid I desired.

One hand remained against my hip while his opposite rose to my hair, his fingers entangling in my strands as he tilted my head to better receive his kiss.

Some part of me was screaming at us to stop.

But I couldn't hear her over the roar of *need* in my thoughts.

Heat unlike anything I ever remembered feeling seared my insides, pulsing through my veins with one driving thought—*more*.

His arousal grew between my thighs, his slacks rubbing the thin barrier of my lace panties. My skirt was up around my hips, my blouse unbuttoned to reveal my bra, and I couldn't remember how it happened. Except it was my hand running down my shirt, my fingers unfastening the final button.

I shivered. "What are you doing to me?" I felt possessed. Owned. Hypnotized by this male. Yet completely lucid and aware. "How are you doing this?"

"This is all you," he whispered, his lips brushing mine. "You bit me, Aflora."

"To make you stop," I remembered, though I couldn't recall *why*. "I don't like you."

He smiled. "Likewise, baby. But that only makes this so much hotter." His mouth recaptured mine before I could reply, his touch robbing me of my ability to think.

His hands were everywhere and nowhere at the same time.

His kiss a brand against my lips.

His dick throbbing against the place I needed to be touched most.

Too many clothes.

My wrists were caught in one of his hands and hoisted above my head. "Not yet," he breathed. "Not here."

"Not what?" I replied, dazed.

"Shh," he hushed, his refreshing scent surrounding me in a jungle of sensation.

Trees.

Water.

Flowers in full bloom.

The familiarity of the aromas had me sighing in contentment while my body hummed to life with renewed passion.

I kissed him with all of my being, gifting him with the life thriving in my soul, only to be ensnared in his dark web in return. He tugged me under, filling me with a venomous energy that felt wrong beneath my skin.

"Shade," I whimpered, writhing against him.

"I've got you," he promised.

But I didn't believe him.

I couldn't trust him.

Just as Zephyrus said—I'd be wise to develop a similar armor. One outlined in distrust.

My limbs began to shake.

Tears slid from my eyes.

The world rumbled around me, and I couldn't make it stop, even while an inferno built inside me, begging to be released.

It terrified me.

Enthralled me.

Owned me.

Shade's tongue dominated mine, his cock a thick presence against my core, pushing me to the precipice of something terrifying. I clung to him with all my strength, horrified and captivated at the same time. Nothing I could do would stop this. I felt it in my very blood, an unerring compulsion to give in to Shade's ministrations.

A part of me rebelled.

The other part… rejoiced.

I hated him more in that moment than anyone else in my entire existence. Yet my craving for him won.

Ecstasy erupted inside me, drawing a scream from my throat that was filled with self-loathing and pain. And also represented the most powerful orgasm of my life.

I wasn't a complete innocent.

I'd played with Glacier countless times, and while the Water Fae was good in bed, he *never* made me feel quite like this.

Like liquid ice.

Hot on the inside, frozen on the outside.

A tremor rocked me from head to toe, my rapture subsiding beneath a fresh wave of horror.

I couldn't discern up from down, right from wrong, or passion from hate. Shade's lips were at my neck, his kiss far too tender for my liking. I'd prefer his bite so I could hate him more. Only, he held me with worship in his touch, his warm body wrapped around me in a false blanket of protection.

"I hate you," I whispered, my eyes wet. "I hate you. I hate you. I hate you."

"I know," he replied softly. "I hate myself, too." He nuzzled my throat, sighing. "I'm not supposed to be here, but I wanted to make sure you were okay."

"I'm not okay," I told him, shuddering. "Not okay at all."

He kissed my jaw before pulling back to meet my gaze. "You're strong, little rose," he said softly, the new nickname underlined in a deep caress. "We'll both be okay in the end. You'll see." He pressed his lips to mine once more as he carried me to the chair. Lowering me into it, he hovered over me with a sinful look. "I need to go before Guardian Zephyrus finishes his spell. But I'll see you again soon. In your dreams."

Shade vanished into a cloud of smoke that seemed to take up the entire room, his existence touching every article of clothing and all the walls, until all I could see was darkness.

"Aflora!" Zephyrus's furious voice slapped me across the face, jolting me from the chair. He stood before me with a livid expression, his wand in his hand.

I frowned at him, then whirled around the unfamiliar room. *Wait…* I glanced down to find myself fully clothed and wrapped up in a cloak like a blanket.

My skirt looked brand new, my blouse fully buttoned, and I even had on knee-high boots.

I blinked. "What…?"

"A sleep enchantment," Zephyrus hissed. "That little prick." He shook his head, a curse falling from his full lips. "He's circumventing the rules with mind play. I'd be impressed if he wasn't breaking a hundred protocols to do it."

"So he wasn't… That didn't… I…" My cheeks heated, unable to finish. My damp panties were the only thing on me that matched my supposed dream. So either I'd woken up turned on or I'd orgasmed in my sleep.

Which meant Zephyrus had probably seen it.

Oh, Mother Earth… Warmth touched every inch of my being at the thought of what he'd witnessed.

Fortunately, he didn't seem all that keen to mention it.

"We're done shopping," he said instead, turning on a wave of superiority, an array of bags forming around him. "I assume that's your cape of choice. Same with the wand. The other items will be in your wardrobe by the time we get back." He glanced at my boots and skirt. "A little schoolgirl for our trip back, but I doubt anyone will notice. Let's go."

"Wait, what wand?" I asked. "I didn't pick one."

"Check your pocket, Aflora. One already picked you."

I patted the side of my cape, my eyes widening. "They do that?"

He just gave me a flat look and gestured with his chin toward a mirror. Assuming he meant for me to walk through it, I did and found myself in the cloakroom once more.

My cape billowed around me as I twisted in a sharp circle. "How…?"

"You have so much to learn about our world," Zephyrus replied as he retrieved his cloak and wrapped it around his shoulders with a flourish. "Also, a wand isn't a magical being. It's an extension of our power."

With a wave of his hand, a keypad appeared, and he punched in a code that I caught this time. Of course, it was to the place I didn't really want to go, so not all that helpful.

"We use them as a conduit," he continued, his arm sliding around my shoulders to hold me close while the portal began to whirl around us. "As I said, it's an extension of your power. It helps you focus on a single book on a shelf rather than an entire collection."

Cawing pierced my skull as the crows took over, welcoming us back to the Academy grounds.

In minutes, they were back to their rocky forms, dotting the courtyard.

Flames ignited along the paths again, illuminating the otherwise quiet campus.

"When do students start to arrive?" I asked as he led the way back to Kolstov's building.

"Some are already here but keeping to themselves. The majority will return in five days' time to attend the annual autumn bonfire." He flicked his wrist, sending the bags ahead in a train that moved toward the residence. "Let's take a tour before heading back. We can stop by the cafeteria as well and grab something to eat."

My stomach grumbled at the idea, agreeing.

Aside from the tea he'd forced on me after waking up, I hadn't eaten at all.

"Just be warned," he added, already walking. "The food on Academy grounds is of the human variety. So either you're going to have to learn some meal-conjuring spells or you're going to need to change your tastes. I recommended the latter." He snapped his fingers, a torch appearing in his hand. "Now try to keep up, Aflora. I'm going to give you a crash course in Academy life, and I won't be repeating myself."

CHAPTER TEN

I did not miss this place.

The food.

The lounging crows.

The general aura of misery.

In a week, this place would be the definition of hell, brimming with students all eager to continue their studies.

I envied them.

My entire life had been determined before my birth, my duty to a family I'd grown to loathe. Anything and everything Malik Nacht told me to do, I did.

Including taking a job as a headmaster at the Academy when I had no interest or desire to teach.

I took a sip of my coffee, enjoying the way it scalded my mouth and throat on the way down. Pain made me feel alive. Unlike my current surroundings.

Aflora sat across from me, a pout on her full lips as she eyed the contents of our trays. I'd selected an array of my favorites for her to try, yet she didn't seem keen on any of them.

Impossible female.

She didn't belong here any more than I did.

I set my mug down and folded my arms on the table, leaning toward her. "Want a magic lesson?"

We hadn't spoken much during the tour. Mostly just me gesturing at buildings and telling her what courses were held where, as well as pointing out the various residential units. She remained studiously quiet the whole time, probably because she didn't plan to stay here long.

Given what I witnessed inside AcaWard earlier, she'd be here a lot longer than she anticipated. Because Shade clearly possessed a hold over her psyche, something that suggested their blood bond was a lot stronger than it should be.

Which meant their powers were going to grow together.

And that would very likely lead to their deaths.

A disappointing thought, but realistic.

"What kind of lesson?" Aflora asked, referring to my query.

"Well, as you don't seem keen on the food here, I'll teach you an easy spell for acquiring alternatives." And in turn demonstrate why she needed to change her attitude about our sustenance offerings.

Acquisition spells required energy.

Something that would become quite evident to her in a matter of minutes.

I pulled out my wand and set it on the table. "As I mentioned earlier, wands are not the source of magic. We merely use them to help focus the energy. I'll give you an example." We had an entire table to work with, the other twenty chairs around it empty, therefore providing me with the room to exaggerate this lesson a little. "The spell for creating something edible is *Tareero Tamida* and then the item."

Pretty simple, really. But her expression told me she didn't agree.

"So I just say the two words and the food I want, then it pops up."

"Well, you need to put some magic behind it. But yes, that's the general idea."

She frowned at me. "And I use the wand?"

"It's not required, no. As I said, a wand focuses our magic." Her creasing forehead told me she wasn't following. "Here. I'll provide an example. Give me a food item you're craving."

"Uh, I don't know. A sandwich?"

Now I was the one frowning. "You have a sandwich." I pointed to the ham and cheese melt on her plate.

"That's not a sandwich."

"It's definitely a sandwich."

"This has bread and meat and cheese. A sandwich is leafy greens baked to perfection with yammock filling, berries, and sometimes a sliver of hartmint, if you're feeling gluttonous."

Right. I didn't know what any of those things were. "How about another loaf instead?" That I at least knew how to make as I'd eaten one before.

Her lips twisted as she shrugged. "Sure. That works. Can you make a coldberry loaf?"

"There are different types of loaves?"

After studying me for a long moment, she said, "A shroom loaf is fine."

Good because that was the only one I knew how to make. Rather than waste time on explaining the plan again, I just performed the spell. "*Tareero Tamida loaf.*"

One the size of her entire plate appeared, causing her eyes to widen.

"That's huge," she gasped out.

"Yeah. Because I didn't control the size with my wand." Not exactly true. Children could perform this kind of magic in their sleep and still make an appropriate loaf, but I wanted to exaggerate the results for teaching purposes.

Hey, look at me living up to my headmaster role, I thought sourly.

Wouldn't King Malik be so proud?

Arrogant fuck.

Clearing my throat, I pushed the negative thoughts away and refocused. "Using the conduit, you can control the magical outcome." I picked up my wand and performed the spell again, this time creating a perfectly proportioned loaf. Then I muttered a cleanup spell that dissolved all the food on the table—including the items we'd picked up from the chef—and said, "You try."

She considered for a moment, then nodded. "All right." Taking her wand out of her cloak, she gave it a little wave while saying, "*Tareero Tamida sandwich.*"

Nothing.

Not even a twitch of magic.

I leaned back in my chair and watched as she tried again.

And again.

And again.

All without any kind of result or a single hint of feeling.

After her tenth go at it, she huffed, "This isn't working."

"Clearly."

She stared at me, waiting.

If she expected me to give her more directions, then she had another think coming. I already explained how the process worked. If she couldn't figure out how to apply it, that was on her, not me. Besides, I shouldn't even be here.

"Is my wand broken?" she asked, holding out the magical conduit.

I didn't even look at it. "No." *Because it's not about the wand*, I added to myself. She needed to figure that out on her own. Magic came from the blood. I couldn't really help her find the link. She needed to do that herself.

"Well, that's helpful," she muttered, putting away her wand. "Could you at least explain how I make it work?" she asked slowly as if speaking to an idiot.

I answered her in the same tone with, "You access your magic."

"Right. How?"

"How do you call on your earth essence?" I countered.

"It's a natural connection through my soul."

"Then there you go," I replied. "Class dismissed."

She pointed to the collar at her neck. "I think you're forgetting this."

"You're letting a necklace hold you back? How disappointing." It only blocked her earth magic, not her access to the dark arts. I could admit that out loud, but that would belittle this exercise.

"Holding me back?" she repeated. "It cut me off from my gifts!"

"And?"

She gaped at me. "Wow. You are the worst teacher I've ever met."

"It's my first year," I offered in explanation. "And I technically haven't started yet."

"Well, you're off to a horrible start," she muttered.

I lifted a shoulder, unbothered by her attempt at an insult. This wasn't my career choice. And if I had it my way, I'd be done before I even started.

"So you all expect me to perform magic with a handicap," she drawled. "Oh, but I may not have any dark magic at all, which this exercise seems to confirm."

"Yet you dismantled a high-level spell inside your mind yesterday, which suggests otherwise," I pointed out. "Not just anyone can outmaneuver a Nacht binding charm."

"The little web, you mean?"

"There was nothing little about it." Yet, that she considered it *little* said quite a bit. "How did you dismantle it?" I'd wondered the same thing last night but had been too amused by her attacking Kols with a thwomp. Dangerous, yes. And entertaining as fuck. I was almost disappointed when she lost.

Alas, she always would.

"I found a piece of my light and followed it," she answered vaguely. "I don't see any light now because of this." She gestured to her throat again.

"That cuts you off from your elements, not the dark magic growing inside you." Which I sensed humming just beneath her skin. Another hint I could provide her with, but to what purpose? The best way to learn was by doing, not being led. If she wanted any hope of surviving in our world, then she needed to start thinking and acting for herself. Not relying on others to protect her.

Even if that was technically my job for the time being.

She shook her head. "This is a waste of time."

"Is it?" I drawled. "I had no idea."

"Wow. This is really not the right career path for you."

I smiled. "Your reasoning skills are outstanding, Aflora." I leaned forward. "And you couldn't be more right."

"Then why are you here?" she demanded.

"Because I'm serving my duty to the crown as prescribed." *Whether I like it or not,* I added to myself. But enough about that. "Regarding your powers, Midnight Fae pull through our blood, not our souls. So try that instead."

There. I'd tossed her a bone. Now no one could accuse me of not trying to help.

"Through my blood," she repeated, her tone skeptical. "Right."

"Look, if you don't want to try, then eat the shit offered up at the buffet and let's head back. I could use a nap, and you have a pile of textbooks to start reading." Not that any of them would help her.

This poor girl was utterly fucked.

And so not my problem.

Then why are you trying to teach her? some unhelpful voice in the back of my mind asked.

I shoved it away. I wasn't helping her, just providing some guidance to get her started.

Aflora glowered at me, her blue eyes glittering in a way that reminded me of sex.

Hot.

Passionate.

Fierce.

Sex.

The kind of fuck I enjoyed.

Not. Happening.

Except I always did favor the forbidden. And nothing could be more forbidden than the female sitting across from me. With her full, pouty mouth, delicate jaw, slender throat, and, mmm, that body. She might be wrapped up in a cloak right now, but I'd already noticed her ample assets—pert tits, slender waist, and a heart-shaped ass.

I wasn't blind.

Aflora was a stunning woman. And strictly off-limits for a myriad of reasons.

Which only made her more appealing.

"*Tareero Tamida sandwich,*" she said suddenly, her tone underlined in power.

My lips parted as a giant, wrap-like green blob appeared, its front end landing between us as it stretched across the entire length of the very long table and down onto the floor.

Aflora's narrowed eyes quickly widened. "Oh… wand."

Yeah. Wand.

But I wasn't so much worried about the still-growing sandwich as I was concerned about the pale shock spreading across her cheeks. "Aflora—"

She began to tremble, her cerulean irises rolling into the back of her head as the energy wilted from her small frame.

Shit.

I jumped out of my chair and across the table—and the ever-growing monstrosity on top of it—and landed at her side in time to catch her before she went down.

"*Qalto,*" I snapped, my spell overpowering hers and dissolving the green atrocity into dust.

Aflora moaned, her consciousness fighting for life as her body gave out completely.

"This is why I recommend you eat our food," I informed her softly. "Magic requires strength, and strength comes from proper nutrition."

If she heard me, she didn't reply.

With a sigh, I lifted her into my arms. "I guess we'll continue this lesson later."

Whenever she woke up.

CHAPTER ELEVEN

AFLORA

Five days of reading and I still didn't understand how dark magic worked. It felt unnatural and wrong, like I had to access an inappropriate part of myself to activate my abilities.

Because I don't belong here, I thought for the millionth time.

Not being able to ignite the Midnight Fae influence inside me was probably a good thing. It meant this forced bond with Shade wouldn't amount to much. Maybe it would disappear soon.

When I suggested that hopeful sentiment to Zephyrus yesterday, he'd remained as stoic as ever, never giving anything away.

He was the worst teacher in all the fae kingdoms and totally unapologetic about it.

Obviously, neither of us wanted to be here. Which gave us something in common. Not that it brought us any closer.

No, Zephyrus was a closed book.

And I didn't try to pry him open.

Instead, I spent most of my time reading alone in my new room. When my stomach complained, either I joined him for meals in the living area or we walked to the cafeteria. At some point he'd gone shopping, or perhaps had food delivered, some of which were items I recognized. However, most were human meals.

Ugh.

My insides still crawled from the breakfast he'd forced upon me. Eggs with cheese and onions. *An omelet*, he'd called it.

Gross.

I preferred to label it as *torture*, but I ate the monstrosity because he refused to make anything else, and my wand didn't want to cooperate. Turns out, his whole lecture about magic requiring energy was right. The less I ate, the worse I performed.

While part of me preferred not to be able to access the dark powers, the other part of me recognized that I needed the magic to survive in this world.

Because yeah, Midnight Fae Academy was proving to have a dangerous campus. Not only were those snakelike vines watching my every move, but I also had all types of wildlife eyeing me with curiosity. And I learned pretty fast that none of the plants or animals in this realm were kind.

My shoulder winced with the reminder of the fire gnat I met last night.

Not a pretty lightning bug, but a beast with sharp teeth and a fiery after-bite.

Zephyrus had watched the entire thing with a bored expression, not once helping me. When I demanded to know why, he merely shrugged and said, "It won't kill you."

Just thinking about it brought a scowl to my face. Again.

Headmaster Zephyrus served as proof that beauty on the outside did not equate to beauty on the inside. Because his exterior sure was gorgeous, but inside him lived a dark, unhelpful jackass of a man who considered me more of a burden than a project.

Well, fine. He could take his uncooperative behavior and shove it up his muscular butt. Not that I'd spent a lot of time admiring said butt. Or thinking about how many hours he had to clock at the gym to maintain such a fit physique.

Right, so that was a lie. But not many Elemental Fae were warriors, so Zephyrus's fighter build intrigued me a little. *Strong* didn't seem like an adequate enough adjective for him. He practically oozed power from his pores without even trying. Kind of like Kolstov, but in a different way.

With a shake of my head, I pushed away thoughts of the two males and focused on the textbook in my lap. It explained Midnight Fae hierarchy and all the bloodlines. Zephyrus had told me there were only five, but according to my book, there were actually six types of Midnight Fae.

I spent yesterday reading up on the Elite Bloods and Kolstov's family legacy as the oldest royals of that line. As primary conduits for the dark-magic source, Elite Bloods were considered the most powerful of Midnight Fae kind, hence their leadership over all the others.

The Warrior Bloods were particularly gifted in physical strength and agility, allowing them to serve as Guardians of the Elite Bloods. Ergo, Zephyrus's role. What I still didn't understand was why he'd been relegated to the Academy when his family had a long-standing history of protecting the Nachts. From what I'd read, him being here was a demotion of epic proportions. If he wasn't such a jerk, I'd ask him.

Opening my book, I started reading up on the next bloodline.

The Death Bloods.

Shadow's family served as the monarchs, with Aswad as the current king. Their powers were linked to necromancy and the harsher sides of dark magic.

It seemed they also maintained access to the source, but in a much different way, through the art of—

A crash inside the suite jolted me upright and off the bed.

The sound of feminine laughter followed.

I frowned. Zephyrus had mentioned that students would be moving back in today. Something about a bonfire kickoff later tonight. Apparently, it was the thing to do. I'd considered using the massive distraction on campus as a potential time to escape, but I had nowhere to go.

The fact that Claire hadn't reached out to me yet confirmed the Elemental Fae Council's fear in having me return. Given what recently happened in that realm, I understood. The last notion they would want to entertain at the moment was a potential hybrid Elemental-Midnight Fae.

Except I didn't feel any different.

Other than the fact that I couldn't access my earth.

I really hoped Sol and Claire were holding the source together in my absence. They were the only others in existence who could access earth magic in a similar way to me. Their connections weren't as strong as mine but should be enough to help the Earth Fae maintain their powers.

Blowing out a breath, I started reading again, when male voices trickled down the hallway.

Kolstov, I thought, recognizing the deep tone.

A knock sounded at my door, followed by, "That's my five-second warning, princess. Try not to be naked again."

I glowered at the door. "Dick," I muttered, putting my book off to the side and standing just as he followed through on his five-second promise.

His bright gold irises slid over my shirt and jeans, amusement shining in his depths. "I'm almost disappointed to find you clothed."

Uh-huh. "Well, I *am* disappointed that you're back," I returned, adding a saccharine smile at the end.

He chuckled. "Yeah, I missed you too, sweetheart."

I rolled my eyes. "I bet."

"Stop flirting and introduce us." The smooth voice came from the hallway just as a male joined Kolstov in the doorway. I recognized him from my textbook.

"Trayton Nacht," I said. "Huh. So the photos really do update in real time." I'd wondered that when the images kept shifting around last night, some sort of magic allowing them to update with each passing moment.

"Have you been studying already?" Kolstov asked, a teasing note to his voice. "I suppose you did have a lot to catch up on."

Not this again. "Yeah, I've had some time in solitary this week to read, and since my wand doesn't work, I decided to study the different bloodlines instead."

He leaned against my doorway, arching a haughty brow. "Learn anything interesting?"

"Yeah, the Death Bloods have more intriguing powers than the Elite

Bloods." I'd read in the texts that the two types of Midnight Fae had been at war for centuries, and Kolstov's darkening expression confirmed it.

Score one for Aflora, I thought, smirking inside.

"I suppose you're obligated to say that as the illegally chosen mate of the future Death Blood Monarch. Pity you couldn't have been claimed by a worthier bloodline."

And Kolstov evens the match by volleying an equally hurtful statement back at Aflora, my mental voice added, killing my inner victory lap. "Like yours?" I countered. "No, thanks."

"Don't knock it 'til you try it, baby," he drawled.

Trayton shook his head. "Stop flirting with our new roommate."

"That's like telling Kols to stop breathing." A petite female popped up at Trayton's side, her white-blonde head barely clearing his shoulder. Her bright blue eyes met mine. "I'm Ella. Let me know if these two assholes are bothering you, and I'll set them straight."

Trayton gave her an indulgent grin as he wrapped his arm around her waist. "Yeah? Tell me how you plan to do that."

"Now who's flirting?" Kolstov put in.

"Oh, I'm not flirting." Trayton faced Ella and started to back her up against a wall. "We're way past our flirting stage."

Ella snorted as she grabbed his lean hips. "Always so romantic."

"You love me anyway."

"Do I?" She tapped her chin thoughtfully. "Sometimes I don't know why."

"And you chose the room beside theirs," Kolstov murmured to me, having entered my space. He glanced around with a curious gaze. "It's boring as fuck in here."

"I'm sorry. Was I supposed to decorate?" I asked, batting my eyes. "Because I missed that memo."

He pulled out his wand. "Allow me to help."

I grabbed his wrist before he could wave it around. "No. I don't plan to stay long."

"Yeah?" He stared down at me with those piercing irises, causing my breath to catch in my throat.

Why were all the Midnight Fae so good-looking? Even his brother was a sight to behold.

"Where do you plan on going?" Kolstov asked softly, taking a step closer.

I didn't release his wrist, even though I probably should have. But his nearness had me frozen before him. His rich, masculine scent swathing me in a cloud of intoxicating male.

"I..." I trailed off, my throat constricting tightly.

His gaze dropped to my lips. I licked them on impulse, my mouth going dry. Something about Kolstov called to my inner fae. His power was a worthy mate to my earth essence, only because we both possessed royal bloodlines. I'd felt it when our energy danced in the living area a few days ago.

But he wasn't an Elemental Fae and therefore not truly an ideal match.

Even if my instincts said otherwise.

"Hmm, I think you do want a taste," Kolstov whispered, his free hand going to my hip. "If you're good, maybe I'll allow—"

"Why is my new suite next to yours?" Zephyrus demanded from the doorway. "The whole purpose of this new assignment, according to your father, is to provide students with my superior knowledge. Students, being Warrior Bloods, not Elite Bloods."

Kolstov released me, his wrist easily leaving my grasp as he spun around, giving me his back. "We both know it's a temporary assignment."

"My living next to you? Or my playing the role of teacher?" The bitterness in Zephyrus's tone matched his expression.

"The latter."

"Right. Because you plan to fix it when you become king."

"Are we really going to have this argument again?" Kolstov suddenly sounded tired. "Come on, Zeph. You know why this happened."

The headmaster's eyes narrowed for a long moment before he turned and left without another word.

Kolstov sighed, following him. "You can keep punishing me all you want. It won't stop me from—"

"Don't," Zephyrus interjected. "Just. *Don't.*"

"Then stop being a dick" was the reply.

"Fuck you."

A crashing sound made me jump. I poked my head around the door just in time to see Trayton leaving a freshly kissed Ella behind in the hallway. She blinked after him, then glanced at me. "Welcome to the Nacht family drama. Never a dull moment."

Sounds of a scuffle came from the living room, which suggested the guys were fighting. An image of Zephyrus pinning Kolstov entered my mind, provoked by the first time I'd seen them together.

Zephyrus struck me as the stronger of the two, but I'd tasted a glimpse of Kolstov's power, and yeah, they were definitely evenly matched.

"Don't worry. Tray will make sure they don't destroy anything too valuable," Ella said, moving past me into the room. She glanced around, much like Kolstov had. "Boring maybe, but I get it. You don't want to be here. Shade's a fucking prick for biting you."

My lips twitched. *Finally, someone who gets it.*

She faced me, adding, "My mate at least introduced me to the Midnight Fae realm before biting me."

"Introduced you?" I repeated, her statement confusing me. "You mean you weren't born here?"

"I'm a Halfling," she informed me, then paused as if waiting for a reaction.

"So you grew up in the Human Realm." It was a guess based on her earlier claim about entering the realm.

"I did." The challenge in her tone confused me.

"Did you know you were part fae?"

"No, not until Tray told me."

My eyebrows rose. "Well, that must have been quite a shock."

"Yeah, I imagine it's similar to being bitten against your will and forced to attend an Academy in another realm." She glanced at the book on my bed and smirked. "Ah, the Midnight Fae factions. What chapter are you on?"

"I just started reading about the Death Bloods."

She nodded. "Want a crash course in the bloodlines? It'll be faster than reading that boring thing."

"You're offering to teach me?" I shook my head at how stupid that sounded out loud. "Sorry, the others haven't been very… helpful." Technically, Zephyrus had tried a little. And Kolstov, well, he was just being a pompous ass about me not studying Midnight Fae kind while growing up.

Ella snorted and collapsed onto the edge of my bed. "Kolstov's a bit preoccupied with his future, and Zephyrus is, uh, not teacher material."

"Yet he's a headmaster."

"Yeah, he's going to make our lives hell this year," Ella muttered. "Anyway, enough about that. What you need is a quick overview, something I'm very equipped to provide considering I had to learn all this myself recently." She patted the bed beside her. "I promise I don't bite. All my blood intake is through food."

I gaped at her, the comment so tongue in cheek that it took me off guard.

Which caused her to laugh. "Your expression is priceless and probably similar to mine when Tray first told me about Midnight Fae drinking blood. Oh, but that reminds me. Lesson number one: Don't call them vampires. They hate that."

"Yeah, Kolstov may have mentioned that after I called him a bloodsucker."

Her lips twitched. "Bet he loved that."

"Not so much."

She laughed. "Well, don't let him bother you. He's a womanizing jackass, but deep down, he has a heart. You just have to really dig to find it."

I finally joined her on the bed, feeling somewhat at ease for the first time in almost a week. Something about Ella relaxed me. Maybe it was her calm demeanor or, more likely, her frank assessments. I enjoyed her candor and her politeness.

She didn't judge me for not knowing everything about the Midnight Fae.

And I appreciated it more than she could know.

"Okay, so let me break this down for you," she said, tucking one leg underneath her while the other bounced off the side of the bed. "There are five main bloodlines. You know the names?"

I nodded. "Death Bloods, Elite Bloods, Sangré Bloods, Warrior Bloods, and Malefic Bloods."

"Do you know what they do?"

"I've only read that Elite Bloods maintain the central source of dark magic and Death Bloods access the harshest resources from a different entry point. They prefer lethal magic and dabble in necromancy." I picked up the book.

"One thing I don't really get is how they access the source indirectly. That was the part I was reading when you all arrived."

Ella picked up the book and tossed it to the side. "Yeah, no. Trust me, you want the verbal lesson, not the text one. All bloodlines access dark-magic sources, but the Elites have the most access, which is why they're considered royalty. They're the strongest. All those black lines pulsating on Kols's neck and arms, leading to his heart? Yeah, that's the source transferring reign to him one stroke of power at a time. Scary shit, if you ask me."

I had noticed the writhing inky vines along his neck and hands but didn't realize they stretched up his arms. "Is it permanent?" I wondered out loud.

"No. Apparently, it disappears after he ascends." She shrugged. "I guess we'll see. Anyway, the Death Bloods access the darkest sections of the source. They literally thrive on Death Magic. So, like necromancy, as you said. It's rumored they're just as powerful as the Elite Bloods, which explains why Malik and Aswad hate each other."

The two reigning monarchs, I thought, recognizing the names.

"Then there are the Warrior Bloods, like Zeph, who specialize in defensive magic. They're usually carved out of stone in the sense that they are all hard lines, muscular, athletic, and stoic as fuck. So if Zeph was a dick this week, don't take it personally. They're all like that. And he's particularly moody after having been removed from Kols's personal guard. The whole headmaster position is a demotion of sorts."

"And why did that happen?" I asked.

Ella's lips twisted to the side. "Uh, so, Kols and Zeph… they like to share women. And let's just say, they shared the wrong one. Things went to hell from there."

"They both fell in love with her?" I guessed.

Ella laughed loudly and shook her head. "Oh, God no. Nothing like that. Kols? Love? That's like a bad joke." She shook her head, her shoulders vibrating from suppressed laughter. "But yeah, nothing like that. Anyway, the Sangré Bloods are next. Their power lies in intelligence. They're pretty much wizards when it comes to playing chess." She pointed to the collar around my neck. "That was developed by a Sangré Blood. I can tell by the power swirling around it."

Her not-so-subtle change of subject back to our lesson left me curious about the truth between Zephyrus and Kolstov, but I allowed her to continue.

"So the Sangré Bloods are highly intellectual," I inferred.

"Yep. You'll be able to identify them by their bald heads. They draw these patterns on their skin, and the more intense the design, the more powerful the fae. It's sort of their way of showing off, or that's the way I see it, anyway. The Warrior Bloods wear their muscles and scars, the Sangré Bloods paint beautiful patterns on their heads, the Elite Bloods dress in expensive jewels and robes, and the Death Bloods love their skull shit."

"Sounds… charming."

She scoffed. "Yeah. Shade is the lead asshat on campus, but trust me, the rest of them are just as dark as he is."

"Great. I can't wait," I deadpanned.

Her lips curled. "I like you. As much as I know you don't want to stay, I'm looking forward to having your around for a bit. You can help me keep Tray and Kols in line."

"Yeah, I doubt they'll listen to me at all."

"Oh, I'll teach you my ways," Ella promised. "You'll see. We can tame them together."

I doubted that but smiled anyway. "So what about the Malefic Bloods?"

"Ah, yes, the final of the five. The Malefic Bloods specialize in offensive magic. They're like the polar opposite of the Warrior Bloods. The latter defends, the former prefers spells that create damage. When I first learned all this, I called them the malicious ones, to help remember that their magic is dangerous and often intentionally cruel."

Right. Avoid that sect of Midnight Fae, I noted to myself. "Is there a way to tell them all apart? I mean, the Sangré Bloods will be obvious, from what you've said. What about the others?"

Her blue eyes captured mine, a grin forming in their depths. "Actually, how about we continue this lesson tonight during the bonfire. That way, I can show you more than tell you."

"Zephyrus mentioned the bonfire."

"Yeah, it's an annual tradition," she replied, bouncing off my bed. "It's actually pretty fun. But a word of advice? Don't drink the beezlepunch. You'll regret it." She started toward the door. "I'm going to make some sandwiches if you want any. I'm sure the idiots will be starved from throwing all that magic around. Feel free to join us whenever you're ready."

CHAPTER TWELVE

AFLORA

I didn't join Ella for sandwiches but did agree to follow her down to the bonfire with Trayton. Kolstov and Zephyrus had disappeared, whether together or apart, I wasn't sure. I also didn't care.

Or that was what I kept telling myself.

I *shouldn't* care.

They were just two hot fae handling their own problems. It had nothing to do with me. My curiosity as to what the hell happened between them paled in comparison to my need to survive this new world.

Yet, a part of me kept hearing Ella's casual statement about how the two men used to share women.

It wasn't uncommon in the Elemental Fae realm for us to mate more than once, especially when a fae had access to multiple elements. Our new queen had access to all five elements and therefore required five mates to satisfy her ever-growing power. Yet, that wasn't what Ella had meant.

She'd implied they shared women for pleasure.

And now I wondered what that entailed. Because being sandwiched between those two beautiful, fierce males? Yeah, that painted a pretty hot picture.

One I quickly doused water on because it would never happen.

At least, not outside my head.

Because in my head, it was definitely already happening.

And I really, really needed it to stop so I could properly focus on whatever Ella was saying beside me. Something about the bloodline colors.

Despite everyone wearing casual clothes, they all seemed to be dressed in similar shades.

"The Malefic Bloods wear solid black all the time. They never wear color," she said, nodding toward a group of Midnight Fae socializing on one side of the bonfire.

"Because we're at the Academy?" I wondered out loud. I'd opted for one of the Academy-regulated black skirts and a plain white button-down top. Nothing too fancy, but appropriate for the school grounds. Ella had chosen jeans and a tank top. Most of the others were in their cloaks, the females in skirts, the guys in slacks.

Except for the Elite Bloods. They all seemed to be showing off their fashion sense with a variety of different colors. I'd recognized them almost immediately because of the power swirling around them—it reminded me of Kolstov.

"No. They wear black everywhere regardless of the event or occasion. It's their signature color." She shrugged. "All the bloodlines have one. Death Bloods are purple. Sangré Bloods are navy. Warrior Bloods prefer a deep green, like the color of the LethaForest that surrounds our campus. Elite Bloods wear dark red. And Malefic Bloods…" She nodded toward the same group, finishing her statement.

Wear black, I translated. "What's a LethaForest?" I asked, glancing around the open meadow and searching for trees. We weren't near the campus buildings anymore, but we weren't in a woodsy area either.

"Beyond the walls," she explained. "We're still in Academy proper. But if you go past the gargoyle-guarded gates, you'll quickly find the LethaForest. Don't go in there alone. There's a bunch of scary shit that lives in there, and it's filled with wild thwomps." She shivered with the statement, something that caused Trayton's lips to curl down as he approached with two glasses of some sort of drink.

He handed her one. "Are you okay?"

"Just warning Aflora about the LethaForest."

His frown disappeared into a knowing grin as he held out the other cup for me. I accepted it with a softly uttered "Thanks."

"You're welcome. And yeah, Ella isn't a fan of things that go bump in the night. When I mated her, I didn't realize she was afraid of phantoms. Had I known…" He let that hang, and Ella elbowed him in the side.

"Shut it. You grew up in this world. I didn't. And those *phantoms* are freaky as fuck."

He lifted a shoulder. "That's why I don't go near them."

"Yeah, yeah. I'm never going to live that down, am I?"

"Nope."

She rolled her eyes, refocusing on me. "I may have gone exploring my first year here. And I may have found myself surrounded by ghostly knights with swords that weren't corporeal, but very real. They were not happy with me for disturbing their nest, or whatever they called it."

"Haven," Trayton corrected. "You totally slept through our Wild Creepers course last year, didn't you?"

"No. But your world is full of so many make-believe critters that it's hard to keep them all straight."

"Uh-huh. I think—"

I dropped my cup as Shade appeared across the way, flanked by two male Midnight Fae. His gaze instantly met mine, his icy blue eyes smoldering from the embers of the flames separating us.

"Grr, I have things to say to you," I growled, mostly to myself since Shade couldn't hear me yet.

"What?" Ella's forehead creased.

Trayton bent to pick up my glass, the contents all over the obsidian grass below. I couldn't even take a moment to consider how improper that color was for *greenery*. "Aflora?" he prompted, arching a brow.

I could see the pair watching me from my peripheral vision, their expressions ones of matching confusion. Until Trayton followed my stare. "Oh."

Yeah. Oh. "Hold my flowers," I said, taking off toward my now smirking Midnight Fae *mate*.

"Hold her flowers?" I overheard Ella repeat behind me. "Is that supposed to be like holding a beer?"

"Maybe?" Trayton replied.

I ignored them.

My colloquialisms clearly didn't belong in this realm. Just as I didn't. But nothing could be done about that now.

Except maybe kick the tulip arse of the Midnight Fae who had forced me into this situation.

He watched my approach, amusement dancing in his features. "Hello, gorgeous."

His expression and words infuriated me so much that I couldn't stop my fist from landing right in his face.

A hush fell over the air around us, shock displayed on the faces of those flanking Shade. I didn't care. I wound up my fist, ready to hit him again, only to find my wrist caught in his hand.

His smirk died behind a mask of annoyance as he used his grip on my wrist to yank me into his hard body. "It seems you need a lesson on how to properly greet an old friend."

"Old friend?" I huffed a laugh. "Yeah, you're certainly not that."

My knee angled upward, aiming for his groin.

But I hit his thigh instead.

His eyes narrowed threateningly. "Who taught you how to fight? A flower?"

He whirled me around in a cloud of smoke that clogged my lungs and blinded my vision. I spun, searching for freedom, only to find my back pressed against something hard. Squirming, I tried to escape, but another wall hit my front, two strong palms grasping my hips and holding me in place.

"Let me go!" I demanded.

"Too late for that, princess," he replied, his lips against my ear. "You're already mine."

I grasped his shoulders—confirming Shade was the wall in front of me—and tried to use the surface at my back for leverage to shove him away.

But he remained immobile, his strength overpowering mine far too easily.

A whimper caught in my throat. He'd ensnared me in less than a minute, capturing me in this thick, smoky blanket. "Don't you dare bite me again," I snapped, feeling utterly helpless and infuriated at the same time.

"You came at me, baby," he whispered menacingly. "What kind of mate would I be if I didn't punish you properly, hmm?"

"I'm already being punished, you willow stump!"

He chuckled, shaking his head against my neck. "Darling Aflora, we really do need to improve your vocabulary." He kissed my racing pulse, sending a shiver down my spine that seemed to settle in my lower belly.

No, not a shiver.

A tremble.

One that ignited a subtle quake inside that terrified me even more.

Because it meant some sick and twisted part of me enjoyed his touch.

I squeezed my eyes shut, forcing that sensation to subside. *No. No. No.*

His teeth grazed my skin, stirring goose bumps down my arms. "Please don't," I begged, my nails digging into his cloak.

If he bit me again, it would deepen the bond. Kolstov said Shade had only initiated the bond and a second bite would seal it. Then a third… I shuddered, unable to finish the consideration because I couldn't allow that to happen.

Or any of it.

I needed to stop him.

To fight.

To *escape.*

He murmured something that I didn't hear beneath the chaos rattling around inside me. The noose around my neck kept me from accessing my earth essence. But somewhere within, there was a link to dark magic—because of Shade. I just needed to use it against him.

Pushing away from reality and ignoring the shadowy smog cloaking my vision, I searched deep in my mind for some sort of link. Anything that didn't belong. Anything that I could *use.*

His tongue danced up the column of my throat, his touch temporarily drawing me back to the hands on my hips and the growing arousal pressing into my lower abdomen.

The flame inside me inched higher, yearning to dance with him in an intimate way that neither of us could afford. It had to be the bond. This compulsion to give in to him sexually and do whatever he requested.

I clenched my jaw, refusing to cave.

I'm stronger than this.

Don't let his mind tricks overwhelm you.

Focus.

With a deep breath, I dove back into my mind, frantically searching for a path to follow that would lead me out of this complication. Because giving in to him and these indecent urges wasn't an option.

Tying myself to him more would harm us both.

Not that he seemed to care.

"I don't want to hurt you, Aflora," Shade murmured. "I know I have, but it was never my intent."

"Lie," I choked out, torn between what he was doing and saying and my desire to fight.

"No, darling. I've never lied to you, nor will I ever lie to you." He kissed my jaw, working his way to my mouth. "You can hate me—and you should—but I promise there's a reason."

"What reason?"

"Fate," he replied cryptically before sealing his lips over mine.

I refused to open for him.

Refused to kiss him back.

Refused to fall into this lustful trap.

He made no sense. Had ruined my life. Wouldn't give me any details on what he wanted. And now had me trapped against some tree or wall, surrounded by a thick essence I couldn't see through. Were we still at the bonfire? Or somewhere else entirely? He seemed to be able to teleport, in addition to controlling my mind. What else could he do?

Heck, was this even real?

I'd dreamt of him almost every night this week, waking up in a variety of orgasmic states, all brought on by his mouth and hands. Were the dreams a response to his bite? Or was he manipulating me?

I hated that I didn't know.

Hated more that I didn't know how to stop him.

His tongue danced along the seam of my mouth, requesting entrance.

I denied him.

His grip on my hips tightened, causing me to wince. I grabbed his neck and dug my nails into his scalp in response, needing to harm him in some way.

Yet all it did was make him smile against my lips. "I love that you're not giving in," he admitted softly. "Proves you were the right choice all along. An easy mate would bore me significantly."

"I'm an *unwilling* mate," I snapped. "You ra—"

He took advantage of my retort, sliding his tongue into my mouth and stealing my breath away. I nearly bit down, then remembered what that did in my dreams. His blood made me crazy with lust.

No.

Allowing his kiss made more sense.

Only, I didn't want any of this, even if my body seemed to crave his touch.

I returned to my inner search, navigating the complex webs of my mental state for anything out of place. When I found nothing, I dove into my soul, desperately seeking out my link to earth.

So dark.

Black.

Wrong.

Wait, what's that? A glint of cerulean blue light caught my focus, drawing me nearer. It blended into the inky abyss but began to glitter as I approached. Tugging on the thread, I followed it into the deep recesses of my spirit.

A chill slithered over me, followed by a wave of warmth as Shade deepened our embrace. For as much as I hated him, I had to admit the male knew how to work his tongue. I couldn't help responding, my body arching into his as if being pulled upward by a string.

"I hate you," I muttered against his mouth.

"You've said that before," he acknowledged. "And I've admitted to hating myself for what I've had to do to you."

"Yet you won't tell me why."

"Because I can't." He recaptured my lips, silencing our conversation, and drew his palms up my sides as if memorizing my body for the first time. And maybe he was. I really had no way of knowing if he visited my dreams or if they were all in my mind.

I couldn't even tell if this was real or not.

The glimmer of cerulean drew me deeper, dividing my focus between Shade's touch and the mysterious puzzle unfolding inside my soul. Something was unraveling, a lock of sorts that I seemed to be distorting with this odd wisp of beautiful blue.

"I can feel that," Shade whispered. "Whatever it is you're doing."

I ignored him.

He couldn't possibly be this deep into my soul.

Dancing in the darkest recesses of my being.

"We're mates," he added. "My bite sealed us together for eternity. The sooner you accept that, the better."

"I'm not a Midnight Fae," I replied, irritated all over again.

"Are you sure about that?" he countered, causing me to blink up at him.

The smoke had dissipated, allowing me to catch his azure irises. *I am pressed up against a tree*, I thought, finally able to see my surroundings.

We weren't anywhere near the bonfire.

So either he'd teleported us or I was lost in a dream state again.

"Release me, Shadow."

"I can't."

"That seems to be your favorite phrase," I replied coldly. "You can't tell me why you bit me. You can't release me. You can't explain—"

"You talk too much." He kissed me again, causing me to growl in frustration.

The cerulean rope in my mind tightened suddenly, causing me to stiffen just before a wave of power rippled across my skin. Shade flew backward, landing on his ass a few feet away, his eyes wide in shock.

And the tree behind me withered to dust.

I gaped at the bright blue flames dancing along my palms, then shivered as they disappeared.

"What the fuck was that?" a sharp male voice demanded.

"Her power awakening" was the drawled reply.

I spun around to find Kolstov glaring at me and Zephyrus leaning against another tree. "I didn't mean to do that," I said, a note of pleading in my voice. "I just wanted Shade to release me."

"Well, it worked." Zephyrus seemed amused.

Kolstov definitely did not share that opinion.

Neither, it seemed, did Shade as he shoved off the ground to stand at my side. "Touch her, and I'll fucking destroy you."

I blinked, surprised by the protective quality in Shade's tone. He'd just been taunting me moments ago, refusing to explain anything and kissing me without my permission. Now he wanted to stand up for me? How ridiculous.

"I'd love to see you try," Kolstov replied, folding his arms. "You're handicapped and alone."

Shade lifted his arms, revealing the leather cuffs against his wrists. "Oh, you mean these?" The bands disappeared a second later. "Yeah, I deactivated those almost as soon as Chern put them on. But thanks for the accessory."

Energy rippled around Kolstov, his expression thunderous. "Do you have a death wish, Death Blood?"

"Is that meant to be some sort of oxymoron?" Shade asked conversationally. "Because you'll have to be more direct. I skipped a lot of my language courses throughout the years. Well, those and other classes."

"Your arrogance is going to get you killed."

Shade grinned. "Is it? Good to know."

"Can someone tell me what just happened?" I asked, interrupting their little testosterone-filled fight. "Why did I turn blue?" The fire had since dissipated, but I felt it roaming through my veins, waiting for me to call upon it again.

"Blue?" Kolstov repeated. "I saw purple."

Zephyrus frowned. "It was red to me."

The two males shared a glance as Shade looked down at me. "Blue?" he asked softly, his tone different from the one he'd used with the other males.

"Yeah. Bright blue."

"Like a lighter shade?"

I nodded.

"Interesting," he mused, glancing back at Kolstov. "Are we going to have a problem here?"

"We already have one," the prince replied on a snarl. "You bit her against her will."

"Is that what she said?" he returned, sounding far too entertained. "Well, she might be right. But our laws still make her mine. Fascinating how that works, yes?" His smile was cruel. "It is your family who stands behind those archaic politics, Kolstov. Can't go breaking the rules now, can we?"

Kolstov appeared ready to murder Shade.

But his words were rolling around in my thoughts.

Kolstov's family allows the males to claim females in the manner Shade did? Without reprimand? Why?

"Elemental Fae choose their mates," I said out loud. "It's a much better practice. And I will choose mine."

Shade chuckled, his expression indulgent. "An adorable thought, but impractical in our world. You already belong to me, Aflora."

"I don't belong to anyone."

He grabbed the back of my neck, pulling me to him. "Keep denying it, baby. That makes our dance so much more fun." He pressed a quick kiss to my lips before releasing me and refocusing on Kolstov. "So I'll ask again. Are we going to have a problem here? Because she's mine and I protect what's mine."

"I don't need you to protect me," I corrected him. "I've survived a lot worse than this, and I'll continue to survive, thank you very much."

He ignored me.

As did Kolstov.

Some sort of strange conversation happening between the two males.

"It was a minor explosion of power," Kolstov said after a beat. "She's safe from reprimand."

"Good." Shade's shoulders seemed to relax a fraction, suggesting he'd been tenser than I realized.

"Why would I be reprimanded for protecting myself?" I asked, confused.

"In a normal situation, you wouldn't be. But nothing about your circumstances is normal. Any and all signs of you morphing into an abomination will be considered and taken into account by the Council." Kolstov arched a brow at me. "I don't think I need to tell you what will happen should they decide you've grown too powerful as a result of this mating."

I swallowed. *Oh.*

"Well, this has been fun," Shade interjected. "Aflora and I will be going now."

Wait, wh—

"No." Zephyrus finally pushed off the tree, his expression still bored yet somehow holding an edge. "I'll escort her back to the Elites, as she's under my protection."

"Yeah? And who protects her from Kolstov should he decide to make a regal decision in regard to her life?" Shade countered.

"Perhaps that's something you should have considered before you jeopardized her life for your own selfish need," Zephyrus returned, avoiding the question. "Let's go, Aflora."

I stared at all three of them and shook my head. "Yeah, no. I'm good. I'll just escort myself, thank you." I turned on my heel, heading toward, uh, darkness. Then spun around again, only to find another thick layer of ink painting my vision. Not because Shade was messing with my mind, but because he'd taken us somewhere without a lot of light.

When I turned around, it was to find three pairs of amused gazes.

"Lost, sweetheart?" Kolstov prompted.

My jaw clenched. "Just point me in the right direction." As soon as I said it, I realized the error in my words.

Even if they gestured a certain way, I couldn't trust them to tell me the truth. With my luck, I'd end up in that LethaForest Ella mentioned earlier. Or somewhere worse.

Gritting my teeth, I caved and refocused on Zephyrus. "Fine. Escort me back."

His lips actually twitched as if he approved of my downfall.

Dick.

"This way, *princess*," he said, gesturing to the path behind him.

I didn't reply or look at the other males as I followed the headmaster in silence.

Maybe Shade and Kolstov would kill each other in my absence.

One can only dream, I thought. Then grimaced at the realization that everything Shade had done to me tonight had been real.

And with my luck, he'd probably go much further as soon as I closed my eyes.

"This world stinks," I grumbled to myself.

"Sucks," Zephyrus corrected. "Or you could say it's shit."

"What?"

"Consider it a vocabulary lesson," he tossed over his shoulder. "I am a headmaster, after all."

I rolled my eyes. "Yeah, you're a brilliant teacher."

For a brief second, he almost appeared entertained by my jibe. But it disappeared a second later behind his usual expression of stoicism. "Do me a favor, Aflora. Try not to explode in class tomorrow. Another display of power like that could be your death sentence."

With that, he led me back to Kolstov's suite without another word.

Ten minutes later, he left me in the living area, and I felt even more alone than I had every night this week.

Because his words had served as a not-so-subtle warning, one that told me my life was very much in danger here. Something I already knew, but the reality still stung.

How could I control a power I knew nothing about?

And worse, what if I couldn't control it at all?

CHAPTER THIRTEEN

KOLS

"Did she wonder how we found her?" I asked as I entered Zeph's suite without knocking. His gargoyle hadn't batted an eye, which told me I was welcome.

Zeph confirmed it by entering the living area with two bottles of beer, one of which he tossed to me. I caught it by the neck.

"Aflora was too consumed by her explosion of power to ask questions," he replied, collapsing into one of the room's recliners. "If she thinks about it later, she'll probably assume we followed her from the bonfire."

That wouldn't necessarily be too far from the truth. When her locator jumped positions, I knew something had happened. Tray's text message confirmed it when he said Shade had used a smoke spell to remove her from the bonfire. The bastard clearly didn't know how to abide by any rules. Not only had he removed his cuffs—something he should not have been able to do —but he'd also interacted with Aflora after being expressly told to leave her alone.

"I should report him," I said out loud, referring to Shade.

Zeph popped the cap off his beer and took a long swig, his throat working with each swallow. "Wouldn't do much."

Leaning against the wall a few feet away from his chair, I sighed, "I know." If I reported Shade, they might expel him. Then he'd just lurk around the shadowy edges of campus anyway. "What game is he playing with her?"

Zeph set his bottle off to the side, his expression thoughtful. I'd almost forgotten about this side of him, what with all the animosity he'd thrown my way these last few months. Part of me hoped our earlier brawl meant we were finally moving forward. The other part of me knew better.

Things between us would never be the same.

"You really saw purple flames?" He glanced at me.

"Yeah, the kind I'd expect from a Death Blood." They were vibrant and violet flared.

"Well, I saw red, like the kind of flames you create."

We frowned at each other. "And she called them bright blue," I added. "Which is impossible. No Midnight Fae burn bright blue."

"Maybe she meant navy, like the Sangré Bloods?"

"How the fuck would that even be possible?"

"No idea. But she's not exactly normal. Could it be an influence from her elemental power?" Zeph suggested.

I flicked the top off my bottle and took a long sip while considering that. Then slowly shook my head. "She's an Earth Fae, not a Fire Fae. The flames are tied to her awakening connection to dark magic."

"Suggesting her mating bond with Shade is indeed turning her into an abomination," Zeph pointed out.

We both fell silent, me drinking my beer, Zeph swirling his around on the table in that thoughtful way of his.

"Fuck, this isn't good," I finally said. "This isn't good at all."

"Are you going to report it?"

I nodded. Then I shook my head. "I don't know what the hell I'm going to do. It might still be temporary. Maybe she expelled what little power she has inside her and now she'll go back to normal." I heard the lie in my words, saw the confirmation of it written in Zeph's features.

"It's not like you to play the naïve card, Kols."

Kols. Not Prince Kolstov or Kolstov, but Kols. He hadn't used my preferred name in months. I swallowed another sip to keep myself from commenting on it or allowing him to see the glimmer of hope that small word provided.

We might not be able to go back, but I wasn't opposed to moving forward.

Zeph was the one who cut off all ties.

Not me.

"I know you want to fuck her, just like you do every other hot, unattainable female to cross your path," he added, destroying the moment. "But that shouldn't hold you back from doing what you have to do. Just do the deed and end her afterward."

Such a cruel approach. Although, I knew he didn't mean it that way. Not completely, anyway. Zeph thrived on logic. And to him, feeding the lust before completing the task struck him as practical.

Except nothing about this assignment was practical.

"I can't just kill the last remaining Earth Fae Royal," I reminded him. "And maybe my approach is naïve, but I need to hope this power mingling will just go away."

"Wrong. What you need to do is prepare for the inevitable. Her power is growing. I've been watching her all week, and she's not growing weaker. She's growing stronger. Almost as if Shade's bite flipped a switch inside her. Something's not right, and her little power display tonight proves it."

He picked up his bottle and finished it off in a few deep gulps. Then he waved his hand over the glass, refilling it with a muttered spell.

I pulled up my phone, checking the app linked to Aflora's tracker, and noted her presence next door. She hadn't tried to run yet, which actually made me admire her a bit. It implied that she put her people before herself. To return in her current state would thwart the balance. She also wouldn't be safe there given that the Elemental Fae recently took down an insane abomination. They wouldn't be all that accepting of her return.

So maybe it wasn't so much that she put her people first as it was her survival instinct kicking in.

Regardless, the intelligence in her decision to stay boosted her appeal in my eyes. Which was exactly the wrong response overall because I could not—and should not—entertain the possibility of fucking Aflora.

She was a forbidden fruit.

Off-limits.

As Zeph already said, *unattainable*.

Yet I couldn't deny the urge to kiss her earlier. I'd also enjoy sticking one to Shade in the process. The asshole had disappeared into a cloud of smoke before I could give him a piece of my mind. However, I felt his residual presence all the way back to my building, suggesting he'd followed Aflora.

"He seems to care about her," I mused out loud.

"Who?"

"Shade," I clarified. "He traced after you and Aflora to the Elite Residence."

Zeph considered for a second, then lifted a shoulder. "I think he cares more about the bond than he does her. If something happens to her, he'll be the one living in pain for eternity."

"Probably should have thought about that before biting her," I grumbled.

"True, but I think there's a bigger scheme behind it all." Zeph set his mostly full bottle down and braced his arms on his thighs. "Shade's a dick, don't get me wrong, but that fucker doesn't do anything without a reason."

"I don't know. He seems to do things all the time just to piss everyone else off," I muttered in reply. "That's part of what makes him such an ass."

"Yeah, but those are small irritants. Taking an Elemental Fae mate—specifically, Aflora—is a catastrophic decision for him and her. Why would he do such a thing? It has to be more than just wanting to piss off his father, or your father, or the Council. He's up to something."

Which brings us full circle, I thought, recalling the way our conversation began about what game Shade was playing and why. "Something tells me we won't know until his plan unfolds."

"Which is precisely why I suggest you say nothing and observe. Let's see what he does with her."

"You want to use the Royal Elemental Fae as bait?"

He flipped his hands, palms up. "Shade signed her death warrant the second he bit her, and we both know it. This whole observation game is just for the paperwork so they can validate killing her. We might as well figure out what the hell Shade is up to in the process and make use of what little remains of her life."

I released a humorless laugh, his words a repeated punch to the gut. "You're a cold son of a bitch. You know that, right?"

"I'm thinking defensively. It's what I do."

"Yeah, and while you're great at it, could you for a moment try to remember that she's a person, not a pawn?" *Technically, she's a future queen,* I corrected myself. *Much more important than a pawn.*

"Shade put her in this mess, not me. I could choose to pity her, or I could choose to use her to ensure he never pulls that shit again. I vote for the latter. You should, too."

"It's not black and white, Zeph."

"Why? Because you want to fuck her? Just get your dick wet, sate the need, and move on. It's what you do best."

My jaw ticked at the barbed insult. "Right, and you're not at all interested in fucking her?" I knew he was, because I'd caught the flare of intrigue in his gaze while looking at her. Oh, he hid it well, but I knew him better than he gave me credit for. A few months apart would never change that.

Besides, we both had a type, and Aflora checked all our boxes in spades. She also posed one of the biggest challenges I'd ever encountered, mostly because flirting with her was akin to flirting with death. One wrong move and we'd end up on the chopping block right beside her. Which only made her more alluring as a prospect since it added the element of true danger.

"We're not talking about this," Zeph said, his voice deepening.

My lips quirked up. "You're right. We don't need to. I already know you want her. And you brought it up—twice—not me. I'm just throwing the ball back in your court. If you want to share her, just say the words."

"Stop."

"Why? Because I'll push your limits?" I taunted. "Because the whole headmaster role adds yet another element of the forbidden to an already intriguing situation?"

His green irises swirled with embers. I'd either just royally pissed him off or turned him the fuck on. Probably both.

Zeph enjoyed harsh sex.

Anger was his aphrodisiac.

Fighting served as foreplay.

And we'd fought a lot these last few months, both mentally and physically.

Our earlier quarrel still simmered between us. He'd gotten in a few good hits, but so had I, and it'd left us both infuriated and a little bruised on the inside. Hence, I'd opted to avoid the bonfire. But the alert on my phone, activated by Aflora's collar, had sent me to Zeph's door. Then Tray's text had forced us both outside.

Now Zeph and I were alone again.

Two decades of experience hanging between us.

Five years of that spent between the sheets with multiple women and occasionally just each other.

I didn't date or do girlfriends. Yet Zeph had always been my one constant.

Until six months ago when we seduced the wrong chick. She'd used the sexual distraction to try to take advantage of me and my power, and she'd caused a lot of damage in the process.

Needless to say, my father had not approved of the outcome or Zeph's inability to "properly protect me."

And here we were.

"I need you to leave," Zeph finally said, his hands balled into fists. "Now."

"No." What we needed to do was have this out once and for all. Six months of this bullshit was long enough. "What do you want me to do, Zeph? Apologize again? Promise you I'll fix it? Because I've already done both of those things. What more can I do? You want me to suck your cock all night? Let you take me up the ass? Go seduce Aflora for us both? Find a human that fits nicely between us? Tell me what I need to do to fix this."

"You can't fucking fix it. You let me take the fall for *your* choice."

"I told my father that I picked her and invited her into our bed. He blamed you for not vetting her. Which, yeah, is sort of your job as my Guardian."

His gaze narrowed. "He denounced me in front of the fucking kingdom over a fuckup we both shared equal blame for."

I flinched at the memory of my father's cruelty. Because yeah, he'd been a major dick over the whole issue. Then turned around and told me to grow the fuck up. "We both suffered that day."

"Yet you'll still ascend, and I'll remain here as a headmaster. And don't tell me you're going to change that. I don't want any favors from you."

"You're my best friend, jackass. It's not a favor. It's a reality. No one can replace you as my Guardian. I refuse."

His lips curled into a harsh grin. "Yeah, well, I can and will refuse the assignment."

I matched his grin with one of my own. "You can try, Zeph. But we both know my word will be law."

"Which makes you just like *him*," he retorted. "You must be so proud."

Fuck, I hated when Zeph took on the asshole act. "I'm not my father."

"Then prove it and stop threatening to force others into positions they don't want to be in."

The bottle almost slipped from my fingers, his words hitting home. "You really don't want to be my Guardian anymore." Not a question, but a statement. "All because of one fucked-up experience?"

"It was more than a fucked-up experience, and you know it. We were reckless and stupid, and lives were lost in the process when that bitch borrowed your access to the source. How can you not feel guilty about that?"

My lips opened and then closed. Because I suddenly understood.

This wasn't about punishing me but about punishing himself for a failure he felt responsible for.

"Those women died because of Dakota, not because of you or me."

"You really are naïve if you believe that. It's your duty to the Midnight Fae realm to protect that access, and you didn't. Just as it was my duty to protect you from harm, and I failed when I let that bitch into your bed." He pushed off his chair and rolled his neck. "I'm done for the night. It's your turn to play babysitter. I'm going for a run."

"Zeph—"

"No." He cut me off with a thunderous expression. "I'm done, Kolstov. Absolutely and resolutely. It's time for you to believe that and move on." He pushed past me, heading toward the door and not once looking back or even asking me to leave. Instead, he left, his angry aura burning the air in his wake.

But for the first time in months, I knew why.

He wasn't mad at me.

He was mad at himself.

No, he was mad at *us*. For all the damage we'd caused. And while I understood the guilt and responsibility for what had happened, I also knew dwelling on the past fixed nothing.

Instead, I'd learned from the experience.

I rarely fucked Midnight Fae before the event, and now, I never would.

Only humans.

And I intended for it to remain that way, even after I mated Emelyn.

I shuddered at the thought of her and our intertwined destinies. Not fucking her would be the easiest task of my life.

Unlike Aflora…

I pulled out my phone again, noting she was still next door. Probably in bed. It'd be far too easy to join her and use her as a distraction from my growing frustration.

Except, with her increasing powers, it was possible she could also access my source.

Which firmly placed her in the *will never happen* pile, where she belonged.

"Fuck," I muttered, rubbing a hand over my face.

I set my bottle down in Zeph's sink and gripped the counter.

I could really use an outlet of relief right about now. Rather than fuck around like I'd intended to this last week, I'd spent the majority of my time with Cyrus and Exos—two Elemental Fae Kings—talking about Aflora. They were adamant that I protect her, stating she wasn't just a Royal Fae but also a friend of their Claire. Which meant any harm befalling the beautiful princess would put me on the shit list of a queen and her two kings. Not to mention her other three mates.

Talk about a rock and a hard place, I thought, sighing. Right, well, standing in Zeph's kitchen wasn't going to do anything for me. Knowing him, he wouldn't be back tonight.

I'd work on him more tomorrow.

Because, while I agreed with his bait idea, we needed something more solid that allowed us to keep Aflora safe.

Even if her death was indeed inevitable.

CHAPTER FOURTEEN

AFLORA

"All right, this is where I leave you," Ella said, stopping in front of an ominous-looking building with tall, black, moving spires. Well, not moving, exactly. More like the vines wrapped around it were moving.

Because of the snakes.

I suppressed a shudder.

"You just go up to the gargoyle there, give your name, and he'll allow you to pass," Ella added, gesturing to a snarling stone statue a few feet away.

"Yeah, he looks friendly," I muttered.

Ella snorted a laugh. "They're all like that. They think they own the campus." She started to walk away backward while saying, "I don't recommend kicking one. I made that mistake early on, and it tried to eat my foot off. Annoying little assholes, if you ask me." She shrugged and turned away with a wave. "Good luck."

I wrapped my cloak tighter around me as if it were a blanket rather than a piece of my Academy wardrobe. The jabbing of my wand in the inner pocket made it impossible to forget the true purpose.

Nibbling my lip, I wandered up to the gargoyle and said, "I'm Aflora of the Elemental Earth Fae."

Two pinpoints of bright red scanned over my outfit, the unfriendly expression turning even meaner. "Your energy signature is a puzzling mix of magic—part Royal, part Midnight Fae." The grating of stones deepened the being's voice, giving it a harsh quality that made me flinch.

"I have a class in here today for death magic," I told it. "If you would please allow me entry, I'll be on my way."

"Such a polite one. So abnormal. Just like your magic. You're a bit of a quandary, aren't you?" Those sharp points of red light met my gaze. "This is not the course or field for you."

"Just let her through, Sir Schmahl," Shade said as he materialized beside me. "As my chosen mate, she has Death Blood running through her veins. This is an appropriate course for her, even if she's too weak to handle it."

"Too weak?" I countered, focusing on the willow stump to my left. "I'm not weak."

"We'll see, won't we, love?" He refocused on the bristling gargoyle. "Come on, Sir Schmahl. You know you want to see the outcome of this little test just as badly as I do. It'll be fun to watch her fail, won't it?"

"Hmm, yes. Yes, she will fail," the gargoyle agreed.

"Seriously?" I gaped between them both. "Bullying me on my first day of classes? How charming." It didn't escape my notice how many times I'd called Shade *charming* in a sarcastic sense.

"No bullying, just speaking practically," Shade replied, his dimples flashing. "What do you say, Sir Schmahl? Are you up for a bit of rebellious fun?"

"If she dies, I am not responsible" was the gargoyle's dark reply.

The door swung open beside him, showcasing a tunnel lined with torches. *Great. The inside matched the ominous exterior.*

Shade pressed his palm to my lower back, giving me a nudge. "Don't worry, Sir Schmahl. I'll clean up any messes she creates."

A snort followed that comment. Or maybe it was just the gargoyle shifting positions. I couldn't really say, the sounds the being made hard to decipher.

"Come along, pet," Shade whispered against my ear. "I'll escort you to the lecture hall."

I bristled but didn't argue. Mostly because I had no idea where we were going. The schedule Zephyrus had given me didn't list room numbers, just buildings. And on our tours this week, he said nothing about where to go once inside each castle-like structure.

Shade's warmth seeped through my cloak, his peppermint scent swirling around me in a wave of refreshment. Every inhale increased my alertness, waking me up to this new world of Midnight Fae while also soothing me in a way it shouldn't.

It's the bite, I told myself. *He's hypnotized my blood.*

"The halls change," he said, his hand moving to my hip to stop me from taking another step. He placed his arm around my lower back in a decidedly intimate manner. When I tried to move away, his grasp tightened. "Hold on."

"Stop manhandling—"

Shifting rocks cut off my statement, freezing me in place as the corridor warped into a new dimension of dungeon-esque walls. My throat went dry at the windowless wooden doors and the flames crawling along the different torches.

"Every student creates a different path," Shade explained softly. "Our age dictates what course we should take and leads to the appropriate classroom. You can see ours outlined in purple fire down there." He pointed ahead to the violet glow.

"Are all the buildings like this?" Because if they were, this was going to be a very long week of finding my courses.

"There are similarities, but every subject has its own nuances. Defensive arts, for example, requires you to battle a figment to enter. Your experience and skill are determined by how well you do, and you're placed accordingly. So I suspect you'll be in a beginner-level Warrior Blood course." He winked down at me.

I scowled. "You know nothing about my abilities. And it's not my fault your Council handicapped me." I pointed to my collar, then recalled his statement last night about his cuffs. "Wait—"

"Oh, no. I know where you're going, and no, I won't help you remove it. Prove your own worth and figure it out yourself. I have faith in your failure, baby."

Ugh! "You're such an ignorant, impossible jerk of a willow stump!"

He laughed loudly, shaking his head. "I can't take you seriously with words like that, Aflora. Try calling me an asshole and we'll talk."

"How about I call you a bloodsucker instead?" I threw at him, livid by his callousness and hot and cold behavior. "A manipulative, impulsive *bloodsucker* who uses cruelty as a flirtation tool."

His smirk died. "Careful."

"Or what?"

"Or you'll piss off every Midnight Fae in this building. That term isn't one we allow here."

I scoffed at that. "Well, it's what you are, so I'm not sure why you'd shy away from it. *Bloodsucker.*"

He studied me for a long moment, his evil grin returning. "You know what? I changed my mind. Go ahead and use that term. Let's see what happens."

With that, he turned and headed toward our supposed class. It was probably a pitfall directly into hell, yet I followed him anyway.

And paused on the threshold when I found a normal-looking lecture hall inside with desks and chairs and windows that overlooked a courtyard of burning thwomp trees.

This place was like a riddle. The hallway resembled an underground cavern meant for criminals, and this room reminded me of something from a human college campus. There was even a chalkboard at the front.

I stepped inside, half expecting it to morph into a nightmare, but nothing changed.

Shade had taken a seat amidst a group of students, their expressions filled with adoration as they spoke to him.

He must save his "charming" act for me, not the others.

Or maybe they enjoyed that side of him.

I sat on the opposite side of the room, keeping him in my peripheral vision while assuring an ample amount of distance.

As more students entered, they greeted him with a variety of weird handshakes, some bumping his fist, and all took seats near him, leaving me very alone. Which was fine. I preferred it that way.

At least until they started glancing at me and whispering things to him that made him chuckle.

I narrowed my eyes. This game of his had proven to be very dangerous, mostly because I didn't know how to properly play it. He bit me, seduced me, pretended to protect me last night, and guided me today, all the while issuing insults, and now it appeared he was making jokes about me.

Were they taking bets on how quickly I would fail?

Well, I'd just have to prove them all wrong.

Except I had no idea what I was doing or how to use my wand.

And the choker around my neck resembled a noose.

Shade's words echoed in my mind. *"Prove your own worth and figure it out yourself. I have faith in your failure, baby."*

Pompous jackwad, I thought at him now. His goading fueled a fire inside me, one that blended with the cerulean energy I'd created last night. I felt it humming beneath my skin, having not quite died even while I slept. As if it now belonged despite the foreign sensation of its presence.

I studied my fingers, half expecting to see them glowing, when a loud crash at the front of the room sent my focus upright.

A burly male appeared from a cloud of smoke, his cape flapping around him like bat wings. An appropriate entrance considering his small head. It didn't quite fit his robust physique. Not fat, so much as solid. His neck bulged with strength, his thighs the size of my waist. And he had to stand at least a foot taller than me.

He reminded me a bit of Sol, causing my heart to skip a beat in my chest. Not in the way it used to when I had a crush on him, but in a familial way. The male had practically raised me with his mother's help. And his sister had been my best friend before she died.

It felt like a lifetime ago.

A distant memory when faced with my current reality.

Which included a pacing giant at the base of the classroom, his hands holding a scroll. Everyone had gone quiet, waiting for him to speak.

A pair of midnight irises scanned the room, landing on me.

Here we go.

But rather than say anything, he shrugged and went back to his scroll. The parchment went up in bright purple flames a moment later, and he clapped his hands. "Welcome to Advanced Conjuring. Most of you are familiar with my teaching methods. For those of you who are not, I prefer pair teaching. Now, get your wands ready and we can begin."

All the students pulled out their conduit tools, so I did the same.

"You know the spell," he added. "Well, maybe not." That last statement was for me, something he confirmed when he met my gaze. "When I count to three, wave your wand in a crisscross pattern three times and say *Sharikana.*"

I nodded to display my understanding, but he'd already looked away.

"And go," he said.

Echoes of the spell chanted from around the room, and I quickly followed suit, only to startle as energy zipped around me. A lasso of sorts formed around my wrist, the magical substance roped directly to Shade across the room.

His lips curled and he blew me a kiss.

I tried to yank myself away from him, which only tightened the connection and sent a piercing whistle through the air.

Cringing, I ducked into my desk and nearly dropped my wand.

Then felt Shade's subtle tug back. A taunt. And it shoved me right over the cliff into a puddle of fury.

Angling my wand at him, I snapped, "Let me go."

Which did absolutely nothing other than amuse him.

So I sent a blast of blue fire down the rope, directly to his wrist.

He jumped out of his chair, dropped his wand, and wrapped his hand around the flaming line. This time I fell out of my chair when he yanked.

I screamed and sent another blast of my cerulean magic at him, until the link severed.

And a raging professor stood before me. "Have you lost your damn mind, girl?!"

Yes, I thought at him, wiping my hands against my black skirt and fixing my white blouse. "He lassoed me," I explained dumbly. Because he had to have seen that, right?

"Because that's the purpose of the spell!" the professor roared. "*Pair magic*." He gestured around the class, indicating the ropes tying other students together. "Your magic chose his magic. Then you tried to burn him up with your power, which is not acceptable behavior for my class."

My jaw hit the floor. "My magic chose his?" That was impossible. I would never in a million years choose that willow stump!

Another realization struck me just as quickly. *My spell worked. Oh, this can't be a good sign. It's supposed to stop, not start working.*

Pixie sticks, this was bad. *Very* bad.

Shade stood a few feet away, his entertainment over our situation clear in his icy gaze. "Perhaps we should try again, Headmaster Irwin? It seems Aflora isn't interested in being my partner for the year."

The robust male spun on his heel. "The spell cannot just be undone, Shadow. She's your partner, and you will learn to work together. Starting in detention after we're done here today."

"Detention," I repeated, familiar with the term but never having experienced it.

"Yes. Where you will work on pair-bonding exercises until I'm satisfied you understand the purpose of teamwork."

He uttered a spell and waved his thick branch of a wand, and the world righted around me as he sent me back to my chair with some sort of floating spell. I tried to bat it away, uncomfortable with the inky presence coating my being, but it disappeared as soon as my butt hit the seat.

Shade was not provided the same treatment.

He merely collapsed beside his desk into a lazy sprawl befitting a king.
I hated him.
Loathed him.
Could not stand the mere sight of him.
And now I was stuck with him as a mate *and* as a class partner.
This year could not get any worse.

CHAPTER FIFTEEN

AFLORA

I lied.

This year could absolutely get worse.

As I found myself literally bound to Shade's side in Headmaster Irwin's version of detention, all I wanted to do was die. But we had an essay to write together. He'd joined our hands with some sort of magical pen that required our agreement on the words for it to work.

The topic? *Define partnership.*

I gritted my teeth as Shade tried to write something about partnership falling to the stronger of the pair to lead.

When the script vanished, he sighed and glared down at me.

"You try."

"Screw you," I tossed back.

"He won't let us leave until we're done."

"Then I guess we're living here now." A childish thing to say, but there was absolutely no way I could work with this monster. "You only have yourself to blame, really. Not like I asked you to bite me."

He snorted. "Are we back to that old argument already?"

"It's not old," I countered. "It's very fresh and new and *wrong*."

His arm flexed against mine, the rope tying his left limb to my right limb tightening with the movement. There was another band of magic around our torsos, gluing my right side to his left side. Every time he breathed, I felt the strap pull against my chest.

This would have been intimate with anyone else.

With Shade, it only made me want to kill him.

But we were forbidden from drawing our wands.

Not that I knew how to use mine anyway. Today's class had consisted of a series of insane tasks involving conjuring deathly objects like skulls and bones and *hearts*.

As Shade had predicted, I failed every task.

Mostly because I refused to try. Playing with the dead went against every principle I possessed as an Earth Fae. I conjured life, not death.

Shade, however, excelled in a frightening manner. Each spell he uttered resulted in perfection, his aura an essential cloak of darkness. If only I could turn him into a ghost and make him disappear.

"Look, if I promise to tutor you, will you stop acting like a brat?" he asked, his genuine tone almost comical.

Except his words had me seeing in shades of red.

"You are the absolute last fae in all the realms I'd seek tutoring from. And I am *not* acting like a brat."

"That entire statement was the definition of *brat*, Aflora," he replied, sounding tired. "I'm the best conjurer in this Academy. Hell, I'm one of the best, period. Saying no to my tutoring offer is both impractical and stupid. You're only denying me because you're mad at me. Hence, brat-like behavior."

"Well, excuse me for being a little miffed by our current predicament. *You* put me here."

"And what's done is already done. It's how we use the past to move forward that defines us, and so far, you're not impressing me."

"Aw, well then, it's a good thing I'm not trying to impress you, Shade," I replied sweetly, batting my eyes.

His jaw popped from clenching his teeth, the first sign of frustration I'd ever seen in him. "We need to finish this damn assignment, Aflora. Unless you intend to join me in more intimate locations like the bathroom or the shower." His gaze dropped to the top button of my blouse. "Actually, that sounds like a beautiful plan. Shall we go?"

I tried to elbow him but couldn't, thanks to the binds.

Instead, I growled at him low in my throat. "Not happening."

His lips twitched as he bent to press his mouth against my ear. "That's not what you say in your dreams, little rose."

I gasped and tried to face him, only to be yanked right back into his side by the powerful spell. "You are in my head!"

"No, I'm in your *blood*." He kissed my neck before I had a chance to realize his intention, then nipped my pulse. "You're mine, princess. Forever. Now either work with me or let's go play in bed."

"Never."

"Stop lying to yourself," he said softly. "I know how you really feel and so do you. The sooner we get past this brutal courtship period, the better. Because I'm dying to fuck you."

"Shade!"

"What?" he demanded, his blue eyes glowing with power. "Would you rather I lie, too? Pretend my cock isn't hard as granite right now from your flowery perfume and seductive curves?" He snorted. "And I don't even like flowers. Yet all I can think about is exploring your petal-soft skin and dipping my tongue into your damp pussy. Because let's be honest, we both know you're wet. I can *smell* it, Aflora."

My jaw nearly hit the floor, his crude words doing things to me that they most certainly shouldn't.

And with Headmaster Irwin lurking in the other room.

Oh, Mother Earth, save me from this cruelly handsome fae!

"Mmm, and now it's intensifying," he mused, leaning in to nibble my neck once more. "Did Glacier not speak to you like this, baby? With intention and lust-filled promises?"

I shivered, his nearness messing with my mind.

Until his words fully registered.

Glacier. I couldn't recall ever mentioning my *boyfriend's* name. Well, ex-boyfriend technically. He never prioritized our time together, our last missed date being the final straw for a lot of reasons. Not least of all because of Shade kidnapping me.

"How do you know about Glacier?" I asked, my voice taking on a husky quality I pretended not to notice.

"I know everything about you, Aflora," he whispered into my ear. "You've been mine for longer than you know."

"What does that even mean?" All these cryptic words about a fate he seemed to know everything about were driving me crazy. "Why did you bite me?"

"Because I was told to," he replied against my jaw, his free hand coming up to cup my face.

I allowed him to guide my mouth to his, only because I was too flustered to stop him. And a small part of me wanted to taste him again, to feel the caress of his lips against mine.

Because Shade knew how to kiss.

Really, *really* kiss.

His tongue mastered mine in a single move, silencing the conversation between us while providing me with a distraction I didn't realize I craved.

He had this bizarre hold over me, one that drove logic out the window and replaced it with mind-numbing *need*.

In this state, I longed for another bite. Not that I'd admit it out loud. Although, something told me I didn't have to. Shade claimed to be in my blood, but that somehow linked to my mind. I could feel him infiltrating every square inch of me, taking over my existence with his own.

"I hate what you're doing to me," I admitted on a whisper, my attempt to pull back thwarted by his hand sliding into my hair and holding me in place.

"Your racing pulse and arousal say otherwise," he replied, taking my mouth once more.

His earlier kiss paled in comparison to this one. He'd gone easy on me before. Now he demanded submission with each stroke of his tongue, his grip falling to my nape, where he squeezed and held me in place for his domination.

The binding around us seemed to slacken a little.

His arm moving against mine.

But I was too busy trying to keep up with the assault on my mouth to consider what else was happening.

He'd stolen my ability to breathe, his lips turning violent in a way I should hate. Yet my legs clenched in reply. My abdomen coiled. And the intimate parts of me wept for attention.

Wet didn't begin to cover it. Why was this turning me on so completely? Because of our bond? Another spell? Or did I enjoy this love-and-hate pull between us?

I whimpered, conflicted.

My mind loathed this male.

Whereas my body succumbed to his every touch, almost as if he'd trained me in my dreams to respond this way.

His lips curled against mine. "There. That wasn't so hard, was it?" he asked softly, causing my brow to crumple.

"What?"

He brushed his mouth against my cheek before settling back into his chair. "We're done," he called out.

I blinked at him.

Then down at the paper he'd written *while* kissing me.

It disappeared before I could read it, and Headmaster Irwin appeared in the doorway holding the essay. His surprised expression told me whatever it said was not what he expected and probably not something I'd agree to at all. Shade had done something to override the lesson, in addition to kissing the life out of me.

"Very well," Headmaster Irwin said, releasing us from his bonds. "I expect better behavior during our next session." That last bit was aimed at me before he disappeared into a cloud of smoke.

Shade stood and stretched, his impressive bulge inches from my face.

He wasn't lying about the *hard* part.

"My tutoring offer still stands for whenever you decide to consider logic over emotion," Shade said, then caught my chin and lifted my gaze to his. "As does my shower and bed offer." With a wink, he turned toward the door. "I suggest you follow me, little rose. Or you'll end up lost in the building until the students start arriving tomorrow, which will throw off your schedule completely."

He disappeared through the glowing doorway, not giving me a second to gather my thoughts or my things.

Except they were all gone.

Headmaster Irwin had passed out a class text and notebook during the class, along with pens. The others had left with them. But mine were nowhere to be found.

I chased after Shade and found him waiting against the wall, his books and mine tucked under his arm. "How...?"

"As I said, conjuring is my specialty." He canted his head, causing his dark hair to fall over his forehead and into one eye. "They'll be in your room when you get back. Consider it my version of an olive branch. Accept it at your own peril."

He didn't allow me to reply, merely continued down the corridor. I stayed close to his side, pausing when he did to allow the walls to shift. Then breathed a sigh of relief the second we exited into the dark evening.

Until I found Zephyrus waiting with a scowl beside the gargoyle.

"What the fuck took you so long?" he demanded, scowling first at me and then at Shade.

"Detention," Shade replied. "She attacked me with green fire. Impressive, really, but does make me wonder where she's getting that Warrior Blood influence from." He cocked a brow at the headmaster. "Any ideas?"

I frowned at Shade. "It wasn't green. It was blue. And you deserved it."

"I think you might be color-blind, babe. Maybe we'll check that out later." He tossed a grin over his shoulder, apparently deciding this conversation was over despite his question to Zephyrus. "See you in your dreams tonight, little rose."

"Stay out of my head!"

"Blood, baby," he reminded me, the words a whisper against my ear despite the distance his legs had put between us.

I batted at the vacant space, trying to get rid of whatever residual presence or spell he'd left in his wake. And found Zephyrus staring at me with an arched brow. "Blue fire?"

"Yeah, blue."

"Can you show me?" he asked.

Sighing, I held out my hand, calling the power to my fingertips. And of course, nothing happened. "I think Shade sucked out all my energy for today," I muttered.

Zephyrus considered me for a long moment, then nodded. "Perhaps tomorrow, then. We're late for the dining area anyway, and you need to eat."

"Is it your job to feed me now?" I wondered out loud.

"No. I just want you to survive," he replied. "Follow me if you feel the same way."

Unable to fight that logic, I did what he asked.

Ate a disgusting humanlike dinner in silence.

And found my books waiting for me on my bed when I returned to my room. Beside them was a black rose and a note that read: *Sweet dreams.*

CHAPTER SIXTEEN

AFLORA

Day two of my schedule centered around Warrior Class.

Because apparently Midnight Fae enjoyed fighting.

At least the wardrobe worked for me—stretchy black pants, a T-shirt, and my hair thrown up into a ponytail. I even had on tennis shoes. All the guys were similarly dressed, including Kols and Shade. Only the Malefic Bloods wore black T-shirts instead of white.

"You were right," I said to Ella. "The different types are becoming easier to identify." The Sangré Bloods were the easiest with their colorful heads, then the Malefic Bloods because of their penchant for obsidian. The Death Bloods I recognized because of class yesterday, and the Elite Bloods seemed to be gravitating toward Kolstov.

The Warrior Bloods weren't in this class because it was defense basics and they would slaughter us all. Or that was how Ella explained it, anyway.

Regardless, I was ready for a physical course. I had a lot of pent-up annoyance to burn, thanks to Shade's mental gymnastics last night. He'd taunted me with his tongue over and over, never letting me orgasm, and I woke up panting and hot and *very* frustrated.

His smirk now told me he knew it, too.

"I can't tell if you want to fuck him or kill him," Ella remarked, following my glower to the source of my anger.

"Kill," I said. "Definitely kill." I tugged on my collar, irritated by its presence. I'd give anything to be able to create a tree and use its branches to smash the willow stump's head into the ground.

Of course, it'd probably be a burning thwomp.

Uh, yeah, I didn't want to play with those again.

A hush fell over the students as Zephyrus appeared in a pair of loose pants and a sleeveless shirt. He didn't acknowledge me or Kolstov, just picked up a thick wooden stick from the ground, gave it a twirl, and ignited both ends with green flames.

"You all know who I am. You all know why you're here. Defensive magic is a key part of your continued education. But I'm not going to waste your time teaching you spells from a book you can read. Instead, we're going to practice them. However, before I can assign you to groups, I need to assess your skills. So today will be about what you know and what you can handle."

Ella and I shared a glance.

I was pretty sure what *group* I'd be assigned to.

"We'll go for old-fashioned duels with winner and loser circuits. I've already assigned your first pairings." He snapped his fingers, and names began scrolling through the air in emerald script crafted from fire.

"Ha. Well, our friendship was short-lived," Ella remarked, pointing to our pairing. "You'd better bring more than flowers to this fight, earth chick. I've been practicing with Tray." She wiggled fingers lined with dark red magic, her gaze taunting in a playful manner.

Her teasing warmed me slightly, making me relax just a bit.

Until the first fight began.

Vibrant sparks flew through the air as physical attacks were blocked with defensive spells.

Defensive spells I didn't know.

"Uh, this is going to be a really short fight," I told Ella.

She smirked. "I know. But I promise to go easy on you. Trust me, I was a newbie not too long ago. I get it. We can review some common defenses tonight or during one of our break days."

I nodded absently, my focus falling to Shade as he stepped into the ring with a lanky Malefic Blood. The male narrowed his gaze. "I'm so glad we're paired, Shadow. I've been dying to kick your ass all week for disgracing my sister."

"Is that what she told you?" Shade mused.

"That would require her to be able to speak, which—"

"Stop flirting and get to it," Zephyrus said, interrupting the Malefic Blood.

"Gladly," the lanky male replied, a sharp, translucent blade appearing in his hand.

I jumped as he charged Shade in a whirl of power, his aim going right for the other male's heart. It was a brutal attack, one clearly meant to kill.

But Shade sidestepped with ease, stirring a dark cloud in his wake and wrapping it around the other male's throat. "If you want to play like that, then properly challenge me," he said sharply, yanking on the hold and bringing the male to his knees.

"Enough," Zephyrus snapped.

Shade released the male with a little wave of his hand and shrugged. "Stiggis started it."

"Bastard!" The Malefic Blood flew through the air toward Shade, additional weapons falling into his hands, but he ran headfirst into a wall of magic and bounced backward to collapse to the ground.

My eyes widened as Zephyrus put away his wand, the block disappearing with it. "Chig, take this idiot to the medic."

"Yes, sir," another Malefic Blood said, his body width twice the size as that of the male on the ground. He lifted the unconscious man and tossed him over his shoulder as if he weighed nothing, then headed off the field.

"I'll move you into the winner's circle, Shade. But I expect to see defensive magic in your next match." Zephyrus dismissed him before he could comment and gestured for the next pairing to come forward.

Which was Kols and a petite female wearing a wicked smile. "Ready, future lover?" she asked him, her catlike eyes glowing red with power.

"If you think I'm going to go easy on you, Emelyn, then think again."

Her resulting laugh reminded me of nails on a chalkboard, her expression nowhere near amused or kind in any way. She flipped her long black braid over her shoulder and fell into a fighter's stance. "I've been practicing."

"I'm sure you have," Kols replied, his stance relaxed as they squared off. "Give it your best shot, Jyn."

"Is her name Jyn or Emelyn?" I asked Ella in a low tone.

"Emelyn Jyn," she replied, her tone sour. "She's Kols's future mate."

My eyebrows lifted. "She is?" Didn't he say something about not doing girlfriends?

"Yeah. Assigned by the Council. Some sort of agreement between Malik and Lima."

"Yes, our Council fancies arranged pairings," Shade added as he came to stand with us. "I was assigned to Cordelia, Stiggis's older sister."

I frowned at him. "Then why did you bite me?"

"Why indeed?" he mused, his lips curling. "Maybe I wished to avoid my arrangement. Or maybe it was for another reason entirely. And maybe, if you're a good little rose, I'll tell you one day." He touched the tip of my nose with his index finger and sauntered off just as Kols pinned Emelyn to the ground beneath a wall of power. It reminded me of the one Zephyrus had used to block Stiggis's attack on Shade.

Emelyn screamed in pain, but Kols didn't stop.

And Zephyrus merely watched.

"Isn't he going to stop him?" I demanded, torn between Shade's commentary and the action unfolding before me.

"Who? Zeph?" Ella asked, snorting. "Yeah, no. He'll let this continue until Emelyn gives the signal, which should happen in about three, two, there it is."

A cloud of red smoke puffed out around them, and Kols released the brick of magic. "Practice harder, Jyn," he said, walking away.

"We're next," Ella informed me.

"Great." I followed her into the ring and noted how several fae fell silent around us, their intrigue palpable.

Too bad for them this would be a short show.

"I have no idea what I'm doing, so go ahead and start," I said, owning my inexperience.

Ella smirked. "Already am, princess."

I almost asked what she meant, when I *felt* her energy swathing me in a cloak of immobility. The thought of being bound triggered me into action, that blue light within me igniting to life and easily cutting through her invisible ropes while also memorizing the magical feel of them.

Using the knowledge, I tried to weave my own spell to wrap around her and nearly smiled when her legs locked in place.

"Holy shit, you're a fast learner," she said, pulling out her wand. "*Italaka.*"

My spell dissolved.

I took out my wand as well, unsure of how that would help me, and waited for her next attack. Which came in the form of a water figment shaped like a lion. I jumped to the side as its jaws yawned wide, its teeth far too real. They reminded me of crystal fragments. Sharp, precise, and turning right for me.

A cerulean wave of power billowed out of me, destroying her fragment and sending Ella to the ground.

Zephyrus stepped in with one of those walls, except it went around me while he and Tray knelt to check on Ella. I stood frozen on display, unable to move, and confused as hell.

"Did I do it wrong?" I asked, but my words echoed around me in my makeshift prison. I pressed my palm to it and jolted at the zap. Then cocked my head as the energy signature seemed to unravel in my head, allowing me to absorb the knowledge just like I did with the binding spell.

Strange, I thought, even as I memorized the spell Zephyrus had woven and, more importantly, how to undo it.

Closing my eyes, I disentangled the threads, removing the enclosure and allowing me to hear the chaos erupting around me.

Questions and accusations flowed from every inch of the courtyard, followed by someone screaming, "Zephyrus! She's escaping!"

He spun around to find me free of his cage and narrowed his green gaze. "You. Come with me. *Now.*"

I wasn't given an option to comply, some sort of invisible noose tightening around my waist and yanking me forward.

Kolstov fell into step on my other side, his jaw tight. "Why didn't you tell us you could do that, Aflora?"

"Do what?" I asked. "All I did was dismantle her water monster."

"You attacked her with WarFire," Kolstov snapped.

"What? I don't even know what that is."

"It's the giant purple ball you just threw at my brother's mate," he returned through his teeth.

"Purple?" I blinked at him in confusion. "It was blue."

"And again, I saw red," Zephyrus added, opening a door to a nearby building and ushering us inside. "What role do you want? Peacekeeper or guard?"

"Peacekeeper," Kolstov replied. "I'm the only one with the right bedside manner for it." His focus fell to me. "Do exactly what Zeph tells you to do, or I'll be left with no choice but to reprimand you publicly."

He turned on his heel, leaving us just inside the archaic stone structure. I gaped after him, startled by both the threat and the plea in his gaze as he uttered it. "I don't understand."

Shade materialized beside us, his amusement palpable. "Well, that was exciting. You sure do know how to make friends, little rose."

"Did you know she could do that?" Zephyrus demanded.

"No, but I'm thrilled by the prospect."

"Would someone tell me what I supposedly did?" I cut in before the headmaster could reply.

"WarFire," Zephyrus said. "You created WarFire and threw it at Ella. It's a lethal flame meant to kill. And it requires high-level magical skill, something you claim not to possess, but that little act suggests otherwise."

"I…" I wasn't sure how to reply to that. "All I did was destroy her water lion."

"What color did you see?" Zephyrus asked, ignoring me in favor of Shade. "I saw red. Kolstov swears it's purple. You?"

"Green," Shade replied. "Just like yesterday."

"It's cerulean blue," I insisted, annoyed that they kept talking about the color of my flame and not focusing on what the heck just happened. "Is Ella all right?"

"Cerulean…?" Zephyrus repeated, trailing off and sharing a glance with Shade. "That's impossible."

"Why are you all so obsessed with the color? You're telling me I almost killed Ella. Is she okay?"

"Tray's healing her," Shade replied, still holding Zephyrus's gaze. "And I agree; that's impossible."

"Do you have Quandary Blood in your history?"

"No. It's a dead line."

"I know that."

"Then why bother asking such a question?"

"Just tell me what's going on," I interjected, tired of these conversations about colors and bloodlines. There were more important things at play here. "How could I possibly create WarFire? I don't even know a standard defense spell."

"WarFire is an advanced offensive spell." Zephyrus finally gave me his attention again. "It's exceedingly difficult to conjure and requires a lot of energy. It's also extremely illegal."

"Great." I threw up my hands and paced in the small stone space, wary of the dusty walls and cobwebs in the corners. *Beautiful place*, I thought, pinching the bridge of my nose. "You realize Earth Fae don't fight, right? We're very peaceful beings."

"Could have fooled me," Shade murmured.

"I learned how to duel at a young age because of my birthright, but I rarely took defensive or offensive skills in school. My method of fighting is through power. *Earth* power. And we don't create fire."

"Yet here we are," Shade replied, leaning against the wall with his arms folded. "How did you pick up her bondage spell? Or did you read that in a book?"

"I don't know. I just… absorbed it."

"Which is how you dismantled Zeph's force field?" Shade guessed.

"Is that what that was?"

"Yes." Zephyrus narrowed his eyes at me. "A powerful one, too, that you took down faster than anyone I've ever seen."

I swallowed. "Oh." That wasn't good for a lot of reasons. Well, none of this was good. It showed a growth in dark magic, which I definitely didn't want. "I really am becoming an abomination, aren't I?"

"So it would seem," Zephyrus replied, not mincing words. "The question remains: Is it permanent or temporary?"

I had no answer for that and neither, it seemed, did Shade. He merely remained as nonchalant as ever, not a single inkling of remorse tainting his features.

Because he didn't care at all that he'd put me in this situation.

"What about you?" I asked. "Are you growing elemental gifts?"

He lifted a shoulder. "Everything feels normal to me, apart from my link to you. That's new."

"Yeah, you put it there."

"I remember."

"And you don't care at all that you did it."

"Of course I care. Why else would I be willingly standing in this outdated shack of a former classroom with you?" He pushed off the wall to stalk toward me. "This isn't exactly the most comfortable of spaces, but I didn't want to leave you alone with Zeph and Kols."

I glared up at him. "I'm in this mess because of you."

"I know."

"And you're completely unapologetic."

"Am I?" he countered, cocking his head.

"Are you?" I demanded.

"Shall we play the 'maybe' game again?"

"Ugh!" I wanted to slap him. "You're impossible and cryptic and such a… a… bloodsucking willow stump!"

He chuckled and shook his head. "You're so close, Aflora. So close."

Apparently, *bloodsucking* had lost its damning effect from yesterday, leaving me as the butt of his joke yet again. "Fine. You're a fucking asshole," I told him, the words tasting wrong in my mouth.

And of course, they only amused him more. "Oh, I do like that word from your lips, little rose. Say *fuck* again."

I threw my hands up in the air and turned to Zephyrus. "Can you make him leave?"

"It would be a waste of a command. Shade doesn't follow rules."

"Indeed, I don't," the Death Blood confirmed. "Besides, I'm here for your protection against the angry mob outside. If Kols can't calm them all down, we're going to have a fight on our hands. And I'm not ready to lose you yet."

"Don't feign selflessness." Zephyrus folded his arms, causing the muscles to clench and flex in the process. "We both know you just want to avoid the pain of losing a mate."

"I never claimed otherwise," Shade replied casually. "But my reasoning is neither here nor there. I'm here to protect her, and protect her, I shall."

"Or I could just create another ball of *cerulean* flames," I muttered, not really meaning it.

"Do, and I'll kill you myself," Zeph warned.

A chill swept down my spine at the truth in those words.

His green eyes glowed with sincerity, too.

I swallowed and nodded. "Then maybe you could use this time to teach me how to control it."

"I'm going to need more than a few minutes for that lesson." He considered me for a long moment. "But I'll talk to Kols about your schedule. I think your independent study should be reevaluated and scheduled with me. You're going to need all the defensive-magic help you can get after that little display out there."

Shade nodded, his agreement clear.

Something told me my reply wouldn't matter, so I remained quiet and waited instead.

What felt like hours later, Kols joined us once more, his expression wary. "Ella's fine. Tray's irritated, but understanding. And the others, well, let's just say Aflora hasn't made any friends."

Not like I had any here anyway, I thought sourly.

"No one is escalating the issue, but I had to agree to enhance her collar with more power restrictions," he added.

Zeph's chocolate-colored eyebrow inched upward. "How are you going to do that?"

"I have no idea." He looked at me. "For now, I need you to stay in the suite. No going to the cafeteria. No socializing."

"What about class tomorrow?" I asked.

"You'll be with me, so that'll be fine. But going forward, we need a better device to keep your powers in check."

So, a tighter leash. Awesome.

I sighed. "All right." While I hated the prospect of it, I understood the reason behind it. If my powers continued at this rate, I might actually hurt someone, and then I'd never be able to live with myself. Restraint made sense. I'd rather bear the pain myself than inflict it on another.

"You're not going to fight me on it?" Kols asked, his expression surprised.

I shook my head, swallowing. "I know what an abomination can do, Prince Kolstov. If that's truly what I'm becoming, restraint is a requirement." My shoulders fell as I looked toward the door. "If you lead me back to the suite, I'll stay there until you tell me otherwise."

Because escape was never going to be an option at this rate.

Not with the fire still licking a hot path beneath my skin, begging to be unleashed.

The power inside me seemed to be searching for an outlet, a way to explode. There had to be a way to temper it. Because if not... I shivered, refusing to consider that outcome.

I will survive this, I promised myself. *Somehow.*

CHAPTER SEVENTEEN

KOLS

"I swear to God, if you apologize again, I'm going to hit you with another jaws creation," Ella threatened as I finally returned home.

Dealing with Aflora's little power display had cost me more than I wanted to admit. Mostly because of Emelyn. She'd gone to her father, which meant I'd been called into an emergency Council discussion regarding Aflora's development. I assured them all that I had her under control and reiterated the complication of her status as the last Earth Fae Royal. Killing her now would provoke a war. They needed to come to terms with the Elemental Fae Council before that could even be considered as an option.

Several wanted to lock her up.

But my father stood by my side and reminded everyone that this task served as one of my ascension trials.

An ascension trial that was proving to be my most difficult test yet.

Aflora sat on a couch beside Ella, her shoulders caved inward as she held a mug of hot chocolate between her delicate hands. "I had no idea I could do that."

"I know."

"Maybe I shouldn't go to any more classes," Aflora continued. "The power seems to be growing, not dying, and that can't be a good thing."

"Classes are a requirement," I interjected, making my presence known since neither of them seemed to hear me walk through the door.

Aflora jumped, her blue eyes rounding as she looked up at me.

Ella didn't react at all. So maybe she had noticed my arrival.

"How'd the meeting go?" Tray asked as he walked out of the kitchen with a beer. He did a good job of hiding his anxiety over what happened today, but I caught the hardening of his jaw as he took in Aflora's close proximity to Ella.

That wasn't an incident any of us would soon forget, even if Ella seemed fine now.

"I have an upgraded collar for Aflora to wear," I replied, pulling the item from my pocket to show him and the rest of the room. "But they've agreed to let her stay for now, as long as she continues to attend her courses as scheduled. Her independent study day will be with Zeph, where he will attempt to teach her more about defensive arts and control."

"Bet he loves that assignment."

"Actually, he volunteered," I replied.

Tray's dark eyebrows shot up into his hairline. "Did he attend the meeting?"

I nodded. "He served as a witness in her trial."

"Wait, there was a trial?" Aflora asked. "Why wasn't I allowed to testify?"

"Because you're a female," Ella muttered. "The Council is full of sexist assholes." She looked pointedly at me and Tray with those words, the argument a common one between us.

"It's how our world functions," I replied, more for Aflora's benefit than Ella's. The latter already knew full well how we did things around here. "Only males are allowed to present to the Council. If you have something to say, you send your mate."

Aflora snorted. "Because I can trust Shade to speak on my behalf." She shook her head, giving me a look. "I'm technically a queen, Prince Kolstov. I speak for myself."

"From what I understand, you still haven't accepted your ascension, which makes you a princess," I corrected. "And as I said, our Council does not allow females to attend our proceedings." As I agreed with her concerns regarding Shade, I didn't comment on that part. But I did feel it was necessary to add, "That said, Shade did speak on your behalf today. And he did well."

Her lips parted. "*What?* What did he say?"

"It's not important. What you need to know is, the Council ruled to allow you to continue attending classes, but they want you to wear this upgraded collar. Shade, Zeph, and I have also been charged with monitoring your power growth, so you'll be partnered with at least one of us in each class." I glanced at Ella and Tray. "Do you mind giving us a minute to sort out the power exchange? Just in case there is a fallout from the swap?"

Normally, I wouldn't mind their presence, but I wouldn't risk Ella again.

Tray clearly agreed because he set his beer down without a word and walked to his mate, extending a hand.

"Really?" she said, giving us both a sardonic look. "Aflora's not going to explode."

Neither of us replied because we both knew that Aflora could indeed explode at any moment, and I was the only one powerful enough to handle the fallout.

"It's fine," Aflora murmured, pushing off the couch. "Let's go to my room instead. I won't fight the exchange."

After her easy capitulation earlier, I assumed she'd say something like that. Because Aflora put everyone else's safety above her own. This collar could very well suck the life right out of her, for all we knew, and yet she would willingly let me put it on her if it meant she'd suffer instead of those around her.

I admired the hell out of her for that.

Because I would do the same thing in her situation.

It was the responsibility of a royal to put others first. Which, consequently, was exactly why I loathed Emelyn Jyn. She only thought of herself, not others. When I told my father that, he merely shrugged and said it was my future duty to keep the woman in line. So, yet another task to fall on my shoulders in my future role.

Pushing the annoyance away, I focused on Aflora's thick black hair falling in waves down her back as she led me to her room without another comment. She really was beautiful, in an otherworldly way, with her creamy skin, soft curves, and heart-shaped ass.

Any other lifetime, and I'd bend her over her bed, plunge deep inside her, and make her moan my name for hours.

But this life denied me the ability to follow through on that lust-crazed fantasy.

I caught her hand as she entered her room and led her to mine instead, desiring the familiarity of my personal space for the conversation we needed to have.

She didn't fight my nonverbal request, just allowed me to take her into my quarters and shut the door. Stopping a few feet inside my room, she turned and watched me warily.

"I have no idea what this is going to do when I put it on you," I admitted in the stillness between us.

Her throat worked as she swallowed. "I guess there's only one way to find out."

"Actually, I see there being two approaches here." Hence the reason I wanted her in my room for this discussion. I was breaking about a dozen rules, but the idea came to me while on my journey home.

Collaring her felt wrong. Like a steep path I didn't want to risk going down because I probably wouldn't enjoy whatever I found waiting for me at the bottom.

However, I'd give her the choice of where we went from here.

"My concern with this upgraded collar is that it's going to handicap you completely, leaving you unable to defend yourself." Something I suspected she was going to need now that she'd proven herself capable of producing WarFire. That was an advanced, difficult skill to master. And she'd displayed it beautifully in the worst possible way.

Aflora stepped backward to my four-poster bed and sat down without an invitation. Not that she really needed one. "If you don't put it on me, I could lose control and hurt more people."

"Yes," I agreed. "But how are you going to learn control if you are shackled so completely?" I pushed off the door to join her on the bed and handed her the upgraded device. She flinched as it shocked her skin, much the same as it'd done mine when Chern had given it to me. "You can feel it, right? How it's sucking the power right out of your fingertips?"

Her throat worked again, her tongue slipping out to dampen her full lips. "I'll do what I have to do."

"I know." I reached out to tuck a lock of her dark hair behind her ear, then ran my fingers over her current collar. "But sometimes the safe way isn't the right way."

Bright blue eyes met my own. "What do you mean?"

"I mean that in order to survive, you need to learn control, and none of us can teach you that while you're handicapped." I allowed my hand to drop to cover the device in her palm. A zing of discomfort immediately drove up my arm. Placing it around my neck would suffocate me entirely.

I suspected it would utterly destroy Aflora, likely belittling her to a near-human state.

"How about we hide the collar for now and save it as a backup plan. Then, in the interim, you can work with me and Zeph on how to master your new gifts. It won't be easy, and we certainly won't perfect this overnight, but with a little trust and guidance, I think we can make this work."

"That's an option?"

"It can be one, yes." It was a huge risk on my part, especially as it went against the Council's decision. But my father had trusted me with this assignment, claiming it as one of my trials, which allowed me to do this my way. And that collar just felt wrong on so many levels.

"Your Council didn't approve this option," she said after a beat, her intelligent gaze reading my face a little too well. "Why would you risk this for me?"

"I'm the future king, and sometimes kings make unpopular decisions." That was a lesson my father taught me at a young age. "This would be included in that category."

I released my hold on the item in her hand, kicked off my shoes, and twisted around on the bed to face her. It placed my back near my mountain of pillows and the headboard. I relaxed against the silky haven, pulling up one knee to wrap an arm around it while my opposite leg dangled off the edge of the mattress.

Much more comfortable.

"Have you never had to make an unpopular decision for your people?" I wondered out loud, studying her and catching the grimace my question evoked. I knew her answer before she admitted it.

"Yes." She mimicked my pose, only she didn't have a headboard to relax against, just air or the dark wood post. She chose neither and set the collar aside, her fingers wiggling as if to regain feeling. I understood because I'd felt the same twinge of loss in my hand from touching that power-sucking choker. "When Chancellor Elana attacked last spring, I absorbed a lot of her dark energy into myself to protect my people."

Well, that was an interesting detail.

"How did you do that?"

She nibbled her lip, then cocked a shoulder upward. "Honestly, I don't know. It was a natural impulse to take the brunt of her assault and dismantle it."

I considered her for a long moment. "Describe to me what you mean by *dismantle*." Zeph had told me what she said about the cerulean flames earlier, as well as her comments about picking apart spells and putting them back together. Her comment about Elana suggested something else at play here. Something that had nothing to do with Shade biting her.

"It's like a web." She twisted her lips to the side, her gaze turning inward as if she were searching for the design inside her mind. "I can see all the strands and pick them apart to morph into whatever I need them to be. Or, like today, I memorize how it was created and replicate it."

Well, shit. "Have you always been able to do this?"

"Yes. No. Well, sort of." She blinked, coming back to me. "I rarely had a need for it before, but I've always been able to think that way about power. It's natural, which is why I reacted to Elana the way I did. And also today. I understood the magic in a weird way, crafting it to suit me, but I had no idea it would produce WarFire. I just released some of the flames burning under my skin."

Her shoulders fell on a sigh, and I fought the urge to reach across the bed and pull her into a hug. I could see how troubled she was by everything that happened today. It marked her as an abomination, a threat to fae kind. Yet she clearly wanted to do the right thing. Unlike some fae in her position who would go after the power to use it to their advantage, to protect themselves at the cost of others.

Aflora wasn't like that at all.

If I told her to wear that choker, she would, even if it killed her in the process.

And it had nothing to do with her need to survive and everything to do with her desire to lead properly.

"I want to try something." I pushed away from the headboard to sit cross-legged on the bed.

"Um, okay." She copied my position again, facing me with our knees almost touching.

"I'm going to release a spell—nothing violent—and I want you to try to manipulate it without using your wand or your voice. Just like you did with Ella earlier. But don't use any fire."

She nodded slowly. "Okay."

"Good." I held my palms up and indicated for her to do the same. "This is a simple spell for creating an object. You saw Stiggis do it earlier with Shade. Ready?"

"Yep."

"*Ajamee* apple." A bright red apple appeared in my hand. I brought it up and took a bite, waggling my brows.

She frowned. "I thought the spell for creating food was *Tareero Tamida*."

"Ah, yeah, that's one way to do it for food. *Ajamee* will create anything you want." I set my apple on my nightstand and opened my palm again. "*Ajamee* dagger." I visualized the knife I wanted, and it appeared a second later, glistening beneath the moonlight shining through my windows. "You have to envision what you want when you say it, and the object appears."

"Zephyrus told me not to do this without a wand."

"Well, I don't want you to use a wand or your words at all. I want to see if you can make the magic work without uttering a sound, like you did today when dueling Ella."

"But that was different because the magic was used on me. I can't sense your spell at all like this."

"Hmm. All right, we'll go about this a different way, then. Lie down," I said, a dangerous idea forming in my head.

I couldn't touch her the way I wanted to, but I could use my gifts on her in an entirely different way. I had promised not to unleash a violent spell. I said nothing about erotic ones.

Aflora stretched out her long legs and laid her head on a pillow while I shifted to my knees to sit near her abdomen. "Okay, I want you to try to absorb what I'm doing, the way you did with Ella, and use it back on me." *This'll be fun*, I mused. "Ready?"

She nodded. "Yes."

I hovered my palm over her midsection, noting the way her shirt had ridden up to display a taunting sliver of her creamy skin. I focused my energy there, murmuring a spell meant to induce heat in a sensual manner.

Aflora's fingers dug into the comforter on either side of her hips, a sweet little sound catching in her throat.

"Do you feel that?" I asked softly, compelling the sensation to spread across her stomach and higher to her breasts.

She shuddered, her eyes falling closed.

"Focus on the spell, Aflora," I whispered, using my power to send a wave of it downward to the apex between her thighs. "Try to unweave it and send it back into me, sweetheart."

Goose bumps pebbled down her arms as she squeezed her legs together in a manner I recognized all too well.

It took physical restraint not to bend over and place a kiss above the waistline of her pants. Mmm, then I'd tug down the fabric to explore her dampening arousal with my tongue. I bet she tasted sweet, just like how she smelled. Her alluring scent called to me, confirming her interest and telling me how ready she was to receive.

My spell wove deeper into her, seeking the places on her body that required a skilled touch and heating them even more.

"Kolstov," she breathed, arching up off the bed.

"Kols," I corrected, giving in to the desire to press my palm to her abdomen. I pushed her down into the bed and hovered above her. "Now manipulate the spell and re-create it, just like you did with the binding curse from earlier."

"O-okay," she managed to reply, her voice husky with need.

Oh, this was a hazardous game because now I wanted to hear her moan. To watch her fall apart. To slide my thickening cock into her and bring us both to a climax neither of us would soon forget.

I clenched my jaw to hold back a groan, my balls aching with the prospect laid out before me. It would be so easy to slip out of our clothes and lose ourselves in the sheets for hours. Days, even.

Fuck, I need to get laid.

Preferably by a writhing, dark-haired goddess with bright blue—

My eyes widened, the scene unraveling before me an impossible sight.

Holy shit, it's cerulean.

I could *see* her magic unfolding as she mentally stroked my spell, learning and manipulating the ends and crafting it into a spell of her own.

"You're—" A jolt of heat directly to my groin had me falling to the mattress beside her on a spasm so violent that my heart seriously stopped.

Aflora's beautiful gaze captured mine, her smile that of a seductress with her enchantment wrapped around my dick. Literally. She gave it a stroke, and I grabbed her hip in response, our bodies turning toward each other on the bed. "Fuck, Aflora."

Definitely not a virgin or inexperienced.

Not with a grip like *that*.

"You said to use the spell against you," she replied, her tone still husky but this time filled with feminine pleasure. "How am I doing?"

"Wonderfully," I admitted on a hoarse exhale, jolting as she did it again. My grip tightened as I fought the instinct to push her to her back and truly take over. To kiss her deeply, rip off her clothes, and fuck her until my heart stopped again.

But that sliver of cerulean magic taunted my senses, grounding me in the reality of our situation. Not only had she just learned a spell through touch, but she'd also unwoven it and reapplied it in a way only a Quandary Blood could. And the color surrounding her magical essence proved it.

Aflora was absolutely an abomination.

A problem I would eventually need to slaughter.

If I were smart, I'd end her now and not wait for her to grow any stronger. There was a reason the Quandary line died out.

The Midnight Fae had slaughtered them all.

This female posed more risk to my ascension than anyone I'd ever met.

Yet my instinct had me pulling her closer, not pushing her away.

The urge to protect such a precious gift overwhelmed me, consumed my ability to think clearly. "Aflora," I whispered, my lips suddenly dangerously close to hers. "You have no idea how unique you truly are."

She released her mental grip on my cock, her energy vanishing as she captured my gaze. "I know more than you realize."

"Can you tell me about your parents?"

"What about them?"

"Did they have any Dark Fae heritage?" I wondered out loud, trying to solve the mystery of her creation. Because these talents couldn't have come from Shade. He was one hundred percent Death Blood. "You're displaying Quandary Blood gifts, and I have no idea how that's possible."

"Quandary Blood?" she repeated, frowning.

"The sixth line," I explained, ignoring my twinge of annoyance at her not thoroughly having researched our kind. Every fae kingdom treated politics differently. And she was right about her upbringing being vastly different from mine. I grew up with parents. She grew up fighting for her existence against some unknown plague that later turned out to be abomination related.

How ironic, given her situation.

"My parents were Earth Fae," she said slowly. "Not Midnight Fae."

"Either that's not true"—which was my suspicion—"or Shade's bite somehow infected you with the rarest gifts among our kind. Quandary Bloods haven't existed in over a thousand years."

"What happened to them?"

I wasn't going to lie to her. "We killed them all."

Her eyebrows shot upward. "What? Why?"

"Because Quandary Bloods, when they existed, could manipulate energy in a way no one else has ever been able to do, including turning off any link they desired and leaving the fae powerless. The web you mentioned is your connection to the spell. And—"

"I can undo it and piece it back together," she finished for me, her body tensing beside mine. "That's not normal."

"No, it's not."

"Shade can't do that?"

"Not that I'm aware of," I replied. "It's not a Death Blood function." But I had to wonder if he somehow knew or sensed this gift inside Aflora. Maybe that was why he picked her as a mate—to wreak havoc on our kingdom.

"My family fell into power because of a Quandary Blood," I continued, thinking about the history my father once told me. "There was an uprising that ended in the overthrowing of a Death Blood from rule—Shade's ancestor, actually—and a Quandary Blood transferred the source connection from the fallen royal to my grandfather." Which initiated a millennium of animosity between our families.

"And then you killed all the Quandary Bloods?"

I frowned, considering. "I didn't, but the Midnight Fae did."

"Why? If they helped, then why would you kill them all?"

"Because they were dangerous. As I said, they could dismantle a Midnight Fae's power and render him no better than human."

"Did they do that?" she asked.

"Yes. The Death Bloods used them to try to regain power about a thousand years ago. The Quandary Bloods were dismantled and exterminated in response, serving as a warning to keep the Death Bloods in line."

"Sounds like a rather murderous approach," she replied, her displeasure written into her features. "Maybe some of them were innocent."

"Like you?" I suggested, arching a brow. "Are you innocent, Aflora?" I gave in to the impulse to press her back into the bed, my thigh sliding between hers as I moved over her, our lips still dangerously close. "Because I think you're a lot more experienced than you let on."

The double entendre was intentional. It applied to both her magical skills and sexual talents. Because the way she'd used that spell on me without even blushing told me a lot about her confidence in the bedroom. Which only made me want to explore her more.

"I don't even know how to use this power," she whispered, her big blue eyes guilelessly gazing up at me. I almost wanted to call it an act, but I sensed her sincerity in those words. "I have no idea where it came from or why."

"Your parents, most likely," I replied, resting my elbows against the pillows on either side of her head. "Now the question becomes, what should I do with you?"

Kill her was the obvious choice.

But if Shade somehow knew about her bloodline, that implied a much deeper motive at play than him just wanting to avoid his mating duties.

I could practically hear Zeph in my head telling me to use her as bait, to determine exactly how far Shade planned to go.

That plan seemed more practical with every inhale, and not just because it would grant me answers. It would also allow me to keep this beautiful creature alive for as long as possible. I still couldn't have her, especially now that I knew what kind of power she seemed to be harvesting in her blood. But that didn't mean I couldn't have a little fun, right?

"We're going to keep this secret between us for now," I told Aflora, nuzzling my nose gently against hers. "But it means you need to do exactly what I tell you in regard to your growing talents. Understood?"

"Why would you do that for me?"

"Because I'm not done with you yet," I admitted on a whisper, my lips brushing the corner of her mouth.

Dangerous. Very dangerous.

But, oh, it felt good.

Too good.

This female was an ideal mate in every way. Or that was what my instincts told me.

However, my mind knew otherwise.

I'd made a mistake months ago of following my dick into a bad situation. I wouldn't be allowing that to happen again, no matter how much it hurt to stop this little game.

Which was precisely why I rolled off of her and onto my back, my body tense with the need to do a lot more than chastely kiss her. "Now would be a good time for you to leave," I said, my jaw clenching with each word. "We'll talk more tomorrow."

Aflora seemed to pause, but I couldn't risk looking at her. Because if I saw even a single ounce of desire reflected in her gaze, I'd do a hell of a lot more than taste the edge of her mouth.

While I adored stretching my limits and testing my resolve, something told me this female would destroy all my maintained control.

Worse, I'd welcome it.

As the door softly shut behind her, all I wanted was to go after her, push her up against the wall, and devour her entirely.

And allow her to do the same right back to me.

CHAPTER EIGHTEEN

ZEPH

"A Quandary Blood," I mused.

The news didn't surprise me. I had suspected it when we all saw different colors in her fire. That was a trademark Quandary Blood trait, a way to complicate their magic.

"I wonder what kind of wand the figments gave her at AcaWard." I never actually looked at it, but I imagined it held traces of her heritage. "Have you asked to see it yet?"

Kols shook his head, his expression tired. "I was too focused on keeping her magic under control in Elite Class today. Emelyn has decided Aflora is a fun target for practicing her mean-girl bullshit, which put Aflora in an immediately defensive position." He sighed, relaxing into my couch, and lifted a bottle of beer to his lips.

At this rate, we were going to go through my entire stash our first week. Good thing we had two break days coming up. Just had to get through another class tomorrow first, then I could pop into the Human Realm to pick up more. Except it would be on Kols's dime. He came from money. I did not.

"We could ask for her wand now," I suggested. "She's next door, right?"

Kols took a long swallow, his golden irises flaring in a way I recognized. It told me what he was going to say before the words left his lips. "I need a break before I do something stupid."

"Like fuck her?"

"Yeah, exactly like that." His gaze narrowed at me. "And don't tell me you're immune from the pull. We may not have played together in a few months, but I know your type. You want her just as badly as I do."

I lifted a shoulder. "It's not going to happen."

"I know. Now, if only my dick could get the message, we'd be on the same page."

"Your dick always did get you into trouble," I muttered. *Technically, us,* I corrected. His dick always got *us* into trouble.

He set his bottle down on the coffee table and leaned forward to rest his elbows on his knees. "Yeah, if you need to blame me for what went down with Dakota, then do it. But I need your help here, man. This is a big fucking deal. If Shade mated her because he knows what she is, then there's a lot more going on here than just an act of rebellion."

I don't blame you. I blame myself, I thought. But it didn't matter, because he was right. We needed to focus on Shade and Aflora and whatever the hell was going on there.

"What did you read from her when you discussed her Quandary Blood?"

"Genuine surprise and a hell of a lot of confusion," Kols replied. "She's either an amazing actress or she had no idea about her abilities. I'm going with the latter because she seems to think it's Shade's fault. She was pretty adamant that her parents were pure-blood Earth Fae."

"Her gifts prove that to be a lie."

"I agree, but that doesn't mean she believes it. Regardless, it shows innocence. I think she's a pawn in a much larger game. What I want to know is, who is the master on the board? Is it Shade, his father, or someone else entirely? Because we both know the Death Bloods and Quandary Bloods share a dark history."

"Hence the reason your grandfather killed them all off a thousand years ago," I said, recalling the lessons from my history courses here at the Academy. It was a subject that always left me uneasy—the extermination of an entire bloodline to send a message to all the others.

Behave or you'll be next.

The Quandary Bloods were seen as the villains of the story, but I always suspected there was more to the history than what we were told. It was a topic most of us avoided, something I assumed was done with a purpose. If no one questioned the events of the Midnight Fae Dark Age, then the secrets remained safely buried.

Maybe that was Aflora's purpose here—to help disinter some of those rumors.

"We need to keep her alive," I said, lifting my ankle to rest over my opposite knee. "She's worth more than bait." Because she might be the key to unearthing a truth long hidden.

"My father would want her dead immediately." Kols stared at the floor, his expression hard. "I should kill her, Zeph. She's an abomination. I have proof of it."

I considered him for a long moment. "Then why haven't you executed her?"

He continued to focus on the black carpet. "I promised Exos and Cyrus that I would look after her," he admitted softly. "Not because it's the right thing to do, but because I want to." He exhaled a long breath, his golden eyes finally lifting to mine. "I feel this strange urge to protect her, Zeph. I barely know her and yet..."

"You feel obligated to shelter her from the harsh future you know awaits her," I finished for him, my voice equally quiet.

Because yeah, I understood. That bizarre inclination to watch over her tied into my strange need to teach her, to help her survive. Yet I knew her death was inevitable. The need to take care of her hit me right in the gut, and I had no idea where it came from or why.

"Do you think it has something to do with her being an abomination?" I wondered out loud. "Maybe she has some sort of enchantment woven into her existence that's forcing us to act in her best interest."

"Like some sort of self-preservation instinct?"

"Yeah, exactly." I rubbed the scruff dotting my jaw, a stiff reminder of my need to shave again soon.

I'd let myself go this week as a result of my misery pertaining to my new vocation. Teaching was not for me. I had little patience for idiocy, and half the new students were too green to know their left foot from their right. They'd learn. Eventually.

"It's possible," Kols replied, considering my enchantment theory. "I feel half-crazed with lust every time I'm near her. And before you say I'm always like that, this one is different. The others were just challenges I enjoyed conquering. Aflora poses more than just a challenge. She's a real threat to me and this kingdom. And it goes against all my training to let her live, let alone *help* her."

"You're talking about the choker." I gave him a hard look. "Tell me you put it on her."

"You know I didn't," he muttered.

"Fuck, Kols." This was bad. Really bad. "That was a direct order from Malik."

"You think I don't know that?" he countered, shaking his head. "I realized my mistake about thirty minutes after I allowed it to happen."

"You mean after you jacked off," I translated, knowing him all too well. He'd told me about the heat spell when explaining his findings about her powers.

"Yeah, twice, but that's beside the point. I know it's wrong, yet I still couldn't put it on her this morning. Instead, I focused all my energy on keeping her under control today."

"Which, I imagine, only brought you that much closer to her power." That was how our abilities worked. We fed off the power waves of others. Kols was the strongest among us, the black lines dancing along his arms and chest an indication of his ties to the source. If we practiced our spells together, my strength would grow tenfold. Implying Aflora's would as well.

"You have no idea," he muttered. "My power is hungry for hers, and not just in an ascension kind of way."

"She's an ideal mate, isn't she?"

He picked up his beer and took a powerful pull before nodding solemnly. "I've felt it from the moment I laid eyes on her. Her personality isn't helping matters."

"Meaning?"

"She's selfless and intelligent, has a backbone of steel, and, let's not forget, she's stunning." He set his bottle back down and dropped his head to his hands. "This is wrong on so many levels."

I allowed him to wallow for a moment while I contemplated everything he'd said. A few thoughts kept popping back into my mind, most of them dangerous to utter out loud. Similar to the historical secrets I suspected were hidden for reasons that might not be in everyone's best interest.

However, since we were already having a conversation that could land us both in a dungeon, why not push the boundaries?

"We've been told our entire lives that abominations are vile creatures," I started, considering my wording carefully. "But isn't it how we use the gifts that matter? Not necessarily who our parents are?"

He lifted his gaze just enough to catch mine, his palms still hovering over his mouth. "What are you trying to say, Zeph? Speak plainly."

"Aflora is an abomination, but she doesn't strike me as evil at all. I'd actually call her *sweet*."

"We barely know her," he pointed out.

While I agreed, I couldn't help saying, "You've always prided yourself on being a good judge of character. Would you trust Exos's and Cyrus's opinions of her?"

He lowered his hands, clasping them between his legs as he continued to rest his elbows on his thighs. "Exos and Cyrus would do anything to protect their mate. And their mate is friends with Aflora. That alone means I can't trust their opinions because they're inherently biased."

"All right, well what does your gut say about Aflora? Because mine says the girl grew up playing with flowers, not plotting world domination."

He snorted. "Oh, she's innocent. But not entirely. The way she used that heat spell on my cock spoke volumes about her lack of innocence."

"Always thinking with your dick," I mused, amused despite the serious subject matter. "Just because she knows her way around your pants doesn't mean she wants to take over the Midnight Fae kingdom."

"Yeah, yeah, I get your point. But I would have bet money a week ago that she was a virgin, and before you say that's irrelevant, it's not. If I misjudged her experience, then I could easily be misjudging *her*."

"Fair," I agreed. "However, I never picked up a virginal vibe from her, just a lack of experience with multiple partners. Which is still my assumption in that realm of conversation. Regarding the more important one, however, I don't think Aflora could ever invoke harm intentionally. Hell, she looked ready to cry when you destroyed her burning thwomp last week."

Kols chuckled. "Yeah, she wasn't at all happy today when Headmaster Jenkins used a crow in her compulsion spell. There were tears in Aflora's eyes when the poor thing died. I lied and told her the bird was a conjured being, not real."

"She believed you?"

"Yeah." His lips curled. "I made her a crow on our way back to the suite. She still has it in her room."

"And this woman is a threat to our kind?" I scoffed. "You're using that bird to spy on her right now, aren't you?"

"Not presently, but yeah, I can see through its eyes."

I smirked. "I'd call you brilliant, but your ego doesn't need stroking."

"You're right. I already know I'm brilliant." He finally cracked a smile. "So what are we going to do?"

"I should think that's obvious," I replied, lifting my ankle off my knee to sprawl lazily in my recliner. Despite hating the location of my suite, I couldn't deny the comfort in the furnishings provided by Kols's family. They kept my fridge stocked—except for beer—and provided me with all the luxuries I grew up with in the Nacht Estate. Not a bad life. I just hated the new teaching part of it.

"We're going to protect her," Kols said, referring to the future plan.

"Yeah. Until we figure out what the hell is going on with Shade." And possibly glean some historical answers in the process. "He tasted her, so he has to know what she is."

Kols bobbed his head in agreement. "The question is, did he know before he bit her?"

"That's my guess."

"Mine, too."

"One thing that perplexes me—"

"Only one?" Kols joked.

I didn't remark on it, just continued my thought. "He had to know we'd figure this out. Why hasn't he tried to keep us away from her?"

"He hasn't had a choice."

"He's Shade," I reminded him. "He's a dick who doesn't play by the rules, yet he's been waltzing the peaceful line all week. Why?"

Kols frowned. "I... I don't know."

Neither did I, hence the reason I brought it up. "We need to keep him away from Aflora."

"Easier said than done. He keeps visiting her dreams." Kols grimaced. "I overheard her moaning his name last night."

I arched a brow. "Overheard?"

"Okay, I may have tried to play with her in her dreams. It's safe and an easy way to burn off some lust. But Shade was already there."

My lips twitched. "Maybe you should try shoving him out tonight and see what happens."

"Don't think I won't."

"Oh, I know you will." Just the thought of it had my dick awakening in my pants because I knew what that scene would look like from Kols's point of view. And yeah, I wanted in on it. But I'd never give in to it. Even if I went to bed the last few nights to thoughts of Aflora's full mouth wrapped around my cock.

I cleared my throat. "Right. Well. I'm going for a run."

"Another one?" Kols asked, arching a brow.

"A man has to exercise."

"Uh-huh." He gave me a knowing look. "Good luck."

"Given that you're the one who has to sleep next to her every night, I think you're in need of luck, mate." I stood and stretched, smiling as Kols observed the movement beneath his hooded gaze. "Feel free to add me to your little nighttime fantasy. You know what I like."

With that taunt—one I shouldn't have allowed to slip from my lips—I left to explore the Academy grounds again.

All the while thinking of a dark-haired beauty with pouty lips and tits made for a man's hands.

Thinking about her wasn't exactly a sin.

Even if it felt like one.

Too bad that distinction only made me harder.

CHAPTER NINETEEN

AFLORA

"Okay, so this time, try not to kill me, 'kay?" Ella stood across from me on a mat, her hands up in the air. It didn't escape my notice that Trayton hovered near the edge, his gaze holding a lethal warning in them.

"No magic," he said, his tone holding a royal inflection I recognized all too well.

Annoyance flashed in Ella's features. "She knows, Tray. That's the point of this makeshift gym class."

"Physical training," Kols corrected, joining his brother. They both wore sleeveless shirts that showed off their athletic physique. I could definitely see the family similarities between them in their regal postures and aristocratic jaw structure. But Tray resembled the night, while Kols reminded me of the sun.

A sun I very much missed.

Starting classes in the evening really messed with my concept of *days*. We finished closer to the time I used to wake up, then slept during the light hours and started all over again each night.

No wonder the Midnight Fae were pale.

Well, except Shade. He had a slight tan, which I suspected linked back to his penchant for disappearing into shadows.

He winked at me from across the gymnasium where he stood waiting for his turn on the mat.

I scowled at him in response.

His dreams at night were killing me, and he knew it. I argued with him every time he entered my head, yet I still ended up mostly naked and writhing beneath him.

Except for last night.

My cheeks burned at the memory of the things I'd done with Kols while asleep. It'd also been in my head, a coping mechanism that helped me force Shade out, and I was a bit embarrassed by how thoroughly I'd used the Royal Fae. He was supposed to be helping and mentoring me, yet I spent the night doing wicked things to his sculpted physique.

A physique that flexed as he took a step forward and lightly took hold of my arms. "You can do this, Aflora. It's just a tumbling exercise. Ella will show you how it works. Just don't call on your fire, okay?"

Mother Earth, even now he was trying to help me and had no idea how I'd used him last night. My hesitation on the mat had nothing to do with fear and everything to do with guilt.

Just don't think about it. Or how good his hands feel on my arms right now. In fact, you should take a step back, I coached myself.

Except I didn't listen at all.

Instead, I looked deep into his golden irises and thought about how they glowed while I went down on him. I swallowed, his taste a lingering memory in my throat. "I can do this."

"I know you can."

With a nod, I forced myself to look at Ella. She arched a light blonde brow. "Oh, are you finally ready? Because I'm bored and growing fairy wings over here."

Trayton snorted. "You wish."

"I do!" She threw her hands up in the air. "Fae should have wings and pointy ears."

My own ears twitched at the thought, and I brushed my dark strands behind them to show off the tips. "I have pointy ears."

Ella spun around to face me, her lips pulling into a huge grin. "There! That's what we should look like. All she needs is wings."

"Fairies have wings," Trayton explained calmly. "And they're not real."

"Well, technically, pixies exist and they have wings." Amusement briefly touched my chest as I thought of Claire's obsession with the little creations brought on by her connection to the spirit element.

"We have our own version here," Trayton muttered. "Ella loves them."

"But he won't let me keep them as pets," she pointed out.

"Because they bite and like to set fires all over the damn place."

"Are you all going to stand around and chat all day or get down to work?" Zephyrus's voice came from right behind me, the heat of his body sending a shiver down my spine. He'd worn gray sweatpants and a white T-shirt today, something several of the females seemed intrigued by throughout the gymnasium. Myself included.

I firmly blamed Shade for my runaway hormones. If he hadn't spent every night taunting me with his touch and tongue, I wouldn't be having all these illicit fantasies about Kols, and I wouldn't find Zephyrus particularly irresistible today.

"Am I invisible?" the headmaster demanded.

"N-no," I stammered, spinning to face him and having to look up to meet his smoldering green eyes. There was a hint of brown around the pupils that captured my attention for a long moment before I shook my head. "We were just getting started."

He arched a brow. "Yeah? Because it looks like you're all over here gossiping. Maybe I need to reassign pairings." He glanced to the left, his mouth already moving before I had a chance to respond. "Shade! Get your ass over here."

The Death Blood shadowed over to us in a wave of his black smoke, his expression bored as he appeared. "The whole headmaster thing seems to be going well for you, Zeph. Bet it feels nice to be able to issue commands for once rather than constantly taking it up the ass from Kols."

"Oh, please assign me to him," Kols said, stepping forward. "I'll show him what it feels like to take it up the ass."

Zephyrus shrugged. "I was going to give him to Tray, but go for it." He looked at the other royal. "Help me manage the match between Ella and Aflora, then go spar with Fang."

Glancing over my shoulder, I mouthed, "Fang?" at Ella, hoping I'd heard that wrong.

She burst out laughing, nodding. "Yeah, original. I know."

"Stop goofing around," Zephyrus snapped, his hand grasping my hip and forcing my attention back to him. "I need to see what I'm dealing with so I can better plan our independent study next week. Unless you want me to assume that all you know how to do is pick flowers from the ground?"

I bristled at the negative insinuation in his tone. "I'm not a helpless pixie, Zeph."

His eyebrow arched again, saying nothing and everything with that look alone. We weren't familiar enough for me to use his nickname. It just sort of slipped out.

"Headmaster Zephyrus," I corrected softly.

"Don't be a dick, Zeph," Ella cut in, stepping up to my side. "We were just about to start. And we don't need to be managed."

"That remains to be seen," he replied, his eyes still holding mine. "Go on then, pixie flower. Show me what you can do. I'm waiting."

"Do you think it's wise to goad the chick who almost killed me two days ago?" Ella asked, folding her arms. "No offense, Aflora."

"She's fine. She's wearing the new and improved choker, right?" He seemed to see right through me, his green irises gleaming knowingly.

"Right," I said, swallowing. "I'll be fine."

"Then stop stalling and give me a show, pixie flower."

Heat crept up my neck at his words and the tone with which he uttered them. Hard, demanding, and inflexible. Three words that absolutely described Zephyrus.

With a resolute nod, I faced Ella and caught Kols and Shade standing beside Tray, observing the entire exchange.

Great. So I would be giving them all a show.

"Just kick my ass and get it over with," I muttered to Ella as we entered the circle drawn on the mats.

She gaped at me. "Did you just curse?"

"I know how to curse," I said, falling into what I hoped resembled a fighting stance. I'd watched a few Powerless Champion duels in the Elemental Fae kingdom. I knew what to expect. I just hadn't enrolled in any of the Academy courses, preferring solo athletics to combat sports.

"I'm small, but I'm fast," Ella warned me.

"Good, then this will be over quickly." Because I had no idea what I was doing and I refused to hurt her like last time.

It was a miracle she forgave me so quickly. Actually, it made me question her intelligence. But she claimed to like me and said we had a lot more in common than I realized. Not wanting to deny a gift of friendship, I let the lack of common sense slide. After all, it was in my favor.

Her fist flew at my face, causing me to jump backward on instinct. She followed up with a punch toward my middle, which I avoided by spinning out of her reach. "That's how we're going to do this?" I breathed, dodging another fist.

"You said to get this over with quickly. Stand still and I'll grant your wish," she panted, kicking out this time.

"Why the hell would people want to take a course on violence?" I demanded, glancing at Zephyrus. "What purpose does this"—I ducked again, narrowly missing Ella's elbow—"serve?"

"It's physical exercise that also enables you to protect yourself in untoward situations." Zephyrus's arm snaked around my waist as he hauled me backward into his hard body.

"What kind of 'untoward situations'?" I spun and found my wrists caught in one of his hands before I could even consider my next move.

"Midnight Fae frequent the Human Realm regularly." He started backing me up off the mat.

"And there are situations there that require combat?" I asked while trying to find Ella over his shoulder. He thwarted my attempt to seek her intervention by speeding up his pace and practically shoving me backward with his grasp.

There had to be a way out of his hold, which I suspected was the lesson here, but my body seemed to obey him on impulse despite my brain's commands to the contrary.

"Many dangers exist in the Human Realm, Aflora," he murmured as my back met a wall. He pinned my hands over my head, his opposite hand going to my throat. "Weren't you recently captured and overpowered in the Human Realm?"

"By a Midnight Fae," I replied, glaring up at him. "Not a human."

"Hmm, but had you known how to properly defend yourself, maybe you wouldn't be here now," he said quietly, his grip tightening around my throat. "Even now, you're helpless with no idea how to fight me. I can feel your capitulation with every swallow. I *own* you right now, and there isn't a damn thing you can do about it."

The words were soft, his gaze burning into mine.

Everything seemed to fade away around us, the moment stretching as he held me captive in a decidedly inferior position. It should have infuriated me. Instead, it heated my blood, and not in a combat sort of way. Even if I could fight him—which I absolutely couldn't—I wouldn't. Because I *liked* him overpowering me.

The realization swept over me, causing me to melt beneath his hold.

I wanted him to own me, just like he said.

To tell me what to do. To guide me. To teach me in a manner that had nothing to do with this class and everything to do with *us*.

Oh, I'm in trouble.

First, Kols.

Now, Zeph.

And not to mention Shade, who still haunted my every breath.

"You like this," Zephyrus whispered, his heat surrounding me so entirely that I forgot how to properly breathe. Every inhale filled me with his intoxicating woodsy cologne. It left me light-headed and confused and aching for more.

"You shouldn't like this," he continued, his lips falling to my ear. "Is this why you let Shade manipulate you so thoroughly? He gave you a little attention, and you showed him your neck? Are you truly that easy?"

His comment lit a fire in me that ate through the heat his touch had inspired and spurred me into action. My knee connected with his steel thigh, sending a jolt of pain up my leg. That only made me angrier. I stomped on his foot with as much force as I could muster and squirmed in earnest against him.

His hips pinned mine, leaving me utterly defenseless and seething mad. "Let me go."

"But it was finally getting interesting," he whispered, his teeth skimming my earlobe. He nipped me gently, drawing a growl from my throat.

"You're too big to spar with me," I snapped. "It's an unfair fight."

"Fights are never fair," he returned.

"That's what magic is for."

"Ah, but it's against Midnight Fae Council rules to expose our kind in the Human Realm. So what would you do in this situation, pixie flower? Would you let a bigger male take advantage of you? Or would you use magic on him and bury the evidence?"

I stopped trying to free myself and instead met his smoldering gaze. "Are you asking if I would let him hurt me or kill him instead?"

"A male in this position would do more than just hurt you," he replied softly. "He'd destroy you."

"Then I'd have no choice but to truly defend myself."

"Then do it," he encouraged. "Defend yourself."

"You just said magic isn't allowed in a fight like this."

"We're not in the Human Realm."

"No, we're in Defense Without Magic class," I retorted. "Stop trying to convince me to break the rules, *Zeph*."

His mouth went to my ear again, his breath hot against my skin. "We're all breaking rules here, princess. That collar of yours is just the beginning of the quandary we've found ourselves in, yes?"

I froze. My lungs ceasing to work.

And he pulled back with a knowing smirk. "We have a lot of work to do, Aflora. I expect you to come prepared for our independent study course. I suggest you use the next two days off to study."

With that, he released me and stalked out of the room.

I gaped after him, as did several other students.

Kols flashed me an apologetic look, one that confirmed Zephyrus's statement.

He'd told the headmaster all about my bloodline, as well as the collar around my neck. Not that I could blame him, as the two of them were clearly close even when arguing. But it left me even more alone than before, reminding me that I had no allies in this realm. Whatever assistance Kols provided, it would likely come at a cost.

Because he would always choose his own over me.

Just as he should.

I'd do the same thing in his situation.

Which meant I could only trust him to an extent, if at all.

My shoulders stiffened, my spine straightening. I wouldn't let this knock me down.

Zeph was right. I had to fight for myself to survive this, which meant I needed to learn how to properly defend myself. Both in the Human Realm and in this one. Because someday soon, my life would very likely depend on it.

CHAPTER TWENTY

Several weeks of classes sped by without incident, mostly because I locked myself away in my room constantly to study. I had a lifetime of material to read in order to catch up in all my courses.

Death Magic class.

Warrior Magic class.

Elite Magic class.

Defense Without Magic class.

Break day.

Break day.

Midnight Fae Politics—the only class I seemed to be doing all right in, thanks to Ella's tutoring.

Malefic Magic class—my least favorite.

Independent study day—*ugh*.

Break day.

Break day.

Break day.

Today, I had another independent study day with Zeph. Who was a complete ass and way too hands-on for my liking. Mostly because he inspired thoughts that weren't appropriate. Especially when he pinned me to the mat or to the wall. I occasionally caught a glimmer of interest in his gaze, but it always disappeared before I could confirm it. Which meant I probably made it up in my daydreams.

Who could blame me with my nightly sexual escapades? If it wasn't Shade in my head, it was Kols. Causing me to heat up every time I went near the Midnight Prince. So I was pretty much in a constant state of red because he rarely left my side, always helping me in every class and ensuring my magic stayed in check.

Shade, however, seemed to be leaving me alone. Mostly because he kept skipping class. It annoyed the daylights out of me because I needed him in Death Magic class and he rarely showed up, forcing me to navigate the halls and spells by myself. When I asked him about it in my dreams, he kissed me to silence the conversation.

The only positive was that it forced me to be independent and to learn on my own. A benefit and a curse because I had no idea if I was doing anything correctly. I just went with my gut.

My legs buckled beneath me as Zeph swept his foot in an arc that sent me ass-first onto the mat. "You're distracted," he accused. "Do you think I want to spend my time babysitting you? Either show up or get the fuck out of my gym."

"Your gym?" I huffed, pushing myself back up to a standing position. "Are you finally embracing your headmaster role?"

He snorted and changed the subject. "Show me what you learned in Malefic Magic class yesterday."

I knew he was going to demand that.

After weeks of sparring with him during several class days and on a handful of break days, I'd begun learning his expectations. He wanted me to apply every lesson to my sparring. Not only did he want me to master control of my power, but he also wanted me to be able to use it defensively.

Or *offensively* in this case.

Steeling my spine, I held out my hand and murmured the conjuring spell we learned yesterday. Ice picks formed around us almost immediately, all aimed at Zeph. His lips actually twitched as he batted them away with a quick defense spell. "Good. Again."

I repeated the incantation.

He destroyed it a second later.

"Once more."

Narrowing my eyes, I decided to throw him off guard and called up a different spell that I'd read about in my books last night. It was from the next chapter and involved fire. A dangerous move considering my history with the element, but my cerulean flames remained in check as a parade of black embers encircled Zeph.

His eyebrows shot up just enough to confirm I had surprised him. In the next breath, he uttered words that dispelled my creation. "Cute," he muttered. "At least I know you can read."

The jibe made me roll my eyes at him. "I'm not an ignoramus."

He considered me for a long moment. "No. You're not."

"Careful, Zeph. That was almost a compliment." I always called him *Headmaster* or *Zephyrus* around others, but I'd taken to using his nickname when in private. He never corrected me, so I took that as his way of allowing it.

"Well, you seem to be taking well to Malefic Magic, so let's try some more defensive moves. Maybe it'll help you not get your ass kicked next week."

"Praise tied to an insult," I mused. "There's the Zeph I've come to adore."

He glared at me. "Stop talking and start focusing."

"I am focused."

"Then knock me down."

I sighed. "Sure." We both knew I couldn't. Not only did he have, like, twelve inches of height on me, but he was also solid muscle and an expert defender. Hitting him was akin to punching a wall. Making him budge even an inch proved impossible every time we did this exercise.

But I'd try anyway because he demanded it.

Using a technique he taught last week in Warrior Magic class, I tried to circle around to his back to knock out his knees.

He moved with me, his arms folded, his expression bored.

Gritting my teeth, I tried the leg sweep he used on me a few minutes ago.

And nothing.

Not even a flinch.

It actually hurt me more than it probably hurt him.

So I ran around behind him and jumped on his back, my arms around his neck and my legs around his waist.

"What the fuck are you doing?"

"Hanging out," I said, my forearms locking around his throat. "When you get tired of holding me up here, you'll fall."

"You weigh practically nothing," he gritted out, his head twisting in a futile effort to see me. "Get down."

"No."

"This isn't useful at all." He sounded livid, which only made me cling to him more. Pissing him off had become a favorite pastime of mine. He was a dick to me, so I paid him back in kind. "Seriously, let go."

I placed my chin on his shoulder and sighed. "I think I'll just stay here until you fall down."

His resulting growl vibrated my chest through the thin fabric of our shirts. He'd worn another of those sleeveless ones that showed off his arms. It was about the only thing I looked forward to on our sparring days. Oh, and his gray sweatpants. I rather liked those as well.

"Aflora, you have three seconds before I remove you, and you're not going to like how I do it," he warned.

I yawned. "Do your worst, Teach." Probably not the wisest move to goad my instructor, but he didn't scare me. Maybe I'd adopted too carefree an attitude while attending the Academy. My life was still very much in danger, and I took that seriously—hence my endless study hours—yet I had to let go sometimes. And for whatever reason, those times seemed to occur when around Zeph.

And in my dreams with Kols and Shade.

These three men left me—

"Oof," I breathed as my back hit the sparring mat and Zeph sprawled out on top of me, locking my wrists over my head.

I hadn't even felt him move, just suddenly went airborne as he spun me around in a move that should not have been possible.

"Brat," he muttered, his hips pinning mine to the floor.

"Maybe," I managed to say, the word coming out on a winded exhale, thanks to the roughness of my landing. "But I got you"—I inhaled sharply to replenish my lungs—"on the floor."

His irises swirled with dark green, reminding me of the lush forests back home. I nearly sighed, loving that smoldering look and longing to see a real tree again. The dark magic continued to grow while my access to my primary gift remained just out of reach, although lately I'd felt it flaring on occasion, as if begging me to connect to the source.

Kols told me last week that he'd met with Exos while on a break day and learned that Sol had taken up the mantle of managing the source for me in my absence.

I was both pleased and saddened by that news. Pleased because the male I loved like a brother needed to embrace his earth more, and I'd finally provided him with the push he required to do so. But the act saddened me as well because it meant the Elemental Earth Fae were seeking a way to survive without me.

It was the right thing to do. I couldn't lead them as an abomination. Yet that didn't stop me from wanting to try.

Kols believed I grew up with my Quandary Blood powers and that Shade's bite had just provided me with an excuse to access them. Or perhaps my presence at the Academy was what had truly awakened them.

Except I'd used them before when I stopped Elana.

"What put that puzzling look in your eyes?" Zeph asked, reminding me of his presence on top of me. Not that I'd forgotten. His woodsy scent and hard, masculine body were difficult to ignore.

"Nothing."

"Don't lie to me."

I gave him a look. "Because you never lie to me?"

He actually appeared affronted by the statement. "Actually, I haven't. Everything I've told you from the beginning has been truthful. We both know you're not going to survive here. It's just a matter of time. It makes my efforts futile, but at least I tried."

I laughed humorously. "You really have a way with words, Zeph." However, he was right. He always spoke his mind around me, never avoiding the truth. That didn't mean I could trust him, but I could at least rely on him to give it to me straight.

"You're avoiding my question. What were you thinking about?"

"Why do you want to know?" I countered.

"Humor me."

I suspected he meant that literally, as he often found entertainment in my comments. This would no doubt be the same. "I was thinking about Sol taking control of the earth source and how I'm happy for him but sad for me. As an abomination, I can't properly lead my people, no matter how badly I may want to."

Zeph considered me for a long moment and released my wrists to balance himself on his elbows on either side of my head. It effectively caged me beneath him in a decidedly intimate manner that he didn't seem to notice. "Do you know why abominations are killed on sight?"

"Yes. They're evil."

He arched a brow. "Are they?" he asked softly, his gaze dropping to my lips. "Are you evil, Aflora? Or have our Councils trained us to fear what we don't understand?"

I swallowed, the warmth from his body seeping into mine, bringing us closer with each breath. A forbidden desire to kiss him entered my thoughts even while I considered his words. "I don't feel evil," I whispered.

"I don't think you're evil either," he agreed, his voice just as quiet, our conversation one we shouldn't be having. "I believe abominations are destroyed because our Councils fear their power. They claim it will disturb the source balance, but I think what they really mean is that it will disturb *their* balance."

"Why are you telling me this?" I asked as his eyes met mine once more.

"I don't know." He started playing with a loose strand of my dark hair, his long finger coiling it around the end. "Something about you makes me want to protect you. I keep fighting the instinct, yet you pull me right back in. It's a puzzle I can't solve, but I suspect it's linked to your power. Quandary Bloods are considered the most lethal of our kind. Yet, again, I wonder if that label was created by the Council out of fear, not practicality."

He pressed his forehead to mine, inhaling deep and sighing against my lips.

"You're improving admirably," he added, his words nearly silent. Then he fractured the moment by rolling off of me and landing deftly on his feet in one of his expert moves. "Class dismissed, Aflora. I'll see you in a few days."

My heart pounded in my chest as he walked away, my breathing ragged from both his words and his nearness.

If my power doesn't kill me, these males will, I thought, unable to move. I felt hot and cold and so incredibly turned on.

And my dreams tonight would only make it worse.

CHAPTER TWENTY-ONE

ZEPH

*T*hank *fuck for days off from class.*

I had three days—technically, three and a half since I dismissed Aflora early—to work off this intense need throbbing inside me.

Every damn time I closed my eyes, I pictured Aflora beneath me, writhing on the sparring mat, or my bed, or against the damn wall, all the while moaning my name.

This mounting desire to fuck her was a problem. I nearly acted on it today, my dick rock hard as I pinned her to the floor. Talking had been the only way to remain focused and keep from doing something colossally stupid.

Glaring at my reflection in the mirror, I took in the dark hollows beneath my eyes and the stubble already growing against my jaw. It seemed that no matter how often I shaved, that perpetual shadow existed. One of these days, I'd just stop and let the beard come.

Maybe.

"Fuck," I muttered.

What I really needed was blood. The supplements on campus were enough to keep a Midnight Fae going, but nothing compared to a fresh human vein. I'd spent the last month and a half living on the shitty substitute because I didn't feel like fucking around.

Tonight, that would change.

A hot vein and a warm, slick cunt were on the menu.

Because I needed to fuck before I did something I'd regret—like go next door, strip Aflora, and take my fill of her.

The damn female had gotten under my skin in the worst way. All these one-on-one sessions only made it worse. I had my hands all over her daily, memorizing her curves and feeling her body quiver against mine.

She read like an open book. It'd be so easy to take her. She wore her interest in her eyes. Not to mention the floral perfume of her arousal, which seemed to be a constant aphrodisiac between us these days.

New plan, I decided, ripping off my shirt and removing the jeans I'd just put on.

If I went to the Human Realm in this shape, I'd last all of a few seconds inside a woman. Especially if I found one that resembled Aflora.

I turned the water on in the shower, gave it about two seconds to heat up, and stepped beneath the cool spray with my arm braced against the marble tile. No amount of jacking off was going to fix this growing obsession. But it would prepare me properly for tonight, then I'd fuck Aflora out of my system.

And think of her the entire time.

It was so wrong, which only made this indulgence more right.

"Fuck," I cursed again, my head falling to my forearm as I gripped my shaft with my opposite hand.

I'd been hard since I set foot inside the gym. Aflora had pulled all that gorgeous hair up into a ponytail, just like she always did. It elicited all sorts of fantasies every time. I wanted to grab hold of all that hair and jerk her head to the side to trail my lips up the column of her neck and nibble her sweet flesh. Mmm, then I'd use my grip to guide her down to her knees and drive myself deep into—

"Hey, Aflora said you cut your session short. Did her magic...?" Kols trailed off as he entered the bathroom, my walk-in shower wide open in an unintended invitation because I hadn't bothered to close any doors. His attention shifted to my hand and the angry hold I had on my cock, his eyes heating at the sight. "Oh."

A single sentiment, filled with understanding.

I stroked myself while he watched, an entire history of intimacy sparking between us in the flash of a second. This intensity between us only grew over the years, blinding us to our actions and how they impacted others.

Now was no different.

I knew I shouldn't.

I knew giving in to this impulse would be a mistake.

Yet I couldn't deny the flaring of his pupils or the sharp intake of breath as his arousal quickly caught up to mine.

He wanted me like he always did.

And right now, I was too far gone to fight it.

I shoved away from the marble, took hold of his nape, and yanked him into the shower. He grunted as his back hit the wall, his gold irises on fire as he boldly met my gaze. I took his mouth in a punishing kiss meant to draw blood, and he gave it back in kind, his palm grasping the back of my neck and squeezing as he fought my dominance with his own.

He'd lose.

We both knew it.

But part of the allure between us was the battle each time we fucked.

I released his nape to grab his shirt, the buttons tearing beneath my hand as I wrenched the fabric away from his chest. He growled. I snarled. And his shirt fell in tatters to the floor of the shower.

He kicked off his shoes, the leather ruined from the water. His pants and boxers soon followed, leaving us naked and panting against each other. "Tell me about the dreams," I demanded. "Because I know you've been in her head every night."

Kols arched into my palm as I grabbed his dick, his breath shuddering over my lips. "Not every night," he replied. "Just most of them."

"What does she do? How have you fucked her? I want details. All of them." I tightened my grip, giving him a firm, harsh stroke to underline my demand.

"*Fuck*, Zeph."

"That's the idea," I replied, pressing my forehead to his. "Tell me what she likes."

"She likes everything," Kols panted, his back bowing off the wall. "I've had her so many different ways over the last month, and she loves all of it. Sometimes she even takes control, allowing me into her fantasies. Yet she has no idea that I know or that it's all a mutual exchange. She thinks she's using me against Shade to kick him out of her head to indulge in her own desires."

"Mmm, if that were true, then I'd be there, too." Because I knew she wanted me, had seen the glimmer of interest countless times in her beautiful blue eyes.

"I think she's tried, but I'm always the one available," he admitted. "She fucking keeps me up at all hours with my hand on my cock, stroking endlessly until she's satisfied."

"Do you come?" I asked him, our eyes locked together.

"Every time."

"Do you imagine her coming over to lick you clean afterward?"

"Yes."

"Which makes you come again." It wasn't a question but a statement. Because I knew Kols. We both were drinking blood supplements because we hadn't fed properly in ages. And it was all Aflora's fault. Her fucking enchantment, her allure, her sweet floral scent. "She's driving me mad."

"I know."

"Tell me about the dreams," I said again, wrapping my fist around both our cocks and stroking them together. "I want the details, Kols. Tell me how she tastes, how she screams, her favorite position. How does she like to be fucked?"

He swallowed roughly, his palm still on the back of my neck, his opposite hand on my arm as if he wanted to help me guide the pace below. I thrived on control, and so did he. Poor Aflora would be helpless between us, our needs dictating her every move.

And she'd fucking love it.

We'd make sure of it.

"She sucks cock like a queen," Kols said, his head hitting the shower wall as I squeezed our shafts together on a violent upward twist of my wrist. "I haven't taken her ass yet, but I want to. She looks amazing on all fours and cries out when I fuck her from behind. Shit, she's insatiable, Zeph. I can take her for hours, at least in her mind. I made her come four times against my tongue the other night, and she orgasmed a fifth time around my dick only minutes later."

I released a harsh breath, my hand moving faster. "She'd fit perfectly between us."

"I know. Trust me, *I know*." He bucked into my palm, his eyes falling closed. "But it's never going to happen. She's unattainable."

My dick throbbed with his words, which was entirely the point.

He knew how to spur me on.

Just as I knew how to ramp him up.

"If she were here, I'd command her to kneel and watch us play," I told him, my wrist twisting once more. "Then I'd make her lick us clean when we finished."

Kols cursed, his exhale sharp and heated. "Would you let her come?"

"I'd *make* her come," I replied. "But I'd tell her to do it herself. She hasn't earned our mouths. Not yet."

"Because she's forbidden."

"She's a disobedient brat."

"Who is also completely out of our reach," he added, his taunt sending a hot jolt of lust down my spine. "She's dangerous, Zeph. A toy we're not meant to touch."

"I know."

"Walking down that path would be akin to flirting with death," he continued, stoking my flame even higher. "She's the most complicated challenge we've ever met."

"I know," I repeated, my forehead falling to his. "*Fuck*, I know."

"We can't have her, Zeph."

I growled at his declaration, prepared to fight.

He grabbed my shoulders to shove me up against the other wall, reading my cues as he always did. And I took hold of him to push him back, my grip on us relentless. "You're going to come all over my hand. Then you're going to lick it off."

"Fuck you."

"Not today," I replied with a sharp yank, eliciting a guttural sound from him. I'd let him take me once, after a long quarrel that equated to savage foreplay. But it was almost always the other way around.

"You're killing me," he groaned, shoving me backward once more.

I grunted as I hit the wall, then spun us around to place his back to the hard surface, keeping my chest pressed against his.

He growled. "You're in a fucking mood."

"I didn't ask you to join me," I said, my lips falling to the corded muscle along his neck to skim his pulse.

"No, you grabbed me and ripped off my clothes."

"You knew I was in the shower," I whispered darkly. "You could hear it."

"I didn't expect the door to be wide open."

"I didn't expect you to barge into my suite, but here we are." I ran my tongue over his raging pulse, felt his dick respond with a throb against my palm. "This is what you wanted, right? To fuck around?" It was what we both needed. All because of *her.*

He grabbed my hip with one hand, his opposite palm still around my nape in an assertion of false control. We both knew who was alpha between us. He just liked to fight it. And I loved that he did.

"She screams when she comes," he whispered, arching into my touch. "It's the most beautiful sound. I listen for it every night, knowing her fingers are buried deep in her pussy, and each time, I imagine my cock taking her deep while you drive into her ass." He hissed out a breath as I squeezed in response to the vivid vision painting my mind from his words. "Fuck, Zeph, she'd make the most arousing noises just for us."

I pictured it perfectly, us driving into her from two different angles and taking her to new heights of pleasure, all the while teasing and taunting and making her beg for more. More images flashed through my mind of her on her knees sucking Kols off, my hand in her hair to dictate the pace. Kols going down on her after I've fucked her, my cum on his tongue mingling with her fresh arousal. Aflora licking him clean after he blew his load all over my abdomen, like he was about to do now.

His forehead hit my shoulder, my lips still near his pulse. "Do it."

"You haven't fed recently," I replied, my breath ragged from my hand and our discussion.

"I'm fine. Fucking do it."

My incisors ached at the prospect, Kols's bloodline an aphrodisiac to my senses. As his pledged Guardian for life, I could drink from him without worrying about the mating link snapping into place, because we were already bonded in a different way. I pledged my fealty to him nearly a decade ago, sealing our fates.

That was what marked this assignment as temporary.

No one could protect Kols like I could.

We were literally linked in an ancient ceremony very few knew about outside of his esteemed lineage.

"Now, Zeph," he demanded, his voice hoarse with the strain of his impending climax.

I sent him over the edge by biting down hard on his neck and piercing his vein. His power flowed into my mouth on a wave of molten energy that revitalized my connection to the dark arts in an instant and shot me into oblivion with him.

Our groans reverberated around the marble walls of my shower, his seed mingling with mine against our abdomens and coating us in the forbidden lust that constantly brewed between us.

That was why we enjoyed this—the wrongness of it.

We were both equally fucked up and embraced the insanity.

Nothing could ever exist here beyond mutual satisfaction, his destiny and mine already tied up in a fucking bow of Council-sanctioned perfection.

A perfection Aflora endangered, which only enticed me more.

She had the potential to change everything.

And destroy us all.

In likely the best way possible.

I released Kols's neck, my eyes finding his as our minds melded together in a temporary infusion. This always happened when I bit him, our mental states fluctuating.

Those thoughts about Aflora hadn't been mine, but his. Only, I echoed the sentiment now that I'd heard it. "You want her to fuck it all up," I whispered, having seen the darkest secret lurking inside his mind. "You welcome her chaos."

"It's a dark fantasy." He licked his lips, his voice hoarse from our joined pleasure. "It'll never happen."

"But you want it to."

"As do you."

I didn't deny it.

Because he was right. The depraved part of me that connected so deeply to Kols longed to see his wicked thoughts come true. Which was precisely why I released him. "Get out." This never should have happened anyway. I owed it to him—to *everyone*—to remain distant and avoid a repeat of the Dakota experience.

And Aflora posed the biggest risk in the history of my existence to Kols's safety.

We shouldn't even be discussing her, let alone fantasizing about her.

Kols narrowed his gaze, ignoring my command to leave. "Look, I get it. You're losing sight of your control around her. But being a dick isn't going to solve this problem."

I ground my teeth together, my urge to punch him rising with every breath. "This has nothing to do with my control." *And everything to do with protecting you,* I added to myself.

"It has everything to do with your control. You want her, and it's becoming harder and harder not to fuck her. The fact that she could derail a future we both despise only makes her that much more intriguing. But we can't. We both know we can't."

"I'm not the one considering that fantasy," I pointed out.

"Maybe not, but you like the idea just as much as I do," he tossed back as he bent to pick up his sodden clothes. "Next time, I'm in charge."

"There won't be a next time, Kols."

He gave me a look. "When did you start lying to yourself?" he asked.

He didn't wait for an answer, instead stepping out of the shower to throw his ruined wardrobe into my trash bin, and grabbed a towel.

"Thanks for the hand job," he said at the doorway. "But we're both going to need a hell of a lot more than that to survive Aflora."

I couldn't think of a single retort, his words truer than anything I'd ever heard.

So I leaned back against the wall, closed my eyes, and allowed the water to trickle over my skin, washing away the evidence of our pleasure.

He left with a towel around his waist, his accusation hanging between us.

When did you start lying to yourself?

The day Aflora first arrived, I thought back at him now, not that he could hear me.

The admission was more for me anyway.

Including the realization that I'd always been interested in the pretty little Royal Earth Fae, even when I claimed not to be.

Only now, my control was slipping, just as Kols had stated, proving he still knew me better than I knew myself.

I'm so utterly fucked.

CHAPTER TWENTY-TWO

"Ugh, Zeph is in a mood," Ella groaned as we finished our fourth lap around the courtyard. He'd started today's class with cardio fitness, claiming it would help fire us up for whatever defensive spells he had in store.

But I agreed with Ella. Zeph was just doing this to be cruel. "It's too hot for this."

"I know," she panted, grabbing her water bottle off the ground and downing half of it in one go. "I swear the moon is really a sun in this place, because fuck, it's burning up out here."

All the exploding burning thwomps nearby didn't help.

Zeph blew hard on his whistle, calling everyone in and pairing us off like he did for each class. Kols joined me in his sweats and sleeveless shirt, looking refreshed despite our heavy warm-up. "He's being a dick," he muttered.

"I know." I just didn't know why. We hadn't seen each other since my independent study day that he'd ended early. That was five days ago. Usually, I saw him at least once during our break days, but he'd either left the Academy or avoided me the entire time. I suspected it might be the latter since he wouldn't even look at me today.

He stood with his arms folded in the center of the courtyard, his legs braced, as he explained today's exercise in an emotionless tone.

"Playing with familiars," Shade mused when Zeph was done, his arm brushing mine as he moved to stand beside me. "This part should be new to you, yes?" He didn't wait for me to reply, instead adding, "I wonder what's going to show up to protect you. Maybe a pretty flower?"

"Attack me and find out," I taunted.

As I'd practiced the conjuring spell last night during my preparations for today's class, I already knew what would arrive to defend me. And I'd love to watch it claw Shade's eyes out after the dream he'd inflicted upon me last night. I could still feel the scrape of his teeth taunting the flesh between my thighs. And I hated how just the image of it had me clenching my limbs, my arousal mounting all over again.

For as much as I loathed him, Shade knew how to use his tongue.

At least in the mental visions he continued to force upon me.

I asked him last night if it was all just for show, a fantasy he created to live through since his reality didn't measure up. He'd taken that as a challenge to drive me mad, and he'd thoroughly succeeded.

"Mmm, you do know. Now I'm intrigued," he said, referring to my taunt.

"You're paired with Stiggis," Kols reminded him. "So fuck off."

"Sadly, Stiggis isn't in class today. Some sort of family emergency involving Cordelia. Tragic, I'm sure. Anyway, I came over to play with my little rose instead," Shade replied.

"She's my partner, Shade. Find someone else to irritate."

"Hmm, maybe I should just join you both," Shade suggested, a grin in his voice. "Unless you're afraid it might be too much for her to handle, what with the sensations and all that." I flinched at his suggestive tone and the way his icy blue eyes glimmered with knowledge.

"I—"

"Stop fucking around," Zeph interjected, cutting me off. "Shade, work with Kols. I'll handle Aflora's lesson for today." He grabbed me by the elbow, leading me away before either male could reply.

I twisted out of his grip when we came to a stop in the corner of the courtyard and lifted a brow. "Is everything all right?"

"We're not here to chat," he snapped. "Take out your wand and perform the spell so I can see how much I need to correct before the next exercise."

Right, someone's in jerk mode. An ivy plant must have crawled up his butt this morning and latched on.

Not wanting to pry or make things even more uncomfortable between us, I pulled out my wand and muttered the incantation. A gorgeous bird with black and white feathers swooped down from the sky to land beside me, its yellow-and-black beak parting to release a sound of welcome.

I smiled at the beautiful creature. "Good morning to you, too, my darling Clove." I bent to run a finger along her soft feathers, having named her last night. She blinked big obsidian eyes at me, then leaned into my touch, her only confirmation of comfort.

"A falcon," Zeph mused, eyeing my familiar. "I would have expected a snail or something else slow and easy to kill, not a bird of prey."

I narrowed my gaze at him. "I'm not easy to kill."

He snorted. "Yeah. You are." He had his wand out in a flash, the same spell murmured beneath his breath to call his own animal protector to life.

I jumped as a slithering snake appeared, its tail long and as thick as my wrist. But it was the *heads* that grabbed my focus. There were three of them, all split at the proverbial snake neck—if a snake even had such a thing.

My falcon shifted, noticing my unease, the feathers along the wings beginning to flutter with power as the wings flexed outward. "Your familiar is a snake?" I asked, taking an unsteady step backward.

"Obviously."

The black and green scales began to move as the snake slithered toward me, three sets of beady red eyes seeming to glare at my existence. "I don't think it likes me," I whispered, sliding back another few inches.

"It's my familiar, not yours," he replied, folding his arms. "He senses how I feel and acts accordingly."

Which meant his three-headed creation would be in a similar mood to his master.

"Maybe this isn't a good idea," I said, eyeing the murderous glare coming from his familiar. Zeph might maintain a bored exterior, but inside, he appeared to be furious over something.

And that fury was definitely being reflected in his pet snake as it slithered toward me.

My falcon bristled again, letting out a warning caw of a sound that scattered goose bumps down my arms.

"Zeph," I whispered.

"Headmaster Zephyrus," he returned, his tone dripping ice. His snake hissed in response, the three heads echoing the sentiment and causing Clove to screech angrily.

I jumped backward, the two animals lunging for one another at the same time and squabbling across the ground.

"Stop!" I demanded, trying to pull the slithering monster off my falcon. It had all three sets of mouths latched onto different points, its tail wrapping around the body to squeeze as Clove's talons dug into the scaly rope and tried to use its beak to pierce the slimy beast.

It all happened so fast, the animals quick and sharp and deadly.

They rolled across the courtyard, horrible sounds wrenching from my falcon's throat as Zeph's hideous creation threatened to destroy her. "Make them stop!" I begged him, tears pouring from my eyes. But he merely watched the show with a disinterested expression, his green irises as dead as his soul.

No wonder he created something so vile.

It represented him so completely.

To be able to stand there and watch his *pet* destroy my beautiful falcon without a care in the world.

Her cries slowly died, a piece of my heart seeming to break off and wither away with her.

I fell to my knees, the weight of devastation crushing me beneath a wave of desolation. The textbook didn't talk about this, only commented on the resolute loyalty of our familiars and how they will protect us to their dying breath.

Clove's obsidian eyes met mine with a final blink, her grief at having failed me so palpable that I cried out in anguish. "Please," I whispered, reaching for her and unable to do a damn thing because I didn't know how to help her.

How to stop this. How to *kill* that sickly three-headed *thing* destroying my beloved creation.

"You're pitiful," Zeph said, his voice cold and remorseless. "Just like your familiar." His snake gave a victorious twist, and Clove's body went limp, her eyes falling closed.

I covered my mouth to hold back a sob, the sight before me destroying my will to breathe.

What was the point in inspiring life just to have it taken away so coldly?

The monster refocused on me, those lethal eyes glowing with malicious intent.

"What will you do now?" Zeph asked. "Run away? Build a fortress of flowers to hide behind?"

I didn't reply, my grief suffocating my ability to move. *How could you?* I wanted to ask him. *Why did you do this to me? What lesson are you trying to teach me?*

The snake slithered off my dead familiar, pinpoints of evil watching me with obvious intent.

I just held its gaze, waiting for the inevitable. Even if I knew a spell that could hurt the creature, I wouldn't use it. "I don't take lives. I create them," I whispered to it, defeated and broken. "So do what you must."

"That's why you won't survive in this world," Zeph replied, his voice dark with some unspoken emotion. "There's no one here who will protect you. Only yourself. And without the will to survive, you'll merely perish."

I swallowed thickly, his words battering my already destroyed heart. "Better to perish than to become a monster." I met his gaze and found death staring back at me from his dark green depths. "A monster like you," I added, finally seeing him for the first time.

Whatever demons he harbored, I wanted nothing to do with them.

If he wanted to break me with this exercise, he'd succeeded, but not in the way he probably intended.

"Killing and hurting others isn't the only way to survive," I told him, pushing to my feet and ignoring his bristling pet. If that thing wanted to attack me, so be it. I wouldn't fight back, at least not in the way Zeph anticipated. Instead, I'd go about it my way—by undoing his spell. Maybe I'd tame a new pet in the process. Or maybe I'd die trying.

At this point, what did it matter?

I turned on my heel, leaving him behind.

He called my name. I ignored him.

He shouted after me. I stopped listening.

Several students watched me leave the courtyard. I didn't acknowledge any of them.

I'm done, I thought. *I just want to go home.*

CHAPTER TWENTY-THREE

KOLS

"What the fuck?" I demanded in a low voice, stepping into Zeph's path to keep him from pursuing Aflora. After that little display of jackassery, the dick clearly needed a moment to breathe before he made the situation worse.

"Move," he ordered me.

"No."

His green orbs flashed with emerald fire, his shoulders tensed for a fight.

I arched a brow, daring him to hit me. Class or not, I'd happily duel him in front of the entire school. Even if it meant having my ass handed to me. Anything to protect Aflora from more of Zeph's bad mood. "You could have at least told her that familiars can't really die." Well, unless the owner died, too. Then the familiar passed as well.

A muscle ticked in his jaw as he looked over my shoulder in the direction she'd gone. "She needs to learn."

"Is that how you justify what you just did to her?" I wondered out loud. "Fascinating."

"I taught her a lesson she needed to learn."

"And what was that exactly? That she can't trust you?"

"Yes. Nor should she rely on me."

I shook my head. "Something tells me that lesson was more for you than it was for her," I muttered, turning around.

"Where the fuck are you going?"

"To fix the pretty little flower you just ripped apart," I tossed back at him.

"Class isn't over yet."

"Then fail me," I retorted.

"Don't tempt me, *Your Highness*."

I ignored him and followed Aflora's energy signature toward the Elite

Residence. Zeph could kiss my left nut. Then spar with Shade, assuming the Death Blood bothered sticking around. He'd probably disappeared at his earliest chance, choosing to skip class rather than attend. Given Zeph's behavior today, I wouldn't blame anyone from jumping ship and telling the *headmaster* to fuck off.

Dick, I thought, irritated all over again. When I saw Raph, Zeph's pet snake, ripping into Aflora's falcon, I nearly intervened. But then Shade's damn bat went after Night, and nobody messed with my familiar.

Sensing my unease, Night settled on my shoulder, his black wings brushing my neck in a sign of affection. We'd met years ago when I first learned how to conjure him, as would be the case with most Midnight Fae. But Aflora would be brand new to the bond created with the protector spell, which only made what Zeph did that much worse.

"You can help me give her a demonstration, Night," I told my crow. "Then I'll release you to the wild once more." Most Midnight Fae had a relationship with their familiars where they only called upon them in time of need, or in this case, during a course discussion. They were considered a defensive arm, mostly used in combat. But I suspected Aflora wouldn't feel that way about her falcon.

I entered my suite, noted the stillness of the living area, and went straight for her room. She hadn't bothered closing her door, just went to her bed and curled up in a ball to stare out the window.

After everything she'd endured, this exercise had been the one to fracture her strength. Knowing that had my hands curling into fists at my sides, my irritation at Zeph mounting by the second. He'd taken this strong, beautiful creature and belittled her to a ball of sorrow. All because of his own emotions over his losing control around her.

My crow cawed, startling Aflora into a seated position, her blue eyes filled with hope.

Only to die when she found me in the hallway. Her focus went to Night on my shoulder, her expression clouding over. She returned her gaze to the window, her shoulders caving inward in a way I recognized immediately. Usually, that sort of response would send me running. But I stepped forward instead to sit beside her on the bed.

She trembled in response, her quiet sadness piercing the air and prickling my heart.

"You can bring him back," I informed her softly, referring to her falcon. He'd started stirring around the time I'd stepped into Zeph's path, which meant the beast would be back to full health soon. "Just use the same spell, and he'll find his way up here. It just might take a few minutes to get through all the doors. Sir Kristoff will let him through since he's tied to your essence."

"I don't want a new familiar," she said, her voice barely a whisper.

"It won't be a new familiar. We only get one."

She shook her head, her cheeks glistening with fresh tears. "Zeph killed her."

Her? I thought, frowning. I hadn't gotten a good look at the falcon, but

Aflora would know better than I would. Just as she would be able to sense that the bond still thrived if she went looking for it.

Night flew off my shoulder to perch on her nightstand, taking my mental cue through our connection.

"Aflora," I murmured, sliding my arm around her shoulders. It was an awkward angle with her legs tucked partially beneath her, but she melted into my side, her body curling into mine as a single tear slipped from her eye.

"I thought the squawk..." She trailed off, her shoulders beginning to shake.

I followed her train of thought. "You thought Night was your falcon." I didn't bother pointing out that falcons didn't sound the same at all. Her heart didn't know the difference because Zeph had broken it with his cruelty.

"I'm sorry. This is... I'm being..."

"A familiar creates an unbreakable bond with its host," I whispered, my lips brushing her temple. "That's why you felt the pain from your falcon, sweetheart. But I promise you he, or rather *she*, is fine. A familiar can't die unless his or her owner dies. Zeph was an asshole for not telling you that."

Well, he was an asshole for a lot of things.

I gave her a reassuring squeeze and added, "Our familiars are created with the protector spell, meaning your falcon was born from the incantation. She's tied to your existence, so she'll always regenerate for as long as you're alive." Which, if I had it my way, would be for a very long time.

I swept her hair over her shoulder to palm the back of her neck and forced her to meet my gaze once more.

"Say *Ahaminee*," I told her. "You don't need your wand, just the spell." It was a more advanced phrase than the one her textbook would have taught her initially, one I only knew because of my unique upbringing.

Becoming King of the Midnight Fae required a certain amount of defense instruction early on in my life. While I learned some things at the Academy, I mostly attended as a formality or a rite of passage.

Aflora studied me for a long moment as if debating whether or not to put her faith in me. I allowed her the time to consider her alternatives. She either believed me or she didn't.

"There's only one way to know the truth," I whispered, catching the distrust in her gaze. I couldn't blame her for being wary. While I might have gone out of my way to help her these last two months, it wasn't all out of the goodness of my heart. I wanted her to survive for a multitude of reasons, one of which existed in my pants.

Hence our frequent dream sessions.

Which worsened my cravings for her rather than satisfying them, as tasting her only made me want to experience reality with her that much more.

"*Ahaminee*," Aflora said, incredulity written into her tone and features. But there was enough power tied to it for the incantation to work. I felt the spell shimmering over the air, reaching out for her creation and beckoning her to join us.

When nothing immediately happened, Aflora's gaze narrowed in suspicion. "It's not a trick," I promised her. "Just be patient."

Her jaw clenched, but she gave me a stiff nod, choosing to believe me for a little bit longer.

I released her neck to stroke my hand up and down her back, lending her my strength in the process and caressing the energy vibrating around her aura.

It was a dangerous game to allow my power to mingle with hers. An intimacy I shouldn't grant her. One that would infuriate the entire Council if they ever found out. Yet it came so naturally to me that I couldn't stop it, my connection to dark magic thriving when in her presence because of our mating potential.

She relaxed considerably, her expression softening. "What are you doing?" she asked, her pupils dilating.

"Something I shouldn't be doing," I murmured, my fingertips trailing up to her throat to brush her quickening pulse.

She leaned into my touch, her eyes falling half-closed. "Why does it feel so good?"

"Because it's meant to soothe you." My thumb traced her jaw, my gaze tracking the movement. She had such soft skin, reminding me of a flower petal. Her lips were soft, too. Or I imagined them to be in our shared dreams. They looked soft now, plump and ripe. I licked my own, my mind wandering to a place it shouldn't as I increased the intimacy of our connection.

She shivered, the power humming between us in synchronization. It'd be so easy for her to reach out, to take a sliver of my access to the source, but she didn't. She merely basked in the glow, her eyes now fully closed in contentment.

Until a cooing sound caused them to spring open in surprise. Our link weakened as her focus went to the falcon swooping in from the hallway, her expression opening in excitement and pure joy. "Clove!"

Aflora's familiar landed on the bed and shook out its feathers before peering menacingly my way.

Night cawed out a warning, but I sent a blast of security through our link, calming the animal before it picked a fight with the much larger bird. I wasn't concerned about Night's success—I knew he would win, as he always did—but I just didn't want a repeat of the experience outside.

The falcon shifted closer to Aflora, its black eyes on me the entire time.

"I'm not a threat to your fae," I informed the bird, lifting my hand for inspection. Not that it helped.

Familiars were resolutely protective of their owners, refusing to submit even to a Royal Fae of my caliber.

"The first rule you need to learn is how to communicate with your familiar via the bond you formed at the time of creation," I said softly, careful not to provoke any emotions from her that might inspire retaliation from her new pet. "For example, I'm currently reassuring Night that you and Clove are not a threat to us. You should do the same for your falcon."

"How do I do that?" she asked.

"Here, I'll show you." I slowly covered her hand with my own and opened our connection to begin a new tutorial on familiars and how to control them.

We covered a variety of spells all meant for calling our familiars to us. I also gave her some hints on how to properly defend herself and Clove when needed and even went into a handful of offensive incantations.

A hint of danger niggled at the back of my mind throughout our entire exchange, the notion that the method of my instruction posed significant risk to the crown, but Aflora never once tried to push, only using our link to learn and improve her own skills.

It took several hours, our familiars watching and bonding the entire time.

By the time we were finished, Aflora had propped herself up against her headboard, legs stretched out and crossed at the ankles, with me right beside her. She wore the most satisfied grin, her blue eyes sparkling with life once more and confirming I'd more than completed the task of improving her mood.

She sighed in contentment as her falcon preened between us, its large wings feathered outward in a display of black and white. Aflora stroked the tips, her lips twitching. "You know you're pretty, don't you?"

"I do, yes," I replied, fully aware she meant the compliment for the bird but accepting it for myself as well.

Aflora laughed and shook her head. "You're so modest, Kols."

"Extremely." I waggled my brows at her. "We both know I'm attractive."

"Do we?" She scratched her jaw, her gaze appraising me slowly. "Hmm, I guess you're all right."

"All right?" I repeated, arching one eyebrow. "Is your vision failing?"

She snorted, her carefree attitude warming me inside.

Because *I* did that.

I put that smile on her kissable lips.

I improved her day.

And it pleased me to no end to see her resulting happiness now.

She held my gaze, her smile slipping into something more heated as she considered me with a growing seriousness. "You're more than all right," she whispered, her tongue slipping out to dampen her lips. "You're very much more."

"More what?" I asked her, aware of the risky tightrope we both stood upon and daring to take a step forward. "Much more what?"

She angled toward me, her palm falling to the small space on the mattress between us. "Handsome," she whispered, her glimmering blue eyes falling to my mouth.

"Just handsome?" I asked, leaning into her magnetic pull.

She swallowed, her hooded gaze lifting to mine. "More than handsome." She brought her hand to my cheek, her opposite one still situated between us. "You're gorgeous, Kolstov."

"No." I cupped the back of her neck, angling her head to the exact place I wanted it, my lips very nearly brushing hers. "You're the one who is gorgeous, Aflora," I corrected her. "Fucking irresistible."

She shuddered, her sweet breath a kiss I could no longer deny. I captured her mouth on her next inhale, my tongue sliding in to duel with hers a hairsbreadth of a second later, and our worlds came crashing down together in unison.

I felt the intrusion deep inside, the rightness of our embrace locking us together in an intimacy that would never end.

She was beneath me in the next moment, my hips settling between hers as I pinned her to the bed. Months of foreplay between our minds led to this, our bodies coming together like two magnets that had finally removed the barrier between us.

That barrier was a reality I felt slipping away.

Cascading us both into a dangerous oblivion neither of us could deny.

"Aflora," I murmured, my teeth skimming her lower lip.

I should stop this.

Should roll off the bed and walk out the door.

But fuck if my body would listen to my mind.

There'd been ample opportunities for her to access my power. Why would she do it now?

Because you're distracted, a dark part of me reminded.

Only, she appeared just as distracted beneath me with her eyes closed, her body arching up into mine, seeking *more*.

I kissed a path down her neck, my incisors achingly close to her seductive pulse.

No, I told myself, quivering deep within. *That's not for you.*

Oh, but the rest of her I could taste. Could lick. Could nibble. Could explore.

"Tell me to stop," I whispered, my hands on the hem of her shirt, clenching harshly against the fabric. "Tell me to leave."

She shook her head, her little pants of need music to my ears. "I've dreamt of this so many times," she admitted, her voice breathy and so fucking sexy. "I want you, Kols. I know... I know the risk. I know this is wrong. I know we shouldn't." She groaned, her nails biting into the back of my neck as she caught my gaze. "But I need to *know* this. Please."

CHAPTER TWENTY-FOUR

KOLS

Aflora's grip tightened as she yanked me downward, her lips reclaiming mine, causing me to lose myself to her all over again.

Only this time, I welcomed the forbidden nature of our embrace.

I reveled in the sweet danger brewing between us.

Allowed it to seduce my senses and jerk me into the licentious promise of pure sin.

Her shirt disappeared, allowing me my first real glimpse at her pale skin. "So beautiful," I mused, kissing a path downward to the lace of her bra. Her blue eyes burned with passion and need, eliciting a smile from me as I licked a delicate path along the crease of her breast. Her nails dug into my scalp, her breaths quickening as I drew the fabric aside with my teeth to reveal one stiff, rosy tip.

I gave it a tentative taste, a groan catching in my throat at the pure lust dilating her pupils in response.

"More," she begged.

"More what, sweetheart?"

"Just *more*." She writhed beneath me, her sweet body primed and ready from all our nighttime flirtations. I could almost *feel* her need inside me as if we were connected in an intimate pool of thought.

Her whimpers were music to my ears, encouraging me to suck her nipple deep into my mouth. "Kols!" she cried out in response, tossing her head backward on the bed in a rapturous wave.

I nibbled the tip before repeating the action on her other taut peak, my palm cupping her opposite breast and giving it a tender squeeze. Fuck, she was responsive, her entire body vibrating with desire beneath mine from barely any attention to her tits.

All those fantasies taught me what she enjoyed.

But they also gave her insight into my preferences as well, which she proved by hooking her fingers into the waistband of my pants and shoving them downward in a bold move. That exposed my cock.

She didn't apologize.

Didn't look to me for approval.

Just used her foot to guide the fabric down my legs, leaving me bare below the waist. "Fuck, Aflora."

"Yes," she replied, her hands moving to my shirt to tug it upward. "Yes, please."

A growl morphed into a groan in my throat, my forehead falling to her collarbone. "Don't say that unless you mean it."

She trembled, her grip tightening in the fabric still wrapped around my shoulders. "Please, Kols." Her legs wrapped around my waist, placing my shaft right against her heated center. I could feel her warmth and dampness through the fabric of her black stretch pants, her need seeping into my skin as she rubbed herself shamelessly against me.

I cursed.

My dick throbbed.

My balls tightened.

And I nearly forgot how to fucking breathe.

Because I wanted her. *Badly*.

Take her, a dark voice whispered. *Fuck her raw*.

Just the image of it nearly had me coming all over her.

That I could sense her own mounting need only intensified the experience, urging me to take what I wanted, to indulge in the forbidden fantasies lurking between us.

Her heels dug into my ass, demanding action. My lips hovered close to her breasts, my forehead still against her collarbone.

And then she moaned.

The sound went straight to my groin, wrapping around my cock and giving it a figurative stroke that removed reason from my thoughts.

I wanted her.

She wanted me.

We were consenting adults.

This is going to happen.

A forbidden blanket swathed us in a cocoon of lust and illicit cravings, my mind running rampant with all the ways I wanted to take her. But first, like this, with my cock buried deep between her thighs.

I kissed her again, my tongue spearing her mouth, my resolve crumbling into dust.

She welcomed me with a sweet, needy noise.

And the rest of our clothes disappeared with a muttered spell under my breath.

"Oh," she marveled as the magic shimmered over her skin. She arched into me, her hot pussy welcoming my dick in a wet kiss.

"Last chance, Aflora," I warned her, my shaft sliding through her damp folds.

"Fuck me," she demanded, just as I'd taught her in our dreams.

Because I loved those two words from her lips.

She made them sound so inappropriate, thus serving as a reminder of how wrong this was between us and inviting my darker instincts out to play.

I wanted to do wicked things to her.

Teach her how to fuck in the best ways.

Explore every inch of her.

Degrade her.

Claim her.

Fucking mark her.

Fuck, I was so hard it almost hurt. Every part of me ached to finish this, to make her mine, to claim her so resolutely that no one else could ever satisfy her again.

"Please," she breathed. "Take me, Kols. I need this. I need *you*." The plea in her voice sliced through the final barrier between us, snapping my control in half.

I slammed home inside her, a jolt of electricity zipping up and down my spine. Fuck, I'd never felt so connected to a woman. Her sensations were mine and mine were hers, only heightening the experience and spurring us onward into a wicked dance between skin and spirit.

She screamed as I plunged in and out of her, driving us both into a frenzy of pants and ecstasy that I felt sure everyone on campus had to feel. Because our powers were mingling once more, her gift weaving with mine in an intoxicating manner that I couldn't escape from.

Dangerous.

Must. Stop.

Can't.

Oh, fuck.

Mine.

I fought that last thought, my body tensing against hers, only to be sucked back into her web of delirious energy as her thighs tightened around me. This was wrong. So, so, so wrong.

Ugh, fuck, I can't pull away.

More.

Less.

Destruction.

Beautiful.

My name fell from her lips in a sound of worship that heated my skin, her gorgeous form glued to mine as I fucked us both into a state of oblivion unlike any I'd ever reached. She screamed as she tumbled over a cliff of darkness, yanking me down with her into a rapturous sanctuary of insanity and bliss all mingled as one.

Her pleasure rivaled mine, her mind open to me in a way I didn't understand.

I could sense her earth.

Could smell the trees and flowers she adored from home.

Could feel her safe haven welcoming me home.

What's happening? I wondered, delirious with pleasure and confusion, my cock pulsing on another orgasm inside her and taking me under once more. "*Fuck*," I breathed, my head falling to her shoulder.

She quivered, her own ecstasy rupturing as a result of mine, our joining so much more powerful than any dream ever allowed us to experience.

Only, it left me feeling cold at the end, my soul instantly sensing a disturbance, a foreign presence that shouldn't be inside me. I immediately locked it down, terror screeching through me at the thought of another woman using me so horribly.

Yet my powers surrounded me completely, the energy signature normal and untouched.

Except that unknown essence remained, clinging to my life source and locking around me in a way it shouldn't.

I again tried to sever it, using my power to attack the bond and freezing when Aflora shrieked below me in pain.

Her eyes flew open, meeting my gaze at the same time. Her lips parted. Mine curled into a snarl. "What did you do?" I demanded.

Because I could see in her gaze that she knew something.

Panic and horror and fear all mingled in her expression at once.

Her lips moved without sound.

Her pupils flared.

"What the fuck did you do?" I repeated, going to my elbows on either side of her head. Our bodies were still joined below, my cock still pulsing inside her. But fury overrode the rapturous oblivion, my mind catching up with the sensation pulsating in my heart. "*How?*"

"I-I don't know," she sputtered. "I... It shouldn't..."

I recoiled from her, going to my knees on the bed and realizing with disgust what we'd just done. "Fuck!" She'd bonded me. Not as a Midnight Fae, but as an Elemental Fae. I could feel the ivy of her earth magic tightening around me, suffocating my connection to the source and drowning me in an essence I didn't want. "Get rid of it. Sever it. *Remove it.*"

"I-I can't," she stammered, her expression one of astute horror. "It's the third level."

"*What?*" I knew how Elemental Fae bonds worked. There were four levels, the first two breakable and the third... not. It marked us as betrothed. Until the final ceremony that forever joined two Elemental Fae souls. "That's fucking impossible." It required agreement by both parties, unlike Midnight Fae bonds that could be completely one-sided when driven by the male.

"I don't—"

"How the fuck did this happen?" I shouted, springing off the bed and trying to get as far away from her as possible. "How did you trick me?"

"I didn't!"

"The hell you didn't," I snapped, starting to pace. "I wouldn't bond you willingly." I had a duty to my kingdom, to my people, that always came first. And I knew better than to allow an Earth Fae to initiate a fucking mating bond.

I was the future king.

A royal.

A damn powerful Midnight Fae.

"You tricked me somehow," I accused her.

I just didn't know how or when. Perhaps it'd all been a ploy from the beginning. A ruse to seduce me into something wicked. That would explain the pull.

"Was this your plan all along?" I demanded as another thought quickly followed, one that threatened to pull me into a murderous state. "Did Shade put you up to this?"

"What? No!"

"Then why would you do this? Are you working with him? Trying to bring shame to my family? To me? To destroy my reign before it even begins?"

Her lower lip wobbled, her blue eyes spitting fire as she scrambled upward on the bed. "Fuck you, Kols!"

"Been there, done that, princess," I retorted, livid with myself for my stupidity. I gripped the back of my neck, took in the sight on the bed again, and turned away before I did something idiotic like light it on fire. "Get out." The words slipped from my lips before I could take them back. Then it struck me how right the demand was, how much I needed her to leave right this fucking second before I killed her.

Because that was the immediate solution—her death.

It'd break the bond.

It'd shatter Shade.

It'd be a fitting punishment for all parties involved, myself included because I suspected losing her would hurt me as well, thanks to this foreign shit she'd put inside my chest.

I growled and palmed my pec. "Fucking get out, Aflora," I demanded, needing her as far away from me as possible before I did something I couldn't take back.

"And go where?" she asked, her voice suddenly much quieter than before.

The temptation to look at her, to apologize, hit me so swiftly that I snarled. Because fuck that. She didn't deserve my concern. She'd trapped me in her forbidden web and ensured I couldn't leave without significant pain to us both!

I hated her.

Loathed her fucking existence.

Wished I'd never met her.

"Get out!" I shouted, uncaring of how deranged I sounded. Molten lava boiled in my veins, my power increasing by the second. If she didn't fucking leave, I'd explode and she'd bear the brunt of that eruption.

Her sob pierced my ears.

I ignored her.

Too focused on the mounting anger threatening to shred us both.

I barely noticed her running past me in a pair of pants and a shirt, didn't once consider how she'd dressed so quickly, and instead knelt on the floor to unleash the power that threatened my very existence. Flames erupted throughout every inch of her room, destroying the evidence of our fucking, and eating through all her belongings in a thorough sweep of power.

Objects could be replaced.

I'd figure it out later.

When I could properly think again.

"Fuck!" I bellowed, red flames encircling me and spiraling and screeching across the room. A blast of power slammed the door to keep it from spreading through the suite, leaving me trapped inside the raging inferno.

I welcomed the heat.

The punishment for my actions.

And crumpled into a broken pile of guilt and sorrow.

Not just because I'd let the Midnight Fae down, and my parents, but Aflora as well.

I deserved to burn.

I welcomed the pain.

"Destroy me," I demanded, my forehead meeting the ground. "Just fucking destroy me."

CHAPTER TWENTY-FIVE

H*ot.*
     I felt too *hot.*
Like a volcano on the verge of an eruption.
Heat simmered beneath my skin, inching through my veins, causing me to sweat as I ran aimlessly through the midnight air.

Get out.

Fucking get out.

Kols's fury pierced my heart, his anger a brand lashing at my heart with each step.

I could feel his ire, his anger, his *blame.*

But I hadn't meant for this to happen, didn't understand how it was even possible. *He's not an Elemental Fae,* I thought for the thousandth time. *I can't bond with him.* Yet I felt the unmistakable connection tying us together. We'd skipped levels one and two and blasted straight to the third, our link resolute.

Breaking it would be impossible outside of death.

As if the fae required another reason to kill me.

I need to get out of here, I thought, spinning in a circle somewhere outside of the Academy walls. I'd gone through the open gate, uncertain of my destination, and now I had no clue where I was. A stupid move born of emotional turmoil.

How could a beautiful moment go so wrong?

Kols's essence still warmed my thighs, his seed dampening my core.

Mother Earth, that man could move. He'd taken me to a state of incomprehension. Only to be destroyed by fate showing her ugly head.

It left me mated to *two* Midnight Fae.

I screamed an incoherent word into the void of darkness around me. There wasn't a curse alive that could express my frustration. Nor one that could help. Not even an enchantment. Unless something existed that could undo time, but I doubted it.

"What the fuck are you doing out here?" a deep voice demanded, sending me in a spin toward a shadow lurking near a tree.

I could hardly see, the moon hidden above the thick branches of the forest I'd entered. "Zeph," I said, my heart in my throat.

Clove had followed me outside, only to take flight when I started to run, and I had no idea where she went. Probably somewhere with Kols's crow, as both birds had followed me on my mad dash outside. At least they were safe from Zeph's vile snake.

He moved forward, his steps silent over the earth. "Are you all right?"

I startled, his tone holding a note of concern, but I knew better. Besides, it was such an absurd thing to ask because obviously I wasn't all right.

Just the notion of it had me laughing out loud, the urge to cry hitting me square in the gut.

Answering him would be futile, so I ignored him instead, spun around again, and picked up my path again through the trees.

Only, he caught my arm and yanked me back toward him.

I reacted instinctually, my leg sweeping low to knock him off-balance and my fist cutting upward to strike his jaw.

Both were hits that would have made me proud in defense class. His resulting grunt and growl, however, had me instantly regretting my immediate reaction.

I took off at a sprint, needing to escape him.

But his arms ensnared my waist merely two steps later.

"What the actual fuck, Aflora?" he demanded, his lips against my ear. "Is this about Raph?"

"Raph?" I repeated, lost. "Who's Raph?"

"My tripod snake," he replied softly, his grip tightening as he pressed his nose to my neck. "Why do you smell like Kols?" A soft question, one I couldn't stand to answer.

I hadn't meant for the bond to snap into place.

Hadn't meant to lose myself in the moment.

Get out.

Fucking get out.

"Let me go," I begged, the heat building beneath my skin once more. It'd temporarily subsided due to the shock of his arrival, but it had returned with a vengeance, flooding my veins with liquid fire.

"No." His tone brooked no argument, yet I needed him to release me, this power inside me threatening my every breath.

"Zeph..." I tried to warn him, my breath coming in pants as sweat beaded across my skin. "It burns," I whispered, my limbs beginning to shake beneath the onslaught of energy cascading through my spirit.

"What are you doing?" Zeph asked, spinning me in his arms and catching me as my knees buckled.

"She looks ready to explode, and not in an appealing way," a new voice said as Shade materialized beside us. His palm caught my cheek, his dark gaze searching. "What has you so troubled, little rose? Why do I sense Kols in you?"

"How the hell did you know we were here?" Zeph cut in.

"Her fear called to me," Shade murmured, his eyes still holding mine. "What did Kols do to you, Aflora? Why is his power pouring through our bond?"

I couldn't say it even if I wanted to, my throat tight with emotion and fear as the flames threatened to surface. If Zeph didn't release me, I'd burn him alive. And even if he deserved that after what he did to Clove, I couldn't hurt him. Not like that.

Swallowing thickly, I pushed the heat down, only to have it skyrocket inside me and spark at my fingertips.

"Her eyes are glowing," Zeph said. "Cerulean fire."

"Where's Kols?" Shade demanded.

"Fuck if I know."

"Isn't it his job to keep her powers under control?" He finally released me to focus on the male behind me. "He's done something to her powers."

Is that concern in Shade's voice? I wondered, starting to feel delirious. *Can't be. No.*

"I can sense it, too," Zeph replied, that same note in his tone.

This is bad, I thought, trembling beneath a hum of electricity that ran across my skin. "Burning," I managed to whisper, my knees wobbling violently. "Going to—"

A scream ripped from my throat, cutting off my words, as pain unlike anything I'd ever felt slashed a hole right through my chest. Zeph released me with a hiss, allowing me to fall to the ground in a ripple of cerulean flames that scorched the forest floor.

"*Fuck!*"

"What the fuck is that?"

Their voices mingled, making it impossible to tell them apart. I couldn't hear beyond the roar of power lapping at my essence and overtaking my soul.

Tears slid from my eyes.

Everything ached.

My heart sped up.

Too much.

It's too much.

I didn't know how to balance it all, to find my equilibrium. It reminded me of my first time accessing the source of my earth power, that necessary need to placate both sides between my soul and the core of my element.

Only, I couldn't find that center.

It kept moving out of my reach and showering me in electricity, humming dangerously through the air, warning me of the wrongness of my presence.

"Help me," I begged, not sure if I spoke the words out loud or muttered them in my mind. "Too hot. Dying."

An agonized cry reached my ears, the sound excruciating, one I belatedly realized was my own. Everything glimmered in shades of blue around me, a rippling effect of my overheated aura.

Focus, I told myself. *Rein it in.*

Only, I didn't know how because I was too full of energized substance to accept any more.

I ripped at the choker around my neck, needing my earth, hoping to hide in the source to find my stability once more.

There, I thought, my element immediately responding despite the device encircling my neck. Whether I'd somehow deactivated it or overrode it, I wasn't sure, but my beautiful gifts responded and grounded me with the familiarity of soil and earth.

I rooted myself to the ground, reveling in my birthright and locking onto my royal line to find sanctuary in my home element.

Every inhale filled me with floral aromas, and every exhale calmed the fire, until finally I surfaced enough to survey my surroundings in a burnt courtyard shrouded in sunlight.

Blue embers danced in the air, drawing my focus to the damage around me.

I opened my mouth, but no sound escaped me, only another whimper of pain as the flames began to build once more inside me.

Oh, no...

My stomach heaved, a cramp building in my lower abdomen and churning with unrepressed power.

"We need to ground her!" someone shouted. It sounded like Kols, but that couldn't be right.

"And how the fuck do we do that?" *Hmm, Shade,* my mind supplied, his presence providing a temporary balm to my rioting soul. *Mate.*

"I have an idea." That still reminded me of Kols, some part of me recognizing his aura nearby. Or perhaps in me. After all, he was my earth mate now. Sort of. Maybe.

What have I done?

Everything went quiet once more beneath another pulsing wave of excruciating pain that crushed me to my very soul. I curled into a ball on the ground, seeking the utopia only created by true balance.

It eluded me, my talents too fierce and untamed to heed any sort of order.

I whimpered, then jolted as a hand clamped onto my throat, giving it a squeeze. "We're going to help you," a deep voice informed me.

Zeph.

He guided me to my back, his palm squeezing when I tried to curl into myself once more. "We need you like this," he explained, his thigh settling between mine.

Skin to skin.

I frowned.

Why am I naked?

"This had better work," Shade said, his lips suddenly by my ear as he stretched out alongside me.

"If it doesn't, there's only one other alternative," Kols replied, his mouth near my opposite ear, his warmth seeping into my side.

"Kols," I managed to say, my throat dry as I tried to look at him, to apologize, to ask where he'd come from or how he'd arrived.

"Don't," he replied, his tone harsh.

Pain splintered in my chest, only to be overwhelmed by the lava pouring through my being. I could try again later. Assuming I survived this next blast of heat.

Zeph released my throat, his hand traveling down my torso to my hip as he settled between my splayed thighs.

"What are...?" Another pulsating shock of heat silenced my question, thwarting my ability to focus on anything other than the quakes rocketing my limbs.

"Now!" Kols demanded. "Before she detonates again!"

Again? I thought, wincing as something sharp pinched my neck. *Shade*, I recognized immediately, our bond snapping more firmly into place with his bite.

"No!" I screamed, but it was lost to the ripple of ecstasy his mouth forced through my system. I shuddered, conflicted between the inferno threatening my being and the euphoria trickling into my veins.

I gasped as Kols bit the other side of my neck, his incisors sliding deep into my vein to suck harshly at my blood.

A cry lodged in my throat, the pain mingling with pleasure as a third mouth met my breast, the kiss almost gentle. The slice of teeth followed against my tender skin, causing my back to bow off the ground. *Zeph*. I felt his claim, his bond lashing at my spirit and sinking literal teeth into my soul. Along with Kols.

All three of them pulled in unison, taking my blood and leaving me weak and defenseless beneath them.

And utterly powerless.

I nearly wept, my impending death the most blissful and rapturous experience of my life.

Until I realized I wasn't dying at all, but living.

Thriving.

Balancing.

They were taking on my excess energy, drinking their fill and leaving me depleted in their wake. Creating a new equilibrium, one that allowed me to breathe again, to think, to realize the gravity of their sacrifice.

They'd all three just taken me as a mate at once.

Drinking my essence in an effort to help me create order within my powerful chaos.

And I had absolutely no idea why.

I opened my mouth to ask, but my lips were suddenly too numb to move.

They were taking too much.

I tried to tell them, to warn them, to beg them to stop, but each pull sucked me deeper into a web of euphoria I couldn't escape from. Two mouths at my neck, one at my breast, and a pulsing need blossoming between my thighs.

As if Zeph knew, he released my breast to slide his mouth down to my nipple, his green eyes meeting mine as he gently teased the tip with his tongue.

I weakly arched off the ground, my body responding while my mind fought to catch up. Only, he sucked my nipple deep into his mouth, causing my brain to flicker out of existence.

Kols chuckled against my neck, his tongue dancing over the wound he'd created. "That's fun," he mused, tracing a wet path up to my ear. "If I didn't want to kill you, I'd indulge in that reaction more."

I shivered, uncertain of how to react to that threat.

"You won't kill her," Shade said, his mouth whispering over my jaw as he moved to hover against my lips. "It'll hurt too much." He kissed me tenderly, his tongue slipping between my lips to give me a taste of my own blood.

Zeph nibbled my breast sharply, causing me to gasp, and Kols mimicked the motion against my earlobe. "What the fuck are we going to do now?" he asked.

"Mmm, you're the future king," Shade murmured, speaking each word against my mouth. "I imagine you'll figure it out. In the interim, I'll tuck our sleeping beauty into my room for the night since you destroyed hers."

"Don't you fucking—"

I never heard the end of Kols's statement, his words disappearing beneath a cloud of smoke. One that seconds later unfurled to reveal a bed adorned in rich purple silk.

Shade's bed.

CHAPTER TWENTY-SIX

"Fuck!" Kols shouted, his focus on the space Shade and Aflora had just vacated. "I'm going to fucking kill him."

"That's assuming you'll be alive to do it," I muttered, looking around the field. "You fucking mated her, didn't you?"

Kols expelled a long breath, several curses following before he said, "All three of us just fucking did."

"Oh, I know that part." I pressed a palm to my chest, irritated by the strand circling my heart and linking back to a woman none of us had any business claiming as our own. "I was referring to *before* our little quad formation. Aflora was drenched in your power."

Kols grimaced, his palm gripping the back of his neck as he blew out a long breath. "We, uh, fucked."

I gathered as much by her half-dressed state. She'd run out here without shoes on, her hair a mess, and her shirt on backward. It was part of the reason I'd chased after her from the Elite Residence. The other part was driven by guilt. I'd been hard on her today. Maybe a little too hard.

And now everything had gone to hell.

"I get fucking her"—more than I ever wanted to admit—"but why the hell did you bite her?" I knew Kols. He had better control than that, even around someone as alluring as Aflora.

"I didn't. Not until just now, anyway." He shoved off the ground to his feet, his focus shifting to the damage around us. "Her Elemental Fae bond initiated, taking us to the third level."

My lips actually parted. "That's why I smelled her all over you." I'd known it was deeper than sex, but I couldn't figure out why she practically oozed his magic. Now I understood it. "She mated you."

"She did." Anger colored his tone, but I suspected he was more furious with himself than with her. Kols knew as well as I did that the bond between Elemental Fae required mutual agreement to take form.

Which meant that deep down he'd wanted to mate Aflora.

And that had to be pissing him off.

"It caused our powers to merge," he added gruffly, taking in the destruction. "She exploded as a result."

"Your power sent her over the edge."

"And straight into the deep end." He shook his head, his annoyance palpable. "I have no idea how we're going to fix this. The consequences will be severe."

"They'll absolutely kill her for this, and likely me as well." Because I'd failed to protect Kols yet again. I'd also partaken in the four-way bond, not to benefit Kols but to save an abomination. That wouldn't be forgiven lightly, if at all.

"Yes," Kols agreed softly. "They'll slaughter her publicly to punish the three of us. Then they'll take your life as well to hurt me specifically. And my father will definitely postpone my ascension." He uttered the words in a dead tone, his golden irises flaring with power and knowledge.

I slowly pushed to my feet, then tucked my hands into the pockets of my sweats. "Is that the path you choose?"

He arched an auburn brow. "Are you asking if I'll let them kill you?"

"Will you?"

"No."

"You won't have a choice." Once the Council found out about this, they'd have all our heads on a platter.

"There's always a choice," Kols countered, his gaze holding mine. "Killing Aflora will literally destroy a piece of my soul—thanks to our illegal mating bond—and leave me in a shell of misery. I've seen it done to other fae. It's the worst kind of punishment imaginable." He stepped forward to grab my shirt, yanking me to him. "And losing you is a fate I refuse to ever accept. I won't allow them to take you or Aflora from me."

Aflora, I knew, was more for his own survival. Losing his mate would destroy him, and she'd bonded him as both an Elemental Fae and a Midnight Fae, marking the consequences of her loss as undefinable. It might very well kill him.

However, he could absolutely live without me.

He just didn't want to.

I grabbed his shirt with one hand, my opposite palm going to the back of his neck, and kissed him to return the sentiment.

As much as I sometimes despised this male, I also couldn't live without him.

Even when I wanted to.

He returned the embrace, his tongue laced with Aflora's blood as he delved deep into my mouth in a dominant sweep of power. I returned the move in kind, taking him with a ferocity I knew he couldn't deny, and smiled when he groaned.

Now wasn't the time or place.

I also wanted to add Aflora to the mix. We were all going to hell anyway, so I might as well grant myself the taste I'd craved for weeks.

But first, we needed a plan, and to properly form that, we required time.

"Your father would have felt the disturbance of power," I said, releasing Kols almost as swiftly as I'd grabbed him.

He nodded. "I know."

"Either you tell him the truth and damn us all or you give him a cover story. And if you choose the latter, then we need to do something to hide our connection to Aflora." Because everyone who walked near us would be able to smell her in our blood and vice versa. It would be obvious to them all what we'd done tonight, and word would spread quickly through the ranks. Especially when several Council members' children attended Midnight Fae Academy.

"I can handle the cover story," Kols murmured. "But we need to make sure Shade is on the same page, as he'll be the alibi."

"You're going to tell your father the two of you engaged in an illegal duel," I translated.

Kols nodded. "It'll explain this." He gestured around the burnt clearing that Aflora had created with her explosion of power. "My father will reprimand us both, but it'll be a verbal warning more than anything else. He'll claim it's a rite of passage for us to fight."

A good and fair point. "That'll work, but we need something to hide the bonds."

"That's going to be harder," he muttered.

"No, it's going to cost us," I corrected. "A lot."

"What do you mean?"

"I know a guy," I muttered, massaging my jaw as I considered what I was about to reveal. "He can help hide things, like bonds."

Kols narrowed his eyes. "Like protection oaths?"

"Yeah. Like protection oaths."

He fell silent, his astute gaze holding mine as a myriad of emotions ran through his expression.

Understanding.

Hurt.

Anger.

Pain.

Each emotion hit me in the gut, making me feel worse by the second. Because yeah, I knew the guy as a result of my own research in regard to how to break bonds. Specifically, the protection oath I'd spoken to Kols. He needed someone else, someone better suited, to guard him. And I'd proven more than once now not to be the right man for the job.

Case in point, he'd gone and mated an abomination on my watch.

That marked me as the worst Guardian in Midnight Fae history.

"We're going to discuss how you know him later," Kols finally said. "For now, can you reach out to see if he can help us mask the mating bond?"

I nodded, saying nothing more. He could bring it up all he wanted, but it wouldn't change anything. What was done was done.

"It's a temporary solution that gives us time to figure this shit out." Kols blew out a long breath, his focus shifting to the dawning sky above. A million thoughts ran through his features, each one tied to an emotion I could taste from his aura without him having to say a word.

Because I felt the same way.

This was so utterly fucked up.

When Kols suggested the three of us bite her at once, I didn't hesitate. I'd accepted the solution almost eagerly. *Too* eagerly. To the point where I hadn't once considered the consequences. I'd just wanted to save Aflora.

I should have killed her instead.

It would have made all of this so much easier.

Had I just taken her out when she first arrived, Kols never would have mated her, his future wouldn't be in jeopardy, and he could have lived his life the way it was meant to be lived.

She'd been a weakness to us all from the day she arrived. Part of me hated her for it, hence Raph's behavior in class today. He'd acted upon my aggression toward her, taking it out on her precious familiar.

Wrong, yes.

However, it'd felt good at the time to expel some of my frustration so violently. Until the guilt hit me square in the chest.

The female had some sort of magical pull over all of us, creating a web of dangerous choices that both Kols and I had fallen into almost willingly.

I despised her for it.

And adored her at the same time.

"I'm glad my solution worked," Kols said, his mind clearly following a similar path to my own because I felt the exact same way. "It's wrong, and I hate her, but I hated watching her suffer more."

"Because you don't really hate her." Just as I didn't.

"I know," he agreed quietly. "But I want to."

"I know," I replied, purposely repeating his words.

A moment of mutual understanding fell between us, our minds aligned in that eerie way we'd come to respect over the years. It was why we worked well together, even when we shouldn't.

"I'll handle my father and Shade, while you..." Kols trailed off, his focus falling to the ground. He bent to pick up a discarded wand, his lips curling down. "I guess I'll talk to Aflora, too. This is hers, right?"

I hadn't actually studied her wand much, but it looked right. "Yeah, I think so. But I don't remember her using it."

"She probably summoned it without realizing it." Kols eyed the magical tool with interest, raising it into the light provided by the rising sun, and frowned harder. "Her essence is all over this, so it's definitely hers, but I swear it's changed somehow. See that blue streak? Looks like a crack, doesn't it?"

I studied the sharp gold tip and noted the letters inscribed at the top. "This wand used to belong to someone else. Are you sure it's hers?"

"It's definitely her wand," he said, catching and following my focus to the word. "*Lahaz.* That sounds like a spell."

"Or a name."

"I'll ask her if she knows what it means when I confirm this belongs to her." He tilted the wand again, his brow furrowing. "How have I never noticed the cerulean lines before?"

"Maybe the wand changed formation," I suggested. Magical conduits were known to grow with their masters. "It could be maturing, just like Aflora's connection to the dark arts."

His jaw clenched, his gaze finding mine once more. "She's going to be a handful."

"She already is."

He snorted. "True." With a soft curse, he shifted focus to the clearing again. "Right. You talk to your guy. I'm going to find Shade and give the asshole a piece of my mind. Then I'll make sure we're on the same page."

"And if we're not?"

"Then I really will have a duel to report." He turned on his heel, frustration and irritation pouring off his essence.

All because of a girl.

One neither of us wanted to be tied to.

Yet I didn't really regret claiming her, even though I knew I should.

That nagging little realization followed me as I made my way to the portal and all the way to Ching's place. By the time I arrived, I still had no answers, only a resolute opinion that we'd done what we needed to do and that there was no real alternative.

Which couldn't be true at all.

We'd shattered our futures all for a girl who didn't belong here.

An abomination.

A wrongness.

So why did it feel so right?

CHAPTER TWENTY-SEVEN

AFLORA

Several Minutes Earlier

Silk sheets.

Violet undertones.

Obsidian furniture.

It all matched Shade's usual furnishings when he visited my dreams, the notes of his preferences in every minute detail.

I sat on his mattress, too exhausted to fight him or demand he take me to my room. What did it matter anyway? I wouldn't be alive much longer. Might as well go out in style.

My head fell to my hands, my body shaking from the power exchange in the field. I felt all three of them inside me, their presence somehow grounding me. The question became, was it permanent or temporary?

Not that it would change my fate.

I was absolutely an abomination, my power surge proving it. "I'm a danger to everyone," I whispered, my shoulders caving inward.

"You are," Shade agreed, as helpful as ever. "But we can help you manage it."

I nearly laughed. Except it came out as some sort of half-sob, half-crazed snort. "Fae, I'm hopeless," I mused, broken. "When did I become this weak shell of nothing?"

"You're not weak, little rose," he whispered, his knuckles brushing one of the hands still covering my face. "You're one of the strongest females I've ever met."

This time I did laugh and lowered my hands to my lap while meeting his gaze. "That's not what you said when we first met. I believe you called me a delicate flower, just after saying someone called me beautiful." I frowned with the memory, my focus sharpening. "*Who* told you I would be beautiful, Shade?"

"Does it matter?" he countered. "What's done is done."

"As I'm going to die soon, I'd like to know who subjected me to this fate. So yeah, it matters. Who in the Fae gave me to you as a mission?" Wasn't that what he'd called me when we first met? A "task"?

"You're not going to die soon, Aflora." He caught my chin between his thumb and forefinger, giving it a subtle squeeze. "We won't let anyone hurt you."

We being him, Zeph, and Kols.

Ha. "Yeah, I believe that." *Not.* Had the three of them helped ground me? Yes. But that didn't inspire much trust, not after my last few months with them. "Why did you bite me?"

I meant all of them at once, which he must have understood because he replied, "To save you from exploding again." His tone suggested his response was obvious.

He was right only because he hadn't told me what I really wanted to know.

"Why would you care if I detonated? I mean, why not just kill me? I'm a danger to you, to *everyone*. Why help me?" I should be dead. A buried abomination. Destroyed. Not feeling centered within my myriad of power. Not entertaining mate-bonds to *three* male fae.

None of this made any sense.

He sighed, released my chin, and turned toward one of his dressers. I waited for a reply as he opened a drawer. Continued to wait as he opened a second. Then arched a brow when he turned around to hand me a pair of boxers and a shirt.

"I don't want clothes. I want answers."

His gaze slid downward, heat flaring in his pupils. "Well, that's up to you, but I have to admit my focus is a little distracted with you wearing nothing in my room. Particularly after two months of foreplay in our dreams."

Ugh! I'd forgotten I was naked, my attention divided between my fate and my confusion over what just happened outside. "How did I lose all my clothes?" I'd run out of my room with pants and a shirt on. No shoes. But I had no idea how—

"You destroyed them when you blew up out in the field."

I blinked. "Blew up?"

"You went up in flames, Aflora." He dropped the shirt and boxers beside me. "Bright cerulean flames, I might add, and you destroyed the entire clearing. I'd be impressed if you hadn't nearly killed me and Zeph in the process."

My eyebrows flew upward. "*What?*"

He studied me for a long moment, his icy blue irises thinning as his pupils dilated. "There's too much power inside you, little rose. It required a release, only your explosion wasn't enough and you were gearing up for a larger one. So we reacted accordingly."

By biting me, I translated.

"Why?" I asked.

"Why does there need to be a reason?"

"Because I should be dead, Shade!" I snapped, irritated by his continued evasiveness. This hot and cold game with him needed to end. "Just tell me why this is happening. Why did you bite me? Who put you up to this? What's your—"

His lips captured mine, just as they always did at this point in our dreams.

I refrained from biting him, aware of what that would do.

And instead dug my nails into his neck, deep enough to draw blood.

He flinched and encircled my throat with his palm, pushing me down to his bed. "Is that how you want to play, Aflora?"

"I'm tired of playing," I told him, my voice holding a low growl in it. "I want information, Shade. No more of these half answers."

"A half answer implies I've given you at least a partial response, which I mostly haven't."

"Exactly," I said, exasperated.

He used his grasp on my neck to pull me up the bed until my head met a pillow. He settled beside me, balancing himself on his elbow while his opposite palm remained around my throat.

"How do you feel?" he asked in the softest voice imaginable, his warm game on point once more.

"Irritated. Angry. *Murderous*."

His lips curled, but only slightly. "How about physically? Are you sore? Does anything hurt?"

"Only my brain," I muttered. "What with all the cryptic responses and everything."

His amusement disappeared behind a mask of mild annoyance. "I mean it, Aflora. You went up in literal flames. I thought you were going to burn to ash beneath that wave of power." He almost sounded sad by the prospect, but I knew better than to believe his tone. "Tell me how you're feeling. Please."

I nearly asked if that word hurt him to utter, but instead gave him the truth because I was too exhausted to banter with him anymore. "I feel balanced and tired."

He nodded, his grasp loosening as he trailed his touch downward between my breasts, reminding me of my nude state.

I should have accepted his clothes.

Except it really didn't matter. He'd seen me naked countless times in our dreams.

"Are you in pain anywhere?" he asked softly, rephrasing his earlier question.

"No." *Just my mind.*

Another nod, this one more solemn. He gripped my hip to guide me onto my side to face him as he lowered his head to rest on the same pillow as me. "Has Kols or Zeph told you anything about Quandary Bloods?"

"I know they can take apart magic and rebuild it," I said. "And that they used to work with the Death Bloods until the Elite Bloods had them all killed."

He nodded. "Yes. They fear that which they cannot control."

"Like abominations."

"Just like abominations," he agreed. "Which makes you volatile and dangerous in their eyes."

"Because I'm too powerful for them to control," I whispered. "You said it yourself—I almost killed you and Zeph tonight." I flinched with the words, my heart giving a pang over the thought of harming another soul, let alone two so close to my own.

"But you didn't," he murmured. "I shadowed him out just in time, and you mostly contained your own explosion as soon as it released. Well, apart from murdering all those trees."

If he meant that as a joke, I didn't find it very funny. "Any loss of life is unacceptable. If I can't be controlled, I should be exterminated."

"That's a very narrow view, Aflora," he murmured, his palm sliding up my side, along my rib cage, and back down again. "What if you could learn control?"

"I've been trying that since I arrived, and tonight should tell you how that's been going for me."

"But now you have a support system to rely on."

"I have no one to rely on," I countered. "You never tell me anything of importance. Zeph is the realm's worst teacher. And Kols hates me. Some support system."

"Yeah, he's a shit teacher," Shade agreed, smirking. "But Kols doesn't hate you, and I tell you important things all the time. You just don't hear me."

"Right." I didn't bother arguing with him. No sense in trying when it wouldn't change anything. He wouldn't even tell me why he'd bitten me, let alone who put him up to it.

A tense stillness fell between us, his icy gaze holding mine as he continued to draw his palm up and down my side. Slowly. Purposefully. Tenderly. Goose bumps pebbled across my arms, the intimacy of his nearness eliciting memories of our dreams and the touches that followed this caress. But he didn't try to kiss me. Didn't try to do anything other than softly memorize the curve of my hip and back up again.

"Kols's grandfather ordered the slaughter of the Quandary Bloods shortly after they helped the Nacht family gain access to the dark-magic source over my family. I believe it's because they didn't want to risk that realignment of power ever being undone. It's the ultimate point of contention between the Elite Bloods and Death Bloods. Which is why your existence must be protected."

It was the most information he'd ever given me at once, and still not nearly enough.

"Did you know?" I wondered out loud. "Did you know I could access Quandary Magic?"

He considered me for a long moment before saying, "I was told of your potential, yes. I didn't believe it until I felt you override the choker your first week here, and I've been doing everything I can to help you hide since."

I frowned. "Help me hide?"

"You didn't think Kols was the only one assisting you, did you?" His lips quirked upward. "He's been in your head just as much as I have, Aflora. Surely you've figured that out by now."

"He helps me during class."

"And at night," he added, a sinister grin entering his icy eyes. Somehow that look only made him more handsome, in a sinful sort of way that made my heart pound.

Then his words registered. "He knows about the dreams." Not a question, but a statement, my lips parting. "But I thought that was because of our bond!"

"No, darling. Dream manipulation is old magic. You make it easy because you don't know how to defend against it, and none of us have bothered to teach you how. My reasoning should be obvious, but you'd have to ask Kols for his purpose in your mind. If I were to guess, I'd say it was his way of fighting an obvious attraction. For me, I just want to play with my feisty little mate."

I scowled at him, which only made him smile harder.

"You're a rare diamond among a sea of jewels, Aflora. I can't blame Zeph or Kols for wanting you. I'm even willing to share, but you are mine first and foremost. Because my claim is deeper. And soon, we'll finalize our mating. Then the truth can be revealed. At least in parts."

"More riddles," I muttered, shifting to my back, only to have his hand yank me back to my side.

"Providing all the answers would weaken you, Aflora. Riddles, as you call them, are what make a Quandary Blood thrive. And there are some facts in life that must be discovered on our own in order for us to flourish. But that doesn't make me any less here for you. I've been helping you from the beginning, more than you'll ever know."

"Helping to torment me and taking me against my will," I mused. "Such an amazing mate you are, Shade." I couldn't help the thick sarcasm in my tone, my mind at wits' end. "You destroyed my life, and now I'll die because of it. And you won't even tell me why." This time he let me fall to my back.

I closed my eyes, tired of talking to him.

He wasn't going to give me anything useful.

He never did.

"You weren't the only one not given a choice," he said quietly some time later. "We're all pawns on a board serving a higher purpose. A fate that may or may not come to fruition. Only time will tell."

"What does that even mean?" I asked, opening my eyes to find him propped up on his elbow and gazing down at me with sadness in his eyes. "Someone told you to bite me. Did they not tell you why?"

"I already knew why, Aflora. But that doesn't mean I wanted to take you against your will, that I wanted to force a bond on you without even knowing you." He cupped my cheek, his thumb brushing my bottom lip. "If it's an apology you want, I can't give it to you. Because I don't regret it. Not anymore. Not after learning so much about you. I see now why our fates were destined to intertwine."

"Because of my Quandary Magic."

"No, because of *you*." He leaned in to kiss me, his mouth questing against mine. "I know none of this makes sense, that you blame me for everything that's happened, and you're fully within your right to feel that way. But one day soon, you will understand, and you will thank me for forcing this upon you."

"Not likely," I grumbled, the words brushing his lips.

He grinned. "I very much look forward to proving you wrong."

I knew he wouldn't be able to, that it wasn't possible for me to ever thank him for dragging me into this world and destroying my life. But I couldn't stop the rush of heat that overwhelmed me as he kissed me once more.

I hated him.

Wanted to *hurt* him as he'd hurt me.

Yet the fire he lit inside me stoked higher with each touch, lick, and nip between us. It proved that lust and hatred truly were neighbors in the circle of emotions that dictated us all. Because the passion between us burned hotter and hotter every day.

"I hate you," I whispered.

"I know."

"I wish I'd never met you," I added, a hoarse growl in my tone.

"I know," he repeated, his frosty gaze flicking open to meet mine. "But if you hadn't met me, you wouldn't know about your Quandary Blood."

Another kiss, this one deeper, his eyes holding mine the entire time.

"You never would have explored your other powers," he added, his voice darkening in a way that made my belly flip.

His tongue slipped through my lips, tasting, tempting, and tantalizingly thorough.

I bit back a moan, trying not to show how he made me feel. Attempting to shove away the lust he too easily evoked.

However, the thigh parting my legs knew immediately, his pants brushing my exposed sex, my dampness seeping through the fabric of his trousers in an instant.

"Yet your little display tonight would have been an eventuality with or without my influence," he continued in a gruff tone. "However, unlike tonight, you wouldn't have had anyone to ground you." He flexed his thigh in a way that sparked pleasure inside me, my sensitive flesh pulsating with a need he expertly awoke.

"Shade..."

"You wouldn't have possessed any knowledge of what was happening to you, Aflora," he whispered. "Or how to stop it."

I swallowed, his comments all true, his touch evoking a volcano-like reaction to boil in my lower belly, threatening to consume me completely.

"Without my interference in your life, you would have ended up hurting people you loved." He nibbled my lower lip at the same time his thigh pressed into my weeping heat.

This entire conversation should not be turning me on.

He shouldn't be making me this hot.

I threaded my fingers through his thick, dark hair, clinging to him despite my mind telling me to order him to stop.

Resisting him proved to be impossible.

"You make me feel so..." I trailed off, unable to explain it. My body was on fire in a manner similar to before, but oh-so different.

Kols had ignited me with power and sensation.

Shade somehow caressed my soul with icy flames, an impossible element that seemed to only exist between us.

"Come for me, gorgeous," he whispered against my ear. "I can take it."

I wanted to scream for him to release me, to beg him to take me over the cliff, and to kill him all at the same time. The intensity between us boiled over, my world cascading into a glimmer of oblivion so overwhelming that I nearly forgot how to breathe.

And then I was screaming his name as both a curse and a blessing as energy erupted all around us.

He absorbed it all, allowing me to float in a state of rapture that shook every inch of my being, letting me leave my body and return.

"Shade!" The room glowed, my heart beating a chaotic rhythm that refused to slow, until his mouth brought me back to the reality of our moment.

His tongue stroked mine, his hands gliding up and down my sides once more and his warmth heating up my cool, damp skin.

I shuddered, lost to him utterly and completely, while despising him all over again, yet kissing him as if I required his existence to survive.

"You're beautiful," he praised, nuzzling me in a gesture almost too sweet for our volatile bond. "Sleep, Aflora. We'll discuss more in the morning."

I opened my mouth to argue but found it falling slack from whatever spell he'd woven over me. My eyes narrowed in annoyance, wishing he would stop messing with my dreams and my sleep states.

But he disappeared in a cloud of his intoxicating smoke before I could convey the message.

And my world went black.

CHAPTER TWENTY-EIGHT

SHADE

I sensed Kols's presence in my suite about a minute before Aflora detonated. He'd somehow convinced Sir Black to grant him entry, something no one else had ever been able to do. I suspected our shared mate-bond had helped.

Although, that didn't explain how the Elite Blood had managed to enter the Death Blood residential quarters.

"Did you issue an edict to allow your entry?" I mused, materializing behind him in my living area. He'd paused in the center of the room, likely because he'd overheard Aflora's cries of pleasure. I'd stop to listen, too, if I were him. She truly was a beautiful creature. Exquisitely unique, and absolutely mine.

A flicker of gold flame brightened his gaze as he outwardly relaxed. "She screams louder for me."

"Does she?" I considered what I knew of their tenuous relationship and smiled. "I'll see if I agree come morning."

"She won't be in your bed much longer."

"Yeah? And where do you plan to take her? Back to your bed? What with her own quarters being demolished to ash and all," I drawled, leaning against the wall that led to a slender hallway.

Unlike Kols, I only had one bedroom. Guests weren't really my thing. Unless they were dark-haired and gorgeous, like the female fast asleep in my sheets. I'd tuck her in properly when I returned.

He frowned. "Did she tell you that?"

I lifted a shoulder, giving nothing away. Because no, she hadn't told me that. I'd *felt* it. Kols's display of power triggered Aflora's reaction, overloading her connection to the source of the dark arts. Her cries for help had stirred me from my sleep, dragging me into the dawn hours in search of my agonized mate.

Never in my wildest dreams could I have anticipated finding her in the LethaForest. It was a miracle she'd survived her trek out there.

A miracle, I assumed, that could be attributed to Zeph's interference. He'd clearly followed her out there and likely dealt with a few threats before approaching her.

Or perhaps it'd all been a date with fate.

Aflora seemed to adore those.

"Don't worry, Midnight Prince, our queen is safely tucked into my bed. No need to disturb her or move her."

"You're not even supposed to be near her, let alone sharing a room with her," he replied, folding his arms and doing his best to appear regal.

"Oh, are we playing a game of who can break the most rules? Because I think you're way ahead of me tonight, Kols. How many oaths did you break by mating her? Or shall we discuss the nightly visits to her dreams?" I pretended to consider our situation and scratched my jaw. "No, those were technically within the parameters of the rules. So how about that collar you never put on her after her little magical display in Warrior Magic class?" Because yeah, I knew all about that.

"Have you been lurking in my rooms?" he demanded.

Another shrug because I'd never give away my secrets. Not to him. Not to anyone. "What do you really want, Kols? There's a naked, gorgeous woman in my bed that I'd like to get back to, and soon, if you don't mind."

"And if I do mind?"

"It won't stop me," I admitted with a smile. "Just as my initial claim on her didn't stop you."

"Well, you'll have to take that up with her since *she* mated *me*."

"Is that how Elemental Fae bonds work?" I asked, feigning curiosity. "Because I swore those were mutual arrangements." Yeah, I knew about that, too. Had sensed it the moment it snapped into place. It'd felt like a fire gnat latching onto our bond and refusing to let go. I hadn't understood it until I'd found Aflora.

The moment her power went up in flames, the puzzle pieces had fallen into place. I supposed that as a mixed fae, she would have multiple partners. Kols wasn't exactly my first choice for this venture, but I should have known destiny would require it.

He had probably foreseen it. Just like everything else.

A muscle ticked in Kols's jaw. "What game are you really playing here, Shade? You had to know about her Quandary Blood origins. That's why you chose her. What I can't figure out is your end goal. Was this part of it? Forming a four-way bond?"

"Who says I have an end goal?" I countered. "Maybe someone else is pulling my strings."

He snorted. "That's impossible. You despise authority."

"True," I agreed. "But that doesn't mean I can't seek to fulfill a higher purpose. Perhaps I want to end this age-old feud between our families."

Incredulity darkened his features. "We both know that's bullshit."

"Do we?" I countered, giving him yet another shrug. "I guess we'll find out."

He took a step forward, his calm façade cracking. "Cut the shit, Shade. Why Aflora? What's your play here?"

"Maybe I like her," I suggested. Not exactly a lie. I did quite fancy—

I ducked as his fist came for my nose, and shadowed out of his reach and across the room just as Sir Black bellowed a warning through the room. The cheeky little gargoyle despised violence. It was the only trait I disliked about him. I mean, who didn't enjoy a bout of savagery? Especially between a Death Blood and an Elite Blood.

Kols ignored Sir Black and pulled out his wand, his expression radiating the intent to do damage. A spell graced his lips just as a loud ring came from the device he held aloft in his hand.

The murderous intent fled from his features, replaced by a grimace as he answered the magical call with a flick of his wrist. "Hello, Father," he greeted in an admirably calm voice. He flashed me a look that told me not to say anything. I idly considered disobeying him on principle but decided it was in Aflora's best interest not to announce my presence. The less we did to draw attention to ourselves, the better.

Because this whole quad-bond thing? Yeah, it wouldn't end well when the Midnight Fae found out.

Part of me couldn't fucking wait. I almost dared them to do something about it. Our collective power as a unit had the potential to overpower the entire damn Council.

But our strongest asset didn't have a clue how to use her Quandary powers yet.

Which brought me to the practical part of myself who knew we were nowhere near ready yet. Hence, I leaned against the wall and shamelessly listened to Kols's side of the conversation. His familial magic allowed his father to talk directly into his ear while the wand was engaged. Similar to answering a human phone but without the necessary device.

Personally, I preferred the physical mobiles and carried one with me to talk to my own father. The less that asshole could get in my head, the better.

Kols and Malik, however, had a very different bond than me and my father.

"Yeah, Shade and I got into it," the Midnight Prince said, causing me to arch a brow. "That's the disturbance you probably felt."

Ah. Clever. Blame the rivalry instead of our Aflora. Not a bad tactic. His father would believe Kols won the battle with ease, disregarding the significance of my power as most Elite Bloods did. That was how I ran under the radar so fluidly. They all sat on their high and mighty thrones assuming themselves to be the rightful heirs to the kingdom while the true royals hid in the shadows.

Royals like me.

One day, I'd make a point of demonstrating how wrong they'd been about me and mine.

But not today.

Instead, I gave Kols a nod, accepting his story and listening while he detailed our makeshift duel to his father. To his credit, he awarded me a few positive hits but then boasted about my eventual takedown at the end. It took considerable effort not to snort at the ridiculous conclusion.

As if I would ever go down that easily.

However, to protect Aflora, I'd allow the outlandish tale to exist. I'd even go as far as to thank Kols for crafting it because it meant he'd decided to protect our mate rather than turn her in. At least for now.

That decision could change in a second.

Yet something told me it wouldn't. I'd witnessed his concern for the Royal Earth Fae on more than one occasion. And tonight, he'd taken that concern to a whole new level of *need*. Suggesting the three of us bite her all at once had required a fair bit of sacrifice on his part, something he'd given without thought. He'd renounced his entire kingdom to ensure her survival.

Because there was no question now that everything would change.

He couldn't properly ascend with Aflora as a mate. Not because the source would reject him, but because the precious Council would deny his candidacy and demand he step down. As he had a twin with a mostly proper mate, it'd be an easy solution for them. There would be a handful who frowned upon Ella being a Halfling, but knowing Tray, he'd tell them to kiss his royal ass.

Then he'd be faced with punishing his twin for saving an abomination instead of killing her.

Kols's shoulders were tight with annoyance, his golden eyes glowing as he accepted whatever his father had just said with a contrite "I apologize for my behavior. It won't happen again."

I nearly said, "Don't make promises you can't keep," but I wasn't in the business of offering advice. Instead, I wandered into my kitchen to fix myself a drink.

Kols met me a moment later, his wand carefully stowed. "If anyone asks—"

"You kicked my ass in an unsanctioned duel," I finished for him as I dropped three ice cubes into a glass. "Got it."

He studied me for a long moment, his expression wary. "How the hell am I supposed to trust you not to fuck this up for us all?"

"Hmm." I found my favorite liquor, took it from the cabinet, and poured myself a healthy amount.

"That's all you have to say? *Hmm?*" He appeared ready to retrieve his wand again.

"You can start by letting me keep Aflora for the night," I replied, giving my glass a little swirl to chill the contents. "We'll regroup tomorrow when you bring her something to wear."

He regarded me with a violent glint in his gaze. "If you touch her—"

"Oh, be assured that I already have," I cut in, adoring the way his skin turned red in response. "But I would never hurt her."

"And you just expect me to believe you? To rely on you to keep her safe?"

"Yes," I said, replying to both questions. "She's my mate, Kolstov. I may enjoy taunting her, but I'd never let anyone or anything hurt her. Why else would I have showed up in the LethaForest? It certainly wasn't for a little late-morning stroll. That's for damn sure." I took a long, necessary sip of my drink, adoring the way the liquid burned the back of my throat.

Kols finally relented with a sigh, his head bobbing back and forth in defeated agreement. "I'm going to fucking regret this."

"You absolutely are," I agreed, but I wasn't so much referring to trusting me as I was binding himself to Aflora. He would definitely have moments of regret, followed by sweet moments of reward that made it all worth it.

Or maybe that was just my fate, not his.

Time would tell.

"Zeph went to find someone who can help us hide the bonds," he informed me, his tone low. "Until we can figure out how to move forward, we need to hide this from the Council."

"And they call me the rebel," I murmured, amused.

"This isn't a fucking game," Kols snapped.

"Everything in life is a game to someone," I returned, stepping around him to enter the living room.

"Does her life mean nothing to you?" he demanded, his harsh tone causing me to pause midstep. "Do you not realize what will happen to you if something happens to her?"

I glanced over my shoulder to meet his gaze. "I don't care what happens to me," I admitted, my voice a hush of sound that seemed to slap him across the face. "But I do care what happens to her. Which is why she's staying here tonight. I've given you two months with her, Kolstov. It's my turn to care for her in my own way. You can have her back—unharmed—tomorrow."

I didn't bother giving him anything else, just shadowed back to my room and the beauty resting in the center of my bed. If he opted to stay and listen, that was on him.

What I wanted to do now had nothing to do with Kolstov or Zephyrus or the Council or anyone else.

It all centered around Aflora.

Just as it had since my first bite.

I set my glass down on my nightstand, pulled off my shirt, and crawled into the bed beside her. A few muttered words released her from the sleeping spell, allowing her beautiful blue eyes to open.

Palming her cheek, I leaned in to run my tongue along the seam of her mouth. She opened for me as I knew she would, her mind still caught in the land of fog and dreams and her memories convincing her this might be a fantasy more than reality.

I could so easily take advantage of her in this state.

But I wouldn't.

I wanted to earn her trust in a magical sense, not necessarily in a traditional one. I desired her soul. Her heart. Her everything.

She was nowhere near ready to give me more than physical touch, and that was fine. We had time. We'd work up to what I really craved. She might initially despise me for it, but in the end, she'd fall for me.

Which was all part of the fun.

A Quandary Blood needed challenges and puzzles and riddles. I offered them to her in spades, existing merely to entice her, and one day our powers would mingle to create something so beautiful and amazing that the Council wouldn't dare touch it.

Whether or not Zeph and Kols opted to be a part of that was up to them.

So far, they were following the right path.

But I knew from *him* that our road wasn't an easy one, with a multitude of potential dead ends. My purpose in this life was to ensure the female curling into me survived it.

And I would do everything in my power to see it through.

Even if she hated me for it.

I gently nibbled her lower lip before kissing her deeply, cherishing her in the only way I knew how. She was too exhausted to do anything more, and that was okay with me. I'd hold her all night, guard her in her dreams, and continue watching her from the shadows when she woke.

My mate.

My little rose.

My future.

I adore you, I thought at her, not that she could hear me. *I'm so sorry I have to break you, Aflora.*

The only way for her to truly fly was without restraints, which required sacrifices from us all.

And this one would be mine.

CHAPTER TWENTY-NINE

KOLS

"Why do you still have Aflora's wand?" Zeph asked as he entered my bedroom without knocking. I'd set her magical conduit on the dresser, desiring to keep it safe for when I went back to her tomorrow morning.

"I didn't get to see her. Shade had already tucked her into his bed." I grimaced with the words, not at all pleased about her spending the night with him. Of course, he hadn't exactly given me much of a choice. I could have fought him, demanded he hand her over, but decided it wasn't worth the trouble. As I could sense her emotions now—thanks to the bond—I knew she was safe. If and when that sensation changed, I'd do something about it.

For now, I'd let him keep her.

Just for tonight.

Tomorrow was a whole new day for negotiation.

It also gave me time to replace all her belongings and the bedroom furniture.

Part of me still wanted to kill her for trapping me in this mess with her. Meanwhile, the more logical side of me recognized it'd been a mutual claiming.

I'd wanted her from the moment we first met, and even before that when I saw her at Cyrus's coronation. She was one of the most beautiful women I'd ever seen, her long black hair highlighted with strands of blue. Those gorgeous eyes. Delectable curves. Sinfully sweet smile.

Every attribute she possessed lured me to her.

Coupled with her astounding power and royal bloodline, it was no wonder my fae soul sought her out as a match.

I'd been too weak to fight it, and for that, I would pay the ultimate price.

Hating her was easier than hating myself. That didn't make it right.

"You look like hell," Zeph said, stopping by my bed. I was lounging in the pillows with a bottle of whiskey in my lap. No shirt. No shoes. Just a pair of gray sweats.

"Thanks. I feel like hell." I took another swig, wishing like crazy it would make me drunk already. But the power I'd imbibed from Aflora seemed to be eating at my ability to feel intoxicated.

I'd taken the brunt of her outburst, allowed it to fuel my insides, and fed it directly back into the source. Like some sort of damn siphon.

Zeph and Shade had helped, but they weren't the ones with direct access to the dark arts. So the brunt of it fell on me.

The ink along my arms writhed in contentment, while my insides revolted.

I couldn't believe any of this had happened, had no fucking clue what to do now. I'd straight up lied to my father, something I had never done before. Not over a major situation such as this, anyway. Little lies, yeah. Major ones, no.

"Fuck," I muttered, taking yet another swallow before holding the bottle out to Zeph. "Want any?"

He took the bottle and set it aside rather than taking a swig. "It won't help."

"Tell me about it." I'd been trying to drown my sorrows for over an hour to no avail. "Her power is like a live wire running through my fucking soul."

"Not sure what I can do about that, but my buddy did make us these." He dropped a pair of brown leather bracelets on the bed beside my hip. "Ching said these will help hide our connection from the others."

"Ching?"

"My buddy who specializes in hiding bonds. Apparently, mating bonds are a popular thing to hide, so he already had several tools available at his disposal to create these." Zeph studied the bracelets. "I didn't give him your identity, mostly because I imagine he'd freak out if he knew. Because there's only one reason someone would specialize in this type of magic, and that's to hide things from the Council."

"But he knows who you are."

"He does. Just as he also knows I want out." He met my gaze, daring me to comment.

I didn't.

Mainly because I was too exhausted to fight with him right now.

I just wanted this night to end already.

Besides... "There's no getting out now," I told him softly, my focus falling to the bracelets. "So how do these work?" I asked, giving him a chance to deflect and change the direction of our conversation.

He accepted it. "They're generic concealing spells. Wearing the bracelet cloaks the mating bond, making it impossible to sense or trace."

"What about Aflora? If she wears one, it'll hide her link to Shade, and people will suspect something is up."

Zeph nodded. "Yeah, Ching is making something special for her. He's going to try to have it done by morning. If not, we need an excuse to keep her out of class."

"I'll just say she was hit by some stray magic during my duel with Shade. No one will question it. Hell, Emelyn will probably be thrilled." The bitch had painted a target on Aflora's back solely because of her affiliation with me. Well, that hatred would become a lot worse when she realized we'd mated each other.

Assuming we lived long enough for anyone to find out beyond the Council.

My shoulders slumped as I sunk deeper into the pillows.

"It's not like you to mope," Zeph said, his tall frame towering over me as he stared down at me from beside the bed.

"Fuck you, Z," I muttered, tugging a pillow over my head. Childish, yes, Unhelpful, also yes. But I just wanted to hide for eternity.

"You realize this connection between the four of us is powerful, right?" Zeph asked.

"Haven't had a minute to analyze it." My words were muffled by the pillow.

A pillow that disappeared when Zeph took it from me. "Stop being a lazy, woeful dick, sit up, and start thinking."

I glared at him. "I don't want to think, asshole."

"Well, too fucking bad, jackass," he tossed back. "We broke a few rules. So fucking what? The mating laws are archaic and you know it. You also never wanted to mate Emelyn anyway. Aflora is a much better match. She's hot as fuck, too. Strong. Powerful. A Quandary Blood. That means, with the right training, she can rewrite all this bullshit in our favor. The only truly shitty part of all of this is having Shade involved. I'd suggest we kill him, but that'd hurt Aflora, which would weaken the bond overall."

I blinked at him. "Who made you King Practical all of a sudden?"

"I've always been the practical one, Prince Crybaby," he returned.

"I am not a crybaby."

"You're lounging in a pile of pillows feeling sorry for yourself instead of realizing the opportunity that exists here. She's fucking powerful. You felt it tonight when we grounded her. The Council is going to lose their shit over it because they can't battle it, unless we bend over and take it up the ass. Which I'm not keen to do. You?"

"What happened to *they'll probably just kill her and then you?*" I asked. "Isn't that what you said just a few hours ago?"

"Yeah, and you told me you weren't going to let that happen. And I believe you. So stop feeling sorry for yourself and help me figure out a solution. As you said, there's no getting out of this now. Let's figure out what to do with it, unless you have a time spinner lounging around that I don't know about."

"That's a whole different realm of fae beings," I muttered, thinking of the Paradox Fae. "But they would be so useful right about now."

"Yeah, except they'd never help us. Actually, they'd probably make it worse."

I snorted. "True." They were deceitful little fuckers who loved to play tricks with time. To ask a favor of them required significant payment, and even then, it was never guaranteed that they would follow through without leaving some devious surprise lying in wait. "Still an avenue to keep in mind," I said. Because all options had to be considered.

"Not really. I think we'd end up bonding her regardless of how we played it."

He wasn't wrong. "I felt the pull from the moment I first saw her."

"Me, too."

We shared a long look that ended in a mutual sigh.

"What I still want to know is what Shade has to do with all this," Zeph continued. "He knew this would happen."

"What do you mean?"

"He wasn't surprised at all tonight. Just accepting. What kind of Midnight Fae doesn't mind two other men taking liberties with his mate?"

I frowned. "I'm certainly not keen on her being in his bed right now."

"Exactly."

"Yet I allowed it," I added.

"Because you're not opposed to sharing women. But Shade is notoriously alpha in his preferences and not the type to share."

"True." I sat up, my hand rubbing down my face as I thought it all through. "He didn't seem pleased by my suggestion to bite her, though."

"He seemed worried," Zeph agreed. "But not about our claim. He was concerned for her and what would happen if we couldn't get her power under control. There's a difference."

"Yeah, there is," I agreed, recalling the fear in his eyes as he watched her fall apart before us. "He really does care about her."

"He also saved my life tonight when she blew up that first time. If he hadn't shadowed me out, I would have burned right along with her. Only, I'm not equipped to survive cerulean fire."

That was when I'd arrived, having felt her power mounting through our bond. I'd been able to absorb most of her destruction, keeping the energy centered in that courtyard with an electric current stirred directly from the source.

"This is such a mess," I said, blowing out a breath. "I asked him about his motive tonight. He replied with his usual cryptic bullshit."

"Do you trust him?" Zeph asked.

I scoffed out a "No." Because I absolutely did not trust that bastard.

"Neither do I."

"So what do we do?"

"We monitor him. And we protect Aflora." He locked gazes with me as he said it. "There's something about her, Kols. Something important. And it goes deeper than her Quandary Blood."

"She's an abomination," I reminded him. "That could be what you're sensing."

He shook his head. "I keep feeling like she's the key to some long-buried secret. It's just a sense I get. One I want to understand before we decide how to proceed."

Zeph's instincts had proven reliable over the years, and I wasn't about to deny them now.

"We should start by looking into her origin," I said, thinking about her past. "Her parents supposedly died when she was young. Everyone thought it had to do with the Earth Fae plague, which they later realized was caused by an abomination."

"I'd put money on there being more to that story," Zeph replied.

"Me, too." I'd have to involve Exos or Cyrus in this to request some details. Maybe I could ask them for information on her background and claim I needed it to help exonerate her or something.

"You're thinking about asking the Elemental Fae Royals." A good guess, one born of years of knowing each other.

"I am," I confirmed.

"A good start."

I agreed with a nod before saying, "Well, I guess we need to put on these cuffs and hope your friend comes through with something for Aflora."

"He will." Zeph picked up the brown leather bracelets and handed one to me. "Cheers, Kols."

I huffed a laugh. "Yeah. Cheers." I tapped the band against his, then snapped it over my wrist. Aside from a slight humming sensation, I didn't feel any different, but the nod from Zeph told me it'd worked. When he followed suit, situating his into place, I understood.

The slight traces of the mating bonds were gone.

Now we just had to see how long these things held.

Solve the mystery of Aflora's existence.

And figure out what the fuck Shade was up to.

"This is going to be one hell of a challenge," I said.

Zeph smirked. "Yeah. Yeah, it is." He pulled the sheets back on my bed. "Now scoot over. I'm sleeping in here."

I arched a brow. "Your room is next door, *Guardian*."

"Shut up and move, Kols."

My lips quirked as I obeyed. "Lose the pants."

"In your dreams."

"Or we could play in Aflora's," I suggested, thinking of how fun it would be to fuck with Shade. "Make her moan our names so loud that the Death Blood can't sleep."

A sinister glint darkened Zeph's gaze to a forest-green color. "It's late and I wasn't planning to rest much anyway."

Yeah, it was nearly half past noon outside. "Then let's have some fun. We've earned it after the last twenty-four hours."

"You already had fun earlier," Zeph replied. "Tonight, it's my turn."

"Then have at it. I'll follow along." And jump in when offered the chance.

CHAPTER THIRTY

AFLORA

Rich spices.

Peppermint.

Woodsy cologne.

I was swimming in all three scents, my body well used despite hardly being touched. When night fell, all I wanted to do was sleep since my mates hadn't let me rest at all.

They were all vying for placement in my dreams, their seduction resolute and far too tempting.

I loathed them.

Craved them.

Wanted to kill all of them.

Didn't understand them.

"You hate me," I told Kols, his arms wrapped around me as he pulled me back into his chest, his lips falling to my neck. None of it was real. I knew that. But I didn't know how to stop any of them from playing in my head.

"I don't hate you, princess," he whispered.

"You blamed me for our mating bond."

"Because he's an idiot who doesn't know how to take ownership for his own actions," a dark voice said, directly into my ear and overriding Kols's voice in my head.

"What?"

"Wake up, little rose," Shade demanded, his teeth skimming my throat. "We're done playing this game. For now."

My eyes opened, Kols's chuckle a residual sound in my mind.

Violet curtains were parted to reveal a starry night and silk sheets twined with my legs. Shade rested behind me, his arm tucked around my waist, his bare chest to my back, his lips at my ear again. "Welcome back, little rose."

I swallowed, my heart skipping a beat. "Where am I?"

"My room." He pressed a kiss to my neck once more, then guided me to my back to hover over me. "You need more sleep. How about we skip our classes today and stay here?"

"How did I...?" I trailed off, the events of last night slamming into my mind on a vicious assault of reality.

Zeph's three-headed snake killing Clove.

Sex with Kols.

Him sending me away.

Running into the forest.

My powers bursting.

Shade shadowing me here.

Every memory tumbled through me, causing me to flinch as dread pooled dark and thick inside my belly. "What happens now?"

"We sleep," Shade replied. "Assuming you're taking me up on my offer to skip class, that is."

"No." I shook my head in an effort to clear it. "What happens to the four of us? To me?"

"Ah, I believe the plan is to pretend like nothing happened at all." He lifted a shoulder. "I suppose we'll see how well that works, won't we?"

"I..." *What?* "Will that even work? Won't the Council know? What about our bonds?" I could sense all three males inside me, shredding apart my heart with their various hooks. Their magic rioted around my soul as well, as if each one vied for dominance over my powers, seeking to absorb me entirely.

Grounding me, I realized. *They're absorbing my energy to keep me grounded and stable.*

I poked at them in my mind, rearing back when the lines hissed in response. Shade visibly flinched, his lips curling down. "What did you just do?"

"Touched your... bond?" It was a guess. I didn't really know what to call it, but they felt like anchored chains surrounding my spirit, tying me down.

"You can see them?"

I nodded slowly, looking inside myself once more. "Yeah. I think."

"Can you describe them?"

"Like wispy strands of magic coiling around the core of my abilities," I said quietly. "They're pulsing with power. *Your* powers." I reached for the one with a more solid link, noting Shade's essence as I carefully stroked through our connection.

He shivered in response, his blue eyes gleaming brightly. "That's your Quandary Blood ability," he whispered. "I can't see our connection at all. Not like that."

"What do you see?" I wondered out loud.

"You," he said softly, his palm caressing my cheek. "Or rather, I feel you. Inside me. In my mind, my heart, my soul." He leaned into me, his lips brushing mine. "I can sense your emotions. I know when you're in pain or aroused. Not exactly your thoughts, but close. Like our souls are joined in a way that makes you easier to read. And, of course, I can play in your dreams."

Entertainment teased his full lips, causing them to twitch as I rolled my eyes in response.

"I'm going to prioritize learning how to block you all," I muttered. Maybe Ella could tell me. Or one of my textbooks.

"Mmm, I'll just counter-spell you, little rose. Or maybe I'll just play with you in reality." He drew his teeth along my lower lip, his touch promising.

"I don't know," I replied, wanting to tease him. "You might not live up to my dream expectations."

He chuckled, his breath a kiss of mint against my tongue. "Darling, I'll surpass every single fantasy, including the ones you shared with Kols."

I shivered at the thought, recalling the one the Midnight Prince had inflicted on me last night. "That might not be possible after last night."

"Why? Because he allowed Zeph to join him this time?" Shade appeared darkly amused. "I know my skills, and they absolutely measure up."

"Right now, you're all talk."

"Says the female who came against my thigh last night from just my mouth touching hers," he replied softly, kissing me again, this time with purpose. "Keep this up, little rose, and I'll provide you with a demonstration instead of letting you sleep."

"You'll probably provide one in my mind anyway," I retorted.

He smiled against my mouth. "Likely." Another kiss. "Absolutely." This time with tongue. "Definitely." I drifted off in his arms once more, this time with an odd satisfaction lingering in my chest.

One that disappeared when I awoke alone in his bed to find his half of the mattress cold. A black rose rested on his pillow with a note beside it.

Something came up. Dream of me later, little rose. —S

I snorted. "All talk," I muttered, pushing myself upright to take in the fixtures of his room. They were elegant in a way I sort of expected from him. Dark, too. All obsidian wood with violet furnishings. Very Shade.

But there weren't any personal items. No photos. No little knickknacks, just the essentials required for living.

Perhaps he didn't spend much time here.

As he skipped class regularly, that would make sense.

I stretched and slipped from the sheets. The boxers and shirt he'd offered me last night were folded on his bathroom counter with another black rose. I took it as an invitation to shower and change, which I did, his shampoo smelling minty and fresh, just like him.

Tying my hair up into a knot with my long strands, I pulled on his clothes and studied myself in the mirror.

My collar was gone.

I hadn't noticed it before.

Had it fallen off last night, or had Shade removed it?

Likely last night, which explained how my Elemental Fae abilities had returned. I closed my eyes and smiled as the source welcomed me with an aromatic kiss from the earth. It sort of reminded me of Zeph and his woodsy scent.

Actually, it smelled almost too much like him.

Almost as if—

"Aflora." His voice came from the doorway, his green eyes wild with emotions. "We have to go."

I frowned at him. "What?"

"There isn't time to explain. I need you to put this on, and we need to run. Now." He held out a collar that was identical to the one I'd lost.

"Zeph, I—"

"The Council knows, Aflora. They're searching the grounds for you. We have to go right now."

"I don't understand."

"Neither do we, but they have a recording of you admitting you're dangerous. We don't know where it came from or how."

"A recording?" I repeated, swallowing.

He handed me the collar as he replied, "Yeah. I only heard part of it before I ran here to find you."

"What did you hear?" I whispered, my heart beating a mile a minute in my chest.

"You said any loss of life is unacceptable and that if you couldn't be controlled, then you should be exterminated." He shook his head. "We can discuss this more later, but we need to go. They'll be on their way here next."

I absentmindedly clutched the collar in my hand, my mind too consumed by what he'd just said. "That's what I told Shade last night," I whispered, swallowing thickly. "I told him I should be exterminated."

"Well, then we know where the recording came from," he muttered, cursing under his breath. "I knew we couldn't trust that asshole."

But why? I thought. *Why would he do this to me?*

Why has he done any of this? I countered myself. Nothing about Shade could be predicted. Everything he did was for himself first. I still didn't even know why he'd bitten me.

Something came up, he'd written.

Something like running to the Council to tell them about last night?

"Aflora!" Zeph snapped. "We have to go."

Right. Collar. Snap. Neck. Done. An immediate zing went through my body as the magic fell into place, causing me to tremble. Not only had it removed my access to earth, but it had also significantly weakened my cerulean fire. Almost to the point where I couldn't feel it. "What's in this...?" I trailed off, realization dawning. "Wait, is this...?"

The door to the bedroom crashed open, two Midnight Fae charging in with wands at the ready.

Zeph leaned against the wall, his hands in his pockets, as Kols followed what I now realized were Royal Guardians. They wore the Nacht family crest on their cloaks, the green colors denoting them as Warrior Bloods.

Just like Zeph.

"She's disarmed," Zeph informed them, his tone dead and emotionless. "As requested."

What?

"Excellent. Take her to the Council dungeons," Kols said, sounding as regal as ever.

"Council dungeons?" I repeated, my heart in my throat.

This whole thing had been planned, I realized. From Shade leaving me with the note to Zeph showing up with the collar. And I'd stupidly put it on, too consumed by the comment about the recording.

Now I was defenseless.

And about to be taken to the Council for extermination.

"An anonymous source provided a recording of you admitting to your increased abilities." Kols met and held my gaze. "Your powers will be evaluated by the Council. If they determine this claim to be true, a reassignment may be required."

I translated what he really meant. *Extermination.* Just like I'd said last night. Only, Shade had provided me with a glimmer of hope, something I should have known better than to feel.

He'd tricked me.

They all had tricked me.

Shade recorded a private conversation and shared it with the Council.

Zeph showed up like a knight in shining armor, claiming to want to help me escape, all to lull me into a false sense of comfort while I put on the power-depleting collar.

And now Kols was looking at me like I meant nothing to him. He wanted me dead. He'd told me that last night. It would make his life easier if I didn't exist, would kill the bond between us and free him to pursue his destiny. So, naturally, he wanted me out of the picture. Why wouldn't he?

The spiteful part of me almost laid the accusation at his feet here, but the intelligent side of me held it back. If I spoke out now, he could take my life and claim self-defense. With Zeph at his back as a witness, he'd get away with it, too. Would probably use the guards' lives as cause and claim I had killed them. When, really, he'd do it to silence them.

At least, that was how I would play it.

Which meant I needed to save the declaration for later.

To announce it in front of other Council members.

Because if I was going down, so was he.

Zeph, too.

And Shade, the treacherous bastard.

They were all going to the grave with me.

Kols's pupils dilated, his gaze narrowing with knowledge as if he overheard the plan unfolding in my mind. Or maybe he saw the desire for vengeance flashing in my gaze.

I didn't care.

I let him see my anger.

Allowed him to witness my promise for retribution.
I'm not going down alone, I told him with a look.
Because in the end, they'd pay for what they'd done to me. *I vow it.*
Welcome to purgatory, boys.
You'd better hang on.
It's going to be a wild ride.

EPILOGUE

KOLS

Aflora glared at me with a hatred I felt to my very soul.

She thought we'd betrayed her. Yet everything we'd done was to *save* her.

If Zeph hadn't gotten that collar around her neck in time, the Guardians would have sensed her additional bonds, which would have required me to kill them. Because I couldn't risk them going back to the Council with those details.

Seeing Aflora's expression now, it was clear Zeph hadn't been given a chance to explain.

She appeared ready to kill me. I supposed that worked in our favor in terms of believability, but I could see the wheels turning in her head.

If she breathed a word of our bonds, we were all fucked.

Zeph and I shared a look, his expression telling me he'd caught her resulting animosity as well.

Aflora was a ticking time bomb in so many ways, both in what she could say and in her mounting powers. Not to mention Shade, the bastard who fucking betrayed us all.

Our first order of business would be to free her.

Then we'd deal with the Death Blood.

Preferably with a stake through his fucking heart.

BONUS SCENE

ZEPH

Tracing into Aflora's mind was far too easy, the poor girl having not developed a single barrier to keep me out. The Guardian in me knew we needed to fix that oversight as soon as possible, whereas the male in me wanted to exploit the weakness to the fullest extent.

Tonight, I chose the latter.

The taste I'd gotten of her out in the forest wasn't nearly enough, and after weeks—*months*, if I was being honest with myself—of wanting her, I needed to indulge at least once.

Kols rested beside me, his mental presence nearby without being intrusive. He wanted to watch, as he often did when I played with a female.

I allowed it because I wanted him to watch, too.

Eventually, we would share her.

But for this experience, I needed to have her to myself, to learn her, to adore her, to fuck her the way I craved. Well, maybe not to that extent. That would require this to be reality, not a dream. She also needed to work up to my expectations.

Mmm, yes, this would be an introduction instead. A seduction of sorts. A way for her to get to know my preferences, at least on the surface.

"Aflora," I murmured, pulling her away from Shade and into a dreamland that I controlled.

His amusement touched my mind through the quad-bond we'd all formed, momentarily pulling me from the experience, as having him so near felt foreign and wrong. But I quickly ignited a block, keeping him from interfering, and sucked Aflora deeper into my web.

I suspected he allowed it, as it was far too easy to borrow her presence. He'd probably had his fill of her already since she was in his bed tonight.

Or maybe he welcomed the break.

Was she a needy lover?

A curious one?

Shy?

I couldn't wait to find out, the details from Kols having not been nearly enough. I wanted more, craved firsthand experience, and would acquire that from her tonight.

She blinked up at me in confusion, her beautiful blue eyes showcasing a world of questions she didn't voice out loud. When a flash of pain reached her features, I knew why. My heart gave a subtle pang, my regret over being too hard on her during class hitting me square in the gut. But I wouldn't apologize, refused to give her an inch. The world wouldn't go easy on her, and it was my job to prepare her. As cruel as my lesson might have been, it was a necessary one.

However, her introduction to my version of intimacy would be a softer experience. Scaring her in the real world differed significantly from my preparation in the bedroom.

I gently palmed her throat, choosing action over words, and bent to brush my lips over hers in our first kiss. Technically, it didn't count. Which meant we would have more than one first experience and that only excited me more.

"Zeph," she whispered, a note of wonder in her voice that went straight to my groin.

Innocent, I thought, amused. Except Kols told me she sucked cock like a queen, which meant she could play both innocent and seductress.

The perfect combination.

"Are you manipulating my dream?" she asked, her gaze bright with knowledge.

I smiled. "Shade told you Kols has been in your head, too."

She nodded. "Yes."

"Then you already know the answer, pixie flower." I took her mouth again before she could issue a complaint, needing her more than she could possibly know. Biting her breast had quenched some of my thirst and stirred a whole new addiction that required satisfaction. And only she could relieve me now.

My grasp tightened around her throat, my lips curling as she gulped in response. She must have been naked with Shade because she wore nothing now, her gorgeous curves on display for me to explore and taste to completion.

But I started with her mouth, slipping my tongue inside to dominate hers in the manner I favored. Each stroke served as a lesson, teaching her how to receive me, how to welcome me, and how to kiss exactly the way I preferred.

She was a fucking natural, her moans confirming she enjoyed the exploration as well, her body curving into mine in beautiful submission. "You're perfect," I praised, kissing a path along her jaw and tenderly nipping her pulse before pressing my lips to her ear. "I've wanted you since that first night," I admitted softly. "But you've been the forbidden fruit I couldn't taste. All that ended tonight, pixie flower. You're mine now, and I intend to take you thoroughly."

I pulled back to catch her gaze, noting the reddening of her cheeks and the escalation of her breath. All signs of arousal, except for the hint of fear in her eyes, the one I'd placed there earlier with Raph's demonstration.

I didn't like seeing that glimmer in her eyes.

But I could respect it.

"I'm not an easy lover, Aflora," I warned her. "Pain intrigues me, and I favor control. But you're in charge here. Always. You need to tell me if I push you too far. Until I can trust you to do that, we'll go easy on each other. Both in your mind and outside of it. The kind of relationship I prefer takes time." Kols was the only one in my life who had ever truly reached the level of trust I required, which was why we often shared women. He kept me balanced. Told me when I took it too far.

And in turn, I protected him.

Or I tried, anyway.

Two times I'd failed now, the second of which being the female gazing up at me now.

However, I hadn't failed just him this time, but myself, too.

Worse, I couldn't bring myself to regret it. Not this time. Not with Aflora submitting so beautifully beneath me.

She didn't question my preferences.

Didn't balk at them.

Merely accepted them with a slight nod and an adorable little lick of her lips. It wasn't enough but definitely served as a start.

"Tonight I'm just going to taste you," I told her. "But consider this an introductory warning for what I will eventually want from you. Now grab the headboard and don't come until I give you permission."

She shivered but lifted her arms in the perfect display of obedience. I half expected her to fight me, to argue, to say something to the contrary. Yet she seemed completely enthralled, as if I were acting on a fantasy she long harbored. Maybe she did. We were playing in her mind, after all. She could try to take over, if she wanted to. However, she appeared content to let me lead, and I adored her all the more for it.

I sensed Shade slipping into the periphery of her mind, having found a way around my block.

It'd be easy to kick him out, to eject him yet again, but I let him stay this time. It was my job as headmaster to teach, so I'd show him how this was done.

Kols's amusement touched my mind, his years of experience showing as he guessed my motive for allowing Shade to remain on the edge. He knew I loved to taunt, and taunt I would.

"Are you ready for me, Aflora?" I asked softly.

She nodded.

And I shook my head. "Words, pixie flower. Give me words." That was the first lesson in trust—communicating openly and verbally.

"Y-yes, except I'm still not sure if this is real or not."

"It's fantasy," I whispered, nuzzling her. "A joint fantasy."

"In my head."

"Yes."

"With you being in control, like Kols and Shade."

"With me being in control, but I'm nothing like Kols or Shade, Aflora." I sank my teeth into her lower lip, drawing blood in the process and groaning at the exquisite taste of her.

She sucked in a breath in reply, goose bumps pebbling along her arms and spreading to her delicious tits. Her nipples hardened into beautiful little points that begged for my mouth, but I wouldn't indulge in them until I had her full understanding and consent.

"This is a dream," I murmured. "One I'm influencing in your mind."

"Okay."

"We're both aware that this is happening," I added.

She nodded again and repeated, "Okay."

"Do I have your permission to continue?"

She paused, considering me for a long moment before dipping her chin once. "Yes."

"Good." Because I needed this to be mutual, not one-sided.

"Only, I'm confused," she admitted against my mouth just as I was about to kiss her again.

"Confused about what?" I asked her softly, my lips skating over hers with each word.

Her blue eyes held mine, her brow furrowing. Yet her pulse escalated. She clearly wanted me. It was her mind giving us trouble now. "In class earlier, you—"

"No, Aflora," I cut in, knowing what she wanted to discuss. "What I demand of you during a lesson in the classroom will never overlap with what I require from you in the bedroom. They are two different entities, entirely separate. I'm Headmaster Zephyrus during Academy hours. And after them, I'm just Zeph."

She swallowed, her pupils dilating. "Just Zeph."

"Can you handle that?"

Another nod, this one slightly shallower but accompanied by a heated glance that confirmed her yearning rivaled mine. "Yes," she whispered.

"Then I can proceed?"

"Yes," she said again.

I smiled. *Brilliant.* "No more talking unless it's to tell me how good you feel beneath my tongue." I captured her mouth and swallowed the sweet little noise she made in response to my command.

That little noise blossomed into a moan as I ran my palms up her sides, exploring her supple curves.

Aflora was feminine perfection, soft in all the right places with a warrior's heart underneath. I felt it beat against my hand as I cupped her breast, my thumb flicking her rosy bud and drawing more of those intriguing sounds from her lips.

Fuck, I adored a responsive woman.

And Aflora was definitely that.

She didn't shy away from her pleasure, her nipples tightening in eagerness and invitation. I licked a path down her neck to her collarbone and lower to take one of the stiff peaks into my mouth. She threaded her fingers through my hair in an attempt to hold me there. I bit her hard in response, my gaze capturing her wounded one as I growled low in my throat.

She stiffened, her fuckable mouth parting in confusion.

"Did I give you permission to release the headboard, Aflora?" I asked her.

"N-no," she stammered.

"Then I suggest you grab it again—right now—hold on, and don't let go until I tell you otherwise."

She quickly gripped the wood, her throat working as she managed to reply, "Sorry."

I smiled against her abused breast. "Oh, darling, you're not sorry. Not really. But if you release that headboard again, you will well and truly be sorry."

Orgasm denial was a favorite pastime of mine, and I excelled at it. She'd be in tears before the end of my torment, begging to come, and then I wouldn't stop until she begged me to stop.

Her grip tightened around the headboard, her cheeks going a little white.

The exact opposite of what I wanted to see from her.

And precisely why we would be taking our time getting to know each other.

"I would never injure you," I promised her. "I like pain, but only when mingled with pleasure."

I demonstrated by gently laving the bite mark on her tit, my tongue soothing her wound and seducing her back into the moment.

"Like this," I whispered, closing my mouth around her nipple and sucking her deep while massaging the tip with my tongue.

She bowed off the mattress in reply, her eyes falling shut on a groan as she desperately clung to the headboard.

"Just like that," I praised, switching to her other breast.

She practically panted in response, her heart bouncing wildly against her ribs.

Mmm, her arousal mounted by the second, permeating the air and taunting all my masculine senses. I inhaled deeply, loving the floral scent of her and finding it beautifully appropriate.

While delayed gratification might be a favorite game of mine, I wouldn't do that to her tonight. Mostly because I couldn't. I was dying to taste her, to feel her climax against my tongue, and revel in her pleasure over and over again until sunset.

There would be no sleeping for either of us tonight.

She'd be exhausted and gratified and unable to move later without thinking of me and the memory of my tongue between her thighs.

I slid down, kissing a wet path along her abdomen, pausing to dip my tongue into her navel while studying her reactions.

Parted lips.

Rosy cheeks.

Half-mast eyes.

Absolutely everything I wanted to see in a woman when making this descent. I nibbled her hip bone, smiling when she gasped and bucked in reply. Such a sensitive female, definitely made to be bitten. But I'd save that for our real experience together.

This dream was about satisfaction for us both.

A way to learn more about one another without risk.

Her soft, dark curls teased the hairs along my chin as I pressed a kiss to the top of her mound. I palmed her thighs to push them wide, exposing her slick pussy to my view.

She didn't shy away from me.

Didn't fight, either.

Merely tossed her head back with an eager sound, her excitement palpable and visible in the slickness of her folds.

"You're soaked for me, pixie flower," I whispered, admiring her damp heat. "I can't wait to make you wetter, baby."

She shivered, her lips parting in expectation.

I drew my nose along her seam, inhaling deeply and allowing her sweet nectar to take me completely. My dick throbbed, begging me to rip off my sweatpants and sink myself into her. But this wasn't about me or my needs.

I wanted to do this for her.

And also to fulfill my desire to taste her pleasure.

Something told me she'd be a screamer, unafraid of sharing her ecstasy with the world. Mmm, I bet she'd lock down on my fingers, too, her greedy cunt craving a cock to milk instead. *My* cock.

Soon, I promised us both. *Very soon.*

However, first, I required *this*. I parted her intimately with my tongue, licking upward to her clit and back down to the tight hole that would one day soon hug my shaft. I'd take her ass as well, once we worked up to it. Maybe even while Kols fucked her pussy.

Just thinking about it had my balls tightening in need.

She'd be the perfect puzzle piece between us, writhing in exquisite rapture while we took her to oblivion and back.

All the females we'd shared previously meant nothing, were just passing opportunities we took temporary pleasure from.

Aflora would be different.

Because she belonged to us, as we belonged to her.

Our mate.

Our minds would soon be intertwined—once we bit her two more times.

I groaned at the very real thought of what that would mean for us, how truly intimate it would be to fuck her while *inside* her. Our souls married as one. Our hearts beating in tandem with the other.

Fuck, who knew that could be so damn sexy?

I never desired a mate because it wasn't meant for me. Kols was my future. Serving as his Guardian my only path.

But now Aflora existed between us.

Having her changed everything.

"Zeph," she whispered, her plea a song I wanted to strum all night. I'd paused just under her clit, tasting without pleasing, and she desired more.

Her knuckles were white around the headboard, her restraint admirable as she held on for dear life. I could see her desire to let go, grab my head, and guide me upward to the place she needed me to touch.

I hummed against her flesh, smiling when she jolted. The reverberations would have given her just a hint of satisfaction, only to pull her deeper into a blanket of despair.

"*Please*," she said, her musical voice a proverbial stroke against my shaft. Because I loved the sound of a female begging, especially her.

"Please what?" I taunted her, studying her face as her eyes clenched shut in pleasurable frustration. Because my words had vibrated her once more. "Do you want me to suck your little clit into my mouth, Aflora? Massage you with my tongue until you explode?"

"Yes," she whimpered, her legs trembling around me.

"Say it," I encouraged her. "Tell me to suck your clit."

She gave an adorable little groan, my demand turning her on even more. It helped that my lips were now brushing her clit when I spoke, the heat of my breath stroking her arousal.

Her tongue slipped from her mouth to dampen her lips, a shuddering exhale escaping her as she quivered. "Please suck my clit, Zeph. Let me come."

Clever angel, I thought, amused. Not only had she asked nicely, but she'd also added a comment about being allowed to fall apart. "You're perfect, Aflora," I informed her. "Fucking perfect." And she didn't even know why. She was just a natural at submitting to me, her ability to take instruction displaying gorgeously in the bedroom.

I rewarded her with a firm lick, my mouth closing around her sensitive bud and giving her the suction she craved.

She screamed, her body coming off the mattress as she maintained a death grip on the bars of the headboard. Her admirable display of submission required an ample reward, so I gave it to her. "Come for me, pixie flower," I whispered. "Come hard."

I'd barely uttered the last two words when she fell apart on a scream that I would forever remember. Because it was underlined with my name. Never had I enjoyed hearing it more than in this moment as she repeated it over and over, her head thrashing from side to side as she shattered spectacularly beneath my tongue.

Kols stirred beside me in his bed, his mind attuned to mine and Aflora's, his voyeuristic tendencies shining through as he observed us. He stroked his cock in the real world, just outside the dreamscape, his orgasm mounting.

I reached across to stop him from continuing. "No. Time for you to join us."

"What?" Aflora asked, surfacing from her orgasmic state and hearing me speaking out loud and in my mind to Kols.

He didn't hesitate or argue, his powers mingling with mine as he joined us inside her mind.

I smiled as her eyebrows flew upward, her red cheeks showcasing her recent pleasure. Kissing a line up her abdomen, I returned to her mouth as I settled my body alongside hers. "Kols wants to play, too."

"But he hates me," she whispered to me, causing Kols to chuckle as he settled between her legs.

"This is about fantasy," he told her softly, his lips brushing the same place I just abandoned. "Just lie there and enjoy it, sweetheart." He didn't give her time to protest, his mouth sealing around her clit as he slid two fingers into her tight channel.

She yelped, her hands nearly leaving the headboard to make him stop, but I caught her wrists before she could. "Shh, you'll be all right."

"It's too much," she panted, squirming. "Too much... *sensation.*"

I smiled, knowing exactly what she meant. "Ah, Aflora, but this is a dream," I murmured, kissing her tenderly to silence her continued protests. "Don't you know the best part of dreaming, pixie flower?"

She shook her head. I couldn't tell if it was in response to my question or to the torment Kols was inflicting upon her between her thighs.

Either way, I answered. "The best part about a dream is it can defy reality," I whispered. "Which means we can make you come over and over again, all night, without once having to take a break. Because your body will continue to regenerate to our expectations."

Her eyes widened. "No."

"Oh, yes," I replied, nuzzling her and palming her breast to give her nipple a little squeeze. "It's the worst and best form of torment known to the Midnight Fae. And we're only just getting started."

She began to quake, her next orgasm already mounting, thanks to Kols's expert skill.

"Welcome to my mind, Aflora." I kissed the corner of her mouth and tweaked her peak once more, drawing a shudder from her. "It's a devious, intense place filled with endless ways to pleasure you. Tonight is merely an introduction, a taste of what our future holds."

She whimpered, and I smiled, sensing her mounting rapture.

"Go ahead and scream for us, baby," I said quietly, giving her permission to fall apart. "Once Kols is done, we'll switch places, and I'll drive you to new heights all over again."

And again.

And again.

Which I did.

As did Kols.

Until the sun went down, when I promised her a repeat performance again later.

Only, the moment I opened my eyes, everything went to hell.

And my plans for Aflora disappeared beneath a wave of crushing reality.

The Council knows...

MIDNIGHT FAE
ACADEMY
BOOK TWO

PROLOGUE

AFLORA

Earth Fae reside in a world of peace and flowers. We value life. We encourage growth. We adore vitality and prosperity.

That was the world I grew up in—a universe warmed by the sun and caressed by love.

Now I'm trapped in the darkness, fighting for my existence among a horde of treacherous Midnight Fae. Trust does not exist here. Hearts are often broken. And mate bonds mean nothing to the male fae who reside in this realm.

Those are the lessons I've learned these last few months during my captivity in the Midnight Fae realm.

They promised to teach me how to control my growing dark powers.

They promised to keep me safe.

I naively started to believe them.

Then they lied.

The cold black stone beneath my bare feet is evidence of their betrayal.

The looming cell with iron bars and a cold-faced gargoyle define my fate.

But I won't take this lying down.

If it's a fight they want, I'll give them one. I'm not going down alone. I refuse. They got me into this mess. It's only fair to invite them to the party of chaos.

I'll bite my tongue.

Bide my time.

And destroy them just like they destroyed me.

The jail door clinks shut while two of my mates watch with merciless expressions. I don't bother meeting their cold gazes. I already know what I'll find—unapologetic righteousness.

In the end, I'll burn those smug grins right off their faces.
I'm no longer the meek little Earth Fae they held captive here before.
Now I understand their rules.
And as soon as I free myself from the magic of these bindings, we'll play.
Prepare to bow to the queen, boys. I'm coming for you.

CHAPTER ONE

KOLS

Aflora refused to look at me.

Not that I could blame her.

She thought I'd betrayed her.

That knowledge hurt me almost as much as her resulting shiver to the dungeon air. Shade's shirt and boxers did little to keep her warm, but it was more than her lack of proper clothes. It was her soul reacting to the wrongness of her surroundings.

Elemental Fae weren't meant to stay underground for long periods of time. It'd only been a few minutes since our descent, but I caught the unease radiating from her shoulders. It rivaled my own, because I had no idea what to expect. The news of her trial arrived first thing this morning, and the Council was set to meet within the hour to discuss her fate.

I had no clue what this supposed recording revealed. Hell, I could be facing my own execution, for all I knew. But I doubted it. Otherwise, I'd be in chains right next to Aflora.

Which meant there was still hope.

It all depended on what Shade had told the Council.

I rubbed a hand over my face as the iron bars locked behind Aflora, the gargoyle overhead watching her with severe distaste. "Don't harm her," I told the stone creature. "She's still a guest until the Council deems otherwise."

Aflora snorted before settling on a stone bench, her eyes continuing to avoid mine.

There were things I wanted to say but couldn't with our surrounding audience. So I merely said, "Someone will return should a test of your abilities be required for the trial. Otherwise, you will be notified when the Council reaches a decision."

I met Zeph's gaze as I turned, his green orbs giving nothing away. We'd discuss this more once we were away from all the surveillance cameras and lost our two Warrior Blood guards.

Aflora didn't reply or acknowledge my comments, her stature prim and proper as we left her alone in her cell.

Too bad I couldn't force her into a temporary dream to communicate with her, but we didn't have time for that. So instead, I walked with purpose up the stairs, past the Council Chambers, and into a corridor that led to a room where I could speak with Zeph in private.

The pair of Warrior Blood guards remained at the dungeon entrance, their job to ensure Aflora didn't escape. That alone told me the Council had no idea how powerful she was. If they did, they'd put a lot more than two fae on watch.

Zeph closed the door behind us, his first comment a string of curses that ended in Shade's name. "Did they let you hear the rest of the recording?"

I shook my head. "Only the bit you overheard with her calling for her own extermination." I ran a hand over my face once, fatigue weighing down my shoulders. "We need a backup plan. Because if this goes south…" I trailed off, not wanting to finish that statement out loud.

"Breaking her out won't be hard. Those two nitwits on the stairs will go down in a single spell. But we'll need to alter the security footage."

Yeah, we were on the same page. I'd already begun to think about whom I could bribe to clear the tapes. "Where will we hide her?"

"That's the part I haven't figured out. We can't trust anyone. Not even her Elemental Fae."

True. If they learned about her growing power, they'd have no choice but to end her life. "Fucking Shade," I muttered, livid all over again. "What the hell was he thinking? He has to know this is going to bite him in the ass, too."

"Maybe that's what he wants." Zeph scratched the dark stubble dotting his jaw. "His motives all seem to revolve around creating chaos. If the Council finds out what happened last night—"

The door opened to reveal my father on the other side, his expression one of relief. "Oh, good, you're already here." He joined us without asking, his gold eyes narrowing at Zeph just enough to indicate he still wasn't pleased with the Warrior Blood, before fixating on me. "Is the recording true? Is her power growing out of control?"

"I haven't heard it all yet to comment," I answered carefully.

Disapproval radiated from my father. "You've spent the last few months supervising her. Surely you can make an assessment regarding her power."

"Yes. From what I've observed, her power level remains the same as the first day she arrived." Not exactly a lie. She was born with Quandary Blood abilities; she just hadn't used them much until her forced enrollment at Midnight Fae Academy. And last night, she sort of exploded because of that contained power.

So, yeah, she was losing control. But the quad-bond mating ritual we'd performed as a result of her outburst should help ground her. Maybe.

Which opened a whole new realm of consequences.

We'd solve those problems another day.

One issue at a time.

The first one being to free Aflora from the dungeon.

"Then why is she claiming a need to be exterminated?" my father challenged.

I considered his query and quickly formulated a safe reply. "From what little I've heard of the recording, it was a hypothetical statement—*if* she proves too powerful, she needs to be removed. Aflora feels very strongly about protecting her Earth Fae."

My father studied me for a long moment, his gaze narrowing. "So what caused the inferno in her room at the Elite Residence on campus?"

Fucking gargoyle, I seethed. My brother, Tray, wouldn't report the incident. Neither would his mate, Ella. Which left the damn stone guardian at the front door. "That was my fault. I had a little too much aggression after my duel with Shade and released it inappropriately. I'll repair the quarters myself." By using magic, of course.

The tick in my father's jaw suggested that he suspected I wasn't providing the whole truth, but he eventually conceded with a stiff nod. "The Earth Fae is your ascension trial. I trust you to see it through appropriately."

"And I am," I promised him. I just wasn't doing it the way he'd originally intended. What with accidentally mating the girl during sex and biting her soon after to initiate the Midnight Fae bond.

My father left without another word, never once acknowledging Zeph other than that initial glance. Normally, it would irritate me. Today, I had other, more important matters to address.

"He knows you're lying," Zeph said before I could speak. "But I don't think there's anything incriminating on the tapes, or he'd be angry, not just disappointed."

A fair assessment. If there was anything about the quad-bond on the recording, my father would have reacted differently. Such as throwing my ass in the dungeon and Zeph into an execution chamber. "Whatever it is, it had to be enough to call an emergency meeting and require her detainment."

"That wouldn't be hard. The Council often overreacts."

I snorted. "You would say that."

"Just as you wouldn't," he returned, his tone lacking his usual teasing disdain. He seemed as tired as I was. Likely because we both didn't do much sleeping last night, having enjoyed the new connection with Aflora a little too much.

Palming the back of my neck, I blew out a long breath and looked at the ceiling. "She thinks we betrayed her, Zeph."

"She'll get over it." He clearly didn't share my concern. "Go prepare for the Council meeting. If the findings are dire and she's truly in jeopardy, text me a note about possibly missing a few classes this week. If she's fine, let me know when you'll be back on campus. I'll react accordingly."

I bobbed my head in agreement. "Okay. And if you see Shade before I do, punch him in the face for me."

Zeph grunted, his green eyes blazing with vengeful power. "If I see him first, there won't be much left of his face for you to hit."

"Good." Because the fucker deserved a beatdown for whatever game he'd engaged us all in now.

I just hoped Aflora wouldn't pay the ultimate price for his newest diversion.

CHAPTER TWO

AFLORA

"I don't suppose you can fetch me a glass of water?" I asked the gargoyle.

He snorted in reply.

"I didn't think so," I murmured, sighing as I relaxed into the stone wall at my back.

This place was hell. My own personal purgatory. Earth Fae didn't belong underground. Not that it mattered, I couldn't access my source with this choker around my neck anyway.

Closing my eyes, I returned to my task of trying to unlock it with my mind. The magic caressing my skin itched at my conscious, the cloaking mechanism one that seemed to warm the bonds emanating from my heart.

I tugged on one of them, and a familiar woodsy scent touched my nose. *Zeph.*

Yanking on the other strand filled my essence with rich spice and power. *Kols.*

And the final cord released a wave of peppermint, the refreshing taste one craves first thing in the morning. *Shade.*

I frowned. *Why is the collar connected to them? To hide our links?*

That would explain Zeph's haste this morning in forcing the contraption on me. He wanted to guarantee no one would find out about our bonds.

"I need you to put this on, and we need to run. Now."

His words replayed in my head, causing me to scowl even harder than before. I'd stupidly believed he wanted to help me. Had thought he might even care about my welfare.

But those jackholes only cared about themselves.

Hence my current predicament.

Ignoring my anger, I refocused on the enchantment circling my skin and plucked at some of the other magical strings. They all seemed to be suffocating my powers, which explained the tingling sensation rioting through my spirit. It was a miracle in itself that I could access enough of my essence to investigate the spells on the collar. Undoing them would be another task entirely.

"Ah, there you are." Shade's voice warmed my face, his hands soon following as he materialized in front of me.

I jumped to my feet, my fists ready to meet his face, when he grabbed my wrists with ease and backed me into the wall. The gargoyle didn't seem to care at all, his beady red eyes focused on a space over my head instead of on the Midnight Fae forcing a thigh between mine.

"The Council is about to convene. Do you have any special requests on how I should address them on your behalf?" he asked, his ice-blue eyes capturing and holding mine.

I spat at him rather than reply.

Like I'd trust him to speak on my behalf.

Willow stump, I thought, furious.

His eyebrow inched upward as he released one of my wrists to wipe the spittle away from his face. I used the opportunity to try to shove him away, but he caught my wrist again with ease, holding both above my head beneath one of his palms.

"Are you asking me to spit on them, Aflora?" He cocked his head in an almost playful manner. "Because I'm pretty sure that won't go over well."

"Go to hell," I told him.

"Already there, baby," he replied.

Holy Elements, I hated this male. He'd bitten me against my will, trapped me in this world, nearly convinced me to somewhat trust him, and had me thrown into a jail cell again. "Did you record everything last night?" I asked him, my lip curling into a snarl. "Including the part about our qua—"

His mouth caught mine, his tongue pushing inside before I could think to respond. Fury boiled inside me, my reaction coming a second later in the form of a bite that caused his blood to spill over our lips.

I spat it on the ground instead of swallowing, our residual dreams teaching me the consequences of imbibing his essence.

Fire lit his gaze, causing the ice to melt around his irises into a pool of bright blue flames. "Careful, Aflora, or we'll end up giving the Council quite the show." He cocked his chin toward the corner, just above the gargoyle's head. "They're watching us right now. Listening, too. So if you have something you want to say, do it now."

His eyes flared with warning, some sort of hidden message brewing in his azure depths.

Had they sent him down here to torment me while they observed?

Was I supposed to admit something?

Remain quiet?

Fight him?

I didn't know.

"It would help if I knew what I was on trial for," I said, narrowing my gaze.

"You don't remember what you told me last night?" he countered, his lips curling. "I suppose the sex was pretty intense in comparison."

Sex? We didn't have sex. He'd used his thigh to force my climax. Then Zeph and Kols had taken over my dreams afterward.

What are you trying to tell me? I wondered, some of my ire cooling in favor of confusion. "I told you I should be exterminated."

"Yes, *if* your power can't be controlled," he replied, his emphasis on the word *if* making me frown. "Do you have anything you wish to add to that statement?"

"What would I add?" I countered.

"That's why I'm here." His thumb stroked my wrist. "Is there anything you want me to say on your behalf?"

"I don't want you to speak on my behalf."

"That's not how our rules work."

"Well, your rules are archaic."

"Perhaps, but that's a discussion for another day, Aflora. I need to know if there's anything else you want me to tell them. That's why I'm down here—at the Council's request—and why some of them are watching us right now."

There it was, a reiteration of a warning.

They can hear and see us.

Okay.

I expected that.

But why did it concern him? Because he didn't want me to mention the quad-bond? How would that impact him? Everyone knew we were mates already. Kols and Zeph were the ones who'd suffer if I mentioned what happened last night.

Well, and me.

However, I didn't matter to any of them.

Just as Kols and Zeph didn't matter to Shade.

So why would he care?

"If you have nothing to add, then I'll handle it from here," Shade said, his voice lower as his thumb continued to massage my wrist. "I know exactly what happened last night, little rose. But don't worry. I won't go into specifics on how good you feel around my cock."

My brow started to furrow. "What—"

His lips caressed mine. "It's okay, sweetheart. They won't ask for specifics. They just want clarification on the recording. I know what you meant, and I'll make sure they do, too."

Another riddle.

Another game.

Another way to betray me.

"Like I'd ever trust you to speak on my behalf," I whispered.

He smiled. "There's my fiery mate." His lips went to my ear, his voice dropping to a whisper as he added, "Don't lose her, Aflora. We have many more trials to dance through together." His teeth skimmed my throat in a display of Midnight Fae affection before he released me, his eyes glazed with power. "Wish me luck, little rose. I'm about to either exonerate you or ensure your demise. Personally, I hope for the former. It'd be such a loss of talent otherwise."

He disappeared into a wave of smoke before I could reply, causing me to growl in annoyance at the empty space around me.

Then I focused on the camera. "You're a bunch of archaic flower petals," I muttered. "When you're ready to join me in the present, I'll give you a statement. Until then, go fluff yourselves."

I started to pace, my mind rattling with notions of Shade's intentions. Whatever his goals, they were self-fulfilling at best.

Which meant I needed to be ready for a fight.

Something that would be hard considering my lack of sleep last night— thanks to my jackhole mates.

That was probably why I couldn't focus enough to unweave the power from my neck. Well, that, and inexperience.

Sighing, I collapsed onto the floor mattress and pounded my fist into the soft material while envisioning three different male faces. They were probably watching me and chuckling, which only made me strike the fabric harder.

They continued to underestimate me.

That would change today.

I lay back on the makeshift bed and closed my eyes.

Time to tackle this collar, I told myself. *Once you're free, they'll never know what hit them.*

CHAPTER THREE

SHADE

"Any loss of life is unacceptable. If I can't be controlled, I should be exterminated." Aflora's voice played throughout the Council Chambers, followed by my recorded response.

"That's a very narrow view, Aflora. What if you could learn control?"

Several snorts replied to that question while I maintained my calm demeanor against the wall, one leg crossed over the other, hands in my pockets. My father wanted me to sit beside him. I'd sooner accept a position in hell.

"I've been trying that since I arrived," Aflora replied, the rest of her sentence altered for the purposes of this meeting. I'd play along only to an extent. Which was why I'd doctored the tape before handing it over.

Convince them you're playing by the rules, and they'll give you more freedom.

Not exactly a prophecy, but solid advice. As *he* had been right about everything thus far, I chose to listen to him. Because now more than ever, I needed the flexibility to blend into the shadows and help Aflora hide the truth.

"Yes, and now you have a support system to rely on." Another doctored section of the recording, this one easier than the other since it was my response.

"I have no one to rely on." Aflora sounded so disgruntled. Not that I blamed her. "You never tell me anything of importance. Zeph is the realm's worst teacher. And Kols hates me. Some support system."

"Yeah, he's a shit teacher." I smirked, just as I had when I originally spoke those words. "But Kols doesn't hate you, and I tell you important things all the time. You just don't hear me."

"Right."

"Here, I'll make it better, little rose. Just close your eyes and—" The recording cut off, causing several gazes to swing my way.

I shrugged. "What can I say? She's a gorgeous woman." I allowed them to form their own opinions on what had happened next. If they wanted to judge me, I welcomed it. Because that would deflect them all from the truth of what actually occurred after her last word.

When I told her about Kols's grandfather ordering the slaughter of the Quandary Bloods.

And admitted I knew about her heritage before we met.

Two very important details I did not want to share with the Council.

"That's it? That's the entirety of the recording?" King Malik demanded.

"Oh, there's more," I drawled. "But it's mostly just grunts and moans. Without the visuals, it lacks the finesse of the moment."

Kols narrowed his gaze at me, his golden orbs flashing with disdain.

Yeah, I could have given him a heads-up about my intentions. But I didn't want him to develop a false sense of leadership over me. I played by my own rules, no one else's. It would be best for us all if he learned that lesson now.

"So she believes herself to be an abomination." Tadmir's white hair flickered with blue flames, the only outward indication of his current mood. "That's enough for me. Kill the girl. It'll free up Shadow for the mating bond, and he can carry out the agreement between our families."

I remained quiet, not trusting myself to reply to that out loud.

Kols wasn't so restrained, his tone underlined in authority as he replied, "Aflora didn't call herself an abomination. She's just being a martyr because she cares about her people. If anything, that only marks her as a worthy queen to the Earth Fae throne."

The blue flickers grew around Tadmir's head. "There must be a reason she wants to be exterminated." His beady black eyes turned to me. "Where's the beginning of the recording?"

"Nonexistent," I lied. "We began the discussion in the hallway, out of range. I guided her into my room mid-conversation to catch at least part of her words for the use of the Council." Complete and utter bullshit, which only Kols seemed to know. Fortunately, he kept his royal mouth shut.

"What led to her proclamation?" Chern, ever the wise fae, played right into my hands the way I'd hoped he would.

Sangré Bloods could be so predictable sometimes in their penchant for logic. Today, that worked in my favor beautifully.

"She was upset about my little tiff with Kols." I met and held the prince's burning gold eyes. "She didn't appreciate the flare of power our duel created and was lecturing me about the loss of life in the LethaForest."

Releasing Kols's gaze, I took in the room of blank stares.

Idiots.

"She's an Earth Fae," I reminded them all. "She values all life, including the destroyed burning thwomps."

I lifted a shoulder, done with my mouthful of untruths.

Though, I did mention the dead trees to her during that conversation.

And technically, her extermination reply followed right after.

So it wasn't all a lie, just a bit jumbled.

Kols's jaw ticked, but he didn't correct me. The duel had been his brilliant cover story for what really happened between the four of us last night. I'd only enhanced his explanation and also provided the Council with a different rabbit to chase, just in case they came back to question the destruction in the LethaForest.

"And that led to her calling for her own death?" Chern prompted, his gray eyes intelligent.

"Yes, because I told her sometimes things die, and she launched into a debate on her own powers and fate. Then she said if she can't be controlled, she should be exterminated. I believe she meant it hypothetically, but I thought it wise to share the recording with my father. It was this Council, after all, that demanded I report back any findings no matter how small. I'm merely complying with the edict."

There. Flowery bullshit for the table. Isn't it beautiful? I thought, fighting a smile.

King Malik didn't appear all that impressed.

Neither did Tadmir.

I mean, honestly. Did they really expect me to waltz in here and request the death of my mate? I suppressed a snort. That would never happen.

"That was the request of the Council," my father agreed, his tone flat. "And the recording itself is incriminating."

True. But my explanation exonerated her without fail. I just needed them to believe me. Which was the only potential weak point in my strategy.

And exactly why I had a backup plan should the Council vote negatively against Aflora.

"You've spent the most time with her, Kolstov." King Malik turned toward his son. "What are your opinions on the matter?"

"As I mentioned earlier, Aflora puts her people above herself. If she truly believed herself to be a danger to them, she'd demand her execution."

Clever wording, I mused.

"What I heard on the recording is exactly the kind of statement she'd say to me," he continued. "But it remains an *if* scenario, not a resolute one. To exterminate her now would be a false preemptive measure without proper merit and likely earn retaliation from the Elemental Fae."

All very logical without an ounce of emotion.

If we were alone, I'd applaud him for the outward stoicism.

"She's your ascension trial," King Malik replied. "If that's your decision, I stand behind it."

Oh, if you only knew what Kols had been doing to his little "ascension trial" yesterday around this time, you wouldn't be so quick to agree, I thought.

Outwardly, I remained as calm and cool as Kols, never once showing an opinion either way. The Council thought I only cared about fucking Aflora. I preferred it that way. Made things easier.

"So we just send her back to the Academy?" Tadmir's tone matched the embers floating around his oval-shaped head, his annoyance piqued.

"A hypothetical conversation is not grounds for execution." Chern rubbed his bald head, the designs along his scalp flaring with magic. "We should continue to monitor her developments through Kolstov's reports."

Kols's jaw ticked once more, the only indication of his discomfort.

Yes, young prince, how does it feel to lie to the room of your intended peers? To know that the truth would have you ousted from that precious throne and potentially killed in the process? I wondered.

I almost pitied him.

That cuff around his wrist might hide his truth from the room, but he'd made his bed when he chose to invite Aflora to play between his sheets.

Of course, destiny wrote that act into the cards long ago.

And there was no escaping fate.

I yawned as the Councilmen began their usual debates, with Tadmir on one side, Chern on the other, and my father and Malik in between while Svart remained dutifully silent. Some of the Seconds spoke up, but most were in agreement that Aflora should be allowed to return to the Academy with Prince Kolstov as her warden.

There were so many innuendos on the tip of my tongue regarding Kolstov's method of guardianship, but I swallowed each one.

"Continue to report back anything useful," my father told me after the meeting adjourned. "It doesn't matter how small."

"Sure," I replied, acting as though his request didn't faze me in the slightest.

My goal was to convince him I resided on his side, that my duty was to him and the Council. Because I needed him to stop watching my every move.

The pride in his eyes now suggested that perhaps I'd won some favor with him, that maybe he would remove the surveillance he had on me at the Academy. I'd know soon enough, as I'd spent the last few months skillfully avoiding them.

That was one of the many benefits of my bloodline—my ability to detect *paths*.

If only I could find the quickest way out of this new mess.

Alas, the prophecy stood, and things were about to become a whole hell of a lot worse before they ever improved.

Ah, my poor, darling Aflora. This is only the beginning. Please don't hate me too much.

CHAPTER FOUR

AFLORA

"We really need to stop meeting like this, little rose," a deep voice murmured into my ear.

I sighed, not wanting to move, my body cocooned in a blanket of comforting warmth. Yet something about those words nagged at me, dragging me back to a reality I didn't want to face.

To the hard mattress beneath me.

To the stale air of a dungeon.

To the beady red eyes of the supervising gargoyle.

I sprang upward, my head aching with the desire to return to my dreamless sleep. *Ugh.* The exhaustion had won while I was messing with the magic around my neck, leaving me in the same position as before—powerless.

Shade's palm ran up my side in a soothing gesture undermined by lies. Leaping to my feet, I backed away from him. He remained on the mattress, his athletic form balanced on his elbow. "The Council concluded that your theoretical commentary was not enough to require action, and I've been instructed to return you to the Academy. So whenever you're ready, let me know."

I gaped at him. "Theoretical commentary?"

"Yes. I explained to them how you were merely theorizing what should be done if your powers were to grow out of control. As they haven't actually proved uncontrollable, the Council saw no reason to act." He lifted a shoulder. "Classes resume tomorrow—well, later today, really—as scheduled."

"I'm… I'm free?"

"Not really. The Academy is just a fancier prison, in my opinion." He pushed off the ground and landed deftly on his feet. "Shall we, princess?" He extended his hand with the offer, his dark brow waggling in a taunting manner.

"Is this a joke?"

"If you think it is, then my ego's wounded. Because I swear I'm funnier than that."

I stared at him.

He stared back.

Time ticked on between us with his hand dangling in the air.

The gargoyle huffed in agitation, his stone wings beating rapidly as he shoved through the door and left it wide open in his wake.

Either I was dreaming or Shade had told me the truth.

"Take a chance," he dared, a sinful promise teasing the edges of his lips. "I promise not to bite you today."

"I think it's a little late for promises," I muttered, stepping around him to reach the door.

Shade caught me by the waist, pulling me back against him. "I said you were free." His lips brushed my ear with the whispered words. "I said nothing about using doors."

"Wh—"

The world shifted around us in a thick gray cloud, causing my stomach to roll with uncertainty.

Then the scent of fresh-cut grass tickled my nostrils.

Followed by flowers in bloom.

And the kiss of a morning sun.

I'm dreaming, I thought, spinning in a circle as the inky smog evaporated into a blue sky. Plush green blades met my bare feet, the sensation of earth breathing life into my being and sending me to the ground in a sob of unfiltered joy.

Earth.

I'm surrounded by earth.

The essence beckoned me to play, but the mechanism around my neck halted my reaction, yanking me back to a reality of pain and suffering. I clawed at the offending leather, longing to be rid of it, and screamed in frustration.

This was the definition of hell—being surrounded by the element I craved just to be cut off from it because of black foreign magic.

More torture.

More games.

More wicked intent.

I growled, ready to kill the being who did this to me. I lunged for him, only to find myself caught up in his much stronger arms, his lips at my ear. "Breathe."

The single command had me snarling. "*I hate you.*" It came out hoarse, my emotions spilling from my pores in ripples of convoluted fury.

"I didn't put that device around your neck," he reminded me in a calm tone that only infuriated me more. "But you have the tools to undo it. So stop freaking out and use your Quandary Blood to unweave the magic around your source." He released me and took a step back.

I spun around, ready to slap him, when his comment registered.

You have the tools to undo it.

He was right.

I did.

Assuming I didn't fall asleep again.

Frowning, I prodded at the spells enchanting my collar once more and found them waiting eagerly for my manipulation. Odd. They hadn't done that in the dungeon. Why could I see them more easily now?

"The cells are laced with protective spells that make magic difficult to access," Shade said, reading either my mind or the confusion on my face. "You should find your Quandary Blood skills are much easier to access, even with that thing choking the life out of your magical spirit."

He took another step away from me, his back meeting the trunk of a nearby tree.

"Just try to remember how to put the spell back together. We can't have Kols or Zeph finding out that you can circumvent their little masterpiece, yeah?" He slid down to the ground, still braced against the tree, and closed his eyes. "I'll just be over here having a nap while you play."

I blinked at him. "A nap?"

"Mmm," he mumbled, clasping his hands in his lap. "You're not the only one who requires beauty sleep, little rose."

"Wait, where are we?" I asked, taking in the array of fields and trees and flowers around us. "In the human world?"

He snorted. "I have no idea where we are. While trying to return you to the Academy, my exhaustion kicked in and we accidentally ended up here. Too bad, really. It's so bright. Alas, I didn't want to risk getting us more lost, so we decided to nap here for the day before trying again. I'm sure Kols will understand. He has a room to fix, after all."

"Do you always talk in riddles?"

"Only when I'm tired." He yawned dramatically. "And, man, am I tired. Hope you don't mind spending some time here, Aflora. Sorry for my lack of coordination and direction."

He didn't sound apologetic at all.

But that was the point.

He'd purposely brought me here and was telling me the lie he intended to give everyone else.

My fingers unfurled from the fists at my sides, realization threatening to breach the icy confines of my heart. *He brought me here to play with my earth.*

He'd given me the gift of the sun. The grass. Trees with real leaves. Flowers in full bloom. And while he wouldn't tell me where we were, he'd also provided me with subtle instructions on what to do.

All in his cryptic little way.

I studied the chiseled features of his handsome face and caught the slight twitch of his lips—the only outward sign he was pleased. Then his expression slowly fell into one of contentment, his closed eyes unmoving. "Use your

Quandary Blood to set your earth source free, little rose," he murmured. "I've always favored floral scents."

Me, too, I thought, slowly kneeling once more as I engaged the part of my spirit that loved solving puzzles. It felt so foreign and yet familiar. A conundrum of energy that I didn't quite understand, but I applied it to the collar around my neck and slowly picked at the various strands of magic. I didn't touch the ones tied to my Midnight Fae mates but focused on the black web surrounding my elemental gifts. Pulses of the source peeked at me from below the dark strings, demanding freedom.

It was an intricate dance woven through my mind, the powers blending in a manner that surpassed logical form. This shouldn't feel right, but it did. The essence mingled inside me, my problem-solving skills mating with my love for the earth as a spark of light stirred behind my eyes.

There, I thought, seeing the source of my elemental power beckoning me forward. I followed it knowingly, bathing in the rays of welcome it shined through my spirit, and lifted my eyelids to find myself rolling across the earth in a blanket of flowers.

An exuberant giggle bubbled from my chest, happiness kissing my soul after what felt like months of despair.

This was my rightful place.

My home.

My earth.

A breeze trickled through the trees, sending me their warm welcome as more blossoms sprouted from the grass in an array of my favorite colors.

The dark one is watching, one of the trees whispered, drawing my attention to where Shade lounged beneath the green limbs. His eyes were indeed open, his expression amused.

"You remind me of a nymph," he said softly, his voice deep and soothing. "A gorgeous little nymph."

"I've heard that word used to describe Earth Fae before. It's appropriate."

His lips twitched, his eyes falling closed once more. "Wake me when the sun falls, little rose." He fell into true sleep then, his breaths even as he remained seated against the tree trunk with his legs crossed at the ankles.

I let him rest while I explored the meadow, my heart soaring with the song of beauty and nature's grace.

This place wasn't part of the Human Realm, the life surrounding me unfamiliar with mortal essences. So it was a fae world of some kind, but I couldn't determine which one. Every time I asked, the trees whispered of something different, something new, distracting me from my questions and urging me to exhaust my earth essence instead.

I created a myriad of plant life, played with the grassy roots and soil, and luxuriated in the foliage of life.

By the time the sun began to descend, I felt full of vitality, my soul thriving in a way I hadn't felt in far too long.

All because Shade brought me here to play.

Under the excuse of having lost his way back to an Academy he'd shadowed to thousands of times before.

Maybe this was his way of apologizing.

Maybe this was all just a trick, a last dance with life before death consumed me.

I couldn't know for sure, my faith in him nonexistent.

But that didn't stop the inkling of gratitude from entering my heart. He'd given me a gift. I just didn't know his intentions for it.

He stirred as night graced the horizon, his arms stretching overhead as he took in the twilight meadow. His lips curled. "This is beautiful, Aflora."

A compliment.

Not a taunt.

Or it didn't sound like one, anyway.

I remained cocooned in my sea of flowers as he stood, his head cocking to the side upon finding me beneath a shield of earth. He stepped forward, only for one of my tree roots to lift and stop his path. "Impressive," he replied, eyeing the obstacle before shadowing around it to appear at my side.

I considered wrapping a vine around him to secure him to the earth, but he knelt beside me and plucked a flower from my hair. He brought it to his nose and inhaled deeply, then released a sigh.

"Unfortunately, we need to return to the Academy, or they'll send Warrior Bloods after us. My excuse will only get us so far." Rather than hold out a hand to demand we leave, he sat down and settled into the flower bed I'd created. "For your own safety, you need to rewrite the spell, Aflora." His blue gaze met mine. "But maybe you can weave it in a way that allows for a little flexibility in the restraint."

Another riddle.

Another clue.

A suggestion.

"And maybe we can come back here in the future," he added, his knuckles brushing my cheek.

"That implies I can trust your word, which I know I can't."

"You can't?" He arched a brow. "Why not, Aflora? I've never lied to you."

"Your actions are louder than your supposed truths."

"My actions," he mused, his hand falling from my face to the flower petals around him. "You mean how I doctored the recording to save you from the Council's wrath? How I brought you to this special place to give you a day of freedom at the expense of my own?" He phrased both as questions. "Are those not actions in your favor?"

"You gave them the recording."

"An altered version of it, yes."

"Why?" I demanded. "You had me essentially arrested for what purposes?"

He scrutinized me for so long that I was surprised when he actually replied, "To lull the Council into a false sense of security. If they think I'm playing by their rules, they'll give more freedom—something we could all use at the moment. I also wanted to distract them from looking into the explosion of power from the other night. Kols's little story about the duel wasn't going to satisfy my father. He knows I'm not the losing sort."

His explanation shocked me for a multitude of reasons, not the least of which being that he'd actually given me a factual reply. The question was, did I believe him?

"You believe actions prove integrity," he continued, arching a brow. "Then ask me to bring you back here in the future. We'll see what happens. In the interim, I need you to enchant your collar again. But if you want to program in a backdoor to access your earth, I'll look the other way and pretend not to notice."

He stood and wiped his palms against his pants.

"I'm fucking starving," he added, abruptly changing the subject. "Did you happen to make anything edible around here? Like fruit?"

My lips curled at the thought of home and the Elemental Fae Queen's favorite peach trees. "No. But I can." It was one of the only human fruits I knew how to create, thanks to Queen Claire's obsession with the juicy treat.

Shade faced me, his expression expectant.

So I gave him what he wanted by calling the seeds to the soil and expediting the growth through my access from the source.

He watched in fascination as the tree grew, the branches sprouting with leaves first and then luscious circles of fruit. He plucked one off the tree and took a bite, his moan of approval holding an erotic appeal that I pretended not to hear.

"Fuck, this is delicious." He leaned once more against the tree he'd used for his nap and devoured the peach. Then he walked over and snatched another one.

"Throw the pit over there," I instructed him, pointing with my finger to where I wanted it.

He did as I requested, and I used the core to create another tree. "Earth is a continuous cycle of life."

"While Midnight Fae are known for the darkness of death," he returned, his blue eyes alight with knowledge. "But Quandary Bloods are rumored to be more than just dark magic. They're conduits of The Source. The one that controls all others, I mean. That's how many of them were able to hide during the mass extermination—they assimilated as other types of fae. Even Earth Fae. Or that's the theory, anyway."

"Are you saying that not all Quandary Bloods perished?"

"I think your existence answers that question, little rose," he replied before finishing off his second peach. "Now we have to stop stalling. If we don't return soon, we'll be back where we started—in the dungeon—and we can't have that. Not after I went through the hassle of having that tape altered to suit our needs." He pushed off his tree, hopped over the root I'd left in the ground, and came to stand over me. "Snap the magic in place and let's go."

He made it sound so easy.

Which, now that I knew how to unravel the spell, actually was pretty simple to put back together. But the confident manner in which he spoke made me wonder how he knew it would be such a quick task.

"Do you know any Quandary Bloods, Shade?" I asked him while I mentally began the process of closing off my connection to the earth source.

"Now you're asking interesting questions," he praised, his gaze alight with mischief. "If I told you yes, would you believe me?"

"Maybe."

"Then maybe I do. I mean, I know you."

"Other than me," I clarified.

He merely smiled, his hand finding mine as he pulled me to him and pressed a quick kiss to the corner of my mouth. "Did you create a way to access your earth through the spell?"

I took a page out of his book and didn't reply other than to grin.

"My perfect mate," he whispered, pressing his forehead to mine. "Hold on tight, little rose. I suspect we're about to endure a rough Academy welcome."

CHAPTER FIVE

SHADE

If I wasn't holding Aflora, I would have ducked.

For her, I took the punch waiting for me upon our arrival.

"Your actions are louder than your supposed truths," she'd said.

How's that for an action, princess? I thought now as I shifted my jaw to ease the pain.

When Kols went for round two with my face, I shadowed myself—and Aflora—to the other side of his royal suite.

The gargoyle chose that moment to appear with a screeching sound, his distaste at my Death Blood presence causing a shrieking alarm to blare throughout the audacious four-bedroom apartment. I blasted the damn thing with a silencing spell by issuing a command from my mind, causing it to sputter and collapse on the ground in a cluster of rocky wings.

Its red eyes breathed fire as it came for me in all its stone-filled glory.

Determined little badass, I thought, trapping it beneath a net of shadows I conjured with a flick of my wrist.

Its lips parted in a bellow that my silencing enchantment fortunately caught.

I smirked at the tiny idiot. "Not so tough now, are you?"

Rage blazed from its gaze, just as it did from Kols's gold irises as he charged across the living area.

"This isn't beneficial conversation," I pointed out, ready to shadow again.

Only, Aflora stepped in front of me and slammed her fist into Kols's jaw as soon as he was within distance.

My lips actually parted.

"Razzleberries," she breathed, shaking out her hand with a hiss of pain.

Kols's residual anger subsided beneath a wave of shock tinged with dismay as he prodded his jaw with two fingers. "You hit me."

Her shoulders tightened and her chin lifted. "You threw me in a cell."

"To protect you, Aflora," he growled.

A laugh bubbled out of her as she shook her long waves of black hair. "I felt very safe there. Thanks, Prince Kolstov." She turned on her heel to leave, and he caught her wrist.

"What was I supposed to do, Aflora?" he demanded. "Shade's the one who gave them the recording, not me."

I snorted. "Don't bring me into this."

"Are you fucking kidding me? This is *your* fault," he seethed. "And where the fuck have you been? You were supposed to bring her directly here."

"Oh, was I?" I pretended to think. "I suppose that order didn't register correctly."

"Where did you take her?" Another command. One of these days, he'd realize that I didn't consider myself one of his precious subjects to be dictated to.

"Let go of me," Aflora interjected, twisting her arm.

He tightened his grip. "Where did he take you?"

She gave him a defiant look. "While trying to return me to the Academy, his exhaustion kicked in and we ended up in an unknown location. He didn't want to risk getting us more lost, so we stayed there for the day while he napped. Now I'm here. Happy?"

Kols's jaw ticked while my lips canted into a delighted smirk. My clever little mate had used my riddled explanation without even blinking. "Exactly," I agreed just as Zeph burst into the suite.

His gaze narrowed, a flash of anger crossing his features as he headed right for me.

Great.

"What the fuck were you thinking, Death Blood?"

"That my father would never believe Kols's little duel story and I needed to give him something to distract him," I replied coolly. "It worked."

Zeph paused midstep, his calculative gaze raking over me as he considered the reason. That was one thing I liked about the Warrior Blood—he preferred logic over emotion. Some of his fury melted, but not completely, his green irises whirling with notes of annoyance. "A warning would have been fucking appreciated."

"A warning could have impacted the fate of events." They weren't meant to know my intentions. Not yet. And I refused to alter the scope of Aflora's path just to appease her other mates.

"Fate of events," Kols repeated, his voice holding a mocking quality. "What are you, a Fortune Fae now?"

I merely smiled. "Do I look like a Fortune Fae?"

He scoffed. "You do love your—"

"Aflora!" Ella ran into the room, her blue eyes rimmed with relief. "Thank God you're okay."

God, I thought. *How human.*

Ella stopped short at seeing Kols's death grip on Aflora's arm, her expression going from relieved to livid in less than a second. "Let her go, jackass," she snapped.

Both his eyebrows flew upward. "Excuse me?"

She poked him in the chest, her petite form raging. "It wasn't enough that you destroyed all her things, so now you're going to manhandle her? Fuck you, *Prince*."

The fiery little Halfling just went up a peg, in my opinion.

"Destroyed my things?" Aflora repeated, her brow furrowing. "What do you mean? He had me locked up, but only for a few hours."

"You didn't tell her about the little tantrum you threw in her bedroom?" Ella sounded like she was ready to kill Kolstov, something I wouldn't mind watching unfold. He'd have a hard time protecting himself, what with her being his twin's mate and all.

How fun, I mused, folding my arms and settling in for the show.

At least until I saw Aflora's lower lip give a subtle wobble as she whispered, "You destroyed my room?"

"Technically, it's my room," he muttered, killing any sense of amusement I felt over the situation. Because that was precisely the wrong thing to say.

"You're un-fucking-believable!" Ella screamed, causing Tray to run out into the living room.

"What the fuck did you do, Kols?" he demanded, looking at his mate in dismay.

But my eyes were on Aflora, on the way she held her head high despite the heartbreak radiating from her eyes. "He's right. It's his room, his suite, his world. What an amazing king you'll be someday, Prince Kolstov. Now, if you wouldn't mind releasing me, I would very much like to take a shower. Assuming I still have a working bathroom that I'm allowed to use."

"Fuck, Aflora. I—"

"You can use mine," Ella cut in, her expression radiating murder. "Let her go, asshole, or I'll make you let her go."

"I suggest you listen to my mate," Tray added, his features as cold as ice.

Kols considered the room before grumbling out a curse and releasing Aflora's arm. "We need to talk," he told her. "Have a shower and get dressed. We'll talk on our way to Defense Without Magic class."

"And what's she supposed to wear?" Ella asked, arching a light blonde brow. "*You destroyed all her clothes.*"

Aflora flinched.

Kols ground his teeth together in annoyance. "I'll buy her new ones."

"Damn right you will," Ella agreed. "Today. But I'm taking her shopping, not you."

"She has class," Kols argued, his golden irises flaring with power. "And she can't leave the Academy without supervision."

"Then I'll be her 'babysitter.'" Ella was not backing down, and I sort of loved her for it. Aflora needed a strong friend, one capable of keeping up with her own feisty side. It seemed this little pixie of a female was the perfect partner for her.

"She almost killed you in an academic setting, Isabella," Kols reminded her in a harsh tone. "You're not suitable to guard her."

"God, she's not a monster, Kolstov! She doesn't need to be watched twenty-four seven."

"I'm also standing right here, and I'm capable of making my own decisions," Aflora interjected, silencing the room. "I need clothes. If Prince Kolstov doesn't trust me to purchase them by myself, then he can supervise. I'm not afraid. I'm not a damsel. I'm not a threat. But I am tired of this debate. I want to take a shower. And I would really like to eat something at some point, assuming I'm still allowed to eat Prince Kolstov's food."

She issued him a challenging glare with that last comment, and his jaw clenched.

At this point, the guy was going to grind all his teeth into dust by midnight.

"I can make you breakfast while you take a shower," Zeph said.

Aflora looked at him, her blue eyes flaring with power. "The last time I accepted a gift from you, it paralyzed my powers and I ended up in a dungeon. So, no, thank you. I would rather eat a burning thwomp."

He scoffed. "That's just childish, Aflora."

"You say that like your opinion matters to me." She cocked her head. "It doesn't." She dismissed him in favor of Ella. "May I please use your bathroom?"

"Yep. And you can borrow some of my clothes, too. Then we'll go shopping and have brunch somewhere."

"Again—"

"I'll go with them," Tray said, cutting off his brother's likely complaint about Aflora leaving the Academy without a *guard*.

"Have you all forgotten that you have class today?" Zeph asked, his tone holding an edge to it. "*My* class."

"Oh, I haven't forgotten," Ella quipped, her lips curling. "Consider this our notice that we're taking a free day."

He folded his thick arms over his crisp white button-down shirt. "You can't just take a free day."

"Stop. Just stop." Tray looked between Kols and Zeph, his black eyes simmering with fire. "I don't know what the fuck has gotten into the two of you, but figure it out and fix it. This bullying bullshit isn't you." He refocused on Aflora. "Come on. I'll show you that not all of us are assholes around here."

She gave him a nod, took a step, and then paused before glancing back at me. "Thank you for today," she said softly.

"Anytime," I told her, meaning it. "Actions prove integrity, right?" It was my way of letting her know my offer still stood. All she needed to do was ask, and I'd whisk her back to that field in a heartbeat.

She studied me for a long moment, her gaze filled with distrust. But she nodded in understanding.

That look alone told me she wouldn't request a return visit to our secret place until she possessed an inkling of hope that I might follow through. Which she didn't have at this moment. That gave me a goal to achieve.

I *wanted* her to trust me. To rely on me. To believe I always had her best interests at heart. Because I did. Everything I'd done these last few months was for her; she just couldn't see it because of the way fate had unfolded. But one day, she'd piece together the riddle I'd left for her and finally understand our purpose together.

Our fates were woven together through an event that occurred many, many years before our births.

Telling her wouldn't work.

She had to see it for herself, to learn her path on her own, to accept her destiny in this wicked world.

I'd keep pushing her because I had to. I'd hold her when she cried. I'd cherish her every breath and strengthen her from the shadows.

Because this was only our beginning.

And I refused for us to ever end.

She must have seen some of that knowledge in my expression, because her eyes narrowed just a bit. Then she gave another little nod and turned to follow Ella out of the room.

"Well, that went splendidly," Kols muttered.

"Were you expecting different results from your brutish approach?" I asked him, arching a brow.

"You're the last person I need or want advice from," he replied.

Well, that's just too bad, I thought. *Because I'm about to lay into you anyway, Prince Jackass.*

"You can blame her for the mating bond all you want," I told him, switching topics to the true issue at hand. "However, we all know Elemental Fae bonds require two willing participants to form, especially on that level. But maybe that's your chosen path to leadership—blame others for your faults rather than own them. In which case, I agree with Aflora's commentary about your future rule, *Your Highness*." I gave him a mock bow with the derogatory words.

Then I glanced at an unamused Zeph.

I couldn't even get started on his issues.

"If you'll both excuse me, I have a class to prepare for. Hopefully, this one won't end in a needless death of a familiar." My comment was pointed at the dick who'd killed Aflora's falcon just because he couldn't control his own yearnings.

And these two idiots thought I was the volatile one.

I shook my head and disappeared into a cloud of smoke before they could reply.

If they didn't get their shit together soon, I'd have to consult my grandmother about the future again. Just to find out what might happen to the end objective if I accidentally killed one or two of Aflora's mates. Because at this point, it was a fair expectation that I might have to end them.

CHAPTER SIX

ZEPH

F_uck._ I knew Aflora would be upset, but I hadn't anticipated it bothering me.

Not like this.

I rubbed my fist over my chest, frowning at the hallway she'd just walked down moments ago with Tray and Ella. Shade's words didn't bother me. Aflora's, however, did.

You say that like your opinion matters to me. It doesn't.

Did she truly mean that? Or was she just being a brat?

I wanted to think it was the latter, but her overall demeanor punctuated the former. She'd _dismissed_ us, her distrust evident. "What the hell was I supposed to do?" I wondered out loud. "Tell her the guards were coming?"

Kols's brow furrowed. "What the hell are you talking about?"

"Yesterday. The arrest. Was I supposed to warn her?" I actually wanted to know. Our plan was hasty but solid. We needed her in the choker before the Warrior Bloods captured her, or the Council would sense the mating bonds on her. And that would lead to a whole world of questions we weren't ready to answer. "There hadn't been time to explain."

"We also needed her shock to look real," Kols pointed out. "It was the only way."

I considered that, my frown deepening. "Similar to Shade saying our knowing would have deviated from the path he intended us to walk down." He'd referred to it as fate, but I read through his statement. "Our anger at Shade—"

"Is probably similar to how Aflora feels about us," Kols finished for me.

"Only worse. She was all alone in that cell, uncertain of her fate. And we did nothing to convince her we were doing this to protect her."

"Which explains her hating us now." He palmed the back of his neck, giving the tendons a squeeze before glaring up at the ceiling and shaking his head. "Fuck."

"Yeah," I muttered. "*Fuck.*"

We shared a long look, a thousand words traveling between us without any defined meaning. But the end thought was the same—we had to fix this.

"I need to give her a free pass today," I said.

"And I need to not press the shopping trip issue."

I nodded, agreeing. "I'm giving you a pass today, too, so you can clean up *her* room."

Kols grimaced. "That just came out. I shouldn't have said it."

"Obviously," I deadpanned. "What the fuck is wrong with us? We're not this bad with women."

"It's *her*," Kols growled. "She's… she's…"

"Gorgeous," I suggested.

"Yeah, but it's more than that. She infuriates me just by existing. And not because of anything she's done, she's just so…" He trailed off on another growl.

"Irresistible. Headstrong. Powerful. Forbidden. I can play this game all day, Kols."

His lips twitched. "Sexy. Intelligent. Pretty much perfect, aside from the whole off-limits part."

"She's also ours," I added, arching a brow. "And we're doing a shit job of making her understand what that means." Which, to be fair, was all pretty fucking new. We'd also had the minor detail of her imprisonment to deal with before we could talk to her about what happened in the LethaForest.

"What do you suggest we do to help her along?" Kols asked, a glimmer of amusement brightening his golden irises.

"Well, for starters, we need to convince her to forgive us." Which would be a challenge in and of itself. *I would rather eat a burning thwomp.*

Ouch.

"Yeah, that'll be fun." He ran his fingers through his auburn hair, gripping the ends and blowing out a breath. "I'll start with her room."

"And I'll figure something out." No idea what. Not only did I have her holding the collar trickery against me, but her falcon's temporary death, too. Both were done with good intentions, albeit harsh ones. Although, I doubted she'd accept the logical reasons.

We'd burned through her trust.

Now we had to earn it back.

Easier said than done.

"I don't recommend breakfast," Kols said, his lips twitching.

"Yeah, clearly not." Maybe I'd try for dinner, just to poke fun at her statement. However, she probably wouldn't find humor in anything I did right now. I also wasn't the humorous sort. "I need to get to class. Maybe I can kick Shade's ass today as a demonstration." Just the notion of it cheered me up considerably.

Kols snorted. "Hit him hard for me."

"That, I can do." Meanwhile, I'd figure out how to fix this with Aflora. Because yeah, my earlier assumption that she'd just get over it was obviously wrong.

And it was going to take a lot more than a meager apology to work my way back into her good graces.

CHAPTER SEVEN

AFLORA

"Don't I need a new wand, too?" I asked after the AcaWard figments finished wrapping up all my purchases into boxes. Ella had chosen the expedited shipping method so the items would go directly to the Academy, freeing up our hands for the afternoon.

"Kols didn't destroy your wand," Tray replied, leaning against the wall with a bored expression. "It's impossible to do since they're gifts from the source and conduits of our magic, not actual items. He probably has it somewhere. I'll ask him for it when we get back."

"Oh." I suppressed the urge to grimace for the thousandth time today.

Kols destroyed all my things.

Because he hates me.

Because we're mated.

I swallowed the feelings whirling around in my throat, compliments of my churning stomach. I didn't want Ella or Tray to see the mess I was inside, so I'd spent the better half of our day holding myself together and pretending not to care about what Kols had done.

Yet my heart fractured a little more each time.

Technically, it's my room.

What a lovely reminder of my lack of a place in this world. My presence was deemed temporary, a life to be snuffed out at the earliest sign of trouble.

Except the Council had let me go because Shade doctored the tapes. Which implied Kols had gone along with his explanation.

Why?

I didn't understand their choices. We all knew I was an abomination and a threat, but none of them took the opportunity to turn me in. Maybe because they feared the Council's reaction to our quad-bond.

Frowning, I accepted the cloak hanging before me on some invisible hook and draped it over my shoulders to cover my skirt and blouse combo. My new boots hit me at my knees and added a few inches to my height. The outfit proved suitable for our plans this afternoon, which included food and drinks. Apparently, Tray knew of a little place in the village that catered to all types of fae appetites, not just Midnight Fae. They even carried spritemead on tap.

A little jolt of excitement zipped through me at the reminder, helping to distract me from my more morose thoughts.

Kolstov could rot with the willow stumps for the afternoon.

I had other plans.

Lifting my head high, I looked at Ella and Tray. "I think that's everything."

"All your books have been sent on as well," Tray said, his arm automatically lifting to accommodate Ella as she sidled up to his side.

"Thanks, Nacht." She brushed her mouth against his square jaw, and he caught her mouth with his own for a sweet kiss before nuzzling her neck.

The two of them fit together like two petals on a perfect flower. My heart gave a little pang that I swiftly ignored, not willing to let my not-so-perfect *mates* sour my mood once more.

I was done moping.

Not that I'd really ever started.

So Kols burned all my things. They weren't even mine to begin with. Just like the room. Let him throw his inferno tantrums and destroy the items his family had bought. Fine. It didn't matter.

They betrayed me. Locked me up. Didn't tell me what the hell was going on.

Okay, also fine. They could play their games with themselves from now on because I was done.

No more mates.

No more dreams.

No more anything.

Totally not practical resolutions, but I'd figure them out. Somehow.

"I need a spritemead," I announced, interrupting Ella and Tray's adorable little moment.

He stopped nibbling her jaw to smirk at me. "Then I know just the place."

The packages all whirled around us in a wave of magic before sailing straight through a solid wall toward whatever enchanted express would take them back to the Academy. Hopefully, they would remain untouched until my return. Not likely, but I'd deal with that later.

Along with all the other issues in my life.

For now, I wanted to indulge my Elemental Fae tastes.

The walk through town revealed a lot of cloak-clad fae wandering the streets in pursuit of a late midnight lunch, just like us. But the tavern Tray led us to wasn't overcrowded with patrons, leaving several booths open near the windows for us to pick from. The wooden tables were dark in color and adorned with candles that illuminated the darker interior. No ceiling lights or lamps, just fire, and the occasional torch near the corner bar.

Slightly spooky, but oddly homey because of the fireplace in the opposite corner lined with bookshelves. A gargoyle crawled up onto our table, his expression bored. "What'll it be?"

"Three spritemeads, please," Ella said. "And some menus."

"Yeah, yeah," the stone creature grumbled before jumping down with a loud crunch as his stone feet met the marble floor.

I winced, thinking that sounded rather painful, but his wings crinkled at his back as he strutted off toward the bar. He seemed to weave pretty easily between the array of high-top tables and stools, so it must not have hurt at all.

"Three spritemeads, hmm?" Tray asked.

"Aflora swears it's good, so we're going to find out."

"I've already tried spritemead," he replied, touching his index finger to the tip of her nose from across the table. He'd chosen one side of the booth, while we shared the opposite bench.

"And is it good?" she pressed.

"I guess you'll find out soon enough." He winked at her. "But I'm getting a proper beer to go with mine."

"Proper beer," she echoed, glancing at me and wrinkling her nose. "He likes human beer from Germany best. I'm not a fan of any of it."

"I'm not a fan of human drinks in general," I replied. "No offense."

"None taken. But hot chocolate is divine."

"On that, I agree." We had our own version as Elemental Fae, but it was similar enough. Just with a few additional spices.

Three pints of spritemead appeared before us on the table with an array of menus cascading across the top. Tray slammed his palm on the top of them to stop the colorful array of papers from flying to the floor, their windy arrival kicking up quite the little tornado across our booth. It disappeared with a flourish, but not before brushing the hair from our faces and leaving us all with a windswept kiss across our foreheads.

"Well, that's different," I breathed.

Tray snorted. "That's a gargoyle being an asshole." He glared over his shoulder at the stone creature in question. "Find a new occupation if you don't want to wait tables."

"Oh, it's my fault. He's in a mood from having to man the counter for me while I whipped up some stir-fry in the back." A woman with long white hair and dark green eyes seemed to appear beside us, her features young yet oddly old at the same time. Like she'd lived a long life and had seen a lot, too. But there wasn't a single wrinkle marring her otherwise lovely face. How interesting.

"Hey, Anrika," Tray drawled, his easy grin creasing into a pair of dimples that seemed to make Ella swoon a little. Or maybe it was the way he seemed to know everyone. He'd addressed all the figments by name in AcaWard as well, despite them being invisible. "How's the family?"

"You mean Seif?" she asked, snorting. "He's reckless and stubborn and just like his father."

"Which is why you adore them both."

"Absolutely." Her expression radiated pride. "But yeah, he's good. I'll tell him you were asking after him. He's been a bit busy lately with his errant Omega. She's giving him hell, which, of course, means I approve."

"Omega?" I repeated, frowning. "Like a Fortune Fae?"

"Yeah, Seif chose the seer life over his dark magic and blood. Crazy, right?" Tray winked at Anrika as he spoke.

I took a sip of my spritemead as Anrika replied, "He's always had a mind of his own, that one. But Gina'll be a good match once he calms her down."

I coughed, the liquid going down the wrong pipe, causing Ella to thump me on the back. Three sets of eyes looked at me in confusion, Tray arching a brow. "Not up to your standards, princess?"

"No, not that," I managed to say, my voice hoarse from the drink flowing in an inappropriate direction. I cleared my throat twice before asking, "Gina?"

"Yeah, that's his reluctant mate's name. I've not met her yet. Why? The name mean something to you?"

The vision of a coffee shop and a dark-haired Fortune Fae sprang into my mind. *Gina,* she'd told me. Just before adding something about our paths crossing as a happenstance of fate.

"It's going to be an interesting year for you, Aflora," she'd said.

I hadn't thought much of it at the time.

But now…

"You're in his thoughts now, after all."

I blinked and found all three of them staring at me expectantly. "Uh, I may have met a Fortune Fae named Gina recently. In a coffee shop in the Human Realm."

"Huh, well, I'll be," Anrika murmured, a distant gleam giving her that elderly aura once more. Such a strange contrast to her otherwise youthful features. Like her age was somehow trapped in a young Midnight Fae form.

Of course, all the Midnight Fae appeared young. They stopped physically aging in their twenties. This woman could be thousands of years old. Perhaps that was the reason I caught such an ancient quality to her appearance.

It would probably be rude to ask, so I didn't.

"You're Aflora," she said suddenly, that odd aura disappearing in a flash, replaced by her young self once more. "Ah, yes, I've heard all about you."

"From Gina?" I asked, slightly taken aback by her age-shifting trick. *Am I the only one seeing that?*

"Oh, no. From a very old friend." Her eyes sparkled. "I'm most excited to have you here, sweetheart. And I imagine you're in the mood for something from home, yes?"

A very old friend? I wondered. However, she'd asked me a question. Etiquette dictated I needed to answer that first. "Yes, please. I would love a proper sandwich."

"I have just what you're looking for," she beamed. "Wings for Tray, yes?"

"Always."

I almost asked what wings were, when Anrika asked, "And what about you, Ella darling? Wings, too?"

"Sure. It's been a while since I had some good buffalo sauce."

"Anrika's wings are the best," Tray vowed.

"Yeah?" A glimmer of humor entered Ella's gaze. "All right. I trust you."

Anrika clapped her hands, causing the menus to disappear before we ever had a chance to read them. "I'll be back in a shuffle," she announced, vanishing into a cloud of glitter that left me coughing in her wake.

Tray laughed.

As did Ella. "Well, she's fun. Why haven't you brought me here before if her wings are so amazing?"

"Because we've been on our tour of chicken around the kingdoms, Isabella. I had to save the best for last."

"Uh-huh." She gave him a fond look before glancing at me. "He has a thing for chicken wings. It goes back to our very first date, actually."

"Ah, that was a fun night. Your first visit to the Midnight Fae realm."

"Fun? I wanted to kill you that night."

"But you didn't. You even let me kiss you. Twice."

Ella grumbled something unflattering at him before adding, "I didn't like Tray much when we first met. He was kind of a dick."

Tray snorted. "She misunderstood my intentions."

"Because you were an asshole."

He lifted a shoulder. "My plan worked in the end, didn't it? You're mine."

"Yeah, yeah," she scoffed, rolling her big blue eyes. But I caught the happiness radiating beneath her expression, her absolute joy at having him in her life.

They really were a fine couple.

Very unlike me and my mates.

Whom I refused to think about.

No. No. No.

"So her son is a Fortune Fae?" Ella asked Tray, providing a fantastic distraction from my mind. "Like one of the Midnight Fae Alphas I learned about last year?"

"Yep. He chose to abstain from blood and magic all his life and turned Fortune Fae as a result. An Alpha, as you said. Fangs and all." He bared his teeth at Ella, causing her to snort.

"Still don't understand why you *vampires* don't have fangs," she muttered.

"Actually, I've never understood that either," I admitted. "Anatomically speaking, it makes sense since Midnight Fae drink blood."

"Exactly," Ella said, waving a hand in finality.

"Our incisors are sharp enough without the additional fang point," Tray drawled.

"Yet Midnight Fae males who don't drink blood end up getting fangs as a Fortune Fae Alpha. Yeah, that makes sense." The way Ella said it implied it didn't make sense at all. Which I agreed with her on. Then again, I had pointed ears and that seemed silly, too. They served no purpose, and I heard just as well as any other fae.

"Fortune Fae are a different breed of puzzles," Tray murmured.

"So what happens to female Midnight Fae who reject their dark source?" Ella asked, frowning. "We never covered that in class."

"Because they become Norms," he replied. "Not as exciting."

"What's a Norm?" Ella asked.

A type of Fortune Fae, I thought, while Tray dove into a political lesson that more than intrigued his mate. She peppered him with questions that took up the majority of our meal, which was fine by me. I sat by and listened while I enjoyed my sandwich—which was indeed a proper one with shrooms and all the fixings. Anrika brought me a second spritemead without asking if I wanted one, giving me a wink before disappearing into glitter once more. The magic reminded me a bit of Shade's, only he preferred the dark smog to happy confetti.

I sipped my drink while thinking about him and his promise before he left.

Anytime.

A hopeful part of me wanted to believe that he meant it. The intelligent part of me refused.

None of the guys could be trusted.

That much I knew with certainty.

Yet, Shade had given me a glimpse of home today. Had even coached me a bit on how to handle my collar.

Not the signs of a male who wanted to hurt me.

"Ready?" Tray asked, drawing me from my thoughts. "It's an hour before dawn, and Kols is probably ready to come find us."

I glanced out the windows and noticed the mostly vacant streets.

"Oh." I hadn't realized how late it'd gotten. We'd spent a good chunk of the midnight hours in this tavern, indulging in food and conversation. And spritemead. "I would very much like to come back here." *Wait…* I wanted to find out what Anrika had meant about her old friend.

I glanced around for the woman and frowned at the empty surroundings. "Ah, we're the last ones here."

"Yeah, Anrika closed up an hour ago," Tray said with a chuckle. "She left right after giving you that last mug of spritemead. Told her irritated pet to see us out." He gestured with his chin toward the stone-faced gargoyle standing absolutely still by the door. All eighteen inches of him seemed to bristle with irritation without actually moving. Impressive.

"Pet," it muttered, the stones grating with astute annoyance. "Leave."

Tray smirked. "Sure."

We exited the booth, and Tray bent to pat the little gargoyle on the head. "Have a good night, little guy."

The thing growled in reply, the sound far more ferocious than any being that size should be able to make. Ella squeaked and practically shoved Tray out into the cool air of the night, with me right behind them.

He bent over laughing, clearly having indulged in more than a few beers and spritemeads combined.

Oh, but we all had.

What a fun night.

I actually felt warm. Sort of like I was floating on a cloud. I started to hum as we walked, the song one my mother taught me long ago. A sad little ballad with words I didn't quite understand, but ones I'd memorized nonetheless.

It wasn't until I hit the second verse that I realized both Ella and Tray were gaping at me. "What?" I asked, my cheeks heating at their open perusal. "My voice isn't that bad."

"No, it's the song. It's haunting," Ella whispered.

"It's forbidden," Tray corrected. "Where did you learn those words?"

"What?" I asked, startled by his sudden vehemence. "How could a children's ballad be forbidden?"

"Because you're singing about spells used to realign the source," he replied, glancing around as if to make sure no one else heard. "We need to go." He moved with urgency toward the cloakroom I'd used with Zeph a little over two months ago during my first week in this realm. Only, we all already wore our cloaks this time because of the cooler weather.

Tray activated the portal and took us directly to the crow field at the Academy.

A few students watched our arrival with interest but didn't stand in our way or try to speak with us. Which was good because Tray didn't appear in the mood for conversation. He practically stormed down the obsidian sidewalk, past the burning thwomps and bare bushes, ignoring all the writhing snakes along the various posts and fences, and led us up the stairs into the Elite Residence.

The doors parted with a flourish, not needing a code because of whatever Tray did with his hand. And up the master staircase we went to the third floor.

"What's wrong with you?" Ella demanded as we approached the gargoyle at the end of the hall. Apparently, Kols had undone whatever spell Shade had cast over the creature. Its beady red eyes glared upon seeing me, as if blaming me for the earlier incident.

Join the club, I thought at it. *Everyone in this place seems to think I'm at fault for something.*

"We'll talk in the suite," Tray muttered, his voice holding an edge to it.

Ella frowned at him. "Fine."

Great.

There went my happy evening. All because of a song. I shook my head and followed them inside, ready to face whatever else waited to be thrown my way. Because at this point, what was one more mark on my record?

CHAPTER EIGHT

KOLS

I glared down at the message from Emelyn, not in the mood to deal with her bullshit. Alas, I had no choice but to appease the bitch. I couldn't risk her finding out I mate-bonded Aflora. Not because I cared about Emelyn's emotional reaction—which, I imagined, would be violent considering I was supposed to mate *her*, not Aflora—but because I knew Emelyn would go straight to her father with the information.

And he would go to my father.

Sighing, I typed out a response regarding her outfit question and hit Send. Then added, *Not that we're going together*. Because no, we were not attending the Blood Gala as a couple.

Talk to your father, she replied. *He's the one mandating we make a public appearance, Prince.*

I rolled my eyes because I heard the derisive snort on the end of that sentence. *Consider it done. We're not going.*

Good, she shot back.

Good, I repeated at her.

Then I put my phone down on the coffee table and ran my fingers through my hair. "Fuck," I muttered, exhausted. My father had been trying to force my hand with Emelyn Jyn for several years. Neither of us was keen on the arrangement, nor did we have much say in it.

Her father, Lima, was Malik Nacht's right-hand man. They'd established the agreement between our families years ago, deciding that crossing the birth lines would produce one hell of an heir.

Sure, Emelyn and I would create a powerful child.

But that required us to fuck, which would never happen.

She despised me almost as much as I despised her. And there was only one female I wanted in my bed right now—the one walking through the door with my brother and his mate. Mmm, I loved her legs in that skirt and boots combo. But I didn't particularly care for the wary expression upon finding me sitting in the living area.

Aflora was not going to forgive me easily. I hadn't betrayed her trust, at least not intentionally. However, her blue eyes said I'd destroyed every bridge we'd built, landing me near the top of her dislike list.

I cleared my throat and stood. "Your packages arrived and have been put away."

"By you?" she asked, sounding displeased at the prospect.

"Yes, but you can reorganize however you want."

She lifted her chin a notch upward, lengthening her regal neck. "I will."

Yep. Definitely not going to forgive me anytime soon.

Tray cleared his throat before I could reply, not that I really had a response. "Aflora, sing again."

My brow furrowed at the bizarre request. "What?"

"Quiet," he snapped at me, focusing on my gorgeous mate instead. "Sing again."

She cleared her throat. "It's just a ballad my mom taught me."

He nodded. "And I want Kols to hear it. Please."

Uh… I looked at Ella for an explanation, but her concerned gaze was on Aflora. My mate twisted her hands in front of her and cleared her throat. Then she began to hum, and I swore my heart stopped at the hypnotic sound.

I gaped at her, amazed by the sweet notes leaving her mouth. *Ballad* was an understatement. Aflora resembled a siren, her voice tugging at my very soul.

Mine, I thought. *This beautiful creature is mine.*

Except she hated me at the moment.

We weren't supposed to be together.

And our little mating quad might end up killing us all in the end.

Minor details.

I nearly snorted at my mental gymnastics, only Tray's intense expression caught my attention. He was trying to tell me something with his gaze. I frowned, not understanding.

Aflora was a gifted singer. So what?

Except then her words began to register.

The ancient language she spoke was one I'd only heard in whispers throughout my upbringing. It was an ancient dialect of Midnight Fae that supposedly died with the Quandary Bloods.

The Council had maintained hints of the spells in our historical documents. Particularly, the most violent of potential enchantments.

Which was what she uttered now—a string of promises to realign the source through an incantation only Quandary Bloods understood. It sounded so hypnotically beautiful coming from her mouth. I could almost feel myself slipping into her thrall, willing her to carry out the threat lurking behind her bewitching melody.

"Aflora," I breathed, stepping toward her as if to pull her into my arms.

But then the music stopped, and her blue eyes clouded over in distrust, her own feet carrying her backward and into Ella's side.

I blinked. *Right.* Tray and Ella didn't know about my attachment to Aflora. And I needed to keep it that way to protect them, because if they found out about what happened the other night, they'd be forced to speak to the Council or face severe punishments for conspiring to hide us.

This whole thing was a fucking mess.

"Who taught you that song?" Tray demanded, his dark gaze hard.

Aflora swallowed. "My mother did, many years ago."

Tray glanced at me, his brown brow cocked upward. I stared back at him, telling him with my expression that I'd handle it. This was my job, not his. I'd go to Exos and Cyrus, see if they could give me some history on her background. The Earth Fae she grew up with was part of their mating circle. Maybe he'd know something useful.

"How could Aflora know a forbidden song about the realignment of power?" Ella asked, telling me that Tray had explained what the song meant before they arrived. Great. I hoped he was at least quiet about it.

"Maybe her mother heard it from someone," I suggested, thinking on my feet. "And she didn't understand the meaning, so she hummed it to Aflora as a little girl. The Elemental Fae wouldn't recognize it, so her mother wouldn't have thought much of it."

"Sure. That's one theory," Tray said, still looking at me.

I dared him with my gaze to voice another. The tick in his jaw told me he wanted to, but not in front of Ella and Aflora. Likely because his speculation would be damning to my mate. Not that he knew we'd mated.

Well, he suspected it.

While he hadn't expressly admitted it, I knew he was aware that I'd slept with Aflora. My twin had taken one look at the aftermath of her room, glowered at me, and stalked off. There was really only one thing that could have made me react like that, and it'd come from a very emotional place, brought on by sleeping with Aflora.

I only hoped he didn't suspect the bond, or we'd be in a world of hurt. Not because I didn't trust him, but because he'd end up risking himself and Ella to protect my actions. And I couldn't let him suffer on my behalf.

I cleared my throat. "Look. It's been a long fucking night. Hell, it's been a long fucking week. We can worry about the song later. Just... don't hum or repeat the words in public, yeah?" That part was directed at Aflora.

She nodded in reply, then pulled her cloak around her like a blanket. Or maybe she considered it a shield. Regardless, there wasn't much we could do right now. I explained that to Tray with another look, one he conceded to with a nod.

Then I refocused on Aflora. "Come on. I want to show you what I did to your room." I didn't wait for her to acknowledge my request, just turned and headed to the hallway off to the left of the living area.

I passed the study area, guest room, and Tray's quarters and paused at Aflora's upgraded door. She appeared a minute later, her shoulders bowed a little as she met me alone in the corridor. Ella had probably told her to yell if I caused any trouble.

Given the tension in the air, that wouldn't take much.

With a whispered spell, I called for the new key I'd created earlier and sent it to hover in front of her. Her blue irises swirled with power as she studied it. "What's this?"

"Your key," I told her. "It's programmed to recognize your magic. I tied it to your wand, which is on your bed inside."

"Why do I need a key?"

"Because I put a lock on your door, and that"—I gestured to the ornate metal rotating in the air between us—"is the only thing that can open it."

Her ebony lashes flickered. "You made me a lock?"

"Yes."

"One you can't override?" She sounded disbelieving.

"Yes," I repeated. "I never should have said it was my room. An excuse won't make up for it, so instead, all I'll say is I'm sorry and I hope you'll accept my apology in the form of reinforced privacy."

She gaped at me. "You're apologizing?"

"Yes," I said for a third time.

"Really?"

"Do you want me to go onto my knees, too?" I asked her. "Beg a little?"

Her lips twitched. "Actually—"

"No." The only way I'd kneel for her was if she spread her legs and welcomed my tongue between her thighs. I allowed her to see that knowledge in my gaze, the very real fire burning inside me just for her. *My mate.*

Fuck, that was going to take some getting used to.

Yet I couldn't deny how right it felt between us. Maybe because of her Elemental Fae influence. We were level-three bonded, which, in her world, made it pretty fucking permanent. As did my bite as a Midnight Fae.

Yeah, Aflora and I were tied together indefinitely.

Whether we liked it or not.

Her vibrant eyes held mine for a beat, then she swallowed and grabbed the key to try it in the door. Magic hummed around us, the mechanism searching out Aflora's identity before allowing her entry. "It's similar to a gargoyle but without the added nuisance," I explained softly.

"What happens if I misplace the key?" she asked as the wood whispered open.

"There's a spell you can use to call it to you, like the one I just recited." I spoke the incantation again, this time slower, and she murmured it back to me, which caused her key to jump out of the door and hover in front of her face again.

She smiled at it. "That's handy."

"I'm glad you approve."

Her amusement dimmed a little, whether at my words or the thought of entering her room, I wasn't sure. But I suspected it was the latter when she steeled her spine and stepped through the threshold. I waited by the entrance, not wanting to disrupt her perusal of the room.

She set her key on the nightstand, admired the new bed, draped her cloak over the blue comforter—the same shade as her eyes—and then focused on the shimmering magic near her window.

I waited for her reaction, unsure of what she'd think of the enhancement. "What is this?" she asked, squatting down beside the makeshift pot.

"It's, uh, a gift," I replied, palming the back of my neck. "Our flowers and general vegetation are a bit different here, but Mistress Marigold said this will bloom with a fairy plant if properly cared for. And so, I bought you one." It seemed lame now, like some sort of lackluster apology present. But it'd felt right when I was working on redecorating the room.

"Mistress Marigold?" Aflora glanced at me. "Who's that?"

"One of the Academy caretakers." I swallowed the lump growing in my throat, irritated by its presence. Since when did I feel nervous around females? *Ridiculous.*

With a shake of my head, I focused on my surroundings instead of on Aflora.

"Mistress Marigold is in charge of the residence halls. After I finished cleaning everything up in here, I consulted with her on ways to make it a little more Elemental Fae friendly. She suggested the plant. So I ordered it. But if you don't like it, I can take it back. Actually, if there's anything you don't like, just let me know. I'll return it. This is your space. You choose."

And, wow, since when did I fucking ramble?

This chick was giving me a headache just by existing.

I winced. Yeah. Not the best thought. Right. "I'm going to bed," I announced. Some sleep would help me sort out my behavior. Maybe a hand job, too. With thoughts of Aflora.

Ah, fuck. Just the notion of it had me hardening in my pants. *This mating business sucks!*

"Kols!" she called after me. I'd already gotten to the door of my room, my feet carrying me away from her as if I were running from a fire.

I paused and didn't look at her. "Yeah?"

"Thank you," she whispered, the two words making me cringe.

I didn't do this for her gratitude. I did this because… well, I couldn't say why I went through all the trouble I did today other than I wanted to make it up to her. An apology of sorts to right a handful of wrongs. And I doubted I'd even achieved that. But at least she seemed to like it.

Rather than reply, I just nodded, not trusting myself to speak, and disappeared into my quarters.

I needed some sleep.

Tomorrow, I'd dig into her past.

Starting by meeting with a pair of Elemental Fae Kings.

I sent a notification off to Cyrus, knowing it might be a few hours before he caught it. His kind weren't as big into technology as Midnight Fae, but someone would pass along my request.

Then we'd chat.

Likely in the Human Realm.

At least I'd get some much-needed blood. Sex, not so much.

I winced and picked up my phone again and shot Zeph a text. *Celibacy isn't my thing.*

His response arrived a minute later. *No shit.*

Come over. He would know why I sent the text.

Just as I understood his response. *Be there in five.*

Playing with each other didn't break any mating rules, particularly as we were all set in this quad together. Besides, if Aflora wanted to come over and join us, we'd both be game. But something told me it would be a while before she'd even consider the opportunity.

Which meant we would just need to work that much harder to convince her.

I always did adore a challenge, especially a forbidden one. As did Zeph. Together we'd break her resolve. Not just in her dreams, but also in her bed, with our mouths and tongues and hands. Until she couldn't stand the thought of breathing without us. And then we'd truly make her ours.

Because fuck the consequences.

Aflora was already mine.

CHAPTER NINE

AFLORA

I sat in my Midnight Fae Politics classroom, trying to ignore the whispers around me.

Everyone knew about my arrest, but the reasons behind it were all wrong.

Some said I attacked Kols.

Others claimed I'd lost my shit after Zeph killed Clove, and stated I tried to burn down the Elite Residence.

"Kolstov is fine," I heard someone say behind me in response to someone else's comment about me trying to kill him. "Altrina saw him in the Human Realm last night, working his magic on a pair of mortals."

My teeth clenched. *Is that where he ran off to?* I wondered.

I hadn't seen him since the night he gave me the key to my renovated room. Not that I'd really gone looking for him. I needed a few days just to decompress and was thankful my mates had allowed me the time alone. But when I woke up for classes and heard from Ella that Kols still wasn't back, I'd begun to wonder where he went.

Is he meeting with the Council about me?

Has he told his father about our mating?

Is he trying to find a way to undo what happened?

The thoughts had run rampant through my mind, making me uneasy and distrusting. I kept waiting for a horde of Warrior Bloods to descend upon the Academy and take me back to that dungeon. However, the primary assault I'd received so far was in the form of rumors.

And now this.

"Sounds like Kols," another girl replied. "I swear he's fucked his way through half the mortal population."

"Well, if I had my fate promised to a chick like Emelyn, I'd do the same." That came from a male in the back of the room.

"You could only be so lucky, Slag," a prim female sniped with a flip of her long blonde hair over her shoulder. "And if I were Emelyn, I wouldn't want to be anywhere near Prince Kolstov's cock. He's a walking disease. I hear he even fucks Halflings."

Someone snorted. "You're confusing Kols with Tray."

"Oh, no, it's a Nacht family tradition at this point." The prim fae practically purred the words, her penchant for cruelty written into the sharp angles of her too-perfect face. "I mean, Tray took the Halfling human mutt as his mate, and his brother has no doubt fucked the Elemental abomination. To each his own, I suppose."

"Aw, are you not getting enough dick in your life, Justine?" Ella asked, her expression one of mock concern. "Is that why you have to focus on others? Live vicariously through those you envy? That's a shame."

A flicker of magic singed the air, but Ella caught it easily with her wand and returned it to the sender just as our headmaster entered.

"Isabella Cinder!" Headmaster Vayera snapped, her cloak billowing around her in a flurry of annoyance. "What do you think you're doing?"

"Practicing defensive arts," Ella replied, not at all contrite.

"Not in my classroom, you're not." Headmaster Vayera pointed to the door with a sharp black nail. "Out."

"It was one spell," Ella argued.

"*Out!*" she shouted, not bothering to give Ella a chance to explain.

"Ella was just protecting herself," I interjected. "Justine started it."

"I did not!" the blonde perfectionist fae retorted, sounding affronted.

"Oh, come on," Slag drawled. "We all saw you send that firefly at the Halfling. Aflora's right, Headmaster. Ella was just protecting herself."

Headmaster Vayera pulsed with irritation, her beady blue eyes searching the room. "Anyone else care to add to this delightful discussion?"

"Ella insulted—"

"That was a rhetorical question, Corrine," Headmaster Vayera cut in, then took out her wand to wave it through the air with a muttered spell. Thick texts landed on each of our desks, all opening to various sections littered with legal jargon.

Groans filtered through the air.

"You will read and decipher each point, then present your section to the class by midnight. There will be no break today, as it's clear you all enjoyed your fresh air a little too much yesterday and the day before. We'll have a quiz instead that will cover all of the presentations, so I suggest you pay attention and be thorough in your translation."

Ugh, academic punishment, I thought glancing down at my section regarding Paradox Fae time manipulation laws. This wasn't even related to Midnight Fae at all. Well, except for the bit about how it was illegal to work with a Paradox Fae to change a timeline. But that was the case in all the realms.

I blew out a breath that turned into a vibration between my lips. Ella snorted in response.

And so began our very long day of reading, deciphering, and articulating into essay form. Because yeah, that was the test method Headmaster Vayera selected.

"She's just evil," Ella said as we entered the residence hall several hours later.

Tray stood waiting for her at the stairs, his eyebrow cocking upward at her statement. "Who?"

"Headmaster Vayera." Ella drew out the *a* on a long groan. "She made us read Midnight Fae ordinances, Tray. Then she quizzed us on it afterward, and it was awful."

His lips quirked upward. "Sounds like my childhood."

"Ugh, not the same." She walked into his open arms and accepted his hug. "It felt like law school," she mumbled into his chest. "Not that I've been, but it's the hell I imagined."

"Mmm," he hummed, holding her close and kissing the top of her head. "Need me to make it better, baby?"

And that was my cue to keep moving. "You two have fun," I called, racing up the steps to the third floor and heading toward the gargoyle at the end.

"Sir Kristoff," I greeted.

"Abomination," he returned in his chilly tone. It didn't help that the stones churned together in his mouth every time he spoke.

At least he allowed me to enter. I suspected if he had a choice, he'd close off all the doors and keep me trapped in a room with no entrance or exit. Similar to his *master*.

I scowled at the memory of the Council dungeon and moved through the threshold into the suite. Kols and Zeph were inside, their attention snapping to me as their conversation came to a halt.

"Don't stop talking on my account," I said, noting Kols's flushed appearance.

Blood, I realized. *It's from drinking blood*. Zeph had the same look about him, suggesting they'd both gone into the Human Realm for a snack. And probably sex.

Fine.

Just fine.

We were mates, but we hadn't discussed anything about being committed. I mean, they betrayed me not twelve hours after biting me. So. What did that say about our *bond*?

I snorted and stomped off to my room, not wanting to talk to either of them. If they wanted to seek pleasure elsewhere, I couldn't stop them. I didn't even want to sleep with them anyway.

At least I knew why my dreams were vacant the last few nights. It wasn't out of respect for me or their way of giving me time. No, they were too busy playing with mortal females and using them for blood and pleasure.

My bedroom door slammed behind me.

"Not my business," I muttered to myself.

Who was I to even judge anyway? I had three mates. There was one of me. Of course, I wouldn't be enough to satisfy them. Not that they'd bothered to try. But I didn't want them to anyway, so this worked out well for all parties involved. They could mess around and leave me alone, and maybe we'd find a way to break this link between us.

I was a Quandary Blood, right? My gift literally unraveled magic. Why not try it on the mating connection?

I hung my cloak in my closet and stared at my reflection in the mirror Kols had affixed to the back of the door.

"What's the point of any of this?" I asked myself. "Why am I even here?"

Because Shade had bitten me.

I narrowed my gaze.

Shade.

I hadn't heard from him in a few days either. Had he joined the guys in their little human orgy? Doubtful. So where was he? Why hadn't he reached out?

"Stop it," I chastised myself while taking off my blouse and skirt. "Just. Stop."

The guys didn't matter. My future did. Whatever that meant.

I put on a pair of flannel shorts and a soft white T-shirt, then shut the closet and walked over to flop onto my bed. "Enough," I muttered into my pillow. "Enough. Enough. Enough."

CHAPTER TEN

I cleared my throat, attempting to dispel some of the tension in the air caused by Aflora's abrupt entrance and subsequent exit.

"She's still pissed," Kols noted, vying for the role of Captain Obvious.

"She needs to get over it," I replied. "We gave her three days to cool off. Now she's just acting like a brat."

Kols gave me a look. "We destroyed her trust."

"By protecting her," I pointed out.

"But she doesn't get that."

"Because she's being a brat and choosing not to talk to us. Instead, she's stomping around and throwing a fit." As if she overheard me, a door slammed from her room, causing me to roll my eyes. "It's as though she wants me to spank her."

Kols grunted. "Yeah, good luck with that."

"She'd be wet for me in a second and you know it."

"And she'd hate you every step of the way." Kols shook his head. "Seriously, we fucked up. It's going to take time to fix that."

"Something we don't have on our side."

"Well, tell her that," Kols said, gesturing to the hallway. "Let me know how it goes."

I huffed out a breath. It would go well until she came all over my cock. Then she'd go right back to hating me. While the former would be enjoyable, the latter wouldn't help us move forward.

My elbows fell to my thighs as I leaned forward. "This is ridiculous. All we've done is to help her."

"She doesn't see it that way."

"Clearly." And while I could admit to some fault in the matter of the approach, she wasn't exactly giving us a chance to explain.

Or maybe I hadn't tried hard enough to be heard.

Or really at all, I thought to myself.

But that wasn't the point. "Tell me what Sol said." Kols had been in the middle of detailing his meeting with the Elemental Fae when Aflora stomped into the room. I'd been about to suggest she join us for the discussion, but her little temper tantrum reaction to seeing us in the living area had me biting my tongue.

Kols cleared his throat. "Right. Well, first, he threatened to kill me."

"You told him about the mating?"

"No. He sensed it. Not sure he approves."

I smirked. "I bet not. But he can't do anything about it."

"That's exactly what I said. Then I asked him to help me help her."

"And?"

"He told me to fuck off." Kols picked up his beer and took a long swig. "So Cyrus stepped in and reminded Sol how I helped them with their Chancellor problem by providing dark-magic texts. And Exos commented on how working together would only help Aflora, not hurt her. As her Earth mate, I'm duty-bound to protect her and yada yada, so eventually Sol caved."

He stood up to retrieve his suit jacket and pulled something from the pocket. "These are Aflora's parents." He handed me an old-fashioned-painting-styled photograph, one depicting a couple staring down at the baby in the female's arms.

"Is that baby Aflora?"

"Yep." Kols snagged his beer bottle by the neck and enjoyed another swallow while remaining on his feet.

I studied the photo. "She looks so much like her mother." Gorgeous. Dark hair. Pale complexion. Beautiful smile. I felt my own lips curve at the sight, my heart warming a little at an innocent Aflora being loved on by her parents. Did they know then what a powerful child they'd created? I imagined they did.

"Do you recognize them?" Kols asked.

I studied both parents and slowly shook my head. "No. Should I?"

"No. I was just curious."

"Wouldn't you already know what they look like through all your royal training?" I meant the question earnestly. Kols had grown up studying fae politics. Surely he'd seen a photo of the Elemental Fae royals at some point.

"Elemental Fae are not known for capturing photos. They prefer to live life and enjoy the moment, and they balk at technology."

"So why did her parents have a photo?"

"Exactly," Kols replied, collapsing in the recliner once more. "Sol said that a lot of things about Aflora's childhood were abnormal, including that photo. And when I asked him about the ballad, he recognized it. Aflora used to hum it often when she was younger, usually in moments of happiness."

"But he didn't recognize it otherwise?"

"Nope. None of them had ever heard it before, so it's not like some Elemental Fae nursery rhyme."

"Well, that's something at least." It would cause a lot of political strife if our kind found out that the little Elemental Fae were running around humming about how to realign the source of dark magic.

"It's still troubling, and what I dislike even more is that Sol couldn't tell me anything about Aflora's grandparents. She's a descendant of the royal Earth Fae line. How do they not know anything about those who came before her parents?"

I frowned. "Do they not believe in keeping records, in addition to their dislike of technology?"

Kols snorted. "I asked the same thing. Sol didn't appreciate the comment."

"It's a fair statement."

"I agree, as did Cyrus. He felt it very strange that not much is known about the Earth Fae royal line. They rely so much on whom the source has favored that they don't focus much beyond that. And while they know the names of her ancestors, they couldn't say much about them. Everyone who would have known them died in the plague that abomination caused."

"Their former Chancellor?" I asked, seeking clarification. There were several abominations throughout our history, but she was the latest to cause issues among the realms.

"Yeah. Elana."

I considered that. "Do you think she took out the Earth Fae on purpose?" I wondered out loud. "I mean, she targeted their element first. What if she did it to erase the history?"

"Why attack Aflora as a girl, then?"

"To cover up her actions?" I suggested.

Kols finished his beer in silence, contemplating my comments. Then his head bobbed side to side slowly. "Doesn't feel right."

While I agreed with his assessment, I still said, "But it's worth keeping in mind."

"True." He set his empty bottle on the end table. "All right. So we know she has Quandary Blood in her. We know her lineage doesn't have great records. And we know her powers are unraveling."

"She feels grounded right now," I replied, sensing my mate-bond with her. It tugged at my heart a little, mostly because I could feel her displeasure. Knowing I helped cause that emotion irked me. But I couldn't change anything we'd done. It was all to keep her safe, whether she realized that or not.

"She does," Kols agreed. "We need to keep her that way."

"Is that why you fed while in the Human Realm?" I asked, arching a brow.

"You're just as well fed as I am."

"I ordered a catering service," I admitted. Digesting food infused with blood wasn't the same as feeding from a neck, but it did the trick and rejuvenated my magic.

"How was it?" Kols asked, genuine curiosity in his gaze.

"Different. Not nearly as enjoyable as biting Aflora."

His lips curled. "I doubt much is as enjoyable as biting Aflora."

"Did you think of her while you fed?"

"No. I didn't want to make it intimate, and feeding without sex is hard enough already."

I nodded, understanding. "Did you just enchant them?"

"Pretty much. They'll have a memory of a heavy make-out session that left them light-headed afterward." He lifted a shoulder. "There were a few other Midnight Fae roaming about, so I created a glamour for them as well. Have to keep up appearances and all that."

"It worked," I told him. "I overheard a few of them gossiping about it outside."

"Good." Then he frowned. "Do you think it got back to Aflora?"

"Probably."

"Do you think it'll bother her?"

"That her mate was seen in the Human Realm fucking around with mortals?" I asked. "Would it bother you if we heard Aflora was doing that?"

He scowled. "She doesn't need blood."

"What about sex?"

"Are you trying to piss me off?" he demanded.

"No, I'm trying to get you to see the obvious, idiot," I replied. "Your reaction right now is your answer."

He started to snap something back, only to pause, then he growled in annoyance. "Fuck."

"Yeah." I understood because I wouldn't like hearing that about Aflora at all. In fact, I'd probably find the human who dared to touch her, and kill him. She might not feel like she was mine yet, but that didn't make it any less true. I claimed her the moment my incisors met the plump flesh of her breasts. She just hadn't accepted it yet.

"I suppose that's another apology for my list," Kols muttered.

"Maybe we should just give her a dozen orgasms instead. Most women prefer that to flowers."

Kols snorted. "She's an Earth Fae. You know she prefers the flowers."

"Only because she doesn't know any better," I mused, finally taking a sip of my own beer. "I'll happily show her when she's ready."

"In her dreams?" He sounded hopeful, but I turned him down with a look.

"No more dreams for her. Not until we've worked this all out." It was what I'd said the other night, and I stood by it. We needed our mate to trust us before I could continue her sexual education. Otherwise, I risked pushing her too far, and I didn't want to chance harming our already fractured bond.

"Ugh," Kols groaned, his head falling back against the chair. "You have no idea how much I want to fuck right now."

"You always want to fuck," I pointed out. "And I'm very aware of that."

He grunted. "Dick."

"Not a good way to woo me into some temporary relief, Kolstov."

"I'm not getting on my knees again," he said, glancing at me. His reference to the other night in his room had my lips quirking upward in amusement.

"Then I guess you're not getting fucked," I replied.

"I said I want to fuck, not be fucked."

"Semantics."

"You're an ass," he chastised, standing up and tossing his bottle into a nearby trash can. "I'm having a date with my hand tonight. You can fuck off."

"Enjoy," I murmured, not moving from the couch.

"You can go now."

"I'm good."

He shook his head and grumbled a curse under his breath, then focused on the kitchen. "Leftover pizza?" he asked, changing the subject.

"Sure."

"Good."

I watched as he worked, the banter between us reminding me of an easier time between us—a time I wasn't sure we'd ever experience again. However, as he pulled a box out of the refrigerator and slid the contents onto a tray, I started to entertain the notion of a different kind of future. One where we were friends like before, only closer.

Because of Aflora.

Or maybe it would all go up in flames and burn us all to the ground.

I rubbed a hand over my face and shut my eyes, the vision of a dark-haired beauty with cerulean magic flashing in my mind.

What am I going to do with you? I thought at her, aware that she couldn't actually hear me. That wasn't how the initial bond stages worked. I could sense her and manipulate her dreams with magic, but I couldn't yet access her mind.

Soon, though.

Soon.

CHAPTER ELEVEN
AFLORA

I stared at the black rose on my seat before glancing across the room at Shade. He winked and returned to his conversation with one of the other Death Bloods. Then the flower disappeared into a purple mist, the illusion gone.

"How romantic," Emelyn drawled, having witnessed the entire exchange from her spot a few seats over. "He sends you dead flowers as gifts."

"Shall I do the same for you, *my beloved*?" Kols asked as he took the chair beside mine.

Emelyn narrowed her black eyes at him and ignored the offer. "Why does your father still think we're going to the Blood Gala together, *darling fiancé*?"

Blood Gala? I repeated to myself as I took my seat.

"I told you I'd handle it," he replied with a hint of annoyance.

"Is that what you were doing while gallivanting all over the mortal realm, fucking everything with two legs?" she asked, her long lashes batting demurely at him. But the violence radiating from her dark irises told a very different story. One I understood very well as my stomach clenched with her words.

Murderous, I mused. *That* was how I felt as a result of her statement.

I wanted to throttle Kols for being so disrespectful to our bond.

Which was ridiculous.

I had to get over this. We weren't exclusive. We didn't even like each other. Maybe I'd tell him later about my idea to use my Quandary Blood gifts to unravel the mating. He'd probably jump at the chance, what with all his other obligations. Including the female staring at him now, waiting for his response.

He didn't give her one.

Rude.

Headmaster Zankry cleared his throat from the front of the room, his hazel eyes boasting a bluish color today. They tended to change with his mood. Green meant angry. Black correlated with irritation. Brown indicated boredom. And blue typically suggested excitement.

Which meant he had a dangerous task for us to complete today.

I wondered if anyone else noticed that his class plans matched his irises or if they were all too busy talking to each other to pay attention.

"Aflora," Kols murmured.

I ignored him. Just like I did during breakfast when he asked me to wait for him before going to class. I didn't see the point, so I'd gone on ahead. He'd caught me at the entrance to the academic building but had wisely stayed quiet.

It seemed that bout of wisdom had come to an end.

Fortunately, Headmaster Zankry cut in with his trademark clearing of the throat to signal for our required attention. Black tendrils of power slithered like a snake up and down his arms, his Malefic magic on full display. "I hope you all followed the course assignment list and read the chapter on hallucinogen charms, because that's our task for today."

Excited murmurs broke out in the room, causing the hairs along my arms to rise.

Oh, I'd read the chapter all right.

He wanted us to play with optical magic, the kind that disrupted the mind and created dangerous illusions. If not properly deflected, the opponent could be rendered completely useless in seconds.

"And I'll be matching you all through a compatibility enchantment," Headmaster Zankry continued. Magic swirled through the air, the strands reminding me of that day in Advanced Conjuring class when Headmaster Irwin linked me to Shade for the entirety of the course.

His ice-blue eyes caught mine from across the room, his lips curling as if to confirm he had the same thought. The notion of being tied to him again didn't upset me like it did that first day. Actually, I really wouldn't mind—

"Oh, you have got to be fucking kidding me," Emelyn snapped as the ropes connected my wrist to hers.

My eyebrows lifted in surprise.

"How is *she* compatible to my magic?" Emelyn demanded, taking the thought right out of my mind. Because we were nothing alike. At all. The only thing we had in common was Kols. Sort of.

"No shit," a male said from across the room. It was the guy Shade always seemed to hang out with during classes. His name started with an *A*. Ajax, maybe? "There is nothing compatible between me and the friggin' Midnight Fae Prince." He held up his wrist, the magic strand attached to Kols.

My Elite Blood mate snorted. "I think your enchantment needs some work, Headmaster."

Shade just yawned, his magic cord linked to Stiggis. The latter appeared thrilled to be tied to my Death Blood mate. He clearly hadn't forgiven Shade for turning his back on the mating to his sister, Cordelia.

It was like everyone in the room was tied to someone they disliked, making them the opposite of "compatible."

The dark-haired fae snapped his fingers from the front of the room, forcing our attention back to him. "I said nothing about these being pairings based on friendship qualities. This class is about dueling and offensive magic. Now stop messing around and get to work."

Kols glanced warily at me before he stood. The warning in his eyes was clear. *Don't give anything away,* he was telling me.

I didn't dignify the look with a response and instead watched as our desks disappeared into mist, the room shifting forms to resemble a gymnasium-sized arena with marks along the floor. The first time this happened, I'd gaped at the transformation.

Now, I'd expected it and waited until it was done before allowing the illuminated cord to guide me to the appropriate sparring ring. As soon as Emelyn and I were in position, the magic vanished and she readied her wand.

The spell left her lips before I even had a chance to prepare. Bright red flames engulfed me, the heat shocking the hell out of my system. It felt *real*. It *burned*. My knees buckled on instinct, my hands frantically seeking a wand that didn't exist. Somehow, she'd cloaked it. I couldn't find it. I searched futilely while the fire ate through my clothing, leaving me naked and hot and mortified as everyone turned to watch me fail.

Then they all evaporated into a cloud of smoke, the infamous death fields in the Spirit Kingdom taking their place.

Screams.

Terror.

Death.

I couldn't breathe. This place had haunted my nightmares as a child. Every Earth Fae feared this place—the one where plagued souls went to die.

And I had firsthand experience battling at the entrance in soul form. Sort of. In a weird metaphorical way.

This isn't real, I promised myself, closing my eyes. *This isn't happening.*

And then I heard a whisper against my ear that had me spinning on my heels. Just my name, but it sounded unmistakably like my father.

Impossible.

"...forest," he whispered, the words before it lost to a subtle breeze scented of pine and lavender. "My sweet, beautiful flower. I've missed you. Meet me, my darling. Meet me soon. Join us. Come home."

I whirled in a circle, searching for the source of those words, my heart in my throat. "Dad?" I shook my head. No. It couldn't be him. This was all a game. A trick. A mind illusion, one I needed to break. But I couldn't. Not without my wand.

Then I recalled Zeph's earlier training. Conduits were used to focus control and weren't the source of magic. That came from within.

I searched inside, fighting to untangle the spell Emelyn had woven through my aura. All around me, trees wept, her newest attack an illusion of killing the element I held dear—my precious earth.

Flowers wilted.

Branches burned.

Leaves fell like tears against the ground.

And all the while, my father's spirit hovered nearby, murmuring words I didn't understand. A warning, maybe. But no. This was all tied to Emelyn's cruelty, her wicked intent to destroy me in the harshest manner possible by attacking everything I cherished, including my memories of parents I barely had the chance to know.

She'd taken the mean-girl act too far, had made this personal and shown her vicious nature.

Vindictive.

Evil.

Bully.

I crossed my arms and pretended to cower on the floor, then fought the binds she held on my mind, unweaving them one at a time while carefully keeping my magic hidden. I didn't want her to feel my approach, preferring to take her by surprise.

"Meet me," my father whispered once more.

His voice was a shock to my system, causing tears to well behind my eyes.

I focused on that link next, ripping the anchor out of my heart, unable to take another second of his torment. *He's not real. Not real. Not real. Not real!*

Power blasted out of me, the focal point on Emelyn. I threw her vision into the death fields of the Spirit Kingdom, forcing her to see and feel every spirit's pain of being trapped there. She thought to use it against me, not realizing I knew more about that realm than most Elemental Fae. I'd been taken there by a horrendous abomination who tried to plague my entire kind. I'd stood at the gates, blocking their entry in spirit form while I fought to dismantle her powerful hold and thwart her attempts at accessing the earth source.

I knew pain.

I knew death.

I knew torture.

And I allowed Emelyn to feel every ounce of it now, my anger singeing the air around me.

She deserved this. How dare she try to hurt me. To make me believe for even a second that my father might still be alive. It was wrong. Unacceptable. She—

"*Aflora!*" A wave of defensive magic accompanied my name, the source coming from beside me and knocking me off my feet.

I blinked, unsure of when I'd stood up to begin with, or even how I'd managed it. And at some point, I'd returned to the reality of the gymnasium-style classroom, but now I gaped up at a seriously pissed-off fae prince.

"That was fucking hot," Shade praised as he stepped into my line of sight. Kols glowered at him, which only made Shade smirk. "What? Powerful females don't turn you on?"

The fae prince didn't appear at all amused. "I'll handle it," he said, the words confusing me.

"You'd better," Headmaster Zankry stated. "Or she won't be permitted in my class again."

"Emelyn started it," Shade drawled. "Can't punish one fae and not the other."

"I can when one is knocked out cold and the other is just dazed," Headmaster Zankry retorted.

"I said, I'll handle it," Kols repeated through his teeth. He held out his hand, his gold irises narrowing down at me. "Come. Now."

Part of me wanted to tell him to fuzz right off. But as I glanced around the room and noticed everyone staring at me, I decided not to make matters worse by fighting him.

Pressing my palm against his, I allowed him to yank me forward, my body tingling at his touch. *What magic did he use to pull me out of that spell?* I wondered, electricity humming beneath my skin. It felt like a web of heat encasing my body from head to toe. A static net of sorts, yet my legs moved without any trouble as he guided me out of the Malefic Blood Education Building and back to the Elite Residence.

I didn't speak.

Neither did he.

But I felt Shade following, his presence a security blanket against my senses.

It was strange to realize I felt secure around the male who'd forced me into this mess to begin with and nervous around the one who claimed to want to help me.

They had all hurt me.

Betrayed me in some way.

Yet Shade was the one I sought now as I allowed Kols to guide me upstairs. I glanced behind me, needing to reassure myself that my Death Blood mate still trailed after us. His ice-blue eyes met mine as he winked, completely unfazed by the anger vibrating off the Midnight Fae Prince.

As soon as we were inside Kols's suite, he released me, and the weblike sensation left, bringing me to my knees as a burst of energy puffed out of me.

"Dick," Shade snapped before bending down beside me to press his palm to my lower back. "Are you okay, little rose?" he asked softly, his other hand going to my cheek to tilt my face toward him.

"What happened?" The words were hoarse, my throat suddenly parched.

"Kols cast a cocoon spell to trap your power beneath his. Then he released it without warning because he's a fucking prick."

Kols snorted at the summary from somewhere farther away. The kitchen, maybe? I couldn't tell because my vision was clouded by a sea of enchantment dust. At least, it looked like magic dust. Whatever it was, it made me sneeze and fire off another bolt of electricity.

I shivered from the sudden coolness flooding my veins, the humming from before disappearing.

Shade wrapped his arm around me and pulled me to him, his hand moving up and down my arm while his opposite palm guided my face to his chest.

I melted into him on instinct, absorbing his comfort and allowing it to pull me back into the land of the living.

My father's whispers still lingered in my mind, making me tremble with memories of my past. I rarely dreamed of my parents anymore. Mostly because I trained myself not to. There were so many mornings I'd wake up with the hope that that day might be the day they returned to me, only for it never to happen.

They were dead.

I felt it in my soul the moment the earth source became mine. That only occurred when the former anchor perished.

So it'd all been in my head. Because of Emelyn and her cruel—

"Here." A bottle of water appeared in front of me, courtesy of Kols.

Shade took it from him, removed the cap, and brought the rim to my lips. "Drink, little rose. It'll make you feel better."

For whatever reason, I listened to him, and the second the cool liquid touched my tongue, I was glad I did. Because, mmm, that felt nice. So nice that I closed my eyes and just let him hold me while I accepted the refreshment down my throat.

He chuckled against me. "I think this is the most agreeable you've ever been in my presence."

He wasn't wrong.

But I didn't have it in me to comment on it. I was too tired of everything. The bickering. The feelings. This whole experience. I just wanted it all to go away and leave me alone.

Shade took the bottle away from my lips, the liquid gone.

Silence followed, the noiseless activity blissfully welcome. I inhaled his peppermint scent, allowed it to cling to my lungs and fill me with comfort.

It was wrong. I should push him away and tell him not to touch me.

Instead, I leaned into him more, seeking his strength.

The death fields always drained me; just the notion of their threat hurt my heart. They were gone now, thanks to Queen Claire and her mates defeating the abomination who'd created the vacuum of trapped souls.

That didn't stop me from remembering its existence.

Shade's lips met my forehead, his strong arms holding me tightly in the foyer of Kols's suite. The reality of the moment should have drawn a disbelieving laugh from me, but I felt too dead inside to utter such an amused sound.

Footsteps echoed around us as someone stepped through the threshold, the woodsy aroma warning me of Zeph's presence. I snuggled deeper into Shade's chest, longing to disappear.

I felt weak.

Alone.

Just so *done* with it all.

This helplessness would pass, the emotion residual from the illusions Emelyn had created. I hated her in that moment, despised her ability to make me feel so worthless and meek. She'd gotten off easy because Kols had stopped me.

Why? Because she was his betrothed?

My jaw clenched with the thought. How ridiculous that he would stand up for his *fiancée* after spending days in the human world bedding mortals.

A growl threatened my chest, my annoyance mounting by the minute.

He was a horrible mate.

He denied me after our bond snapped into place, accusing me of planting the seed on purpose. Like I could control an Earth Fae connection on my own. A level-three placement meant he wanted it, too. But he burned all my things in response, sent me running into the LethaForest, and filled our bond with such exquisite power that I felt as if I were about to burst.

Then he claimed not to hate me and, less than a day later, had me imprisoned.

Well, technically Shade had me imprisoned with that recording.

Kols and Zeph had just orchestrated the arrest and the collar around my neck.

I frowned, touching the leather now with the tip of my index finger.

It'd done nothing to stop me from blasting Emelyn's power today. Or had it tried to thwart me and I'd just moved around it?

A consideration for later.

What was I even doing here, allowing Shade to hold me like this? The three males were conversing around me, their words slowly trickling into my ears.

"…dismantled Emelyn's spell," Kols was saying. "Then she put the bitch on her ass."

"It was beautiful," Shade put in helpfully.

"She used her Quandary Blood abilities."

Shade shrugged, his hand still rubbing my arm gently. "No one noticed. She didn't utter a single spell out loud. From what they could tell, she just sent Emelyn into a vision, which was today's exercise, right? Not Aflora's fault that Emelyn couldn't handle a dose of her own medicine."

"Is Emelyn all right?" Zeph asked, his voice low.

"She'll be fine," Shade replied. "Our mate will be, too, by the way. In case you were wondering." The hint of annoyance in his tone created a tense atmosphere that caused the hairs along my arms to stand.

"Are you trying to imply that I can't see, Shadow?"

"No, I'm suggesting you redirect your concern to the right female, Zephyrus. You know, the one who is our *mate*."

"Say that a little louder," Kols snapped.

"Is that a dare?" Shade countered. "Because you know I will. Unlike you two idiots, I've embraced my destiny. Perhaps you should try it."

"Or I could undo it," I muttered, more to myself than to them.

Shade froze against me, the air chilling in the room. "What did you just say?"

Right. Time to tell the boys my thoughts on this whole mating business. As we were all together, why not now? It'd already been one heck of a day. Might as well end it with a bang.

I pulled away from Shade so I could see all three of the males bound to my life and cleared my throat.

"I said that I could just undo it." They all gaped at me as if I'd lost my mind. "What? I'm a Quandary Blood, right? Redirecting power is apparently my thing. Why not apply that logic to the bonds and sever them?"

CHAPTER TWELVE

ZEPH

Ice drilled through my veins. "Absolutely fucking not."

Aflora blinked up at me in surprise. "Excuse me?"

"No. The answer is *no*." I'd claimed her. Planned or not, she was fucking mine, and I wouldn't allow her to undo it now.

She bristled at my tone, some of her inner fire climbing into her gaze. "No?" she repeated. "*No?* I'm pretty sure that's not your call to make."

"I'll just bite you again," Shade interjected, sounding bored already by the discussion. But I caught the hint of hurt in his icy gaze. He very much disliked this line of thought. For once, I agreed with him.

Kols, however, remained quiet.

I glanced at him, expecting to see rage but catching a glimmer of intrigue instead. "You can't possibly be considering this," I told him.

"It'd solve a lot of problems," he admitted with a shrug.

"Yes, it would solve several problems," Aflora agreed as she stood on shaking legs.

"And create a thousand more," I inserted, folding my arms.

Kols gave me a look I knew well. The one that told me he was up to something. Then he returned his focus to Aflora. "Can you undo the Earth Fae bond?" he asked, the question making me realize his intent.

He wanted to test her resolve and see how far she'd go.

Which meant he didn't actually want to dismantle the bond.

Thank fuck for that.

We didn't go through all this bullshit just to undo it.

The bonds existed for a reason. If Aflora fractured our ties, she'd implode, and none of us would allow that to happen to her. She belonged to us. End of discussion.

"Um." She winced, causing me to narrow my gaze. *That*, right there, told me she didn't actually want to do this. Something else was driving her to suggest this insanity. "I'm not sure, but I'm going to try."

"No, you're not," I replied, done with this conversation. "You're not going to do anything."

"Again, that's not for you to decide," she bit back.

I grabbed the back of her neck and tugged her to me. "You're upset. I get it. You don't trust us. Fine. But those are not reasons to break a blood vow. Relationships require work. And I'll be damned if I let you just Quandary-magic your way out of this, pixie flower."

She pressed her palms against my chest and tried to shove me away. "Don't touch me."

"Too late." I clamped my opposite arm around her lower back. "You're angry. You think we betrayed you, but everything we've done is to protect you."

She huffed a laugh, her nails digging into my button-down shirt. "Right."

"Do you think I liked seeing them take you away?" I asked her. "It wasn't my recording that landed you behind bars, Aflora. I did what I could to protect you."

"You mean you did what you could to protect you and Kols," she corrected. "Without the collar, the Council would have sensed our connection. So don't lie to me and pretend it had anything to do with me, because I know it didn't. You will always look out for Kols first and foremost. Now I'm suggesting we find a way to free you both so you can go back to guarding him without me being in the way."

"The collar protected you as well," I pointed out.

"But it wasn't me you meant to protect," she tossed back. "Stop toying with me, Zeph. This whole thing is a big mistake. I'll figure out how to undo it, and we'll go our separate ways."

"What about your balance?" Kols asked, confirming my earlier assessment. He wanted to test her resolve and see if she'd truly thought this through. "Our biting you is what helped you stop imploding the other night. If you remove the bonds, you risk imploding again."

"Exactly," I agreed.

"So put me out in the middle of the LethaForest and let me explode," she retorted. "I mean, really, it's not like you care, right?" She tried to extract herself from my hold again, but I didn't budge.

"Stop telling us how we feel, Aflora," I chastised her, annoyed by her inaccurate assessments.

Her blue eyes rolled in response, causing me to tighten my grip on her neck. "Let. Go." She uttered the words through her clenched jaw.

So I uttered one back at her. "No."

Power flickered through her, and I welcomed the fight, but Kols chose that moment to speak again. "I would care." The soft words had me glancing at him. "I would care a great deal, actually."

Aflora snorted. "Sure. Is that why you spent the last few days humping your way around the Human Realm?"

Ah. There it is—the real reason she's suggesting this.

She was hurt, not just by our perceived betrayal but also by Kols's notorious behavior. He realized it at the same moment, his nostrils flaring as his golden irises pulsated.

I released her, knowing he would grab her in turn, and he did, his palms going to her hips as he walked her into the wall.

"What are you doing?" she demanded, her hands flying up to his shoulders as if to force him back.

"There's a problem with your theory, *mate*," he said, his thigh sliding between her legs as his palms slipped up her sides to slowly memorize her curves.

Her scent began to change as interest darkened her blue eyes. "What problem?"

"Midnight Fae bonds occur when a male bites another Midnight Fae." One of his hands shifted back down to her hip while the other lifted to cup her neck, his thumb brushing the underside of her jaw to ensure she held his gaze.

"I'm aware," she replied.

"Yes, and it's a permanent claim that your Quandary abilities might be able to unravel," he conceded. "But you can't unweave our Elemental Fae mating, princess. We're already mated on the third level, which required agreement from both of our souls. Do you understand what I'm telling you?"

"You don't think my magic can dismantle Elemental Fae bonds."

"No, sweetheart," he murmured. "I'm saying I know it can't."

She shook her head, the movement stilted thanks to his grip on her neck. "I haven't even tried yet, so you can't know that."

"But I do, Aflora." He pressed his nose to her cheekbone and drew his lips across her cheek to her ear. "You would need my cooperation to even attempt it, and you don't have it. Because my soul wanted yours, just as yours desired mine. Our spirits won't allow us to break the vow now. It's too late. Which makes you mine, *mate*."

Her lips parted on a quick breath, her pupils dilating. "I want to break it."

"No, you don't," he replied softly, pulling away from her ear to meet her gaze once more. "As Zeph said, you're upset. I'm sorry. He's sorry. Fuck, I think even Shade's sorry. None of us meant to hurt you. And before you accuse me of not caring again, why do you think the three of us went to the LethaForest, Aflora? Why did we bite you?"

"To hide my growing powers," she answered without hesitation. "Everything you've done is to protect yourselves."

He shook his head. "How did forming an Elemental mating bond protect me?"

"That was an accident. You blamed me for tricking you, remember?"

"Because I was shocked," he admitted. "But that doesn't change the fact that I wanted you and still do."

"Is that what you told the humans this week? The ones you played with and fed from?" She narrowed her gaze at him. "Do they all get false promises, Kols? Or just me?"

"Just you," he murmured, his lips going to her ear. "But they're not false, princess. My vows to you are every bit true."

She snorted, not buying it at all. "Right." Those blue eyes met mine over Kols's shoulder. "And what about you, Zeph?"

I arched a brow. "What about me?"

"I saw you last night, looking refreshed from blood consumption. Did you give her false promises, too? Or do you just tie up your playmates and gag them?"

A vision of her tied up in my bed entered my mind, intriguing me. "Do you want to be tied up, Aflora?"

"Is that really all you heard?" She shook her head and searched out Shade.

He'd hopped up off the ground some time ago to lean against the wall and observe. His expression now dared her to taunt him with her exquisite mouth.

"I don't even want to know where you've been the last few days," she muttered.

"Miss me in your dreams, little rose?" he asked, amused.

"No."

"Liar," he murmured.

She growled, then went back to trying to shove Kols away from her. "Let me go."

"Never," he promised, his hand gliding to her throat to force her attention back to him. "Our souls are engaged, Aflora. You can't change that."

"Watch me," she snapped.

His lips curled. "It's not possible, sweetheart. Your soul claimed mine and vice versa. Even Sol saw it, despite the glamour tied to my wristband. He about killed me for it."

Aflora stopped fighting, her eyes widening. "Sol?"

"Yeah, big guy with rocks for fists," Kols drawled. "He introduced one to my face. Thankfully, I heal quickly." He released Aflora and took a step back. "He gave me a few things for you. They're in a bag in my room."

"What? Why didn't you give them to me when you returned?"

"Because you stormed through the room last night, slammed your door, and refused to come out afterward," he replied, crossing his arms over his chest. "You haven't exactly been all that chatty lately, Aflora."

"Because you were off playing in the Human Realm."

"If by 'playing,' you mean meeting with Exos, Cyrus, and Sol, then sure. And before you ask, yes, I fed. Something I can do without fucking, by the way. But I'm really glad we're having the exclusivity discussion because if you so much as touch another male, I'll kill him."

"Same," I agreed.

Shade merely shrugged. "You two have it covered."

Aflora gaped between the three of us, acting as though we'd all grown multiple heads. "How…? How did this conversation become about *exclusivity*? I just told you all that I want to undo the mating."

"And we told you that's not happening, pixie flower." I cocked my head to the side. "Three votes against one."

"Hardly seems fair," she muttered.

"Welcome to Midnight Fae society," Shade drawled. "Where men make the rules and women are expected to follow them. Isn't that right, Prince Kolstov?"

Kols ignored his commentary, his focus on Aflora. "You chose me."

"Yeah, and you rejected me," she countered. "And then, to add insult to injury, you set all my things on fire. Which, I guess, didn't matter since none of them belonged to me anyway." She shook her head, her exasperation palpable. "Why are we even debating this? None of us want to be in this situation."

"You're right," I agreed. "None of us want to be in this situation."

She flinched, the movement slight but visible. And then she waved her hand at me. "See? Zeph admits it."

"I admit to not enjoying our current situation," I clarified. "The one where you're mad at all three of us and punishing us with hurtful comments about breaking our ties to you. I strongly dislike this situation and would like it to cease. Now."

She gaped at me, her mouth working without sound.

"Much better," I praised, stepping toward her and brushing her dark hair behind her ear. "How about we go sit in the living room and try to discuss this like adults, hmm?"

"I-I don't understand." She seemed to be talking to herself more than to me, but I answered her anyway.

"We don't want to break our quad, Aflora. Well, I might be okay with removing Shadow, but something tells me he's staying."

"I am," he put in, seemingly unperturbed by my comment. If anything, he appeared amused.

I'd evaluate that later.

"You're upset, and I know we hurt your ability to trust us. But we can't change the past, Aflora. We can only fix the future." Shade coughed, causing me to level a glare at him. "Is this entertaining to you, Shadow?"

He cleared his throat. "I can't even begin to explain that reaction. Just. Yeah, continue." He still appeared to be fighting a grin.

I sent a question to Kols with my eyes, and he just shrugged as if to say, *It's Shade. What do you expect?* Which, yeah, what did I expect?

Rolling my eyes, I refocused on the female before me. "I'm sorry for not telling you what was about to happen. There wasn't time, and I worked the situation to the best of my ability to ensure *your* safety, in addition to mine and Kols's." I cupped her cheek and tilted her head back as I stepped into her personal space. "I'll prove to you over time that your best interests are important to me. But I need you to allow me the opportunity to try."

She swallowed, her pretty eyes still holding a touch of that fire I adored. "Why should I?"

"Because I'm your mate, Aflora," I replied, lowering my lips to brush a chaste kiss against the edge of her mouth. "Whether you want me or not, we're bound together. And this will be a lot easier if you just accept that our fates are intertwined."

"What if I want to undo them?" The breathless quality of her voice belied her words, yet her stubborn side refused to back down. I really did adore that about her. I just wished she'd direct that fight to another topic, one less hurtful.

"You don't," I whispered, rubbing my nose against hers. "So stop suggesting it." I nipped her lower lip hard enough to hurt without breaking the skin. A gentle reprimand for her cruel words. Maybe I deserved them, but I didn't have to like them. "You're mine, Aflora. And one day, you'll trust me again. If you allow yourself to try."

"I can't," she admitted. "I can't trust you."

"Not yet," I agreed, pressing my forehead to hers. "But soon. You'll see." With a final kiss to her cheek, I released her once more. "Let's continue this discussion over midnight lunch." I held Aflora's gaze as I added, "I'm cooking. I hope you like burning thwomp."

A muscle in her cheek twitched, one that told me I'd almost earned a smile from her. Better than nothing.

"I need to take care of something first, but I'll be back," Shade said, disappearing into a cloud of smoke before any of us could comment.

A second later, Sir Kristoff ran into the room, red eyes glowing. "Where are they?!" he demanded, spinning in a circle, his little hand holding a stone dagger. Well, I supposed it was a sword for him, considering his size.

"What are you talking about?" Kols asked the little hellspawn.

The gargoyle growled, low and menacing. "The Death Blood and his sword-wielding friend. *Where are they?*"

Kols and I shared a look. I had nothing.

Aflora seemed just as lost. "Are you talking about Shadow?"

"Yes," the stone demon hissed. "And his sword friend. The ti—"

Shade appeared once more and shot a puff of purple dust at the gargoyle, causing the little hellion to sputter and cough, its red eyes blinking repeatedly. Then he frowned and glared up at the Death Blood. "*You.*"

"Aww, did you miss me, li'l buddy? I'd be happy to tie you up again. I know how much you enjoyed that last time."

Sir Kristoff growled and stalked off, returning to his duty at the door while mumbling something about killing Shade in his sleep.

The Death Blood just watched with deep amusement and shook his head. "I think your gargoyle is broken, Kols."

The gargoyle in question raised his dagger like a middle finger and disappeared into the door.

"What the hell?" Kols snapped. "What did you blast him with?"

"A chill pill," Shade drawled. "Seems to have worked."

"Why was he going on about a sword-wielding friend?" Aflora asked, her brow furrowed.

Shade just shrugged. "Fuck if I know."

I didn't believe him. Not for a second. But I also knew Shade wouldn't tell us unless he wanted to. Kols must have come to the same conclusion because he didn't bother to argue. Knowing Shade, it was what he wanted anyway. Maybe he'd gone out into the hall to enchant the gargoyle into acting like an idiot. A distraction to the bigger picture.

"Oh, right. Not done yet. But I promise to be back soon," Shade said, disappearing again.

"What the hell is he up to?" Kols demanded, staring at the place Shade had just vacated.

I just shook my head. "I'm going to make lunch. Then we're having a quad meeting."

"A quad meeting?" Aflora repeated.

"Yeah," I replied, locking my gaze on her. "We're a quad, pixie flower. And you had better get used to it because you're stuck with us. Now I'm going to go make you a burning thwomp sandwich. Would you like that with a side of fire gnat juice?"

Her lips twitched this time. Briefly, but I caught the little movement, and my heart gave a thump in response. "Sounds lovely," she deadpanned.

"Good." I winked at her and turned for the kitchen, leaving her to talk to Kols alone. He still had some groveling to do.

Hell, we all did.

But I'd let him go first.

I was honorable like that.

CHAPTER THIRTEEN

KOLS

Aflora watched Zeph through wary eyes, then shifted that look to me. She still stood against the wall, right where I'd put her, but she appeared a lot less feisty now. If anything, she reminded me of a wilted flower with her shoulders caving inward in insecurity and her arms curling around her middle.

I sighed, hating myself a little for making her feel this way. "I have a reputation for fucking around," I told her softly. "I upheld that image during our break days to deter the others from asking any questions. But I used glamour spells to do it. Exos and Cyrus were there the entire time, if you want to ask them. They were immune to my enchantment, mostly because they knew I'd bonded to you and would have killed me otherwise."

It'd been hard enough to calm them down when they sensed my new mating bond—something that had shocked the hell out of me.

Apparently, my wristband only applied to Midnight Fae links, not Elemental Fae ones. However, the Council didn't seem to have the same ability to sense my connection to Aflora. Which made sense because, according to Exos, it was a link on the spirit plane that gave me away, something only Spirit Fae could see.

And Sol, apparently.

Because he knew right away.

Although, I suspected his was earth source related.

Elemental Fae were fucking complicated.

"If they know about our mating link, then they know I'm an abomination," she whispered, her eyes filling with tears. "They're never going to let me back, are they?"

I immediately pulled her into my arms, needing to soothe her. She'd been so strong, fighting every step of the way, but the helplessness always weighed on her. I saw it peek at me whenever she second-guessed herself. Yet she always pushed it back.

Until now.

"Shh," I hushed, leading her to the couch to sit.

She didn't even try to stop me, her breaths coming in short bursts as the weight of everything seemed to crush her at once. "They shouldn't take me back," she admitted on an exhale, her shoulders trembling. "I'm… I'm…"

"One of the strongest females I've ever met," I told her as I pulled her into my lap to hold her.

That she didn't even object told me everything I needed to know about her current frame of mind.

She'd given up.

Just for a moment.

But that moment broke my heart.

I pressed my lips to her forehead and drew my fingers through her hair.

"Actually, I think you might be the strongest female I've ever met," I corrected, smiling to myself. "It's what drew me to you initially. That, and your altruistic nature. You put the safety of your people before your own needs and desires, just as a royal should. I admire you for it."

She said nothing for so long that I thought perhaps I'd lost her to the sadness, only her eyes were shimmering with unshed tears when she pulled back to look up at me. Aflora hadn't truly broken, just been on the verge of it.

"It's my duty to protect them," she replied softly. "To do otherwise is to fail. It's why I need to talk to Sol, to officially relinquish my power. Because I can't be trusted as an abomination, something I imagine you confirmed with him, Exos, and Cyrus, yes?"

I tucked a lock of hair behind her ear, then drew my fingertips down her neck. "Not exactly."

"But they know we've exchanged a mating promise to each other."

That must have been her definition for the third level. Seemed appropriate. "Yes. They know I'm your intended mate, and they're aware of the complications involved with such a vow. Particularly as it's well known that Shade has also claimed you and that I'm betrothed to another Midnight Fae."

Her delectable mouth twisted to the side, the tears glimmering in her gaze slowly subsiding to an intelligent gleam that told me she was considering every angle of the puzzle before us. "This is why I need to break our bonds. It's one thing to sacrifice myself. Entirely another to take you all down with me."

I slid my palm to her nape, my thumb dancing along the pulse point at her neck. "Maybe I want to go down with you, Aflora." *Or on you*, I added in my mind, my lips curling at the thought.

She snorted. "You accused me of tricking you into our mating, Kolstov. I know you don't really want this."

"Then why did we connect?" I countered. "From what I understand of Elemental Fae bonds, they require mutual agreement." Very unlike Midnight Fae connections.

"We connected because we're compatible," she said matter-of-factly. "We're both royals of very strong lineages, and we got carried away."

"We did," I agreed. "Because I knew from the moment I met you that you were a worthy female of mating potential. I tried to fight it, but I was too weak to resist you. And while the connection shocked me, thus causing me to act like a fucking idiot afterward, I don't regret it. Which is why I won't allow you to remove it."

I pressed my lips to hers, silencing whatever argument brewed inside her thoughts. Because I meant it. I refused to let her break this bond.

Would it make things easier for us all? Maybe.

Would it save me from certain punishment? Absolutely.

But somehow I just knew we'd end up right back here, with my soul tied to hers and a whole hell of a lot of bad blood between us as a result.

I didn't see the point in fighting the inevitable. "I want to find a way to make this work," I told her in a breath, my mouth brushing hers with each word. "We may not have meant to tie our souls together, Aflora, but it already happened. And rather than fight it and each other, I'd like to figure out how to move forward. Together."

She shook her head. "It's impossible, Kols. I shouldn't exist."

"But you do," I replied, kissing her again, this time with more force than before. Her lips yielded to mine, her body betraying her mind. "You exist and you're mine," I added, then fully claimed her mouth with my tongue. My grip shifted from her neck to her hair, my fingers tangling in her thick blue-black strands and holding her to me as I devoured her.

If she didn't want to acknowledge my words, then she could listen to my body.

My opposite hand went to her hip to guide her across my lap and encourage her to straddle my thighs. She followed my lead and wrapped her arms around my neck, then began to return my kiss as if to say goodbye.

I saw right through it, felt her magic humming to life to test her resolve, and tugged on her hair to expose her neck. "Try it," I dared her, my incisors already at her throbbing pulse. "I'll just bite you again and again, Aflora. And you can't break our Earth bond unless I allow it, which is never going to happen. Our souls are already welded together."

At least that was what I understood after talking to Exos and Cyrus. They said something about my essence weaving around hers, similar to how theirs always gravitated to Claire's in the Spirit Realm.

"Don't you see that it's for the best?" she whispered, her body shaking over mine with a convoluted mixture of arousal and resolve.

"You'll implode," I warned her before licking the tempting point of her neck. "I'm the one absorbing most of your magic right now, Aflora. If you release me, you'll detonate." It wasn't a lie. I'd absorbed the brunt of her power the other night, my connection to the dark source forcing me to serve as a funnel.

Her fingers threaded through my hair, her grasp tightening as if to yank me away from her neck, but I didn't budge.

"You'll have to try harder than that, sweetheart."

She growled in response. "You're being impossible."

"And you're being unreasonable," I retorted, nipping her neck. "I won't make excuses for myself, Aflora. I reacted badly and I'm sorry." I nibbled my way up her throat to her ear. "Our relationship is forbidden. It breaks all the rules. It's probably going to cost me my crown. But you know what?"

She swallowed, her nails biting into my scalp. "What?"

"That all only makes me want you more," I admitted. "And if given the opportunity to do it all over again, I would, even knowing what it would cost in return." I nuzzled her tender skin, my lips skimming her pulse once more. Her blood called to the predator within me, urging me to bite, to *claim*. But I wouldn't. Not without her permission.

Unless she tried to unweave our bonds.

In which case, I'd bite her repeatedly until she stopped.

"Why?" she whispered.

"Why what, sweetheart?"

"You're risking everything, Kolstov."

"Am I?" I replied, drawing back to meet her gaze.

"You are," she insisted. "You just praised me for being altruistic by putting my people before myself. What are you doing? You're putting an abomination before your ascension. You're going against everything you've been working for. I want to know why."

"Because it's time for change," another voice replied on my behalf.

I glanced sideways to find Shade lounging in my favorite recliner chair with his feet propped up on the coffee table. As I hadn't sensed his presence, I assumed that meant he'd just arrived. Unless he'd been lurking in smoke form.

His Death Blood abilities irked me greatly.

"Change?" Aflora repeated.

"Yep," he drawled.

"Care to elaborate?" I asked, arching a brow.

His icy blue eyes flashed with knowledge and secrets. "Do you believe all abominations are evil, Kolstov? That they should be exterminated on sight without any trial or cause aside from their mingled blood and powers?"

"Abominations have historically proven problematic," I pointed out, avoiding his direct questions like he did mine.

"Have they?" he countered, arching a dark brow. "Or is that what our Council wants us to believe?"

"It's an international directive to execute abominations," I reminded him. "Not just our Council's."

"Fair," he conceded. "But who proposed that mandate originally?"

"My grandfather," I replied, aware of the history involved. "Shortly after a certain issue a millennium ago."

He nodded. "Yes. Right around the time he also had all the Quandary Bloods executed." He cocked his head to the side. "Now, I might be overthinking this, but it seems to me your family has a history of fearing those with the potential to be more powerful than them."

I narrowed my gaze at him. "If you're trying to accuse me or my family of something, Shadow, then I suggest you stop hiding behind riddles and spit it out."

His lips curled. "I see I've struck a nerve."

"With your cryptic bullshit, sure."

"No. With my concise recollection of just why all this started in the first place. Your grandfather didn't want to risk the source being realigned again, so he exterminated the Quandary Bloods—or at least those he could find—and also strongly encouraged the fae community to execute all abominations. Which, when you think about it, is a very strange choice indeed when Midnight Fae males can become Fortune Fae Alphas by just refusing to ingest human blood. Thereby suggesting fae are actually somewhat related across the species. But I digress."

He kicked his feet off the table and leaned forward, all signs of amusement leaving his features.

"Our Council requires change," he continued, his blue irises landing on Aflora. "So you want a reason, little rose? That's your reason. Our quad is going to change everything, including rebalancing a power source that has long been abused by the Nacht family. With, or without, Kols's knowledge."

"All right." My hands went to Aflora's hips to remove her from my lap, but her thighs clamped down around mine.

"Hold on," she said.

"No. He's just insulted—"

Her palm covered my mouth, shocking the hell out of me. "Why do you feel it's been abused?" she asked Shade.

"Because the Quandary Bloods were removed from the equation, thereby dismantling the balance and allowing the Elite Bloods unfettered access to the source via the Nacht family line. Kolstov's grandfather destroyed the Midnight Fae who were meant to protect the balance, all because he feared the source would be redirected to another line."

I moved my mouth away from Aflora's hand. "Is that the bullshit your father tells you?" I demanded with a humorless laugh. "Un-fucking-believable."

"Yes, he's told me this version of events, and he's also droned on and on about how the source was stolen from our family." Shade lifted his hand, palm up, in a version of an odd shrug, then let it fall back to his lap. "He wants it back for all the wrong reasons. As do all the members of the Council. Which brings me back to the need for change."

Zeph chose that moment to enter with a tray of food. He set it down on the coffee table and fixed his gaze on Shade. "You have my attention, Shade. Elaborate on your suggestions for change."

Of course Zeph would want to entertain this nonsense.

This time Aflora allowed me to lift her off my lap and into the space beside me. Zeph took the spot on her opposite side, his forearms going to his sprawled thighs as he leaned forward to focus on Shade.

"Well?" my Guardian prompted.

Shade studied him for a long moment. "Did you enjoy being demoted to headmaster as a result of your sexual shenanigans?"

Zeph merely smirked. "Nice try at evasion. Tell me your ideas for change."

"It's not my ideas that will matter," he replied cryptically. "It's our mate's."

Aflora had been staring intently at the tray of food, but Shade's words pulled her gaze sideways. I stretched my arm out across the back of the couch so my fingertips could lightly brush her shoulder. It was a natural move, similar to Zeph widening his legs to ensure his thigh touched hers.

Shade noticed but didn't comment. Nor did he seem bothered by it. Actually, he appeared almost content with the possessive display, as if it satisfied some part of him.

"I will never understand you," I decided out loud.

Mischief danced in his features. "You will. One day. Just not today." He looked at Aflora. "I'll see you in your dreams later, little rose." And then he disappeared into smoke once more.

"I hate when he does that," I said, irritated as hell.

"Which part?" Zeph asked. "Accusing your family of hoarding magic, or the vanishing act?"

"Both," I admitted on a huff. "He's infur—"

"Is that dragon steak?" Aflora's attention was on the tray again, her blue eyes wide.

I followed her gaze to the dark gray meat surrounded by leaves. The other two plates just had sandwiches. I assumed one of those was meant for me, the other for Zeph. Shade was definitely not on our guest list, despite being able to get past my gargoyle. Which was a discussion I'd need to have with Sir Kristoff later because I hadn't given approval for the Death Blood to enter at will.

"Yeah, with salad patty," Zeph replied, palming the back of his neck. "Kols asked Sol for some meal suggestions since you're not fond of our meals. This was what he recommended."

"He also told us to get you some scurbuttle snacks," I added. "After he left, Cyrus informed me that would be a bad idea and suggested I stick to dragon steak. He also recommended I not give you bacon."

"Bacon?" she repeated.

"Yeah. I guess it's like troll fat?"

Her eyes rounded in horror. "Why would you eat troll fat?"

"I wouldn't."

"Then why eat bacon?"

I shook my head. "It's not the same, it's just... Never mind. He recommended dragon steak. So." I waved to the plate as if to say, *There it is.*

"I hope I cooked it right," Zeph mused. "Reminded me of beef, so I grilled it the same way."

That explained why it took him so long to prepare the food. "What kind of sandwiches did you make us?"

"Turkey and cheese," he replied. "I added mayo to yours since you like it." He grimaced with the comment, causing me to grin.

I covered my heart with my hand, my other arm still draped over Aflora's shoulder. "You do love me, Z."

He snorted but didn't deny it.

"You made me dragon steak," Aflora said, still focused on her plate. "Because Sol suggested it."

Zeph glanced uneasily at her. "Yeah, he suggested it to Kols. Did I make it wrong?"

"And you added salad patty."

"Yeah, that part just seemed appropriate based on what I know of Elemental Fae cuisine. Seems like a popular side? But I had to use magic because we don't have a lot of those root vegetables here. So, uh, I hope it's okay."

She finally looked at him. "I thought we agreed on burning thwomp and fire gnat juice."

My lips twitched at the mock condescension in her tone. Teasing had to be a good sign, right? Maybe it meant she was past the idea of rewiring our connection, or had at least put it on hold. Regardless, I'd take it.

"Yeah, sorry, all out of burning thwomps, I'm afraid," Zeph replied, his tone contrite. "But if you don't want the dragon steak, I'll eat it, and you can have my turkey sandwich."

He made to reach for her plate, and she batted his hand away. "Don't you dare."

Zeph smirked at her. "Oh, you want it now?"

"Did you poison it?" she countered.

He nodded. "Yep. Laced it with an agreeable charm so you'll do everything I say for at least a week."

"I actually think you might mean that," she replied.

He grunted, grabbed her plate, and set it in her lap. "Eat, Aflora. Or I really will enchant you."

Rather than snipe something back at him, she plucked a leaf off her plate and used it to rip a piece off her dragon steak, then made a show of putting it in her mouth.

Suddenly, food was the last thing on my mind.

And her lips were all I could see.

"Fuck," I muttered.

"No," she replied without missing a beat. She finished chewing and swallowed before looking at me. "I'm not ready to do that again yet."

Zeph met my gaze over her head, then we both gazed down at her. "All right, sweetheart," I conceded. "That's fine."

My Guardian nodded in agreement. "I'm not ready to fuck yet either."

She glanced at him. "You're not?"

"No." He leaned in to whisper in her ear just loud enough for me to hear as well. "I won't fuck you until you beg, pixie flower. And even then, I still might not fuck you. Do you want to know why?"

"Why?" she asked as if hypnotized by his voice. And maybe she was.

"Because you haven't earned it yet." He kissed her on the cheek, then reached for his plate and began to eat.

"He's a dick," I told her conversationally as I grabbed my own sandwich. "And, unfortunately, he means it."

When Zeph set his mind to something, there would be no changing it. He was a stubborn ass like that. But on this, I sort of agreed with him. Until we were in a better place with Aflora, sex was off the table.

However, that didn't mean we couldn't play in other ways.

Such as in her dreams.

I smiled at the memories of all the times I joined her in her mind. Mmm, that was fun. Maybe we'd do it again later. After Shade finished toying with her.

Or perhaps I'd kick him out and take over.

Zeph caught my gaze again, the knowing flicker in his green irises telling me he agreed with my plan. We didn't even need to talk about it; he just knew.

Poor Aflora. Now she had three mates hungry for her dreams.

I pressed my lips against her temple, showing affection because I wanted to, then returned to my midnight lunch. "I'm glad to see you eating a healthy meal, Aflora," I told her. "You're going to need that energy later."

"What?" she asked, her mouth full of dragon steak.

"For your dreams," Zeph replied. He lifted his hand to draw his knuckles down her cheek. "And for your independent training tomorrow."

She groaned, the sound going right to my cock. "Stay out of my head."

"Never," Zeph and I replied at the same time.

"Willow stumps," she muttered to herself. Then she dug back into her meal, the argument forgotten.

Well, one thing was clear—I needed to order more dragon steak.

CHAPTER FOURTEEN

AFLORA

Seven nights of sexual torment.

With no orgasms.

To say I hated my mates right now would be an understatement.

And they knew it, too, the three of them all watching from different corners of the yard with matching expressions of amusement. Even Zephyrus smirked, his lips reminding me of the way he'd held me down last night and devoured me to within an inch of my life.

Just to stop and wake me up seconds before I exploded.

I glared at him, not caring at all that he was in headmaster mode today.

Physical Training with No Magic. Yeah, I'd show him some *physical training*, all right.

That Shade and Kols had chosen to go shirtless for today's sparring activities only added insult to injury. Because yeah, they looked good and they knew it. And while Zephyrus's torso was covered, his arms were fully exposed in his sleeveless shirt. He made a show of stretching, his muscles bulging and inviting me to lick him.

I preferred it when I thought they all had betrayed me.

This was worse.

Much, much worse.

I was even starting to dream of some random guy with long white hair and silver-blue eyes. He at least let me come in those fantasies, which was how I knew I'd made him up. Because it hadn't escaped my notice that his traits were the opposite of my mates'—clearly, my mind's way of retaliating.

Tulip-burning willow stumps, I thought, glaring at the males in question. *I hope you all fall into a burning thwomp.*

"You okay?" Ella asked, appearing out of nowhere at my side. Or maybe she'd been there the entire time. As my focus was entirely on the eye candy across the yard, I couldn't be sure.

"I'm fine," I replied, my voice sharper than I intended.

"You sure? Because it sounded like you just growled at Zeph."

"I probably did." I'd been growling at him a lot lately.

"I thought you were getting along better," Ella murmured. "You've all been studying a lot."

"Yeah, they're helping me with control," I muttered. *And then tormenting me in my dreams afterward.*

"Come spar with me, little rose." Shade's voice came from my left, drawing my focus to his toned physique. The moon played off his tan skin, making me wonder what he'd look like under the heat of the sun. Gorgeous, obviously. And wicked.

I almost refused, but then a better idea entered my mind. I couldn't be alone in my agony here because the guys hadn't orgasmed either. Which meant they'd been teasing themselves, too. Maybe it was time I returned the favor a little.

"Okay," I replied.

"Hey, I thought we were sparring together," Ella cut in.

Tray scooped her up into his arms before I could comment, his lips brushing hers as he murmured, "I guess you're all mine, El."

She sighed. "I'm already yours, Nacht."

"I know." He waggled his brows at her. "How about we ditch sparring and do a little of our own physical activity back at the suite?"

"How about you do the exercises I gave you and stop trying to get laid in my class, Trayton," Zeph deadpanned.

Tray just smiled. "I prefer my plan."

Zeph did not share his amusement. "Put her down and start running. Ten laps."

Ella groaned and Tray cursed.

"Okay, fifteen," Zeph amended.

"Put me down," Ella snapped.

Tray did reluctantly and gave Zeph a look that spoke volumes. "You're a cockblocking dick, Zeph."

"Shall I make it twenty?" he countered, that famous eyebrow of his inching upward into his hairline.

"I'm only listening to you right now for Ella because twenty laps would piss her off," Tray replied before taking off after his mate.

"Goading my brother?" Kols asked as he jogged up to join us, his abs flexing seductively with the movement. And now I wanted to lick him.

"He just makes it so easy," Zeph drawled.

Shade wrapped his arm around me, pulling me back into his hot form. "I thought we were sparring?" he whispered against my ear.

"You all are killing me," I muttered, more to myself than to them.

"Ready to beg already?" Zeph pitched his voice low so the others couldn't overhear. "That's a shame, Aflora. I expected to have to try harder."

Kols chuckled, but Shade just pressed his nose to my neck and inhaled softly.

My blood was on fire.

And I wanted to choke all of them.

"Stop stalling and come play with me," Shade breathed, causing goose bumps to trail down my exposed arms.

He pulled me backward by several feet, drawing me into one of the sparring rings. His flirtation captured the attention of several students in our class, including the two standing in the circle beside ours.

"Well, aren't you two cute," Emelyn drawled, her tone holding a touch of derision.

"Someone's jealous," her partner replied, smirking at Shade and giving him a friendly nod. Yeah, these two were definitely friends. Which had me wondering how Emelyn had found herself partnered with Ajax for today's assignment. Elite Bloods didn't tend to mix with Death Bloods.

"I'm not jealous," Emelyn snapped back.

"Yeah? Could have fooled me, Your Majesty," Ajax replied, executing a mock bow.

"Ugh, why am I partnered with you again?" she demanded.

"Because your friends didn't want to fight you today. You're too moody for them." He folded his arms. "So are you going to try to hit me or what? I'm getting bored over here."

Emelyn charged him with a roar that made me wince.

Moody was an understatement.

She had Ajax flat on his back in less than a second, his expression registering shock, which quickly morphed into determination as he wrestled her across the ground in several skilled maneuvers.

"I don't know how to do that," I admitted, watching him twist and pin her. But Emelyn wasn't one to be outdone. She had him in a headlock two moves later, causing my eyebrows to shoot up.

Shade yanked me backward, away from their violent game, and drew me around to face him. "Then show me what you know how to do."

"Earth Fae don't fight," I told him. "There's no need."

He gave me a look that said he wasn't impressed. "I know Zeph's been training you."

"Yeah, mostly with magic."

"And I've seen you and Ella spar, so I know you're learning how to fight," he added, undeterred.

"Okay, she's shown me a few things, but—"

"Show me what you've learned," he interjected. "No excuses. I need to know what I'm dealing with here."

"Why did you want to spar?" I asked him, deflecting. "You rarely talk to me during class. I mean, you barely even acknowledge me in Death Class, and we're partners in that one. Why today? Why now?"

He cocked his head to the side. "I'm tired of giving you space. You're mine and I want to play. Now stop deflecting and give me a preview of your abilities. Then we'll go from there."

"I gave you a preview that first time you bit me."

"Yeah, and you played with your elements and still lost," he replied, unimpressed. "Now you have that collar around your neck hampering your abilities. Which makes this class a lot more important than you seem to realize."

"Why? Because you're anticipating I may need to fight you off again soon?" I countered.

He swept his leg across my knees, sending me to the ground on a whoosh of air. I coughed and sputtered as he landed on top of me, his hands easily capturing my wrists to bring them above my head as his hips pinned mine to the black grass below.

Not green, but black.

Like all the other vegetation in this realm.

"I'm anticipating that you're going to need to fight others," he whispered against my ear. "And soon. So I need you to stop flirting with me and actually pay attention, Aflora."

"I'm not flirting with you," I managed to say on a harsh exhale, my back throbbing from his unexpected attack. "I think… I think I hate you."

He chuckled and pressed a kiss to my jaw, then drew his lips to my ear. "Best me and I'll make you come later."

I snorted at the offer. "Did that when I woke up, so I'm good, thank you."

Only after I uttered the words did I realize what I'd just admitted out loud. My cheeks heated as Shade went to his elbows on either side of my head, his lips curled in amusement. "Yeah? And did you scream my name?"

"Get off of me."

"Not until you detail the experience for me," he replied, his wicked gaze falling to my mouth. "Did you think of me?"

"I'm not talking about this."

"Then I guess we'll be lying here all night. Works for me, as I find this position to be rather comfortable for all parties involved." He gave a little thrust, allowing me to feel his growing arousal against my heated center.

My thighs clenched, my insides doing all sorts of weird somersaults in response to his small action. I'd told him the truth about my earlier release, but it hadn't done anything to cool the flames burning inside me.

All because my mates wouldn't leave my dreams alone.

And now this!

"Off," I snapped.

He merely smiled. "Make me."

I growled and tried to shove him off me, which did absolutely nothing. Well, no, that wasn't true. Pressing my palms to his bare shoulders sent a zap of electricity through me, making me that much hotter for him.

Because he was shirtless and on top of me.

A fae could only take so much skin-to-skin contact after all these nights of sensual torture.

Or, at least, that was what I told myself. It had absolutely nothing to do with the fact that my three mates were irresistible males with the bodies of gods. And it definitely wasn't because of their skills in the bedroom.

"Your squirming is only turning me on more," Shade whispered, his lips brushing the shell of my ear as he trailed his mouth down my neck to my thundering pulse.

"Why are you doing this?" I asked him, desperate for a way to *remove* him. I also wanted to ask him to shadow us somewhere more private so I could join him in the shirtless department.

Not voicing that desire. Nope. Nope. Nope.

"You're not the only one amped up from all the dreams, love," he said softly, his mouth teasing the sensitive spot behind my ear now. "I've waited for you to come to me all week, and you've stubbornly remained in your room. So I'm increasing the stakes in the game."

"Wh-what?" I stammered. "You never—"

"Stop making out and get to work," Zeph snapped. "Unless you need a more thorough demonstration of today's sparring activities?"

"Seems to me you need a lesson on what making out means," Shade drawled, rolling off of me and popping up to his feet. "Shall I go fetch Kols for you?"

"Cute," Zeph replied.

I pushed off the ground and brushed the strands of grass—if it could even really be called that—from my pants. The razor-like edges sliced across my fingers, making me grimace. *Definitely not grass.*

"All right, Aflora. Let's try again," Shade suggested.

"No. You're out. Go spar with Kols. I'm up."

"You mean, you want me to make out with Kols?" Shade sounded surprised. "All right."

Zeph snorted and shook his head. "Fuck off, Shadow."

"You're an amazing headmaster, Zeph. It's a real wonder that you didn't go into this profession right after finishing up at the Academy."

"Now," Zeph said through his teeth.

"I'll see you later, little rose." Shade winked at me and wandered off in the direction of Kols and one of the other Elite Bloods. Tray and Ella were training beside them, their cheeks pink from exertion. Or maybe something else.

Because I'd woken up with a similar look this—

"Aflora," Zeph snapped, his broad chest suddenly blocking my view as he stepped in front of me. "What the hell is wrong with you?"

"I've not been sleeping very well," I replied primly.

He coughed to hide a smile, but I caught the twitch of his lips. "Well, that's not an excuse to slack off in my class. We fight even when exhausted."

"Oh? Are you also having difficulty sleeping?" I asked him with false innocence.

His green eyes narrowed. "Stop flirting with me and get to work."

"I'm not flirting with you."

"You are," he insisted, taking a step closer to crowd my personal space. His lips went to my ear as he whispered, "And if you continue down this path, I will punish you later."

I shivered, my damn body thrilled by the notion.

Why was it so damn hard to control my reactions to these males? I hated them. Well, not really. Maybe. I wasn't sure. I *wanted* to hate them, but they'd been wearing down my defenses over the last week with their soft touches and—

Zeph grabbed my ponytail and tugged it sharply to expose my neck. "Are you purposely being disobedient?"

I considered that. "Well, no. But sparring is still new to me. Elemental Fae don't really fight unless it's in the Powerless Champion arena."

"Maybe ask her to go pick some flowers instead, Zeph," Emelyn suggested. "She's not really cut out for athletics."

I frowned. "Fighting is only one form of physical activity."

"Yeah, and it's a crucial one that you're terrible at," she spat back. "Just like everything else in this realm. When are you going home?"

"Enough," Zeph cut in, shooting her a bored expression. "Go back to your assignment. I'll deal with this."

Emelyn heaved a dramatic sigh. "She's like a full-time job, constantly requiring a babysitter to hold her hand through even the simplest of tasks."

I bristled at her condescending tone. "I'd like to see you try to perform with a collar around your neck." I pointed to the thin leather choker sitting against my throat. It probably had Shade's lip prints all over it from his date with my pulse a few minutes ago, but I didn't care. "Maybe I should take it off and let you wear it for a day," I suggested.

She laughed, the sound lacking proper humor. "I don't need a leash, because I already know how to control my powers. But the same can't be said about *abominations*."

"Emelyn!" Zeph barked, his tone harsh.

"Oh, did I accidentally admit out loud what we're all really thinking about her?" She pressed a hand to her heart and gave me a mock-apologetic look. "My bad."

My teeth ground together, mostly because I didn't know how to reply. Since everything she said was true.

I was an abomination.

A powerful one.

And I didn't know how to control my abilities. Not completely, anyway.

My heart squeezed at the knowledge, a part of me feeling helpless all over again. But I couldn't let her beat me.

I'm stronger than this.

I can learn.

I don't want to hurt people.

I have anchors to ground me.

I—

A ripple of energy danced over my skin, causing the hairs along my neck to rise. I frowned down at my arms, noting the static electricity humming across my being. It wasn't visible, but I *felt* it. The warmth familiar in a strange way, reminding me of my own magic.

Yet it wasn't coming from me.

"That's enough, Emelyn," Zeph bit out, oblivious to the sensations swirling around me. "You're excused for—"

An explosion rocked the ground, sending us all to our knees. Another boom shook the surface, causing shouts to sound throughout the yard. Zeph yanked me to him, his stance protective, his gaze sharp as he glanced around seeking the source.

Ravens screamed through the air, followed by a cloud of smoke as the burning thwomps around campus unleashed fire into the sky.

And then came the gargoyles, their screeches reminding me of nails against a sharp stone.

I pressed my palms to my ears as Zeph pushed me flat onto the ground, his larger body covering mine.

Shrieks, heat, and a flutter of wind whipped through the Academy. "What's happening?" I shouted at Zeph.

"The Academy is protecting itself," he shouted back.

My eyes widened. "It does that?" But my words were lost to the new wave of chaos swimming around us. The hisses on the wind sent chills down my spine.

Snake vines, I realized, horrified. Those things didn't like me on a good day. This wouldn't go over well.

Zeph's grip tightened around me, his warmth bleeding into me, wrapping me in a cocoon of safety. *Literally.*

I blinked, realizing his magic poured out of him in a defensive shield, covering not just me but all the students in the field. I peeked around him to find Kols at the other end, his own power connecting to Zeph's to bolster him in his effort in protecting the entire class from the debris and insanity flying overhead.

It rippled around us like a tornado, reminding me of an Air Fae activity gone bad.

More of that familiar power buzzed through me, then fled, as if kissing my soul goodbye on its way out. The sirens above grew louder, the slithering snake creatures heading right for me. I cringed, waiting for their impact, only they slid over Zeph's shield and took off into the wind to chase some menacing figment.

My blood ran cold, my heart stopping in my chest. The creatures had sensed the dark energy running through me.

What would happen when Zeph lifted his protection? Would the Academy attack me with the same brutal force?

I shivered and felt Zeph's lips ghost across my temple, the touch brief but there. "I've got you," he vowed, the words meant for my ears alone.

How would I explain to him what I felt? Had it even been real?

He slowly started to sit up, his palm against my breastbone keeping me down on the ground as he glanced around. After several moments of searching, his touch eased, and he moved his hand to my shoulder to pull me upward.

"It's done," he said gruffly, the words carrying across the now silent field.

"The source is calm," Kols replied, his statement clear despite the distance.

No one uttered a sound, everyone gaping at the rocks and ash littering the grounds.

Then someone screamed in the distance, causing Zeph to jump to his feet.

"Go," Shade said, appearing beside me. The statement must have been meant for Zeph, because he took off at a sprint, Kols hot on his tail, along with several other students.

Cries pelted the air, all coming from the same direction. Shade practically yanked me to my feet, his palm finding my lower back as he guided me through the wreckage toward the commotion rising ahead. It didn't take long for us to find the cause.

The Death Blood Education Building had been reduced to a pile of rubble, the once proud spire a cascade of obsidian rocks without any structure.

And above the destruction was a single word written in red flames, the smoke spiraling up into the sky in lethal ropes that resembled chains.

It was a word I knew well.

Because I'd sung it many times before, as had my mother.

"*Alqisian*," I whispered.

"Yes," Shade replied just as softly. "Do you know what it means?"

"Not the translation of it, no."

He swallowed, his focus shifting from the rubble to me. "Retribution."

"Retribution," I repeated, my voice just as low as his. "Meaning what?"

Shade gave me a grim look, his icy blue eyes holding a myriad of secrets underlined in pain. "It means the future is officially now."

CHAPTER FIFTEEN

AFLORA

Silence.

It started after Shade's revelation and continued long after he left with Kols and Tray to attend an emergency Council meeting. I sat on the couch between Zeph and Ella.

None of us knew what to say.

Ella glanced at me, her lips twisting like she wanted to say something, only she kept deciding not to speak. I understood why.

She'd recognized the word because of my song. It was one of the primary phrases repeated throughout the ballad. And it'd been written in fire above the destroyed Death Blood Education Building.

I couldn't explain that. Just as I couldn't explain how I'd recognized the magic. It wasn't mine but felt so familiar. Like I knew the fae who cast the spell.

Impossible, I thought for the millionth time. *It's just not possible.*

Who could it be? My parents? I nearly laughed at the thought. They were dead. I felt their souls depart when the earth source moved to me. And why would they attack the Academy?

However, I'd sensed something ancestral about the magic, like it was somehow connected to me, yet not.

I didn't know how to articulate it, so I kept the knowledge to myself while we waited.

And waited.

And waited some more.

Ella picked up her phone for the millionth time to check for any updates, then set it down again. Zeph did the same. I just sat with my hands clasped together on my lap, useless. Elemental Fae didn't really do technology. We preferred more natural methods of communication.

I pinched my mouth to the side and glanced around for the thousandth time. Zeph looked at me, his dark green eyes sheltered and not giving anything away. I wanted to ask him if this had ever happened before. I also wanted to tell him what Shade had said about the future being now. And I sort of wanted to confide in him about what I felt out on that field.

What if he betrays me again?

Can I really trust him?

A few nights of sexual torment didn't really mean much, and while he'd been against me unweaving the bond, there still wasn't a lot of evidence that he cared about me.

Except he'd guarded me on the field today.

No, he'd shielded the whole class.

Hmm, however, he'd yanked me beneath him in a protective gesture, and I'd felt his concern for my safety. Unless that had all been in my head.

His gaze narrowed at me now, my emotions probably running across my face with reckless abandon, making it obvious what I thought about.

Because I was still staring at him while I ran through all my considerations about trusting him or not.

I swallowed and looked away just as a cawing sound echoed through the suite. Clove swooped in through the threshold, her black and white feathers splayed in a manner that showed off all her falcon glory. My lips curled at the sight of her, my heart warming from the nearness of my familiar.

"Hello, Clove," I welcomed her.

She cooed in response, then dropped something in my lap from her long talons. I glanced down at it, curious, then froze at the sight of blood on my blouse and skirt.

"Oh," I breathed, my eyes widening.

"It seems your familiar brought you a present," Zeph said, his amusement palpable.

"What the hell is it?" Ella asked, clearly horrified by the dead, uh, *thing* in my lap. It was definitely an animal of some kind, but it seemed to be a cross between a rodent and a bird.

Zeph reached over to pick up the item by its long, wiry tail and held up the grotesque sight before us. "It's a stonepecker," he marveled, his tone suggesting we should be impressed.

"A *what?*" Ella gaped at it. "It looks like a possum mated with a… a…" She squinted at the sharp-looking beak. "A woodpecker?"

Zeph considered and nodded slowly. "I can see the resemblance, yeah. They're a bit of a nuisance, yet incredibly powerful. And they're known to absorb enchantments from whatever rock or stone they choose to destroy by pecking, hence the name *stonepecker*."

He set the dead little guy on the coffee table, then glanced at Clove. She'd perched on the back of the recliner chair and was busy preening her feathers.

"Seems someone's been playing in the LethaForest," he mused.

"The LethaForest?" I repeated.

He nodded. "Stonepeckers are nearly extinct as a result of them being a nuisance to Midnight Fae housing structures. Their ability to absorb enchantments also enables them to be used for nefarious purposes, such as circumventing wards or runes."

"What do you mean?" I asked, not understanding.

Zeph brought his ankle up to rest on his opposite knee and stared thoughtfully at the animal, his brow furrowing. "Many important Midnight Fae establishments are protected by wards. You've seen the Academy walls; they're riddled with protection charms."

"The snake vines," I said, nodding.

"And many others," he replied, his expression darkening. "They're controlled by a variety of spelled runes to ward off any evil intentions. But if a stonepecker were to peck at some of the surrounding walls, it could absorb the magic, which could then be used by a Midnight Fae to create a counterspell."

"A counterspell," I repeated. "Like to dismantle the protection spells?"

He nodded, his focus still on the stonepecker. "Yes. It would essentially create a safe portal for the fae to enter and exit through. It may also allow the fae to craft a shield of sorts to deflect any and all counterattacks that may be incurred after harming someone or something inside of the protected structure."

"Such as blowing up a building and writing *Alqisian* in flames above the destruction," I suggested, following his train of thought.

"Yeah. Just like that." He looked at Clove, then at me. "Your familiar just brought us evidence."

"That can't be good," Ella interjected. "I mean, especially after Aflora sang about..." She trailed off, her hands twisting in her lap.

"I didn't do this," I promised.

"Oh, I know you didn't," she replied without missing a beat. "I'm just..." She cleared her throat and looked past me at Zeph. "Is someone setting her up?"

My eyes widened as I glanced back at Zeph.

His expression turned grim. "That's certainly what it seems like. Why else—"

"We have a problem," Shade announced as he materialized across the room. He started toward us, then paused at the sight on the table. "Why the fuck is there a dead stonepecker in the living room?" Then his gaze widened. "Oh, shit. You need to dispose of that. Right fucking now. Before the Warrior Bloods arrive."

"She didn't do it!" Ella blurted out, jumping up to her feet in a defensive stance. "She was with us the whole damn time. I will go in front of those Council idiots myself if I have to. And fuck their male chauvinist bullshit; I will bang down their damn doors and scream at the top of my lungs."

Shade blinked at her, then glanced at me and Zeph. "What is she going on about?"

"Clove brought the stonepecker to Aflora," Zeph explained, gesturing at the blood residue on my uniform. "We believe someone is trying to set her up for this."

Shade huffed a laugh. "Close, but no. The attack has Elite magic all over it, and my father is blaming Kols."

My jaw dropped. "*What?*"

"There's no time to explain. The Warrior Bloods are on their way to conduct a thorough search of the premises, and *that* cannot be here." He pointed at the stonepecker.

"That's ridiculous," Zeph scoffed. "Kols was in my class during the explosion. There's no way he did this."

"While I agree, the scene reeks of source power. And Kols—"

"Is the one closest to the source," Zeph finished for him, cursing under his breath.

Shade dipped his chin once in confirmation, his icy gaze holding a touch of unease. "He looks good for the setup, Zeph. Which means someone is trying to take down the future king."

"Where's Tray?" Zeph asked.

"With Kols. He's the second potential suspect for obvious reasons." Shade ran his fingers through his dark hair and blew out a breath. "I need to get back before they notice I'm gone. I came to warn you that the Warrior Bloods are on their way to conduct a search, authorized by the king himself. So I suggest you hide anything incriminating." His expression flashed with meaning.

Then he vanished into a puff of smoke.

Zeph immediately pulled out his wand and uttered a spell that incinerated the evidence on the table. Then he uttered another one after it that caused the surface to shimmer. He spoke so quickly and efficiently that I couldn't even decipher his words. When he focused on me next, I opened my mouth to stop him, but the magic was already working its way over my outfit and destroying all evidence of the creature from my lap.

I gaped at my pristine uniform.

"Well, that's one way to do laundry," Ella muttered, then shook her head. "Okay, there's something I don't understand."

"Only one thing?" I asked, completely taken aback by the last few minutes of conversation and the revelations Shade had dropped on us.

"Well, many things. But what I really want to know is, why did Shade just come here to warn us? He hates Kols. I'd expect him to be gloating and celebrating the accusation, not"—she waved her hand around the space he'd just vacated—"you know."

Zeph cleared his throat. "Well—"

A commotion at the door interrupted his ability to reply as three Warrior Bloods entered the suite with an irritated Sir Kristoff right behind them. "Fucking royals overriding royals," the stone creature muttered. He waved at them and looked at Zeph. "I'm taking the night off." His stone wings bristled and crunched, then he disappeared into a cloud of white chalk.

"They can do that?" I asked, shocked.

"Unfortunately," Zeph muttered, standing up. At some point, he'd put his wand away, but I sensed his magic lingering in the air. "What the hell are you doing here?" he demanded, his attention on the three male fae in the foyer.

"We're here on order of the king to search Prince Kolstov's suite for anything related to the attack today," the one with white-blond hair to his shoulders replied, his tone devoid of emotion.

"You can't be fucking serious." Zeph folded his arms. "What the hell could Kols have to do with any of this?"

"That's Council business," another of them replied, his chin notching upward in clear dismissal. "You're no longer privy to that information, *Headmaster.*"

"Oh, fuck you, Danqris. I'm Guardian-bonded to Kolstov, which makes me your superior by default. A temporary demotion will never change that."

Danqris's lips pulled back into a snarl. "It will if I find anything that incriminates his ass."

Zeph scoffed at that. "Yeah, be my guest, asshole. But when you don't find anything, and Kols returns to see that you've destroyed all his shit, I'll be sure to tell him who to thank."

The Warrior Blood seemed to take that as more of a challenge than a threat and proceeded to rip apart the suite. When he reached my room, he demanded I unlock it.

And then began to destroy everything inside.

Including my new plant.

Zeph vibrated with anger by the end, but it was nothing compared to Ella. She actually slapped two of the Warrior Bloods after they rummaged through her personal items. Then she kicked the one called Danqris when he went for her underwear drawer.

I watched in amazement as they actually backed off, the blond one even looking a tad contrite as he sidestepped her to exit the bedroom.

After what felt like hours of unnecessary damage, the three Warrior Bloods left without a shred of evidence.

Clove hadn't moved from the recliner, having chosen to nap there while they rummaged through the suite. But I sensed her alertness, as if waiting for me to call her to my aid should I need it.

I wondered why she brought me the stonepecker, if it was something she found outside the walls or if she was trying to tell me something.

My suspicions told me it was the latter, but I couldn't figure out what she wanted me to know aside from the obvious—the perpetrator had used a stonepecker to breach the Academy walls.

"I'm going to fucking kill those assholes," Ella seethed as soon as they left, her eyes flashing with blue fire as she took in the mess they left behind.

"Kols will take care of them," Zeph promised. "But in the interim, we should probably clean this shit up."

Ella muttered a few more choice words before pulling out her wand. "I'll be in my bedroom."

Zeph nodded, his gaze catching mine. "Come on. I'll help with your room."

"Oh, you don't have to do that. I can, uh, well, I can pick up everything," I finished lamely, my lips twisting to the side.

I totally had this. I would just put everything away by hand. How hard could it be?

CHAPTER SIXTEEN

ZEPH

"I totally do not have this," I heard Aflora mutter to herself on the threshold of her room.

My lips twitched as I took out my wand and created a pair of figments. "Put everything back where it was two hours ago." They would be able to sense the history of objects to know where each item went.

The two invisible entities started immediately, causing items to essentially float across the room as they followed my edict.

"When you're done in here, work on the kitchen, then the study area and the other guest room."

They didn't reply, but I felt their agreement through my magical bond to them.

I left them to it and followed Aflora's scent down the hallway to her room, where I found her standing in the center of a disaster zone with her hands on her hips. "You sure you don't want my help?" I asked her softly.

She studied the shattered pot in the corner, her brow furrowing. "Why did they destroy the fairy plant? I mean, what could it possibly have been hiding?"

"They were being assholes," I told her from the entrance of her room, my hands in my pockets. "Want me to teach you a spell that can fix it?"

She glanced over her shoulder at me. "We can fix it?"

I smiled. "Magic can fix almost anything, Aflora." I pushed off the door frame and walked toward her. "Here, take out your wand and face the plant."

Surprisingly, she did exactly what I requested, her focus intense as she surveyed the corner. "Okay. Now what?"

I lightly pressed my chest to her back, then drew my fingers down her arm to the hand holding her wand. "Lift it up to about here," I explained, guiding her wrist upward. "You want to aim at the plant and draw a U just like this." I demonstrated while I spoke by moving her hand subtly into the shape I described before leading her back to the beginning point and releasing her. "Now repeat that action while saying, '*Illa'shala.*'"

She cleared her throat, then followed my instructions to the letter. Excitement hummed through her as the object adhered to her command to repair itself.

"Try it again on your closet door," I suggested.

"But the plant isn't done."

"Don't worry. The spell will continue until it's finished or until you tell it to stop. Trust me."

She shot me a look over her shoulder, one that said she didn't trust me in the slightest, then grimaced upon realizing what she'd just done.

I didn't comment, allowing the moment to pass, and waited for her to try the spell again.

After a few seconds, she conceded, her shoulders tense as if expecting the enchantment to backfire. When it didn't, she visibly relaxed.

"Now say, '*Badan clothes,*' and do a zigzag motion over the closet," I murmured.

"Zigzag, like this?" She drew her wand through the air in a Z pattern.

"Yes, but don't exaggerate your wrist that much." I reached for her again, this time placing a hand on her hip while my opposite reached for her hand. She didn't tense, so I took it as an invitation to press my chest to her back again, then brought my lips to her ear. "Like this." I guided her through a much smaller Z, then drew my fingers up her arm to rest on her shoulder. "Try it."

She did and grinned as her wardrobe pieced itself back together. I was about to tell her to repeat the command for her shoes when she beat me to it, her boots and other articles lining themselves up in the same place they'd been before Danqris had sent a tornado through her things.

Aflora focused on her dresser next, using the same command, then looked at her books. "Do I restack those manually?"

"You could, or try the same spell and see what happens." I still had my hands on her with my chest pressed to her back, so I felt her hesitation once more. But rather than look at me questioningly, she chose to utter the incantation.

All her school supplies returned to her nightstand and to her spot in the corner where she seemed to keep her books.

"You need a desk," I realized, frowning at the space.

"There's not enough room for it," she replied.

She was right. "Okay." I considered for a moment. "I want you to draw a square in the air and say, '*Kala'key bookcase.*' And when you do it, picture the kind of bookshelf you'd like in the corner."

"I thought *Tareero* was the spell for wanting something?"

"Only food. *Kala'key* is how you create something, but you have to be very specific in your mind and make sure to push that knowledge to your wand. Otherwise, nothing will happen. Or you'll get something you don't want. Depends on how it's done."

"That's… promising."

"Do as I said and you'll be fine." And if she didn't, I'd help her fix it.

"Right." She took a steadying breath, then muttered something about tulips under her breath.

My lips twitched in amusement. "Not flowers, a bookshelf."

"I'm concentrating," she chastised.

I released her shoulder to grab her hips with both hands. "Okay. I'll be right here."

She didn't seem to hear me, or perhaps didn't care, because she continued to stare at the corner like she could will the bookcase to appear without a spell. Which would be a neat trick and entirely possible for an older Midnight Fae, but she wasn't quite there yet.

After a few moments, she nodded, lifted her wand, and spoke the enchantment out loud while drawing her box. Then she added, *"Badan books."*

A floor-to-ceiling shelving unit appeared, the wooden poles on the sides decorated with vines of gorgeous blue blossoms that reminded me of her eyes. And on the shelves sat all her books, including the ones from her nightstand.

"Beautiful," I praised.

She gave a little clap and spun around to face me. "I did it."

"You did," I replied, smiling at her. Then I gestured with my chin to the ceramic pot in the opposite corner. "Looks like your plant is appreciative as well."

Aflora twisted toward it, her eyes widening. "Oh! How pretty!"

Hmm, I'd have to mention to Kols later that she'd finally figured out how to access her earth magic through the collar, which implied our earlier enchantment that diminished her power had finally worn off. We'd discuss it right after I told him how Clove delivered a stonepecker moments before the Warrior Bloods arrived.

My jaw ticked as I considered the situation. "When you're done in here, we need to talk about your familiar." I realized the mistake of my comment the minute I said it because Aflora froze, her excitement over the plant dying in an instant.

Fuck.

We still hadn't discussed that day in class when Raph killed Clove. I'd been in a mood, and it seemed right at the time to teach her a lesson about familiars and etiquette.

And yeah, that hadn't gone as planned.

She practically hated me after that.

"I mean in regard to the present she brought you," I amended quickly. "I want to make sure she's not enchanted or under the influence of another fae."

Aflora frowned at me. "You think someone cast a spell on her?"

"Why else would she bring you the stonepecker?" I countered.

My little mate didn't speak for a moment, her expression going from confused to wary. "What do you have to do to her to determine if she's been enchanted?"

I sighed. "I'm not going to hurt her, Aflora."

Her eyes told me she didn't believe me. "Okay."

Right. I'd have to prove it to her, then. "Are you done in here, or do you have other things to straighten up?"

"It's mostly good, I guess," she replied, noting the rumpled bedding, skewed rugs, and ripped blinds.

I called forth a third figment and told her to tidy up the mess.

Aflora's eyebrows lifted. "Why didn't you just show me how to do that?"

"Because the other spells provided a teaching moment."

"Since when do you like to teach?" she asked, her gaze holding a touch of humor that lightened the atmosphere a little between us.

"Never," I admitted. "But I don't mind teaching you." It was the truth, but I didn't expect her to accept it. Rather than wait around for another of those distrusting looks, I said, "Come on. Let's go have a chat with Clove."

"A chat," she repeated with notable sarcasm. "Sure."

"I've been an ass and you don't trust me. That's fine." I wrapped my arm around her shoulders and hugged her to me, my lips going to her ear. "But keep it up and I'll torment you for the rest of the evening and day with my tongue."

"You do that in my dreams already," she pointed out even while her cheeks blossomed into a beautiful shade of pink. "Nothing new there."

"Mmm." I drew my nose across her pretty flush until my lips hovered a scant breath away from hers. "Who said anything about dreams?" I pressed a chaste kiss to the corner of her mouth—the only place I'd allowed myself to truly kiss her outside of her mind. "I'm in your room, Aflora. Right now. Right here. None of this is a dream, and I will absolutely tease you with my tongue on that freshly made bed. Just say the word, pixie flower."

She shivered, her arousal scenting the air in a sultry aroma I longed to taste.

But I wanted to prove myself first.

And for that, I needed Clove.

With a lingering kiss to the same place as before, I released her, grabbed her hand, and tugged her into the hallway without another word.

If we stayed in her room for a second longer, I'd forget all about my task and make undressing Aflora my sole priority. But she wasn't ready yet, and I refused to push her more than I already had.

"You still have your wand, right?" I asked her.

She waved it in response, her knuckles white from clasping the end of it so harshly.

I smirked, understanding why. She'd been teased all week and desired a climax, one I would give her if things went well later.

Clove hadn't moved from her perch on the recliner, her feathers smoothed back and her eyes alert. She watched me with a similar wariness to her master's, confirming everything I already knew about Aflora's confidence in me.

"Raph isn't here," I assured both of them. "Last I saw him, he was sleeping in my closet on a bed of shirts he'd taken off the racks." He was a dick like that and enjoyed creating nests out of my clean clothes.

Clove bristled at our approach, her dark eyes narrowing at me.

I let go of Aflora's hand and stepped away from her slowly before holding out my palm for the falcon to sniff. She didn't budge, her displeasure evident.

"You're going to have to get used to me," I murmured. "I'm one of Aflora's mates."

This didn't seem to placate Aflora's familiar. If anything, she appeared even more anxious.

I tried for a different tactic and kneeled before her, making myself appear inferior, then held out my palm again. "I'm sorry for our first introduction. I promise not to harm you again."

If Kols saw me right now, apologizing to a bird, he'd lose his shit. But this wasn't about the falcon. It was about Aflora.

I had hurt her.

For us to move forward, she needed to see that I knew how to apologize properly. Which required me to get this falcon to essentially forgive me.

Clove tilted her head slightly, her intelligent gaze on my hand.

She shifted forward and snagged my fingers with her beak, biting down hard enough to warn without breaking the skin.

I didn't move.

I didn't even flinch.

Instead, I continued to stare at her. "If you need to exact blood, then fine. I'll give it." Mostly because one taste would tell her who I was to her master and she'd immediately release me.

"Don't," Aflora said, talking to Clove. "Zeph is… a friend."

Just a friend? I nearly asked her, amused. But I kept quiet, allowing her to run the show. It was what the situation necessitated.

Clove slowly released my hand, her gaze flicking affectionately to Aflora.

"Yeah, I like her, too," I admitted softly.

The falcon let out a gentle caw that I interpreted to mean she approved, so I slowly reached out to touch one of her plumes. She didn't react or try to bite me again, which was a good sign. She even leaned into my touch a little, allowing me to win her over with a few gentle strokes down her wings.

I glanced at Aflora to see her staring at me in surprise. "What?"

"You… you…" She shook her head. "Never mind."

"Surprised your falcon forgave me?" I asked her.

"No. I'm surprised you said you liked me. I'm pretty sure you implied the opposite just a few weeks ago."

I frowned. "I never said I disliked you."

"No, you're right," she said, her blue eyes flickering with fire. "You called me pitiful, like Clove."

I flinched. "I was trying to teach you a lesson."

"That you have to kill to protect yourself. I remember."

We were never going to move past this if she wouldn't allow it. And I could only apologize so much.

I sat back on my heels and stared at her. "The Midnight Fae world isn't like your Elemental Fae one, Aflora. I'm only trying to prepare you for survival, something I'm going to take even more seriously now that our souls are tied together."

"I already said I could try unbinding us."

"And I already told you no," I snapped, irritated that she'd even think to bring it up again. "If you release us, you'll implode."

"That's not really your concern, is it?" she retorted.

"That's where you're wrong, Aflora. It *is* my concern. I'm a Warrior Blood. It's literally my job to guard and protect." I ran my fingers through my hair and sighed. "At some point, I vowed to keep you safe. I can't say when it happened, but I suspect it was shortly after we met. I claimed you before I allowed myself to realize it."

I really didn't know what else to say to convince this female that all I ever wanted was to help her survive. Maybe I'd been hard on her, but I didn't know any other way. Warrior Bloods weren't exactly known for their gentle touch.

She stared at me for another long, hard moment. Then looked at Clove. "What was it you needed to check?"

Part of me admired her for yanking us back to the important topic at hand. The other part was disappointed because it left our conversation unfinished, and I was really tired of her holding the past against me. We couldn't move forward if she continued to hate me for what I'd allowed Raph to do to Clove.

Rather than harp on it, I followed her lead, knowing full well we'd return to this topic again soon.

"We need to see if she has any energy strands circling her," I replied. "If someone enchanted her, their signature would be left behind for a few hours."

"And if someone didn't?" she asked.

I shifted my focus to Clove. "There really aren't many options. It could be a coincidence, which I doubt. Or someone asked her to take it to you as a message."

"Fae can do that?"

"Fae that are close to you in some way, like a mate." I almost wanted to suggest that Shade could have done it, but I knew that was impossible considering he was at the Council meeting and had been clearly shocked by the stonepecker on the table. He also wouldn't have popped in to warn us if he wanted to set up Kols.

"Close to me," she repeated. "Like a mate… or family?"

I lifted a shoulder. "Yeah, I think a family member could call a familiar." I studied Clove, searching for any traces of magic. Most fae wouldn't be stupid enough to leave visible evidence, but it was worth checking.

Unfortunately, I saw nothing.

"You'll need to do a tracing spell," I told her. "Or I can do it, if you prefer." I glanced at her, expecting her to agree to the former.

However, she surprised me by saying, "You do it. I'll watch and learn." My face must have registered some shock, because she added, "If you hurt her, I'll make you eat a burning thwomp."

"You seem really fond of the notion of eating burnt wood," I replied. "It's making me question Elemental Fae diets."

"Ha. Ha." She rolled her eyes, but I caught the hint of amusement teasing her lips. "Go on and test her for energy strands."

I grinned. "Then afterward, I'll make you some fire gnat juice."

"Or another dragon steak," she offered.

"Or that," I agreed, winking. Then I took out my wand and gave Clove my undivided attention. "Let's see who sent you, shall we?"

CHAPTER SEVENTEEN

KOLS

What a fucking night.

I blew out a disgruntled breath as I entered my suite, expecting to see the whole thing shredded to hell and pausing upon discovering the pristine interior awaiting my entry.

"They cleaned," Tray explained from the couch, catching my confusion. He had a content Ella snuggled up against him, her head pillowed against his shoulder. "Zeph and Aflora are actually in your room finishing up, and there are some leftovers on the stove, if you want any."

He had an empty plate on the table, suggesting he'd just finished eating. As he'd only left about thirty minutes ahead of me, that timing made sense.

"I'm not hungry," I admitted, still riled up and pissed off from the bullshit the Council had thrown at me.

The only reason they hadn't locked me up for observation was because of Aflora. My father had argued that I needed to be on campus with her to continue her monitoring. Others had suggested she be locked up with me. Then he'd reminded them of my role as future king and the importance of completing this task for my upcoming ascension.

It was all a fucking mess.

And I really just wanted to take a damn nap.

Tray nodded in understanding, then kissed Ella on the forehead, holding her close. "I'll put the leftovers in the fridge for you," he said.

"Thanks," I muttered, meaning it despite my gruff tone. "I'm going to go make sure Zeph hasn't rearranged my room."

"Good idea." He returned his focus to the blonde in his arms, his palm cupping her cheek as he angled her face upward to receive his kiss.

I had spent the last three and a half years envying him and his ability to choose. Not that I'd ever admitted it out loud. My destiny was to serve the crown, a future I'd taken seriously and devoted my entire life to fulfill.

However, tonight the Council rewarded my fealty with an unwarranted accusation followed by a search of my private quarters, all to hunt for evidence that didn't exist.

No one had believed my innocence.

Not even my father.

After everything I'd given up for those assholes, they'd refused to take me at my word.

And that fucking burned.

I yanked on the knotted tie at my throat and started down the hallway to my room, only to pause on the threshold at the sight of Aflora giggling. She sat cross-legged on my rug with a plate in her lap, while Zeph stood over her with his hands on his hips.

"Seriously, I'm going to start feeding you bark," he was saying. "Maybe topped with some charcoal blades."

"Is that what it's called?" she asked. "The black grass in the fields?"

He snorted. "Yeah, that's not grass, pixie flower."

"Well, I know. It's sharp and brittle and… charcoal-y."

His lips twitched. "Hence the name—charcoal blades."

Her nose scrunched upward. "I'm not eating that."

"Yet you'll eat a leafy salad patty monstrosity with mussleberries."

"They're mouseberries," she corrected him. "And yes, I would eat that." She held up her plate. "Please."

"I've already fed you dragon steak and the other version of salad patty. If you want more, you can make it yourself."

I leaned against the doorjamb, entertained by this entire exchange. But my movement drew both their eyes to me and caused Aflora to jump up off my rug and onto her feet. "Oh! You're back."

"I am." I tucked my hands into my pockets and glanced around my room. "Seems like you did a good job cleaning."

"Figments," Aflora said quickly. "Zeph made figments. We were just making sure it's all sorted. So, uh, looks good. I'll leave you two to it, then." She started toward the door, and I moved to block her exit.

"I'm nearly arrested for an explosion at the Academy, and you're going to leave me with a 'looks good'?" I arched an eyebrow at her. "Seriously?"

Zeph came up behind her, effectively caging her between us. She lifted the plate to her chest like that would be able to protect her.

"Um." She bit her lip, considering. "I'm glad you're okay. We know you didn't do it. Oh, and Clove had no magical ties that Zeph could find. So we're not sure who gave her the stonepecker or where she found it, but we're pretty sure it was done on purpose to set you up. It's a good thing Shade stopped by to warn us about the search."

That was a hell of a lot of information in a handful of seconds. I gaped at Zeph. "Stonepecker?"

"Yeah. Aflora's familiar brought it to her as a gift and dropped it in her lap. We're guessing it's how the culprit entered the Academy grounds, but I had to destroy it because of the Warrior Bloods."

Of course. "What about my other things?" I asked him, knowing he'd interpret my question.

He jerked his chin at the closet. "Sir Kristoff did his job."

I nodded. "Good."

Aflora's brow creased. "I thought Sir Kristoff took the night off?"

I grunted and put my hands on her hips to walk her backward into my Guardian's chest, then kicked my door closed behind me. "Sir Kristoff doesn't take time off," I said, releasing her to Zeph. He promptly wrapped his arms around her, knowing I didn't want her to leave. The two of them watched as I walked over to my closet. As soon as I opened it, the gargoyle in question came strolling out with my box.

"Here you go, My Prince," he drawled, holding it up for me.

"Thank you, Sir Kristoff," I murmured. "You're excused."

He bowed and disappeared into a white cloud of dust, his trademark exit.

"Now he's taking the night off?" Aflora guessed.

"No, he's gone back to the front door," I replied, my focus on the box in my hands. I opened it to check the contents inside and nodded. "All here."

"Then the gargoyle did his job," Zeph murmured.

I nodded. "He did."

"What's in the box?" Aflora asked, unusually bold tonight. Or maybe she was just getting more comfortable with us, in which case, I approved.

"Your real collar and a few other items I don't want the Council to know about." Such as the photo of her parents from Sol.

I went to my closet to return the container to the rightful place, one Sir Kristoff knew about so he could hide it again should the need arise.

While my father commanded the kingdom, the gargoyle's allegiance belonged to me. I'd seen to that minor detail the day I started attending the Academy. It was an easy task, mostly because I treated Sir Kristoff with respect and listened to his requests. A few negotiations later and his loyalty was mine.

"My real collar?" Aflora asked, touching the thin leather around her throat. "I thought that's what Zeph put on me before the guards came for me last week."

I met his gaze over her head, wondering if he wanted to explain it or if I should. He gave a subtle nod for me to go ahead.

"This isn't the collar from the Council," I said softly, stepping in front of her again. I lifted my finger to the leather encircling her neck and traced it along her throat. "Remember how there were two before?"

She nodded. "I destroyed one in the LethaForest."

"Yes. So Zeph and I created a new one to replace it, but we had to make it match the one from the Council. We added a temporary enchantment to mask your powers—specifically, your Quandary Blood abilities—and also created a concealment charm to hide our bonds to you. It was done hastily, but it worked."

I pressed my thumb to the side, near her pulse, and unsnapped the leather to bring it away from her neck to see it.

"The spells have slowly worn off over the last week, bringing the concealment to a dull thrum that should only be protecting our bonds, not diminishing your power. Have you felt it weakening?" I asked her softly.

She frowned at the item in my hand. "I hadn't thought much of it after that initial zing."

"I imagine that hurt," I replied, regretful. "But we didn't know what else to do, and there wasn't time to explain."

"So you never put the real collar on me."

I shook my head. "No. Just touching it zaps all the energy right out of me. I can't imagine what it would do around your neck." Which was precisely why I'd never make her wear it.

Zeph bent down to kiss her freshly exposed skin, his eyes holding mine the entire time. I read the message in his depths, just as I noted her sharp inhale.

"Oh," she breathed, her lashes fluttering a little. "I… I didn't realize they were… different."

I set her collar off to the side and returned to brush my knuckles down her flushed cheek. "The primary purpose of that collar is to hide your connection to me and Zeph." I showed her the band around my wrist. "Zeph and I have to wear these, or others will sense the mating claim. Shade doesn't need one since everyone already knows he bit you."

"I think we can remove them for a bit," Zeph mused, his lips still at her neck. "Assuming we're all staying here for the next few hours."

My lips curled. "I think we're staying here for a while."

Aflora swallowed, her pupils darkening. "Are you going to bite me again?"

"Do you want us to?" I countered, removing the cuff around my wrist and setting it beside her collar. Zeph held out his for me to add to the pile, then grabbed her hips to hold her between us as I returned to my position in front of her.

"Do you, uh, need blood again?" she asked.

"Not really, no. I had a shake just yesterday."

"A shake?" Her brow furrowed. "You call humans 'shakes'?"

I smirked. "No. I mean a literal milkshake. Tray and Ella make them all the time instead of feeding on mortals."

"They do?"

"You've never noticed?" I countered, arching a brow. "Ella has a protein shake flavored with blood every evening."

"I thought it was just a human food."

"It is, mostly. With the added nutrients Midnight Fae need to remain connected to the source. Zeph's been ordering blood-laced food as well."

"Not my favorite, but I need to get used to it," he said, lifting a shoulder.

"Why?" Aflora asked.

She tried to glance back at him, but he pressed his mouth to her ear to murmur, "Because Midnight Fae with mates typically don't feed on humans. It complicates matters, as you found out last week with your reaction to

Kols feeding in the mortal realm. We're territorial and we don't like to share."

"So no more drinking blood from the vein, unless it's from your vein," I said, closing the space between us. "And I won't bite you again until you ask me to." Or if I needed to suck power out of her, but I didn't add that part, because it would be implied consent like it was the first time.

"Yes," Zeph agreed softly. "We heard you loud and clear last week, pixie flower. No more sharing."

"I-I didn't say that," she stuttered, her chest rising and falling in fast pants against mine.

"It was implied by your reaction," I informed her. "And we did discuss exclusivity, if I remember correctly."

"We never agreed to it," she pointed out.

"Again, it was implied." I drew my finger down the center of her torso, fondling the buttons of her blouse along the way. "I've had one hell of a night, Aflora. There's really only one thing I want to do right now, and that's to make you come with my mouth. May I?"

Aflora's eyes widened. "Like, really come? Or just tease me more?"

"There will definitely be teasing involved," I promised her, unfastening the top button of her shirt. "But it will lead to a climax that will blow your mind."

An arrogant assessment, but that didn't make it any less true.

The glimmer in her flaring pupils told me she knew it, too.

"Okay," she whispered, leaning back into Zeph. "But if this turns into a dream where you leave me unfulfilled, I really will break our bonds."

"Then I guess we'll need to bite you again, too," Zeph replied, his tongue tracing the shell of her ear. "Can't risk having you force us out."

"Please me and you won't have to worry," she countered, causing my lips to curl.

"Mmm, I rather like this bolder side of you," I mused, popping another button to expose her lacy bra. "Take off your panties for us, baby. Then give them to Zeph."

She shivered, her irises smoldering with intensity. "Yes, My Prince," she whispered, the title going straight to my cock. Zeph had told her to call me that the other night in one of our fantasies, and hearing her use it now made me want to kiss the ever-living fuck out of her.

But instead, I focused on the next button while she lifted her skirt to take hold of the lace between her thighs. She slowly drew it down her legs. I stepped back to allow her to bend while Zeph watched from behind, his green eyes glimmering with anticipation.

Aflora pulled the soft white material over her bare feet, then straightened and held it over her shoulder for Zeph. He took them and nodded at me to finish removing her blouse.

Each button revealed more and more of her creamy skin, drawing my focus downward to admire her subtle curves and flat abdomen. She really was beautiful. It almost hurt to look at her.

Her shirt fell to the floor, leaving her in a bra and skirt, the picture of "naughty schoolgirl." My mouth twitched at the thought of all the ways I could make that title come true, but instead I allowed Zeph to walk her backward to the bed.

"Remove your bra," I told her. "Zeph wants it."

I didn't move from my spot, my hands going to my tie instead to finish unknotting the silk and remove it from my neck.

"On the bed," Zeph said, taking over as soon as her gorgeous tits spilled into view.

She handed him her lacy bra without an ounce of nervousness and hopped up onto the mattress.

"Lie on your back and grab the bars of the headboard," Zeph instructed her.

Aflora frowned but did as she was told. He'd slowly introduced her to his tastes over the last week, exerting his dominance at every turn. This experience would be similar, his methods mostly gentle as a result of not wanting to frighten her.

And this would be the first time he truly touched her.

To my knowledge, the two of them hadn't even kissed yet. Because the dreams didn't really count. They were just erotic fantasies driven by playing minds.

I walked forward to lay my tie over her abdomen as Zeph secured her wrists above her head with the lace of her panties and bra. She watched him with surprise in her gaze, then flickered her focus to the silk on her stomach, her brow pinched.

But she wasn't entirely concerned.

No, she was equally turned on. Her nipples had stiffened to taut little peaks that begged for a man's mouth. Goose bumps stampeded an alluring path down her arms. And her arousal sweetened the air, forcing me to inhale her aromatic scent with every breath.

She liked this.

She wanted this.

Something she confirmed by clenching her thighs and fighting a moan as Zeph drew his fingers down her arm and over her breast to the tie waiting for him near her belly button.

"We're going to play a game, Aflora," he informed her softly.

"What kind of game?" she asked, her voice holding a sultry quality to it that made my blood pump a little faster.

"One where you guess who is touching you," he murmured, trailing my silk tie up her neck. "If you're right, we'll reward you." The garment met her cheek. "And if you're wrong, we'll teach you."

"Teach me?" she repeated, her tongue sneaking out to lick her bottom lip. "Teach me what?"

"You'll see," he replied, draping the fabric over her forehead, preparing to slide it down. "Now close your eyes. We're about to begin."

CHAPTER EIGHTEEN

AFLORA

My heart thumped wildly in my chest, my breathing escalating with each passing second. My mates had gone quiet after Zeph had slid the silk over my eyes. I could hear their clothes shifting, the sounds of zippers unfastening, and fabric dropping to the floor. But I didn't know who was where or what they intended to do.

Heat warmed my insides, the intensity mounting with each inhale and subsequent exhale.

What did they plan to do?

What if they left me like this?

In my dreams, they often teased for hours and hours. They might do the same now and deny—

I jolted as a palm gently wrapped around my ankle, then slipped slowly upward, tracing my leg all the way up to my inner thigh where a single finger brushed my slit. A moan escaped my mouth, only to be swallowed by one of their mouths.

Oh…

The tickle of hair against my chin told me who this was.

Zeph.

My assumption was confirmed in the next breath as his tongue parted my lips and demanded control inside my mouth. His woodsy scent poured over me, claiming me, overpowering me, *devouring* me. I'd thought he was dominant in my dreams, but the reality was so much *more*.

His strength became mine, emboldening me and making me long to free my hands to thread my fingers through his hair.

My thighs squeezed together, drawing my focus back to the hand between them. That had to be Kols, or I'd feel the heat of Zeph's arm across my torso, but all I could sense was his mouth on mine.

Dear Fae, he was a good kisser. He led me every step of the way, his lips a confident presence against my own, teaching and taunting and hypnotizing me with every move.

I groaned as Kols's finger slid inside me, drawing my focus back to him.

Then someone grabbed my breast, his thumb flicking over my nipple and drawing a gasp from my throat.

Their hands were suddenly everywhere, confusing my senses and overwhelming my instincts. My veins burned with need, my lungs forgetting how to work, my throat raspy and dry.

Zeph's lips left mine, moving downward to my breast as Kols sealed his mouth around my clit. They sucked in unison, just like in my dreams, only the scrape of teeth against my core reminded me of Zeph more than Kols, leaving me confused.

Had they switched places? Zeph's mouth hadn't skimmed my neck on his way to my chest; he'd left me completely but only for a brief second. Or that was how it felt before sensation overloaded my—

"Oh!" I cried out, arching off the mattress.

That was *definitely* Zeph between my thighs. I recognized that rasp of his beard, teasing my sensitive lips. However, Kols had left his finger inside me.

No, not one.

Two.

He scissored them back and forth, enticing me closer to the edge with each twist. I lost myself to the heat and longing induced by their touch, their intimate kisses, and their licks and bites and nibbles.

A week of sensual torment created a maelstrom in my lower abdomen, shooting flames through my veins and forcing moans to tickle my throat.

I couldn't focus.

Forgot how to breathe.

Let go of all my thoughts and feelings and fears.

And allowed them to pull me into an oblivion that literally stole my consciousness for a brief moment, introducing me to the afterlife and beyond before pulling me back to the reality of their presence. One of them was chuckling. *Zeph.* The other had slipped down to feast on my arousal.

They were everywhere at once, driving me close to the edge again. "Not yet," Zeph said, pulling back. "We need to play our game first."

I growled in response to his idea of *playing a game*. I wanted to come again. *Right now.*

"Don't be greedy, little mate," he murmured, stretching out alongside me. Kols took my other side, the heat of their bodies bathing me in a lust-induced ecstasy that I longed to swim in forever.

They were naked.

I couldn't see them, but I could *feel* them. Zeph's impressive length met my hip, his cock pulsating with a desire I knew too well. He'd remained clothed in all our shared fantasies, never once allowing me to *see* him. And oh, how I yearned to see him now.

Then Kols pressed his groin to my opposite side, his arousal more familiar, yet not. We'd only been truly intimate once, and it hadn't ended well.

Now I had them both.

In reality.

Naked.

And I couldn't see either of them. Or touch them.

I must have growled again, because Zeph tsked. "None of that, Aflora. We let you come once—without my permission, mind you—so now we'll play a game."

I bit my lip, recalling all the times he'd demanded I ask for permission to orgasm. He had to be in control at all times, his dominance written into everything he did. And I'd broken one of his rules.

Which meant he intended to punish me for it, probably by denying more orgasms—another of his favorite activities. Or so I assumed, given everything he'd done to me over the last week.

"I'm sorry, Zeph. I forgot," I admitted.

He leaned in and pressed his mouth to mine in a tender kiss. "You're forgiven, pixie flower," he whispered, nuzzling my nose. "I loved watching you come in your dreams, but this…" He ground himself against my hip, then palmed my breast and gave it a sensual squeeze. "Mmm, this was so much sweeter and *real*."

His mouth captured mine, forcing me to taste my own arousal from his tongue. I moaned, my grip on the headboard tightening as I fought the urge to rip free from the lacy bondage around my wrists. His knots were loose— something I suspected was done for my benefit—but I didn't want to displease him by pulling away from the bonds too soon.

Something about Zeph made me want to obey him.

And so I did, kissing him as he kissed me and allowing him to guide me into the intimacy he craved.

However, I couldn't stop the sound of protest that left my lips as he pulled away, his mouth my new favorite addiction. He chuckled in response, his teeth nipping my chin. "Don't worry, pixie flower. I enjoy kissing you, too. But you need to answer a few questions for us first."

"Okay," I agreed, my cheeks warming.

Kols leaned in to kiss my neck, his lips finding my pulse as he hummed his approval against my skin. "I hope you answer correctly, sweetheart."

"Who kissed you first tonight?" Zeph asked, beginning the game.

"You," I answered without hesitation.

"Good girl," he replied, leaning down to take my mouth again, this time as a reward.

Kols continued to lick a path up and down my neck while Zeph possessed me with his tongue, the combined intensity forcing me to squeeze my legs together in search of necessary friction.

"Whose fingers slid inside you first, princess?" Kols asked against my ear. "Were they mine? Or did they belong to Zeph?"

I swallowed, this one not as clear. But I felt pretty sure it was Kols.

"Yours," I said. "You touched my ankle and slid up my leg and beneath my skirt, then Zeph kissed me."

He pressed his palm to my stomach before gliding down to repeat the action beneath my skirt, his two fingers sliding into me with ease to scissor once more, confirming I was right because it felt the same. "Who sucked your clit?" he asked. "Me or Zeph?"

"Zeph," I whispered, recalling the way his stubble felt against my flesh.

"And who brought you to orgasm?" Zeph asked, his lips still hovering over mine.

"Both of you," I replied on a moan as Kols hooked his fingers to stroke a spot inside me that caused stars to blink behind my eyes.

"You're amazing at this game," Zeph praised, his lips sliding to my ear. "Now we're going to feed you our cocks, and you're going to guess which one of us is inside you based on taste alone."

Kols removed his touch from below and brought his hand to my mouth. "Suck," he instructed, dipping his fingers into my mouth.

The wantonness of tasting myself on his skin had me groaning in approval, my heart hammering inside my chest. Then they were moving again, rearranging themselves on the bed and pulling my wrists free of the restraints.

I allowed them to guide me to where they wanted me, aware of who held me based on their scents alone. First, Kols guided me up onto my knees. Then Zeph twisted me around and urged me to bend forward until my palms met the mattress.

Neither male released me until they were sure I was steady, their palms tracking over every inch of me and lighting my skin on fire along the way. They shifted again, one of them moving behind me while the other positioned himself at my head. I recognized Kols's spicy scent as he nudged my chin upward to the angle he preferred.

Then the head of his cock kissed my lips.

I opened for him on instinct, allowing him to enter and indulging in his familiar flavor.

Cinnamon, spice, and man.

I groaned, swallowing him as deep as my throat allowed. His fingers twined in my hair, stilling me when I started to pull back for air. He seemed to be trying to catch his breath, perhaps even not make a sound, but I already knew it was him, something I would have told him if I could.

After a beat, he allowed me to move, my nostrils flaring to inhale much-needed oxygen, but he didn't let me pop him out of my mouth. Instead, he drove back in, his grip tightening as he forced me to take more of him.

I relaxed my throat, allowing him to drive while a hand slipped between my thighs to test my arousal. The kiss against the base of my spine told me Zeph approved of what he found.

That little gesture gave the game away, confirming what I already knew about their positions—Kols being in my mouth with Zeph behind me.

Zeph always guarded me in my dreams, his gaze ever watchful as if needing to reassure himself that I was enjoying the act. And he frequently touched me to gauge my interest in certain things, like he did now by sliding his finger through my damp folds.

It made me trust him, even when he took me outside of my comfort zone.

Kols left my lips slowly, drawing me back to him and eliciting a complaint from my throat. He caressed my cheek in response, then moved to switch places with Zeph.

I considered telling them I already knew who was where, but the velvety kiss of Zeph's arousal against the edge of my mouth distracted me.

Oh, yes, please. I wanted to taste him. To learn his likes and dislikes. To please him. To swallow his pleasure just as he did mine.

My lips parted for him, my tongue already moving to greet him as he slid inside far gentler than I expected. I could feel the tension in him, the way he held himself back, and for some reason, that made me want to push him. To see if I could dismantle some of his control and set him free.

Because I wanted to experience *him*, the man behind the dominance, the one who craved me without remorse. I'd seen that male lurking in his gaze, had felt him rising in my dreams, but had yet to experience him in the flesh.

I needed to devour him, to know him, to feel him inside me.

I wanted him to *come*.

I hollowed my cheeks, my throat working to take him deeper, only his palm gripped the back of my neck to pull me away from him instead. Kols's palms burned against my hips as he held me in place, the tip of Zeph's cock whispering against my lips.

I leaned forward to lick him, only to be held back by his hand around my neck. "You already knew it was me, didn't you, pixie flower?"

"Yes," I admitted. "Kols went first, but I wanted to taste you, so I didn't say anything."

He released my nape and drew his knuckles across my cheekbone in a tender manner. They both seemed keen on that little motion.

Actually, there were a lot of similarities between Zeph and Kols.

I knew they shared women, the rumors were rampant about it, but now I understood why. They worked well as a team. Even now with how Zeph gently stroked my face while Kols's thumbs drew hypnotic patterns against my hips.

Always touching and ensuring my comfort. Minus the orgasm denial bit.

Zeph slipped his thumb beneath the makeshift blindfold, slowly guiding it upward and over my head to allow me to see.

I blinked a few times, my eyes unadjusted to the light.

He pressed his palm to my cheek when I swayed a little, his strength providing me with the stability I needed to find my bearings once more. Meanwhile, Kols's thumbs continued that delirious pattern against my skin, the heat of his groin a firm presence at my backside and exciting my nerves.

I wanted them both inside me.

Now.

I looked up at Zeph, my lips parting on a demand. Only, whatever I'd been about to say died in my throat, my gaze hypnotized by the marvelous display of muscles and sinewy skin before me.

Oh, Fae… Removing the blindfold had been a really bad idea. I couldn't think, let alone speak.

Because wow.

Zeph was all man, every inch of him perfectly proportioned and sculpted from stone.

No wonder he could move so fast. He was solid muscle in warrior form. I felt small in comparison, almost inadequate, but equally intrigued.

What would he feel like inside me?

He drew his thumb over my bottom lip, which served as a notification that I was gaping at him with my mouth open. Not my proudest moment, but I was beyond caring at this point.

"I want to properly taste you," I told him. He'd barely been in my mouth at all.

"Do you?" he mused, his fingers gliding back into my hair to knock the blindfold the rest of the way off and onto the bed beside us. His gaze left mine to focus on Kols behind me. "She played our game very well. I think she deserves a reward."

CHAPTER NINETEEN

AFLORA

"I agree," Kols said, one of his palms moving to smooth over my back. "What did you have in mind?"

"A choice," he replied.

"Yeah?" He paused to consider, his finger gliding down my spine to rest at the bottom. "Hmm, yes. Give her the options, let her decide which way to go."

I shivered, intrigued by whatever they weren't saying out loud.

Kols's touch returned to my hips as he pulled me back to sit on my heels, his arms wrapping around me from behind in a cocoon of comforting warmth. Zeph reached forward to widen my legs, his gaze dropping to my core before slowly tracing up my torso to my breasts and eventually to my face.

My palms rested on my thighs in a natural position, something he seemed to approve of.

"She's perfect," he marveled.

"Yes," Kols murmured, his lips going to my neck to trail kisses up to my ear. "Gorgeous, too."

"A bit stubborn," Zeph added.

"Mmm, true, but also regal and intelligent and loyal," Kols whispered.

"And ours," Zeph said, his palm finding my cheek again as he leaned down to kiss me. "Fuck, I love your mouth, Aflora."

He didn't give me a chance to reply, his tongue dueling with mine in the next breath as he lost a fraction of his steadfast control. I reveled in it, excited that I held this mystical power over him, if only for a brief moment.

And then he snapped back, his green eyes blazing with lustful fire.

"You have two options," he said, finally addressing me again.

I would have commented on their penchant for talking about me like I wasn't in the room, but a darker part of me had enjoyed that a little. Almost like they'd provided me with a voyeuristic glimpse into their minds and what they truly thought about me.

"The first option is for you to stay just like this while Kols and I jack off onto your pretty pussy. Then Kols will lick you clean afterward and make you come until you can't speak anymore."

My heart kick-started at the visual his crass words created in my mind, and a fresh surge of warmth tickled the sensitive space between my thighs. *Yes. Yes, I want that.*

"Or," he continued, his gaze twinkling with dark secrets, "you can suck me off while Kols fucks you, then I'll go down on you and make you come so hard you'll lose consciousness for the night."

I stopped breathing.

The second option.

Definitely the second option.

He arched a brow. "Aflora?" he prompted, clearly unable to read my mind.

"Second," I managed to force out, my throat suddenly dry.

"Full sentences, pixie flower. Tell me what you want, or I'll decide for you."

Kols tugged on my earlobe before whispering, "Zeph has a thing for communication. Tell him explicitly what you want, and he'll give it to you."

Which meant I had to repeat the option I desired. Out loud. My legs clenched, the urge to touch myself hitting me hard in the chest. *Need. So much need.*

All driven by my mates teasing for nights on end.

And now I had the ability to soothe some of that aching fire. I just had to *speak.*

Zeph didn't push, his expression patient as he waited for me to gather my courage. I peeked down at his impressive length before allowing myself another thorough perusal of his sexy form.

Mine.

All mine.

I cleared my throat and met his smoldering gaze, my pulse pounding in my ears. "The second option," I said, my voice husky and nearly unrecognizable. "I want Kols to fuck me while I suck you off, then I want you to lick me clean."

His nostrils flared at hearing his words repeated back to him, and Kols's arms tensed, his breath shuddering out against my ear.

"I love hearing you say the word *fuck*," Kols admitted softly. "So damn hot."

"Get back on all fours," Zeph said, his dominance taking over once more.

Kols kissed my neck before helping me into the position. I trembled with need, my thighs quivering as he parted them to accommodate his larger form. The heat of his groin seared my insides as he aligned himself with my entrance, his hands smoothing down my sides.

I only had a second to ready myself before Zeph grabbed my jaw and drew my focus forward to the precum lingering on his tip in welcome invitation. "Lick," he ordered. Not that he needed to. I was already moving forward to taste him.

The second his essence met my tongue, I groaned, yearning for more, and took him into my mouth with an eagerness I didn't know I possessed.

Kols pushed inside me at the same time, his girth stretching me and forcing me to accept him as he slid home in a single thrust.

Zeph seemed to like the idea, because he replicated it in my mouth, forcing himself deeper than before and giving me my first real introduction to his strength and preferences.

I'd been right about him going easy on me before, and I suspected this was still his version of gentle, but his fingers knotted in my hair to guide me into his preferred rhythm. Kols must have known, because he matched the pace between my legs, both of them going long and deep and thorough, their groans aphrodisiacs to my senses.

"Make her come," Zeph demanded, his voice deeper and causing my thighs to spasm.

Kols kept one hand on my hip while smoothing his other along my side to my belly and lower to the place that burned for his touch. I jolted at the first stroke of his thumb, my body far more primed than I realized.

"I want to feel you moan around my cock," Zeph murmured, his thumb ghosting over my jaw as his opposite hand continued to drive the tempo. "Open your throat a little more, baby." He tilted my head to a new angle, his touch coaxing me to submit.

My body bent to his will, allowing him deeper access just as Kols pressed down on my clit. I screamed at the sensation, rapture shaking my limbs and lighting my soul on fire.

"Fuck," Zeph groaned, his movements increasing in time with Kols's. "That feels amazing."

"So damn tight," Kols breathed, his grip on my hip gentle while his opposite hand continued to strum out my pleasure below. "Fucking wet, too. *Shit*."

"Not yet," Zeph breathed.

"Fuck you," Kols bit out.

"I will do exactly that if you come before I'm ready."

Kols convulsed behind me, his body stilling against mine. "*Fuck*." He throbbed deep inside me, hitting a point that had me crying out in pain-induced pleasure. I wanted more of that.

So. Much. More.

Zeph pistoned between my lips, his green gaze capturing mine as my own eyes began to water from his harsh thrusts. I didn't dare tell him to stop, my throat parched and ready to accept his warmth.

"Your irises are alive with power," he whispered, his own irises flaring with wonder. "I've never seen anything so beautiful in my entire existence." His movements slowed, as if he were drawing out the moment, lost to the sensations of our embrace. Color flushed his cheeks, his abdominal muscles tensing. "Now, Kols."

"Thank fuck," Kols breathed, his hips picking up the pace and hitting me in that delicious place that made my legs go weak.

"She's going to come again," Zeph marveled, his voice strained.

Kols responded with his magical touch, his fingers and cock working me in tandem to draw me closer and closer to that edge of oblivion.

I felt drunk on their lust, their masculine growls, their mounting ecstasy, and their sensual knowledge. They knew exactly how to move and where to stroke me, their bodies working mine toward a realm of rapture only they had the keys to open.

Zeph groaned my name, followed by Kols, the two of them dragging me into a sea of sensation with them. Their hot essences bathed my insides, Zeph erupting down my throat at the same time Kols released deep in my channel, their joint exaltation yanking me into a world of bliss I'd never recover from.

They'd destroyed me.

Claimed me.

Made me theirs without having to bite me again.

Because I'd never be the same after this experience.

These two males had ruined me for anyone else.

No, not two.

Three.

Because I felt Shade inside me, too, his essence a shadowy kiss against my spirit. He wasn't here, yet he was at the same time.

I sighed in contentment, my eyes flickering open only to realize I'd been moved to the center of the bed, naked and warm and fully sated. Kols's palm rested on my belly, his opposite one propping up his head as he stared down at me.

"There you are," he murmured, leaning down to run his tongue over my mouth. "Zeph was worried we'd already exhausted you."

"I'm not one for incomplete promises," Zeph added from between my splayed thighs.

My eyes widened, my legs immediately threatening to close, but he held me open with ease, his body much larger than mine. Kols eased backward to allow me to better see the view and kept his palm firmly on my abdomen as if to hold me in place.

"I promised to knock you out with my tongue, Aflora," Zeph said softly. "I meant it." He leaned in to kiss my mound while his gaze held mine, then his mouth slid lower, forcing my back to come up and off the bed.

Kols pushed me back down, his chuckle a breath against my ear. "You're the one who wanted orgasms, love," he whispered, then drew his lips down to my throat and lower to my breasts.

"I can't... I'm not... Oh, Fae..." I couldn't form a single thought, let alone speak. The two of them were driving me insane, their mouths everywhere at once, their tongues wicked instruments of torture that they knew how to use all too well.

And before I knew it, I was flying once more, utterly captivated by them both and falling into an oblivion of insanity underlined with rapturous quakes.

My body hummed.

I screamed.

Their names resembled curses and prayers as they left my mouth.

Darkness consumed me, followed by light, and still I trembled, my world shattering over and over again. I lost track, unsure of who touched me where. All I knew was that I felt owned by them both.

And Shade, whose presence lingered in my mind.

What am I going to do? I wondered, overwhelmed.

A firm lick between my folds drew my attention downward, a plea on my lips for him to stop and grant me a reprieve. Only, the head between my thighs wasn't the one I anticipated.

Long white-blond hair.

Sinful silver-blue eyes.

I jolted, scooting backward until I hit the headboard of an unknown bed behind me, then brought my knees upward to my chest. Kols and Zeph were gone, and the sheets were a silky black very unlike the dark red ones I'd been in moments before.

"What are you doing here?" I breathed, gaping at the figment of my imagination.

"You called for me," he replied, prowling forward like a predatory cat, his upper body fitted muscular perfection. He even had those little muscles by his hips. I knew because I'd created them in my dreams. Just as I'd ensured he was well-endowed to round out the package. Yet tonight he wore black pants.

I cocked my head to the side. "You shouldn't be here."

"Why not?" he asked.

"Because I don't need pleasure right now." I frowned. "And… well, it's sort of wrong, I think. I mean, it wasn't before because my mates were being dicks. But now…" I trailed off, thinking. "It sort of feels like cheating."

His lips curled, amusement shining in his hypnotic gaze. "Cheating, hmm?"

I nodded. "I created you to avoid them."

"Did you?" He paused right before me on the bed, his chest pressing against my shins as he planted his palms on either side of my hips.

So big, I marveled. Even more muscular than Zeph, his shoulders broad and taking up my view of the room. "You shouldn't be here," I repeated on a whisper.

"Probably not," he agreed.

My brow furrowed. "So why are you here?"

"You tell me, little star." His voice dropped to a dark whisper that teased my senses. "Why do you think I'm here?"

"Because I've dreamt of you every day this week," I thought out loud. "So it was only natural to call you to me again."

"Definitely natural," he agreed, his face a few inches away from mine. "Did you think of me when they made you come?"

I shook my head and bit my lips. "No." But now I felt like I should have, which was ridiculous considering I made this guy up for my own personal satisfaction.

He didn't appear disappointed, just curious. "Did they bite you again?"

Shouldn't a figment of my own imagination already know the answer to that? "No."

Now he seemed pleased. "Good."

Odd. "You don't want them to bite me?"

"Not particularly, no," he admitted. "Do you want them to bite you?"

His words gave me pause. *Is this my subconscious's way of telling me I don't want them to mate me?* I wondered, the thought making me uneasy. "I... I don't know," I whispered. "Do I?"

"That's not for me to tell you," he replied, easing backward just a bit before moving to sit beside me with his long legs stretched out and crossed at the ankles.

He reminded me of sex. Dangerous, hot, sweaty sex. Not that we'd indulged in any of that in my fantasies. It'd always been him pleasing me, never the other way around.

Hence, fantasy.

I glanced at him. "Why are you here?"

"You already asked me that," he replied, amused.

"You never answered me."

"No, I didn't." He smiled. "Then again, I rarely do."

"Because it's all in my head," I muttered, understanding. "Are you supposed to be my conscious? Because that'd be kind of weird."

"Why is that?"

"Because I'm not sure what it would say about my mental state if, uh…" I shook my head, the consideration making me dizzy. "Never mind. You're just too attractive to be my mind."

"Oh, I don't know. I find your mind rather fascinating," he replied.

"You would say that as a figment of my imagination," I drawled back at him.

He chuckled. "And is that what I am?"

"What else could you be?"

"Maybe I'm one of your mates," he suggested.

I giggled. "Oh, what fun that would be. Zeph would just love you. Kols, too." They already wanted to kill Shade. Why not add Fantasy Guy to the mix? I giggled again. "That'd be entertaining."

"Wouldn't it?" He smiled, a pair of dimples appearing at the edges that made me giddy. He really was an attractive figment.

"I suppose you can stay around, but no more, uh"—I waved to my naked body—"no more of this. No more sex."

His silver-blue eyes lazily ran over my nudity, his palm reaching out to push my knees away to reveal my breasts to his view. "What if I want sex?"

"That can't happen."

"Why not?"

"Because it's cheating," I decided out loud. "I… I don't want to be unfaithful, even if it's just in my mind."

"What if it's me you are cheating on?" he asked, arching an ash-blond brow.

I snorted. "Cheating on my own mind. There's a riddle for you."

"Maybe it's true."

"You know it's not," I replied, amused. "I can't cheat on someone who isn't real."

"Then, by that definition, playing with me isn't cheating at all. Since you don't see me as real."

I considered that for a moment before saying, "No sex."

His lips curled again. "All right, little star. We'll play by your rules. For now." He reached for me and leaned in to kiss my forehead, his touch warm and tender and kind of perfect.

A sigh escaped me, something about his presence familiar and calming.

Maybe that was the real reason I called him to me—I needed some normalcy after being destroyed so completely by my mates.

Funny that a figment could make me feel *normal*.

"Sweet dreams, darling star," he whispered against my ear.

"Sweet dreams," I mumbled back to him, falling back into my delirious state.

An oceanic kiss met my senses, drowning me in a sea of bliss.

One that reminded me of my childhood and a memory just out of my reach.

Then, finally, I slept.

CHAPTER TWENTY

SHADE

I hid in the shadows, watching Aflora's lips curl as she slept. Kols and Zeph were passed out on either side of her, oblivious to her dreams.

But I knew.

I sensed his presence inside her, the dark power thriving through her veins. It'd been growing all week, culminating in tonight's events, and would continue to seduce her until fate forced her to make a choice.

It was only a matter of time before he came for her. I'd just hoped to have a better hold on her heart before it happened. However, her song had called for him in the village, the haunting melody carrying a spell with it that she hadn't understood.

Tray and Kols had been just as oblivious.

Similar to how Kols and Zeph were now.

I wanted to tell them, to shake them awake and point at the magical essence hovering over Aflora. But they wouldn't even be able to see it, let alone believe me.

Hell, they'd probably lose themselves to a fit of rage at realizing I was in the Royal Prince's bedroom without permission. But this entire situation went beyond the formalities of our society.

If we weren't careful, Zakkai would win.

My fists curled, failure a nagging sensation that churned in my abdomen.

This wasn't over.

Not yet.

She could still choose us.

I just hoped that when she did, it wouldn't be too late.

The darkness eventually lifted, the powerful fae releasing his hold on Aflora's dreams and dissolving into nothingness. I watched her for a beat, debating on entertaining a date in her mind, but her sigh of contentment had me stepping away from her, not forward.

She needed rest.

We'd play another day.

And I had business to tend to.

I cloaked myself in smoke, using it to pull me through time and space to the LethaForest where Kyros stood waiting for me in his trademark leather jacket and jeans.

"Huh. I timed you to arrive thirty seconds from now," he drawled in welcome. "I guess you were a bit less preoccupied with your pretty flower than I anticipated."

I rolled my eyes. "Let's just get this over with."

"So eager," he taunted, pushing away from the tree, the sword against his hip flaring with violet flames. "All right, my shadowy friend. We'll start in New Orleans, as I have a few idiots to question there first. Then we'll move on to Dallas."

I narrowed my gaze. "How long is this going to take?"

"How many times did we work through that whole bonds-realignment discussion with you and your mates?" he countered, tapping his chin thoughtfully. "Five? Six? No, seven times. So I think seven days' payment is more than kind on my part, really."

"Yeah, minus me having to go in and wipe the gargoyle's memory after the fact," I retorted, still irritated by that not-so-minor mishap in our arrangement.

Kyros's head tipped back on a laugh, his amusement at my expense evident. He sort of reminded me of Ajax a little in muscular size and angular features. They also both had the same thick black hair that always fell into their eyes no matter what they did. However, Kyros had tattoos from his neck all the way to his fingertips, covering every inch of his torso, while Ajax just had the lip ring.

That was the difference between Paradox Fae and Midnight Fae—our bodies healed all wounds, including those inflicted by colorful needles. Meanwhile, Paradox Fae could be injured and remain injured. Although, they carried around magical time-wielding swords that allowed them to fix themselves by falling into the past, so it evened out in the end. Mostly.

"That little bastard was so pissed," Kyros mused, wiping tears away from his near-black eyes.

"Yeah. Ha." I folded my arms. "New Orleans?"

He grinned. "Yep."

"Then hold on. It's going to be a smoky ride."

He latched onto my forearm, and I began my journey to the Human Realm to raise the dead.

～

Kyros made me help him for all seven fucking days, the bastard only allowing me to sneak back to campus a handful of times to check on Aflora and her other mates. Fortunately, they seemed to be getting along just fine.

Although, I sensed her distress at my continued absence—a fact she made evident now with her expression upon seeing me in my seat in our Advanced Conjuring class.

Her eyes widened in surprise, then narrowed in annoyance.

Yeah, I was in trouble.

Luckily, I had an excuse. "Hi, little rose," I murmured as she slid into the seat beside me. "How was your week?"

"Fine," she replied, then grimaced at the word she'd used to describe a week of intense sexual activity. Because that was how she'd spent her time outside of class and during her free days—exploring with Zeph and Kols. From what I could tell, they hadn't bitten her again; they were just playing and introducing her to their preferences, which were a bit darker than mine.

Zeph, specifically.

He had a penchant for bondage. Fortunately for him, Aflora didn't mind. She also didn't seem to mind that Zeph and Kols enjoyed sexual activities with each other—something they'd demonstrated for her thoroughly last night.

Her cheeks flushed as if she was recalling the memory now, her tongue slipping out to dampen her lips. "Where have you been all week?" she blurted out, her face darkening to a pretty red shade. "Sorry, I mean, uh…"

"You're allowed to ask me where I've been," I told her softly. "I'm your mate, Aflora."

"Then why didn't you tell me you'd be gone?"

"Would you like me to let you know in the future if I intend to leave the Academy?" I asked her, genuinely curious.

"Um, only if you want to."

"There are a lot of things I want," I admitted, catching her gaze.

"Ain't that the truth," Ajax muttered as he arrived to claim the chair on the other side of me.

I held out my fist for him to bump, the way we usually greeted each other. His knock was a bit harder today, telling me what kind of mood he was in.

No doubt a result of his latest rendezvous with a certain female who was deemed off-limits to him. It seemed we both had a proclivity for picking women we shouldn't want.

"You and Kyros have fun this week?" he asked me, not at all concerned by Aflora listening on my other side.

"*Fun* is not the word I'd choose," I said, cringing at the number of ghosts I'd spoken to this week on the Paradox Fae's behalf. "But I'm out of his debt again."

Ajax grunted. "Maybe you should stop asking him for favors."

"I wish that were possible," I replied, knowing full well I'd need to use him again, and soon. "But he's a useful ally to have."

"Most Paradox Fae are," he agreed, causing Aflora's eyebrows to shoot upward.

"You've been dealing with a time-dweller?" She seemed both impressed and mortified. "They're tricksters."

"I'm very aware," I drawled, shifting my attention to Headmaster Irwin as he arrived. He ignored the class in favor of taking in the freshly renovated surroundings. The Council had restored the Death Blood building with an abundance of power shortly after its destruction, but the magical kinks were still working themselves out.

The gargoyles were having a field day trying to keep order within the building. Students continued to find themselves lost or in the wrong place, snake vines were uprooted and trapped, and a horde of fire gnats had been released from Headmaster Jericho's lab.

I would have been entertained by the chaos if I hadn't known *who* had caused it.

My mood soured at the thought of Zakkai, mostly because I knew Aflora had dreamt of him every day this week again. Was that what caused the hint of guilt in her eyes now? Or was it related to her bedroom gymnastics with Zeph and Kols?

"What did you do all week?" I asked her, curious to see how she'd reply.

"I, uh, studied a lot," she offered, her cheeks revealing that was a lie.

Well, not entirely.

"Zeph is a thorough headmaster, hmm?" I couldn't help teasing her, and the horrified expression she gave me in return said it was worth it.

"I... I mean... I don't..." She cleared her throat, her beautiful eyes conveying an intoxicating mixture of apology and annoyance that made me smile.

"Yes, very thorough indeed," I murmured, winking at her.

Headmaster Irwin chose that moment to begin class, leaving Aflora blushing beside me and unable to reply.

I smirked, amused.

"Today, we are going to practice psychometry," Headmaster Irwin announced. "As you all know, objects have histories, just like souls. But sometimes, calling up the past of an item is harder than that of a person." He used his wand to produce a box with a slit on the top. "Everyone will pick something from this box at random, then work with your partner to decipher the story behind the item."

The container floated to his desk at the center of the room, landing with a flourish amid a stack of papers and spreading them everywhere like confetti.

"I'll go first," he continued, sauntering up to his creation and sticking his hand inside. The older Midnight Fae pulled out a watch that belonged in the Human Realm more than in this one and held it up for all of us to see.

Ajax snorted beside me.

I agreed with his sentiments completely.

What a colossal waste of time, truly. Our building was attacked a week ago, and Headmaster Irwin wanted to teach us all how to look at objects. We should be focused on defensive spells, such as calling up former warrior spirits to help protect our school. But everyone was too busy acting as though we hadn't been attacked last week.

Ridiculous.

At least Kols seemed to be favored as innocent by those on campus. If only the Council had the same faith in him as all the younger Midnight Fae had.

Prats, I thought, not at all impressed by our governing structure—a fact my father very well knew. As did my mother.

"Guess I need to go partner with Janice," Ajax muttered, drawing my attention to the shifting chairs. "Wish me luck."

"You don't need it," I replied. "She does." It was no secret that the Death Blood female had the hots for my best friend. Unfortunately for her, he preferred another fae—one he shouldn't.

Ajax twirled his lip ring with his tongue, then heaved a sigh. "You're a dick."

"I know." I smiled at him. "Yet you hang out with me anyway. What does that say about you?"

"I prefer bad company," he drawled, his amusement palpable as he gathered his things and headed for the petite, dark-haired female waiting for him with stars in her eyes.

Aflora cleared her throat beside me. "Are you going to get the item, or am I?" she asked.

As I'd totally blanked out on the demonstration, I suggested she go first so I could see what spell we were supposed to utter. There were several related to psychometry, and I had no idea which one Headmaster Irwin had chosen for us to explore today.

My mate left her chair, her skirt distracting me as she moved.

Such a fine ass.

Long legs.

Mmm, I liked the little boots she chose today, too. Yeah, I'd let her leave those on while I took her against the wall.

But the blouse could stand to lose a few buttons. And I much preferred her in this outfit without the undergarments. I had nothing against silk and lace; I just wanted to see her tits through the thin white fabric.

A crass consideration, but it'd been a long fucking week of watching without touching.

And I really wanted to touch her.

"Why are you looking at me like that?" she asked, standing in front of me with a rock in her hand.

I glanced down at it. "That's what you picked from the box?"

She shrugged. "It was the first thing that fit in my hand."

My lips twitched. I'd happily give her something else for her hand, but it might not *fit,* as she put it.

"Seriously, why are you looking at me like that?" she demanded.

I stood so I could step into her personal space. Then I leaned down to whisper in her ear. "Because I'm thinking about all the things I'd like to teach you with my tongue."

She stopped breathing.

I kissed her throat—right above her collar—and lifted my head to gaze down at her. "Now let's get this assignment done so I can play with you properly."

She shivered, her pupils flaring. Her lips formed an O without sound, then she swallowed.

Seconds passed.

Then our moment was destroyed by Headmaster Irwin clearing his throat. The entire room had emptied around us. "Get to work," he snapped.

I frowned. "Where did everyone go?"

Aflora sighed. "Did you listen at all when he gave instructions?"

"No, I had other things on my mind." I allowed her to hear the innuendo in my tone and enjoyed her resulting blush.

Then she shook her head, grabbed her things, and said, "Follow me."

"Happily," I agreed, picking up my only notebook and trailing after her into the hallway. "Please tell me we're going to find a dark corner to make out in."

She scoffed at me, leading me out of the building and into the night rather than to a quiet room without windows where I could devour her. "Headmaster Irwin told us to spread out and find a safe place to practice so our spells don't overlap. Then we're supposed to report back with our findings."

"Well, that's much more boring than the idea I had in my head," I admitted, disappointed.

"I bet," she replied, but I caught the flicker of amusement in her features. "How about over there?" She pointed to a bench beside the building, directly across from a new dragon statue guarded by two gargoyles. One of the Death Bloods had probably put them there to protect the building from another attack. It wouldn't help, but they wouldn't know that.

"Shade?" Aflora prompted.

Right. She wanted to know if we could sit there.

So I heaved a shoulder. "Sure. Why not?"

"Good." She plopped down on the charcoal blades decorating the paved path rather than on the bench, then set the rock on the ground.

I glanced between her and the bench but decided to join her on the ground, because why not? She was an Earth Fae, after all. She probably preferred the grasslike substance more than a metal seat. So I indulged my little rose by sitting beside her with my legs stretched out and crossed at the ankles.

"What spell did Headmaster Irwin tell us to use?" I asked her.

"You really weren't paying attention at all," she muttered.

"Nope." I stared at her mouth. "As I said, I had other things on my mind." I couldn't remember what those things were now, but I was reasonably certain they had something to do with her delectable assets. Zeph and Kols had played with her all week, while I'd barely touched her since the night she'd slept in my bed.

"Focus, Shade."

"I'm very focused, Aflora."

She huffed out a breath, but I caught the lingering amusement in her expression. She liked my teasing, which was good because I intended to tease her a hell of a lot more.

I reached out to brush her long black strands over her shoulder. Kols had been allowing her to sleep without her collar in his room, just as he removed his own band. I'd studied how he removed the mechanism the other night, just in case I needed to replicate the action. It was tempting to do so now, simply to expose her pretty throat, but I didn't want to risk anyone sensing her bonds to Kols and Zeph.

They weren't gifted enough to hide their links.

Unlike certain other fae.

"All right, princess. Show me what we're doing," I said, dropping my gaze from her mouth to the rock on the ground. Aflora already had her wand out, her lips moving over the spell without saying it out loud. When she seemed confident in her words, she waved her wand over the rock and uttered the incantation aloud.

Perfect form. Perfect spell. Perfect female.

The way her eyes fluttered closed confirmed she'd executed the assignment accurately and was now deep in the history of the rock. I went back onto my elbows to wait. Depending on how much that little stone had to say, we could be here for a while.

I dipped my head back to admire the moon overhead, my thoughts starting to drift to more intriguing topics, when Aflora began to shake beside me. Frowning, I sat up. "Aflora?"

She didn't reply, her teeth beginning to chatter as if she were freezing. I touched her arm and cursed at the droplets of ice water covering her skin.

"Aflora!" I snapped at her.

Nothing.

Just more shaking.

And then she collapsed.

CHAPTER TWENTY-ONE

AFLORA

Several Minutes Earlier

"*Arie Anni Tarikh Nuk*," I said, drawing a star in the air over the rock. Energy hummed around me as the spell activated, drawing me into a world of heat and despair. I flinched at the sudden change, my lips parting on a scream that didn't escape.

Where am I? I wondered, spinning in a circle and frowning as the Academy unfolded around me.

A raven clucked overhead.

Students giggled as they gossiped in the corner beside the Death Blood Education Building entrance.

"How did I…?" I trailed off, whirling around once more and searching for Shade.

He was gone.

I blinked.

Had he left me in the middle of our assignment? It would be just like him, as he seemed to have a penchant for disappearing. What business did he have with a Paradox Fae, anyway?

I blew out a breath and shook my head.

Oh well. Now, where did my books go?

I took a step forward, only to be snapped backward by some invisible force. My brow furrowed. "What…?"

Then my feet began to walk, as if I were possessed by someone else.

"What's happening?" I demanded. Only then did I realize my voice wasn't resonating and my lips weren't actually moving.

My body continued to operate on its own, my hand drawing out a wand—

one I recognized, yet didn't—and waved it over the gargoyle outside of the Death Blood Education Building.

"*Nahni Haki Aldukhi,*" a deep voice said.

Everything inside me froze at the sound because it came from *my throat*. But it wasn't my voice at all. However, I recognized it. Sort of. From long ago, a song—

The doors opened with a flourish, distracting me from my thoughts as I stepped unwillingly into the building. I ducked immediately into the shadows, creeping along the walls and pausing with every shift of magic around me.

A glimpse of a mirror caught my eye, but my head refused to turn toward it.

Wait...

I caught a glimmer of a shoulder that was far too wide to be my own.

Then I heard the voice speaking again, this time in a low hum of musical energy I recognized. It reminded me of my mother's ballad, only different. Darker. Deeper. *Hypnotic.* I swooned a little, the power warming my veins, the sound a reverberation against my throat.

It's me.

I'm humming.

No.

Not me.

Him.

My eyebrows shot upward. *I'm trapped in someone else's body!*

How? How did this happen? And what were we doing here?

Had I uttered the spell wrong? It'd been a rock, not a person, so why...?

Oh... Oh, Fae... No!

Fire ignited around me, my wand the source of the power. I paused to listen, then more of that ballad hummed from my lips as I whispered enchantments to urge the students to flee. *There will be no casualties today. Just a warning. A message. To let the Council know it's time.*

I tried to shake my head to clear it, confused by the thoughts taking over my own. They were much deeper, masculine in nature, and not at all mine.

This isn't me.

It will be, a deep voice replied, shocking the hell out of me.

Who are you?

You know me, he vowed. *You'll see.*

I didn't understand, but an inferno blazed all around me, making me hot and cold at the same time. Shivers racked me from head to toe, my lips parting on another one of those silent screams.

And then we were outside, our hand rising into the sky to script out a word I already knew was meant to be written.

"*Alqisian,*" I whispered at the same time as the male, our voices commingling into a beautiful song I couldn't help but hum.

My heart began to break, memories of a past long buried tickling my mind with glimpses of my parents.

"Sweet darling flower, we love you so much," my mother breathed, her arms tight around me. *"We're doing this for you, to ensure you survive."*

"It's the only way," my father agreed, his palm against my lower back. *"...take care of you, baby."*

"Who?" I wanted to ask them. "Who will take care of me?"

But they were already gone, the aftermath of destruction blazing before me in a furious wave of devastating power.

A rock tumbled out of the debris, bumping my boot. I bent to retrieve it, then brought it to my lips.

"I'll come for you soon, Aflora," a gruff voice whispered to it. "I vow it."

I couldn't stop trembling, confusion mounting with each passing second as a cloud of thick smoke surrounded me from the wreckage. The rock fell to the ground and I took to the air, swirling in a cloud that reminded me of Shade.

"I've got you," I heard him say. "It's going to be okay."

"Shade?" I couldn't see him, but I *felt* him, our shared bond yanking at my essence. "Shade!" I tugged on that strand, our frail, initial link, following him through the sea of darkness to a place where his peppermint scent surrounded me in a fog of familiarity.

Tears tracked down my cheeks, my heart hammering in my ribs, my consciousness lost somewhere in the abyss, but his voice carried me to the present.

"Wake up," he demanded. "Show me your eyes, beautiful."

I wanted to.

But I didn't know where to look, or which way to go, until I felt another tug, his intoxicating essence swimming all around me. I breathed him in, my mind working through the trickery and blackness left behind by the other entity, my heart racing against my ribs.

"That's it," Shade coaxed. "I'm right here, little rose. Come get me."

"Shade," I whispered, my voice sounding hoarse but finally coming through my own body. *I'm me again.* Only, I couldn't see.

"Hi, sweetheart," he replied, his lips brushing mine.

Mmm, I felt that.

I yearned for more.

But I needed to see him, to know this was real and not another game or spell gone awry.

"I'm right here," Shade promised, his warmth seeping into me and drawing me out of the stillness of my mind and into his arms. "There you are, gorgeous." His thumb drifted across my cheek. "You had me worried for a moment."

I stared up at the sun, then at him, and finally at the tree behind him. "Our meadow," I breathed, my throat sore and scratchy. "How?" *Am I dreaming? Am I still trapped inside that man?*

"I shadowed us here to get you away from that rock," he replied, his lips curling down. "What happened, Aflora? What did you see?"

"Destruction," I told him, shuddering at the images flashing behind my eyes. "He destroyed the education building after making sure everyone got out alive. Then he kissed the rock. He… I was him and he was me. And then I destroyed the building. But I didn't. He did. Except it was me, Shade. I was… I was *him*."

I sat up abruptly, only then realizing Shade had been cradling me in his lap. But he let me move, his gaze guarded as I jumped to my feet and spun around the familiar field. "Is this real?" I demanded.

"Yes," he replied, standing up as well. "This is the meadow I took you to a few weeks ago, after the recording incident."

"And it's real?" I asked again, needing to know if I was somehow trapped in my mind.

He grabbed me by the waist, yanked me to him, and pressed his mouth to mine.

A zing of energy zapped through my system, my eyes widening at the unexpected power.

Then his tongue parted my lips, forcing me to *feel* him. To see him. To be with him.

I wrapped my arms around his neck to better align our bodies and allowed him to ravage me with his mouth.

This, I thought. *This is real. So, so, so real.*

"Mate," I whispered, recognizing the fervor burning between us. "I need you."

He walked me backward *into* the tree. I glanced around, shocked by our new surroundings of wood and leaves. A secret house with windows that overlooked our meadow.

"What is this?"

"Our place," he whispered, continuing to walk me backward. "I enchanted it just for you."

His lips met mine once more, drowning me in sensation and lust and yearning. I moaned, needing this more than I needed to breathe.

We'd yet to truly explore each other, all the dreams leading to a few orgasms that he usually inspired without even really touching me. At least not with his hands or mouth.

Well, sometimes with his hands and mouth.

But it didn't count. They were fantasies of the mind.

This was real.

Our bodies touching, the mattress meeting my back as he pushed me onto the bed, his groin settling between my splayed thighs.

Yes, yes. *This* was my ultimate craving, the forbidden yearning I hated to admit. He was the one who tricked me into this entire mess, the one to bite me without permission, and while I should hate him, deep down I couldn't.

Because I felt connected to him.

That connection was what drew me out of my nightmare and into our dream meadow. Then he'd pulled me into this house. Oh, how I adored this house! Flowers scented the air. Fresh cypress trees, too. And, mmm, something very sweet like chocolate.

"Cookies," he whispered against my neck, his hands roaming up my sides. "They're cookies."

I must have spoken that out loud, and I couldn't bring myself to care. "I need you."

"I know," he said, his lips tracing a path up to my ear. "I need you, too."

"Will you bite me?" I asked, arching my neck backward in invitation. I barely even recognized myself, this wanton energy flowing through me and captivating my every move. Yet, it felt entirely right. I wanted him inside me in all ways. "I missed you," I realized out loud. "Please don't leave without telling me again."

Who am I? Who is speaking these words?

Oh, who cares!

I felt high on life, our bond thriving inside me and pulsating with an intense craving.

Shade kissed me instead of answering, his tongue sparring beautifully with mine. My blouse fell apart, his hand ripping it from me in an eagerness to expose my breasts. I followed his unspoken suggestion and tried to tear his own shirt off, but I lacked the finesse required to mimic the movement.

He chuckled against my throat, then went up to his knees and began the tedious task of unbuttoning his dress shirt. I went up onto my elbows to enjoy the show as he displayed his tanned torso one slow inch at a time.

He truly was a work of art, his lithe form lean and strong, his muscles flexing as he removed the fabric from his shoulders and arms. I admired his alluring display and eyed the trail of dark hair that led to the button of his dress pants. He flicked it open and drew down the zipper while I watched, his intentions clear.

You have a choice, he was telling me with his unhurried movements. He wanted me to be sure, to not rush into my decision, but we both knew I'd end up here with or without today's events.

"I want you," I told him earnestly. "I have for a while."

"I know," he replied, a wickedness in his gaze that lit my blood on fire. "But I need you to be sure, Aflora."

"I am." I meant it. Maybe it was the insanity of the moment or the very real power I felt thriving between us, but I was done fighting the inevitable. He'd bitten me for reasons I still didn't understand, but one thing was abundantly clear to me.

Everything Shade did, he did for me.

To others, it may seem like he had ulterior motives that were self-serving, and maybe some of them were. But somehow, I knew in my gut that all his decisions revolved around me.

He considered me important.

And it was time for me to show him I felt similarly.

"I should hate you," I admitted out loud. "And part of me does."

"Yes," he agreed.

"But another part of me…" I trailed off, my heart beating rapidly in my chest, my mouth suddenly dry. "Another part of me needs to finish this." And he'd ignited that part of me when he'd used our bond to draw me back to him, to save me from whatever hellish ride I'd been on through the Death Blood Education Building tour. "I want you, Shade."

CHAPTER TWENTY-TWO

SHADE

Aflora was high on our bond, her pupils blown wide with lust.

It took every ounce of willpower I possessed not to take advantage of the situation and fuck her the way her body begged me to.

I needed her mind to catch up with the emotions, for her to realize *what* she demanded of me.

"Will you bite me again?"

Those words were music to my ears when she uttered them, but I couldn't be sure she actually meant them. Not in her current state.

I leaned down to kiss her again, my muscles tensing with restraint as she rubbed her hot center against my groin.

Shit, I thought, my heart threatening to burst out of my chest from beating so hard. I really shouldn't have unfastened my pants, but fuck, I needed to *breathe.* She was killing me.

"Aflora," I whispered, fighting for control. She bucked against me in response, her skirt pooling around her hips.

"Take me," she breathed.

"I want to," I assured her, my lips trailing down her neck to her breasts. "You have no idea how much I want to."

It physically hurt not to bite her, to not finish our bond, but everything else had been forced upon her. I wanted this final step to be because she truly desired it, not because she was lost in our connection.

The only way to ground her was to give her an outlet for the power mounting inside her.

And I knew just the way to do that.

Her bra disappeared with a snap of my fingers, revealing her pert tits to my mouth. I took a nipple between my teeth while I palmed the other one.

She hissed, her arousal perfuming the air in a luscious scent of *need.* I'd only ever tasted her in our dreams, not in reality. And I longed to rectify that now.

My palms slid down her sides to her skirt, my fingers finding the zipper and dragging it down. When it hit the end, I ripped the rest of the fabric away from her, earning me a moan from my little mate.

Her fingers threaded through my hair, holding me against her breast. I responded by taking her other stiff peak into my mouth and twirling my tongue around the tip.

"Shade…" She uttered my name like a plea, her skin heating beneath my touch.

She wasn't cold now, but *hot*.

Energy sizzled beneath her skin, seeking an escape. She didn't seem to notice, too lost to the sensations and drunk on the way they made her feel.

I continued my path downward with my lips, stopping to dip my tongue in her adorable belly button before situating myself between her thighs. Her lacy white panties were soaked through, leaving nothing to the imagination. I took the bands on either side of her hips and yanked on the fabric, snapping it with ease and leaving her naked on the bed.

Well, mostly naked.

She still had those adorable ankle boots on.

Her fingers tightened in my hair as she tried to guide my mouth to the place she wanted it, causing me to smile against her slick folds. "You're in a demanding mood, aren't you, pet?"

"Please, Shade," she whimpered, her limbs trembling with the electricity humming through her veins.

Whatever had happened with the rock, coupled with me yanking her out of the enchantment, had awakened her Quandary Blood with a vengeance. That paltry collar around her neck would do nothing to help her now.

But I would.

"I'm going to make you come, Aflora," I told her softly. "I want you to give me everything and let it all go, okay?"

"Yes," she groaned, her nails digging into my scalp.

My cock pulsed in response to her throaty moan, my mouth aching to taste her. I needed this almost as much as she did, but for entirely different reasons.

She was mine, and I wanted her to know what that meant.

So I showed her with my tongue, licking her deep and thoroughly and fully introducing her intimately to my mouth. She sucked in a surprised breath and released it on a sound I wanted to hear from her again and again and again.

I hummed in approval against her slick flesh, then slid two fingers inside her. She bowed off the bed on a cry of pleasure, her cerulean flames glimmering across her skin.

Beautiful, I thought, adoring this unrestrained side of her.

No concerns.

No distrust.

Just lost to the heat of the moment and allowing her mate to take care of her in every way. I fucking loved it and wanted to stay in this place with her forever, but I knew it wasn't the right thing to do. She needed her mind back, and there was only one way to return it to her.

"Come for me, Aflora," I whispered, laving her throbbing clit.

She whimpered, her grip tightening in my hair as she chased her pleasure against my tongue. "Shade!" she cried out, her power erupting in a hot wave of energy that illuminated our bond.

I growled at the onslaught of electricity thrumming through my veins, my incisors aching to bite her and absorb as much of her as I could.

Not yet, I told myself, my muscles tensing in protest.

Our bond was on fucking fire. Her other mates had to feel it, but I couldn't think about them right now, not with her quivering with rapture beneath my mouth. I feasted on her essence and vitality, driving her to the edge again with a few clever swipes of my tongue and groaning with her as she came again.

Glorious, I thought, marveling at her display of ecstasy. She reminded me of a goddess with her blue-black hair spilling across the pillows and her creamy skin highlighted by enchanting blue flames. Aflora didn't seem to notice, too lost in her oblivion to realize she'd lit herself on fire with her outburst.

I crawled up and over her, reveling in the heat pouring off her and into me, and took her mouth in a passionate kiss underlined in possession.

She owned me as much as I owned her.

Fate put me in her path, and duty forced me to remain despite the rocky course ahead. And this moment made that all worth it.

Every secret. Every choice. Every dark doubt. All of it disappeared beneath a cloud of rightness as I parted her lips with my tongue and devoured her.

She wrapped an arm around me, her opposite hand still in my hair. "More," she whispered. "Give me more."

"Aflora," I replied, my voice harsh with my necessary restraint.

But she seemed oblivious to it, her mouth trailing along my jaw to my neck in seductive little caresses I couldn't ignore. I palmed her cheek, then slid my hand back into her hair, intending to pull her lips back to mine, when her teeth pierced my skin.

An inferno blazed across my conscious, my heart thundering in my chest.

Aflora had just *bitten* me.

Tasted my blood.

And swallowed.

Her moan of approval shattered something inside me, spurring me into motion. My fingers tightened around her dark strands, holding her to my neck as she ingested more of my essence.

It was so fucking wrong yet felt too damn good to stop.

I'd never been bitten before—the action was typically reserved for mates during sex—and damn, I was glad I'd waited for Aflora. She could sink her teeth into me anytime she wanted.

"Fuck, little rose," I groaned, my shaft aching with the desire to slip into her velvety heat.

I released her hair to work on shucking off my pants and then my boxers. There'd been a reason I wanted to wait, but hell if I could remember it now.

Her legs parted from my hips, her teeth releasing my neck as she tossed her head back on a throaty demand to take her. I lined myself up and drove inside her to the hilt, our cries of satisfaction mingling in the air.

Home, I realized. *I'm finally fucking home.*

And what a place it was because I'd never really had one. In all my years, I stuck to the shadows, lurking and playing the games set out before me. How fucking appropriate that the biggest task of all was the one writhing beneath me and welcoming me into her with open arms.

"You're everything I didn't know I needed," I breathed, completely lost to the beauty unraveling in my arms. My heart beat for this woman and this woman alone. She was mine, and I never wanted to let her go.

"Bite me," she begged. "Finish it."

"Yes," I agreed. It was time. Our vows were incomplete, and that needed to be rectified.

I pressed my mouth to her throbbing pulse and licked the cerulean magic heating her skin. Mmm, she tasted like power and sex and everything I could ever desire.

Our connection hung in the balance, a weight on both our spirits, waiting for this final thread.

And I granted it the climax of our lives by piercing her vein.

She screamed, her hips driving upward to meet mine, our pace becoming frantic as we both fought to find our release in a wave of insurmountable gratification. Time fucking stopped. Yet our hearts continued to beat, her blood pouring into my mouth as I took her with brutal thrusts that she responded to in kind.

It was animalistic.

Hot.

Ferocious.

Fucking.

No, a claiming. Her nails scraped down my back, drawing blood and causing me to hiss against her neck. I bit her again, her essence giving me the gift of life and completion and binding us on a path to insanity.

We were one.

Together.

Forever.

We were destined to overcome the agony of our existence, to fight in a war neither of us had signed up for, or to die trying.

Every thought, emotion, concern, sacrifice, and sensation traveled from my mind to hers, igniting a marathon of information for my mate to access.

She trembled beneath the onslaught, her eyes widening in shock as her pussy spasmed around me on an incredible climax that I *felt* through my own spirit.

I tumbled into oblivion after her, the orgasm ripping a hole through my chest and damning me to hell in the space of a breath. Everything burned in the best way, our powers dancing on a plane we could sense without seeing.

Our mating was complete.

Done.

Embedded in our spirits for eternity.

And I'd never felt more alive.

Aflora shook beneath me, her blue embers starting to fade as the heat of the moment began to subside. I pulled away from her neck to stare down at her in wonder. None of the prophecies prepared me for this intensity or the feelings that followed.

Pride.

Adoration.

Fear.

Because I knew what lay ahead of us. I knew what we would have to face together. And I knew what decision she would eventually have to make.

What if she chose *him*?

What if she followed the path fate originally set out for her before I stepped in the way?

There were so many unforeseen consequences of altering someone's destiny, but I had to try. It was the only way for us to pursue the alternative future, the one Midnight Fae kind required of us to survive.

Her palm pressed to my cheek, her gaze searching. "There are so many secrets in your eyes right now," she breathed, her voice a rasp against my lips. "I can sense the burdens you carry."

"It's all for you," I admitted softly, my throat working to swallow. "No one should have to know what I know. And to tell you could alter everything."

"Who are you?" she asked, her tone one of fascination, not displeasure. "I feel you inside me, Shade. A mix of fae. And so much *pain*."

I grimaced, not wanting anyone to ever experience the weight of my emotions but knowing it was the price she had to pay for our mating. "I'm sorry," I told her, pressing my forehead to hers. "I'm so sorry, Aflora."

"Don't be," she said softly, her arms wrapping around me. "Share with me instead. Let me help you."

I shook my head slowly. "I can't. Not yet." *Not until you choose*, I wanted to add but didn't. Because it was unfair to lay that burden at her feet now. She wouldn't understand it, not until Zakkai decided to reveal his true intent.

And then the future would realign again.

More prophecies would be born.

Allegiances would change.

Fae would die.

I closed my eyes and pressed my nose to her neck, inhaling the sweet scent of my female. One breath calmed my mind. A second drew me back to her and the reality around us. The cabin I'd built for her. A safe haven no one could find.

How easy it would be to just remain here, to keep her all to myself and let everyone else fend for themselves.

But that wasn't me.

Everyone thought I only cared about my personal satisfaction. Little did they realize how much I'd sacrificed to be where I was today.

Yes, I took Aflora.

However, it was done with a purpose—to protect those I loved. Including her. An impossible claim, but I'd known about her for years, been aware of our intertwined fates, and had fallen for her after seeing dozens of prophecies all revolving around her fate. *Our* fate.

I couldn't even begin to explain that to her.

All I could do was continue to guide her and allow her to make her own decisions. Like she did tonight when she bit me.

I drew my mouth to hers once more, kissing her thoroughly and thanking her with my tongue for the gift of her bond. She would never know how much it meant to me. Or maybe she'd sense it.

Regardless, it was done.

We belonged to each other.

And I intended to spend the rest of the evening thanking her for accepting me.

CHAPTER TWENTY-THREE

AFLORA

Shade's mouth mesmerized me. I could kiss him for hours, and I did. We lost time in the seclusion of his cabin. He brought me berries and the cookies he'd mentioned. He gave me a fruity drink to quench my thirst. He introduced his mouth to every inch of my body. And then he took me again and again.

If this was all a dream, I no longer cared, because it was perfect. A fantasy come to life, with the most unlikely of males at my side.

Yet I felt the bruises of his past echoing in his spirit. So much agony. Selflessness. A caring man hidden beneath a perpetual shadow.

No one knew him.

And for a few brief moments of time, he allowed me to truly see the real Shade—a strong, intelligent, conniving male who put everyone above himself.

Including me.

I couldn't see everything, mostly because that wasn't how our bond worked, but I sensed his sacrifice. "Do you regret biting me?" I asked him, my palm resting against his sculpted abdomen as I snuggled into his side.

He drew his fingers through my hair, tucking the strands behind my ear. "No."

The bond confirmed he meant that. Yet… "I sense so much sadness in you."

He said nothing for a while, his fingers drifting through my hair as he studied the wood beams on the ceiling. "I'm not sad," he finally replied. "I'm just tired. There's so much I want to share and can't, not without initiating substantial risk. And if I have to choose between your safety and my comfort, I'll pick you every time."

I shifted upward to rest my head on the pillow beside him. "Is that why you won't tell me why you bit me?"

"Yes." He rotated toward me, so he lay on his side rather than his back, his icy blue eyes holding mine. "Do you hate me for it?"

"Yes," I said. "And no."

He seemed to understand that, not needing me to voice anything more. "One day you'll understand. One day soon."

"And will I hate you when the truth is revealed?" I wondered out loud.

"Possibly, yes."

I was afraid he would say that. "I don't want to hate you."

"I don't want you to hate me either," he whispered. "But I'll accept your disdain, as is my due."

"You're used to people hating you," I realized aloud.

"I am."

I pressed my palm to his cheek and drew my thumb across his lower lip. "I see you, Shade."

"Do you?"

I nodded. "Yes." I leaned in to kiss him softly, craving his touch with an abandon I couldn't ignore. "I feel you, too."

He palmed the back of my neck and allowed me to slowly explore his mouth with my tongue. It was a lazy embrace filled with unspoken words.

The bond had opened a connection to him unlike any I'd ever felt, yet something about it was familiar, too. I suspected it had to do with the roots we'd already established inside each other with his initial two bites. Now that he'd finished our mating, our link had blossomed into a world of color and sensation.

His pain became mine.

His fears, too.

Yet I didn't fully understand them or why they existed. I just knew it had something to do with whatever he'd *seen*.

"You have Fortune Fae in you," I realized suddenly, pulling back.

"Yes," he admitted softly, sliding his hand down from my neck to rest against my hip. "On my mother's side."

My lips parted. "That makes you an...?" I couldn't finish, surprise rendering me speechless.

"An abomination," he whispered. "Of a sort, anyway. Fortune Fae Alphas are former Midnight Fae who refused to drink blood, making us all related at our origin. Yet we're not allowed to crossbreed, why?"

"Because it makes powerful kin," I breathed.

He nodded. "Yes. And those who are in power right now don't appreciate the challenge cross-species pose. But a thousand years ago, that wasn't an issue. My grandmother mated my grandfathers without much prejudice. One was a Fortune Fae Alpha, the other a Death Blood—the former king before the Nacht family took over."

I frowned. "Wait, but you said your mother's side had Fortune Fae?"

Another nod, his expression grim. "My father married into the familial line of power, then claimed it as his own because females are not allowed to lead."

"An archaic law," I muttered.

"Actually, no, it's not. The Nacht family—Kols's grandfather, specifically—enacted it. My mother would have been on the Council had it not been for his chauvinistic actions. He used my grandmother as an example of why women shouldn't lead."

"How?" I wondered out loud, captivated by his history. This was the most Shade had ever revealed about himself, and I felt through the bond how much this all meant to him. And instinct told me it all tied into our fate as well.

"She went into hiding shortly after the call for Quandary Bloods to be eradicated." A shadow touched his features, one that darkened his ice-blue irises to a dark gemstone similar to sapphires. "Constantine Nacht stated that my grandmother's emotional state forced her to choose family over duty. He said all women were born with that loyalty flaw and therefore were not fit to lead. Thus, my father was marked as the Death Blood incumbent over my mother."

"He didn't object?" I asked, shocked.

"No. Actually, he fully supported it." Shade's jaw ticked, showing how he felt about that. "And the rest, as they say, is history."

"But what happened to your grandmother and her mates?"

He studied me for a long moment. "They suffered a similar fate to the Quandary Bloods."

"They died?"

"Not exactly," he replied cryptically. "What happened with the rock, Aflora?"

His abrupt change in subject took me aback, some sort of wall going up between us. He didn't want me to know about his grandparents, which meant he was hiding something.

As much as I wanted to press him, I sensed the importance of letting it go.

His Fortune Fae relations explained so much about him, particularly his penchant for secrets. He knew things others didn't, giving him an advantage underlined in a myriad of liabilities. No wonder he kept me in the dark so often; he didn't want to influence my choices, and yet, for some reason, he'd taken some of my decisions away from me.

Such as our mating.

"You bit me that day to prevent something else from happening to me," I said, ignoring his rock comment for the moment. "Gina told me I had two paths, that I was already in your sights."

"*His* sights," Shade corrected. "Yes."

My brow furrowed. "Are you saying she wasn't talking about you?"

"She was, in regard to the paths," he replied. "But I can't tell you more. The rest you'll need to learn on your own."

"Why?"

"Because there are some choices I refuse to take from you, Aflora. This is your destiny to follow, not mine to dictate."

"Yet you stole my ability to decide when you bit me that day," I pointed out. "So you'll alter some of my paths, but not all of them."

"I alter the ones I'm destined to alter," he replied, slipping his palm upward to cup my cheek. "Our paths were meant to intertwine. I just upped the timeline."

I wanted to ask him what that meant, but I knew he wouldn't tell me.

Fortune-telling was a tricky game. If he told me too much, he risked disrupting the balance and changing our fates to an unforeseeable future. Which was why he mostly focused on facts I already knew, detailing the past decisions and how they'd already impacted our lives.

But he carefully avoided anything that could explain what tomorrow held for us both, despite the fact that I could sense he knew perfectly well what to expect. Or, at least, he had an inkling.

Because that was how Fortune Fae worked—their visions didn't often make sense, the images a cluster of thoughts that may or may not form a coherent prediction. And from what I gathered of Shade's comments, there were multiple avenues for our futures to take. He only dictated the ones he could control, like that day outside the coffee shop.

"The rock," I said slowly, returning to his question and giving him a reprieve from the fate discussion. I cleared my throat. "It, uh, showed me something devastating. The fire."

His brow came down. "The fire?"

"Yeah. At the Death Blood Education Building." I closed my eyes to consider what I'd seen and relayed the information to him. He remained silent the entire time, allowing me to tell him what I saw, how it felt, the horror of realizing I was trapped inside someone else, and the eventual kiss against the rock. "He said he'd see me soon, like he knew I'd have that vision."

I shivered at the memory, my blood running cold as I opened my eyes again after several minutes of reliving the nightmare.

"How could he know that?" I asked. "Or was it...? Did my mind change it?"

He shook his head slowly, his expression holding more mysteries that I longed to decipher. "He must have placed the memory in the rock, knowing it would fall into your hands."

"How is that possible?" It didn't make any sense. "There's no way he could have known I'd pick that rock in class or that we'd be playing with psychometry."

"Unless he planted the idea in Headmaster Irwin's head," Shade suggested grimly. "Did you pick up the rock, or did it fall into your hand?"

"I..." I paused, thinking back on how I selected the item from the box. "I told you—it was the only thing that fit..."

"Because the other items were enchanted not to," he replied, falling to his back. "Fuck." He pressed his palms to his eyes and muttered a string of curses.

"You know who he is," I said. "Don't you?"

He didn't reply. Because of course he wouldn't.

"Shade, I need to know who he is."

"You already do," he muttered, shaking his head. "Or you should, anyway."

I frowned. "What do you mean?"

"Does he feel familiar to you?" he countered, arching a brow.

The moment he said it, my heart stopped. "The magic…" I trailed off, thinking about the day of the attack. "I… I recognized it."

Shade nodded. "Yeah. You would."

"Why?"

He just stared at me, sad. "We should get back, Aflora. I'm sure Kols and Zeph are worried about you."

"And you suddenly care how they feel?" I countered, actually curious.

"You say you see me," he replied, his eyes still holding that touch of despair that broke my heart. "But do you, Aflora? Do you really see me?"

My soul squeezed in torment, his tone and expression killing me a little. "Shade…"

"It's okay," he replied, his knuckles brushing my cheek. "But we really should go. They can't sense or find us here, which has to be driving them insane."

"They can't?" I glanced around the cabin, noting the windows revealing a dimly lit field outside. *Nightfall.* "We've been here a while."

"We have," he agreed, his hand leaving my skin.

I immediately reached for him, not wanting to separate. Not yet. "Just a few more minutes?" I asked, pleading with him through my eyes.

He seemed reluctant but finally agreed with a subtle nod. "For a kiss."

"No," I replied, causing him to frown. "For more than a kiss." I moved on top of him to straddle his hips, then leaned down to take his mouth with mine. His hands immediately found my waist, his palms gently sliding up and down my sides.

"Shade," I murmured against his mouth.

"Aflora," he whispered, one of his hands gliding up my spine to my neck and higher into my hair.

"I know you care," I informed him softly, my lips whispering against his as I pressed a palm to his heart. "I feel it here."

"Yeah?"

"Yeah."

"Well, I'll deny it if you tell anyone."

I smiled against his mouth. "Don't worry, *mate*. Your secrets are safe with me."

He returned my grin and deepened our kiss. Then I felt the trickle of smoke surrounding us, the only indication he gave me of his power enveloping me to return us to the Academy. I almost protested, but his tongue silenced my ability, his grip tightening as he whisked us away in his trademark cloud.

And then I felt the familiarity of my sheets hitting my back, my room materializing around us. I giggled in amusement, and Shade nibbled my lower lip. "We can go back anytime," he whispered.

"Promise?"

"Promise," he vowed. "I made it for you, Aflora. Only you."

"For us," I corrected. "Our own little—"

A banging against my door made me jump. "Aflora! Open this door right fucking now!"

I blinked. "Zeph?"

"Told you they would be worried," Shade drawled, rolling off of me.

"Don't you dare go anywhere," I told him as I scooted off the bed to find something to throw on. I'd left everything at the cabin, including my boots after Shade finally let me take them off. Apparently, he had a thing for heels.

I grabbed a plain white shirt from my closet, as well as a pair of sleep shorts, and pulled them on while Shade made himself comfortable in my bed. "You could magic yourself some clothes," I suggested, then frowned. "Wait, what about—"

Our wands appeared on my nightstand while I spoke, Shade following my train of thought before I could speak. From what I understood about our new bond, we literally could communicate via telepathy but hadn't yet.

Can you hear me? I asked him.

His lips twitched. *Yes.*

Good to know.

He winked. *Answer the door before Zeph has an aneurysm.*

Right. I cleared my throat and twisted the knob. Kols and Zeph stood on the other side wearing matching expressions of annoyance. "Well, at least I know the lock works," I offered.

"Cute," Kols drawled, looking over my shoulder at the male in my bed. Because of course Shade hadn't accepted my suggestion to put on some clothes. Instead, he sat up with his back against my headboard, the sheets pooling in his lap in a very inviting manner.

He seriously looked like he belonged in my bed. Which, yeah, as my mate, he sort of did.

Are we going to give them a show, little rose? he taunted. *Because I'm game.*

Stop.

I'm not doing anything.

You're... you're...

"Aflora?" Kols cut into our mental conversation, drawing my gaze back to the hallway. "Can we come into your room?"

I wasn't sure what shocked me more—that he actually asked for permission or that he seemed uncertain of my answer. We'd shared a bed together every day this week. Why would that suddenly change? Although, it was his bed we'd slept in, but the principle still applied.

Clearing my throat, I stepped aside. "Yeah, please."

Zeph's jaw ticked, but he entered.

Kols followed.

Then Shade narrowed his gaze. "What happened?" he asked, suddenly serious and very alert.

I shut my door and leaned back against it, nervous.

"There's been another attack," Zeph said, his tone flat. "And it has Kols's essence all over it."

CHAPTER TWENTY-FOUR

ZEPH

"Why wasn't I alerted?" Shade asked, his presence irking me immensely. Mostly because I'd been worried sick about Aflora for the last several hours, just to find out he'd been playing with her somewhere out of reach.

When we were done discussing this incident, we'd be having another conversation about not stealing our mate away without any sort of notification.

Wherever he'd taken her, we couldn't sense her at all. Or him. Which had me wondering what realm he'd taken her to, because it definitely wasn't a Midnight Fae location.

"The Council is meeting right now," Kols replied. "Without Seconds or heirs apparent. I suspect the Elders have been called in."

"Great," Shade drawled. "It's always a pleasure to hear from Constantine Nacht."

Kols bristled but didn't take the bait.

"Now isn't the time to provoke each other," I interjected. "We have a serious problem."

"There's more." Kols cleared his throat, his intense gold eyes landing on Shade. "The attack was in the village near AcaWard at the tavern Tray took Aflora and Ella to the other week. Ajax's parents were injured."

Shade's taunting aura disappeared in a breath. "Are they all right?"

"We don't know yet," Kols admitted. "My father tried to wake them, but they appear to be in a magically induced coma. Ajax is with them now."

"And no doubt blaming you for it," Shade added, running his fingers through his dark hair.

"He's not my biggest fan," Kols agreed solemnly. "But I didn't do it."

"I know you didn't," Shade replied, surprising me.

"How do you know that?" I wondered out loud, suspicious. "Where were you and Aflora?"

He arched a brow. "Are you asking if we did it?"

"No, I'm asking how you know Kols didn't do it and also where you took Aflora."

"Sounds like an inquiry underlined in an accusation," Shade drawled. "What do you think we were doing, Zeph?" He glanced down pointedly at his bare abdomen. "Frolicking around the village?"

"He's just surprised that you'd so readily believe my innocence," Kols said, folding his arms. "And frankly, so am I."

Aflora pushed off the door, drawing Shade's focus to her. She arched her brows at him, her eyes intense, but didn't say anything. He gave her a similar look, then cocked his head to the side as if he were indulging her.

Several beats passed, the intensity between them mounting by the second.

My lips parted as understanding sliced a hole through my chest. "You finished the mating."

Kols jolted as if he'd been shot, his eyes widening. "You bit her again?"

Shade grunted, then twisted to show the opposite side of his neck and the healing mark on his throat. "She bit me first."

Aflora's cheeks reddened as Kols and I turned to gape at her. "You bit Shade?" I asked, the question stabbing me in the gut.

She chose him.

She chose him and not me.

My abdomen clenched with the realization. It was one thing to watch her with Kols, but to know she enjoyed Shade, too... I wasn't sure how to accept that.

"I... yes," she whispered, her tongue snaking out to dampen her lips. "He pulled me out of the spell, and, um, things got heated."

Shade smirked at her description, while Kols narrowed his gaze. "What spell?"

Yeah, I was still on the realization that Aflora fucking bit Shade.

And not me.

Or Kols.

After a week of playing.

She still doesn't trust me, I realized. Not that I could blame her, but the knowledge of it hurt a bit. Even if I did deserve it.

"Headmaster Irwin had us practice psychometry in class today. Aflora's object took her on a ride through the past, and not one she was particularly prepared for." He gazed at our mate, his blue eyes flickering with comments unspoken.

Because they could communicate telepathically now.

Because they were fully mated.

I palmed the back of my neck. *Get a grip*, I told myself. *This isn't the end of the world. She's still mine.*

But somehow she didn't feel very connected to me. If anything, I felt... removed. I frowned, not liking this sensation at all. It made me want to grab her and bite her again, to stake my claim and ensure she still felt me inside her.

Since when did I feel possessive over women?

Since this one stepped into my life, I thought sourly, annoyed.

"You're right," Aflora said, breaking the silence.

"I know," Shade replied.

"So modest." She rolled her eyes, but I sensed her humor. They were teasing each other, their relationship having moved to a level of intimacy that was much deeper than the one I shared with her.

I glanced at Kols to see if this bothered him as much as it did me, but he seemed more intent on whatever our mate intended to say. Was he not even the slightest bit jealous? Or was he hiding it better?

Oh, but wait, he had his elemental bond to her as well.

Because she'd chosen him as her mate.

Which meant he had nothing to fear, because she wanted him, just like she wanted Shade.

So where did that leave me? And why the hell was I spending all this time pondering such trivial bullshit? Emotions weren't my thing. I preferred actions.

Except that was precisely the problem—Aflora's actions proved her desires for Shade and Kols, while I remained third. The male who had bitten and claimed her without her reciprocation, all to save her from imploding.

It'd been a required reaction to her situation.

Perhaps that was all it meant to her.

No.

She at least desired me a little, because our passion was off-the-charts hot. That couldn't be faked. I read women well. I knew their tells. And everything Aflora's body said during our sexual interludes confirmed she wanted me.

Maybe her mind just hadn't realized it yet.

I nodded to myself. All right. A challenge. I liked challenges. If she needed me to prove myself to her, then I would.

Although, I was doing one hell of a job of that right now because she'd been talking for the last few minutes and I didn't have a fucking clue what she'd just said.

This woman is destroying me, I thought, irritated.

I wasn't a man who held conversations in my head or thought about how to woo a female. I fucked them. End of discussion.

Yet Aflora was different.

I actually cared about what she thought of me, and I didn't quite enjoy that revelation. Not giving a damn was far easier.

And utterly impossible where she was concerned.

"Shit," Kols said, drawing me out of my head.

Because yeah, I'd missed whatever Aflora had just said since I was too lost in my feelings. *Who the fuck is this jealous fool in my head, and how the hell do I get rid of him?*

"So whoever enchanted the rock wanted you to find it," Kols continued, palming the back of his neck.

"And somehow convinced Headmaster Irwin to do a psychometry lesson," Shade added.

Okay, clearly I'd missed something important. If I kept listening, maybe I'd figure it out.

"While ensuring Aflora picked it from the items," Kols muttered, then whistled. "That's…"

"Unnerving," Aflora whispered, wrapping her arms around herself. "But that's not all."

"I'm afraid to ask," Kols said.

Aflora looked at Shade for a moment, the two of them sharing some hidden message. "I recognized the magic during the attack," she whispered as if uttering the secret out loud.

Shade didn't look surprised, which meant he already knew this or had suspected it.

Which was big fucking news to me because I had no idea, nor had I come close to sensing Aflora's connection to it. And given that I'd been the one spending time with her after the incident, I should have at least had an inkling about it.

"Why didn't you say anything?" I demanded, angry more at myself than at her. However, my tone came out scolding, causing her to flinch. Yet I couldn't apologize, because she should have said something.

"I… I wasn't sure if I should mention it," she admitted softly. "I wasn't even sure what I felt."

"A simple comment stating you recognized the magic would have sufficed," I chastised her.

"And when should I have told you?" she countered. "When the Warrior Bloods were searching the suite?"

"Oh, the two-hour wait before that would have been just fine. Or, I don't know, before you sucked my cock. That would have worked, too."

She bristled. "What? Do you think I hid it because I'm guilty?"

"I'm honestly not sure what to think, Aflora."

"This isn't helping," Kols cut in, stepping forward as if to get between us. Only then did I realize I was pretty much squaring off with Aflora in the middle of her room.

Great, Zeph. Really taking that whole "wooing the female" thing to the next level, I thought sourly.

I backed off, my hand scrubbing over my face as I forced myself to cool down. My annoyance wasn't with her but with myself. Taking it out on her wouldn't fix the situation. "You should have told us," I said, my voice softer now. Well, softer than before. It still came out sounding gruff and displeased.

"I told you now," she replied, fire flashing in her eyes. "But your reaction makes me wish I hadn't."

Ouch.

And also deserved.

"I'm glad you did," Kols interjected, stepping in front of her and forcing her to look at him and not me.

Always the hero.

He was a prince, after all.

I just served him and his entire family.

And now Aflora.

"When you say 'familiar,' do you mean it was elemental in nature?" Kols asked her. "Or maybe it felt similar to your Midnight Fae abilities?"

I couldn't see her face, but I imagined she had a contemplative gleam in her gaze—the one that always conveyed her intelligence and ability to strategize. That look always intrigued me. But as much as I wanted to see it now, I stared at the back of Kols's head instead.

He often grounded me.

Which I unfortunately needed at the moment.

"It reminded me of my Quandary magic," she finally replied. "And I sensed it before the chaos began, almost like the being had warned me of his presence before attacking."

My brow furrowed. "How do you know it was a male?"

"Did you miss the part about her journey in his body through the Death Blood Education Building?" Shade asked, arching a brow. "She heard his voice."

Right. That'd been when I wasn't paying attention. Now I really regretted the trip through my head. "She heard him?"

"She *was* him," Shade corrected, his icy gaze turning glacial. "He imprinted the memory on the rock for her to find, even left her a message. And I'm guessing it wasn't a coincidence that today, of all days, he attacked the village. Because he set it up for her to travel back in time with that rock just before making another statement. Oh, and I'm also going to venture a guess to say the tavern was done on purpose."

"Why don't I believe those are guesses?" I countered, narrowing my eyes. He spoke with confidence, telling me he knew a lot more than he was letting on. "There's something you're not telling us."

"There's a hell of a lot I'm not telling you," he retorted. "And I can't. That's not how the future works."

"Oh, for fuck's sake, not this shit again about the future." I wanted to beat some sense into his cryptic ass, and probably would have if Aflora hadn't stepped out from behind Kols and directly into my path.

Her palm found my abdomen as she ensured that I didn't step any closer to the bed, her gaze burning into mine. "Zeph."

My inner turmoil ceased in the space of a breath, my hands grasping her hips to pull her closer as if I craved her comfort. And maybe I did. "Aflora," I murmured, utterly lost to her.

Surprise flickered through her features as if she expected more of a fight. But I didn't want to argue with her or upset her. I merely needed to protect her.

"I wish you would have told me," I admitted, my voice far less combative than earlier. Hell, I sounded downright contrite. And the shock rolling off Kols told me just how out of character this was for me, but I couldn't seem to help it. "I can't protect you if I don't know what's going on, pixie flower."

Her features softened considerably, her irises flaring with emotion. "I should have told you."

I nodded in agreement. "But at least you did now," I conceded.

She lifted up onto her toes to brush a kiss against my jaw. "I'm not used to relying on others," she whispered.

"I know," I replied just as quietly.

"Well, I think it's pretty clear what our next steps are," Shade drawled from her bed.

"Yeah? Please share because I have no idea what the hell is going on," Kols said.

Shade grinned, the cocky bastard enjoying our torment just a smidge too much. "We need to take Aflora to the village and see if she senses the same energy signature. If she does, it'll prove it's the same person who attacked the school."

"The Council is already sure of that," Kols pointed out.

"Maybe, but they also think you're responsible. So if we're going on what they believe, then..." Shade let that insinuation hang in the air.

"He's right," I said, hating that I agreed with the Death Blood but also respecting the hell out of his reasoning skills. "We need to see if Aflora can sense anything at the attack site. She might be able to give us a hint about who it is, or maybe see something the Council hasn't."

Shade nodded. "Exactly."

Aflora glanced over her shoulder at the male on her bed, and they engaged in another of those secret conversations that ended with the Death Blood smirking. She shook her head in response, clearly exasperated.

"What are we missing?" Kols asked.

"He's leading us," Aflora said in a tone that sounded both amused and irritated at the same time. "He can't tell us what he actually knows, so he's ensuring we wander down the right path instead."

Shade dipped his chin in acknowledgment, causing me to frown. "Why don't you cut the cryptic bullshit and just tell us what you actually know?" I suggested, irritated with this game.

"He can't," Aflora replied, drawing my attention back to her. "Just like he can't tell me why I recognized the magic."

I gaped at her. "That doesn't make any sense."

"It does now that I know his history," she whispered.

"History?" Kols repeated. "I don't understand."

"It's a long, drawn-out story," Shade replied. "But your grandfather knows it well."

"What the fuck are you talking about?" Kols demanded, taking the words right out of my mouth.

"Ask him," Shade encouraged. "Tell him you want to know what really happened to Zenaida, Kodiak, and Vadim all those years ago. If he tells you the truth, you'll have your answer."

"Or you could enlighten me now," Kols suggested, his tone indicating he knew Shade would never oblige.

"And what fun would that be?" the Death Blood asked, clearly amused.

"Okay, that's enough," Aflora said, turning in my arms. Rather than leave me, she pressed her back to my chest, allowing me to wrap my arms around her.

"We're going to need to learn to trust each other." She looked pointedly at Kols and Shade, but I knew she included me in that statement. "There's someone trying to frame Kols, and whoever that person is has an energy signature I recognize. So I agree with Shade that we should visit the village, but it'll need to be on our next free day to avoid anyone wondering why we're there."

My chest warmed at her taking charge and thinking everything through logically. Kols and Shade seemed to approve as well, their gazes reverent.

We really were royally screwed when it came to this woman.

Our only saving grace was that she didn't seem to know it yet.

"Obviously Kols can't go with us," she continued. "So it'll need to be me and Zeph. Shade, too, if he wants to go. And we can just say I wanted some spritemead and proper Elemental Fae food from the tavern. That can't be too far-fetched an excuse, right?"

"It's believable," I agreed, thinking about her obsession with dragon steak and loaves.

"I'll use my next free day to talk to my dad," Kols said. "And maybe Constantine." The latter was spoken for Shade's benefit.

"A sound plan," Shade agreed, his lips curling. "And I'll definitely tag along to the tavern. Anrika's an old family friend."

"Of course she is," Aflora deadpanned.

Shade winked at her, another secret passing between them.

Rather than let it bother me, I pressed my nose to Aflora's hair and inhaled her familiar perfume, content to have her in my arms. She might not have claimed me yet, but she would. I'd make sure of it.

And in the interim, I'd protect her as best I could.

Including on our mission to the village.

Because something told me there was a lot more to this than just framing Kols.

It couldn't be a coincidence that Aflora arrived when she did, her Quandary Blood powers flickering to awareness right before these attacks began.

Shade met my gaze, his eyes telling me a story I longed to decipher. "I'm going to figure you out," I promised him.

"Good," he replied, welcoming the challenge. "I'm counting on it."

Aflora yawned, drawing all of our attention to her. I lifted her into my arms and set her on the bed beside Shade, deciding to offer him my own version of an olive branch.

"We'll leave you two to rest," I said, pressing my lips to Aflora's temple.

"I'll be in the guest room tonight, and Kols will be right next door. Sweet dreams, pixie flower."

Shade's glimmer of surprise was worth my boon.

Yeah, I could be a good guy when I tried.

Remember that, I told him with my eyes, then turned and let Kols say his good night.

Rather than wait for him in the hall, I went to the guest room and closed the door. There would be no dream-walking tonight. Aflora deserved her time with Shade. Even if it did make me want to break something.

CHAPTER TWENTY-FIVE

AFLORA

I clasped my cloak around my neck, my fingers drawing over the collar beneath. Kols had taken it off me again last night, then held me while I slept in his bed. Zeph hadn't joined us, choosing to stay in the guest room for the fourth day in a row.

It sort of felt like he was avoiding me. Although, I'd seen and spoken to him several times because he'd essentially moved into Kols's guest suite. And he'd led class yesterday, as well as two days before that, so he wasn't entirely evading me. He just had this distant air about him that I didn't understand.

We also hadn't been intimate since the day I returned with Shade—an oddity only because we'd spent every day for a week prior to that getting to know each other between the sheets. Then this week, he'd barely kissed me.

Something was definitely bothering him.

Which, in turn, left me uneasy.

Shade had sent a message saying he'd meet us in the village later. He wanted to check on Ajax because he hadn't been in class since the attack on the tavern. I'd told him not to worry about me, that I'd be fine with Zeph. But as I studied myself in the mirror, I wondered if that were true.

Then the male in question knocked on my door, his voice soft as he uttered my name from the hallway. "Are you ready?" he added in that same tone.

I swallowed and nodded, more to myself than to him since he couldn't see me. "Yeah," I called back to him, then grabbed my wand from my nightstand, tucked it into my cloak, and met him at the threshold of my room.

His green eyes roamed over me with interest, his lips curling a little. "Casual looks good on you," he murmured, noting my jeans and cream-colored sweater. I had on a pair of boots as well that covered my calves up to my knees. It seemed a bit strange, but Ella showed me how to wear them on the outside of my pants. She claimed it was all the rage in the Human Realm.

Some days I really missed my Elemental Fae roots and the wardrobe that came with it. Those outfits were far simpler and nature friendly. Mostly because I used to make my clothes out of the earth.

These were… not as natural.

But Zeph seemed to approve.

He wrapped his palm around my nape, drawing me to him for a long, sensuous kiss that had me wondering if I'd just misunderstood his behavior these last few days. Because wow. His tongue really knew how to engage mine. I hummed against him in approval, my body melting into his as one of his arms cradled my lower back while his opposite remained against my neck.

Minutes passed, his warmth bleeding into me and claiming me in a sensual manner. I pressed my palms to his black sweater, the soft material gliding across his hard abdomen beneath.

He nipped my lower lip, then deepened our kiss with a groan before walking me backward into my room. It was the wrong direction, but I didn't mind. I'd missed him. I'd missed *this*.

And it was our first time doing this without any sort of audience.

Because we were finally alone.

Pleasure zipped down my spine, my heart racing with excitement.

Yes, yes. More, please.

Zeph must have read the need building inside me, because the arm around my back slid lower, his palm grabbing my ass to yank me flush against his growing arousal. I moaned in response, my fingers gliding up his sweater to his broad shoulders.

The back of my knees hit the edge of my bed, when a giggling in the hallway interrupted our moment. Zeph broke away from me so quickly I nearly fell onto the mattress, but my legs locked into place, keeping me upright.

"You think that's cute, do you?" Tray asked, sounding genuinely amused by whatever Ella had just done.

The door to their bedroom closed as Ella replied, "I do, yep. If you're nice to me, I'll consider handling that issue for you later."

"Oh, you'll be handling it all right, El. I guarantee it."

"Now who's being cocky?"

"I called you confident, not cocky."

"Uh-huh," she replied, her voice growing fainter as they walked toward the living area and away from the bedrooms. "It held the same implication."

"We should probably go," Zeph said, his voice low.

I swallowed, nodding. "Yeah."

Ella and Tray didn't know about our quad-bond, something Zeph made apparent by leaving my room ahead of me and leading the way down the hall in his usual aloof manner. His presence in the guest suite didn't seem to raise any questions. He shared a history with Kols, so Ella and Tray had just sort of accepted his staying here even though he had a place next door.

"Where are you two heading off to?" Tray asked as we entered the living area. He had Ella's hips pressed up against the counter that divided the kitchen from the rest of the room. It was set up like a little eating nook with stools, but most of us used the dining table beside the kitchen instead.

"Aflora wants a proper loaf," Zeph replied, sounding annoyed. "Because apparently my magicked ones aren't good enough for her."

"Well, if you just figured out what mouseberries were, this wouldn't be a problem," I shot back, playing along.

He grunted and grabbed his cloak from the back of the couch. "Let's go, Earth Fae."

"Hold on," Tray said, stepping away from Ella to give us an incredulous look. "Are you going to the village?"

"Where else would we go?" Zeph asked, arching a brow. "New York? London? Oh, no, I know—we'll just go visit Elemental Fae Academy. I'm sure no one will mind at all."

"Don't be a dick," Tray snapped. "Why the hell would you go to the tavern right now?"

Zeph waved at me. "Because Aflora wants some mustard berries."

"Mouseberries," I corrected him.

He gave Tray a look that said, *Do you see what I'm dealing with here?*

Tray wasn't amused, nor was he buying the excuse. "Kols is with my father right now trying to convince him that he's innocent, and you're heading off to the scene of the crime. Don't think for one second I believe your bullshit about *mouseberries*."

"You're right," Zeph drawled. "It's the spritemead she's really after."

Ella cleared her throat. "Guys, Tray has a point. The village has to be crawling with Warrior Bloods right now, and I doubt the tavern is even open."

"It is," Zeph replied. "I already spoke to Anrika. She said it's perfectly safe for us to come in, so we're going for a midnight lunch. You can believe whatever you want, Tray. As for the Warrior Bloods, then I guess it's a good thing I'm one of them. Now let's go, Aflora." He walked through the threshold before either of them could comment, clearly done with the conversation.

"Bastard," Tray muttered. "This is a horrible idea."

"I'll be okay," I promised him.

"I don't know what you two are up to, but be careful," Ella pressed, obviously seeing right through our excuse as well.

At least we tried. "We'll be fine," I told her, forcing a smile. "See you in a few hours."

Taking a page from Zeph's book, I slipped through the threshold before they could argue and found him waiting against the wall for me in the residential hallway. He arched a brow, then cocked his head to the side as if to say, *Let's go.*

I followed him silently past all the creepy gargoyles and continued to trail after him down the two flights of stairs. He led me outside and along the various paths to the raven field without saying a word and called up the portal for us to step through.

It wasn't until the birds began to swarm around us that he touched me, his palm a brand to my lower back as he pulled me close under the guise of keeping me safe during transport. But I felt the lingering need in his embrace, just as I sensed his lips in my hair as he gifted me a kiss where no one could see.

My mouth curled upward.

This side of Zeph—the quietly affectionate side—excited me. Mostly because he didn't let anyone else see this part of him. He sometimes revealed it in front of Kols and had sort of showed it to Shade the other night, but it all tied back to his tenderness with me. I suspected it was a foreign reaction for him, which only made it more special.

"We're here," he whispered, drawing my attention to the cloak closet around us.

I glanced up at him and went to my toes to kiss the edge of his mouth. "They're mouseberries," I informed him softly, earning a smile in return. "And I'm going to make you try one today."

He smirked. "Can't wait." His lips captured mine unexpectedly, his tongue dominating mine in a sweep of power that left me weak in the knees.

Just as quickly, he stepped back, leaving me reeling in his wake, and opened the door to reveal the exit into the street. He winked and turned, expecting me to follow.

"Willow stump," I muttered, stepping out of the closet and onto the cobblestone streets. He was only a foot ahead, his gait intentionally slow to allow me to keep up.

The village was less busy than my last visit, most of the Midnight Fae walking with a businesslike briskness rather than meandering and socializing with one another.

My stomach twisted at the change in atmosphere and the resulting sense of unease in the air. It reminded me of why we were here, especially as we rounded the corner to see the tavern's exterior. While the stones resembled the same restaurant I'd visited a few weeks ago, I could feel the newness of it and the residual magic left behind from the restoration. Just like the Death Blood Education Building.

I swallowed, my palms dampening with each step.

Dark power lingered in the air.

Quandary magic, I recognized with a breath. That was why it felt familiar. It reminded me of a puzzle recently undone and put back together, only the strings were left behind for a Midnight Fae to tease and unwind.

A Midnight Fae like me.

I paused on the sidewalk, a few steps away from the tavern.

"He knew I'd come," I said to myself, glancing around, trying to find what other clues he left for me to unravel.

"What?" Zeph asked, coming to my side.

"I can feel him," I whispered, startled by the realization. "His energy signature is thick, like he left it for me as a clue to find. But why would he do that?"

Was it even intentional?

I frowned.

Yes. It was definitely intentional. Just like the rock.

"We should—"

"Ah, you're here!" Anrika rushed outside with a giant grin on her face that didn't quite reach her eyes, silencing what I'd been about to say. "When Guardian Zephyrus called to say you wanted to stop by, I prepped my kitchen and have quite the buffet of items for you to enjoy. Come on in and I'll get you both settled."

Zeph made a gesture with his hand. "After you, Aflora."

This was where having the mate bond in place would be really handy because I could tell him with my mind how bad an idea this was, but I had no way of communicating that without alerting Anrika. So I gave him a tight smile and followed our hostess inside to the same booth I'd sat in with Tray and Ella a few weeks prior.

The gargoyle who served us, however, was nowhere in sight.

I frowned, wondering where he'd run off to, but Anrika distracted me with a large glass of spritemead a few seconds after I sat down.

"I had this waiting for you," she explained with a twinkle in her eyes.

"Thank you," I said, uncertain of how I felt about that.

She called up some American drink for Zeph. "Your usual," she drawled. "Be back in a jiffy." She disappeared into a puff of glitter that made me sneeze.

Zeph's lips curved upward, his amusement palpable. "I think you have a fan."

"Something's not right," I rushed to say, my voice quiet. "I think he's here, Zeph." Because I still felt him. *Everywhere.*

Yet the tavern was empty—the complete opposite of my last visit here. There'd been Midnight Fae coming and going throughout our meal, everyone jovial and chatty.

Today felt like... a funeral.

I shivered at the thought, the hairs along my arms rising on end.

What's wrong, little rose?

I jumped at Shade's mental interruption, my eyes flying around the room to search for him. *Where are you?*

With Ajax, he replied. *I can sense your panic. What's going on?*

The tavern, it feels—

"Aflora?" Zeph said, his brow creased. "Are you listening to me?"

"Shade," I replied, shaking my head as my Death Blood mate began talking again.

It feels like what?

It feels like he's here, I rushed to say to him, then focused on Zeph. "He's—Shade's—in my head. He..."

Are you sure? Or is it his energy signature you're sensing? Shade asked, his voice sounding rushed in my thoughts, like he was pacing while speaking.

It feels fresh. Too fresh. Like the day of the attack. I hadn't felt him at all at the

Death Blood Education Building that day we worked on psychometry spells, yet I sensed him *everywhere* here. *This feels intentional. Like he knew I'd come.*

I'm on my way.

I opened my mouth to let Zeph know, when his phone began to ring. With a frown, he pulled it from his cloak pocket and brought it to his ear. "Zephyrus." His expression gave nothing away as whoever it was spoke on the other line, his green eyes holding mine the entire time. "I see." The masculine tones of the speaker created a deep hum.

Did you call Zeph? I asked Shade.

No reply, suggesting it was him.

"Understood. You know where we'll be." Zeph hung up the phone, sliding it into his pocket once more.

"Shade?" I guessed.

"No. Kols. He's been called into an emergency Council meeting with the Elders." His lips flattened. "It doesn't look good, Aflora. We should go."

I nodded, agreeing, just as Anrika appeared with a tray of delicious-smelling loaves. My mouth practically watered for them, but my pulse thrummed a warning in my ears that I couldn't ignore.

"Can we wrap these up to go?" Zeph asked her softly. "I just received a call from Prince Kolstov, and we've been requested at Nacht Manor."

The Council is convening with the Elders, Shade informed me, his mental voice annoyed. *Get the hell out of there, Aflora. This can't be a coincidence.*

We're working on leaving, but Zeph just said we're needed at Nacht Manor? I phrased it as a question because it seemed strange to me.

He must be lying to protect you. Trust him, Aflora. He won't let you down.

Famous last words, I thought back at him. *The last time I trusted Zeph, I ended up in a dungeon.*

I won't let anything happen to you, little rose, Shade vowed. *And neither will Zeph. Trust your mates.*

It said a lot that Shade wanted me to put my faith in Zeph. They constantly bickered with one another, but it seemed, on this point, my Death Blood mate trusted my Warrior Blood mate.

Anrika had been in the middle of talking to Zeph, her excitement lost to a cloud of concern. "Of course," she was saying, picking up our untouched glasses. She disappeared without the glitter this time.

Zeph sighed and rubbed his hand over his face. "I hate doing this to her."

"Doing what?" I asked, wondering what else he had planned.

"Everyone is too unnerved by what happened here to come in for a bite, and I'd hoped to provide her with a little bit of normalcy today. Unfortunately, I've just further driven the proverbial stake through her heart." He shook his head. "Things are changing. It unsettles people."

I leaned forward, dropping my voice to a whisper. "Can you feel the magic?" I asked him. "The lingering spells?"

He frowned. "From the restoration?"

"No, the at—"

"Here you are," Anrika announced, reappearing with a floating bag beside her and two plastic cups. She tried to smile, but it turned into more of a grimace. Her disappointment was palpable.

"Thank you, Anrika," Zeph murmured, holding out a card. "Aflora has been craving food from home, so I'm wondering if there's a way to start ordering a few meals a week. I'll talk to Kolstov to see if Sir Kristoff is open to picking it up for us."

"You don't need to do that, Zephyrus."

"Oh, but I do," he replied, grinning. "Aflora needs the sustenance and hates the Academy food."

Well, he wasn't wrong about that. But I also knew he was doing this to be supportive, and seeing that side of him warmed my heart.

He stood and kissed her on the cheek. "Thanks again," he said to her before waving his hand over the bags. "I'll be in touch soon."

Anrika nodded, tears glistening in her eyes. I stood to follow him, but she stepped into my path, her hands finding my shoulders. "Be careful," she said in a voice so soft I could barely hear her. "If they find out what you are, they'll come for you, too."

I froze as she disappeared.

Zeph turned with an arched eyebrow, having missed her words.

I opened my mouth to tell him, when a strange energy caressed my skin, causing all the hairs along my arms to stand—just like it did that day at the Academy. Right before the attack. "We need to run," I told him urgently, my eyes rounding.

Chills skated up and down my body, that familiar magic kissing my senses.

Zeph grabbed my hand and yanked me forward, the food and drinks forgotten as he pulled me outside and into the empty street.

Not a soul in sight.

Similar to what I'd seen in the vision after the mysterious male had woven spells to vacate the building.

Zeph didn't seem to notice, his focus on getting me to the portal, but the cobblestones began to shake beneath a wave of harsh power.

I jolted to a stop, my essence reacting to the incoming attack. *No!*

Electricity hummed over my being, crafting an enchanted net of cerulean blue. I didn't allow myself a moment to consider the repercussions, my instincts roaring to life and forcing me to wrap the buzzing cloak around myself and Zeph to block the incoming meddlesome energy.

Wind soared around us, the familiar caw of alarms and stone shifting to fight.

I caught the glimpse of white, there and gone in a flash, a warm chuckle brushing my ear. I whirled around, searching for the culprit, only to find air.

Zeph was speaking, his tone insistent, but I couldn't stop hunting for the source of power.

Who are you? I demanded, the words in my mind rather than out loud.

Your destiny, a deep, sensual voice replied. *My darling Aflora, you truly have grown into a beautiful woman. Just like your mother.*

Another kiss of power touched my heart, working its way through my blood, heating all my frozen limbs beneath a ripple of authority and awareness. I tried to track him, but he lingered in the shadows, his presence there and gone in the breeze.

We'll play again soon, he promised darkly. *Retribution will be ours.*

He started to hum the song my mother taught me as a child, the haunting melody weaving an enchantment through my spirit and drawing out the memory of my past.

Only it was no longer my mother singing to me, but another—a male without a face, his voice hypnotic and empowering. I closed my eyes, lost to the sound, to the moment in my history that seemed forever changed.

I began to sing with him.

A promise.

Our futures forever intertwined.

He owned half my soul.

"I'll protect her," I heard him saying. "Always."

"Then our deal is done," another voice replied. Lighter. Feminine.

"Mom?" I asked.

But no one heard me. They were too busy enacting a blood vow, with my life at the center of the puzzle.

Something sharp bit into my neck. His teeth. He swallowed. Binding us as one in a forbidden claim.

"Aflora!"

I couldn't open my eyes, my world painted in shades of black. Of a destiny I never desired, but chosen for me by another.

"Aflora!"

The voice had begun to change, the deep quality one I recognized.

My vision wavered, someone shaking me to awareness once more.

And I opened my eyes to see bright green orbs of horror staring down at me, his beautiful lips reddened by my blood.

"Zeph?" I whispered, my voice a rasp of sound. Had his been the bite I felt?

"Fuck," he breathed. "You scared the shit out of me."

His mouth touched mine, my essence sweet on his tongue.

He'd bitten me again, tying us closer together.

Yet it wasn't his image in my mind but one of a male cloaked in white.

My other half.

Then everything went black once more, Zeph's curse the last sound to grace my thoughts.

CHAPTER TWENTY-SIX

KOLS

Tadmir was late again. He sauntered in with a muttered apology to my father, then took his seat with a flourish, his white hair sprawling haphazardly against his shoulders.

None of the Seconds were invited to this emergency meeting, but Shade and I were included. I met his icy gaze across the table and noted his trademark boredom. The Death Blood really was skilled at hiding his intentions. Unlike his father, Aswad, who appeared to be brimming with annoyance beside him.

"Right, now that we're all accounted for, we can begin," my father announced, drawing the focus to the head of the table, where I sat beside him. Tray hadn't been allowed to attend, which prickled my nerves. My twin usually kept me grounded, and his absence only seemed to enhance the sense of foreboding in the air.

Something's coming.

Something I'm not going to like.

The Council rarely called upon the Elders, but this was the second time this week they were requested to join us.

My father reached out to them in the old ways, using his magic to summon the guidance of the ancient ones who ruled before us.

It was the only time I ever saw my grandfather, as well as my great-grandfather. I'd actually only met the two men three times throughout my twenty-four years, indicating how rare it was for them to be called to our chambers.

Midnight Fae lived forever unless killed via very specific means, which was why we only ascended once in a millennium. The oldest of our kind often slept to pass the time, eternity being a long time to live. Sometimes it impacted viewpoints of morality as well, causing the ancients to go mad with sadism. Those Elders were put down if they refused to sleep.

My grandfather had yet to require the mandate, his mind still sharp, as was evidenced in his gold eyes now as he appeared in the Council doorway. My great-grandfather followed behind him, their appearances similar in that they held the forever appearance of a thirty-year-old male, but I could see their ages in their gazes and in the way they carried themselves.

So incredibly old.

Several others followed them, their presence bringing with them a coldness that drilled ice through my veins. I looked at Shade again. He just yawned, like he was ready for a nap.

Never in my wildest dreams would I have imagined a time when I considered him to be my ally, yet I felt the pull to trust him today.

Because of Aflora.

This quad-bond had affected me in ways I never could have anticipated, starting with my desire to follow a Death Blood's lead.

I did my best to feign boredom as well, all the while hoping the band around my wrist concealed my forbidden connection to my mate. There was nothing I could do about the Earth Fae bond, but as none of them could see the elemental sources of power, I assumed I was safe in that regard.

The Elders sat in the available chairs, the rest choosing to stand around us. There were two dozen of them, all varying in age up to ten thousand years old.

I fought the urge to shiver, their presence always reminding me of a necropolis with their lifeless gazes and still forms. Some of them didn't even appear to be breathing.

My father cleared his throat, taking charge of the room in his classic manner. "Per our vote earlier this week, it's time to bring Kolstov into the fold," he announced.

My heart stopped beating. *What?* He couldn't be calling forward my ascension. My trials weren't done. And the Seconds would need to be here to witness it.

I didn't dare give away my confusion. Instead, I glanced at my father with an arched eyebrow, feigning confidence and curiosity at the same time.

"As you all know, Shadow was brought in on our efforts four months ago when we provided him with an induction task that solidified his membership," my father continued. "He's proven himself at every turn, and it's time to grant Kolstov the same opportunity."

Okay, I really did not like where this was going. Particularly at the mention of Shade already being on the inside. He didn't meet my gaze now, his focus on my father. "I've done what's best for Midnight Fae kind, Your Majesty," Shade said, the words probably the most respectful ones I'd ever heard leave his mouth. "And I'd do it again in a heartbeat."

Aswad dipped his head. "You've made our bloodline proud, son."

"I know," Shade agreed.

Several members of the Council nodded in agreement, while the Elders merely observed.

"Shadow's reports have indicated that Kolstov has behaved admirably in his handling of the Earth Fae Royal," my father said. "It serves as further proof of his acceptance of his future responsibilities, marking him as a loyal observer of our laws with the leadership qualities to carry out justice as we see fit."

"Hear, hear!" several Councilmen cheered, saluting me while I fought the urge to frown.

What the hell is going on? I wanted to demand but instead forced myself to remain silent. Something told me I was about to find out Shade's true motives. *Finally.* And I'd probably want to fucking kill him afterward.

"The recent attacks framing him as the culprit have made this even more important, which is the true purpose of today's meeting. We'll need his cooperation in bringing the revolutionaries to justice once and for all."

Fists pounded on the table, the excitement of the Councilmen stirring an ominous energy in the air. This wasn't going to end well.

"Bring him in, Warrior Danqris," my father said with a wave of his wand, sending the message to somewhere else in the building. Given the context of his words, I suspected it was the dungeon.

I swallowed and dared to meet Shade's gaze again, but he was too focused on his nails as he lounged like a king in his chair, oblivious to the growing animosity in the room.

"You see, Kolstov, we've been fighting a war for over a thousand years," my father explained. "Some centuries are quieter than others, but we caught wind of a growing revolution about fifteen years ago. Our Elders, the ultimate protectors of Midnight Fae kind, handled the disturbance for us, then advised us on what to do next."

"What kind of disturbance?" I asked, forcing a calmness in my tone that I didn't quite feel.

"One involving Quandary Bloods," my father replied.

Forcing surprise wasn't required, mostly because hearing him mention Quandary Bloods shocked the hell out of me. "Quandary Bloods?" I repeated. "How is that possible? They're dead."

"Exactly what I said a few months ago," Shade put in unhelpfully.

He and I would be having a serious discussion after this, one that would likely end in my fist meeting his arrogant face. I knew the bastard was hiding something, but never would have expected that it involved the Council and the Elders.

Fucking prat.

"The Quandary Bloods were mostly eradicated by Constantine Nacht and his Councilmen," Aswad said. "However, several escaped and went into hiding throughout the fae realms. Rather than worry Midnight Fae kind about the lingering threat, he wisely chose to safeguard the details with the Council and the Elders. And we've been working in secret ever since to eradicate the issue."

"Most of the problems have been dealt with," my grandfather added, his tone flat. "However, a stronger resistance has risen over the last two decades, and they've caused a few more issues than usual. We attempted to cut them down roughly fifteen years ago, but we weren't as successful as we would have liked. Which is why we allowed the Royal Earth Fae to live."

My father nodded. "Yes. Her parents were known loyalists, and we suspect she is, too."

"*What?*" I couldn't stop my reaction, my blood thrumming in my ears. *Known loyalists?*

And did they just admit to being the ones who killed Aflora's parents?!

"Why the hell didn't you tell me that from the beginning?" I demanded. And, holy fuck, did they know about her Quandary Blood abilities?

Yes. They had to. Because Shade had been informing them the entire time.

Which meant they knew about our bonds as well.

"For what it's worth, I've yet to see any evidence to support that theory," Shade said calmly, his gaze catching mine. "You've been living with her. Have you seen anything to suggest she supports the resistance?"

I stared at him. *Is this a trap to test my loyalty to the Council? Or is he trying to tell me something?*

"I didn't even know there was a resistance until right now," I replied through gritted teeth. Technically, that was true. It also avoided the direct question he'd just asked me, something he seemed keen on doing. Time to repay him the favor. "So how would I know what to look for?" I countered.

What the fresh hell is happening here? I wondered, my mind whirring with a multitude of ideas at once.

Did Shade play us all from the beginning? Did he never care about Aflora? I knew he'd been hiding something, as did Zeph, yet the Council didn't seem to know all the details.

Unless they were biding their time with me?

"It's true. She's shown no signs of linking to the resistance," my father said, drawing my attention back to him. "Between Kolstov's and Shadow's reports, I have seen no evidence of a connection."

"That's why you had her attend the Academy," I realized, thinking out loud. "To use her as bait."

He dipped his chin in affirmation. "Yes, we felt sure the Quandary Bloods would come for her out of loyalty to her parents. We suspect that was the point of the attack last week as well, but you and Zephyrus thwarted the attempt to collect her, which is the other reason we needed to bring you in—so that doesn't happen again."

I blinked. *Out of loyalty to her parents? Because they helped Quandary Bloods?* No, those weren't the most important questions to ask. Instead, I focused on the more prevalent issue at hand. "You want her to be taken?"

Another nod. "Shadow's bonding with her allows us greater insight into her mind, and now that they've completed their mating, he can fully track her. So if the resistance takes her, we can use her as a beacon to take them down."

He glanced at my grandfather. "It was Constantine's idea, and a brilliant one at that."

"You told Shade to bite her," I said, feeling numb inside.

"Yes, we did," my father confirmed.

That doesn't make any sense. "Then why did the Council almost vote him out afterward?" I asked, unable to mask my confusion.

"It was all for show," Shade informed me. "They suspect that one of the Seconds is working with the resistance and feeding them information."

My father nodded. "Yes. So we're using them to stay one step ahead, which is why we had to make it look like Shade was being punished for his forbidden actions."

"You were really convincing," I said, looking pointedly at Tadmir.

The Malefic Fae lifted a shoulder. "We all make sacrifices for the greater good. Mine is to temporarily hold off on a powerful alignment. Shadow's will be to kill his Elemental mate and take my daughter at a later date."

My stomach twisted at the casual way he just informed me of Aflora's pending assassination. But what really bothered me was Shade's bored expression, like the thought of hurting her didn't impact him in the slightest.

Yet he hadn't said anything about our quad-bond.

Which indicated there was more at play here than I knew, unless this was all leading up to that major reveal. Maybe he intended to take my throne, and that was his trump card.

Hmm, no. If that were the case, my father would be simmering with anger toward me. Instead, he seemed pleased to be bringing me *into the fold*, as he'd called it.

A knock sounded through the chamber, drawing my father's gaze to the door. "Ah, that must be Danqris with our guest." He glanced around the room as if to determine our readiness, then called out, "Enter."

Danqris and Warlow entered with Headmaster Irwin clamped between them. The Death Blood professor's eyes were wild as he took in the audience before him, his skin paling to a sheet of white. "I-I didn't—"

"Silence," my father bellowed, his cheeks reddening with anger. "You will speak when spoken to." He shot a spell through the air, aimed at the headmaster's mouth, physically silencing the fae. "Put him in the chair," he instructed, gesturing to the lone visitor chair that no one ever wanted to find themselves in.

I swallowed and risked a glance at Shade.

He didn't give anything away, yet somehow, I sensed his unease.

Yes, something was definitely not right here. *What game are you playing?* I wanted to ask him, but the attention in the room had shifted to the sweating headmaster. He appeared ready to pass out.

"Shadow, enlighten everyone with the information you provided me," my father instructed.

I already knew what story he intended to share with the room—the one Aflora had given us the other day about her psychometry experience.

Only, as Shade spoke, I noticed he left out key details of her encounter. Such as how the power felt familiar and how she sensed the energy during the initial attack. He did include the bit about the fae sending her a message, but he changed the message slightly, making it less personal and more of a warning.

"He informed her that they would be coming for her soon but didn't say when" was Shade's summary. "I'm monitoring the situation."

My father nodded at that last sentence, pleased with Shade's supposed acquiescence.

Yet I knew the real story and saw how he morphed the truth to give the Council just what they wanted to know, without revealing the crucial points.

Just like he frequently did with me.

I took that as a sign to not write him off just yet. He seemed to be playing a role here, as he did with everything.

All right, I thought. *I'll play along. For now.*

"Do you believe Headmaster Irwin knowingly provided her with the item, or was he enchanted?" Chern asked, speaking up for the first time today. The intricate patterns woven into his bald scalp seemed to thrive with power as he engaged his Sangré magic to determine the various logical avenues of this situation.

"I believe he was enchanted," Shade admitted. "He seemed rather out of it that day in class, like he was speaking without really being there."

Headmaster Irwin started to nod, but a look from my father froze the male in place.

"There are ways to determine what he knew and what he didn't," Chern murmured. "I would need a few hours with him."

"Would you mind allowing Kolstov to join you for the interrogation? I feel it would be a good learning experience," my father said. "It'll also provide a reasonable introduction into what we know about the resistance, too."

Chern nodded. "I would be happy to bestow my experience upon him."

I suspected that would include a magical transfer of knowledge, given that was what Sangré Bloods were most well-known for doing.

"May I join as well?" Shade asked. "As the key witness, I may have some additional suggestions for your line of questioning."

"Of course," my father replied, glancing at Chern. "Assuming you agree?"

The Sangré Councilman bobbed his head in confirmation once more. "It would be a wise move, yes."

"Then it's settled," my father said, clapping me on the back. "Welcome to the inner circle, Kolstov. There's not a grand ceremony for this, I'm afraid. But you'll get that when you ascend." He winked.

I forced a smile, my heart in my stomach. "Understood. Does Tray know any of this?"

My father shook his head. "He doesn't."

"You don't suspect him of feeding information to the resistance, do you?" I asked him, incredulous. "Because I can assure you, he's not."

My father chuckled. "No. We know it's not Tray, or you. We only kept you in the dark because this is usually considered an ascension privilege, and you have enough to worry about with your ascension trials. However, the recent attacks framing you required us to move up our time frame. And you also did too good a job protecting the bait, leaving us no choice but to bring you in so it doesn't happen again."

"Yes, the next time there's an attempt to collect her, we need you to allow it to happen," my grandfather added, his gold irises whirling with uncanny power. "It's our best lead to tracking them."

"Right," I replied. "Because of her mating bond to Shade."

"Exactly," my father murmured. "The Elders had originally wanted it to be you, but we feared no one would believe you'd disregard such a fundamental law on a whim."

"So they tapped the one known for rule-breaking," Shade drawled. "Me."

My grandfather grunted. "You didn't even balk at the request."

"Of course I didn't. You gave me permission to taste an Elemental Fae, and a gorgeous one at that. Why the hell would I refuse?" Shade sounded so flippant, as if we were discussing the damn weather. But I was starting to recognize his tactics for avoidance. He made jokes to deflect, and in this case, he wanted everyone to believe Aflora meant nothing to him.

However, if that were true, then he would have told them all about our united bonds, and he hadn't.

"Yeah, yeah," Tadmir replied. "Enjoy it while it lasts, Death Blood. You're still promised to my daughter."

Shade smiled. "I'm aware of my obligations, Malefic Blood. Just enjoying my freedom while I can."

"Shall we give Chern the room?" my grandfather suggested, gesturing to the patiently waiting Sangré Councilman. "Or do you prefer the dungeon for your interrogation?"

"The room is fine," Chern replied.

"Then we'll reconvene in three hours," my father announced, standing and squeezing my shoulder. "Try to learn what you can. We'll talk more over dinner later."

That wasn't a request but a demand. "Of course, sir. Thank you."

He smiled, pleased, and led the others from the room, leaving me alone with Shade, Chern, and Headmaster Irwin.

"Shall we begin?" Chern asked.

Shade kicked his feet up on top of the table and crossed his legs at the ankles, the picture of uncaring. "Sure. Have at it."

I didn't mimic his pose but instead laced my fingers on top of the wood and gave Chern my undivided attention. "Teach me."

CHAPTER TWENTY-SEVEN

ZEPH

It was a testament to humanity that no one seemed to notice or care that I carried an unconscious female through the streets of New York City. There were a few glances here and there, but not a single human tried to stop me or raise questions.

Which was precisely why I chose Manhattan to lie low.

"Good evening, sir," the doorman greeted me as I approached the familiar residential building. I'd spent a good portion of the last year here before returning to the Academy. No one really knew about this place, aside from Kols. He knew I enjoyed hiding here, mostly because of the added convenience of available blood walking around everywhere.

"Is everything all right?" the doorman asked, eyeing Aflora in my arms.

Of all the mortals, of course this one would ask. "She's fine, just had a bit too much to drink. Bringing her back here to sleep it off."

He nodded solemnly. "Ah, yes. I understand. Good luck, sir."

"Thank you," I replied, heading toward the stairwell. My flat was on the third floor, making it easy enough to reach by foot, even with the precious cargo in my arms.

She didn't stir or make a sound as I walked, her head pillowed against my shoulder as she slept off whatever magic she'd tapped into back at the village. I'd felt the burn of it, the imminent danger surrounding us both, and her mental defensive measures.

It'd all happened so quickly that I hadn't been prepared to fight, and the next thing I knew, power exploded out of her. My only option was to bite her, to try to ground her. It'd resembled an electrical wire hitting my bloodstream, spiraling me into a dark-magic whirlpool that nearly drowned me alive. Then she surfaced, bringing me up with her, and we were back in the village again.

The whole thing had felt like a dream. But I knew it was real because of the energy humming through the cobblestone street and dancing along the wood beams of the surrounding light-colored buildings. Flares of magic had lit up the night like lanterns, drawing a straight path to Aflora.

I hadn't waited around to see if anyone else felt the disruption, and instead headed right for the portal to bring her to the Human Realm. We'd stay here until I heard back from Kols—who'd been silent since going into the Council meeting.

Balancing Aflora with one arm, I reached for my wand and muttered an unlocking spell at my door. It opened with a slight creak to reveal my one-bedroom home.

The interior didn't boast elegance or wealth, the kitchen being sorely outdated compared to the Academy accommodations, but I rather preferred this place to my Elite Residence suite. Mostly because it was mine.

I'd purchased it using my credits as a Guardian to the Nacht family. The credits could be traded in for human cash at an exorbitant amount—a good thing because owning a place in New York City required a lot of mortal money.

I kicked my door closed behind me with the heel of my boot, then took Aflora into my bedroom to lay her on the bed. Her blue-black hair sprawled beautifully across my dark green pillows, her face holding a pale glow that reminded me of the Midnight Fae moon.

Gorgeous, I thought, smiling down at her. Then I carefully removed her knee-high boots and set them in the corner of my walk-in closet. Her cloak was next—which I hung beside mine. They weren't normal accessories in the Human Realm, but no one had seemed to notice. I slipped off my own shoes, placed them beside hers, and returned to tuck a strand of her hair behind her ear.

"Be back in a few minutes," I whispered, kissing her forehead. I could feel her slowly slipping back into consciousness and wanted to be prepared to welcome her back to reality.

Since I'd left all our food back at the village, I opted to whip up a few things for us in the kitchen. It required a bit of magic, as my fridge and shelves were pretty empty—I lived primarily on blood when I visited the city—but I managed to create some of those mouseberries Aflora kept talking about.

She was awake when I returned to the bedroom, her gaze on the windows that broadcast boring views of the residential building across the street.

I liked Upper Manhattan for the location, not so much for the scenery.

Her nose twitched as I approached, her focus shifting to the plates in my hands. "What happened?" she asked, her voice hoarse.

I set the plates down on my nightstand, then magicked a cup of water for her and held it to her lips for a sip. "I'm not sure, but I think you saved our asses in the village," I told her.

She took the glass and drank half the contents in one go.

"Someone or something attacked us, and you fought back." Or I thought that was what had happened. "Do you remember it?"

She appeared to fall into her thoughts for a moment, her throat working as she finished the drink. A spell refilled it for her, something she seemed to appreciate given the glimmer in her blue irises. "I felt him," she finally said after finishing the second cup of water. "He… he was there." She brought her hand up to her neck, frowning as she felt the healing mark against her skin. "Did you bite me?"

"Yes," I admitted, taking her glass and setting it on the nightstand. "You were buzzing with power, like that time in the LethaForest." I sat on the edge of the bed near where she lay on her side. My knuckles whispered over her cheekbone to her throat. "I had to call you back to me, Aflora. The energy seemed like it was going to swallow you whole."

She frowned, making me wonder if I'd done the wrong thing. I was the one she hadn't yet accepted as hers, and I supposed she could see my actions as a way of forcing her hand—a common male behavior of Midnight Fae kind.

"I… I had to anchor you, Aflora," I said, uncertain of how to explain it. "I could feel you slipping away, almost as if another entity had forced the power to explode out of you. If you erupted in the village, fae would have died. It was the best way to protect you, as well as the others."

Her blue eyes flickered with confusion as she met my gaze. "Did you not want to bite me?"

"No, that's not what I mean." I palmed the back of my neck, frustrated.

Why is this so damn difficult? I wondered. Probably because I never cared what a woman truly thought of me before. Really, I rarely cared what *anyone* thought of me. But Aflora was different. I needed to win her over for reasons I didn't quite understand. They went deeper than our bond. Like my very spirit required her approval, yet I had no idea how to acquire it.

"Zeph," she said, reaching out to lay a hand on my forearm. "Do you regret mating me? Is that why you've been distant all week?"

"What? No." *Fuck, what a shit show.* "This whole situation is so far outside my comfort zone, it's… I don't know how to handle it." And that was the rub right there, the reason this mess infuriated me.

I couldn't control the outcome.

"I lead," I told her. "It's who I am. I make decisions every day. Everything I do is driven by logic. But none of my training has prepared me properly for…" *For you,* I wanted to say but wisely chose not to.

I blew out a breath, released my neck, and dropped my head into my hands. I was totally fucking this up. And I hated that I had no idea what to say.

"Talking isn't my strength," I admitted. "Neither is giving up control."

This seemed ridiculous. Fretting over the bullshit would get us nowhere. So I'd just be blunt. She might not like it, but it would be better than dancing around these asinine thoughts.

"I've never agreed with the Midnight Fae mentality associated with mating," I told her. "But I never really cared too much because I never intended to take a mate. I'm independent and I do my own thing. However, you changed that, and now I've bitten you twice without your permission.

Which is technically fine by our societal laws, but that doesn't mean I feel right about it."

My logical side argued that it wasn't *convenient* at all, more of a burden. Especially considering the consequences of that action.

But that was all beside the point.

"Anyway, you chose Kols with your earth magic. You even chose Shade by biting him. Yet I essentially forced myself on you. Yeah, it was for the right reasons in the end, but that doesn't change the circumstances for biting you."

Okay. I was done rambling now. It left me feeling vulnerable and weak, two adjectives that were very much not me. And I sort of hated that Aflora drew that side out of me.

Avoiding relationships had worked well for me.

Maybe I'd go back to that.

Leave Kols and Shade to handle Aflora, protect them all from afar, and just—

"Zeph," Aflora said, her hand curling around my wrist to tug my hand away from my face. "Look at me."

I was tempted to glare at her in response but chose not to make this worse and gave her my attention instead. She studied my expression, her lips curling at whatever she saw there. Probably a scowl because this was fucking uncomfortable.

"I think that's the most emotion you've ever displayed in my presence." She sounded amused, which only made me want to glower again. But she distracted me with her tits as she sat up, her sweater stretching deliciously across her chest.

Removing her cloak had been a fantastic idea.

Actually, no. I should have just taken everything off.

"You made me mouseberries?" she asked, gaping at the plates on the nightstand.

"Don't get too excited," I cautioned her. "Pretty sure they're just mustard berries or something."

She snorted. "You know what they're called."

"Do I?" I asked innocently. "Huh. Well, I guess you'll have to taste them and find out if I did it right." I knew I had, as they were pretty much the same thing as sour green grapes, but I enjoyed teasing her anyway.

She flashed me an amused smile that made my heart race. Aflora was a gorgeous woman, but when she smiled at me like that, I forgot how to think.

Because I'd made her happy.

A rarity, it seemed. But for a brief moment, I'd pleased her, and that made me want to puff up in pride.

Kols would laugh hysterically at the sight. Fortunately, he wasn't here to witness it.

Aflora took the plate, settled it into her lap, and propped her back up against the headboard. "All right, Headmaster. Let's see if your chef skills measure up, shall we?" She waggled her brows at me playfully, then lifted the loaf to her mouth and took a sensual bite.

Well, it was sensual to me, anyway. Hell, everything she did with her lips and tongue seemed to hypnotize me.

And that moan she released after tasting the food I'd prepared?

Yeah, that was hot, too.

I adjusted myself on the bed, my jeans suddenly a little too tight, and busied myself by eating the loaf off the other plate. It was okay. Sort of like having a sour fruit salad in a soggy tortilla. Not my favorite, but I knew better than to voice an opinion out loud on the topic.

"So where are we?" she finally asked, glancing out the window again.

"New York City," I told her.

"In the Human Realm?"

While she voiced it as a rhetorical question, I responded with a nod. "Yeah. We're lying low until we know what the Council meeting was about. And, well, also until we know if anyone noticed what happened in the village." Because that could go bad quickly if anyone witnessed that explosion of power.

She visibly shivered but indulged in another bite.

A comfortable silence fell between us while we finished our meal, her gaze far away with thoughts I couldn't hear. We needed to discuss what happened, but I wouldn't push her.

Instead, I considered an alternative that might provide us both with a necessary reprieve from all the chaos surrounding our lives.

"Do you want to see Central Park? It's only a few blocks away from here and should be pretty empty because of the late hour." I checked my watch. "Actually, I think it closes to the public soon as well, or might already be closed. We'll just enchant a guard or something."

"Central Park?" she repeated, her eyes lighting up. "I've never been."

I figured as much. "I'm sure it's not the same as the Earth Fae Kingdom, but it's probably more similar to it than our version of nature in the Midnight Fae realm."

Her lips twitched. "Yours is about as opposite as you can get with black grass and burning trees."

"Charcoal blades are not grass."

"Oh, I know," she said empathetically. "They're closer to knives."

I smirked. "Not like knives either."

"Sure." She set her empty plate to the side. "Do you want to go now?"

Given the eagerness pouring off her, I suspected a negative reply would upset her. Not that I wanted to refuse her. Actually, I rather liked the idea of making her smile again. "Sure," I replied, placing my dish on top of hers. "We'll need coats instead of cloaks, just to better fit in. Let me see what I can find."

Aflora released a small chirping sound that had me glancing over my shoulder at her. She had her hands clasped in her lap like she wanted to clap them together, her eyes sparkling with excitement.

I arched a brow. "If all it takes is the mention of a park to earn your happiness, then I should do all right with this mate shit."

She snorted. "I have a feeling there will be a lot of parks in our future, Zeph. With comments like that, you'll be apologizing to me all the time."

"Probably," I admitted, but I couldn't stop the grin from spreading over my lips. "Sometimes I'll make it a little more interesting, though."

"Yeah? Like how?" she asked, genuinely curious.

"Make-up sex, Aflora," I told her. "I hear it's fun. We'll try it sometime." I winked at her and left her gaping at me from the bed as I wandered into the living area to find some jackets.

This whole "normal activity" thing would be fun.

We'd have to try it more often.

CHAPTER TWENTY-EIGHT

SHADE

Four fucking hours of interrogation later, Councilman Chern ascertained the same thing I'd done in a matter of seconds the other day. "Headmaster Irwin was acting under an enchantment. My suspicion is that a Quandary Blood is to blame."

The Council members and Elders listened while Chern detailed his tactics for pulling that information from the Death Blood's mind, then the Sangré Councilman continued with his suggestions for how to handle the situation. "His psyche is vulnerable, so until we apprehend the Quandary Blood who did this, we'll need to keep Headmaster Irwin under close observation."

Meaning he wanted to jail the poor man until the matter was resolved.

Several of the Councilmen bobbed their heads in agreement, while Constantine Nacht pointed out that locking up Headmaster Irwin also served as a suitable punishment for being "so easily corrupted by enemy forces." I nearly snorted at that claim. These imbeciles had no idea whom they truly faced or how many centuries of hatred had piled up toward them.

But they'd find out, and soon.

Kols met my gaze from across the table, his golden orbs flaring with a thousand questions. Fortunately, he hadn't voiced anything that could incriminate us, but I suspected we were due for a long conversation after this was through.

He probably thought I bit Aflora because the Council told me to, which was partially true—I'd done it to maintain my cover. But I knew years ago that my fate would cross her path. This was so much bigger than the Elders or the Midnight Fae Council could possibly comprehend. They would have to see beyond their own bigotry and arrogance to realize the truth, and I wasn't about to help them with that task.

Kols's father made a few closing remarks once the sentencing was done, then looked to Constantine for any further guidance the Elders wished to bestow upon us. The retired king merely advised Kols to allow Aflora to be taken next time, something he agreed to with a mere nod, likely because he was too livid to speak. I understood that feeling all too well.

When the meeting finally adjourned, I stood and stretched my arms, ready to disappear, only a look from Kols told me he'd come after me if I did.

"Your mum is looking forward to having you over for dinner tonight, Kolstov," Malik said softly, reminding his son that he'd agreed to come home after this mess.

My father, on the other hand, left without even looking at me. There would not be a similar invite to come home for a family dinner. We didn't do that, because it would require talking and making false pleasantries, something neither of us could be arsed to do.

And my mother, well, she rarely spoke these days.

"I'm looking forward to it, too," Kols replied. "I just need to talk to Shadow about a few things before I go."

"Does it involve that little power scuffle you two got into last month? Because he told the Council how he nearly beat you." Malik grinned at me while he spoke, clearly enjoying the rivalry between me and his son.

"I believe I said I let him win," I drawled. Because that had been a far more believable story than the one Kols had come up with.

"Let me win?" Kols repeated, his eyebrows popping upward. "Since when?"

Malik chuckled. "I'll leave you two to work that out. See you in thirty minutes or so?"

"That'll be enough time for me to remind Shadow who is closer to the source, yes." Kols sounded so serious that I wondered if he intended to deliver on that threat.

A few others showcased their amusement at our trademark bickering, then left us alone in the Council Chambers. Kols cocked his head toward a painting of Constantine on the wall, then stepped toward it with his wand. A muttered spell caused the colors to shift, revealing an entrance to a room I didn't know existed here.

Kols led the way, his shoulders rigid, and I followed him into a much darker chamber lacking in windows. He uttered a spell to silence the interior, canceling out any listening devices, then he leaned back against a table in the center of a black rug. There were only three chairs, the space about a tenth of the size of the other room.

"What is this place?" I asked him, glancing around.

"Oh, something I know that you don't?" he countered. "Fascinating."

I snorted. "Want to play a game of trading information, Elite Blood? Because I have a feeling I'll outlast you by a mile."

"What the fuck?" he demanded. "What. The. Fuck?"

"You'll need to be more specific," I drawled, then ducked as his fist came for my face. "Well, now there's a positive way to seek answers." I mockingly applauded him and jumped to the side as he tried to strike me again.

Then I shadowed to the other side of the table. "Feel better yet?" I asked him when he heaved a furious breath.

"Hardly," he muttered, fixing his suit jacket and tie. "Start talking, Shadow, or so help me, I will kill you."

I let the false threat go because time wasn't on our side, and bickering got us nowhere. "Do you really think I bit Aflora because of some edict?" I asked him, arching a brow. "You know me better than that. I've never been one to play by the rules, and authority means shit to me."

"So why did you do it?"

"Because fate demanded it," I admitted. "Because I wanted to. Because she was always meant to be ours." There were a thousand reasons I could list, none of which would truly satisfy his quest for knowledge. "I gave them that recording as proof of being on their side, just like I bit her because they asked me to, but I never do anything without a true purpose. They don't know about her collar or her additional ties. They also have no idea who they're truly fighting in this war."

"And you do." Not a question, but a statement.

"Yes." I ran my fingers through my hair and considered what else I could tell him without risking fate. "Look, I know I've not been very forthcoming—"

"Understatement."

Ignoring his interjection, I continued, "But you can trust me to have Aflora's best interests at heart. She'll have a choice to make soon, and that choice will rely very heavily on our ability to get along."

"A choice of what?"

"Which destiny to pursue," I replied.

"Stop speaking in fucking riddles and give me something I can understand."

"I don't know how to do that without risk," I admitted.

"Then you're fucking worthless to all of us," he retorted, causing me to flinch. "How the hell am I supposed to protect our mate if I keep being blindsided by bullshit? I mean, the school gets attacked, and apparently, I was supposed to let her be taken? Fuck that. Now I find out the Council and the Elders have known all along that Quandary Bloods are still alive, and that you've been working with them for months."

He started to laugh, the sound a bit hysterical.

"They've also been killing anyone and everyone associated with Quandary Bloods for hundreds of years," I added. "Don't forget that part, or how they casually mentioned the reason they left Aflora alive."

"Right. Because they killed her parents." He placed his palms on the wood table, his shoulders bowed as he muttered a string of curses under his breath. I would have been impressed by some of them if I wasn't sensing the pain underlining each colorful word. "How the hell are we going to tell her that? She's going to hate us."

"She won't," I promised. "We didn't do it."

"You're right. My fucking grandfather did." He shoved away from the table to begin pacing, his long legs eating up the small space of the room quickly. When he nearly hit the wall, he turned and walked back to me, then rotated again, and did several laps while continuing to shake his head.

"She won't blame you," I said softly, meaning it. "She knows it's not you."

"You say that like you've already seen the outcome," he replied, pausing to look at me. "Are you working with a Fortune Fae? Is that how you know so much?"

"Yes." No point in hiding an obvious deduction. I just wouldn't give him details, something he must have known since he didn't bother to ask me for information on my source.

Instead, he looked at me and intelligently asked, "What can you tell me, Shade?"

"There's a war coming," I said, feeling that was pretty evident now based on everything that had already happened. "And Aflora is going to be forced to pick a side. Retribution or reformation."

"And what side are we on?" he demanded.

"That remains to be seen," I admitted honestly. "I've seen the potential for both avenues." I realized the mistake in my wording the second his eyebrows flew upward into his hairline.

"*Seen?*"

Yeah, that'd be the word I shouldn't have mentioned. Rather than reply, I remained silent. I'd already said too much.

"Explain," he demanded.

"I can't." Not without risking everything. "One day, I will. I promise. But for now, I need you to trust that I have Aflora's best interests at heart."

"It's hard to trust someone who is constantly hiding things and withholding important details, Shadow."

"Just as it's hard to trust someone related to the male who got us all into this mess to begin with," I tossed back, tired of this bantering act. "You've studied Fortune Fae. You know that prophecies can change depending on the actions of others. If I touch or influence the wrong strand in the web too much, it could sever and end and land us on a completely new string of fate."

He didn't reply, just watched me with a tick in his jaw.

I sighed. "I'm walking a tightrope, Kols. I'm trying to help where I can without interfering too much, and it's fucking exhausting. So rather than hold it against me, why don't you try to have some fucking respect and work *with* me? I provide hints as I go along. If you're smart, you'll catch them. If not..."

Then we all fail, I thought with a shrug. I knew I was being infuriating, but I had no choice. If I gave him all the answers, our destinies would be strongly impacted and all the predictions could change.

Fortune Fae weren't supposed to interfere too heavily in the fates of other fae, and I'd plucked Aflora's strands several times within the notorious web that dictated our destinies. My meddling had already impacted the futures for Kols and Zeph, causing their strands to cross Aflora's in the process. It was a consequence I knew about ahead of time, having chosen to go that route anyway, but that wasn't the point.

I'd already altered destiny several times. The more I told him, the stronger the risk that our current strand would end in the web.

And then fate would change. *Again.*

Which would be very bad for all of us involved.

"Tell me you care about her," Kols said after a long, tense beat.

"I more than care about Aflora," I replied. "She's my reason for everything and the driving motivator for many of my decisions. And if I could, I'd take her away from this situation, but I know that's not how any of this works. She's a pivotal element in the future with a destiny only she can choose. And I'll support her, even if she makes the wrong choice."

Because that was what I was destined to do.

And the same with Kols.

"Our futures are aligned, Midnight Prince," I told him softly. "It's time for you to accept it, just as I have, and stop looking for who to blame in all this. Because, trust me, you won't like what you find down that dark alley."

"More cryptic bullshit," he muttered.

"That's never going to change," I replied. "Now go home. I'll let Aflora know we're okay." She'd told me about an hour ago that she was in the Human Realm with Zeph, something about heading to the park. Sounded like a date to me, which had made me smile.

It was about time Zeph worked to win her over.

He'd made a lot of bad turns along the way, but he seemed to be curving the right way now.

"I'll be in touch," I told Kols, disappearing before he could demand I stay. We'd discussed enough. He knew I wasn't on the side of the Council and the Elders, which would have to satisfy his curiosity for now because I had a more important place to be.

A few minutes later, I materialized in the meadow I'd taken Aflora to twice now.

The sun illuminated the flowers, giving the place a beautiful glow I knew she'd adore, but it was the light up on the hill beyond that captured my interest.

I wandered up the familiar path to the cottage lurking beyond the concealing mist, my magic allowing me to enter at will.

"Hello, Shadow," my grandmother called from inside, welcoming me in that eerie way of hers.

Because she'd *seen* me coming.

"Hi, G'ma," I replied, stepping through the threshold into the living area. "I think I screwed up."

Her blue eyes—the same shade as my own—glimmered with knowledge, confirming my statement.

"Come," she murmured, gesturing to the dining room. "We'll discuss it over cookies."

I sighed. Sweets weren't a good sign. They meant she had bad news to share.

And I could only imagine what that would be.

CHAPTER TWENTY-NINE

AFLORA

Zeph's palm covered my mouth as he held me firmly against his chest. "Shh," he whispered in my ear as I giggled against his hand.

Apparently, it was frowned upon to visit the park after hours, something I found out when a rude human barked at me for dancing across the grass. He'd then tried to blind me with a flashlight, which was really quite cruel.

Zeph had responded by grabbing my hand and forcing me to run with him down a path, then ducked into these gorgeous green bushes. I wanted to pet the leaves and branches, but he grabbed me and placed his hand over my mouth, demanding I stay quiet.

For whatever reason, that made me want to laugh, mostly because I was high on life out here. The Human Realm had so many mysterious flowers and plant life, each one uniquely beautiful with its own earthy strand that I longed to follow.

No wonder Claire introduced her earth mate, Sol, to peaches. If I ever had a chance to see the Elemental Fae Queen again, I'd ask her about these azaleas and roses and crape myrtles. Oh, those were like trees, but with flowers, and I yearned to see them bloom. And the daffodils, too! So many beautiful histories, all underlined in color and fragrant scents.

I sighed happily, causing Zeph's arm to tighten around me.

Right. He wanted me to be quiet. But how could I be silent in such a gorgeous place? I wanted to dance around more and play with my earth magic. It'd been so easy to circumvent the collar this time, proving Kols and Zeph right about the enchantments—they'd worn off.

So all my powers were free for me to explore, yet this man with the flashlight had ruined it all.

Evil human.

His boots scuffed against the path as he searched for us, his voice gruff as he spoke into some sort of communication device. "Some crazy flower chick," he was saying. "She was stripping in the middle of the fucking park."

I scowled at him. I was not *stripping*, just removing my sweater because I wanted to roll around in the fresh green grass. Really, some people had no understanding of what it meant to be an Earth Fae.

Which, yeah, humans were oblivious to our existence.

My bad.

But who could blame me when surrounded by all this life? I just wanted to swim in the nature of this place and listen to all the tales of the flowers around me.

Zeph pressed his lips to my ear. "Stop that."

I blinked, confused, then realized the leaves were swaying around us, ready to embrace my magic. It just came to me instinctively, the urge to help them all grow and prosper a part of my base existence as the conduit for the earth source.

The light-bearing human disappeared down the path, causing Zeph to relax somewhat against me. "We should get out of here."

"Why?" I asked against his hand, my voice muffled.

"Because we've already drawn enough attention to ourselves here. There's a division of Warrior Bloods who scan incident reports to spot any signs of supernatural activity in the Human Realm. If that officer files a case about a 'crazy flower chick' dancing naked in the park, it'll raise a red flag."

I frowned. "I wasn't naked."

"Not yet," he agreed, using his wand to retrieve my sweater from the field and handing it to me. "Put this back on, Aflora. Humans don't frolic without clothes on in Central Park unless they're sunbathing, or doing other things."

"I was doing other things," I pointed out as I pulled the sweater over my head. "I wanted to feel the grass."

He nodded, his lips twitching at the sides. "Uh-huh."

"What?"

"Nothing."

"That look isn't nothing, Zeph." I folded my arms. "Tell me."

He shook his head, his mouth curling into a fond smile. "I'm just amused by your Earth Fae inclinations. It's very stereotypical."

"Stereotypical," I repeated. "In what manner?"

He pressed his palm to my lower back to guide me the opposite way down the path, purposely keeping us to the dark areas to hide our presence. "Nymphs are a popular lore in the Human Realm and commonly depicted as nature beings who frolic around naked." He glanced at me sideways. "Which, I'm pretty sure, you were about to do."

"I don't know about naked," I replied. "But maybe. There are just so many glorious scents here, and the magic coming from the ground is very alluring."

"You know what's alluring?" he asked quietly, guiding me into a darker area of the park where the moonlight was hidden by the lush branches above us. He walked me backward with his palms against my hips. This was not the path we'd entered on, and my boot-clad feet were encased in the beautiful green grass once more.

I bit my lip and stared up at him. "What's alluring?" I whispered, continuing to step in the direction he led me, trusting him not to let me fall.

His lips went to my ear. "The idea of stripping you naked right here and fucking you up against this tree."

My back hit something hard, my palms finding the bark behind me and identifying the vivacious American elm tree. So big and full of life. I gave it a little pet, pleased with its sturdy roots and overbearing size. I also rather liked how dark it was beneath the trunk-like branches.

And more specifically, I enjoyed how Zeph felt as he trapped me between his body and the hard surface behind me.

"Yes," I said softly, my hands wandering up to grasp Zeph's shoulders. "I like that plan very much."

"Do you?" he asked, his words a breath against my ear. "It won't be sweet or romantic, but hard and fast. It might hurt."

"Will you bite me?" I asked him.

"If you want me to."

"I do." I hadn't been aware the first two times he'd bitten me, and I really wanted to feel him, to make this moment just about us and our unique connection to one another.

"It'll finalize our mating bond," he warned.

"I know." I wasn't afraid of it. We were already on a wild ride together, so we might as well finalize it and see where it went. That he wanted to do it here, in the middle of my element, only made it that much more powerful and intense.

His lips drew an enticing path along my jaw, leading his mouth to feather over mine. "Be sure, Aflora."

"I am," I promised him, my nails dragging along his shoulder to his neck and then into his hair to hold his head where I wanted it. "I want you inside me, Zeph." I meant the phrase in every way it could be interpreted but decided to seal the deal with the two words I knew he truly wanted to hear. Because Zeph was all about communication and trust. "Fuck me."

He shuddered against me, any restraint he had in place dissolving in a second.

And his mouth took mine.

It wasn't a gentle kiss but a claim, his tongue dominating mine. But I held my own, refusing to bow completely, meeting him as a match, and challenging him at every turn.

If he wanted to own me, he'd have to win me.

And I wouldn't bow easily.

Not tonight.

Not while surrounded by power that fueled the energy source inside me.

This was *my* domain, not his. And queens did not kneel unless they wanted to.

He smiled against my mouth, his amusement palpable. "Oh, Aflora, you just made this that much better." His fingers dug into my hips as he captured my lips once more, his kiss savage and violent in the best way.

A warrior.

My warrior.

There were moments when I hated him, but he more than made up for it during the times when I adored him.

Times like now.

He'd brought me to this place, wooed me unintentionally with the familiarity of the earth, and now I intended to let him claim his reward.

My sweater disappeared again, followed by his own. I hissed as his bare chest met mine, my bra seeming to have vanished beneath his touch. He cupped my cheek, his tongue enchanting mine into a sensual duel I never wanted to end. I ran my palms over his bare back, loving the way his muscles flexed and moved.

He was all strength and man.

Experienced and knowing.

Velvety smooth and hard as a rock.

"Zeph," I moaned, arching into him as he unbuttoned my jeans. My zipper slid down, the sound echoing in the night, accompanied by the shuffle of fabric and boots as he fully undressed me, leaving me naked against the tree. He took a step back to admire the view, his Midnight Fae eyes allowing him to see what a human wouldn't be able to.

It made him predatory.

Cruel.

A sleek panther in the dark.

My skin prickled with goose bumps, my thighs quaking with need, my core slicking in warm welcome.

I loved the vulnerability that came with being naked while he still wore his jeans and boots. I adored the sensations of earth magic humming across my exposed skin. And I craved the masculine scent of arousal tickling my nostrils.

"I can smell you," I whispered, falling back against the tree, my hands roaming my own curves. "You want me."

"I do," he admitted, yet remained still, watching me embrace my element and touch myself in kind.

Prolonging the moment made me needy, had my knees threatening to bend, but I used the earth to keep myself upright, to be the queen I was born to be.

For him.

For myself.

"Zeph," I said, my voice low and sultry.

"Aflora," he returned softly, his thumb flicking open the button on his jeans.

I couldn't see him as well as he could see me, but I caught enough of his movements to recognize his intentions. His zipper whispered through the air, lashing my skin with a fresh wave of warmth and anticipation. However, he didn't kick off his pants the way he'd stripped mine.

Hmm, no. He wouldn't.

This was Zeph.

He needed a measure of control, which would come with him being partially dressed while I stood vulnerable and naked among the trees.

I didn't mind. This was what I wanted. And his proclivity for dominance called to the queen within me. I adored the fight, the push and pull, the need to submit while knowing I could challenge him if I wanted to.

It made this so much more sensual and right.

His hands caught my hips, his arms flexing as he hoisted me into the air. "Wrap your legs around me."

I did and moaned at the feel of his hard arousal situating itself right between my thighs. "Yes, Zeph. Yes."

He didn't enter me but teased me instead, his head stroking my clit with expert ease and causing me to shake against him. His mouth sealed over mine, catching my scream as rapture erupted inside me without warning. I hadn't even felt it mounting, too lost to the teasing air and intensity thriving between us.

I panted against him, an apology on my tongue for exploding without his permission, but his tongue refused to let me utter the words. Almost as if he didn't want to hear them. And maybe he didn't, because I could feel his masculine pride vibrating around us, his obvious pleasure at causing me to fall apart without doing much more than stare at me.

"I love when you come," he admitted, his lips tracing mine with each word. "I'm going to need you to do it again, Aflora. But around my cock this time."

He didn't give me a chance to reply, his hips shifting and causing him to line up with my entrance without so much as a hand between us. His body just knew where to go and how, and he proved it now by penetrating me with a thrust that left me winded.

His name caught in my throat, a cry of pain mingled with pleasure tingling against my tongue, and was swallowed abruptly by his mouth.

He kissed me as if he needed my essence to breathe.

And then he began to take me, truly, with his hips pounding against mine.

He'd been right about it being fast and hard, and it did hurt, just like he warned. But oh, it felt so good, too. I welcomed the scrapes against my back, bathed in the masculine growl coming from his chest as he pummeled into me, and tossed my head back on a sound of approval that probably echoed through the park.

If that guard came back now, I'd tie him up with a vine and stuff a flower in his mouth.

Because no one and nothing was going to ruin this moment.

Zeph had me.

I had him.

All I wanted now was his bite.

"Please," I begged him, referring to the pressure growing between my legs and the ache in my veins. I needed him to finish this, to tie us together as one.

His lips feathered over mine, his hands tightening on my hips as he angled me to receive him even deeper. "You feel so fucking good," he breathed.

"You, too," I replied, unable to say more. I had my arms wrapped tight around his shoulders and my ankles crossed over his ass. The rasp of his jeans against my inner thighs heightened the moment, reminding me of my vulnerability with each stroke.

Yet I felt the tenderness in him, too.

The way he held me with care, his guarded energy as he monitored my reactions to his movements and actions. It hurt in the best way, and I made sure he knew that by gazing directly into his eyes and showing him what this did to me.

"Fuck," he whispered, his mouth taking mine again in a brutal kissed underlined in promise. "I don't know what I did to deserve you, Aflora, but I'll spend every day thanking whatever higher power put you in my path."

I arched into him, my limbs trembling with the intensity growing inside me. "I'm close."

"I know," he said, his tongue tracing a wet path along my jaw to my ear. "I can feel you clenching my shaft, pixie flower, trying to force me to come early with you." He bit my earlobe, sharp enough to pause the mounting orgasm inside me. "Not yet, Aflora."

"Please."

"Soon," he promised, his pace lengthening, smoothing, and drawing out the moment.

I wanted to scream, to beg, to howl in frustration.

But then I felt a burning twist in my gut that curled into the pressure already churning inside me, and power thrummed through my veins. "Ohhh…"

"Yes," he replied. "That's what I want."

The sensation grew, causing my limbs to tighten around him, the ecstasy climbing with each measured stroke inside me. "Zeph," I breathed, my world seconds away from exploding.

"Now," he said, his teeth sinking into my pulse half a beat later and shooting me off into the stars.

My throat burned with the scream I released, Zeph's palm closing over my mouth to silence the echoes of my ecstasy as he followed me into the pleasurable abyss.

His soul intertwined with mine, marrying us in a forbidden manner that felt deliciously right. I felt him enter me in every way imaginable, his mind becoming mine as mine became his. Connections deepened, his thoughts melding and firing signals inside my brain.

I couldn't understand it, similar to my mating with Shade, but somehow I knew that if I tried, I could access whatever history or detail I wanted, just as he could do the same to me.

It was a level of trust and adoration reserved for mates.

A knowledge that I wouldn't enter him uninvited, just as he wouldn't penetrate my mind without my permission.

The door could be closed as well—I sensed it now—but rather than shut him out, I allowed him to *see* me, and he returned the favor in kind.

An opening.

A new beginning.

A relationship underscored in trust and equality.

He craved to dominate me yet desired my backbone and strength as well. All his lessons were meant to empower me, including the ones I hated. Zeph only wanted me to be safe, to be ready for the future, to be aware of my own abilities.

There'd been doubts.

Concerns.

Troubles.

Yet they all came from the right place—his heart.

I kissed him, my own heart lost to his as I embraced our connection and what it meant for us both. There was fear, uncertainty, and dread. But the adoration, hope, and desire outweighed the uncertainties. And that was what I clung to.

"We need to go," Zeph whispered, his Midnight Fae senses picking up on something I hadn't—the approach of humans. "Your screaming caught their attention."

"Why do you sound pleased by that?" I asked him as he slowly pulled out of my body and set my feet on the ground.

"I'm pleased about a lot of things right now," he admitted, and while I couldn't quite make out his mouth, I suspected it was twisted upward into a smirk.

He handed me my sweater, then found my jeans. My boots were last, and by the time I was all ready to go, he had put himself back together as well.

"What about my underwear?" I wondered out loud, trying to find my bra and panties.

"I've got them," he said, causing me to frown.

"Where?"

But the sound of approaching boots silenced his ability to respond. He pulled me behind a tree just before a ray of light hit the area we'd been a second before. His palm caught my mouth again, making me wonder, *Do you just like this position? Or are you afraid I'll make a sound?*

Both, he replied, his lips brushing my pulse. *And your voice in my head is an amazing sound.*

I smiled. *I like yours in mine, too.*

Oddly, it wasn't hard to talk to him without Shade hearing. It was like I had these mental switches that told me whom I was talking to.

That same switch connected to the doors to their thoughts, drawing my attention to Shade's closed one. I hadn't really noticed it before, his mental voice always strong inside my head, but he'd sealed off my ability to see into his mind. Likely because of his Fortune Fae heritage. I'd have to ask him about it later.

Can you use your earth magic to create a safe escape path? Zeph asked. *Preferably one where the humans don't see us.*

You mean you don't want to go invite them to have loaves with us?

He snorted into my mind. *Cute, Aflora.*

Just checking, I replied, smiling against his hand. *Yeah, I can use some tree cover to help us out, but you're going to have to tell me which direction because this place is huge.*

I can do that, he agreed.

Then let's go, I said, already outlining a path through the trees that would take us away from the humans trampling over the earth. *When we get back, I want a shower,* I added, grimacing as I took a step. *My jeans are going to need to be washed, too.*

Feeling a little damp, pixie flower? Too much seed for your lady garden?

I nearly choked out a laugh at the horrible joke. *Don't ever say that again.*

He chuckled into my mind. *Hmm, but I like growing inside you, Aflora. Rooting you so deep you'll feel me all day.*

Stop.

Making you blossom with pleasure around my thick—

I elbowed him in the side. *If you want me to get us out of here, you will stop right now.*

His amusement touched my thoughts, but he ceased his dirty commentary.

Not that I hadn't heard similar puns before. I was an Earth Fae. There was a myriad of sexy statements that could be made using the element as a base.

For the record, I enjoyed you taking root inside me, I told him as we walked. *And I'm open to you doing it again as soon as we return to your flat.*

Good, because I intend to fuck you against the shower wall next, he replied, his puns replaced by his usual crass approach. *And then I'm going to fuck you in my bed.*

I shivered. *Will you bite me again, too?*

Only if you beg.

I glanced up at him and gave him my best innocent look. *Please, Headmaster Zephyrus. Bite me again.*

"Fuck," he muttered, grabbing my hand and yanking me down the path.

I grinned at his sudden haste.

Yeah, begging I could do.

Maybe I'd make him beg, too.

CHAPTER THIRTY

AFLORA

Mmm, I like this, I thought, stretching against Zeph's soft sheets.

Only, they were the wrong color.

Black, not green. I frowned at them, my fingers drifting through the silk as I glanced up into a pair of silver-blue eyes. "Oh," I breathed, surprised. "I didn't realize I'd fallen asleep." The last thing I remembered was Zeph kissing me thoroughly after taking me for the third time in his bed.

He really did know how to knock a girl out.

My blood heated at the memory of his tongue between my thighs, his scruff tickling my skin in the most sensual way.

"You're blushing," my figment mused, his lips curling at the edges. "Is it your newly bonded mate inspiring those thoughts? Or one of your others?"

"Zeph," I admitted, my cheeks burning hotter. "They all make me blush, though."

"I bet," he drawled, lounging on the pillow beside me in a pair of black pants and no shirt. I tried really hard not to admire his physique.

Tried and failed.

Because he truly was sculpted to perfection, something I blamed my mind for doing.

"Why do you keep visiting me?" I wondered out loud.

"Why do you think I'm here?" he countered, arching a brow. "You created me, right?" There was a hint of teasing in his tone that I probably deserved, because yeah, I did.

"Yeah. For sex," I admitted.

He chuckled, the sound a deep reverberation in his chest that hypnotized my senses.

Why did he have to be so beautiful?

Oh, right. Because my mind made him that way.

"I love how honest you are," he mused, his silver-blue eyes glistening with approval. "So am I here now for sex? Because you seem rather sated at the moment, little star."

His observation heated my cheeks once more. It probably shouldn't bother me that my mind recognized my satisfied state, but hearing it out loud—or in my head, I guess—flustered me a bit. "I'm... I don't know why you're here. Maybe to talk about what happened today?" I'd avoided thinking about the village, so it made sense that my subconscious would push me to consider it.

"What happened today?" he asked as he went up onto his elbow to stare down at me. "Anything I should be concerned about?"

"I think someone tried to trap me," I told him, frowning. "We went to the tavern to see if I recognized the magic used during the attack the other day, and somehow he knew I'd be there. He was waiting for me... and then he attacked me."

His white-blond eyebrows shot upward. "Attacked you?"

I nodded. "Yes. Or that's how it felt, anyway."

"Maybe he was just testing your powers, to see how much you know," he suggested.

"Maybe," I agreed. "But it felt... aggressive."

"That could have been the village reacting to your magic," he pointed out softly. "Perhaps he was actually protecting you from a bigger trap set to catch him, not you."

I considered that angle. "The alarms were going off," I admitted, recalling the cawing and sounds of stones shifting. "But I didn't feel like they were trying to attack me."

"It's possible he deflected it away from you and onto himself."

"Yes, that could be true." My brow furrowed. "But I still think he meant to trap me."

"Or see you, yes," he murmured, reaching out to tuck a strand of my hair behind my ear. "Does he feel ominous to you? Threatening? Do you even know who he is?"

"I feel like I know him," I whispered, glad to be talking to my mind and not to someone else. "His magic reminds me of my past, but I don't know why."

"You're missing memories," he replied. "They were stolen from you to protect you."

"What?" I gaped at him. "How could you know that?"

"I'm in your mind, Aflora. I know many things."

"Or you're leading me into a false train of thought," I tossed back, suddenly tired. "The truth is, I have no idea who he is, just that I feel as though I know him. And he doesn't seem to want to hurt me, but he definitely wants to find me."

He nodded. "All true."

"I just don't know why."

"I think you do," he said softly. "And if you look hard enough, you'll see what's right in front of you. When you're truly ready, the truth will reveal itself.

Because every detail you need is here." He covered my heart with his palm, his touch hot against my bare skin.

"You're not very helpful," I accused, sighing.

His lips twitched. "On the contrary, sweet star, I've been extremely helpful. You're just ignoring the obvious."

"You mean your penchant for riddles?" I asked, mock innocence in my voice. "Yes, those are very helpful."

He released another of those chuckles, the reverberation warming my skin as he leaned in to press his lips to my ear. "Do you like riddles, darling star?"

I swallowed, his closeness doing things to my body that I didn't want to acknowledge. Mostly because it was wrong. "Not particularly," I breathed, my voice raspier than I intended. Why did I have to create a male who impacted me so acutely?

"Then maybe you should ask why your mind is so fond of speaking in them," he whispered.

I already knew why. "Quandary magic is all about solving puzzles. You take things apart just to put them back together another way. A riddle at its core."

"Mmm, true," he agreed, running his nose down my neck to kiss the spot where Zeph had bitten me earlier. "But why would your mind choose to operate in riddles when you claim them to be unhelpful? What if I'm not your mind's creation at all, but something else entirely?"

"Then I would have to consider the possibility that I'm going insane." Something I didn't want to do.

"Or consider that I exist." The words were a kiss against my ear, his teeth skimming my lobe. "I'll be back again soon, sweet Aflora." He pressed a kiss to my temple, his sinful gaze glimmering with intent as he forced my eyes to close once more.

Consider that I exist, I thought, repeating his words with a frown. *But that's impossible.*

Or was it?

"There you are," a masculine voice rumbled against my ear, followed by a kiss to my forehead. "I was beginning to worry."

"Kols?" I whispered, slowly opening my eyes to find him lounging beside me on a bed of red silk framed by gold and black fringe.

I blinked, glancing around the opulent room. Floor-to-ceiling windows spanned one wall, a set of doors situated in the middle that led to a balcony overlooking a black sky sprinkled with bright stars.

"Where are we?" I asked him, taking in the expensive fixtures and flickering candlelight.

He followed my perusal, his lips twitching. "My suite at Nacht Manor. It was easier to bring your mind here than to join you since I don't know exactly where Zeph took you. He's not answering my calls."

"He's not?" That seemed odd. "You should wake me up so I can check on him."

"Not needed. I can sense him near you now," he murmured, his fingers clasping my chin to draw my focus back to him. "Are you at his flat in New York City?"

"Yes. He took me to Central Park."

"Did he?" Kols seemed amused. "Well, that's why I'm struggling to connect with him. Our phones don't always work across realms, but apparently dream manipulation does. At least when connecting to a mate." He leaned in to brush his lips against mine. "I missed you today, sweetheart."

"I missed you, too," I replied, feeling warm all over.

"Did you learn anything at the tavern?" he asked, his fingers sliding into my hair to comb through my tangled strands.

Oh, he didn't know what had happened because he hadn't spoken to Zeph yet.

"Um, he was there waiting for us. The one with the magic I recognize, I mean. I… I think he was trying to get to me, but I stopped him. Sort of." I frowned. "It was weird. I could feel his magic, and mine responded to it, then Zeph bit me and I passed out."

"Zeph bit you?"

I swallowed, the intensity in his gold gaze leaving me uneasy. "Yeah. To pull me out of the enchantment."

His gaze went to my neck, a flicker of jealousy flaring in the depths of his soulful eyes. "I'm glad he did," he said, his hand leaving my hair to run his knuckles over my neck. "Protecting you is priority number one. And you're right; whoever the Quandary Blood is that's responsible for these attacks is trying to take you."

The certainty in his tone had me studying his expression. "How do you know that?" I wondered out loud. "And how do you know it's a Quandary Blood?" We'd discussed the familiarity of his power but hadn't decided his fae type. At least, not with the resolve he'd just spoken those words.

"There's a lot I need to tell you, Aflora," he said, sighing and withdrawing his hand. "It's actually why I brought you here. While this conversation would be better in person, I can't leave without looking suspicious, and I didn't want to wait to tell you what I've learned. My father is requiring I stay here through my free days to review some texts that are related to our current situation."

"Oh. I'm not going to like this, am I?"

"No, you're not," he agreed, sounding sad. "I learned today that certain members of the Council and our Elder circle have been hiding several crucial secrets, all revolving around the Quandary Bloods."

My heart dropped into my stomach as he continued telling me all about his meeting today and how they questioned Headmaster Irwin. He told me how he learned that Quandary Bloods were in fact not eradicated, how the Elders had continued hunting them with help from the Council, and how Shade knew about this for months without letting on.

"He bit you because they told him to," Kols added. "Or that's what I thought until I spoke to him later. He's hiding something, and I suspect it's Fortune Fae related because he mentioned *seeing* a future path."

"Yes," I whispered.

"You knew?"

"Not about your Council's secrets or that they told him to bite me, but I know he's working with a Fortune Fae." I didn't know whether or not I should elaborate. It wasn't my story to tell, and while I trusted Kols, I didn't want to put Shade at risk.

"That explains his penchant for being cryptic," Kols muttered, his arm flexing as he shuffled on the bed beside me. It drew my attention down to his chiseled chest. Similar to my figment, he wore only a pair of pajama pants, while I remained nude.

Something about that wasn't quite fair.

And thinking of my white-haired figment reminded me of his final words. *Consider that I exist.*

Do you? I wondered. *Do you exist?*

Then how was he in my dreams? Well, Kols had infiltrated my head without mating. So it was definitely possible. I needed to learn more about how he did it. That would help me determine if I had anything to worry about or if my head was just playing tricks on me.

"There's more," Kols said, drawing me back to our conversation. "It's about your parents."

Ice drizzled through my veins, his tone telling me nothing good would come from whatever he had to say next. "What about them?" I asked.

"There's no easy way to say this, Aflora, so I'm just going to tell you what I learned."

"Okay."

He took a deep breath, his gold irises swirling with remorse. "The Midnight Fae Elders killed them for being known Quandary Blood sympathizers."

I froze, his words not fully registering beneath the thudding in my ears.

No.

No, that couldn't be right.

"They…" I cleared my throat, my voice a rasp of sound. "They were Royal Fae…" I trailed off, my voice still not quite right. It sounded loud now, like a squawk. Or maybe that was just me.

And wow, I was dizzy.

Stars danced around me. Real ones. Huh. That reminded me of Dream Guy again and his nickname for me. I never did ask why called me *star*, of all things, nor did I know his name. I should probably give him one.

You know, after I figured out the whole dizzy thing.

Because yeah, um, the world was starting to go black.

"*Aflora.*" The urgent tone felt like a slap to my senses, yanking me back into… Zeph's room.

I stared at the windows overlooking the building across the street, tilting my head slightly at the strange exterior. "Is that brick?" I asked. Such an inane question but it seemed easier than facing the tumultuous thoughts in my mind.

Zeph's palms burned into my cheeks, forcing me to look at him. At some point, he'd pulled me beneath him, his elbows braced on either side of my head. "What the hell just happened?" he demanded.

I looked up at him, noted the fury in his green eyes. "What do you mean?" And wow, my voice sounded dreadful. I really needed a glass of water because my throat was killing me.

"You just spent the last five minutes screaming," he ground out. "I couldn't wake you the fuck up and had to put my palm over your mouth to silence you before you alarmed all the damn humans in the building."

"Oh."

"Yeah, *oh*. What the hell, Aflora?"

I opened my mouth to tell him, but I couldn't. The words were trapped in my throat.

And then his phone began to ring.

"Answer that," I managed to say.

"Fuck the phone."

"It's Kols," I said, knowing I'd probably scared him by leaving so abruptly. But there was no way his words were true. "My parents were Royal Fae." The statement was meant more for me than for Zeph. "It doesn't make sense. They wouldn't be able to do that. The Elemental Fae Council…" I trailed off, trying to figure out how the Midnight Fae had gotten away with *murdering* my parents.

And what did Kols mean about them being Quandary Blood sympathizers? I didn't even know what that was until recently.

Except…

I am one.

My eyes went wide. "Of course," I whispered. "They… they were protecting *me*."

But that could only mean they knew about my abomination status. Was one of them really a Quandary Blood?

"Not possible," I continued out loud, oblivious to everything around me. "A Midnight Fae can't connect to the earth source. Unless…" My lips parted, my throat going dry. "Unless a Quandary Blood rewired it…"

I reached for Zeph, his heat having left mine when he went to grab his phone. His hand caught my wrist, drawing my palm to his and linking our fingers. "What is it?" he asked softly.

"What if my parents weren't Earth Fae at all, but Quandary Bloods who rewired the earth source to accept their magic?" I asked him, my heart beating erratically in my chest. "What if they weren't sympathizers at all, but actual Quandary Bloods hiding from the eradication? They were old, Zeph. So, so old."

My mind kept working through the puzzle, the pieces falling into place.

"I was their only heir. An heir they left with a single mother and her very powerful son. *Sol.* Maybe they chose his family because they knew his bloodline was the rightful connection to the source, and that's why…" I met Zeph's gaze. "That's why he's connected to it now."

It was incredibly rare for an elemental source to allow a new entity to tap into the power when it already had a powerful conduit.

"I'd thought the earth source welcomed Sol because of his mating to Claire." She had access to all five elements. It made perfect sense. "But what if it had nothing to do with her, and it was the source realigning itself with the appropriate monarch?"

My entire life had been a lie.

My parents were never Earth Fae.

"I'm a Quandary Blood." Yet that statement didn't feel quite right, and my link to my elemental power screamed at the wrongness of that claim, confusing me even more. "I don't know who I am anymore." My eyes didn't well with tears. My heart didn't break. My mind just kept whirring with theories and possibilities.

But at the end of it all, I knew one thing for sure—I despised the Midnight Fae Council and their Elders.

"They killed my parents," I whispered. *"They killed my parents."* And they'd gotten away with it.

They'll pay, I vowed, uncertain of whom I spoke to.

They will, a dark voice whispered back.

Just for a moment, I swore it belonged to my figment.

But that wasn't possible.

He only existed in my head.

CHAPTER THIRTY-ONE

KOLS

"She's asleep again," Zeph said over the line, his voice tired. "Shit, Kols. What the fuck just happened?"

I ran my fingers through my hair and sighed. "A lot. A fucking lot. Hold on."

I cast a myriad of spells around my room to ensure there were no listening devices. After learning what I had today, I no longer trusted anyone, including my own damn family. Because clearly they were holding out on me. At least my father and grandfather were, anyway.

When I finished my spells, I picked up the phone again. "Are we sure this line is secure?"

"Please," Zeph muttered. "The cuffs work, right?"

"Yeah. Fortunately." Because if anyone sensed my ties to Aflora, I'd be royally fucked, and not in a good way. Since the same guy who'd made the band around my wrist also enchanted our phones, I could safely assume our conversation would be private.

I collapsed on my bed and told Zeph about the meeting, ending with the bit about her parents. "That'd been where I was when she woke herself up."

Zeph had fallen silent, probably from shock. Which, yeah, I'd felt the same when I heard it all in the Council Chambers.

"I think it's safe to say she didn't take the news well," Zeph muttered.

"Thanks for stating the obvious," I drawled, pinching the bridge of my nose in frustration. "She's going to hate me, Zeph."

"She's not," he replied. "She knows it wasn't you."

"Does she?" Because it really didn't feel that way. "I had no idea until today."

"I know you didn't."

"And I couldn't not tell her," I added. "It felt wrong to keep that to myself."

"No, it was the right thing to do," he agreed. "She'll see that. Trust me."

I sighed, my hand falling from my nose to the bed while I stared up at my ceiling. "She said you bit her again."

"Yeah," he replied, clearing his throat. "A few times."

I wanted to hate him, to yell at the unfairness of him taking her before I had the chance to, but my surroundings reminded me why I couldn't take that next step. Not yet. Not until I figured out how to finish the mating without jeopardizing us both. "Good thing the bands work," I said after a beat.

"You're jealous."

"Fuck yeah, I'm jealous."

He chuckled. "It wasn't exactly planned."

"But you're not sorry," I pointed out.

"No, I'm not," he admitted without hesitation. "She's mine."

"Ours," I corrected.

"True."

A comfortable silence fell between us while I considered what a future with her would be like. "Maybe we should run," I suggested. "Take her far away from this bullshit and never look back."

He remained quiet for a long moment before murmuring, "You'd never forgive yourself. And neither would she. The reason you're both so compatible is that you share a sense of responsibility for others, and you won't turn your back on the Midnight Fae. Not even for her."

I despised him for being right. Just for a moment. Then allowed the annoyance to leave me because he was correct. "I can't stop the ascension." The black writhing marks painting my torso and arms were proof of that.

"And she wouldn't want you to."

"I know." I heaved another sigh. "Fuck, I know, but it would be so much easier if I could."

"Want to know what I think about easy solutions?"

"They never last," I said, aware of his thoughts on the topic. "Yeah, yeah."

I could *hear* him smirking. "You want me to coddle your ass and pity you?"

"Fuck you," I muttered.

"Then stop whining."

"I'm not, dick. I'm just telling you my hopes and dreams so you can squash them like you always do."

He snorted. "Whatever, Midnight Prince."

"Don't even start that bullshit with me," I muttered. "We're not going back to the title fuckery again."

"You really hated that, didn't you?"

"You know I did." His whole formality kick had served as a punishment to us both. "The entire situation wasn't our fault. She played us and our cocks, end of discussion."

He fell silent again, making me wonder if he was going to revert into his previous depression and tell me to fuck off. But instead, he quietly said, "I should have seen it coming."

"I should have seen it, too," I told him, owning up to my part in the mistake of our past. "I know my father blamed you as my Guardian for not vetting her, but as the future king, I shouldn't have allowed her to lead me by my cock. As soon as I ascend, you'll be reinstated. Actually, no, you'll be higher because of the whole, uh, quad." That would be unprecedented, but fuck if I cared at this point.

"I've been mad at myself, not at you," Zeph admitted after a beat. "She hurt you under my watch, and that…"

"It happens," I replied softly. "You didn't fail me. *We* failed. But it won't happen again." I thought of Aflora while I spoke, pictured her sleeping beside him. "We're going to do right by her, Zeph."

"Yes," he agreed. "Somehow."

"We'll figure it out." Because there wasn't another choice. "She's ours."

"She is," he murmured, his tone filled with wonder. I could practically see him stroking his fingers through her hair, the vision one that had my lips curling, only to freeze as a shuffle of a foot had my eyes flying to the side door.

The one I shared with Tray's quarters, not the main hall.

I hadn't heard it open.

Nor had I heard it shut.

And Tray stood just inside it, arms folded over his chest, expression furious.

"Shit," I said, sitting up. "I need to go."

"What's wrong?" Zeph asked, immediately alert.

"Tray's here, and from the glare he's sending me, I'm pretty sure he heard most of our conversation."

"Try *all* of it," Tray replied, his tone telling me how he felt about me keeping him in the dark. "You enchanted the entire room but forgot the damn door connecting our suites."

"Seriously?" Zeph sounded exasperated.

"I need to go."

"Fix it," Zeph said, hanging up.

"Yeah, sure," I replied to the phone, tossing it to the side. "Tray—"

"You mated her, didn't you?" he accused.

My eyes widened, going to the door I'd apparently forgotten to enchant. *Rookie move,* I chastised myself.

"I already enchanted it," Tray said, referring to the threshold. "It's just you and me. So no more secrets. No more hiding. Talk to me."

I just gaped at him, unsure of where to begin.

And that was apparently the wrong response.

"You think I'm an idiot?" he demanded. "I've known for a few weeks now what happened in her room that day and the real reason you set it on fire. I could *feel* it, Kols. But I waited for you to come to me, to confirm what I already knew. And I had to hear about it *through our fucking door?*"

"Shit," I repeated, clearly out of decent terms. "I didn't want to involve you."

"I'm your fucking twin," he seethed. "You don't think I can feel these things? We're magically bonded by blood, Kolstov."

I rubbed my hand over my face. "I'm sorry." Two meager words that definitely didn't help the situation, but they had to be said. "I didn't want to risk you knowing too much. You know how bad this is, what they'll do if they find out."

"And you thought I'd turn you in?"

"No," I replied without hesitation. "I was worried about what they'd do to you if they found out you knew and didn't report me."

"You think I'm afraid of them?"

"You should be," I muttered, thinking about what I'd learned today. "They've been hunting down a race and exterminating anyone involved, including Royal Fae like Aflora's parents. You think they'd spare me or you if they found out about this?"

A few months ago, I might have thought they'd forgive us because of our bloodlines. Now? Yeah, now I wasn't so certain.

"She's a Quandary Blood, Tray," I whispered. "Or at least part one. We don't really know, but she has cerulean magic and can undo and rewire enchantments."

He gaped at me. "That's how she knew the song."

"Yes, but she didn't understand the lyrics," I replied.

He started to nod, his shock evident.

When he said nothing else, I softly added, "Now do you get why I hid this from you? From Ella? If the Council finds out…" I didn't need to finish that statement, his expression told me he already knew.

"Fucking hell, Kols."

"Sounds about right," I muttered, rolling off my bed to land on my bare feet. Like me, he had on a pair of pajama pants and nothing else. "Is Ella sleeping?"

"Yeah," he replied, sounding defeated. They'd both joined me and our parents for dinner tonight, but Tray hadn't known the reason for the family gathering. "I can't believe Dad kept all of this from us."

"It's definitely raised a few questions," I admitted. "Like how he's okay with exterminating our own kind. I get that Quandary Bloods are terrifyingly powerful, but Aflora…"

"She can't even kill a burning thwomp," Tray replied.

"Exactly." She wasn't weak by any means, just thoughtful. Caring. "She'd never hurt someone for personal gain. Hell, she wants to turn herself in as an abomination because she doesn't see herself as fit to lead anymore. How could the Council vote to kill someone like that? She's honorable and kind."

"I'm still trying to wrap my head around them assassinating her parents. How the hell did they get away with that?"

I shook my head. "I don't know, but if the Elemental Fae ever find out, we'll be going to war."

"Is that why they kept her alive? Aflora, I mean." He frowned. "Wait, no, you said it was because she's bait?"

Yeah, that was how I'd phrased it to Zeph. "They want me to let her be captured."

Tray grunted. "That's never going to happen."

"No shit." But I wouldn't mind going with her to meet whoever was behind the attacks. Not to fight him, just to find out his motives.

Because one thing had become very clear to me today.

The Council couldn't continue to operate as they did currently. "Things need to change," I whispered. "This isn't the way to lead."

Tray met my gaze, his dark eyes reminding me of our mother's. He dipped his chin. "You have my support every step of the way, brother. Always."

No hint of uncertainty, just unerring loyalty.

I didn't question him, because I'd pledge the same to him.

"I just hope I don't get us killed," I admitted, feeling as if I had the weight of the world on my shoulders.

"You won't," he replied. "Something tells me that mate of yours won't allow it."

My lips twitched. "She's a bit of a badass when she wants to be."

"She'd have to be to put up with your bullshit," he tossed back.

"Jackass," I grumbled, but I couldn't stop my grin.

Because yeah, he was right.

She put up with a lot.

And I sort of fucking adored her for it.

"So now what?" he asked.

"Now I pretend like everything's normal and pray to the fae that Dad doesn't find out." I told him.

Tray gave me a look. "Sounds like a brilliant plan, mate. Top-notch."

"If you think of a better one, I'll be all ears," I drawled.

He just shook his head. "I'm going back to bed. Something tells me I'm going to need all the sleep I can get because Dad said I'm joining you tomorrow for whatever discussion he wants to have."

"Try to act surprised if he mentions the Quandary Bloods."

"Trust me, that won't be hard," he admitted.

Yeah, I imagined it wouldn't be.

"Oh, but there is one positive to all this," he said, starting toward his door.

I arched a brow at him. "Which is?"

"You don't have to mate that bitch Emelyn anymore," he replied, clearly thrilled by the realization. "Silver lining and all that."

I laughed. "Thank fuck for small miracles," I drawled.

"I'd call that a major fucking miracle," he corrected.

I grunted. He was absolutely right about that.

As he undid the enchantment to allow himself to leave, I picked up my phone and sent a quick text to Zeph.

Fixed it. But Tray pretty much knows everything.

Zeph's reply came a few minutes later. *Something tells me he already knew and was just waiting for the right moment to catch you in the truth.*

I considered that with everything Tray had just said and replied, *You're right.*

I usually am, he shot back.

I rolled my eyes. *Take care of Aflora. Tell her I'm sorry.*

Will do, he returned.

I set my phone down and slipped into my sheets. Tomorrow would come all too early, and I needed to be prepared, just like Tray said.

And I also needed a much better plan.

CHAPTER THIRTY-TWO

Eight days later and I still couldn't stop thinking about what Kols had told me about my parents.

It was like finding out they'd died all over again, except I never really knew about it the first time. I'd felt their souls detach from the source—a life-altering experience for a seven-year-old—and I'd understood what it meant. Yet I'd never known *why* it'd happened. Or how.

And now I did.

The Midnight Fae Elders assassinated my parents.

Because they were Quandary Bloods? Because they were helping Quandary Bloods? I didn't know. But Kols had promised to find out everything he could, including who, specifically, had killed them and how.

I didn't blame him. I knew better than that. Yet that didn't stop me from feeling uneasy around him and his direct connection to the source.

He was their future leader.

The Midnight Fae King who would be in charge of exterminating Quandary Bloods and anyone perceived to be assisting them.

What violent lives these fae led. I missed my elemental home surrounded by thriving energies and a love for spirits and general existence.

However, I couldn't go back to them.

Not in my current form.

Because I was an abomination of unknown origin. Who knew if my parents were even the rightful earth source heirs?

Shade came up beside me, his palm finding the small of my back as he leaned in to kiss my temple. "Want to skip class?" he asked me softly. "I'm sure Zeph won't mind."

I looked at up at my Warrior Blood mate and watched as he stretched beside Kols across the yard. He'd insisted we return to the Academy after two nights in New York City, saying we needed to present a normal front and pretend we didn't know anything about the Council's plan to use me as bait.

I'd argued that it put the students in danger to keep me near them.

My mates had then reminded me that keeping me safe at the Academy would be easier than out in the open world. Because here they had snake vines and other nefarious wards in place that would automatically guard me as a student. Thereby making it less obvious when they protected me as well.

This whole thing resembled a waiting game—one I didn't want to play.

"Aflora?" Shade murmured, his lips brushing the shell of my ear and sending a shiver down my spine. I'd stayed at his place after Advanced Conjuring yesterday. It had provided a nice change of pace and sort of solidified our new existence where Zeph, Shade, and Kols somehow managed to share me evenly. Shade never joined the other two, but Zeph and Kols seemed to enjoy putting me between them. Or sometimes Kols was in the middle. Those were interesting experiences.

"That look in your eyes makes me want to skip class even more," Shade murmured, drawing me around to face him. "Are you thinking about last—"

A blast of magic from across the yard had both of us jumping apart to find the source.

"What the fuck?!" Kols shouted as he caught the ball of fire with his hand and threw it downward to smother with his shoe.

"That's *my* line, Kolstov," Emelyn snapped, her palm already alight with another flame. "Have you forgotten to tell me something, darling *betrothed?*"

My heart dropped into my stomach. *Oh, no. She knows. She knows we've bonded and now—*

"I'm sure there are many things I've *forgotten* to tell you," Kols drawled, somehow managing to sound both bored and annoyed at the same time. "Care to elaborate on which item you're inquiring about?"

Emelyn huffed and threw the inflamed sphere at his head, only for him to catch it again and dispense of it like the first one.

"Do that one more time and I'll show you how to properly use WarFire." The threat lingered in his golden irises, causing a chill to skate down my spine.

So much power, I thought. *So much beauty, too.*

Emelyn was either oblivious to the threat or didn't care. She stopped right before him, giving me her back. "Why did a dress arrive for me today from your mother? I thought we agreed not to go to the Blood Gala together."

My brow furrowed as I glanced at Shade, my mental connection to him opening automatically. *Blood Gala?*

Political bullshit, he replied. *The Nacht family throws the fancy ball annually. I always skip, but Kolstov will be expected to attend with Emelyn.*

I frowned. *Oh. Right. Engagement.*

A vision of Kols taking Emelyn as his date to the event fluttered through my mind, and I didn't quite care for it. Not even a tiny bit.

Kols sighed. "Fuck. I forgot to talk to my father about it."

"Obviously," she said slowly, annunciating each syllable. "Fix it."

"Yeah, I will," he muttered.

"No, you'll fix it right now," she demanded. "I'm not going."

"I said I'll take care of it, Emelyn."

"Yeah, and that's what you said weeks ago, Kolstov. I want it fixed right fucking now." She put her hands on her hips.

Whatever expression she gave him seemed to irritate him even more, because his golden eyes swirled with red power. "Remember who you're talking to, Elite Blood."

"My betrothed," she spat out.

"Your future king," he corrected, his tone holding a chill in it that caused all the hairs along my arms to stand on end.

Power sizzled in the air as the two of them squared off.

My stomach twisted at the dark-source essence, my Quandary magic flaring to life inside me at the familiar call. I winced, trying to shove it down, but it spread like rapid fire through my veins.

Aflora? Zeph's deep voice trickled through my thoughts.

My mind shut down my ability to reply, the magnitude of energy swimming around me, through my soul, and stealing the breath from my lungs.

Shade grabbed my wrist, his voice urgent in my ear. I tried to hear him, to comprehend his words, but I couldn't understand him over the roar of sound inside my head.

Kols's golden irises snapped up to mine, his expression melting into concern as he tried to harness his power, but it was too late. He'd released too much, his connection to the source thriving between us like the day we first joined.

Only this was worse.

It ripped through me on a level I didn't understand, the dark essence searing my being and bringing me to my knees.

Kols shouted, the inky lines climbing up his neck writhing and stirring a cascade of electricity that sizzled through the air and zapped my skin.

Blue embers flickered across my fingertips, forcing me to lock my fingers into the charcoal blades. Pain shot up my arms and down my spine, causing me to tremble beneath the weight of oppressing magic.

Red fire sprinted across the ground, circling me.

My body reacted defensively, shooting off an array of colors in response. *Blue. Green. Purple.*

How is that even possible? I thought, tears blurring my vision. *Oh, Fae. It burns!*

The blood-red flames fought mine, the power mounting into an array of light that temporarily blinded me.

And then Emelyn was there, her black eyes narrowed with fury as she engaged in a battle I didn't understand.

Everything began to spin, her energy somehow connecting to mine in a savage handshake that rippled through the air. Zeph and Shade yelled inside my thoughts, their collective voices leaving me unhinged and uncertain as a tornado of power swept me up into a cloud, the world disappearing behind a thick smog.

A hand grabbed mine, nails digging into my flesh.

Not one of my mates.

Emelyn.

Her Elite essence engaged mine, battling my power for dominance.

Except, it wasn't my Quandary side that I engaged to fight back, but a new link to unexpected Warrior magic.

Zeph.

I also sensed Shade.

What is happening to me? I asked, suddenly cold and hot all at once. *Stop this madness!*

I threw out my arms, forcing Emelyn to let go of me, and screamed as the cyclone released me from its smoky grip. I landed with a thump, my pants tearing as my knees met the knifelike grass below.

My chest heaved, breaths coming in and out of me in sharp gusts.

Too much magic. There's too much! I expelled my mounting energy into the ground below, forcing wave after wave of the overwhelming surge to go deep into the earth. Only, I felt Shade and Zeph absorbing it through our bonds. Kols, too.

And a fourth source I didn't understand.

A source that reminded me of home.

My eyes widened as I realized what that had to mean—I was feeding dark energy into the earth source! I immediately pulled back, collapsing onto my side into a ball of shivering nonsense.

Abomination, I told myself. *This is why everyone fears us.*

Because I couldn't control it.

I couldn't stop it.

And I'd just attacked *my home.* My element. My very reason for being.

I reached out on a tentative strand, begging whatever fae gods existed that I hadn't done any permanent harm. But as I poked at my earth energy, I found nothing nefarious or changed. Just my deep-rooted connection to the existence of life.

My brow furrowed. *That's impossible.* I felt the fourth link, the—

"Aflora!" Emelyn shrieked, forcing my attention to her and the threats surrounding us.

My lips parted in shock.

We were no longer in the training yard, but in the LethaForest.

And the encroaching shadows whispered danger.

Emelyn sent a sizzling web toward one, which resulted in a sharp, screeching echo to sound through the black tree trunks.

Hot, acrid smoke billowed in the air.

This was not the same part of the LethaForest I'd visited with my mates, but a deeper section that clearly didn't see fae life often. Because streams of fiery liquid slicked the obsidian rocks, one of which was less than a foot from my prone form. Had I landed just a few inches to the left, I'd have been burned alive.

"Fae...," I breathed, glancing around to gather my bearings.

The sky overhead lacked stars, the inky curtain creating an icy atmosphere that the flame streams heated and illuminated in shades of red and orange.

"Aflora!" Emelyn shouted again, fear etched into her voice.

A rock creature of some kind came toward her, the fingertips long talons of black flames. It lashed out at her, catching her wrist. She cried out in pain, her spells no match for the monster.

I forced myself to my feet, careful of the surrounding terrain, and searched for my wand.

Where did I—

The thing's talons whipped out of its opposite hand, encircling her throat and forcing me to act on instinct. A spell left my mouth—one I had never learned—and hit the being directly in the torso. The creature grated out a loud, crunching growl, then exploded into a mound of pebbles.

Emelyn crumpled to the ground, her neck and wrist charred from the creature's grip. I leapt over one of the fiery streams, then a second one, and knelt at her side. Her eyes rolled into the back of her head, the power zapped from her lifeless form.

Adrenaline spiked through my veins, my mind whirring with solutions I didn't understand. They came from a place deep inside, a foreign strand tied to my Quandary magic. I yanked on it, bringing it to the front of my mind, and sorted through the web of magic before me.

Chaos echoed around me.

Two more rock creatures spurred to life with those deadly claws aiming for me and Emelyn. A spell flew from my mouth that created a defensive wall, more of Zeph's energy surrounding us both while I tapped into the Quandary line that provided me with a strand of thought underlined in magic.

Words spilled from my mouth that didn't belong to me but to something else.

No, *someone* else.

The Quandary link.

Who are you? I marveled even while I spoke, my mind fracturing beneath an assault of confusion and reality woven together as one.

Don't think; do, a deep voice replied.

Familiar.

Warm.

Underlined in memories and dreams…

A vision of white hair flickered in my thoughts, there and gone in an instant as my mouth obeyed his command.

Yet he wasn't so much talking to me as he was allowing me access to his mind and power and granting me the knowledge I needed to survive this insanity. It also wasn't willing, more like my spirit demanding his compliance for my own survival.

And I felt him trying to pull back, to resurrect a barrier I'd unknowingly knocked down.

Who are you? I asked him.

But Emelyn gasping back to life distracted my focus, drawing my attention back to her and the spell I'd somehow woven through her, healing the marks on her neck and wrist.

"How did you do that?" she asked hoarsely.

I just shook my head because I didn't know, the powers spiking through me a tangled mess of knots I couldn't seem to unravel.

I flinched as one of the monsters shredded my defensive barrier, his fire hot against my senses. I grabbed Emelyn's hand, ready to run, but the clouds engulfed me again and sent us spinning through time and space.

Shade, I realized, baffled and completely thrown by his interference. Only it wasn't him at all, but me, tapping into a dark-source connection created through our bond—a connection I didn't realize existed until now.

That was where all the magic lived.

A dark orb of power fueled by my mates, allowing me access to strands of energy I intuitively understood.

I frowned at it, confused by the four links once more.

Death.

Elite.

Warrior.

Quandary.

The last was deeply rooted, as if it'd been there for years. Because that represented me and my family line? That notion didn't feel right.

I tried to investigate it more, only to spin out of the cyclone and into a darkened grove with a stunned Emelyn at my side. Her dark eyes flashed to mine, alarm in her expression. "You're… you're…"

"An abomination," I whispered, unable to lie to her. Not after everything she'd just witnessed.

She shook her head. "That's not…" She cleared her throat, her delicate hand going up to touch her unmarred throat. "You saved me."

I winced, not because I regretted it but because I couldn't explain how I'd done it. "I…" I didn't know what to say.

A hint of wonder entered her gaze. "I sense Kols in you." She lifted her hand as if to touch me, only to drop it a second later and spin toward the dark forest around us and the moving trees. "Who's there?" she demanded, her wand already in her palm.

I tried to find mine again, this time successfully, and mimicked her defensive stance.

Nothing immediately approached, but I felt the building energy and the hum of familiar magic in the air.

Something was coming.

No, the presence was already here.

Multiple essences.

All woven with magic my soul recognized on some deep, dark level.

"Well, well, the *queen* finally arrives," a feminine voice drawled from the shadows of a nearby burning thwomp. "And she brought us an Elite Blood to play with as a gift. How incredibly thoughtful."

CHAPTER THIRTY-THREE

AFLORA

Energy crackled from the deadly trees, causing my defensive instincts to flare to life. Zeph was a strong presence in my head, his magic pouring through my senses to surround Emelyn and me in a protective shield of invisible power, one meant to deflect any untoward spells.

Like the one that came from the darkness, aimed right at Emelyn. It bounced back with an emerald spark, causing electricity to sizzle around us.

"Impressive," the female mused. "Why are you protecting the Elite Blood?"

"Who are you?" I countered, unable to see her cloaked in the darkness.

She stepped forward with several Midnight Fae at her back, all of them raising their wands to illuminate the tips in cerulean magic.

My lips parted. *Quandary Bloods.*

Except for the woman at the front. Her wand glowed with red magic, marking her as an Elite Blood.

"Dakota," Emelyn breathed, her eyes widening. "What are you doing here?"

"Oh, you mean after your betrothed banished me for playing with his source?" she asked, her lips curling into a smile. "What do you think I'm doing here?" She sent another spiral of magic toward Emelyn, but my net caught it and volleyed it back to her.

I had no idea how I was holding that up in front of us, but I felt the strands of it tied to my fingertips, not my wand. A fresh burst of power flared from my hand to restructure the shield, ensuring Dakota hadn't damaged the exterior.

The woven threads of magic hummed back at me, confirming their integrity.

It all came naturally to me, like I'd flipped on a switch in my mind that allowed me to suddenly envision every strand of vitality around us. The elements were there just waiting for me to pluck and use them as I required. Which I did now as I reinforced our blockade, the invisible net pulsing with ominous intent, ready to engage at will.

"That's a bit of an irritation," Dakota said after dealing with her backfired spell. She polished her nails against her shirt, then lowered her wand. "I don't understand. Why are you protecting the very being who wants you dead, Aflora?"

"I don't want her dead," Emelyn said quickly, her widening dark eyes looking at me. "I know I've been a bitch, but—"

"Not *you*, but Midnight Fae like you," Dakota interjected, sounding bored. "Emelyn and her betrothed are the future queen and king of a Council that has hunted and killed Quandary Bloods for over a thousand years. How could you guard someone destined for such evil?"

"I can't hold Emelyn responsible for a history she had no jurisdiction over," I replied, not bothering to point out the sexist nuances that would forbid she even be part of it as the Midnight Fae Queen.

"And for a marriage I have no interest or say in," she muttered, causing me to glance at her. She'd lowered her wand, but I sensed her awareness of our situation, her tense limbs ready to fight as needed.

"Condemning Emelyn would be similar to classifying all Quandary Bloods as evil just for being born into a certain bloodline, as I believe it's her father's lineage that made her a match for Kols," I said, thinking out loud.

"It is," she admitted, her eyes holding a touch of respect as she looked at me. And a glimmer of fear.

"Then why wouldn't I defend her?" I asked, returning my focus to the dark-haired fae who seemed to be the leader of the others. "Destinies change every day, and she's not the one pointing a wand at me right now. You all are."

"They're pointing their wands at Emelyn," Dakota drawled. "As I said, she's the future queen."

"And as she pointed out, it's not by choice." A discussion I'd love to revisit with Kols later. "What do you want? Who are you? Why are you here?" But I already suspected the answers involved the recent attacks and the trap from the village.

They were here for me, to take me to someone.

But who?

Because this female wasn't the source of magic I'd felt at the Academy during the assault, and while the others were familiar to me, they weren't responsible for the events of that day either.

"Where are we?" Emelyn added to my list of questions.

"In an alternate paradigm within the LethaForest," Dakota replied, sounding amused. "We were only supposed to take Aflora, but you came with her. Would you like to be sent back? Because I can arrange that for you."

"And what would that require?" Emelyn asked, arching a black brow.

"Leaving Aflora behind, of course." Dakota sounded so nonchalant, as if the terms of my kidnapping meant little to nothing to her.

"Yeah, I'll pass," Emelyn drawled. "Aflora and I are a package deal."

We are? I thought, shocked by her statement.

"Oh? Are you one of her three mates?" Dakota asked, cocking her head to the side. "I thought they were all male." She glanced at the fae around her as if seeking confirmation. "What were their names again?"

My stomach twisted. How did she know about my quad?

"Shadow, Zephyrus, and Kolstov," one of the Midnight Fae replied. He was a shorter male with long black hair—or at least, it appeared black in the night and with the light of his cerulean-glowing wand flaring before him.

"Kolstov?" Emelyn looked at me. "You mated *Kolstov?*"

"Oh, did you not know?" Dakota asked, not sounding the least bit guilty. "Yes, it does cause a certain perplexity, but we plan to teach Aflora how to undo the bond with him, so he'll be free again shortly. Of course, he's going to die in the process, but that's neither here nor there, yes?"

"You mated Kolstov?" Emelyn repeated, her tone not necessarily angry so much as startled.

"I, uh, yes." There was no sense in denying it or explaining how it happened or telling her it wasn't done yet. This situation required honesty and quick responses, not dwelling on things I couldn't change. We'd deal with the nuances later.

"Does that change your stance on the package deal?" Dakota wondered out loud, her enjoyment in our situation palpable.

Emelyn held my gaze as she replied, "No, it doesn't change a damn thing."

My eyebrows shot upward. She couldn't really mean that.

Maybe she only intended for us to remain in this together until she saw a better escape, because I doubted that Dakota's offer to let her go came without caveats. Emelyn must have sensed the same duplicitous notion as well, therefore not trusting the proposal.

"Huh." Dakota sounded amused. "Well, I'll be. Then I guess you're both coming with us."

"Not so fast, Dakota." The new voice came from the surrounding woods, echoing all around us as if the trees spoke rather than a person. Yet the feminine tones resonated in my thoughts from a single source—a powerful one.

The Midnight Fae before us all raised their wands in a new direction, their expressions grim as another group of fae entered the grove led by a female with long black hair, and a male on each side.

Emelyn gasped beside me, clearly recognizing the trio.

I studied their features. They appeared only a few years older than me, but I could almost *taste* the ancient air surrounding them. And the male to her right had a Fortune Fae Alpha appeal to him with his silver hair, larger build, and enhanced jawline—suggesting he had fangs. Yet his eyes weren't slit like a Fortune Fae Alpha's.

The male on her other side held up a wand lit with purple magic, indicating his Death Blood heritage, and as it illuminated his features, I caught sight of a pair of startling blue irises.

Blue irises that reminded me of Shade's.

Thinking of my mate had me automatically opening my mental channel to him.

Where the hell are you? he demanded immediately.

In some sort of paradigm, I replied. *And I'm pretty sure your dad is here.*

That's impossible.

Well, he looks like you, I whispered, swallowing. *Same eyes. Thick, nearly black hair. Chiseled features. Death Blood magic.*

Silence. Then he softly asked, *Is he with a dark-haired female?*

Yes.

And a man with silver hair?

Yes.

Those are my grandparents, he replied. *You can trust them. I'm coming.*

How will you find me? I wondered.

Just keep the connection open, Aflora. And never shut me out like that again. You scared the shit out of us.

I winced. *I didn't mean to.*

We'll work on it, he promised.

"What are you doing here, Zen?" Dakota asked, sounding wary.

"You know exactly why I'm here," Shade's grandmother replied, sounding regal and in charge. "This is not the way." She turned to address the others with Dakota. "Retribution isn't the only path. We can do this without spilling more Midnight Fae blood."

"She's right," the silver-haired fae replied. "Reformation will allow us to lead without the unnecessary loss of lives."

"Unnecessary," Dakota repeated. "You know what was unnecessary? The Midnight Fae Elders killing my parents for helping Cassandra escape the kingdom. You know what else was unnecessary? The Midnight Fae Elders killing Tobias's entire line because a grandparent was a Quandary Blood."

"Violence cannot be countered by more violence," Zen replied softly. "If you continue down this path, so many more innocents will be wrapped up in a war of blood and retribution. How is that a rightful solution?"

"They deserve to bleed for what they've done to our families," one of the Midnight Fae hissed.

Another grunted in agreement. "The Nachts were never meant to rule. They've destroyed our source and polluted it with their false superiority."

"Blood for blood," a female said softly.

"Hear, hear!" the male beside her cheered.

Zen shook her head. "I understand you're angry—we all are—but to kill the lineages entirely will dwarf Midnight Fae kind."

"It's what they did to us," someone pointed out, his voice gruff and lost in the darkness. "It's what they bloody deserve."

"We've chosen our side, Zen," Dakota murmured. "Perhaps it's time you join us once more. I'm certain Zakkai would welcome you home."

"It's not the path I choose," Zen replied sadly.

Aflora? Shade's voice trickled through my thoughts.

I'm here.

Yes, I feel you, he replied. *I'm about to penetrate the paradigm, and I need you to grab onto me as quickly as possible. There's a fleet of Warrior Bloods waiting out here to attack.*

What about your grandparents? I asked, suddenly worried for their safety. Odd, considering we hadn't really met, but I felt a kinship to Zen, sort of like I'd met her in another life.

They'll be fine, he whispered. *She's already seen what's coming.*

My lips parted in understanding. *Because she's a Fortune Fae.*

Yes, he replied. *Ready?*

What about Emelyn?

Ajax will take care of her, he promised.

Ajax? I repeated.

He's with me. And trust me, he'll make sure she's safe.

But he hates her. And while I didn't have a lot of like for the woman, I didn't wish her ill will. Especially after her show of solidarity here, even if it was for her own survival.

Ah, sweet little rose. Hate and love are so closely connected. Surely you understand that by now?

You mean—

I'll explain later, he inserted, an urgency entering his voice. *I need to come in there now. Are you ready?*

I glanced at a pale-faced Emelyn, then took in the growing tensions outside our shield. The Quandary Bloods had begun arguing, with Zen and Dakota on opposite sides squaring off, their postures a strange mixture of defensive and broken at the same time. There seemed to be pain, coupled with a sense of rightness.

Because they couldn't agree on a path forward.

Retribution on one half, reformation on the other.

A Midnight Fae faction driven apart by the greed and violence of the rest of their kind.

The question became, what side did I fall on? The Elder Midnight Fae had killed my parents. "Will the Elders pay for what they've done?" I asked, cutting off whatever some had been saying. "With reformation, will they pay?" I restated, wanting my direct query answered. "They killed my parents."

"Yes," Dakota replied. "They did."

"Will they be punished? My parents were Royal Earth Fae. That assault can't go unanswered."

Zen sighed. "My child, there is so much you don't understand regarding the circumstances and the consequences of our actions. It's not as simple as one might predict."

"That's a riddle that doesn't answer my question," I replied, ignoring Shade's roaring commentary in my head. He'd asked if I was ready, and the answer was no, not without additional information. "Will the Elders pay for what they've done?"

"We will ensure they pay," Dakota said, her expression gleaming with approval. "And you will lead us as queen."

I had no idea what she meant by that. "I don't want to be your queen. I just want the Elders held accountable for their sins."

"What punishment would you give them?" Zen asked me. "How would you see them properly reprimanded for their actions?"

"How would you?" I countered. "By restoring the balance, yet allowing them to live? They didn't afford my parents the same consideration, so why should I give it to them?"

"Because it's our responsibility as the architects of the source to ensure the survival of Midnight Fae kind, not act as jury and executioner," the silver-haired male beside her said, his voice deep and kissed by darkness. "As the last remaining Earth Fae Royal, I would expect you to understand that sense of duty."

"Am I an Earth Fae Royal?" I asked, arching a brow. "Or were my parents Quandary Bloods in hiding?"

Zen's eyebrows lifted in surprise while her counterparts stared at me in confusion, making me wonder if I had deduced that incorrectly. But before I could ask, the ground began to shake, causing the Quandary Bloods to curse and weave their magic through the air in hypnotic shades of cerulean blue.

Shade's grandparents vanished, the world shifting around Emelyn and me in a delirious dance of excessive light, blinding me momentarily before revealing the similar surroundings of the LethaForest once more.

Burning thwomps released an explosion of smoke and fire, causing me to cringe.

And chaos descended as magic wove through the air in a colorful eruption.

Emelyn grabbed my hand, yanking me to the side. I nearly shook off her grip, not wanting to fall into another enchanted *paradigm* with her, but then I saw Ajax on her opposite side, guiding us out of the field as his wand produced a thick black smog that hid the three of us from view.

He took off at a clipped pace through the woods, leaving the war behind us as the Quandary Bloods fought the Warrior Bloods—or I assumed that was the case. I hadn't actually seen who fought whom, my focus primarily on following Emelyn out of the insanity.

Ajax didn't stop until we were under a blanket of darkness, the trees in this area of the LethaForest boasting leaves.

I squinted.

No.

Not leaves.

Bats.

So many that they completely blocked the moonlight above.

If they were bothered by our presence, they didn't show it. Only one seemed to care, his little feet moving along the trunk of the tree as he carried himself down until he was a few inches from my face. I slid my wand back into my pocket and studied the adorable little creature with intelligent eyes. He seemed to be doing the same to me.

"Good job, Draco," Shade said from the darkness, startling me. He stepped forward, and the bat landed on his shoulder with a little clicking chirp. Then his icy blue eyes met mine. "We need to go. Now."

"I've got Emelyn," Ajax said. "Go."

I glanced at the pair, who were locked in a hug that spoke volumes about their relationship. It left me wondering what their history entailed, because clearly one existed here.

Shade grabbed my wrist, a thick cloud enveloping us before I could ask for details or even voice my approval, and a moment later, our meadow appeared. My shoulders immediately relaxed, the flowers and sunshine calling to my element. I wrapped my arms around him, breathed in his familiar peppermint scent, and sighed.

Just for a moment, I allowed myself to calm.

To release the last however many minutes or hours of chaos.

To exist in a world that was me and Shade, surrounded by the familiarity of home.

Only, I sensed another presence, one that had my brow furrowing in confusion.

That was when I realized Shade's arms weren't around me, his body stiff against mine.

I pulled back to study his eyes, noting the coldness lurking inside. *Shade?*

No reply.

My lips pulled downward as I tried to access our link and found it closed, just as he'd done before when keeping me out of his mind.

I shook my head. "I don't understand."

"I know," he replied, his attention on something over my shoulder.

No, not something. Someone.

Because I could feel him.

The familiarity of his magic.

The hint of an ocean kiss.

The faint memory of several sleepless nights.

I turned slowly, already knowing whom I'd face—the white-haired male from my dreams. "You're not real," I whispered.

He stood leaning against a tree, his silver-blue eyes glinting with amusement. "We've had this discussion before, little star. And I suggested you reconsider that thought."

I stepped backward into Shade, begging him with my mind to whisk us away from here, but other than place his hands possessively on my hips, he did nothing.

"Why are you here?" I asked, terrified of the answer, praying he said anything other than what I feared.

"Because this was where Shadow and I promised to meet for the exchange," he replied, killing all my hopes.

How could you? I asked Shade. But our link remained closed, the willow stump doing the one thing he told me not to do only minutes earlier—he shut me out.

Zeph! I called, quickly opening another channel.

Silence.

But not in the same way as Shade's.

Zeph felt... *unconscious.*

"What did you do?" I asked, shivering uncontrollably despite the warm sun overhead. "What did you do, Shade?"

"What fate required me to do," he replied against my ear, his lips brushing my temple. "I warned you that you would hate me. Now you know why."

"Because you're working with *him*?" But I didn't even really know what that meant. This male had attacked the Academy, seduced me in my dreams, tried to trap me in the village, and now stared at me with almost illicit intent. "Who are you?" I asked him. "Why are you doing this?"

"I'm Zakkai," he replied. "As to why I'm doing this, well..." He smiled, pushing off the tree to saunter toward me.

Shade held me in place when I tried to step to the side.

Energy kissed my fingertips as my powers ignited in automatic defense, only a wave of Zakkai's hand calmed my power. I pulled out my wand to try again, and he smiled fondly at the item.

"Ah, I've been looking for that," he murmured, plucking it easily from my palm and twirling it between his fingers. "I should have known those figments at AcaWard would give it to you." He chuckled and canted his head to the side, his silver-blue eyes holding mine as he slid the wand under his cloak. "Thank you for keeping my wand warm for me."

"Your wand?" I repeated, my mouth dry.

His lips curled again, causing little dimples to appear at the edges. "Yes, sweet star. My wand."

"I-I don't understand," I whispered. "How?"

He reached out to tuck a piece of my hair behind my ear, then stepped into my personal space, trapping me between them, with Zakkai in front of me and Shade behind me. "Close your eyes," he whispered.

I didn't want to obey him, but my eyelids slipped shut as if he'd drawn them down with a spell. And then I felt him in my mind, untwisting a strand of magic that led to the root of my mate bonds.

One that finally allowed me to understand and see the connection at the end.

The missing link I'd failed to comprehend all this time.

The real reason I had access to Quandary Blood abilities.

It was never my parents or my own heritage or my lineage.

It was *him.*

Zakkai.

My Quandary Blood mate.

EPILOGUE

SHADE

"Y ou had better be right about this," I muttered to the white-haired male standing in the place Aflora had just stood thirty minutes ago. Before Zakkai took her. Before I betrayed her in the worst way possible.

"How many times must you live the same history to believe my method?" Tadmir asked, his black eyes flickering with a millennium of secrets. "This is the only way. Even Kyros agrees, and he rarely agrees with anything."

"It doesn't feel right," I admitted, pressing my palm to my heart.

"Sacrifices rarely do," he replied softly. "But the outcome will prove our pain worthwhile. Trust me, Shadow."

"The last time I trusted someone, I bit an Earth Fae, fell in love with her, and watched her destroy the world in seven different ways," I said, recalling each version of our lifetimes together.

They all linked back to that pivotal moment in Kols's suite when Aflora threatened to break the bonds. I'd been living the same reality over and over again, several different ways, all of them ending in war no matter what I did to avoid it.

So this time I gave Zakkai what he wanted—our mate.

Which had been the plan all along.

He was the reason I'd bitten Aflora, after all. He'd warned me she would be beautiful, that I would crave her, but that she wasn't mine to take.

Yet I did this time.

Because she bit me and I couldn't help but claim her in return.

I'd expected him to try to kill me after I told him, but instead, he'd shrugged and said it only empowered her more. Which was why I'd guided Zeph down a similar path, providing him with the opportunity to finish the bond with Aflora.

I knew the Council would convene to tell Kols the truth on our first break day—as they'd done every time during the last seven iterations of this sequence.

But unlike before, I hadn't voiced discontent with Aflora and Zeph going to the village. However, I hadn't counted on Zakkai's interference—an error that had almost destroyed everything.

Only, it led to Zeph taking Aflora to the Human Realm and finishing the bond.

That left Kols, who, unfortunately, never took the opportunity to finish the mating before his duty to the source.

Thus leaving Aflora with only two of her anchors and a sadistic third mate.

"I hope it's enough," I whispered to myself. "I hope we can pull her back."

"It's never been just about her, Shadow," Tadmir replied. "That's the piece you've failed to *see*—her fate is tied to Zakkai. To win this war, and to ensure the future we both desire, she needs to convince him to take the appropriate path. That's the key."

"And there's no going back this time," I added.

"Yes," he agreed. "Not without risking your memories and hers, and then we'll be right back where we started when I first approached you about fate."

That seemed so long ago now.

And yet...

"Has that happened before?" I asked him, curious just how many times he'd used his Paradox Fae abilities to yank us through the circle of time. The purple sword on his hip glinted at me, as if in agreement with my thought process.

"You'll never know," he replied, but by the gleam in his gaze, I suspected it had happened at least once.

Which explained my inexplicable connection to Aflora.

Our souls had linked many times before, just as she'd bonded Kols and Zeph to varying degrees. I'd witnessed some, but perhaps not all.

And I'd seen what happened when she cut them off indefinitely as well.

Those were the worst iterations of fate.

The ones I never wanted to experience again.

"Aren't you exhausted?" I asked Tadmir. "So many hundreds of years of masquerading as a Malefic Blood while traversing the realms of time and space in unending loops?"

He lifted a shoulder. "I do what I need to do to ensure that fate follows the correct path."

His existence baffled my mind. He was half Midnight Fae Quandary Blood and half Paradox Fae—the true definition of an abomination—and he'd used his Quandary skills to rewrite his abilities to appear as a Malefic Blood after skipping into the future and witnessing the demise of his kind.

And he'd been plotting for this moment ever since.

The one where Aflora aligned with four mates to right the wrongs of the Midnight Fae Elders and the Council.

I'd originally joined the wrong side, choosing to listen to Zakkai's rhetoric about the need for retribution.

Then I saw where that path ended several times over.

Now it was time to walk in a new direction, one Tadmir had tried to drive me down multiple times before. Only, on this attempt, I'd finally listened.

And broke my heart in the process.

I'm sorry, Aflora, I thought, wishing I could open our connection and tell her everything. But Zakkai was in her mind. Which was why I'd blocked her initially. If he found out what I'd hidden, all the fates I'd lived, the futures I'd *seen*, we'd be doomed.

Keeping Aflora in the dark was the only way we'd have a chance at winning this war before it truly started.

I just hoped she'd be able to forgive me in the end.

MIDNIGHT FAE ACADEMY
BOOK THREE

PROLOGUE

ZAKKAI

I'm not a bad man. Of course, I'm not a good man either. I do what I need to do to survive, and that includes making a lot of unsavory choices.

Like biting Aflora.

Ah, I was only ten then. I didn't really understand why my father wanted me to mate her, and I always assumed we would just sever our ties when the time came. Except, she called to me with her song. And then she pulled me into a dream.

I barely recognized her, the gorgeous woman before me nothing like my childhood memories of the little Earth Fae. But her eyes gave her away.

Cerulean blue orbs blazing with *my* magic.

Fuck, it was a stunning sight.

I'd lost my breath, unable to speak. The next thing I knew, her tongue was doing all the talking on our behalf, her naked body pressed against mine in a sensuous kiss that I refused to deny.

Yeah, I probably should have told her the truth. But I gave her hints. I even told her I wasn't a figment of her imagination. However, she chose to indulge in the fantasy, and who the hell was I to stop her?

She wanted to come, so I made her come. Again and again.

It wasn't what I'd originally intended to do upon reconnecting with my long-lost mate, but I wasn't about to say no to a naked and needy woman in my bed. Her other mates weren't properly taking care of her, so I handled the issue with my mouth and hands, never once requesting she return the favor. I was giving like that.

But as I lay her down now on my bed, I wonder if perhaps I should have approached this differently.

There have been several opportunities to do this in an entirely different way. One of those times transpired in a Human Realm coffee shop where I met a Fortune Fae with far too much to say.

Aflora had been there, her pretty blue-black hair hanging in tantalizing waves down her back, while waiting for her date to arrive.

I'd intended to take her then.

Instead, I sent her to Shade.

He thinks I don't know about his little dates with time. Just as he thinks he's going to change fate by playing with my mate.

But he fails to understand how vengeance works.

So I'll teach him again. Just as I'll teach her.

I sigh, drawing my fingers through her soft hair. She needs so much training for the fight ahead, and rather than prepare her properly, I'd spent all our time together indulging her in bed.

"I'll rectify that soon, little star," I promise her, leaning down to press my lips to her forehead. She'll wake soon. When she does, we'll talk.

I have nothing to hide.

No remorse.

No real regrets.

Everything I've done is for the betterment of Midnight Fae kind. She'll understand that soon, and then she'll join me as queen.

My father won't like it. He only wants the bond to be temporary, a way to protect her until she's of age and capable of helping our cause.

But I don't like the idea of severing our fate.

She's mine.

My pretty little star.

We were best friends once, and we will be again.

"You'll see," I tell her softly, brushing my fingers down the column of her elegant throat. She's naked again, her form the picture of perfection among my black sheets. "I can't wait for you to wake up, little star. We're going to have so much fun together."

However, for now, I'll lend her a robe.

Kindness doesn't come naturally to me, but I'll try for her.

To an extent, anyway.

With another sigh, I leave her on the bed and head out onto the balcony, my mind on the future ahead and what this war will require from us.

Sacrifice, certainly.

Blood as well.

Maybe even death.

We'll know shortly. Just as soon as my little star wakes up. Then our journey together will begin… *again.*

CHAPTER ONE

KOLS

"What do you mean, she *disappeared*?" my father demanded, his golden irises on an unrepentant Shade.

A similar question swirled through my thoughts as I sat in my chair at the Council table. *Where did you take her?* I wanted to ask him. But, of course, I couldn't. I had to feign nonchalance and act like none of this bothered me.

Not Emelyn's little episode in Warrior Magic class.

Or the fact that Aflora had then disappeared into some paradigm with my soon-to-be former betrothed.

Or the aftermath of that paradigm being brought to the ground by a horde of Warrior Bloods, and Aflora vanishing with Shade at her side.

I couldn't reach out to her because we weren't bonded on that level yet.

I couldn't talk to Zeph because he'd been knocked out by the magic.

And I couldn't ask Shade any questions because the entire Council sat in a circle around us.

It took every ounce of strength I possessed not to react.

"Start from the beginning," my father stated, his tone brooking no argument.

Shade's icy gaze slid to mine. "Your Highness?" he prompted, the two words dripping with his usual disdain. I couldn't tell if it was all just an act or if he meant that tone. This evening's events had been mostly my fault, something I explained out loud as I recounted the events to the Council.

I told them how Emelyn had attacked me with WarFire, her ire a result of the upcoming Blood Gala. Which, seriously, what the fuck? Talk about a massive overreaction. Yes, I'd meant to talk to my father about our attendance weeks ago, but I'd been a little busy lately.

Of course, Emelyn didn't know that. Because if she did, we had a much larger problem on our hands since I was betrothed to her, yet I'd mated Aflora.

I cleared my throat and continued with the aftermath of the fight, how Emelyn and Aflora were sucked up into some paradigm. We'd located the heart of it in the LethaForest, which was when the Warrior Bloods showed up because they'd been hunting a similar strand of magic. And then all hell broke loose, ending with Aflora's disappearance.

Because Shade wrapped her up in shadows and they vanished, I added in my head. *And he didn't tell me what happened after that because he's Shade and he doesn't believe in positive communication.* A problem I would be rectifying as soon as this Council adjourned.

"And how did she disappear?" my father pressed, his focus shifting between me and Shade.

I arched a brow at the Death Blood. This was his part to explain because I had no idea what he did with her.

"Don't look at me," the bastard drawled. "She vanished before my eyes, too."

Right, I nearly replied, but I swallowed the comment. If he didn't want the Council to know he'd spirited her away somewhere, then I would keep his secret.

"So where is she now?" Tadmir asked, his white eyebrow inching upward into his matching hairline. "Can't you feel her in your bond?"

"She's shut me out," Shade replied, his easygoing tone taking on a harsher quality that hinted at his annoyance. As far as acting skills went, the Death Blood's were top-notch. "I can't sense her at all."

"How the hell did she manage to block you?" Aswad snapped. The Death Blood King wasn't known for his patience, nor was he known for being all that kind to his son. I'd never cared much before, but seeing the way he spoke to Shade now had my hackles rising for inexplicable reasons.

Well, perhaps not entirely inexplicable.

We were essentially bonded through Aflora, making him an integral part of our quad.

So I supposed being defensive on his behalf came with the territory of our new relationship, but I couldn't let the Council sense it. Shade and I notoriously hated each other—a consequence of our birthrights.

"When I find her, I'll ask." Shade uttered the reply through his teeth, then resumed leaning against the wall with his trademark devil-may-care attitude.

I envied his ability to appear so unfazed.

Because inside I was dying. I could sense something was wrong, but I was powerless to investigate the source of that unease. All I wanted to do was tell this Council—the same one that had hidden the truth about the Quandary Bloods from me for nearly twenty-five fucking years—to go to hell. However, instead, I remained poised and calm and waited for them to deliver a verdict.

Which proceeded to take two hours.

By the end of the discussion, I wanted to kill everyone.

They completely disregarded Emelyn's behavior and focused entirely on Aflora.

"The Earth Fae Royal was obviously complicit."

"Agreed. We need to find her. She's the key to taking down the resistance."

"We can use magic to bolster Shadow's connection to her."

Their words blended together after a while, but the final plan was to use Shade to track her through the bonds and to report back as soon as he sensed Aflora's location. Then the Warrior Bloods would take her into custody and either kill her for running away or use her as bait again and kill her later.

Regardless, their plan was to destroy her.

My mate.

My beautiful, sweet Aflora, who had done nothing to deserve their callousness. She'd been set up to fail from the beginning by this very Council commanding that Shade bite her. All because they wanted to use her as bait.

And now that she'd been taken, they were quick to assume she was aiding the Quandary Bloods on their quest for resurrection. The Council claimed there was only one avenue that made sense—seek and destroy.

I tried to argue that it would cause political strife with the Elemental Fae. I also pointed out that she hadn't shown a single inkling of supporting the Quandary Bloods and that perhaps she'd been kidnapped or taken against her will.

The Council and the circle of Midnight Fae Elders ignored the latter. Then my grandfather—who had taken Lima's usual seat for the meeting— stated that the Elemental Fae wouldn't be a problem. His offhanded commentary reminded me that this was the Council who had killed Aflora's parents and kept it hidden for fifteen years. They didn't care about fae politics. It was all just an act before, one meant to place Aflora at the center of a trap.

My blood boiled, and the inky lines on my arms writhed with discontent.

This was my future—the council I was born to lead.

And I realized as I walked out of the room that I hated every single one of them, including my father, who called my name to stop me on the threshold.

I almost didn't listen.

But a nudge from Shade had me turning around to face Malik Nacht, the Elite Blood King. My father. The man in charge of the Midnight Fae Council. The man I had idolized all my life. I'd spent years trying to win his favor and make him proud.

And for what?

To lead a council of murderers.

The sudden clarity clouded my thoughts, blackening my mood and causing the source to swirl inside me, anticipating my growing need for retaliation.

My father frowned as though he could sense it. "Are you all right?"

No, I am not fucking all right, I thought. "I'm fine," I said instead. "Just irritated over the situation."

My father snorted. "Aren't we all?"

"You should be irritated," my grandfather said, stark accusation darkening his tone. "Aflora is your ascension trial, yes?"

"Yes," I agreed, my fingers curling into fists at my sides as he came to stand next to my father. The two men bore a similar resemblance, their ageless features the same as my own.

Auburn hair.

Golden irises.

Regal bone structure.

We all resembled brothers, except my grandfather held an ancient gleam in his irises that only seemed partially formed in my father's and was entirely lacking in my own.

"Constantine," my father said, always referring to my grandfather by name in formal situations such as this. Considering this was only my fourth time actually meeting the patriarch on my father's side, I should probably adopt the same habit.

This man wasn't family so much as a legacy.

I wasn't even sure where he lived. All the Elders disappeared into their own quadrants of the realms, some choosing to play with humans more than their own kind.

Others fell into deep slumbers for countless years or centuries.

Immortality came with perks and consequences.

"I believe we need to have a further conversation on what happens when an ascension is failed," Constantine continued, his eyebrow cocking upward, daring me to argue.

"I haven't failed yet," I replied, matching his haughty tone with one of my own. "Now, I don't have time to waste on a hypothetical discussion. I have an Earth Fae to find. So, if you all will excuse me."

I didn't wait for them to reply.

I also ignored my father when he tried.

And instead walked straight into a portal with Shade at my side.

He punched in the destination—Midnight Fae Academy.

Seconds later, the gates revealed themselves to us along with the Academy's gothic exterior, and Shade faced me.

"Zakkai has Aflora," he said before I could question him about her location. I'd assumed this whole time that he'd just hidden her in one of his infamous shadows.

"Who the fuck is Zakkai?" I asked.

"Her Quandary Blood mate."

CHAPTER TWO

AFLORA

I*'m naked.*

Normally, that thought wouldn't bother me; Earth Fae frequently roamed around without clothes.

But the silky sheets caressing my skin didn't belong to me. Nor did the subtle aroma of the ocean tickling my nose.

Zakkai.

I recognized his essence all around me, could feel his Quandary powers tickling the hairs along my arms in an attempt to seduce my magic into coming out to play, and could taste his familiarity on my tongue. For a month, I thought he was a figment of my imagination. However, he'd left me clues to the contrary—clues I'd chosen to ignore and laugh away.

I wasn't laughing now.

"I know you're awake, little star." His warm voice came to me on a breeze, followed by another tantalizing scent of home. My mother used to decorate our house with fragrances from the Water Kingdom. It was a secret indulgence of hers, one she claimed paired nicely with our earthy perfumes.

Somehow, Zakkai had bottled up that fragrance and wore it around him like some sort of sensual cloak. Or perhaps it was just his natural scent.

"Aflora," he murmured, the taunt in his tone unmistakable. "Do I need to join you under those sheets and wake you up with my tongue? Because I'm happy to oblige, just like I did in all our dreams."

Ugh. My cheeks flamed with the memories—the ones where I'd completely let myself go because I had thought he wasn't real. The things I'd made him do to me...

I shivered.

He chuckled as though he overheard that thought. And maybe he had since he claimed to be my mate.

The heat of his body swept over me as he sat beside me on the bed—not close enough to touch, but close enough to feel.

His familiarity unnerved me, as did the sensation of his silky sheets moving along my legs as I rolled away from him. He didn't try to stop me, just settled against the headboard and crossed his long legs at his bare ankles. I studied his feet for a moment before dragging my gaze up his pajama bottoms to his bare abdomen.

Because of course he chose to go shirtless.

Just like he had in all my dreams.

The chiseled perfection of his body left no mystery as to why I thought I'd mentally created him. He was too godlike to be real with those long wisps of white hair and silver-blue eyes.

"Keep looking at me like that and I'm going to accept it for the invitation that it is, Aflora."

Ugh, his voice was just as velvety smooth as the rest of him.

The man encapsulated sex.

And the grin curving his full lips said he knew it, too.

"It's not an invitation," I muttered, curling deeper into his silky sheets.

A pair of dimples graced his flawless cheeks.

Yeah, he would have a killer smile, too. Because why not?

Maybe he was really an Incubus from the Hell Fae realm. But no, I caught the flicker of cerulean magic lurking deep in his fathomless gaze.

He took my wand, I remembered, frowning. *No, he said it was* his *wand*.

My heart skipped a beat at the memory and Shade's aloofness as he just handed me over as though I meant nothing to him.

Why? I whispered at him. *Why did you do this?*

He didn't reply. Not that I expected him to. I could feel the block in our bond—the one he'd placed there before giving me to Zakkai.

Zeph? I tried the other mate-strand in my mind, the one connected to my Warrior Blood mate. The ends of our bond felt frayed, his silence deafening.

Shade had created some sort of mental block to isolate me from them.

He'd warned me that I would hate him.

He was right.

I'd trusted him, loved him, *mated* him, and he'd repaid me by handing me over to the enemy.

There has to be a reason, I thought. *He cares for me. I know he cares for me.* I'd felt it in our bond, had witnessed it in his thoughts. Maybe Zakkai had coerced him? But why would Shade block my mating links?

My jaw ticked as I considered the endless possibilities of his intentions. Then I focused on the male beside me—the one who likely had all the answers I needed.

"Why am I here?" I asked, sitting up with the sheet clutched to my chest. "Why didn't you tell me who you were? And *how* are you my mate? You never bit me in the dreams." I also didn't think a Midnight Fae could stake a claim in that manner.

If they could, that would be dangerous.

Fae, who was I kidding? Midnight Fae were danger personified.

The male beside me oozed lethality as wisps of power swirled around him. I could taste his essence in the air and sense it deep within my soul. He embodied the source in a similar manner to Kols. I mentally stroked it with my strands of dark magic, curious and wary.

His lips curled in response, his energy intensifying as though to welcome my prodding. "It's fascinating, isn't it?" His low voice rolled over me on a caressing wave. "Our gifts have more or less grown together over the years, creating an everlasting connection. I think that even if I were to break our bond now, you would still retain my Quandary abilities."

"Years?" I repeated.

"Mmm," he hummed, the response noncommittal. Just like everything else.

"Why am I here?" I repeated.

"Why do you think you're here?" he countered.

My grip around the sheet tightened against my chest. "We're mates."

"Yes," he agreed.

"How?"

He arched a white brow. "Surely you're familiar with how the mating process works by now? I mean, you did recently bond a Warrior Blood, yes? And Shade?"

"Are you always this insufferable?" *Answering every question with a question. Pixie sticks, we will never get anywhere at this rate!* "I think I liked you more when I thought you were a figment."

"That's because you enjoyed my tongue between your thighs, Aflora." He tilted his head. "Would an orgasm calm you down?"

A growl slipped through my lips. "Where are my clothes?" Because I couldn't continue having this conversation while naked in his bed.

He nodded to a silk robe twisted into the sheets. "You can wear that."

"Yeah, I'll take my clothes instead." I couldn't remember if I'd worn them here or if I'd lost them in the LethaForest. I really hoped it was the latter because the former would imply that he'd stripped me. And I really didn't want to think about that right now.

Sure, he was a pale-skinned, godlike fae.

And apparently my mate.

But that didn't mean I wanted to be naked with him.

Even if he did have a wicked tongue and skilled hands.

I cleared my throat. "Clothes."

"No," he replied. "You're lucky I gave you a robe, Aflora. Don't push it."

"*Excuse me?*" My eyebrows flew upward. "So let me get this straight. You dream-raped me, then—"

"Dream-raped you?" he repeated, his expression rivaling mine as he released a disbelieving laugh. "*You* commanded *me*, sweetheart. Not the other way around. I came to you to talk, but you told me not to say anything and to fuck you with my mouth instead. As your mate, I obliged. I would hardly call that rape."

"I thought you were a figment of my imagination!"

"And I told you more than once to consider that I was real," he countered. "We can argue about this all day, or you can accept what happened and we can move on to the reconciliation phase. Your choice."

"How can I accept anything when you won't even tell me why I'm here?!" I couldn't hold back my shrill tone, my patience long gone. "How are you even real? How are you my mate? Stop talking in riddles and give me something useful!"

"How about you stop asking ridiculous questions and look inside your mind for the answers that already exist," he suggested flatly.

My mind? He wanted me to go into my mind for answers? Yeah, all right. I'd go into my mind.

The cerulean embers flared inside me, my magic humming to life in anticipation. I'd spent the last however many months trying to drown the power, to temper and control it, but I called it forward now.

Come play, I urged, closing my eyes as the strands whirled inside my thoughts, flickering with electricity and sizzling in the air around us.

Zakkai said something.

I ignored him.

He'd told me to go into my mind. So I had. And now he would experience the consequences of that suggestion.

Maybe I could knock him out and *run*.

I had no idea where I was, but surely a portal existed nearby. Or maybe I could figure out how to shadow again, or whatever it was I'd done with Emelyn.

While Shade had blocked me from his mind, I could still feel his essence warming my blood. Zeph was there, too. Even Kols.

And also… *Zakkai*.

His presence was the strongest, perhaps because he sat beside me. But I suspected it went deeper than that. Our bond was *old*. I could feel the roots of it in youth, the magic somehow married to my connection to the earth source.

He spoke again.

And I continued to ignore him, too busy trailing along the roots, searching for the beginning, seeking a way to destroy him.

No, not destroy.

Hurt.

Earth Fae weren't violent. We created life.

His kind killed.

That was why I would never be a true Midnight Fae, no matter whom I mated or what powers roamed through me. My spirit was all Elemental Fae. His source inside me was foreign and wrong, had morphed me into an abomination against my will, and I still didn't know how it had happened. Because he wouldn't tell me.

I growled again, my ire mounting with each passing second.

This man played in my head without my permission.

He'd *bonded* me at some point.

Now he refused to explain any of it, instead choosing to kidnap me, strip me, and give me a solitary robe to wear.

And he wanted me to play in my head, to search for answers.

Instead, I found the source of my magic and balled it up into a focal point all aimed at him. He didn't want to explain, and I was all out of patience for this game.

I opened my eyes to find him still seated beside me, his expression one underlined in amusement.

I hated that smile and those dimples. I loathed the crinkle at the sides of his silver-blue eyes. I despised his very presence and the chuckle shaking his chest.

He thought this was funny?

Then I'd give him something to really laugh about.

Flames shot out of my fingertips and directly at his chiseled chest.

Only, rather than burn him, they were absorbed by him, his grin morphing from amused to something else entirely. *Heated.* His irises smoldered with the power I'd just unleashed on him. And then he opened his hand.

I tried to duck out of the way, but he was too quick, the spiraling sphere of electricity nailing me in the chest and binding me in a web of intense power. My lungs halted, my heart stopped, and a puff of air escaped my lips.

"Figure out how to untangle yourself, Aflora," he replied, the bed shifting as he slid from the sheets to his feet. "When you're done, come find me and we'll talk."

A laugh threatened my frozen chest, one lacking humor. *Talk,* I repeated in my mind. *All you do is unleash riddles!*

Try solving them, little star, he shot back, his voice like liquid chocolate in my mind. *Start with the cords around your chest before you suffocate yourself to death.*

Zakkai!

Nothing.

Just the kiss of an ocean breeze to my senses and the soft *snick* of a closing door.

He'd left me to unravel his magical net without a wand or any instructions.

And I was already seeing spots due to the lack of air in my lungs.

Zakkai!

Focus on the strands, Aflora. Then find me when you're done.

I'll find you and kill you, I vowed.

I can't wait to watch you try.

CHAPTER THREE

Aflora lost consciousness as I locked the door to my room, her final thoughts all surrounding the myriad of ways she intended to make me suffer. My lips curled in anticipation.

As an Earth Fae, she was all about life and love and peace.

But my Quandary Blood had provided her with a lethal edge that I intended to exploit.

One moment, she promised never to kill a living thing. And in the next breath, she vowed vengeance and devastation. Namely, my death. But I would morph that train of thought into something more useful.

It was all part of her training.

Just like the web I'd woven around her.

She'd figure out how to dismantle it eventually, and I'd be waiting for her when she did. Her life essence was tied to mine, pulling on my energy to revive her. I allowed it, knowing she would need a few breaths to begin the process.

Her roar in my head widened my grin.

I refused to answer her now, listening as she puzzled through what she needed to do. Her mind fascinated me, her convoluted thoughts so similar to my own. She had no idea how alike we truly were, only I'd accepted my fate and destiny in life, while she was still trying to find her own.

The path would reveal itself very soon.

She eventually quieted, her affinity for solving problems springing to the surface as she began to expertly unweave the magic I'd wrapped around her.

So beautiful and cunning. All my previous intentions wavered, including the steps I took now toward the main rooms.

My father wanted an update.

But all I wanted was to walk back to my room, lean against the wall, and watch the stunning female play with magic in my sheets.

Alas, I had to make an appearance before he ventured to my rooms to search for me.

I snapped my fingers and uttered a spell, beckoning for my wand. It ignored me. The damn thing had a mind of its own and seemed to prefer Aflora for the moment. Fine. She could continue to borrow my conduit while she trained. She needed it more than I did anyway.

With a muttered incantation, I changed my attire into something more suitable for a meeting with the others. It was a lazy approach, but also necessary, because if I'd remained in that room for a moment longer, I would have lost all my desire to leave.

Aflora was a sight to behold in so many ways that went beyond her physical appeal. She was admirably gifted in the dark arts, perhaps because she'd been tied to me for fifteen years.

I'd meant what I'd said earlier—it was fascinating to see how my essence had bonded with hers. She almost resembled a Quandary Blood. Except I could taste her earth magic, too. Just as I felt her element roaming through my veins, kissing me with a breath of her vitality and goodness.

The connection had always been there, even during our separation. Although, my father's enchantments had severely dulled it. Then she'd broken that enchantment with her song and nearly knocked me off my feet.

I'd immediately thrown up my walls, protecting us both, but that hadn't stopped me from playing in her dreams.

"Kai," my father called as he stepped into the hallway, his eyes narrowing at my lingering state. "Is there a problem?"

"No. Just observing Aflora's struggle against my binds," I replied, doing my best to keep my tone flat and emotionless.

"Binds?" he repeated. "You were supposed to talk to her and bring her here to meet the others. It wasn't a difficult task."

I nearly snorted. He remembered the impressionable little flower from my youth and had no idea how formidable Aflora had become. "She required a riddle to properly prepare. Once she solves it, I'll introduce her to the others."

My father's jaw ticked. "That's not what we discussed."

"I have it under control." I underlined my tone in steel, reminding him of my position among the resistance. He might be my elder and father, but I was the Source Architect.

He studied me for a long moment, his silver-blue eyes—the same shade as my own—flaring with power. But it didn't match mine. I'd ascended a little over a month ago, taking over his role as the Quandary Blood King. He stood no chance against me, even with his age and experience.

"How is she really?" he asked softly, a note of concern in his voice. "Did you talk about her parents?"

"No. She tried to kill me with a very interesting mix of WarFire instead," I drawled. "But I'll try for that topic during our next conversation."

"WarFire?" he repeated, his ash-blond brows shooting upward. "Does she not realize you're her mate?"

"Oh, she knows. I think it's her version of foreplay." A complete lie. I'd absolutely taunted her into playing with me. And I hadn't been disappointed. "We're working it out."

And by that, I meant she was working through my web, which would provide her with all the answers she so desperately craved.

"She's safe, Dad," I added as the concern in his features grew. "That's what matters."

He fell silent for a moment, then nodded. "The debt to her parents is officially repaid."

"I'm not sure they would agree with that," I replied. "You let the Council use her as bait." It was a sore topic between us. I'd wanted to take her at the coffee shop several months ago, but he'd convinced me to let Shade bite her.

"We needed Constantine to come out of hiding," he said, repeating the statement he'd used several times over the last few months.

"And you wanted to put a leash on Shade," I added. "Yes, I know. I'm just saying, I don't think her parents would appreciate her being used as a pawn."

"The Council was going to use her whether we approved or not. This just allowed us to make use of the predicament." He shrugged. "Her parents would understand. They signed her up for this fate when they agreed to the temporary mating."

"Fifteen years isn't temporary," I said, disliking the term.

He clapped me on the shoulder. "It'll feel temporary when you reach my age, Kai. You'll see."

I forced a smile. "Sure." He still assumed I intended to undo the mate-bonds. It had always been my plan to do so. Even when I'd seen her in the coffee shop, I'd still meant to shatter our connection.

But then she'd undone the enchantment with the song we'd taught her all those years ago.

And I'd joined her in a dream.

The moment our eyes met, I felt as though I was looking into my very soul and finding my other half. My childhood best friend had grown into a gorgeous woman with sexual needs I couldn't help but fulfill.

Seeing her in that manner had felt like my first time, which was insane. I'd fucked women, most of them human and during a feeding. The enchantment over our bond had muted her to a dull ache, one I'd never intended to keep.

Then she'd shattered everything with a throaty moan and a voice that beckoned sex.

I hadn't been able to look at another woman since, and that'd all just been foreplay in our dreams. It was a total mindfuck that I didn't know how to fix.

Well, I had some ideas. Most of them involving a few nights in the sheets. But my instincts said that would never be enough. There was just something so intoxicating about Aflora. Our history only heightened the sensation, leaving me utterly conflicted about the future between us.

What will she think when she learns the truth? I wondered, checking in on her progress through our bonds.

She was still quietly dismantling the enchanted ropes around her torso.

Soon, she would reach the ones in her mind, and that was when the real fun would begin.

My heart skipped a beat, anticipation thick in my veins.

"Let's go debrief the others," my father said, interrupting my inner musings. "Then Dakota can tell us what Zen said in the clearing."

Zen. My teeth clenched at the name. The infuriating female continued to intrude on my plans, her aptitude for fortune-telling an annoyance I wanted to end.

It was why we'd put Shade on a leash. He was her grandson, thereby tying them by blood. Which meant Aflora now had access to that entire line of power, consequently enabling me to play as well.

I hadn't explored the bonds yet. But I intended to, just as soon as Aflora became a willing participant. Otherwise, I risked hurting her in the process. And I would only pursue that avenue if she left me no choice.

Until then, I'd seduce her my own way—with puzzles of magic.

She wouldn't admit it, but the net she fought now intrigued her. I could feel that excitement thrumming inside her as she unwove another strand.

My little star loved a good challenge. And she'd just met her biggest one yet. *Me.*

CHAPTER FOUR

KOLS

"What the hell happened?" my twin demanded as I stepped through the threshold into our suite. "Where's Aflora?" Tray added as he noted my solo entry.

"That's a great fucking question," I snapped.

Shade had vanished into smoke after dropping the bomb about Aflora's Quandary Blood mate.

No elaboration or explanation. Just *poof!* Gone.

Jackass, I snarled in my head, furious with the Death Blood. I intended to rearrange his face the next time I saw him. Or perhaps kill him. Because *what the fuck?!*

I ripped my cloak from my neck and tossed it over the couch. "Where's Zeph?" He should be awake by now. Hell, he shouldn't have passed out to begin with.

I should have known Shade was up to something.

He'd disappeared with Aflora, and Zeph had collapsed a second later, distracting me from trying to follow Shade. Not that I could. His penchant for shadows was a magic very few of our kind could replicate, including those like me who were tied directly to the source.

"We put him in your bed," Tray said, following me as I headed toward my bedroom. "Talk to me, Kols."

I glanced over my shoulder to find Ella lingering silently behind him and shook my head. I'd already accidentally brought my brother into this. I wasn't going to jeopardize her life, too.

"She already knows everything, Kols." Tray folded his arms. "And I've spelled the suite to cancel out any potential listening devices. Start talking."

"We should wake up Zeph first," a dry voice said seconds before Shade appeared in the hallway.

"*You.*" I lunged at him, only to hit the wall as he shadowed behind me.

"Calm down," he drawled, sounding bored.

"Calm down?" I repeated, spinning toward him. "Are you fucking kidding me? You drop a bomb on me about a Quandary Blood mate and disappear, and you expect me to be calm?" I wanted to kill him. Power singed my fingertips as I considered my options.

First, I needed him to stop fucking vanishing.

Then I could force answers out of him.

Because this whole game of piecemeal details? Yeah, we weren't going to play that anymore.

Shade's eyebrows lifted half a second before I unleashed a bolt of power directly into his sternum, disabling his ability to move, think, or breathe.

But that little tell of his eyebrow shift told me he'd *seen* it coming. Which further added to my theory about his fortune-telling abilities. Yet another item I wanted—

A jolt radiated through my blood, sending me to my knees as Shade retaliated far faster than he should have been able to react. *Fuck!*

I yanked on the source, preparing another attack as he phased behind me *again.*

He shouldn't have been able to do that.

He should have been knocked out, on his ass, for at least another—

"Fine. We'll do it your way," he said against my ear. Then his teeth sank into my neck, causing me to sputter out a surprised curse.

I couldn't move, ensnared by whatever spell he'd woven around me.

Sir Kristoff charged into the suite, energy flaring around him as he engaged the ancient magic only his kind could tap into. Shade fell to the floor beside me, groaning at whatever torment my gargoyle had just unleashed on him. Then Tray trapped the Death Blood beneath a net of power that Ella enhanced with another spell.

I curled into myself, the lasting effects of Shade's attack slowly withering and dying beneath a shock of reality.

He'd *bitten* me.

The bastard had fucking bonded me!

My lips parted as a slew of furious statements lined up on my tongue, only for a Paradox Fae to appear with a glowing purple sword. "Again?" he asked, his tone bored.

"N-no," Shade choked out, his body convulsing beside mine.

My eyes narrowed. "Who the fuck—"

"*You!*" Sir Kristoff unleashed another wave of dark gargoyle energy that the Paradox Fae blocked with his sword.

"Stop," the Paradox Fae said with a yawn as he leaned against the wall. "Seriously, this is getting so fucking old."

Shade coughed a laugh, then grimaced beneath the power holding him down.

I touched my neck, wondering if I'd just dreamt up this whole nightmare. But no. I was bleeding. And Shade's lips were tinged with my blood. "Have you lost your fucking mind?" I demanded. "You *bonded* us."

"Yeah," Shade replied, his voice a rasp of sound. "*You're welcome.*"

I gaped at him, then pushed off the floor onto unsteady feet. My muscles ached as though I'd been hit by a freight train. "Let him up," I said, talking to Tray. "I don't want him handicapped when I kill him."

The Paradox Fae grunted. "Again?"

"No," Shade snapped.

"Again what?" I asked, flabbergasted by his presence. "And who the fuck are you?"

"Kyros," he replied, tipping his dark head at me.

"What are you doing here?"

"Do you always ask the same questions?" he countered.

"The same questions?"

"Yeah, I see that you do," Kyros replied, pushing off the wall to straighten his leather jacket. A hint of tattoos peeked out from beneath the coat.

"Someone start talking," Tray inserted, his arms folding over his sweater. Ella clung to his arm, her blonde hair curling in the tendrils of magic wafting off my brother.

"Release Shade from your magic, and he'll give it another attempt," Kyros said.

I narrowed my gaze at him, then looked at my brother again. "Do what he says." Because I was beginning to understand the situation.

Kyros and Shade had been playing with time—a very dangerous game, indeed. None of us would have any idea how many times they'd shifted through this moment, nor any clue as to what happened before. They also could have jumped back to this second from many days, months, or even years in the future.

My jaw ticked.

As much as I wanted to kill Shade, a part of me recognized that he had a reason for his antics.

Perhaps that was why he'd bitten me—to provide me with a glimmer of understanding regarding his motives. Yet this stage didn't afford me much insight. It actually linked him more to me than me to him.

That realization had me narrowing my gaze.

He was up to something.

He also clearly had a death wish because I strongly doubted that the Council had told him to fucking bite me.

Tray reluctantly removed his spell, allowing Shade to begin the recovery process. Sir Kristoff stood beside my left foot, his tiny stone sword held out before him like a wand.

Gargoyles were small but mighty, their magic potent and long-lasting. Hence Shade's continued weakened condition on the floor. Tray's spell had only prolonged his misery, negating his ability to heal. But it was Sir Kristoff's enchantment that had knocked the Death Blood onto his ass.

Kyros yawned again, then resumed his stance of leaning against the wall, only this time he closed his eyes as though taking a nap.

I could see why these two assholes were friends.

Sir Kristoff growled as if to agree, except I knew he couldn't actually read minds.

Shade, however, might be able to hear my louder thoughts. It was a rare gift that came with some bondings, and given some of his unique abilities, I wouldn't be surprised if that was one of them. Aflora had never mentioned it, but I'd also never asked.

Unfortunately, I couldn't hear her.

Which only added insult to misery in this situation.

"Who the fuck is Zakkai?" I demanded.

"Quandary Blood." The words came out on a cough from the still-wounded Death Blood on the floor.

"Yeah, you said that already."

"Then maybe you shouldn't repeat questions," Kyros suggested, his dark eyes flickering open. "Would you like to wake up Zeph now?"

I flinched, startled by the abrupt subject change. "What did you do to him?"

"Why would I do anything?" he countered.

"I don't know. I don't even know why you're here."

"Hmm, no, I think you do," he murmured.

Right. Not going to continue engaging him because he just made me want to blast a hole of dark magic through him. "Shade."

The Death Blood grunted in acknowledgment, his limbs still spasming from residual gargoyle magic. I would pity him, except I couldn't because I actually enjoyed seeing him in pain. He fucking deserved it.

"Wake up Zeph," Tray said, speaking to no one in particular. "Whoever can wake him, fucking wake him up."

"How?" I asked. "I don't even know why he's still asleep."

Magic hummed through the air from Shade as he twirled his finger in a shaky zigzag, his lips moving over an incantation. I didn't catch the spell, his words soundless.

Kyros cocked his head to the side, then nodded as though satisfied.

And the door to my room flew open with a raging Zeph, who stopped short in the hallway. His gaze immediately fell to Shade. "*What. The. Fuck?*" he demanded, charging toward the already crippled Death Blood.

I folded my arms in amusement as my Guardian unleashed a wave of defensive magic onto the prone male, causing Shade to growl in agony.

"Again?" Kyros asked.

"No!" Shade shouted.

Kyros sighed. "Fine."

I pressed a palm to my Guardian's shoulder, stilling him from continuing his assault on the Death Blood. "Zeph," I said softly. "I need Shade to be able to speak."

"Speak?" he repeated. "I'm going to fucking kill him."

"Okay. After he explains himself," I offered. "Then you can do whatever the hell you want to him."

"I wouldn't recommend it," Kyros interjected, causing Zeph to spin toward him.

"Who the fuck are you?"

"More repetition," the Paradox Fae sighed, relaxing his head against the wall behind him.

"Perhaps you should stop fucking with time, then," I told him, folding my arms. "How many times have I lived this moment?"

His lips curled a little. "Now *that* is an interesting question."

"And that's not an answer," I tossed back.

"No, it's not," he agreed. "I think they might just listen to you this time, Shade."

The Death Blood sputtered out a sound of agreement, then spat blood onto the floor. Zeph's enchantment had been the equivalent of a few stern kicks to the most painful parts on the torso. I knew from experience that it hurt like hell. And Zeph usually held back when magically sparring with me.

With Shade, he hadn't held back at all.

"What the fuck is going on?" my Guardian demanded. "Where's Aflora? Why can't I feel her?"

"You can't feel her?" I stood up straighter. "At all?"

He fell silent, his green eyes flashing as he concentrated. "No. I feel her. But there's… a block. And I can sense her struggling." He went to the ground to take hold of Shade's button-down shirt. "Start fucking talking, or I swear to the Fae, I will—"

"Destroy me," Shade rasped. "*I know.*"

Kyros smirked. "Seriously, Shadow. You're going through a lot of pain for something we both know is inevitable."

"Fuck you," Shade spat out at him.

"Not my type," Kyros drawled.

"Give him a second to breathe," I said, touching Zeph's shoulder again. "I want to hear what Shade has to say." My instincts were firing on all cylinders, the sense of déjà vu a very real presence in my mind.

I'd lived this moment before.

An obvious expectation, given Kyros's presence, but it went deeper than that. I could *feel* the familiarity of this situation.

Just like that time when Aflora threatened to undo our bonds. Sir Kristoff had gone off about a sword-wielding fae. I'd just brushed off his commentary as a consequence of whatever the fuck Shade had done to him that day.

But that hadn't been it at all.

"You've been fucking with our lives for a while," I said to the Paradox Fae.

"Have I?" he countered, his dark eyes glimmering with knowledge.

"You were there the day Aflora threatened to dismantle our mating bonds."

He considered me for a long moment before looking at Shade. "I stand corrected. You were right to bite him."

"She succeeded, didn't she?" I added, my heart racing with the knowledge. "She destroyed our bonds."

"She did a lot more than that," Shade muttered, his rasp lessening with each word. He shoved himself up into a seated position, then scooted over to the wall to lean his back against it as he swallowed on a grimace. "Well played, Kristoff." He saluted my gargoyle with his middle finger, then dropped his hands to his lap on a sigh.

I slid down the wall to sit across from him. Zeph joined me, his stance guarded but his expression carefully blank.

"When did he bite you?" Zeph asked me.

"Just before you woke up," I replied, my gaze on the Death Blood.

"You're bonded?" He didn't sound wounded so much as concerned. And rightfully so. There was no way I would be able to ascend whilst tied to Shade.

Granted, I couldn't ascend while mated to Aflora, either.

And frankly, I wasn't so sure I wanted to ascend anymore after everything I'd learned over the last few weeks.

"On the first level," Shade said quietly. "It provides him with necessary insight."

"Except I can't read your mind."

"No, but you can sense my intentions," he replied, his icy eyes displaying an exhaustion I hadn't noticed in him before.

I don't like this, I thought, uneasy with the insight I seemed to have inherited with his bite.

"I don't like it either," he muttered, confirming he could hear my thoughts. Or maybe he'd read it from my expression. I suspected the former because it was Shade.

Tray cleared his throat, reminding me that he stood at the end of the hallway with Ella beside him. "So. Where's Aflora?"

"Currently?" Shade glanced up at my brother. "She's in a paradigm, battling a spell the Source Architect has woven through her mind."

CHAPTER FIVE

AFLORA

Stars twinkled overhead, each one tied to an invisible strand that I sensed more than saw.

I studied them, searching for a pattern or some reason for the madness. Zakkai had locked me inside this riddled web, his power potent and breathtakingly beautiful. I wanted to roll in his essence and absorb all of it into my senses.

But I refused the inclination.

He'd put me here for a purpose, one I intended to decipher.

I'd successfully removed the invisible ropes suffocating my torso, allowing me to breathe. And I nearly fell into the trap of thinking that was it. But then the blinking had started. It was subtle yet potent. He'd meant for me to find this puzzle. I suspected ignoring it would have left me in a worse state than before.

So I lay absolutely still, my breathing steady as I considered each potential route.

Some stars were brighter than the others. They felt too obvious, so I went for the lackluster orbs, only they gave off a hot sensation, their invisible strands shedding energy that caused the hairs along my arms to rise.

I bit my lip. *Which one?* I returned to the star boasting the most light and gently prodded it. A zap traversed my spine, causing me to jolt on the bed.

Not that one, I decided, moving on to the next and experiencing the same sensation.

I growled.

Zakkai would pay for this insanity. He'd created a land mine in my head! What kind of monster did that? And to his mate, no less.

Not that I intended to remain bonded to him.

No, I'd find a way to undo that. Just as soon as I figured out this maze in my head.

Each star possessed a heat signature that sang to the dark magic inside me. *Zakkai's magic.* He was the source of my Quandary skills. But how? When had we bonded? And why didn't I remember?

I'd been operating under the assumption that my parents had lied to me about my birthright, that I was some sort of abomination. However, it was his power running through my veins. It felt so deeply rooted, similar to my affinity for earth.

Which made no sense.

I could feel Shade's power, too, younger in origin. Same with Zeph's Warrior Blood.

But Zakkai's essence seemed to be braided to mine, as though our lives were connected by a single thread.

My eyes narrowed as one of the stars glimmered brighter for half a second, as if beckoning me forward with that thought.

It was probably a trap.

Or maybe a clue.

I prodded it inside my mind and braced for the electric zap, only to be sucked into a very real image of my bedroom from my childhood—the one I lived in before my parents disappeared.

What in the fae…?

"Aflora?" a young male voice called, causing me to spin toward the door. Silver-blue eyes met mine, set in a frame of boyish features with long white hair tied back into a low ponytail. "Are you hiding?" he asked.

I frowned. "Zakkai?"

His brow furrowed. "Am I in trouble?"

"Uh, yes?" He'd crafted a land mine in my head… and sent me back in time?

"Because of the bite?" His lips pinched to the side. "I already told you that I don't want to do it. But Dad said I have to. It's the best way to protect you in case something happens."

"I don't understand."

He blew out a breath and entered my room with a shuffle of his feet, the movement clumsy. Probably because he was pretending to be a child.

Except, as he moved past a mirror, I caught a glimpse of myself and gasped at my young appearance. *Holy fae!* He'd turned me into a kid, too! "How old am I?"

"Huh?" He looked at me and scratched his head. "Seven?"

My eyes widened. "What?" This was the year my parents died. Did he intend to torment me by making me relive it with this kid version of himself at my side?

"Look, I know. This sucks so bad. But Dad says it's only temporary. And I'll protect you, Flora. I always do." He flashed me a boyish grin with dimples on the sides, and a giggle clawed at my chest. Not one I wanted to release, but the body I possessed was apparently amused.

His smile grew as the giggle escaped. *What is happening to me? And why is he calling me Flora?*

"See, I knew you weren't really upset," he teased. "Do you want to go play with the flowers outside before dinner?"

My mom's garden.

I looked at the door, then at the mirror again, and back at Zakkai.

We were in some sort of memory loop. Except he'd morphed it somehow by being here. I wanted to hate him for it, but it'd been so long since I'd dreamt of my mother's flowers and their beautiful scents.

I could indulge in just a few minutes, right?

It was my head—therefore, my rules.

I nodded. "Yes."

His grin seemed to reach his ears as he hopped around to lead me through the halls of my old home. My parents stood in the kitchen, their tones hushed as we entered. A man who resembled an older Zakkai stood with them, his expression emotionless.

"Aflora," my mother said, frowning at my dress. "That's not the outfit I laid out for you this morning."

Her words nagged at me, a memory forming unbidden in my mind. She'd said this to me before… but when?

"Carmella," my father murmured. "She can wear whatever she wants for tonight."

My mother glanced at him, then sighed. "Yes, yes, of course."

"We're going outside to play with flowers," Zakkai announced, sounding proud.

His father—or I assumed the older Zakkai look-alike was his dad— grunted. "You're not an Earth Fae, Kai."

"I know, but Flora is. And she likes flowers." He beamed at me. "And stars."

Why did this all feel so familiar? I'd never lived this moment before, and yet, I knew what my mother was about to say.

"There's no time for playing in the garden tonight," she said, right on cue. "We've talked about this."

Some of the light seemed to die in Zakkai's eyes. "I just thought… maybe… we could play first."

"We're not here to play, Kai," his father said, the sternness in his voice making me flinch.

"Easy, Laki," my dad murmured, walking up to place a hand on my head. "They're just kids."

"Who are about to bond like adults," my mother added under her breath.

"Temporarily," Laki corrected. "He'll protect her until she's of age, then he'll reverse the bond. I'll show him how."

I frowned. "Bond?" I knew what they meant, but I was having trouble accepting this version of events.

"Yes, sweetheart. Zakkai is going to bond with you to keep you safe," my dad said, his voice soft. "It's just a security measure in case anything happens to me and your mom, okay?"

"Why would something happen to you?" The words fell from my lips before I could hold them back, my mind falling into my seven-year-old form and repeating the question I recalled asking that day.

"Because life is full of unexpected events," my dad replied, then pressed his lips to my temple. "This is just our way of adding some protection."

"But you already protect me," I pointed out in my childlike voice. "And so does Kai."

Kai? I thought, repeating the nickname. *Why did I call him that?* Because that was what my memory required.

Or was this all just a lie? Another twisted test?

"I'll always protect you," Zakkai agreed, sounding proud. "But this will, like, bond us more. So that way I can sense if you're in danger."

Laki nodded. "Yes. And he'll be able to help you even if he's in another kingdom."

Yes, I knew all this. Mom and Dad had explained it last week.

I frowned. *Last week?* I shook my head. This experience was starting to feel a little too real, like I was seven again.

Everything slowed around me, my parents freezing in place as my father began to speak. Laki stilled as well, his face void of expression, but Zakkai merely smiled at me, his dimples flashing proudly.

"I don't understand what's happening," I said.

"It's a memory spell, Flora." His eyes sparkled as he used my nickname again. "It's so you can remember."

"Remember what?"

"Me," he replied as everything dissolved around us into a new image of real stars and the two of us lying on our backs outside, his hand in mine. "I don't want to go," he said, his gaze on the sky above. "But Dad says I have to."

"I don't want you to go either," I replied, the childlike voice one I remembered but the phrase foreign. I hadn't even thought to speak those words; they just left my mouth without permission.

"He says you have to forget me, too," he added, frowning. "I don't want to do it."

"Then don't."

"But I have to protect you, Flora." He squeezed my hand. "You're my best friend, and that's what best friends do."

"Mom and Dad will protect me." My mouth just kept moving without my permission, saying things before I could process the reaction. "I don't want to forget you, Kai."

He sighed. "I know. But I'll make you remember one day."

"When?"

"I don't know. Dad says it might be a while. We have to go hide in a new kingdom." The way his lips twisted to the side told me how he felt about that.

"A new kingdom?" I repeated.

"Yeah."

"So you're leaving me?"

"I have to, Flora. The bad fae are getting too close." He finally looked at me, his eyes misted with tears. "I don't want to go, but Dad says it's the only way to be safe."

"What about me?" I asked, my voice small.

He reached over to place his hand over my heart. "I'll always be here, Flora. 'Cause of the bond."

I felt the connection pulsate in response, the strand tying us together as one. It tingled a little, warming my skin. "You're my best friend, Kai."

"I know," he whispered. "You're mine, too, Flora. I'm sorry you won't remember me."

"I'm sorry, too," I replied softly, his sadness weaving an inky sensation through our link. It wrapped around me like a cloak of despair, his eyes clouding over as magic sprang to life between us. "What are you...?"

"I have to," he said, his throat working as foreign energy slithered across my skin. "Dad said we have to leave tonight."

"But you didn't...?" I trailed off, not remembering what I wanted to say. The snakelike sensation writhed through me, confusing my intentions and my mind. I couldn't tell reality from fiction, memory from trickery.

Was this all part of the game in my mind?

Zakkai, I recalled, thinking of the blinking lights and the web of power he'd tossed over me.

But then an image of him as a young boy flashed again, his eyes filled with tears as his father grabbed him by the shoulders and told him to be a man and finish it. Zakkai shook his head, refusing to lose his only friend. He kept saying he couldn't do it, that he couldn't make me forget.

Everything went white.

Then black.

And I blinked my eyes open to see his bedroom once more.

Silk sheets caressed my skin, the hint of the ocean teasing my senses.

Memories flooded my thoughts of summer nights with Zakkai, playing beneath the stars. Growing flowers for him to collect. Building toy castles out of small rocks. Chasing each other in endless games of tag. Magical games of earth blending with Quandary skills.

The final night played through my mind. The night when he bit me three times, then spelled me to forget him. He'd put blocks in place so I wouldn't sense him, but he could feel me... and the pain that had followed.

Zakkai hadn't wanted to finish it, but his father made him. The little boy had collapsed to the ground on a scream, the agony unlike any I'd ever witnessed.

My parents had been concerned, but Laki had insisted his son was fine. "Rewriting the magic to cut her off and forcing her to forget requires the utmost discipline and skill. It hurts. But he'll grow from the pain." He'd held out a hand to Zakkai. "Let's go."

The young boy had looked at me with heartbreak in his eyes, his face wet from tears.

And then he'd vanished.

My chest ached with the memory, my mind conflicted on whether or not to believe it. *Is it true?* I demanded through our newly restored link. *Is what you just showed me real?*

Come join me and find out, he taunted into my mind. *Your robe is still on the bed.*

CHAPTER SIX

SHADE

I felt Aflora snap out of Zakkai's mental web, her mind free once more. Her confusion bled into ire as she considered all that he'd revealed, her stubborn nature stepping forward as she refused to believe his retelling of their past events.

While normally that would make me smirk in amusement, I couldn't. Not with Zeph and Kols sitting across from me wearing matching expressions of annoyance.

"This information would have been helpful two months ago, Shadow," Zeph deadpanned.

My jaw ticked. "If I'd told you about Zakkai then, the future would have changed." Kols and Zeph hadn't accepted Aflora as their mate two months ago. They'd needed time to learn more about her, to realize she wasn't a threat—at least not to them—and to fall in love with her. Without all that, this destiny would never be able to unfold. And the alternative wasn't pretty. I knew because I'd lived through it seven fucking times.

"So her Quandary magic comes from her mating to the Source Architect —*Zakkai*—not her parents," Kols reiterated. "Which means she is the true earth source heir."

"Yes," I replied, reining in my patience to make it through this conversation. His gargoyle had done a number on me, leaving me much weaker than usual. I was still only halfway recovered. If Zeph and Kols decided to fight me now, they'd win. Especially with Tray and Ella on their side.

Then I'd have to start this conversation over *again*.

Which I really didn't want to do.

We'd already gone through it so many times.

Kyros leaned against the hallway wall, waiting for me to signal him for another loop. But this one was going better than the others, mostly because I'd changed the whole game by biting Kols. Granting him a connection to my soul seemed to temper his magic a little. Perhaps he sensed what was coming, how our lives would be forever altered.

Or maybe it was just enough insight to ground him.

Regardless, I was thankful for the reprieve, as I desperately needed to heal. It was hard enough blocking Aflora from my mind at full strength. Having to do it at half strength just exhausted me that much more.

"But her magic has mingled with his over the last fifteen years," Kols continued. "Which makes her an abomination."

"Also yes," I agreed. "Something you would have killed her for two months ago."

He dipped his chin in acknowledgment. "True."

"And won't now," I pressed. "Hence the reason I couldn't reveal this to you before."

"I get it," he repeated, his tone clipped. "That doesn't mean I like it."

I grunted. He thought this was hard on him? He should try living all these realities and repeating every fucking moment.

Kyros smirked as though he could read my mind. Because yeah, he'd joined me in this hell. His motives were his own, but we shared a similar goal.

"All right, what now?" Zeph pressed. "Where is she? How do we get her back?"

"We don't," I replied. "She has to choose."

"Choose?" he repeated. "Between us and Zakkai?"

I wavered on how to reply to that. His phrasing was too simplistic. The real choice she had to make went so much deeper than a game of this or that. Her chosen path would change the landscape for all of Midnight Fae kind, and potentially other fae as well.

"Shade," Zeph snapped. "What choice?"

Kols pressed his palm to Zeph's thigh. "Give him a moment."

I blinked, momentarily stunned by the understanding in the Elite Blood's tone. He was usually the first to join the Warrior Blood in his pressing for details, the pair of them always teaming up against me. Which was fine, as I could handle it. But this softer side of Kols was unexpected.

Had I known the way to calming Kols's reactions was through a bite, I would have done so ages ago. However, if he knew the real reason I'd done it, he might not be so content with it. But that was a conversation for another day. One that would happen very soon, if my grandmother's vision came to fruition.

"Playing with time carries consequences, Shadow. I believe this fate will be one of yours."

"What did I do to deserve this?" I'd asked, for once just saying what I felt rather than pretending none of it mattered.

"It's fate's burden," she'd replied. "You're the strongest of all of us, Shadow. That's why your destiny is the hardest."

Her words played through my head, making me grimace.

We'll see, I thought.

"Shade," Kols prompted, arching an auburn brow. "How do we get Aflora back?"

"Have you considered that she might be safer with Zakkai?" Tray interjected, his tone quiet yet thoughtful. "What will you do if you find her? Run? Because the Council isn't going to let you keep her, Kols."

"Safer with the Quandary Blood who wants to start a war?" Zeph repeated, sounding darkly amused. "Sure. That sounds positively safe."

"He won't hurt her," I said quietly. "I wouldn't have given her to him otherwise."

"We'll come back to that in just a moment," Zeph replied, his green eyes flashing with power. "As to leaving her with him, the answer is no."

"Where would you keep her?" Tray stressed. "In the Human Realm?"

"We could take her back to the Elemental Fae," Kols suggested.

"To the realm where the Elders killed her parents and got away with it?" Tray countered, arching a dark brow. "Perhaps we need to focus on making it a safer place for her to return to first."

While an admirable idea, I knew it would fail.

Every path led to war.

There was no alternative.

But I couldn't say that. Giving too much away could potentially create more destinies, and we had enough laid out before us to last several lifetimes over. Which was saying a lot since we were all immortals with the potential to live forever.

Everyone fell silent as they considered Tray's statement.

Then Zeph cleared his throat. "I can't leave her with Zakkai. It goes against every instinct." He nailed me with a stare. "You have to be feeling it, too."

"I do. Every day." The block was nothing new for me. I'd resurrected the wall between us from the very beginning in an attempt to keep Zakkai out of my mind. "But if you lower the shield I put up, Zakkai will have access to your mind. And he's powerful, Zeph. You won't stand a chance against him."

"I'm still trying to figure out how he ascended without us feeling it," Kols said, frowning. "You claim he's the Source Architect. Shouldn't I sense that as the Source Heir?"

"You do feel it," I murmured, sighing. "And we all felt his ascension. Actually, we participated in it."

Zeph and Kols both stared at me.

I stared back.

Then Kols's gaze began to smolder as his mind caught up. "The LethaForest."

I dipped my chin, confirming he was on the right path.

"What?" Zeph glanced between us. "The LethaForest? Which time?"

"The night Aflora imploded," Kols said. "When I lost control in her room after we fucked for the first time."

"That was your overreaction to the bond," Zeph said.

Understatement, I thought, rolling my eyes.

"I felt a huge burst of power that night, which I originally assumed was tied to our newly formed bond." Kols blinked his gold eyes back to mine. "But that wasn't it at all, was it? You're saying that was the night Zakkai ascended."

I lifted a shoulder. "It could have been a combination of events. Fate likes to do that. But her need to expel all that energy was a result of his rise to power."

"That's what my father felt, too," Kols whispered.

"Do you think he knows the truth?" Tray asked, shifting his stance beside Ella. She'd remained abnormally quiet at his side, her blue eyes wide with growing trepidation. Her fiery personality had taken a back seat to the heavy conversation flowing around her.

"He might," Kols said. "He knows the Quandary Bloods are still alive. Which means he knows I was trying to hide something by saying I dueled with Shadow."

"I think he knows a lot more than you realize," I drawled, very aware of what Malik knew and hid from his son. But it wasn't my place to engage in that conversation.

Kols's eyes flashed. "Meaning what?"

"Meaning you should talk to him," I suggested, rolling my neck as another shudder went down my spine. *Fucking gargoyle.*

"And what should we do about Aflora?" Zeph demanded. "I'm not leaving her with Zakkai. You say he won't hurt her, but your word is unreliable."

"I've never lied to you." I'd just withheld certain details. Or a lot of them. Regardless… "I would never put Aflora in jeopardy."

His eyebrows shot up as he huffed a humorless laugh. "Yeah, I believe that. She's only been imprisoned twice because of you and then disappeared into a paradigm where I can't mentally reach her at all. All three instances scream safety, don't they?"

My teeth clenched. "She's fine."

"I'll believe that when I see it."

"Then I'll take you to her," I said, throwing my hands wide. "Is that what you need? Because he'll let me into the paradigm. I mean, he might kill you in the process since you're tied to Kols, and he wants the entire Nacht family line to burn. But sure. Let's give it a go. Now, perhaps?"

I was so done with this bullshit about trust and lies and deceit. I didn't enter this role of my own volition. It chose me. Fate decided to make me her bitch and turn my world upside down. I'd spent *years* protecting everyone. And for what? To be attacked by a damn gargoyle and left to suffer beneath an elitist spell?

Fuck this shit.

I just wanted a damn nap.

No, I wanted to hold my mate.

Oh, but she hated me now. *Again.*

This wicked loop needed to fucking end.

"You know how to locate her?" Kols asked softly.

"Of course I do," I snapped, done with this dance.

Kyros cocked a brow, surprised by my tone.

I ignored him.

"Can you work out a way for Zeph to see Aflora?" Kols pressed. "One where he isn't killed by Zakkai? If what you say is true about him caring for Aflora, then perhaps he would be open to a meeting, to discuss how to work this out between us."

Now Kyros's lips parted.

As did mine.

Because *never* had Kols suggested such a notion. He always wanted to charge in there with all his elitist energy and destroy.

But now… he wanted to talk? To seek a potentially diplomatic solution? This couldn't all just be because I'd bitten him. Maybe it had something to do with Aflora, or the Council sharing their knowledge of the Quandary Bloods. That'd been another change in this rendition of events, as had everything that occurred before it.

This entire version of time differed from the others.

It sparked a glimmer of hope inside me that maybe I'd finally gotten this right.

I really hoped that was the case because there was no going back now, not without forfeiting everything I'd learned in the process.

"I can try talking to Zakkai," I said slowly. That wouldn't have been possible in the past since I'd betrayed him in every way. But this time, I'd worked with him, at least on the surface. I still had every intention of betraying him in the end.

Unless…

No. I couldn't think like that. Not after everything I'd seen.

Zakkai was dangerous to us all. And Aflora would be, too, if she chose to join his path.

Hell waited for us all regardless of her decision.

"I want to talk to him, too," Zeph said. "He doesn't scare me."

"He should," Kyros interjected, pushing off the wall. "Because he scares the shit out of me." His dark eyes landed on me. "We good?"

I nodded. "For now."

"Excellent." He stroked the hilt of his sword and vanished.

I wanted to do the same thing, but one look from Kols had me remaining in the hall.

"We need to talk through our relationship going forward," he said.

I frowned and pinched my leg, concerned that perhaps I'd fallen into a dream state after the gargoyle's little attack. Because this wasn't the Kols I knew. Maybe I shouldn't have sent Kyros away.

"I know you're still hiding things," he continued. "And I'm going to overlook it. But we need to work together, not against each other."

My brow furrowed as I glanced between him and Zeph.

When the Warrior Blood nodded in agreement, I knew this all had to be a dream. Because no way in hell would these two ever decide to work *with* me.

"We'll start by you contacting Zakkai to arrange a meeting," Zeph said, his green eyes on me. "I want an introduction to this infamous Source Architect."

Kols nodded. "As do I."

"Maybe I wasn't clear before, but Zakkai wants to kill you, Kolstov." I made sure each word was enunciated clearly so there could be no mistake in the interpretation of my words. "He wants to kill Tray and Ella, and anyone and everyone else associated with the Nacht family. Do you understand that?"

"Then Aflora is in danger," Tray interjected. "Because she's mated to Kols."

"Not fully mated," I replied. "And Zakkai can help her undo that link, something that will be even easier for him to do if Kols goes anywhere near him."

"She won't let him remove our bond." Kols sounded far too confident. "And even if she does, I'll just bite her again."

"If you're alive to do it," I pointed out, shaking my head. "You're asking me to help you commit suicide." And I'd bitten him to prevent that. "I may not like you, but I am not going to help you die."

"I can't be killed by you talking to him, can I?" Kols countered.

No, but I certainly could, and then what? I thought, exhausted from this conversation and several iterations of it before this point.

Of course, the others all ended rather violently, so I preferred this temporary lapse in pain to discuss this cordially.

Except Kols apparently had a death wish in this version of events.

Because I'd bitten him? Was that the catalyst for this madness? Or had I finally determined the right sequence of events?

I shook my head, my mental gymnastics giving me a colossal headache. "I need a nap before I talk to Zakkai."

"Okay," Kols agreed.

I studied him. "Seriously, this whole"—I waved a hand over him, unsure of how to define his behavior—"is alarming."

His lips twitched. "This whole *what?*"

I just gestured at him again because fuck if I knew how to describe it.

The result made him chuckle and Zeph roll his eyes. "Do you two need a room?" the Warrior Blood deadpanned.

"No. I'll be fine in Aflora's bed," I muttered, shadowing to her room before either of them could argue with me. Her floral scent hit me right in the chest, sending a spike of agony through my spirit as I fought the urge to reach out to her again. To apologize for what I'd done. To verify that she was okay.

But I felt her in the bonds, her fury hot and very much alive.

Give him hell, little rose, I whispered to our closed mental door. *Flay him alive.*

Because Zakkai fucking deserved it and worse.

I hated him more than I hated myself.

Or I wanted to, anyway.

If I were honest, I also understood him. Which was why I'd sided with him in previous versions of our history. And also why I allowed a tiny flare of hope to touch my senses now.

Maybe this time we would get it right.

Or maybe… maybe this was the final version that would end us all.

CHAPTER SEVEN

AFLORA

Zakkai didn't want to give me clothes? Fine. I'd make my own with the wand he'd left on the nightstand.

My wand, I thought, my lips curling. I could feel the power whirling through me, recognizing my inner magic. Maybe at one point it had belonged to him, but it was mine now.

"Now, what to wear?" I mused, tapping my lip.

I muttered an incantation and waved the conduit around while studying myself in the mirror. Pants and a shirt were too plain. Hmm, a dress was too formal. No, I needed something rebellious and badass.

Knee-high boots—*yes.*

I paired it with a skirt.

"Hmm." I uttered another spell, changing the fabric to a checkered pattern with dark green as the primary color. I added a white blouse, then magicked a cloak with a three-headed-snake charm as the clasp.

Zeph would be so proud. I resembled a Warrior Blood.

I tapped my chin. *What else?* I added a choker to the mix with gleams of red silk woven between black strands. Kols would appreciate the Elite Blood touch.

And lastly, I created a band for my wrist with violet threads to resemble Shade. I wasn't happy with him, but he'd never hidden his devious intentions from me. He'd even warned that I would hate him, which I'd sensed hurt him deeply. So whatever he was up to held a deeper purpose; I just didn't know what it was yet.

The only missing embellishment was a cerulean flair. Nope. Not adding that. If Zakkai wanted me to wear his colors, he could provide me with more than a robe.

I ran my fingers through my blue-black hair, gave myself a once-over in the mirror, and tucked my wand into the pocket of my cloak.

Where are you? I asked my Quandary Blood mate.

Find me was his coy reply.

I narrowed my gaze. *You really want me to hurt you, don't you?*

His responding chuckle did nothing to alleviate my ire. If anything, it only stoked the flames. I didn't appreciate his little mental mind game or the memories he'd implanted in my head. They weren't real. They couldn't be. Yet, I couldn't find any trace of magic surrounding their existence. It felt as though he'd unlocked them, not placed them there, and that was even more unnerving.

What else existed in my memories that I didn't know about?

I shivered and focused on finding Zakkai instead.

It wasn't hard. He'd practically left me a path of cerulean magic to follow. I couldn't see it so much as feel it, the energy signature familiar and palpable to my senses.

I wound through the stone corridor, noted the fire lamps flickering with magic along the rocky interior, and passed several closed doors.

Two Midnight Fae stood sentry at the end of my path, one of them opening the final doorway for me and revealing yet another hallway, this one lined with glass windows on one side. I peered out of them and noted the array of wildlife and trees below. We were about three stories up, in some sort of castle. The sun rose over a set of mountains in the distance, making me frown.

This landscape wasn't anything like the burning thwomps on the Academy grounds. No charcoal blades, raven-like stones, or fire gnats. Just a meadow of pretty flowers, healthy trees, and a mountain of green.

It's not time for gardening, Aflora, Zakkai taunted in my thoughts, reminding me of the memory he'd skewed.

Stay out of my head.

Afraid I can't do that, sweet star. You're my mate, after all.

For now, I retorted. *We're going to break the bond, at least according to the fake event in my head.*

Who says it's fake?

I do, I replied, trailing after his essence again down the hall. It led me to another stone corridor lined with doors.

A few Midnight Fae mingled, all pausing to stare at me with widening eyes.

I ignored them, holding my head high, and allowed my cloak to billow in my wake. No sense in making friends. I didn't plan to be here long.

A pair of double doors stood closed at the end of the hall, the edges lined in Zakkai's energy. I sent a blast of magic against the center to blow the doors open, then walked through the threshold with the sole intention of finding the man playing in my head.

Only, a room of Midnight Fae paused mid-bite to gape at my rather forward entry.

They were all framed by windows overlooking the mountain, their tables evenly spaced in a cafeteria-style setting with Zakkai at the front of the room.

He sat beside Laki—if that was even his name—and several other fae. All of them stared at me as I approached, the chatter turning to whispers.

I ignored them all, my focus on my *mate*. He'd changed into a button-down shirt and tie, his white hair loose and wild around his broad shoulders.

The picture of sin.

He even had a glass of red wine—likely spiked with blood—to finish off his vampiric appearance. He sipped from the rim as his silver-blue eyes ran over me in clear appreciation. Then he set the glass down as the brunette beside him leaned over to whisper in his ear. It was an unmistakably intimate gesture that she strengthened by sliding her hand under the table, presumably to rest on his thigh.

I studied her familiar features with a frown.

Dakota, I recalled. She'd referred to me as a queen.

And from what I inferred by her current body language, she was very friendly with my *king*. My heart raced at the notion, my eyes narrowing as a result.

She had to know Zakkai was my mate.

Except he intended to break our bond, so maybe she didn't care.

I shouldn't care either.

However, part of me wanted to march over there and remove her hand from Zakkai's leg. A ridiculous instinct, considering I didn't even want him to be my mate.

I already had three; I didn't need a fourth. This was just temporary. If he wanted to make flowers with that dark-haired Elite Blood, then so be it. I'd much prefer to just kill him anyway.

Have you come to play? he asked into my mind, his head cocking to the side—the side that was noticeably away from Dakota.

That's interesting, I thought, ignoring his question.

Her full lips pursed as she straightened, her dark eyes flicking to me. "Nice of you to finally join us," she said, removing her hand from Zakkai's thigh to place it on the back of his chair in a decidedly proprietary move.

He didn't seem to notice or care—likely because she touched him often—and instead smiled at me. "I see you decided on Academy attire. Does that mean you want a lesson?"

A hum of conversation flowed behind me, a hint of excitement touching the air.

"Last I checked, classes with you weren't part of my curriculum. I think I'll stick with the itinerary Kols provided, thanks."

His grin widened. "Oh, but there's so much I can teach you," he said, his voice a sinful caress that seemed to imply so many meanings to his phrase.

"Kai," his father said, a hint of caution in his tone.

"One moment," he replied, his eyes twinkling with wicked intent. "I'm indulging our queen."

"I'm not your queen." I folded my arms. "You're not Elemental Fae."

"No, we're not," he agreed. "But you are most definitely *my* queen." He pushed his chair back, knocking Dakota's hand from it without ceremony. She quickly pulled her arm in, her lips flicking downward in brief annoyance before flattening into a straight, emotionless line.

"Kai," his father tried again, but Zakkai was already moving around the table.

"Did you have trouble sleeping, Aflora?" he asked as he sauntered toward me. "Is that the cause of your current mood?"

"Trouble sleeping?" I scoffed at the notion. "Is that what you call it?"

He smirked and stopped in front of me to tuck a strand of hair behind my ear.

Sweet star, you've insulted me by charging in here while wearing clothes that represent all your mates except me. He cupped my cheek. *If you kneel for me, I'll forgive you.* The words were softly spoken into my mind, a promise underlined in intent.

This was his territory, not mine.

It would be wise to show a little respect.

The problem was, I had no respect left in me to give.

"I'll never kneel for you." I enunciated the words clearly for everyone to hear. Maybe I should have replied mentally, but I had nothing to hide. And I meant what I said. "I bow to no one."

Gasps met my bold statement.

But a glimmer of amusement shone in Zakkai's gaze. "I can make you kneel."

"You can try," I countered.

The crowd broke out in louder whispers, and Laki heaved an audible sigh from the front of the room.

Apparently, my responses bothered him. Well, he could eat a burning thwomp. So could Zakkai, for that matter. "Just break our bond, and I'll be on my way," I said.

"Did you bring my wand?" he asked, ignoring my statement.

"No, but I brought *my* wand."

His lips twitched. "Good. You're going to need it." He began rolling his shirtsleeves to his elbows, his gaze holding mine. "I'll give you the first spell for our duel. I'm a gentleman like that."

"Duel? I'm not dueling with you."

"Oh, but you are, little star. You've challenged me, and I accept. So we'll duel."

"I didn't challenge you."

"Consider this your first lesson, Aflora. When you inform your king that you refuse to bow to him after insulting him with your entry and attire, it results in a challenge." He cracked his neck, his shirt fully rolled to his elbows now. "Either kneel or deliver your first spell."

"You're not my king." Perhaps goading him was the wrong thing to do, but my survival sense no longer seemed to exist.

"I'm the Source Architect. That makes me your king." The patience underlining his tone would have been admirable had I been able to admire him.

"A title doesn't command respect," I informed him in a similar tone. "Actions do."

He arched a brow. "Meaning?"

"You attacked an academy full of students and a village of innocent Midnight Fae. Those are actions I'll never bow to." *Not to mention altering my memories,* I added mentally with a narrowing of my gaze. *I'm not some delicate little flower you can manipulate with your Quandary magic.*

Silence met my words, the entire room seeming to have frozen around me.

Zakkai studied me for a long moment, his silver-blue irises swirling with power. "Respect is an important value here, Aflora. One you seem to be lacking." He took a step backward, his stance one I recognized from Zeph's warrior courses. "Lesson number two, sweetheart. Ask questions before you lay accusations at the feet of others. It's insulting to do otherwise. Now, name your first spell."

"Ask questions," I repeated on a humorless laugh. "I've asked you several questions, *Kai*. Your method of answering them leaves a lot to be desired."

"As does your current attitude," he countered, cerulean flames dancing along his fingertips. *I can't allow this to go unanswered, Aflora. You're insulting me in front of our people.*

Your people, I snapped.

Our people, he said again. *You're one of us.*

I'm an Earth Fae. A Royal. "I will not bow. *You are not my king.*"

His jaw ticked. "Vacate the tables."

Chairs scraped across the ground as the fae jumped to his command. They all moved to the glass wall, their gazes riveted on the sparring match unfolding in the center of the room. Magic whipped through the air as the tables all folded onto one another to create a neat pile in the corner, giving us ample floor space to work with.

"Such confidence, Aflora. I just wanted to see what you could do, but now, I intend to show you what *I* can do." He moved into his defensive stance again. "You have five seconds to utter a spell before I go first."

CHAPTER EIGHT

ZAKKAI

Fuck, she was magnificent.

I wanted to fist my fingers through her hair and kiss her, then bite her in reprimand for her disobedience. No one ever challenged me; they all knew better. But Aflora stood before me in all her royal glory, daring me to react.

"Four seconds," I told her, counting down my warning.

Her beautiful eyes narrowed, her energy flaring to life. I tasted all her mates on the wind and the addictive undercurrent of her elemental birthright. It provided an intoxicatingly potent mixture that I wanted to devour.

But I uttered, "Three seconds," instead.

She'd insulted me countless times. To allow it would make me appear weak, and I couldn't afford that as the Source Architect. I could accept her as my equal, but not as an adversary. Not when our people relied on us to lead.

"Two seconds, Aflora." I already knew the incantation I intended to use. Nothing harsh, just a warn—

Green fire shot across the floor to circle my ankles. The ropes gave a tug, threatening to drag me to the ground as a tree root burst up through the floor to snag my calf. My brow furrowed at the bizarre mixture of magic. She hadn't spoken, just used her mind to unleash the power.

I would have been impressed if that hadn't been such a strict breach of protocol. "Who the hell taught you how to duel?"

"Zephyrus," she replied, sending another blast of magic at my torso that resembled red flames. "And Kols." She disappeared into a cloud of purple smoke, only to appear behind me with a ball of fiery violet energy. "And *Shade*." She unleashed the WarFire directly at my head.

Right.

She wasn't dueling.

She was trying to kill me.

I ducked, then caught the WarFire before it could hit anyone else, smothering it beneath a wave of my own power. Then I snapped the shackles around my ankles and calf with another thought and leapt away from her freshly created sphere of colorful flames.

I caught it with my hand—coated in cerulean magic—and crushed it like one would a physical ball and tossed it away. "My turn."

Her eyes widened a fraction as I flung an electric web her way, similar to the one I'd covered her in earlier.

Only, this time she shadowed away from it, causing the energy to fizzle out upon hitting the stone floor.

Clever, I praised her, spinning to send another to her new location. But she phased again, this time disappearing long enough for me to realize her true intent.

Escape.

I smirked and checked my watch while everyone glanced around in confused silence, searching for their missing queen.

Ten.

Nine.

Eight.

I yawned.

Six.

Five.

Oh, Aflora.

Three.

Two.

She returned with a loud "Oomph" as the spell I'd woven over her upon entry kicked in, yanking her back to me like an elastic band. She landed on her ass, her startled expression amusing.

I didn't give her a moment to acclimate, instead shooting another net at her.

Cerulean flames engulfed her prone form, disintegrating the strands in an instant as she bounced up to her feet in a beautifully defensive maneuver. *Nice,* I told her. She'd completely disregarded all the rules, but that didn't stop me from approving of her overall form.

The woman could fight.

Her skills clearly came from her bond with Zephyrus, which confirmed my suspicions about him being a formidable adversary. If she could channel these maneuvers from him, then he would be a force to reckon with in person.

I looked forward to meeting him. Maybe I'd let him live—if anything, so my mate remained as agile and gifted as she was now.

A burning thwomp sprouted in the middle of the room, causing several Midnight Fae to gasp. I studied the growing monstrosity, wary of her intent. Those were dangerous trees meant for *outside*. They had a penchant for bursting into flames.

She added a sea of charcoal blades beneath it, the grass notoriously sharp.

"Aflora," I warned. "This is a duel, not a death match."

"Free me and I'll let you live," she countered.

"Free you?" I nearly laughed. "You mean like allow your powers to flourish to their full potential rather than drown you beneath a collar?" I looked pointedly at her neck. "You created that, sweet star. Not me. I would never dilute your abilities." Although, watching her now, I could see why Kolstov had felt the need to. She was absolutely out of control, and she didn't seem to understand the full extent of her abilities.

A fact she accentuated by throwing another WarFire sphere at my head. A second came right after it, nearly hitting the fae by the windows.

"*Aflora.*"

She ignored me and sent two more threatening balls in my direction, her control unhinged as she grew more powerful by the second.

Fuck.

I'd wanted to see what she could do, and she'd certainly come out swinging.

If we were outside, that would have been fine, but she'd unleashed WarFire and a burning thwomp in the middle of the damn castle. Upholding the complexity of the paradigm already had me at half my usual power. I couldn't afford for her to disturb that balance, or I risked her hurting someone.

Right. I needed to end this the hard way, then.

I took her next attack and squashed it before it left her hand, then wrapped her in a rope of electricity that sizzled against her struggling form. She screamed and tore through the binds with an impressive wave of power that had my lips parting in surprise.

And all hell broke loose.

Fire poured off her in ripples of purple, red, green, and cerulean, swimming across the floor with dangerous intent. Several of the fae at my back began to scramble, but one of them sent a bolt of lightning directly into Aflora's chest, momentarily stunning my mate and sending her to the ground on an anguished cry.

Another bolt followed, the red hum telling me the identity of the perpetrator.

"*Dakota,*" I snapped. "*Enough.*"

She sent a final enchantment, one meant to paralyze her prey, then looked at me with astute defiance. "You didn't have the balls to do it, so I did it for you."

"I didn't ask you to intervene." Nor would I have asked her to.

"You didn't need to. I knew what you needed."

"Your presumption is out of line," I informed her, striking out a similar bolt of power to bring her to her knees. "Never touch my queen again."

"Kai," my father interjected.

"No. I had this under control." I focused on all the power humming through the room and canceled it out with a single wave of my hand. The burning thwomp disintegrated to ash, and Aflora's ropelike flames sizzled into a calming mist. With another brush of my fingertips, the room returned to normal, the paradigm responding to me—its master—and righting all the wrongs.

Then I turned to Dakota's quivering form on the floor and sent another bolt into her to even the score. She'd hit Aflora twice with that magic before paralyzing her. "While you may have acted with good intentions, Aflora is still your queen and I am your king. You do not attack her without cause."

"Kai, she felt threatened and reacted," my father interjected.

An understatement.

Dakota had felt threatened by Aflora since the first time I mentioned she was my mate. The power-hungry Elite Blood had been after my cock since day one. I saw right through her antics—she wanted to use me for her own gain. Just like she'd used Kolstov and Zephyrus. The difference between me and them? I knew how to think with my head.

She would never be welcome in my bed.

I'd made that clear from day one.

It had nothing to do with my ties to Aflora and everything to do with taste.

Just like Dakota's attack had nothing to do with defending the others today and everything to do with her growing jealousy. I hadn't missed her little display of possession when Aflora had arrived. The only reason I hadn't put the Elite Blood in her place was because of the hint of irritation it had sparked inside my mate.

She didn't like the notion of another woman touching me. I understood that, as I hadn't been all that fond of her taking other mates. But we'd been separated for years, and the intention had always been to break our bond upon our reunion.

I wasn't a saint.

I'd fucked around.

However, I hadn't bonded anyone else. Nor would I.

Aflora was it for me, something I knew the moment I saw her in the dreams. Perhaps even before. I hadn't been able to look at another woman since the coffee shop. It wasn't something I'd spent a lot of time evaluating until she'd commanded me to go down on her the first night.

I'd been hers ever since.

She just didn't know it yet.

Her pain spiked through our bond, causing me to turn toward her. She had curled herself into a shivering ball on the floor, the spell having worn off, leaving her utterly defenseless.

Fuck, she looked so small and fragile like that. A broken little flower, devoid of life.

No one should ever see a queen in this manner.

Yet Dakota had ensured everyone witnessed Aflora's fall.

Power licked through my veins, the inclination to kill her riding my spirit. "Run, Dakota," I said, my voice a low growl. "*Hide.*"

My father heaved another of his infamous sighs, his annoyance palpable. He didn't much care for my temper. Funny, considering I'd inherited that trait from him.

I walked over to Aflora and scooped her up into my arms. "Class dismissed," I informed the room, carrying her to the door and into the hallway. I sensed my father following but ignored him.

He didn't speak until we were alone in my wing of the castle, his disappointment unmistakable. "You let that get out of hand."

"I tested her limits," I countered. "Had you allowed me to recruit her earlier, we would have had time to train your way. But now she's bound to three other Midnight Fae, thereby necessitating my brand of schooling."

"She wasn't ready then."

"She's not ready now," I retorted, fed up with this familiar argument. "She's throbbing with power and has no outlet to expel it. I provided what she needed today, just as I'll do again tomorrow. However, I'm doing this my way. Because I am the Source Architect." I added that last bit for his benefit, reminding him yet again of my position of power. "Trust me to handle this."

"You just threatened a valuable asset," he said through his teeth. "That makes it difficult to trust you, Zakkai."

His use of my full name—in addition to his inane statement—had me rolling my eyes. "Dakota isn't valuable. She's a power-hungry cunt who will betray us all at the first sign of a higher position."

He growled at my bluntness. "What the hell has gotten into you?"

"Dakota attacked my mate," I snapped, stopping outside the door to my room. "I don't take kindly to that." How could he not see the problem with her behavior?

"Temporary mate," he corrected.

"That's always been your plan," I drawled, neither confirming nor denying the intention.

He'd forced this bonding.

Then he'd made me alter her memories of me.

That'd only been the beginning of my hellish existence. Each course he'd administered since had been worse than the last. And now he wanted me to graduate to the next level by removing the only piece of goodness left inside me—my link to Aflora.

"If you'll excuse me, I'm going to run a warm bath for Aflora to help remove the remainder of Dakota's enchantment." I used a mental command to open my door, then attempted to shut it in his face, but of course, he followed me inside.

"We're not done with this conversation."

"Are you really going to hound me over nearly killing Dakota?" I asked, huffing a laugh. "Because it's not the first time I've almost done that, Father." I once found her naked in my bed. Rather than celebrate the discovery, I'd made her return to her rooms in the same outfit she'd walked in with—her skin.

For whatever reason, that just made her work harder to win me over.

"We're so close to our goal," he pressed, laying his hand on my shoulder, his tone softening. "We've done our duty to Aflora's parents by protecting her. It's time for us to move on and finish what we started. That's the only way to truly honor their memory and all the other lives taken at the hands of the Midnight Fae Elders."

I released a long breath, my muscles relaxing in the process.

"Father, I've not changed course from our intentions," I replied. A little sparring fun with my mate wasn't going to alter my destined path. "And Aflora's much more than just a duty. You saw her power today. She's an asset."

I gazed down at the still-trembling female in my arms, her blue eyes wide as she listened without speaking. The paralyzing spell had probably rendered her incapable of making a sound, but I suspected it went deeper than that. She seemed genuinely interested in what we were discussing. I couldn't blame her, given the subject matter.

"Her parents died for our cause," I added, holding her gaze. "We need to give her a chance to decide if she wants to join our quest in honoring their loss. I can't expect her to make that decision in a single night, not after everything she's been through."

"It's that or death," he said.

"Yes," I agreed, noting the way her pupils dilated at the confirmation. "The Midnight Fae Council was never going to let her live. The only reason they did all those years ago was to use her as bait to find us." I added the latter for her benefit, wondering if she knew the truth.

The flare of her nostrils suggested she did.

Did Kolstov tell you? I wondered.

Yes. Her mental voice was strong and completely at odds with her fragile physical state. I suspected she could still fight even in this form, purely from her mind.

"Did he tell you that the Elders killed your parents for helping Quandary Bloods survive?" I spoke out loud, not caring if my father overheard. This wasn't news to him.

Yes, she repeated. *He told me after the Council informed him.*

That… is oddly admirable of him.

He didn't know about any of this until recently. But Shade knew.

Shade knows a lot of things, I agreed before looking at my father. "Kolstov told Aflora the truth about her parents' deaths." The young Midnight Prince had only recently been inducted into the inner circle—a fact my uncle Tadmir had told us about just last week. I'd expected the Nacht family heir to embrace his role as king and accept his position as lead assassinator of my race.

But him telling Aflora the truth was counterintuitive to that notion.

He also hadn't informed the Council about his bonds to her—something I assumed was purely selfish on his part. If they learned about their impending mating, he'd lose his right to the throne. Or worse, they'd kill him for consorting with an abomination.

Of course, he also hadn't told them about her growing Quandary Blood skills. I'd never quite understood why he'd kept that hidden, other than to assume it was to also save his own ass in some way.

"That doesn't change his fate," my father said. "The whole Nacht family needs to die."

"I know," I replied, still lost to my thoughts.

You can't kill Kols, Aflora said, her eyes growing wide.

I bent to press my lips to hers. *Shh, we'll talk more after you rest.*

No, Kai. You can't kill Kols!

It's okay, little star, I assured her. *I'll show you how to break the bonds so his death doesn't hurt you.*

She began to panic in my arms, her body convulsing as she fought the recovery process and demanded her limbs react.

I sighed. "Aflora, that's only going to worsen the side effects." I laid her in my bed and uttered an enchantment to warm my sheets around her. What she really needed was a bath, but I couldn't do that if she continued to squirm. I slipped my hand into her cloak to retrieve my wand, then cast a soft spell over her, insisting she sleep.

No! she shouted into my mind. *Kai, no!*

Shh, I'm trying to help, Aflora. Just relax. I intensified the spell, fighting through her weak defenses and throwing her into a deep sleep within seconds. Then I shook my head. "She's one of the most stubborn females I've ever met."

"The strong ones usually are," my father replied, clapping me on the shoulder again. "Break the bond tomorrow. It'll help you both."

I tensed at the command in his voice, but my father didn't notice. He merely patted me again and showed himself out, all the while expecting me to comply.

No, I thought, tucking a strand of hair behind Aflora's ear. "I'd much rather keep you, sweet star." I bent to kiss her forehead. "Sweet dreams."

CHAPTER NINE

My chest burned, stirring me to awareness beside Kols. He remained studiously asleep, his features void of discomfort. Another pang had me pressing my palm to my pec to massage the throbbing muscle, but it did little to dispel the agony rippling through my veins.

Something's wrong, I realized. "Aflora."

"She's fine," a groggy voice said as Shade materialized in Kols's room wearing nothing but a pair of boxers. He scratched the back of his neck and blew out a breath, wincing as a fresh wave of heat splintered through me.

"Doesn't feel fine," I gritted out through my teeth. And considering his reaction rivaled mine, he obviously felt it, too.

"Hmm?" Kols murmured, blinking awake, then frowned upon finding the Death Blood only a few feet away. "Where the fuck are your pants? And why the hell are you in my room?"

Shade rolled his eyes. "You're lucky I'm wearing boxers," he muttered. "I usually sleep naked in Aflora's bed."

A visual I did not want to entertain. "What the fuck is going on, Shade?" I demanded.

He palmed the back of his neck and dipped his head back to stare up at the ceiling. "Aflora is siphoning power out of us to help herself heal."

That forced me to sit up. Same with Kols.

"You said he wouldn't hurt her," I said, narrowing my gaze. "What happened, Shade?"

"I don't know!" he shouted, throwing his arms up in the air as he lowered his wild eyes to mine. "I can't link to her without risking Zakkai getting into my head, and he already knows too much. I've risked a lot just by lowering the barrier between us to check on her. I can't do it again, but trust me, I wish I could. Fuck, I wish I could do a lot of things right now."

This was probably the truest Shade had ever been with us. And, unfortunately, it wasn't fucking good enough. "Let's try her dreams again," I said to Kols. "Maybe she's asleep now."

"You can't," Shade started, but I held up my hand.

"Your head is a problem because of all your time fuckery. I get that. But I don't know those details. If Zakkai wants to rummage through my thoughts, he's welcome to experience my rage."

"It's more than that," Shade insisted. "He's the Source Architect. He can rewrite powers, Zeph. He can alter *your* powers."

"I'm not afraid of his Quandary skills," I retorted, refocusing on Kols. "We should—"

"He can undo the mating bond," Shade interjected.

We could have heard a pin drop after that pronouncement.

Altering my powers was a consequence I could live with. Altering my bond to Aflora? No, that wasn't an acceptable risk.

Kols cleared his throat. "What about our elemental bond?"

"I don't know," Shade whispered. "But maybe."

"Has he undone our mating bonds before?" I asked.

Shade swallowed. "I don't know."

I frowned. "You don't know? Yet you're positive that he can do it now? Through a dream?"

Shade shook his head. "You don't understand."

"You're right. I don't fucking understand because you're not telling us everything," I snapped, tired of this convoluted riddle of a game. "Either give me something I can work with or get the fuck out of here."

"Zeph." Kols placed his palm on my thigh, the blanket the only thing separating his touch from my skin. "Are there timelines you don't remember?" Kols asked, the question for Shade.

"Likely, yes." Shade's hands fell to his sides in a helpless gesture. "There are certain rules with time. If you bond to another fae—full bonding, not just an initial stage—then you can't go back without taking the bonded mate with you. And the only way to ensure that a bonded mate forgets is if you sacrifice your memories as well. So it's possible I've done that, but I wouldn't remember if I had."

"This is why I don't fuck with time," I muttered.

"You're not helping," Kols said, squeezing my leg. "Shade, has Zakkai ever dismantled our bonds to Aflora?"

The Death Blood stilled. "I already admitted to Aflora succeeding in that endeavor," he said slowly. "Her Quandary magic comes from Zakkai."

"Meaning, if she can do it, he definitely can," Kols translated.

Shade dipped his chin in acknowledgment. "I'm not saying he will. I'm saying the possibility is there, and if you choose to talk to Aflora, you need to be very careful."

"Who put the block in my head?" I asked him, narrowing my gaze. I'd thought it was because of her location in a paradigm, but something about the way he phrased his statement made me think otherwise. *If I choose to talk to Aflora.* Meaning I *could* talk to her.

"It's a safety measure," the Death Blood replied.

"That's not what I asked."

"I know," he replied.

"Remove the block, Shade," I demanded, reading between the lines. "I'll control my own link."

Shade started pacing. "It's not that simple."

"It *is* that simple," I replied, conjuring my wand. "Get the fuck out of my head."

"I'm not in your head." He stopped to stare at me. "I put the block in Aflora's mind."

"Then fucking remove it," I said through my teeth.

"Zeph."

"Stop *Zeph*ing me, Kolstov. I'm not playing into his riddles anymore." I pointed my wand at Shade. "Remove the block. *Now.*"

Shade released an insufferable sigh and sat on the bed, which was not at all what I anticipated. "Torture me all you want, Zephyrus. It's nothing compared to the pain I'm already in."

Kols put his hand on mine, lowering the wand. "He's not going to remove the block, even if you hurt him."

"Maybe not, but hurting him will make me feel a lot better," I muttered.

"No, it won't," Kols said softly. "The only thing that will make any of us feel better right now is Aflora. I think we should try to reach her in her dreams, but tread carefully."

Shade huffed a laugh. "The irony."

"What irony?" Kols asked.

"Zakkai used to visit her mind while she slept between both of you." His lips twitched. "You never noticed. Maybe he won't notice either, except I'm guessing he's waiting for you right now."

"Since you know him so well, maybe you should come with us," I suggested, only half meaning it.

"Actually, that might work," Kols murmured. "You might be able to sense his energy signature."

"His energy signature?" Shade repeated. "Aflora is *drenched* in his energy. They bonded when she was seven, and his magic has been growing with hers ever since." He pulled his knee up onto the mattress and leaned against one of the posts at the foot of the bed.

A strange sort of silence fell between the three of us as we considered what that meant. Shade had mentioned the age of Zakkai's bond to Aflora earlier, but hearing it again really drove the point home.

Fifteen years.

I hadn't even been bonded to her for fifteen days.

"Aflora inherited the earth source shortly after their mating," Shade added, his tone lacking his usual snark. "You can imagine what that's done to her, right?"

"It caused her powers to mingle with his, which is what marks her as an abomination." Kols sounded wary, but he mimicked Shade's position by leaning against the headboard with one leg drawn up, the sheets pooling at his hips.

If Aflora walked in and saw this, she'd probably faint. Three of her mates, mostly naked, sitting in a weird triangle shape on the bed.

I would have laughed if I had a sense of humor.

But nothing about this was funny or okay. And the dull ache in my chest only emphasized that fact.

"You said you were able to lower the barrier to check on her. Do it again. I want to feel her."

Shade's ice-blue eyes glittered even in the low lighting of the room. "My mental block isn't the same as the one I put in her mind."

"Then we go into her dreams," I replied, done with this negotiation. "I need to know that she's okay, and I'm not accepting your confirmation to the contrary." He hadn't earned my trust. Fuck, he was far away from that point.

"Call Kyros and put him on standby. If this goes badly, we'll just shift backward in time." Kols shrugged as though messing with the timeline mattered little to him.

His whole demeanor had changed since Shade had bitten him—an act that made my blood boil.

I was Kols's protector. His Guardian. And a Death Blood had first-stage mated him while I'd been passed out from a spell.

A spell cast by the same Death Blood in question.

There really was no mystery here as to why I wanted to kill him.

The only reason I hadn't touched him yet was because of Aflora. Hurting him would hurt her, and she was in enough pain already.

My eyebrow lifted with the thought. "Wouldn't breaking my bond with Aflora hurt her?" I asked slowly, interrupting whatever the Death Blood had just been saying to Kols. "If your claim regarding his care for her is valid, then would he risk harming her in that manner?"

Shade stared at me. "Breaking the bond would hurt, yes. As to whether or not he would go through with it, I'll just say that he's not opposed to risks."

"Meaning he would jeopardize Aflora if the situation required it," I translated, my irritation renewed. Not that it'd necessarily left. "Right. We're done with this conversation. I'm going into her dreams. If you two want to join me, then do."

I lay down and closed my eyes.

Something was wrong, beyond the obvious. And I wasn't just going to sit here debating when I could get to the heart of the matter.

In Aflora's mind.

CHAPTER TEN

AFLORA

Magic curled around me in a cocoon of color.

Purple.

Green.

Cerulean.

A splash of red.

I reveled in it, soaking up the energy my soul so badly needed, while also prodding at my renewed connection to earth. It smelled fresh and sweet, the source a welcome hive of sunshine that warmed my skin.

Beautiful, I thought, twirling in my bed of flowers and inhaling all the fresh scents. It rejuvenated my depleted spirit. Yet I couldn't recall how or why this rejuvenation was needed.

Strange.

Oh, but the sun! I missed the sun.

I paused. *Why do I miss such a vital element of life?* I tapped my lip, whirling around a little slower now, trying to determine what felt so off about this place.

It reminded me of something.

A safe place.

A meadow of flowers with a home hidden in a tree.

Shade, I breathed, sighing as violet energy flared around me. Sadness overwhelmed me, a sense of betrayal lurking beneath the waves of energy.

"Aflora…" My name came to me on a breeze, the deep, masculine tones reminding me of a Warrior Blood.

Zeph, I thought, my heart skipping a beat. *Oh, yes. Zeph.*

But he wasn't in my meadow. Except his green magic flickered around me, the dark hue reminding me of a forest of evergreens. My lips kicked up at the thought, the scent of his woodsy cologne touching my senses.

I followed the trail created by his masculine presence, searching… searching… searching.

However, a trickle of purple light gave me pause. *Shade.*

His minty aftershave swirled around me, beckoning me toward a darker section at the edge of the meadow. I hadn't noticed it before, the sun having lit up all the corners earlier in the day.

Hmm, something wasn't quite right about this little nook.

But his presence grew with each step, his shadowy energy seducing my inner fae.

Dark magic.

I curled a cerulean strand around it, testing the tendril of smoke, and smiled as he tugged back.

Come dance with me, little rose, he was saying. Or that was how I interpreted the invitation, anyway.

My bare feet brushed the last hint of sunny grass before I stepped through the dark threshold into Kols's Academy bedroom.

I blinked, startled by the shift. Then gaped at the three shirtless men in Kols's bed.

"This must be a dream," I whispered to myself, noting their chiseled features and gorgeous faces.

Kols with his auburn locks of thick hair and golden irises.

Zeph with his dark strands and forest-green eyes.

And Shade with that perpetual smirk and icy gaze. He sat against the bedpost at the foot of the bed, his legs clad in a pair of black boxers.

Kols and Zeph were against the headboard, the silky sheets low on their hips and leaving a suggestion of nudity below.

I glanced down to find myself similarly dressed in a threadbare tank top and boy shorts, nothing else. My lips twisted in consideration. "I'm usually naked in our dreams."

"We're ensuring that we don't deviate from the purpose of this dream," Zeph said.

"Oh." I cleared my throat. "Well, you all are…" I waved a hand at their bare chests and cleared my throat again. "Sorry. What's the purpose of what now?"

Kols chuckled. "I think she's fine, Zeph."

"Come here, pixie flower," my Warrior Blood mate demanded, holding out his arm.

Normally, I'd balk at him, but I really wanted to comply this time. So I shuffled toward the bed and crawled on top of him to steal a much-needed hug. Although, I couldn't remember why I wanted one. And touching him had my eyes welling up with tears.

I buried my face in the crook of his neck, inhaling his familiar scent, and shuddered against him.

"I don't think she's fine at all," he said, his arms closing around me in an embrace underlined in heat and power.

Safe, I thought. *I feel safe here.*

Among my mates.

Except, it wasn't real. This was all in my head, and that caused my heart to ache with a sense of acute loss. "I don't know what's wrong with me," I admitted, swallowing thickly. "I... I... feel... I feel so sad."

"He's enchanted her mind," Shade murmured, his voice low. "I can see the bands of his magic threaded through her thoughts."

"He?" I repeated. "He who?"

"Zakkai," Zeph said, palming my cheeks to pull my gaze to his. "He's taken you to a paradigm. I could feel your pain. Did he hurt you?"

"P-paradigm?" I recognized that term. But I couldn't define it. Just as I knew Zakkai, yet his description remained just out of reach. "This..." I trailed off, frowning.

Everything was so dreamy and perfect and pretty.

My mates were mostly naked.

Mmm, I wanted to lick them all.

Wait, I thought, shaking my head. *That's not right.*

I'd gone from... from something... to... Did they all have to be so distracting? "You all need clothes."

Kols reached for me, the inky lines along his arms writhing with hypnotic power. Zeph released my face, his hands dropping to my hips. I glanced down, noting how I straddled his thighs.

Why am I wearing clothes? I wondered, biting my lip. *That's not the point of dreams. I should be naked. But didn't I just tell them...?*

I flinched as Kols's palm met my cheek. His skin burned against mine, his power a shock wave that yanked a gasp from my throat. *"Oh!"* I arched upward and nearly fell, but Zeph's hand landed on my lower back, holding me steady.

Energy hummed through me, magic warring deep inside my soul.

I closed my eyes, falling into the black hole of whirling energy, searching for the cause of the disturbance.

Red and cerulean battled.

Beautiful colors.

So bright and vibrant.

Only, they were trying to destroy one another.

No, no, couldn't have that. They were too pretty to harm each other.

I plucked at them, tugging the two cords apart, and shoved them to separate recesses of my soul, then jolted awake on Zeph's lap once more.

He was shouting.

Kols had fallen off the bed, and Shade was trying to help him up.

I frowned. "What happened?"

"Zakkai," Zeph snarled the name.

I blinked, then gasped. "He wants to kill Kols!"

"No shit," Shade snapped, his sharp tone startling me. He never spoke to me like that.

And considering how we'd left things, he should be groveling. "You gave me to Zakkai," I said slowly, everything coming back to me in a surge of insanity. That part wasn't important. I needed to tell them about his intentions for Kols. Except, hold on, I already did.

"Are you all right?" Zeph asked, cupping my cheeks once more. "I need to know you're okay. I could feel your pain."

"My pain?" I repeated, trying to pull away to look at Kols, but Zeph held me steady.

"Aflora, did Zakkai hurt you?"

"No," I replied, frowning. "No, Dakota did."

His eyebrows flew upward. "Dakota?"

"Some Elite Blood," I said. "She hit me with a horrible spell. It… it paralyzed me. Zakkai made her stop. Then he took me back… to sleep… in his room." I glanced around as the dream started to blur. "Zeph, he wants to kill Kols." I tried to grab him to ensure he understood, but my hand went through him.

"Aflora!"

"Zeph!" I cried out, lunging for him. "He wants to kill Kols!"

He caught me by the waist as I nearly tumbled to the floor and yanked me back up onto the bed. I curled into his lap, shivering. "I don't know where I am," I whispered. "I don't know where he's keeping me, but there are mountains and sunshine."

I glanced up, a plea for him to find me lining my lips, only his eyes had turned a silver blue. And his dark hair now fell in white waves around his shoulders.

Zakkai.

My limbs froze. My heart stopped beating. My eyes went wide.

He knew about my dream.

He knew what I'd betrayed.

Oh, flowers, I'm a dead fae…

His lips curled. "I'm not going to punish you for loyalty, Aflora," he whispered, cupping my cheek and pressing his lips to my temple. "I actually quite admire that trait in you." He tucked me against his bare chest, the heat of his skin seeming to thaw some of the ice coating my veins.

He… he didn't feel mad.

Maybe he was hiding it? Playing some sort of mental game again? Did he have more memories of mine to alter?

"The memories are real," he said softly. "I spent the first ten years of my life with your family, seven of those years with you. We were best friends, Aflora."

I shook my head, denying every word. "You put those memories there."

"I didn't. But I did remove them initially." He sighed, his gaze taking on a faraway gleam. "We knew the Elders had discovered our location in the Elemental Fae realm, and it was only a matter of time before they came for us. My dad tried to convince your parents to run, but they refused because it would have meant leaving the earth source behind."

He fell silent for a moment, his expression radiating a pain I could sense through our bond. It pinched my heart, causing my eyes to prickle with tears. Not because it hurt, but because I hurt for him.

"We compromised with the bond." He cleared his throat, his voice lower, and huskier with emotion. "Then I erased all your memories of me and my dad to protect you from the Elders. It was quite literally the worst day of my life. The agony of removing all those moments, to know my mate wouldn't know me, was a task no ten-year-old should ever have to endure. But I didn't have a choice. It was either that or put your life at risk. The latter was an unacceptable fate."

I recalled the memory of seeing him on the ground, writhing in torment as magic whirled through the air. "Your dad told you to be a man." The words came out on a whisper, my mind fracturing beneath the image engraved in my memory.

Zakkai grunted. "One of his favorite phrases from my childhood. Pretty sure he still wants to tell me that sometimes."

I shook my head.

It's not real.

Don't believe his lies.

But it feels real.

I couldn't find any evidence of tampering inside my mind. Which was strange because he'd clearly done something.

"All I did was finish unraveling the spell," he said. "You started the process with your song. I finished it with the web. It seemed like the easiest way to convince you of the truth, except you still don't believe me."

"Sort of hard to believe someone who keeps playing mental games with me," I muttered.

"Fair," he agreed, his hand drawing up and down my spine. "But the fact remains that we used to be best friends. You were my Flora, and I was your Kai. We went everywhere together." His lips curled, and he slowly shook his head. "That sometimes feels like a former life. I don't even remember that boy anymore."

I studied his profile, noting the sincerity in his features. Part of me wanted to believe him, but I knew better than to fall for his story this quickly. However, while he appeared to be in the mood to provide details, I decided a question wouldn't hurt our situation.

"If you're not that boy, then who are you?"

He considered me for a long moment. So long that I thought he intended to ignore me, or perhaps respond with another riddle.

Instead, he reached out to tuck a strand of my hair behind my ear, then brushed his knuckles down the side of my neck. "I'm a being of vengeance," he said softly, his gaze following his touch as he traced my collarbone with the back of his hand. "I want justice for what's been done to Quandary Bloods. Justice for your parents. A new reign to right the wrongs of the Elite."

"A new reign?"

"Mmm." His gaze returned to mine. "Have you not considered what it could look like?"

"Honestly, I've just been trying to survive."

He nodded. "Yes. I understand that more than you know." He dropped his hand to my hip, his body relaxed beneath mine. "Do you approve of how the Council operates today?"

"I assume you mean the Midnight Fae Council."

"Yes. I'm referring to the male-driven hierarchy where females are expected to bow and just accept their place. Do you approve?"

"Of course I don't. When Shade bit me, they wouldn't even let me participate in my own trial. They said my betrothed had to speak on my behalf."

He smirked. "It's ridiculous, right? I mean, I prefer logic, but I also understand the role sentiment plays in decisions. Yet Constantine Nacht has created a dictatorship based on harsh resolves alone, without any care as to how it impacts anyone else."

"Constantine Nacht is the cause?" I asked. "Kols's grandfather?"

"He's the one who enacted all the changes a little over a millennium ago. All because he feared feminine emotion." Zakkai rolled his eyes. "Has Shade told you the story about Zenaida? How she chose to follow her heart instead of duty? Because she's the cause for all this. Or rather, she's the scapegoat the Council uses for their hierarchical decision."

"He told me how Constantine Nacht made an example of her. She went into hiding with her mates after he gave the order to eradicate Quandary Bloods."

Zakkai nodded. "Yes. And Shade's father assumed the Death Blood throne instead of his mother because Constantine declared women unfit to lead." He rolled his eyes again. "It was all a ploy to establish his crude hierarchy. From what my father has said, Constantine has always considered females to be the weaker gender since only males can mate via their bite."

"Elemental Fae require mutual agreement for mating."

"Yes, I know," he replied, his lips curling. "You chose Kolstov."

"I did." I wasn't going to deny it. "You can't kill him."

"He's a Nacht, Aflora. They all have to die for the power to be rightfully restored."

"But he didn't do anything wrong. His grandfather did. You can't punish him for another man's sins."

"Actually, I can. Their familial line has tainted Midnight Fae kind for over a thousand years. Those seeking retribution require the eradication of the Nacht bloodline. And I intend to fulfill that eradication."

"That makes you no better than Constantine," I argued. "He attempted to slay an entire race over prejudice. Your kill list might be shorter, but you're still planning to take innocent lives."

"It's a sacrifice we must endure for justice."

"I won't let you kill Kolstov."

He sighed. "When the time comes, you won't have a choice, Aflora. But" —he pressed his finger to my lips before I could snap a comeback at him—"I will agree to consider your side if you agree to consider mine."

I frowned. "I don't understand."

"I want you to give me a chance to explain this war to you, to show you why the Nacht family needs to pay for their sins. And in return, I'll also consider your point of view."

I narrowed my eyes.

Obviously, I didn't believe he would ever uphold his side of that agreement. Just as I knew that I would never agree to him hurting Kols. However, his confidence had me wondering what trick lurked up his sleeve.

"What do you have in mind?" I asked.

He smiled. "I want you to attend the Blood Gala with me."

The Blood Gala?

That was the event Emelyn had mentioned in Warrior Magic class before all hell broke loose.

Fae, when was that? Just yesterday? The day before? I blinked. My sense of time was a mess, thanks to the endless hours of sunshine—which still poured in from the balcony windows of Zakkai's room—and all the bizarre dreams.

I shook my head, trying to clear it.

"You decline?" Zakkai asked, frowning. "I'm not planning to do anything at the event. I just want you to observe the societal event and give me your thoughts afterward."

"I was shaking my head in confusion," I admitted, biting my lip. "You want my opinion?"

"I want to teach you," he corrected softly. "And to do that, I need to show you how the Midnight Fae operate."

"At a gala?" I uttered the words slowly, not fully understanding how a fancy party would explain anything to me about Midnight Fae.

"The Blood Gala," he said.

"Okay. But how will a gala change my mind about Kols?"

"It's not about Kolstov, Aflora. It's about purpose."

"I... I'm not clear on what you mean."

He considered for a moment before saying, "The Blood Gala is a political affair."

"Yeah, I get that part."

"No, I don't think you do," he murmured, his eyes catching and holding mine.

My heart skipped a beat. "Okay." It came out on a whisper. Because the intensity in his gaze told me that I wasn't going to like whatever he intended to say next.

"Aflora, the Blood Gala is an annual event that celebrates the death of the Quandary Blocds. It's hosted by the Nacht family, and the sole purpose is for them to gloat over all the blood they've spilled. *That* is what I want you to observe."

CHAPTER ELEVEN

ZAKKAI

Aflora's silence confirmed she hadn't known the purpose of the Blood Gala. She wasn't a born Midnight Fae, so she didn't grow up with horror stories about the Quandary Bloods and our terrible intentions.

I nearly snorted.

The Nacht family had destroyed the sixth house of Midnight Fae. All for greed and power. Alas, that was a tale as old as time itself. Everyone sought control. However, Quandary Bloods were the ones born with it.

"What do you plan to do at the Blood Gala?" Aflora asked quietly.

"I already answered that," I replied.

"You expect me to believe you only want me to observe?"

"I don't expect anything from you," I admitted. "I'm asking if you'll attend with me so I can better explain our cause. That's all."

I meant it, too.

The Blood Gala was too obvious a place for us to attack. Besides, our disguises would already require an exorbitant amount of power. Adding violence to the mix wouldn't bode well for anyone involved.

She studied me, her blue eyes radiating intelligence. It made me want to peek inside her mind, to hear her thoughts. She often spoke them loudly, making it an easy task.

However, I waited for her to utter them out loud instead, content to continue holding her on my lap. She hadn't put up much of a fight, and I liked how she unconsciously leaned into my touch. Our bond had matured over the years, despite the masking spell.

Breaking it would hurt worse than making her forget—a fact my father seemed to happily disregard. Pain served as a teaching tool to him, one he used to strengthen my resolve.

But dismantling my connection to Aflora lacked a true purpose. If anything, remaining bonded empowered us both.

"I want to talk to my other mates," she said suddenly, causing me to frown. "What?"

"You want me to trust your intentions. I'm giving you a way to earn some of that trust. Let me talk to my mates, and I'll consider attending the Blood Gala."

She really wasn't in a position to negotiate with me. I could easily weave a compliance enchantment around her, then drag her to the event. However, a young, immature part of me longed to have her attend willingly.

That part of me was tied to the boy I used to be.

The boy who considered Aflora his best friend.

"You want to talk to your other mates," I repeated out loud, thinking through her request. This gave me an opportunity to show her my kinder side —a side I would likely only ever reveal to her. However, it would be on my terms, in an environment I could control.

Like the dream she just experienced with her mates.

Yes.

I could allow that.

It would not only win over her acquiescence, but it would also grant me an opportunity to learn more about her mates and their relationships with Aflora.

I nodded slowly, deciding on a path forward that would work for both of us. "All right. You can dream-walk with them. But you can't mention the Blood Gala. And I will be there to supervise."

She frowned. "That's hardly proving you're trustworthy."

"Trust works both ways, Aflora," I replied. "You show me that I can trust you, while I show you that you can trust me. Seems like a reasonable compromise to me."

"You want to kill Kols."

I wasn't going to lie to her. "I do."

"You can't do that in the dreams."

"Actually, I could," I told her, briefly considering the possibility. "But I won't." It would be horribly dissatisfying. And... "I won't use you to hurt your mates. That's not who I am."

Her eyebrows lifted. "Who you are?" She huffed a humorless laugh. "You attacked an academy filled with students, and the village. I'm pretty sure I know who you are by those actions alone."

"I vacated the Death Blood building before I cast a harmless spell that I knew would be fixed in a matter of hours. And I didn't attack the village," I corrected. "So, by your definition, you don't know me at all."

"You didn't attack the village?" Her brow furrowed. "But I felt your energy all over the street."

"The day you and Zephyrus went to visit?" Now it was my turn to release a laugh. "Star, what you sensed was my protection."

"I heard you laugh."

"Yeah, I found it endearing that you thought you could fight me," I admitted. "Similar to the episode a few hours ago."

She scowled, making my lips quirk upward.

When her eyes narrowed, I took pity on her and offered a more thorough explanation.

"The Elders attacked some known Quandary Blood supporters in the village, which is why the essence surrounding the crime was Elite Blood in nature. Then they left an enchanted gift behind, one meant for Quandary Bloods. You felt me protecting you against that spell. And I was amused because you were trying to fight my protection." I smoothed out her frown lines with my thumb. "I didn't attack the village, Aflora. Anrika is an old family friend."

"Anrika? The tavern owner?"

"The very one." I didn't know her as well as my father did, but she was a longtime supporter of our cause.

Aflora's full lips parted, drawing my focus to her mouth. "She said she knew about me… from an old friend."

"That'd be Zenaida," I murmured. "Shade's grandmother. They knew about our bonding, and Anrika actually knew your parents as well. She and Zurik, her mate, were the ones who helped my father and me escape. Only, the Elders discovered their actions, and, well, Zurik paid the ultimate price."

I swallowed, recalling the scene vividly. It was my first real exposure to the cruelty of the Midnight Fae Elders, and the council who bowed to their every whim.

"Zurik told the Elders that he forced Anrika to help him. They made her prove it somehow. I don't know the details, but it surrounded his death. I think they made her do it."

"That's horrible," Aflora breathed.

"That's just the tip of the iceberg," I said, giving her a squeeze. "Constantine Nacht favors the death penalty. In fact, I dare say he enjoys it. Why else would he insist on an annual gala that celebrates the extermination of an entire race of fae?"

Which beautifully brought us back to the topic at hand.

"All I want is a chance to show you why I am who I am, Aflora," I added softly. "I could force you. But I would prefer your willing participation."

"You criticize Constantine for favoring the death penalty, yet your intention is to kill his entire family," she replied. "Do you not see the fatal error in that thought process?"

I sighed. "The Nacht family is responsible for thousands of Midnight Fae deaths, Aflora."

"Kols isn't," she insisted. "He's not even the king yet."

"No, he's just the groomed heir destined to take over the violent reins from his father," I deadpanned. "His destiny is to become my biggest threat. We will duel. It's inevitable."

"You don't know him like I do," she whispered. "He's not okay with what his father and the Elders have done."

"Once he ascends, his personal feelings will no longer apply." I attempted to gentle my voice, but she flinched anyway. "Let's table this discussion for later and focus on our trust exercise. Take me to your mates. I'll behave in your dream. Maybe then you'll consider attending the gala with me."

She swallowed, her blue eyes widening. "R-right now?"

"It's an appropriate hour for dreaming," I said, noting the midday sun outside.

Of course, it was always sunny here. I'd made it that way to better hide our paradigm in this realm.

However, I could read the time because I knew the nuances of my creation. It was close to noon in the Midnight Fae realm, making it the dead of day for our kind. They would all be asleep, or should be, anyway. If they weren't, then her spell would pull them into dreamland.

I set her off to my side and made a show of sliding beneath the sheets before lifting the black silk in invitation.

"I promise I won't touch any of them. Unless they attack me, then I'll only defend myself." Like I'd done with Kolstov the first time around. He'd targeted my enchantment, and I'd retaliated. Seemed only fair, considering our dark fates.

She nibbled her lip again, then she slowly joined me. The sheets moving over her skin drew her focus to her exposed legs, her brow pulling down. "What am I wearing?"

"My shirt," I replied, amused that she had just now noticed. "Now lie down and take us to dreamland, Aflora. Once you're satisfied, we'll sleep."

Her brow crinkled as she settled her head on the pillow beside me, her blue eyes wary.

"I'm not going to hurt them," I repeated, doing my best to hide my irritation. All she needed to do was look into our bond to find my sincerity.

Did I want to hurt her mates? Sure.

Would I? Not yet. Perhaps not ever. At least where Shade and Zephyrus were concerned. The former amused me. The latter provided my mate with defensive magic. Both were worthy reasons to keep them alive.

Kolstov, however, would die. Just not tonight.

"Aflora?" I prompted when all she did was stare at me. "Do I need to repeat my promise a third time?"

"Uh, no." She cleared her throat. "It's just… I'm not sure… Well, I don't know how to…" She trailed off, her nose scrunching the way it used to when we were kids.

My lips curled. I loved that look on her. Part confusion, part annoyance. Not at me, but at herself. Which was how I figured out what she meant. "You don't know how to invade their dreams."

She shook her head slowly.

My smile grew. "How disingenuous of them. I know they've played in your mind countless times, yet no one ever showed you how to return the favor?"

"I learned how to take over, um, in my own ways."

Memories of her naked body beneath me populated my mind, heating my blood. "Oh, I'm very familiar with your methods, little star."

Her cheeks reddened. "I thought you were a figment."

"I know," I replied, slowly leaning forward to give her a chance to move. When she didn't, I lightly brushed my lips against hers in a chaste kiss.

She shivered in response, remaining still.

I considered that a minor victory and a prelude to our long battle ahead.

"Every bit of what I did to you was real," I whispered. "When you're ready for a live performance, let me know, and I'll show you what happens when I'm in control." I kissed her again—a bolder touch, but still soft—and pulled back to study her flushed cheeks.

She'd stopped breathing.

Not out of fear, but something similar.

Rather than push the subject, I decided to offer her another olive branch in the form of a lesson. "Close your eyes, Aflora. I'm going to teach you the dream charms."

CHAPTER TWELVE

AFLORA

My thumping heart made hearing Zakkai's whispered spell difficult. But I eventually caught on to what he wanted me to say, and uttered the incantation in my mind while focusing on Zeph. His proclivity for defensive magic made him an ideal candidate to fend off Zakkai should he choose to go against his promise.

I'm not going to hurt them, Zakkai murmured through our link. *You'll see.*

If you betray me, I'll never trust you, I replied.

I would never use you to hurt them because it would put you at risk, too. He uttered the words with such finality that, for a moment, I almost believed him on instinct.

Then my brain reminded me that he wanted to kill Kols, and I went back to being concerned about this dream.

It's not working, I said.

Because you're overthinking it and worrying about me instead of focusing on your Warrior Blood, he replied. *Just take a breath and relax, Aflora. Imagine where you want to go and try again.*

He made it sound so easy. Under any other circumstances, I would have agreed with him. But having him beside me and knowing what he intended to do made me wary to engage my mates.

A rush of emotion warmed my bond to Zakkai, the sensation catching me off guard as he flooded my mind with his thoughts.

All of them at once.

His frustration over me wasting time fretting over an inconsequential item, followed by his assurances that he meant me and the others no harm, and finalized by a surge of protective energy that highlighted his need to keep me safe.

That final strand of his thoughts displayed the conflict he refused to engage—harming my mates through my mind would harm me, too.

"And I won't do that," he said out loud. "Give me a chance, Aflora. You knew me once. I might not be that boy anymore, but my vow of protection still remains. Which my soul has proved these last few months. You've pulled on my powers more than once. I could have stopped you. But I've never put a leash on you. Or a collar."

Those three words made me shiver. "You know about that?"

"I could feel it," he replied through his teeth. "There were many moments that I wanted to find you, but I knew you weren't ready. That was the whole purpose of the song. The moment you sang those words, the countdown began. And here we are."

"You're being much more forthcoming now," I whispered, thinking about his riddles from earlier. Was that yesterday now? Did time really matter anymore?

"I've always been forthcoming, Aflora. Even in your dreams, I told you the truth."

"You phrased the truth as questions."

"Yes, to make you consider alternatives."

"You could have just voiced those alternatives," I pointed out.

I sensed his grin—something I couldn't see because my eyes were closed, but I *felt* it through our bond. Or perhaps it was just his amusement and my mind had created the image of his dimples. "There are a lot of things I could have done, little star. I think I deserve some credit for not taking advantage of a very willing situation."

My skin heated at the meaning in his tone. "I thought—"

"I know what you thought," he interjected. "Which is why it would have been so easy." His voice was like silk, wrapping around my nerves and drowning me in warm sensations.

I opened my eyes to find him hovering over me, his room no longer around us. Instead, we were lying on a bed of flowers, the earthy aroma heaven to my senses. "Ohh," I breathed, my soul rejoicing at the luscious offerings in the air.

Zakkai ran his lips across my cheek to my ear.

"Do you prefer this dream, little star?" he asked, his breath warm and enticing against my skin. "We could do whatever you want here. A fantasy. No rules. No dark destinies. Just us reveling in a bond we've never truly consummated." He kissed the sensitive pulse point of my neck, sending a jolt down my spine.

My thighs clenched around his muscular hips. He still wore his boxers, but nothing else. And I was naked beneath him—something that should have concerned me, but the bed of earth felt too good against my skin to complain.

"This…" I trailed off on a sigh as his lips met my collarbone.

"You know the spell," he said against my skin. "Either use it, or we'll stay here and play." He started a path downward to my breasts, causing my mind to blink in and out of focus as I fought to hold on to our purpose.

Zeph, I thought. *I'm supposed… to dream… of Zeph.*

"Tick-tock, Aflora," Zakkai murmured, his teeth skimming my nipple with the words. "Make a choice."

I threaded my fingers through his long white hair and pulled him back up to my mouth. "Stop distracting me."

He pressed his lips to mine, his palm resting against my cheek. *Make me,* he taunted into my mind, his tongue tracing a dangerous path along the seam of my mouth.

If I let him inside, I would lose all my senses.

Because Zakkai was a kissing god. I'd learned that in previous dreams. He knew how to render me utterly useless with his skilled tongue.

No, no, no, I thought, fighting for control.

Zeph had taught me better than this.

I focused on our mate-bond and the door blocking me from his mind. *Take it down!* I demanded, irritated by the block.

Not my spell to remove, Zakkai replied, his nose skimming my cheek. "Shade put it there, star," he whispered into my ear. "Dismantle it."

"Why did he put it there?"

"I imagine he's concerned that I might be able to access him and Zephyrus through your mind." He grazed my neck with his teeth, then focused on my pulse again.

"Can you do that?"

"I don't know," he murmured. "However, if Shade felt the need to block me, it suggests he's either foreseen the act or it's happened in another timeline."

"Timeline?" I repeated.

"Has he not told you about his penchant for playing with time?" Zakkai went to his elbows on either side of my head, his white hair falling like a curtain around me. "One of his best friends is a Paradox Fae. *Kyros.*"

"Tricksters," I whispered, recalling the time Shade had mentioned playing with a time-dweller. He'd been talking to Ajax about it before Advanced Conjuring class.

That'd been the day I picked up a rock and lived through the explosion at the Academy.

An explosion Zakkai had orchestrated.

"You planted the rock," I said, cold water rushing through my veins at the memory. "You made me live through the explosion."

Zakkai stared down at me with a note of confusion lurking in his blue eyes. "Which rock?"

"From Advanced Conjuring class."

"I'm not sure what you're talking about."

"Headmaster Irwin taught us a psychometry spell to call on the history of objects. My object was a rock from the explosion. I was you. I waved my wand and said, '*Alqisian,*' and a voice told me that this was my future—that I would one day be you."

Zakkai rolled off of me to lounge on his elbow at my side, his expression clouded. "Who was with you during this class?"

"Shade," I replied.

"Engage him in a dream first. I want to know what he felt."

I blinked at him, confused. "What he felt?"

"It wasn't me, Aflora. I'm curious if he knows who sent the rock or if he still has it. Knowing Shade, he pocketed it. Let's ask him, hmm?"

"But he…? I don't…?" I cleared my throat. "You didn't send the rock?"

"Not my style," he drawled. "Let's talk to Shade. He might be easier to connect to."

"Why?"

Zakkai lifted a shoulder. "Because he's welcome inside my wards."

"He is?"

"Death Bloods have always served Quandary Bloods. Most of them still do." He shrugged again. "It's why Death Bloods used to be the royals of the Midnight Fae. Quandary Bloods used Death Bloods to harness the source power. Many thought—and still believe—that Quandary Bloods were working for the Death Bloods. But that's never been the case."

That was… a lot of interesting information. But my thoughts had already returned to the rock. If Zakkai didn't send it to me, then who did? Was he lying? Maybe. Although, I wasn't sure what he had to gain by such a lie.

Unless he meant to goad me into dreaming up my mates.

No, that couldn't be right. It'd been my idea from the beginning. Well, not an idea, but a demand. And I was wasting all this time debating it rather than acting on it.

I shook my head, clearing it, and closed my eyes to focus on Zeph again. Zakkai had requested Shade, but I wanted my Warrior Blood mate first. He wasn't the one who had willingly handed me over. While I knew a reasonable explanation existed—or I hoped one did—I hadn't forgiven Shade yet. I'd consider it after he told me why he'd made that decision.

The connection between me and Zeph was riddled with purple lines. *Shade's spell.*

I poked at it and studied the structure.

It was a solid enchantment. But I could see the minuscule threads at the end—the ones that allowed me to slowly unweave and learn the spell.

I considered stopping, aware that Shade had put this here to block Zakkai, but if I could unravel it, so could my Quandary Blood mate. That made it all a moot point and more of a hindrance than a necessity.

"Very good, Aflora," Zakkai whispered.

His words momentarily distracted me from my goal, causing the band to snap back in place. "Stop spying on me."

"I'm not spying," he replied, his knuckles brushing my cheek. "I can just feel your magic. You're a natural."

"You mean an abomination," I corrected, peeking at him.

He smirked. "You say that like it's a bad thing. Which I suppose you've been taught to believe, but that's an erroneous assessment driven by those in power."

"Shade once said something similar. He said those in charge don't like crossbreeding."

"He's right," Zakkai murmured, his touch drifting down to my throat. "Go back to your task, Aflora. I promise not to interrupt again."

I considered him for a moment, then closed my eyes again.

Shade's magic reappeared immediately, my affinity for puzzles flaring to life. Zakkai's hand left my collarbone to drift down my arm, where he linked our hands, his magic flourishing through my veins in response.

I engaged my link to him while playing with Shade's threads, my mind memorizing the magic in case I needed to replace it. Zakkai would still be able to undo it, but maybe I could add a few enhancements to slow him down.

If that was even needed.

His protective energy seemed to hum around me, assuring me that he wouldn't put me at risk. It could all be a lie. But a childlike part of me wanted to believe him. To test him. To see if he meant it.

His thumb whispered over my wrist, the touch reassuring.

"If this is all a trick, I'll hate you forever," I whispered as I tugged on the final strand of Shade's spell.

Zakkai didn't reply.

I nearly halted as a result but decided there was only one way to really know his intentions. So I pushed through the link to Zeph's mind and hummed the spell Zakkai had taught me.

Tanoomeen Ma Ana.

Energy buzzed around me as I pictured the place I wanted—the park in New York City that he'd taken me to—and I opened my eyes to find him leaning against a tree in jeans and a button-down shirt. His green eyes narrowed at me before looking over my shoulder. "What is this?"

"I believe they call it a dream," Zakkai drawled as he stepped up to my back to wrap his arms around my waist. "Well done, little star," he whispered against my ear before dropping a kiss beneath my ear.

I tensed, waiting for him to say or do more, but all he did was hold me, his warmth a blanket of comfort against my back.

Zeph studied us beneath his intense gaze, his lips flattened into a line. "Who created the dream?" he finally said after a long minute of silence.

I swallowed. "Um, I did." I thought that would be obvious by the scenery, but I could see where he might think Zakkai had manufactured it from a memory in my head. The Quandary Blood was fond of playing with my mind, after all.

He gently nibbled my earlobe. "I heard that."

"Stay out of my head," I replied.

"That's not part of our arrangement, star. When dreaming, I'll be monitoring all communication and thoughts. It's a trust exercise, remember?"

My lips twisted as Zeph further narrowed his gaze. "Trust exercise?" he repeated.

"He agreed to let me dream-walk with my mates in exchange for—"

"It's a test of trust," Zakkai interjected. "I'm proving that I won't harm you via her connection to you." *You can't tell them about the Blood Gala,* he added into my mind. *They can't know about our plans to attend.*

Oh. Right. I cleared my throat. "He's trying to make me more agreeable."

"You look pretty agreeable to me," Zeph replied, his gaze dropping to Zakkai's arms around my waist. "He's had you for, what, a day? And you're already allowing him to teach you spells?"

The admonishment in his tone made me bristle a bit. "If I recall right, I let you whisk me off to a magical wardrobe shop during our first day together."

"You didn't *let* me do anything, Aflora. You protested everything, even the spaghetti."

"You don't like spaghetti?" Zakkai interjected, sounding amused.

"She doesn't like a lot of things," Zeph informed him flatly, pushing off the tree. "Why am I really here, Quandary Blood? What spell have you woven through her mind?"

"Several," Zakkai replied. "But this dream is all her. I don't even know where we are."

Zeph snorted. "You expect me to believe that? After you put Kols in a magical coma?"

"Kols is in a coma?" I repeated on a gasp. I spun around in Zakkai's arms. "You promised not to hurt anyone!"

Zakkai rolled his eyes. "I didn't hurt him. He attacked my spell and I retaliated, just as I said I would do. And that happened in your initial dream, not this one. He's also perfectly fine."

Zeph came to stand right beside me, his focus on Zakkai. "He was unconscious in his bed seconds ago."

"Last time I checked, naps weren't painful," my Quandary Blood mate drawled. "Bring him into the dream, Aflora. Have him confirm for himself."

"Don't," Zeph warned. "It's a trap."

Zakkai just shook his head. "You should have started with Shade. He's much more agreeable."

I considered them both, my mind reaching through the connection to read both mates. Zeph's innate distrust hit me square in the heart, while Zakkai's essence boasted tranquility and sincerity.

I met his silver-blue eyes, studying him intently.

It was a risk.

One I needed to take to know the truth.

"*Tanoomeen Ma Ana,*" I whispered, my mind focusing on Kols to bring him into the dream.

CHAPTER THIRTEEN

SHADE

I studied Kols and Zeph on the bed and frowned.

Aflora's essence flourished around them, her magic weaving a dream spell that held them both captive to her mind.

Zakkai must have shown her how to do that, but I couldn't figure out why. He'd never willingly allowed her to dance in the dreams of her mates before.

Of course, this was the most she'd ever bonded to any of us. At least as far as I knew.

Would this finally be the rendition of our fate that worked? Or was this a sign of the ultimate failure?

A Paradox Fae couldn't fix death—something Kyros and Tadmir had both warned me about from the very beginning. Once a life strand ended, it couldn't be brought back into a timeline.

Not without an anchor, anyway.

And I wasn't even sure if that could work.

I considered the two men on the bed, debating my next move. I wanted to join them. I also needed to talk to Ajax.

Every other avenue I'd tried had failed, and I finally figured out why—they all revolved around Aflora. So I was playing with a new path that Zakkai wouldn't be able to sense. A path that wasn't tied to him at all.

Another risk.

Another potentially horrid fate.

But I was running out of options.

A tug at my consciousness had me glancing at the bed again. Aflora was unweaving my block, her power seeming to have grown overnight.

Because of Zakkai.

I sighed. She was ahead of schedule. I expected it to take her at least another week to break my barriers. At least she would know how to throw them back up when the time came.

With a wave of my wand, I conjured my phone and shot a message off to Ajax, telling him I wanted to meet up later tonight. I had to handle this dream first, as well as visit with Chern—he expected me to show up in an hour to discuss methods of tracking Aflora—and then I could continue my exploration of the alternative plan.

Rest was for the weak.

And I didn't have time for weakness.

So I lay down on the bed near Kols and shut my eyes, giving in to Aflora's call.

Little rose, I said into her mind as I materialized beside her and Zakkai. *Central Park is an interesting choice.*

So you can hear me, she replied, her blue eyes glowing with power.

I can always hear you, I murmured, sliding my hands into the pockets of my jeans. Another interesting choice. We were all similarly dressed in casual attire, like we were preparing for a stroll around the park. If only it would be this easy. "Zakkai."

"Shade," he returned. "I need the rock from your Advanced Conjuring class."

It was just like Zakkai to deliver a command with his greeting. In this case, it was an unexpected demand. "Are you talking about the one that sucked all the life out of Aflora? The one you gave her?"

"I didn't give it to Aflora," he replied, his brow furrowing. "And what do you mean, it sucked the life out of her?"

"She nearly passed out from the spell. And your essence was all over it."

"You attacked the Death Blood building?" Kols asked, his tone holding a touch of that arrogant annoyance he favored.

Zakkai ignored him in favor of me. "Drop the rock in our usual place. I want to review the magic."

"Sure. I'll just add it to my growing to-do list," I drawled.

The Quandary Blood arched a haughty white brow. "Today."

I lifted a shoulder. "Why not?" I had no intention of sleeping, anyway. I shifted my focus to Aflora, her cerulean gaze guarded. "Is he treating you all right?"

"Do you care?" she countered.

"You know I do, little rose." I reached out to tug on one of her loose strands of hair and gave her a half smile. *It's okay, Aflora. I can take your hatred.*

I don't hate you, Shade, she whispered back. *But I'm not happy with you.*

I can take that, too, I replied, my heart skipping a beat at the softness in her voice. I expected her ire, not her understanding.

She stepped away from Zakkai to wrap her arms around me. *I'm still mad,* she warned as I returned the hug. *But you're still my mate, Shade.*

I kissed the top of her head and met Zeph's surprised gaze. He clearly hadn't expected this. And he confirmed that by narrowing his eyes at Zakkai.

"Okay, now I know this is all bullshit. Why have you brought us here? To lull us into a false sense of comfort?"

Zakkai merely looked at him and walked over to slide down a tree trunk. A hum of energy told me he'd whispered something into Aflora's mind. Whatever it was had her glancing over her shoulder at him.

Silence fell as they communicated, then she nodded slowly and turned in my arms to face Zeph.

"Kai wants to teach me more about Quandary magic," she said slowly. "In exchange for my willing cooperation, he'll let me dream of you all."

Kai, I repeated to myself, glancing at the Quandary Blood. He'd worked much faster to unravel her reservations this time. Because I'd given her to him? Or because he was playing a new game?

He smirked at me, then closed his eyes as though to take a nap.

"I'm supposed to believe that?" Zeph asked, drawing my attention back to him. "Try again, Aflora."

"I don't know what you want me to say," she replied. "He wants me to cooperate. I demanded access to my mates in return for that cooperation. Is this really that hard to believe, Zeph? He won't let me leave. You can't visit. So I'm doing what I can to see you."

"I'm finding it hard to believe that he would allow you to see us without a catch," Zeph replied.

"There's absolutely a catch," I agreed. "But I suspect we don't know what it is yet."

Zakkai's lips quirked up in response, his eyes still closed.

"He wants to kill Kols," Zeph stressed.

"And the entire Nacht line," Zakkai agreed, his tone soft and lazy. "Maybe I want to give Aflora the chance to say goodbye to her mate."

"You're not killing Kols," she snapped.

Zakkai just spread his hands in response as though to say, *It is what it is*.

"As much fun as it is to discuss my impending doom—an experience I will be declining—I have a suggestion." Kols had remained uncharacteristically quiet throughout the exchange.

I suspected it was because of the power circling around him in a cloud of protection, one meant to retaliate the moment Zakkai attempted anything. He was the future king, after all. The source naturally guarded him.

However, the source wasn't actually his to command—a lesson he would eventually learn from Zakkai. Assuming it came to that. Again.

The Quandary Blood opened his eyes. "I enjoy suggestions."

"Good. Because I think you'll approve of this one," Kols replied, his arrogance rivaling that of the Source Architect on the ground. "The Council and the Elders used Aflora as bait. Now they want to track her through Shade. I suspect you already knew that would happen and have safeguards in place to protect yourself and her. My suggestion is we work together to keep Aflora safe. With you. And we'll use the nightly dreams to regroup with next steps."

"So your suggestion is to maintain the status quo by allowing me to keep

Aflora—a situation you have absolutely no control over anyway and can't alter. Sure. That works for me." Zakkai closed his eyes again.

"My suggestion is to accept where we are and not waste time fighting it," Kols reiterated. "And to instead discuss a future resolution."

I blinked, this twist of fate straightening my spine.

Aflora caught my movement because her back was pressed to my chest. *What is it?*

Kols has never offered to work with Zakkai before, I told her, unable to hide my shock. *They usually just… fight.*

The Quandary Blood's eyelids lifted as he studied the Midnight Fae Prince. "Future resolution? And what would that look like for you, *Nacht?*"

"Well, for one, it would be a future where Aflora lives. Which is not what the Council or the Elders have in mind." His tone held a note of irritation that he usually reserved for me. It was rather nice to hear it directed at someone else for a change. "I think we can all agree that some changes in the hierarchical structure are needed. I'm not sure what those should look like yet, as I've only recently become aware of the challenges, but I am open to discussing them."

"And if I say the only way any of this will ever work is for the entire Nacht family line to die, you'll agree?" Zakkai drawled, his eyebrow inching upward once more. He waited a beat before smiling and saying, "Yeah, I didn't think so."

"Death isn't always the solution," Aflora murmured. "Unless you want to take over the mantle of slaughtering and ending lives?"

Zakkai's eyes shifted to our mate. "Retribution requires sacrifice."

"So does reformation," she countered. "Sometimes we have to sacrifice our desire for revenge to find a more efficient path forward."

My lips parted at her statement.

It sounded like something my grandmother would say.

Zakkai's expression said he felt similarly. He snorted and went back to his nap. "Indulge your mates, Aflora. Then we need some sleep before your classes tomorrow. Your new headmaster won't go easy on you."

"Changing the subject doesn't solve anything," she muttered. "And what class are you talking about?"

"Quandary Magic 101," he replied. "With me as your personal tutor."

"What about her other courses?" Zeph asked. "She's still learning defensive and offensive skills."

"Use the dreams," Zakkai said, yawning. "Or don't. But I'm not letting you into the paradigm. Not while you're tied to the Elite Blood."

Kols and Zeph shared a long look. They couldn't speak mentally, but I sensed they were conversing in another way. Perhaps via their eyes alone.

"Aflora will stay where she is," Kols said. "We won't fight about it but will instead help Shade conceal her location. This is for her personal safety more than anything else."

"And we'll train in the dreams," Zeph added. "So she can better defend herself should something change or happen."

"And we will discuss as a unit how to move forward," Aflora said, her focus on Zakkai.

The Quandary Blood held her gaze.

And she held his back, standing before him like the queen she would one day become.

A tendril of hope curled around my heart, the notion that we might all work together a dream that had always been so far out of reach.

I allowed it to flourish for three seconds. Just long enough to spread a trickle of warmth through my veins.

Then I recalled all the histories where I'd failed.

I couldn't afford to hope.

Not until the end.

"Okay, sweet star," Zakkai said softly. "I'll agree to those terms for now."

His words sent a chill down my spine. Not because of the way he spoke them, but because of the implication behind them.

They'd just struck a deal.

One none of us could hear.

But I knew what she'd just agreed to.

The Blood Gala.

In ten days, our fates would be decided.

Again.

CHAPTER FOURTEEN

KOLS

"I don't like this."

Zeph uttered a variation of those four words after every dream session with Aflora this week. I definitely preferred the fantasies where we all ended up naked. But that was impossible to do with Zakkai observing from the corner.

The Quandary Blood rarely spoke. However, his presence was absolutely felt.

This arrangement couldn't last forever, as evidenced by Zeph pacing beside me.

"Come back to bed," I told him. "There are still a few more hours before we need to leave. We should try to get some proper sleep." While the dreams technically allowed our bodies to rest, it kept our minds vividly engaged. Which left us tired after endless lessons in Aflora's head.

"How the hell am I supposed to sleep when that Quandary Blood has our mate?"

"He's one of her mates, too," I reminded him.

"And you're okay with that?" Zeph demanded, spinning around to face me. "How are you not raging over this, Kols? You've been the epitome of calm, like this means nothing to you. I don't get it."

"Like it means nothing to me?" I repeated, arching a brow. "This means *everything* to me, Zeph."

"Yet, you didn't even react to the fact that Dakota is there. Did you miss the part about her attacking Aflora?"

Not this again. "What do you want me to do? Rant and rave? We both know I want to kill that power-hungry cunt. And I will if I ever see her again." Not just because she'd apparently hurt Aflora, but also because of our past experience. She was like a fire gnat that just didn't know how to bugger off.

"Then how the hell do you expect either of us to sleep? I can barely focus, let alone try to relax." He resumed his pacing. "We've just accepted that he took our mate to a paradigm in some undisclosed location, surrounded by fae whom we don't know, and *Dakota* is there. And we haven't done a damn thing to fix it. Not to mention all the bullshit with the Council and the Elders."

He ran his fingers through his dark hair, his torso flexing with the movement.

Zeph had logged a lot of hours at the gym this week, and it showed. He was already solid muscle. But now those muscles were all tensed and fired up.

"Are you even listening to me?" he demanded, his green eyes flaring with power.

"I'm listening," I said. *And admiring,* I added to myself. "I'm not sure what you expect me to do. I don't like the situation, but Aflora is safer with Zakkai at the moment. We can't properly protect her with my father and Constantine breathing down my neck."

As it was, we'd already been summoned for a visit with my father later tonight. He wanted to discuss the final preparations for the Blood Gala. And in a strange twist of fate, he'd required that Zeph travel back with me to Nacht Manor.

"Safer," he drawled, his disdain coloring the word in a darker tone. "I'm not sure I agree with that assessment, given his track record at the Academy and in the village."

"Aflora said that wasn't him, but the Council setting a trap." Considering everything else they'd done, I didn't find that very difficult to believe.

"Yes, bringing us to an entirely different topic and issue—she seems to be buying into his bullshit, which has me seriously questioning her intelligence."

I sighed. "You don't really mean that." We'd come too far for him to truly feel that way about Aflora. "You know she's brilliant. You also know she's not one to trust easily. She's been burned too many times. *By us.*"

"Are you saying we deserve this?" he asked, green fire flickering along his fingertips. "That this is some sort of fucked-up punishment for all the errors we've made?"

"No, Zeph. I'm saying that we need to trust our mate." I rolled off the bed and stepped into his path, forcing him to stop.

"Don't."

I touched him anyway, not afraid of his simmering temper. He could take it out on me however he wanted. We both could use a good sparring session. Or maybe a fuck.

"Look, we've already established that she can't leave him without a fight, and we've also established that we don't have a safe place for her here. The Council and the Elders plan to kill her once she proves unuseful. And from what I understand, Zakkai will track her down even if we manage to rescue her. So why not work with him to protect her while we figure out the larger issue, hmm?"

His jaw flexed as he clenched his teeth. "What makes you think Zakkai isn't the larger issue?"

"I think he'll become one eventually," I admitted. "But the Council and the Elders are more pressing right now." Case in point, the writhing power dancing up and down my arms. "I'm supposed to ascend a throne riddled with corruption."

"You've known that for years."

"Not the extent of it," I replied as my hands drifted down his bare arms. "I've been blind to the larger issues, just accepting it all because there's been no alternative. And now, I have no idea what I'm going to do. I'm partially mated to Aflora. Shade just bit me, too. I still have three ascension trials left, plus the one I'm currently failing. My grandfather wants to postpone my inheritance of the throne as a result, and I think my father is considering it, too. So what do I do, Zeph? Do I run? Do *we* run? Go hide in a paradigm?"

I shook my head and took a step back to sit on the bed again, my head in my hands.

"I have no idea who I am anymore." Everything I thought I knew had been turned on its head since Aflora arrived. Part of me hated her for it. A smarter part of me acknowledged that it wasn't her fault at all. She was just the culminating event that turned my world upside down.

"You're Prince Kolstov," Zeph said.

"And what does that mean?" I asked him, my forearms falling to my thighs as I looked up at him through my mess of auburn strands. "We both know I can't ascend. Not with my links to Aflora and Shade."

"You think the source will reject you as king?"

"Not the source, no," I muttered. "The Council. The Elders. All of Midnight Fae kind. They'll all reject me." I'd be lucky if they didn't kill me for this.

And yet, I didn't regret a moment of it.

"I've given up so much for them. My identity. My *life*. Every moment of every day has been about my future as the king. Yet they put me on trial for the Academy incident, all the while knowing it wasn't me at all. They never apologized or even acknowledged the oversight. Meanwhile, they were busy attacking the village and framing Zakkai?" I phrased it as a question because we had no proof yet, other than what Zakkai had told Aflora. However, it was an easy accusation to believe given everything else.

"He could be lying," Zeph pointed out. It'd been his immediate reaction the other night when Aflora told us what Zakkai had said about the village. He also apparently hadn't left that rock for her in Advanced Conjuring class.

"He could be lying," I repeated, agreeing with Zeph. "But why would he? What does he get out of it?"

"Aflora's cooperation," Zeph replied. "Which seems to be what he wants. Hence, the dreams."

"Maybe, but he has to know she'll hate him if she discovers he lied."

"You assume her hatred would bother him."

I considered it, frowning. "Wouldn't it bother you? As her mate?"

"I'm not Zakkai."

"No, you're not," I consented. "But given everything the Council and the

Elders have been hiding, I find it reasonably easy to believe that they were behind it." I also trusted Aflora's instincts. She hadn't elaborated on why she believed Zakkai, but I didn't need her to.

And neither did Zeph.

It was just in his protective nature to question everything and everyone. My Guardian required control, and there was no aspect of this situation that he could own or manage. *That* was what had him upset.

He resumed his pacing again, his shoulders tense.

Helplessness was not a good look on him. I felt it, too, but I'd grown up in a world where I had no say in my future. Everything had been mapped out for me before I took my first breath. I'd just been walking the path ever since, following each directive to the letter.

And for what?

To find out I stood at the front lines of a war I thought ended over a thousand years ago. Not only that, but they expected me to fight as well. To kill. To harness the source power and use it to assassinate those who technically created it.

Fuck. "I need a distraction," I said, looking around. "*We* need a distraction." Everything around us was going up in flames, and we were sitting in the corner with our hands behind our backs, watching it all burn.

I stood again, stepping right into Zeph as he moved forward midstride. His irises flared with power. He wanted to hurt something. I could see that need lurking in his gaze.

"Use me," I told him. "Take it out on me."

"No."

"Do it, Zeph." I wrapped my hand around the back of his neck and grabbed his hip with my opposite palm. "Destroy me."

"*No.*"

"Stubborn dick," I said, crushing my mouth against his.

He threaded his fingers through my hair, yanking hard to pull me away, but I sank my teeth into his lower lip to hold on.

He growled.

I growled back.

It was either this or we sparred, and the latter would destroy a lot of shit.

This would at least provide us with a necessary release.

My name rolled off his tongue, the warning clear.

I accepted it as a challenge and kissed him again. This time he bit me, drawing my blood. It should have given me pause, forced me to stop, but instead I fed the essence into his mouth with my tongue and tightened my grip on his nape.

He snarled in response, my blood providing the boost of power I knew he craved.

As my Guardian, he could bite me as often as he wanted. Imbibing my essence had been a key part of his fealty bond when we were younger.

But there was one thing I'd never done—I'd never bitten him back.

It would snap a mating bond into place, one that would further tie us together for eternity. My incisors ached to do just that.

Because why the fuck not? If Shade could bond me, then I could bond with Zeph. We were already vowed to one another anyway. Might as well take it to the next level.

I captured his gaze, then sank my teeth into his bottom lip again, this time hard enough to make him bleed.

His eyes widened. "Kols…"

I made a show of licking the wound and swallowing, eliciting a sharp gasp from him. I'd shocked him. Fuck, I'd shocked myself.

This was reckless.

Crude.

So fucking wrong.

But I didn't give a damn.

He shook his head in disbelief, his eyes wide with a myriad of emotions. "You shouldn't have done that."

I shrugged. I'd already ruined everything, so why not create my own inferno to burn in? "Kiss me," I demanded.

"No."

"*Fuck*, Zeph." I sucked his lip into my mouth, laving the wound and holding his gaze as I did it.

His nostrils flared.

So I repeated the action.

Then I created a new wound, biting him again, and he hissed in response. "*Kolstov*."

"Zephyrus," I returned. "Shall I go for a third? I mean, why not at this point, right?"

His nostrils flared, his chest heaving against mine. Then he tightened his grip in my hair and yanked me into a kiss underlined in feral energy. I groaned, the taste of him addictive and perfect and sweetened by Aflora's essence.

I could sense her in him, her energy an addictive flavor I missed with every ounce of my soul.

Her life thrummed through me as I swallowed more of Zeph's blood. I could feel her inside me, as though she blessed our union with her presence.

Except she wasn't here.

And I *missed* her.

"Tell her what we're doing," I groaned as Zeph walked me backward to the bed. "*Tell her*."

"I already have," he replied, his fingers still in my hair, his lips brushing mine. "She can feel it."

"What is she saying?"

"It's making her hot." He smiled with the words, then trailed his tongue along my lower lip. "She wishes she were here."

"I wish she were here, too," I admitted.

"Get on the bed, Kols. Lose the boxers." The command in his tone was one I wanted to counter, but I knew he needed the control right now.

I'd told him to take it out on me, to *use* me. And the look in his eyes told me he was going to do exactly that.

So I followed his command to the letter, kicking off my black boxer briefs and sliding onto the center of the bed. He grabbed the lube from my nightstand and tossed it to me. I caught it in my fist, then arched a brow at him, waiting.

His jaw ticked.

He usually preferred my mouth, but I sensed his need for something else tonight.

"She can feel the new connection," Zeph said.

"Is she okay with it?"

"Yes." He knelt on the bed. "She didn't realize Shade had bitten you, but she sees it now. She says she feels closer to you."

"I feel closer to her, too," I admitted, my gaze dropping to his dick. The fabric barely contained him, his boxers stretched tight across his hardening length.

"I'm going to fuck you," he said, his voice dark with unhindered emotion.

"I know."

"I'm not going to be nice about it."

I smiled. "I know."

"Get up on your knees."

CHAPTER FIFTEEN

ZEPH

If you were here right now, I'd make you suck Kols's cock, I said into Aflora's mind. *He's hard as fuck, pixie flower. Even has a little bit of cum on the tip for you to lick off.*

I reached beneath him to swipe at the moisture with my thumb, then brought it to my lips.

Aflora moaned through my thoughts as I described his essence to her in exquisite detail. *Zephyrus...*

Yes?

You're making me want to… to do things to myself.

Then touch yourself, I said. "Aflora wishes you were in her mouth right now," I told Kols. "Next time we're together, I want her to suck you off while I fuck you."

His shaft visibly pulsed with the words as I settled onto my knees behind him. He looked good like this, up on all fours before me. I leaned forward to press a kiss to his spine, aware that this wasn't his favorite position.

But he was doing this for me.

To give me an outlet.

To provide me with a semblance of control.

Thank you, I said with my mouth, kissing his back again as I stroked my hand up and down his outer thigh. Then I switched focus in my mind, engaging the connection that Aflora had left open these last few days. I could sense her guarding it, waiting for Zakkai to potentially abuse it, but so far, he'd remained out of my head and out of our connection.

Are you touching yourself, Aflora? I asked her as I retrieved the lube from the bed. Kols shivered as I popped the cap. I squeezed a little into my hand, then reached around to stroke his shaft, teasing him. *I'm touching Kols,* I added softly. *He's groaning quite loudly.*

I gave him a little twist on the end, catching more of the precum in my hand.

Then I applied the lube to the crease of his ass and dropped the container onto the bed.

Aflora, I hummed. *I'm starting to prepare Kols's ass for my cock. He's almost as tight as your cunt.*

She breathed something incoherent into my mind, making me smile. It was almost like she was with us, her excitement vibrating our bond.

What are you doing, pixie flower? Are you fingering yourself while I finger-fuck Kols?

"What's she saying?" he asked, groaning as I applied a little more pressure with a scissoring motion inside him.

"She's playing with herself," I said, sensing her mounting pleasure. "She's mimicking my pace with her own hand."

"*Fuck.*" He arched as I gave him a harsher pump, his skin flushing with his restraint.

"Don't you dare come," I said, repeating the words in my mind to Aflora. "I know it's been a while, but we're prolonging this."

"Dick," Kols muttered.

I squeezed his shaft. "Yes," I agreed, shoving my fingers deeper into him, preparing him for the inevitable.

Tell me where you are, Aflora. What you're doing. Describe it to me.

I could feel her swallowing in response, her heat a welcome embrace through our connection. *I'm in the shower,* she whispered, as though afraid of getting caught. *I'm... I'm up against the wall. My legs keep threatening to buckle.*

Where are your hands?

One is holding me up, she replied, her voice husky and so damn sweet. *The other is between my legs.*

Doing what, pixie flower? I want all the details. How many fingers are you using?

Two, she admitted.

Make it three, I said, adding a third digit to Kols's ass.

He clamped down around me in response, so I tugged on his cock a little to loosen him up. "I warned you that I wouldn't be nice."

"*I. Know.*" He ground out the words, his body tense and hot. I leaned down to kiss his spine again, unable to hold back the gratitude in my touch. He was sacrificing a lot in this position, allowing me all the power and essentially bowing to me when it should be the other way around.

I tried to ease my pace a little, but he growled, aware of my intent.

"Don't you fucking dare," he said. "Give me everything, Zeph. We both know I can take it."

"You can," I agreed, removing my fingers to tug down my boxers. "I hope you're ready."

"I am."

He wasn't.

Not quite.

But he wouldn't fight me on this. It'd been too long for all of us, and with Aflora's panting in my mind and Kols's sacrifice below, I was gone to the moment. I aligned myself with his hips and thrust inside, eliciting a hiss of pain from Kols that quickly turned into a groan as I reached around him again to pump his cock.

I draped myself over him, needing his touch, his warmth, his *soul*.

Then I grasped his hip with my other hand and began to move.

I detailed it all to Aflora in my mind, telling her my pace, describing Kols's responding sounds, told her we were sweating and fucking with a raw intensity that threatened to destroy us all.

She had three fingers insides her tight sheath, mimicking the motion, her little moans music through our bond.

"She's close," I told Kols.

"So am I," he groaned, his arousal throbbing against my palm in agreement.

"Not yet." I wanted us to unravel together, to reignite the threads of our bonds and rekindle the dying flame between us.

Perhaps it was all in my mind—a consequence of our distance.

But I needed this shared moment to renew the hope inside me.

Zeph, Aflora moaned. *Please. I need to come.*

Oh, her voice was perfect. That refreshing kiss of fate I needed inside to tug me over the edge as Kols clamped down around me, urging me to fuck him harder and faster.

The two of them together shoved me to the precipice of oblivion, causing me to nearly lose sight of our goal. But my determination snapped into place, reining me in just long enough to say, *"Now."*

Heat swarmed through my veins as Aflora detonated in my mind, then Kols jolted beneath me, his orgasm spilling into my palm and forcing me to fall over the cliff with him into a heart-stopping climax.

Reality escaped me.

Oblivion welcomed me.

The fucking stars brightened for me.

And for one fantastic moment, everything was perfect, as it should be, the three of us lost to the throes of passion in unison with one another.

I fucking miss you, Aflora, I said, falling onto Kols, my energy depleted, my soul calming for the first time this week.

I miss you both, too, she replied as I rolled Kols onto his side to spoon in the bed. He trembled, his back to my chest, and I held him through the aftermath of our brutality. I kissed his shoulder and his neck, whispered gratitude in his ear, and stroked his abdomen.

Submitting didn't come naturally to him.

And I wanted him to know that I understood and cherished the gift.

He'd bitten me. *Twice.* Forced me to fuck him. Knowing it was what I needed to be able to finally relax. "I don't deserve you," I told him softly, kissing the sensitive spot of his neck. "But I'll never stop trying to be good enough for you."

He shook his head. "You've always been good enough for me, Zeph. For Aflora, too."

I could sense her humming in agreement, her mind somehow having caught our conversation. Or maybe I'd played it back to her. I couldn't tell anymore. We were all so connected, so *bonded*, that I gave up trying to understand the nuances of our connections.

Instead, I allowed the security of that link to lull me into sleep.

With Kols in my arms.

Aflora in my mind.

And warmth thriving in my heart.

CHAPTER SIXTEEN

I pressed my cheek to the cold tile of the shower, my legs trembling from the power of the orgasm that had just threatened to consume my entire soul.

Zeph had quieted, his thoughts turning to sleep.

I was supposed to be preparing for another day of training with Zakkai, and I could barely walk. The release hadn't been enough. Not after everything he'd said and done in my mind.

Kols and Zeph were always hot together, but their bond had intensified everything somehow.

I couldn't believe they'd bitten each other.

And Shade? When had he bitten Kols? *Why* had he bitten him? That didn't seem like the Death Blood at all. They hated each other.

I swallowed, shaking my head, and turned off the water. Then I slumped against the wall. "*Fae*," I breathed, my heart racing in my chest. That'd been an intense ride, and I hadn't even been there.

It took several more breaths for me to find enough courage to move.

I wrapped myself in a towel, then stepped out of the bathroom into Zakkai's room.

To find him lounging on the bed in a pair of jeans and a fitted black sweater, his expression knowing. "Have a nice shower, Aflora?" he asked, his silver-blue gaze sparkling.

I cleared my throat. "It was adequate," I replied, my voice huskier than I intended.

"Only adequate?" He arched a brow. "That makes me wonder what you sound like when you're truly satisfied, then."

My cheeks heated. I hadn't exactly held back in the shower, too lost to the moment to remember his presence just outside the door.

"It also leads me to believe that I was only 'adequate' in our previous dreams. Perhaps I need more practice."

"I'm sure Dakota would be happy to oblige," I replied as I went to pick up my wand. The words just sort of slipped from my mouth, the Elite Blood an annoyance lurking in my mind.

She was *everywhere*.

At lunch.

At dinner.

Showing up during my training sessions with Zakkai.

She'd apologized early on, saying I'd frightened her with my power. It was an utter wallop berry, one I refused to swallow. Because nothing about her struck me as genuine.

Zakkai smirked. "Oh, she's offered several times. But she's not my type."

"Pretty, powerful, and willing?" I replied before murmuring a spell to exchange my towel for a skirt and blouse combo. I added boots next and then another collar of green, red, and purple strands.

"I love watching you enchant your wardrobe," he said, his eyes running over me. "I only wish you'd magic them onto the bed, then put them on slowly for my benefit. It's not like I haven't already seen you naked countless times."

"Then you shouldn't mind missing this opportunity." I finished my ensemble with a cloak and slid my wand inside while he watched. "What lesson are you teaching me today?"

"Hopefully one with my mouth."

It seemed he had a one-track mind. Just like my other mates. "Spells usually require oral skills, yes," I told him, smiling. "So I do hope you'll use your mouth and voice."

"Maybe I'll growl instead, right against your clit," he countered, rolling off the bed and sauntering toward me on bare feet.

It was a distinctly sexy look with his long white hair loose around his shoulders, framing his dark sweater that led to fitted jeans.

So casual.

At home.

Comfortable.

He cupped my cheek with his palm, his skin hot against mine. "My offer remains, Aflora. Just let me know when you have use for my mouth, and it's yours for as long as you want it." He leaned in to brush his lips against mine. "As for today's lesson, we're going outside. There's someone I want you to meet."

He slipped his hand into my cloak to retrieve my wand and used it to give himself a pair of brown boots and a leather jacket. Then he returned it to my pocket with a wink.

"Let's go." He turned, expecting me to follow.

Which I did because he'd said one of my favorite words. *Outside.*

I'd been dying to explore the exterior of this castle, but I hadn't been able to find a single door. And whenever I wandered too far away from Zakkai, a spell lassoed my waist and yanked me back to his side.

We wandered through the labyrinth of stone-and-glass hallways, my eyes drifting over the torches and exterior the whole time. It really was beautiful here. Unique, too. The flames danced along the walls like a strand of lights, their underlying color a cerulean blue. Doors sporadically appeared—all with proper handles and no gargoyles—and the windows seemed to be strategically placed to allow for maximum viewing potential of the outdoors.

"Where exactly are we?" I wondered out loud as the wall shifted before us to reveal a secret staircase that hadn't been there seconds ago. I frowned at it. "How did you...?" I trailed off, my lips parting as the flames danced downward to illuminate the stone steps along the floor.

"We're in a paradigm," Zakkai replied. "One I created. It reacts to my wants and needs."

"So it's like the one I fell into when Emelyn and I were in the LethaForest?" It reminded me of being inside a magical bubble. It looked and felt real, and it was to an extent. Like an alternate reality within a reality.

"That was a crude paradigm, but similar," he replied, heading downward. "This one is far more intricate. It's also hiding roughly fifty fae inside of the boundary walls. The paradigm you were *invited* into was hastily created for the sole purpose of providing a safe place to talk. But as you saw, the Warrior Bloods discovered the magic quickly and tore it down."

I frowned. "Can they discover this one?"

"Only if they know where to look." He paused on the bottom step as another set of stairs formed, then continued his descent. "The key to a paradigm is to put it somewhere away from Midnight Fae. We can sense the magic. It also requires a lot of energy to create, which is how the Warrior Bloods found the one in the LethaForest so quickly. Fortunately, that paradigm wasn't meant to remain. This one is fortified by my magic. Just as Shade's paradigm is protected by his grandparents. And both are strategically located."

"You mean his meadow?" I asked, thinking of the sunshine and flowers and the little house Shade had hidden inside a tree.

"Yes. He built that paradigm as an attachment to the one his grandparents maintain."

"So, like a bubble within a bubble... within a reality."

He stopped at the bottom of the staircase beside a large door and stared down at me with an eyebrow arched. "A bubble?"

"It's how I visualize paradigms. Like an alternative reality bubble within a reality."

His lip quirked up on one side. "More like an invisible doorway to another world crafted by magic." He stepped backward through the wood and held his hand out for me. "You'll need to be touching me for the castle to allow you to leave," he said from the other side, his voice muffled by the door.

"Continuously?" I wondered out loud, taking his hand.

He pulled me through and smiled. "For now." He threaded our fingers together and led me into a garden full of colorful flowers.

I gasped at the sight, my affinity for earth flourishing to life. "Oh." I tugged him toward a stunning pink-and-white blossom, my free hand reaching for the magical bloom.

He allowed it, saying nothing as I stroked the petals to learn the name of the pretty flower.

An Oriental lily. "I've never heard of that," I mused out loud. "Where is this from?"

"The Human Realm," he replied softly.

I stroked another flower a few feet away, the fiery embers sizzling along my fingertips. *Acheron kiss,* the essence whispered through my mind. I frowned. "What about this one?"

"Underworld," he replied. "From a Hell Fae."

My eyebrows lifted. "A Hell Fae?" I was familiar with the infamous species. Their realm was considered the land of rejected fae. "You've talked to a Hell Fae?" They were strictly forbidden by all the realms, their powers too volatile and unpredictable. Many wanted them dead, just like abominations. And there were rumors that the Hell Fae themselves were abominations, too.

"I've met a few. They're not very pleasant," Zakkai said, his thumb stroking along my hand. "But I didn't bring you out here for a flower tutorial, Aflora. I have someone for you to meet."

"But how did you find this plant?" I asked. "Are all of these created by magic?"

"My magic, yes," he murmured, gently pulling me back to the path. "This entire paradigm is mine. I've chosen the colors and the landscape, and I've even created the sun to rival that of our exterior. Your description of a bubble sort of works in that sense—I've ensured our sun rises and sets with the outside world, to help us blend."

"The sun never sets," I pointed out. It was a trait I rather enjoyed about his little oasis.

"During this time of year, no, it doesn't," he agreed. "But in six months, it'll never rise."

I frowned. "Ever?"

"Just for a few months, then it'll come back again." He led me through a gate of stunning vines, and I took a moment to appreciate the lack of snakes and cruel creatures. This reminded me more of my home with all the thriving life and happiness.

"What realm has sun for only half a year?" I asked as I gazed at the trees and mountains beyond. They all whispered their species back to me, the myriad of names setting my Earth Fae soul on fire. I wanted to frolic among them, learn all about their roots, and create several of my own.

"There are certain places in the Human Realm with unique lighting. This is one of them."

I paused midstep. "We're in the Human Realm?"

He dipped his chin. "In a place they'll never look," he added. "This continent is mostly uninhabitable for mortal beings, making it a perfect place for me to hide this paradigm."

My lips parted, surprised at his honesty. Unless he was lying just to test me. "I could tell Zeph that."

He lifted a shoulder. "You could, but you won't."

"How do you know?" I pressed. "I've left my connections open to him." Shade had blocked me out again, which I'd allowed because I knew he had his reasons. He reached out once a day to check on me and had joined a few of the dreams this week. However, most of the time, he resisted my pull, something I could have forced but chose not to. Whatever he was up to would become clear at some point.

"You value his life," Zakkai replied simply.

I stopped walking again. "Are you saying you'll kill him if I tell him?"

"Not directly," he replied, tugging me forward once more. "My walls are reinforced. If he tries to force his way through, he won't survive. No one will. Best not to tempt fate, hmm?"

"You're saying he'll try to find me if I say where we are," I translated.

"Won't he?" Zakkai countered, his eyes glittering in the sun as he glanced at me. "He's not adept at hiding his frustrations, Aflora. He doesn't appreciate me taking away his control over you and your fate. But in this case, I'm the only one who can truly protect you. He'll see that eventually."

"For how long?" I asked, eyeing the cluster of trees at the end of the path. We appeared to be heading into the forest.

"What do you mean?"

"How long do you intend to keep me here?" I rephrased.

He lifted a shoulder. "That remains to be seen."

"Okay, so what's the end goal of all this?" I asked again. "You kill the Nacht family"—something I would never allow to happen—"and then what? You kill all the Elders and the Councilmen, too?"

He seemed to consider for a long moment as we walked, the trees eventually blocking out the sun as he guided us into the forest.

I thought he intended to ignore me after several minutes of silence, then he quietly said, "Then we restore order. It'll be my job to realign the source and define a new monarchy."

"A new monarchy to resemble the old one? With Shade being the rightful king?" It was a guess based on their odd relationship and the commentary regarding Death Bloods and Quandary Bloods.

"He'll absolutely be given a position of power, but he won't be in charge," Zakkai replied. "I suspect he'll be appointed to the reformed council by the new monarch."

"And who will the new monarch be?" I prompted. "You?"

"I'm the Source Architect, Aflora. Not a monarch."

"Yet you claim to be a king."

"An appropriate designation, but not the same," he repeated cryptically.

"Where do I fit in all this?" I asked. "As your supposed queen?"

He merely smiled. "You should probably be more focused on the present, Aflora. And the path right before you, not the one miles away."

"If you want my cooperation, then you need to tell me how I fit into all of this," I replied. "Your father seems to think we're breaking our bonds." He'd brought it up again yesterday, asking why it hadn't been done. Zakkai had just changed the subject, as he often did when talking to me.

"My father thinks a lot of things. That doesn't make any of his statements or theories correct."

"That doesn't clarify your intentions or plans."

"No, it doesn't," he agreed, squeezing my hand again before releasing me.

I frowned. "I thought you said we needed to touch for me to be outside?"

"I believe I indicated it was temporary." His lips curled as he pressed his palm to my lower back. "Now focus, Aflora. Look around you."

I used to think Shade was a walking riddle. Now I knew what one truly looked like—*Zakkai*. Everything he said twisted and turned the phrases, confusing me more. It unnerved me how he could reveal so much and yet so little at the same time.

At least he'd finally told me where we were. Not that I could do anything with that knowledge. Because he was right—Zeph would come for me, regardless of the risk.

We needed to move forward, not backward.

And I was temporarily safe here.

As well as… content.

I didn't want to admit that, but this paradigm was much more comfortable than Midnight Fae Academy. I could breathe here, play with my elemental magic, and truly learn. There were no handicaps, no collars, no pretending. I was just me—Aflora. And it left me feeling rejuvenated and *right*.

Rather than push Zakkai for more information—a task I knew wouldn't end in my favor—I decided to play his game and took in the greenery surrounding us. The beautiful trees sang of their history, their life and promise, their happiness to flourish inside this little alternate reality bubble.

I brushed my fingers down the trunks, learning their magic and memorizing it for future use.

Then I stilled as a gentle caw graced my ears. *Clove.*

I spun around to find my familiar on a branch of one of the trees, her glorious black-and-white-feathered wings tucked into her sides. "Oh, pretty girl!" I looked at Zakkai. "Did you call her here?"

"No. She followed you into the paradigm." He studied me. "Familiars are never far away. They're an extension of our power, similar to the wands. Wasn't she close to you at the Academy?"

"I don't know. We've only recently met," I admitted. "Kols taught me how to call her to me. After Zeph's familiar killed her." I scowled at the memory and ran my fingers through her feathers to counteract the memory. "He apologized to her… after she brought me a stonepecker." My brow furrowed. "Was that from you?"

"A stonepecker?" He chuckled. "No. But I suspect I know who gave it to her." He clicked his tongue, then squatted as a beast with fur ran out of the woods toward him.

My eyes widened as the white ball of fluff tackled him to the ground, his muzzle large enough to wrap around a man's throat. But all he did was draw his tongue up Zakkai's cheek in warm welcome.

The Quandary Blood chuckled. "Did you give Clove a stonepecker?" he asked, his voice holding a warm note to it that had me wanting to smile in response. Except his words had me wanting to frown instead.

"You know her name?"

"Of course I do," he replied. "Don't you know my familiar's name?"

"No. But I assume that beast is your familiar?" Seemed appropriate.

"He's not a beast. He's a wolf. A stunning white Arctic wolf who loves the snow, isn't that right, Zimney?" He scratched the beast behind his pointy ears and grinned up at me. "Today's lesson will be about listening to our familiars. We can even ask them about the stonepecker. When did you receive it?"

"The day you attacked the Academy," I replied.

That caused his grin to falter. "Oh." His forehead crinkled. "Do you still have it?"

Eww, no, I thought, shivering from the memory of that poor dead creature on my lap. Then I cleared my throat and said, "Zeph destroyed it after Shade warned him the Warrior Bloods were coming."

"Interesting," he murmured, slowly standing again. "Two incidents of my supposed involvement where Shade has more or less inserted himself. I still need to obtain that rock from him. I'll do that today after our lesson."

"Are you suggesting he's up to something?"

"Oh, he's always up to something," Zakkai replied, amusement lightening his tone. "Whether or not he's meant to interfere this time, I'm not clear. I don't see him purposely trying to upset you, and given the way you've cringed about the stonepecker, it wasn't a positive experience."

"I don't like death."

He nodded. "Yes, I know. He also sounded rather distressed over the rock issue, so I doubt he put that spell on it. But it does leave me to wonder who is pulling his strings this time around." He lifted a shoulder. "Regardless, we'll get to the bottom of it. *After* our lesson today."

CHAPTER SEVENTEEN

SHADE

"How are your parents?" I asked as I slid into the booth across from Ajax. It'd been a few days since we'd last spoken, and while I cared about his family, that wasn't the real purpose of tonight's visit. But I had to play this cool for my plan to work.

I wasn't taking any chances. We were all in too deep for this round to fail. If we did, I'd literally lose everything—Aflora, my memories, possibly even my grandparents.

No.

This had to work.

Which meant I needed Ajax to act as the catalyst for all the other cards to fall into place.

"They're feeling better," he said. "But refusing to go outside." He leaned forward, his voice dropping. "They're terrified of being attacked again."

What wasn't said was, *By them.*

I nodded to show that I understood the implication and also to demonstrate that I agreed with their assessment. Mostly because I had a strong suspicion that it was the Elders who had attacked the village, not Zakkai, something Aflora had confirmed during a dream conversation the other night.

Zakkai's confession also explained the coma Ajax's parents had fallen into —one Malik Nacht had been in charge of monitoring. Or had he put them in that coma? He'd been the one who was supposed to wake them up. Yet it'd taken him several days, something that shouldn't have happened. The truth remained to be seen.

There were three sides of this revolution.

The Elder-led Council.

Those who believed in reformation, like my grandmother.

And those who desired retribution, like Zakkai.

While the latter two parties didn't see eye to eye, they'd never been violent with one another. So it hadn't made sense for Zakkai to attack those in the village who had helped other Quandary Bloods survive. Some of them might be more in favor of working everything out politically, but he'd never hurt them for that in the past.

The Elders, however, had.

So it was far more likely that they were the ones behind the violence. Ajax's parents were pro-reformation, something not many knew. Although, the attack suggested they weren't nearly as careful as they thought.

"Hi, boys," Anrika greeted, her long white hair tied back into a bun today. Knowledge flashed in her soft features, her perception unerringly astute. She always knew what I was up to, just as she did now. I could sense it in the way she evaluated me with her keen green eyes. Her age showed in that stare, giving her an almost eerie appearance—a thousand-plus-year-old soul trapped in the face of a thirty-year-old woman.

"Hi, Anrika," I replied. "We're just here for a quick snack."

"I know. I already told the kitchen to whip up a pair of blood malts. They'll be out in a few minutes."

"You're the best," Ajax said, his cheeks dimpling as he gave her a genuine smile. He'd left his lip ring at home today, perhaps because he hadn't been in the mood to re-pierce himself.

Fae healed quickly, which meant he had to drive the metal through his skin every time he desired the facial accessory. It gave him a badass appeal that went with his dark hair and blue-black eyes. A startling contrast to our buddy Seif, who now had long silver hair, matching silver eyes, and fangs as a result of his recent transition into a Fortune Fae. I'd not actually seen the changes in person, but my grandfather had told me about them.

"How's Seif?" I asked since I was thinking about him and talking to his mother. "Any news on his errant chase around the realms?"

"He's been quiet lately," she replied, thoughtful. "I think he may have finally caught his Omega."

My lips twitched. "I bet she's giving him hell."

"I hope she is," Anrika murmured, her expression amused. "He needs a challenge."

"That he does," I agreed, thinking of my own challenge. Aflora tugged on my mental string as though she knew my thoughts had turned to her, so I opened our connection. *Hi, little rose.*

Zakkai wants to talk about the rock, she said flatly. *Now.*

I frowned. *I put it in his desired location several days ago. What does he want to discuss?*

"Well, I'll leave you two to chat." Anrika's tone implied an underlying meaning that she confirmed by adding, "Say hello to Aflora for me."

"As soon as I find her, I'll pass along the message," I replied carefully.

Then I murmured, *Anrika says hi.* Since, technically, I'd found my mate in my mind and that qualified, right?

Aflora didn't say anything in return, but I sensed her lingering in our connection.

"You're up to something," Ajax said as soon as Anrika was out of range. "Does it have anything to do with a gorgeous Earth Fae?"

"Everything I do has something to do with Aflora." That was probably the biggest truth I'd ever revealed, yet I said it with a twisted grin meant to throw everyone else off.

We had no way of knowing who was listening.

And as the Council was on my ass about locating my missing mate, I wouldn't put it past them to have me surrounded by eavesdropping spells.

Zakkai wants to meet, Aflora said suddenly. *He says you know where.*

Tell him I'll only agree if you're there, too, I replied, my blood humming at the possibility of seeing and *touching* my mate.

I already said that, and he agreed. Was that a hint of amusement I heard in her voice?

It had me smirking in response, a reaction that earned me a raised brow from Ajax. "Something amusing?"

"Always," I agreed as our shakes arrived via a stone-faced gargoyle. "We're going to need these to go," I said with a touch of disappointment in my tone. "Something's just come up."

The gargoyle muttered something about ungrateful fae brats in response and disappeared with our drinks.

"He's going to add pebbles to those now," Ajax said conversationally. "And what's come up?"

"I'll explain on the way," I replied, sliding from the booth. "And a healthy tip will improve the gargoyle's mood," I added, a touch loudly so the rock creature would hear me. I set down double the payment on the table while I waited for him to return.

Sure enough, he was in a much better mood upon arrival. "Thank you, Prince Shadow," he said, bowing low. Not in a mocking way, but in a respectful one that displayed his appreciation of my generosity.

Seriously, gargoyles were the easiest damn creatures to please.

If only certain fae could be as amenable.

I added a few more coins for fun, causing Ajax to roll his eyes.

Then we took our shakes, bid Anrika goodbye, and ventured out onto the cobblestone streets of the village.

"I hope you don't expect me to bow, *Prince Shadow,*" he drawled.

"I don't think you'd look all that great on your knees, Ajax," I said, eyeing his tall, muscular body. "Not my type either." However, Aflora could kneel for me any day, any time. And I'd do the same for her as well.

Ajax grunted. "Like I'd ever offer."

"I recall you saying that about a certain Elite Blood recently," I replied as I led the way back to the cloakroom. "Pretty sure you fall at her feet now." It was a baited phrase, one I hoped he would pick up and give me the update I desperately craved.

"Yeah, well, I did. Then you recommended I tell her to play it cool, and now she's not speaking to me."

"Oh?" I tried not to sound too interested, but my heart skipped a beat at his words. "She doesn't want to lie low?" I knew she wouldn't. Which was entirely the point.

"No, jackass, she doesn't. So thanks for that solid recommendation."

"You know it's best for right now," I said, trying to make him feel a little better. If it all played out as expected, I'd thank him later. And then I would allow him to punch me in the face. Because, yeah, if this plan came to fruition, I'd earn his wrath and worse.

"Try telling her that."

"I would, but I'm reasonably sure she hates me." And rightly so.

"Well, she hates me, too, now."

"She'll forgive you," I said as I stepped through the threshold to retrieve my cloak. "Trying bowing. I'm sure that'll work."

He grunted. "I hate you sometimes."

No, you don't, but you will, I thought grimly as I used a spell to adorn my cloak. It was hard to click the clasp one-handed, and I actually did want my shake. "I need to run an errand."

"An errand that I assume you're not going to explain," Ajax replied as he engaged a similar enchantment to put on his cloak.

"You really do know me well," I drawled.

"Yeah, yeah." He waved me off. "I have homework to do anyway. As do you, but I have a feeling you've forgotten all about our coursework lately."

"We have coursework?" I asked, feigning surprise. "I thought we graduated."

He just shook his head. "I'll see you when I see you, I guess."

"Soon," I promised. "Maybe I'll show up at the Blood Gala."

He snorted. "Now that'd be an entertaining surprise."

"You think so?" I pretended to consider it. "Perhaps I really should go just to shock the shit out of everyone."

"Do you even own a suit?"

"I might," I replied, smirking. "But why would I wear one?"

He huffed an amused laugh and stepped through the glass to use the portal. "Later, Shade," he said over his shoulder, disappearing from view.

"Later, Ajax," I murmured, staring at my reflection for a moment. *I'm sorry,* I mouthed, not able to say the words out loud, but feeling them nonetheless.

Everyone had their part to play.

This was mine.

I palmed the back of my neck and blew out a breath, exhausted and yet eager to see my mate. *I don't hate you, Shade,* she'd said. She had no idea what those words meant to me. I'd replayed them over and over again in my head for the last week, using them to calm myself when fear and resignation threatened to consume me.

We had three more days until the Blood Gala.

Three days before I found out if all this had been for nothing. *Again.*

I swallowed and closed my eyes, then blew out another breath. *Pull it together. You can do this.* Two phrases I was so tired of hearing myself say. But there was no alternative.

I'm on my way, little rose, I finally said, my nerves under control once more. *See you soon.*

CHAPTER EIGHTEEN

AFLORA

"I'm trusting you," Zakkai said, holding out his hand for mine. "Don't take that for granted."

It was what he said before every dream. I usually returned the sentiment, but this time, it was truly about him trusting me and not the other way around.

Because he was letting me leave the paradigm with him.

I nodded, demonstrating that I accepted his terms again.

No running.

No portal-jumping.

No cloaking.

No trouble.

I wouldn't jeopardize my chance to see Shade, so I'd agreed to all Zakkai's rules. He slid his hand into my cloak to pull out my wand and tucked it into his leather jacket.

I arched a brow. "Really?"

"My trust only goes so far," he replied. "But I also might need it."

"What if I need it?"

"Then call for it," he murmured. "It seems to be more in tune with your desires than mine, so it should listen."

It wasn't an argument worth having, so I merely nodded again.

His lips twitched. "I didn't realize seeing Shade could make you so agreeable, Aflora. I should have offered this days ago."

I rolled my eyes. "Seeing any of my mates makes me agreeable."

"Any of your mates who aren't me," he corrected.

"Obviously."

He huffed a laugh and shook his head. "Let's go, little star." He reached down for my hand, and I gave it to him, just like I had when he'd led me outside earlier. It felt natural to accept, like my palm belonged against his. A fact I refused to evaluate and instead saw as a necessity.

We wandered through the hallways again, but in a different direction from before. This time he led me closer to the main dining hall but veered down a new hallway—one that appeared before him like the stairway and door had earlier—only for us to stop short as Dakota stepped into view. She frowned at our joined hands, then took in my cloak and Zakkai's jacket.

"Are you heading out for another lesson?" she asked, glancing out the windows to the left. "I can't tell what time it is, but I think it's late."

"I didn't realize we had a curfew," Zakkai drawled, stepping around her and yanking me along with him.

"Don't we have a meeting?" she called after us. "The Blood Gala is only a few days away."

My heart skipped a beat at the words.

Zakkai had said there wasn't anything planned for the gala, but Dakota's statement suggested otherwise. I glanced up at him and noted the tick in his jaw. "We'll discuss it later."

"Later when?" she demanded, her heels clicking over the marble as she sauntered toward us. "I understand that you're a little infatuated with the abomination at the moment, but we need a plan, Kai."

I flinched at the term *abomination*.

"*Infatuated* is a childish term," he replied, pausing to look over his shoulder at her. "And there's nothing to plan. I've already said no."

"Yes, but as your father said—"

"My father is no longer the Source Architect. His opinion is his own. Mine, however, is law. I won't be discussing this further. Feel free to provide that report at the meeting." He resumed our pace, ignoring her protests at our back.

"You're losing your mind over this childhood crush!" she shouted as he took another turn. "You're supposed to break—" A wall formed behind us, blocking her from following.

I glanced at him.

His expression gave nothing away, but I sensed his irritation in the bond.

"What's supposed to happen at the Blood Gala?" I asked as a portal panel appeared.

"Nothing is going to happen," he said, punching in a code that I ignored. There was no point in trying. I knew his paradigm would never allow me access to this area without him. "I've already said it'll be hard enough to attend in disguises. I won't be adding more magic to the mix. There will be far too much power present to risk it."

"Do they know we're planning to attend?"

He lifted a shoulder. "It's not for them to decide."

"That doesn't answer my question."

"No, it doesn't," he agreed as the walls melted around us to reveal miles of snow.

My lips chattered at the sudden drop in temperature. *What…?*

Zakkai yanked me into his arms, covering me in the warmth of his body as the portal engaged to whisk us away. But not before my hair turned brittle from the subzero climate.

I was still shivering when the magical swirls ceased around us.

I buried my face against Zakkai's chest, seeking his heat, my body chilled to the literal bone.

"What did you do to her hair?" a familiar voice asked from behind me as fingers combed through my icy strands. "Did you accidentally drop her in the snow?"

"I miscalculated the shift from paradigm to reality before the portal engaged," Zakkai murmured, his arms tight around me. "My spell didn't cover her in time."

"Hmm." Shade stepped closer, his body providing another layer of warmth that I desperately craved.

More, I begged, still frozen and trembling from the shock of the cold.

He aligned his chest to my back as Zakkai dropped his hands to my hips, the two men doing their best to provide me with the heat I needed to function.

It was a shock to my system, my legs locked in some bizarre combination of terror and ice.

"Antarctica is cold, even during their summer," Zakkai said, pressing his lips to my temple. "Sorry, Aflora. I'm not used to taking others with me."

I couldn't reply, my lips numb despite my chattering jaw.

Shade ran his palms up and down my arms, his mouth brushing the pulse of my neck. "It'll pass in a few minutes, little rose," he whispered.

"Maybe now you understand how I know that you won't tell Zeph our location." Zakkai lowered his forehead to mine. "He wouldn't last more than a few minutes outside my walls."

I wanted to nod but didn't try.

Shade kissed my throat again before saying, "Aflora said you want to talk about the rock. Did you figure out who enchanted it?"

"No, because I haven't seen it yet."

Shade stilled behind me. "What? I put it on the table."

"It wasn't there when I dropped by."

"Then someone else picked it up," Shade said slowly.

"Just like someone sent Aflora a stonepecker via her falcon," Zakkai added, his gaze leaving mine to focus on Shade. "She said it was destroyed after you warned them the Warrior Bloods were coming?"

"What are you implying?" Shade countered. "That I'm fucking with you?"

"Oh, we both know you're fucking with me, Shadow. It's what you do best. But in this case, I think someone is fucking with *us*. Who have you been talking to?"

"I talk to a lot of people."

"I know. Who?"

"Hello, Zakkai," a female voice interjected, her tone holding a magical lilt to it that I recognized from the LethaForest.

Zakkai sighed long and hard. "Of course you took the rock."

"It was the only way to ensure you ended up where I wanted you," the woman replied as she moved toward us. I still couldn't move, but I caught her image in the corner of my eye—her long, dark hair unmistakable. *Zenaida.* Shade's grandmother. "It's not who you think, Zakkai. And the intentions were well meaning, not unkind."

My Quandary Blood mate heaved another sigh, his eyes finding mine before dropping to my mouth. "We may need to use a spell to warm her up faster." He cupped my cheek, his thumb drawing a hot line along my lower lip. "You're still tinged blue, little star."

"He exposed her to the Antarctic climate," Shade explained.

"Accidentally exposed," Zakkai corrected in a clipped tone as his magic poured over me, thawing my icy limbs and removing the binds freezing me in place.

I inhaled a deep breath, his oceanic scent a calming cologne that I welcomed into my lungs. Then Shade's essence added to the mix, his refreshing aroma adding a layer of tranquility that had me relaxing between them both.

Thank you, I whispered into their minds.

I'm sorry, Zakkai replied, pressing his lips to my temple again before looking at Zenaida. I followed his gaze to take in the petite female Shade called *Grandmother.*

"I have nothing to say to you," Zakkai said flatly.

"That's fine. You can listen instead." Her tone was very matronly for a female who appeared to be no older than thirty. She wore a navy top of thick band-like straps around her torso that left her midriff exposed. And below her waist was a matching skirt that flowed all the way to the ground.

She was stunning.

I hoped I could pull that off in a thousand years. Assuming I was still alive.

"Hmm, well, I also have no interest in listening to you," Zakkai added.

"Just hear her out, Zakkai," a gruff voice said as a silver-haired male appeared at the tree line. A second man stepped into the clearing beside him —the one who resembled a slightly older version of Shade.

Zakkai looked sharply at my Death Blood mate.

Shade lifted his hands as he stepped back from me. "I had nothing to do with this. I wasn't even here when Aflora called into my mind."

"He didn't know I took the rock," Zenaida murmured. "I did that all on my own. Just give me thirty minutes."

"You think a half hour will change my views?" Zakkai sounded amused. "All right, Zen. I'll take that bet."

"It's not wise to bet against a Fortune Fae," the silver-haired man said, his blue eyes flashing as he smiled to reveal his fangs.

"We're not betting," Zenaida said, her skirts rustling as she turned toward the two men. "Follow me. I have cookies."

"Cookies?" Zakkai repeated, glancing at Shade.

"That means she has troubling news," he muttered. "She always bakes cookies when she's upset about something."

"She makes them for Shadow to help him feel better," the dark-haired man corrected. His icy eyes met mine. "Hello, Aflora. Lovely to meet you under better circumstances."

I cleared my throat, the last of Zakkai's and Shade's enchantments leaving my body and returning me somewhat back to normal. "Hi."

"This is my grandfather," Shade added, stating the obvious. "Grandpa Vadim." He gestured to the silver-haired man, who had turned to walk with Zenaida. "That's Grandpa Kodiak. They're my grandma's mates."

"I thought Fortune Fae required a circle of Betas," I said, recalling my brief knowledge of Fortune Fae and their societal structure.

"Not everything is black-and-white, my dear," Zenaida called back to me, her tone again not matching her attire or physical age. "Now come along. I only have twenty-eight minutes left."

Zakkai smirked and shook his head. Then he pressed his palm to my lower back. "Twenty-seven, Zen."

She waved a hand in the hair over her head, dismissing his comment.

"Next time I need something, you'll be coming to me," Zakkai said to Shade as we started walking. "I want that rock when you're done, Zen," he added, his voice too soft to carry the distance she'd put between us. I couldn't even see her through the trees now.

"Yes, yes," her voice came back to us on the breeze, surprising me.

Fortune Fae, Shade whispered into my mind. *Never underestimate them.*

I never underestimate anyone, I countered. I'd been burned too many times to easily trust a soul. But I did feel a strange sort of kinship to Zenaida, one I'd picked up on when I met her in the LethaForest. It had me moving a little faster, curious to know what she had to say.

Then we stepped into a clearing surrounded by homes.

Several of the fae poked their heads out to gape at us.

I swallowed. *Um, Shade?*

It's okay, Aflora. He linked his fingers through mine, stepping into my side while Zakkai walked on my other side, his palm still against my lower back. *Everything's going to be okay.*

You don't sound very sure about that, I remarked, hearing the hesitation in his tone.

He didn't reply, just squeezed my hand.

Then he led us to Zenaida's door.

Let's get this over with, Zakkai said into my mind, pushing through the threshold. "Twenty-five minutes, Zen."

"I only need ten," she replied. "Sit."

CHAPTER NINETEEN

ZAKKAI

I yawned, already bored by Zenaida's usual spiel about reformation being the more appropriate path forward. It would save more lives. Create a more inclusive council. Realign the source with all the Midnight Fae factions.

Blah.

Blah.

Blah.

As the former Midnight Fae Queen, she deserved my respect. She was also mated to a Quandary Blood—Kodiak.

Well, technically, Kodiak had turned his back on the source by rejecting it in favor of turning into a Fortune Fae, but his transition had been halted by one of Zenaida's visions. They'd interfered with fate by trying to stop Constantine's annihilation of the Quandary Blood race a thousand years ago and had been trying to fix it ever since.

I pretended to check my wrist as though looking for the time, but Zenaida plowed forward without concern.

Her ten minutes turned into fifteen minutes because she'd felt the need to rehash history for some reason.

"So your father was a Quandary Blood?" Aflora asked, engrossed in the story.

"A former one, yes. He fully transitioned into a Fortune Fae Alpha. But I technically have Quandary Blood in me as a result of his origin," Zenaida replied. "Even though I'm considered a pure Omega. I think they do that to avoid the truth about the Fortune Fae ancestry coming from Midnight Fae."

"Yes, because all forms of abominations are frowned upon," I drawled. "So we must excuse any and all crossbreeding as natural, hmm?"

"Exactly," Zen agreed.

"But that would make Shade part Quandary Blood, right?" Aflora pressed, looking at her Death Blood mate. "And Fortune Fae?"

"We've already established that I'm an abomination, little rose," he replied before popping a cookie into his mouth.

I'd avoided the treat, concerned Zen might try to poison me.

She'd never kill me. But she would do what she could to control me.

We'd been dancing around it for years. There was a time when I'd agreed with her, as did everyone else. Then the Elders had shown me their penchant for death. And I'd realized there was only one way to end this.

Retribution.

"So you think there's a way to align all the factions?" Aflora was saying beside me. She sat between me and Shade at Zenaida's dining room table. The Fortune Fae Omega and her two mates were seated across from us.

It was almost like looking into the future to see where we would be in a thousand years, except Aflora would argue that we were missing Zephyrus and Kolstov.

I nearly sighed, but Zenaida was launching into her political plan, bringing us near the twenty-minute mark of this conversation.

Which was when I finally realized that the point of all of this had nothing to do with me and everything to do with the female beside me.

A laugh escaped me as I shook my head and interrupted her midsentence. "Oh, Zen."

Her gaze sparkled as she glanced at me. "I honestly thought it would take ten. But your arrogance provided me with additional time."

"I don't understand," Aflora murmured, glancing between me and Zenaida.

"She's recruiting you," I said, holding Zen's gaze. "There's only one thing she's failed to mention in all of this, and that's her knowledge of your parents' deaths. How about you regale us with that tale, Zen. About the deadly weekend where the Elders slaughtered her parents without an ounce of remorse before coming for countless others."

Silence met my words, Zen's eyes hardening.

"Shall I start naming them all?" I asked, arching a brow. "Or have you forgotten all the suffering and pain in your continued quest for diplomacy?"

"Killing the Elders won't bring them back, Zakkai," she said softly. "Death is a fate none of us can escape." She glanced at Shade with that comment, but the Death Blood was too busy eating his cookie to notice.

"How did my parents die?" Aflora asked, drawing my attention to her gorgeous features. She looked back at me and then at Zen. "I want to know."

I waited to see how the former queen would reply. She knew more than I did. I'd been with my father that day, running for our lives.

However, Zen had foreseen their fates. She'd been the one to warn us the Elders were coming. She'd also been the one who'd tried to talk sense into Constantine that day.

Tried and *failed.*

He'd nearly killed her in the process, but her triad with Kodiak and Vadim had proven too powerful for him. Which was why I wished she would join our side. They had the power to take the Council down but chose to continue to pursue a diplomatic course instead.

The only way reformation would happen was with Constantine Nacht out of the picture.

"Your parents were caught shortly after leaving you with Primrose and her two children," Zen said softly. "The Elders consumed them with dark magic, severing their ties to the earth source. Which is why you ascended early."

"You mean they tortured her parents," I clarified. "By forcing the dark source essence into them, something I *felt* through Aflora and absorbed on her behalf to protect her." Then, shortly after that, I'd protected her again when that half-crazed abomination tried to take the source from her.

I didn't regret it. Nor would I have changed a second of it, other than to perhaps have taken her with me rather than leave her with the Elemental Fae.

"That was a burden you never should have had to bear," Zen interjected. "I told Laki that, but he insisted on you bonding Aflora." She shook her head. "I know you saved her life, but there were other options, Kai."

"Other options," I repeated sourly. "Like trying to talk Constantine off a ledge and nearly dying in the process?" I snorted. "Sure, Zen. That's worked well."

"At least I tried," she replied, sounding sad. "More death isn't the solution."

"Tell that to Constantine," I suggested. "I'm sure he'll listen. What, between attacking the village to draw us out of hiding and using Aflora as bait, he's done a fantastic job of proving he's willing to *talk things through*." I couldn't believe I'd wasted the last thirty minutes on this nonsense. "There's only one way forward, Zen. And it's by responding to violence *with violence*." I stood and held out my hand. "Rock."

She heaved a sigh, and Kodiak wrapped his arm around her. "It's not too late," he said softly.

"But it is," she whispered, shaking her head. "This path leads to death, Kai. I urge you to step off of it and consider alternatives."

"My path started with death," I countered. "It's fitting that it'll end similarly." I glanced at Shade. "Out of curiosity, in all the renditions of this conversation, has it gone exactly the same? Or was this any different?"

He didn't bother trying to hide his antics from me, his icy gaze exhausted as he stared up at me. "Always the same."

"That's what I thought." I returned my focus to Zen. "Rock. Now."

"It's in the top drawer," she said, gesturing to the cabinets beside the kitchen sink. "And your uncle created the spell. I'd ask him why before you attack him."

"Uncle?" Aflora repeated, the chair moving as she slowly stood as well.

"Tadmir," I said, a slight growl in my tone. "My mother's half brother." I should have known he was fucking around in my affairs.

The lack of a reaction from Shade told me he wasn't surprised by this news either, suggesting he knew a lot more about my uncle than I'd anticipated.

Which raised several suspicions.

I studied the Death Blood for a moment and noted his vacant expression. "I could use her to dig through your mind," I said softly.

"You could," he agreed. "But I think she'll give you one hell of a battle to fight in response."

Yes, I'd felt her toying with his initial spell in her mind, learning how to create blocks of her own with cords of Quandary magic. I could break them if I had to. But it would hurt her in the process, and I really didn't want to do that.

"Well, send my regards to Tadmir. Perhaps I'll pay him a visit soon," I replied, retrieving the rock purely to run my own magic over it.

Within seconds, I confirmed Zen's statement to be true. With a shake of my head, I set it on the counter. "For the record, the spell at the Academy was a message for the Council. No one was hurt—something I personally assured —and I didn't send the stonepecker to Aflora. I would never risk her in that way. And the village also wasn't me."

The statement was more for Aflora than anyone else.

But it felt right to include them all.

"It's time to go, Aflora." I held out my hand for her. "Unless you have more questions about the differences between reformation and retribution?"

"No, I think I got it," she said, stepping toward me. "One side wants to negotiate. The other side wants to draw blood. The problem is, neither side is one hundred percent right."

I arched a brow. "Oh?"

She looked at Zen. "Zakkai's right. You can't negotiate with a misogynistic council of men who refuse to listen to anyone other than themselves. They have already chosen to kill anything and everything they fear, which includes your Quandary Blood lineage. That alone ensures that they will never agree to a truce."

A fair assessment, one I would have applauded, but she faced me in the next second, her blue eyes alight with censure.

"And killing them all makes you no better than them. You're just annihilating the threat without giving them a chance to defend themselves or talk things through, which is exactly what they've done to the Quandary Bloods. You'll kill just as many innocents, perhaps even more."

Shade smiled as he stood and came to hug Aflora from the side. "Well said, little rose," he whispered into her ear before kissing her on the cheek.

Part of me almost agreed with him. The other part had seen too much to buy into such a high-level assessment. She assumed I intended to kill blindly, but I had a specific list of targets, all of whom had earned their fates.

She'd understand soon.

After the Blood Gala.

Then we would talk it through. Because I needed her on my side, and once she realized what we were truly up against, I knew she'd see reason.

She had to.

There was no other clear alternative. The Elders refused to listen to reason, so why should I? They needed to pay for what they'd done.

I met Zen's gaze, her expression one of defeat. She knew I'd never align with her again, not after the way she'd failed my mother and so many others. "Take care of yourself, Zen," I said, meaning it.

I didn't wish her ill will.

She was a powerful fae with good intentions. She just didn't have the inclination to do what needed to be done. Fortunately for her, I did.

And soon, Aflora would, too.

Time to go, star, I whispered into her mind.

Can I have a few minutes to say goodbye to Shade?

I nodded. "Of course." I squeezed her hand and left her to it, knowing there was nothing she could say that he didn't already know.

And if he shadowed her off somewhere, I had a spell waiting to bring her right back.

But it wasn't needed.

After a few minutes of hugging and several intimate kisses, she joined me outside and took my hand again, her gratitude warming our bond.

"I don't want to keep you from them," I admitted. "But your safety matters most."

She nodded. "I'm starting to understand that." She glanced at me. "I think I'm starting to understand you, too."

"I don't think you do yet, but you will," I murmured, leading her to the portal. "I'll make sure not to let you freeze this time."

"I would appreciate that," she replied, releasing a shiver from the memory.

My lips curled. "Or maybe I should so I can warm you up the old-fashioned way afterward."

Her cheeks flushed a pretty pink. "Just take me home, Zakkai."

Home, I repeated to myself, my chest warming at the term.

I knew it was just a slip of the tongue, a thought she hadn't meant to voice. Regardless of the cause, I liked the sound of it.

So I nodded.

And took her home.

Then released her to dream of her mates, where she told Kolstov and Zephyrus about her visit with Zen.

What a strange little circle we'd created here, one where I indulged my queen far more than I ever anticipated. Yet, I couldn't seem to stop. She was just too special to ignore.

My father wanted me to break the bonds.

Several of the Quandary Bloods, and Dakota, wanted to attack the Blood Gala.

And here I was, lounging in a corner while she sat between an Elite Blood and a Warrior Blood, telling them all about her day.

I closed my eyes and relaxed, listening to her voice and thinking about the future.

Wars required sacrifice.

What would mine become? And when the time came, would I be willing to make it?

Two questions that chased my thoughts, round and round, neither of them providing me with a solid answer.

Aflora was changing me. That realization should have caused me to take several steps back. But instead, I peeked at her in the dream again and smiled.

Maybe change could be good.

Or maybe it would force me to pay the ultimate price.

CHAPTER TWENTY

AFLORA

I studied myself in the mirror, frowning at the bright blonde ringlets falling to my shoulders. I had green eyes to go with them, and a deep red dress cut low across my chest and fitted at my waist.

"Do you have a fetish for Winter Fae?" I wondered out loud as Zakkai entered in a tuxedo, his hair dark and cropped short on his head. "I look like a Royal Elf." Minus the ears. He'd rounded my pointed tips to match his.

He ran his sapphire eyes—a startling color change from his usual silver blue—over me and smirked. "You look nothing like a Royal Elf." He stepped behind me, his arm wrapping around my waist as he set his chin on my shoulder. "You're stunning, star."

I glanced down at my cleavage. "You're only saying that because you upsized my boobs and put them in this very uncomfortable top." They were practically overflowing, almost indecently.

He followed my gaze, his pupils flaring as he whispered a spell to return my breasts to their normal size. "Better?" he asked softly.

I swallowed, the intimacy of his hold and nearness causing my heart to skip several beats before I whispered, "Yes. Thank you."

He kissed my neck and released me. "For the record, you're gorgeous no matter what you wear or how you look."

I felt his sincerity through the bond and thought the same about his own appearance. He pulled off the short, dark hair and sapphire-eye look rather well. He'd also altered his face a bit, giving himself a rounder chin and thinner eyebrows. My face was more angular with several freckles on my cheeks and nose.

We looked completely different.

But I could feel the enchantment writhing across my skin like a live wire, my true self lurking beneath and waiting to be revealed.

Zakkai buttoned his suit jacket just as someone knocked at the door. He stepped toward it and greeted his father with, "We'll be fine, Dad."

"Famous last words," Laki replied.

The tall male stepped into the room in a pair of charcoal dress pants and a white button-down shirt. No tie. This style of dress seemed to be his preferred attire. I rarely saw him in anything else.

"Have you come to argue some more?" Zakkai asked as he slid my wand into his jacket pocket. He still claimed it was his, but the magical strands responded to me, not him. Ergo, *my* wand.

His father slid his hands into his pockets. "No. You've made it clear that you have no desire to listen to reason."

"As I recall, you took me to a Blood Gala after my eighteenth birthday, saying it would provide me with perspective. I'm doing the same for Aflora."

Laki's gaze slid over my dress before returning to his son. "She's a beacon, Kai. They'll recognize her power."

Zakkai walked over to his dresser to retrieve a small jewelry box. He opened it to reveal a gold necklace with a diamond star pendant hanging from the end. "May I?" he asked, approaching me with the necklace.

"Will it be like the collar?"

"Sort of, but no." He held it up for me to inspect. It looked like an ordinary chain. I touched the metal, expecting it to zap me, yet I felt nothing.

"Okay," I said slowly and gathered all my wayward curls into my hands, exposing my neck.

Zakkai gently drew the chain around my throat, allowing the pendant to hang along my breastbone, and clasped the chain at my nape. "How does it feel?"

"Like a necklace," I whispered.

"Dad?"

Laki pursed his lip. "The beacon of power has dimmed."

Zakkai grinned. "This will hide your mating bonds as well." He showed me a watch on his wrist. "Just like this is hiding my link to you, in addition to dulling my power."

I frowned down at the beautiful charm. "But I don't feel any different."

"Good. That means my spell worked." He stepped to my side, his attention on his father. "Anything else, Dad?"

"It's a risk."

"So was taking me seven years ago," Zakkai murmured. "She needs to see this just like I did."

"Our duty to Aflora was to keep her safe, Kai. This is the opposite of safe."

"As was letting her be bitten by Shade and taken to the Academy," Zakkai retorted. "Yet you deemed that an acceptable risk despite my protests to the contrary. At least I gave her a choice in this instance."

His comment jogged a memory, one where Shade indicated that someone had sent him to me. Something about how *he* had warned Shade that I would be beautiful.

I never did find out whom Shade was referring to. Had it been Zakkai or someone else?

The Midnight Fae Council had told Shade to bite me. But knowing Shade, he'd only complied because he wanted to.

Which left me wondering who really told him to bite me initially. And why.

Shade, I said softly, mentally knocking on the door he'd created. I could push through it, but I preferred him to answer willingly.

However, he didn't this time, his mind oddly quiet.

I was about to try again when Zakkai linked his fingers through mine, distracting me. "Ready?"

"Yes," I replied. None of my mates knew I was attending tonight. I'd kept Zakkai's confidence in exchange for my ability to dream-walk without his interference. He'd upheld his part of the bargain, so I would now uphold my part of it.

These last two weeks—or that was my estimation of the time, anyway— had been eye-opening and engaging. Zakkai had spent almost all of his time teaching me more about Quandary magic while also explaining various points in Midnight Fae history. He was patient and disciplined. Kind yet stern. And a walking riddle who somehow managed to explain everything while explaining nothing at the same time.

We shared a bed each night, where he allowed me to play with my other mates in my mind. Not sexually, really. None of them were comfortable doing anything in front of Zakkai. He'd also kept his hands mostly to himself, aside from a few touches here and there.

Like tonight when he'd wrapped his arms around me from behind. He showed affection without making me uncomfortable. And he never demanded anything from me in return.

Our fantasies had been the same. He'd always provided me with pleasure without asking for reciprocation.

It left me feeling conflicted. I should hate him. He'd bonded me as a child and left. And yet, he'd been a child, too. None of it had ever been our choice. He was supposed to undo it now but refused. However, I suspected that if I demanded it, he would eventually allow me to break the bond.

I wasn't sure if I wanted that or not.

So I allowed him to steer me toward the door. His father's behavior more or less confirmed that Zakkai had nothing nefarious planned for tonight. Of course, it could all be an act, a notion I held in the back of my mind as we stepped out into the hallway.

"Be careful, Kai," his father said. "You, too, Aflora." His tone held a touch of emotion when he spoke my name, one that flickered in his gaze—there and gone in a second.

"I'll keep her safe," Zakkai replied. "Just as I always have."

His father dipped his chin in acknowledgment. "I'll be waiting up for an update."

"I know." Zakkai reached out to touch his father's shoulder in an almost comforting gesture, then he used his opposite hand—which still held mine—to gently tug me along beside him down the hall.

We took a similar path as we did the other day when going to meet Shade. I hadn't spoken to my Death Blood mate since, his connection closed and quiet. I tried again now, wanting to ask him about the biting, but he still didn't answer, making me frown.

"What's wrong?" Zakkai asked as the magical hallway appeared before us, granting us access to the portal near the end.

I didn't immediately reply, unsure of how to phrase my concern.

But as he pulled me close inside the portal, he used his finger on my chin to draw my gaze up to him. "Aflora, tell me what's wrong." He didn't punch in the code, instead holding me inside the cocoon of his body heat, his dark blue eyes possessing his familiar intensity. It seemed no spell could hide that look.

I cleared my throat. "I… I'm thinking about Shade. I've not spoken to him since we saw him the other night. And I wanted to ask him something."

"Ask him what?" Zakkai asked softly, his thumb tracing my jaw.

"The Council told him to bite me," I whispered. "But he once told me that someone had warned him about me. And I was wondering…" I trailed off, biting my lip. Then I decided to just go for it. Either he told me the truth or he deflected. What would it hurt to ask? "Well, I was wondering if that someone was you."

"I see," he replied, his touch drifting to my hair before wrapping around the back of my neck. "Shade and I have known each other for a long time. But I didn't tell him to bite you. The Council did. And I suspect my uncle Tadmir played a hand in this as well."

"Who is Tadmir?" I asked, searching his gaze. "I mean, I know he's your uncle, but I've not met him."

"He's a Midnight Fae Councilman," Zakkai replied.

My brow furrowed. "What? How? If he's related to you, then isn't he a…?"

"Quandary Blood?" Zakkai suggested for me, his lips curling. "Yes, partly. He's my mother's half brother. They shared a Quandary Blood mother. But his father was a Paradox Fae."

I blinked. "An abomination."

"Yes. One who can rewrite power, which is how he's currently parading around as a Malefic Blood. He mated into the royal line and took the mantle from his mate—because women aren't allowed on the Council."

"So… so… he took the Councilman position from her by mating into her bloodline and using his Quandary Blood abilities to rewrite his magic to, uh, match? And everyone thinks he's a pure Malefic Blood?" I wanted to make sure I understand that convoluted piece of history.

"Yes, that's right," he replied. "And what's more, he did all this before Constantine initiated his quest to destroy Quandary Bloods. Which tells me he knew all this was going to happen and used his Paradox Fae abilities to jump back in time to alter history."

"That's… wow. I'm not sure what to say to that," I admitted.

"He's played the long game," Zakkai murmured, his thumb brushing my pulse. "Which is why I'm not surprised he's working with Shade. He's clearly seen something unfold that he wishes to change. And so, I suspect he's the real reason Shade agreed to bite you."

"But you knew he was going to bite me."

"Yes." His eyes clouded over with a darker emotion. "My father informed me of the plan after a Councilman, maybe even an Elder, or perhaps Tadmir, had told him about the Council's intent for Shade to bite you. He wanted it to come to fruition and told me to cooperate. As I wasn't the Source Architect yet, I had no choice but to do as he said."

I swallowed, speechless.

My entire future had been stolen from me via a handful of events where I was given no say in the matter. All because my parents had decided to help the Quandary Bloods.

No. Not that.

It was all because Constantine Nacht ignited a genocide among the Midnight Fae. My parents had done what they felt was right—they protected *lives*. And it'd crafted a path for me, one entangling me in a war I was never meant to be a part of.

Or maybe it'd always been my destiny to be bonded to four Midnight Fae. The center of a conflict. An Earth Fae who favored vitality amid a sea of violence.

"Shade and I have a long history," Zakkai said softly, drawing me from my thoughts. "When I found out the Council's intentions, I went to him and demanded he protect you. He already knew all about you because I'd told him about you when we were younger—when I was still recovering from the spell that separated us. That was actually how I first met Shade. He found me in a ball on the floor and asked me what the hell I was doing."

He huffed a laugh at the memory, one I would have shared, except I didn't feel humored by any of this.

"I told him all about you. Said you were beautiful, loved flowers, and talked about how much I missed our friendship. He'd nodded solemnly in understanding, then said he knew what it was like to have others demand actions that hurt."

He fell silent for a moment, his amusement vanishing as his gaze took on a faraway gleam.

"We weren't exactly friends after that, but we understood each other in a unique way that has carried throughout the years," he continued. "I wasn't thrilled with the idea of him biting you, but I'll admit that I preferred him over anyone and everyone else."

There were others? I wanted to ask, but I couldn't find my voice.

And he wasn't done talking.

"Shade's always known you were mine. However, he fully mated you anyway. I'm not exactly surprised by that. He's defiant by nature. But I also know it goes much deeper for him than that." He pressed his forehead to mine, his eyes closing. "It goes much deeper than that for me, too."

"You warned him I would be beautiful," I whispered, recalling Shade's words that day.

"No, I told him you were beautiful. I must have said it a thousand times when I was younger. I told him all about your flowers, your love of life, and how beautiful you were. It'd been a childlike comment at the time, because I meant you were a beautiful person. Now I would call you stunning."

He lifted his forehead from mine, his eyes opening as he slid his gaze over me.

"Even with the spell, I can still see *you*, Aflora. And you take my breath away every time, even with the blonde curls and green eyes. You're still my Flora beneath it all. My bright star. I'll never see anyone else but you."

A lump formed in my throat, my mind conflicted on how to respond. It was such a moving story, and yet, so incredibly wrong.

They'd all made so many decisions about my life, removing all my choices.

However, I also understood those decisions.

And if I were to truly evaluate them, to decide for myself, I wasn't sure how much my choices would have varied from the outcome. Perhaps, initially, I would have fought for a different outcome, but knowing what I did now, I couldn't see another path for me to have walked down.

It seemed like years ago that I sat in that cafe waiting for Glacier to arrive. I was no longer that delicate flower, pining after a boy who didn't value my worth.

Now I stood in the arms of a man who had given up so much to protect me.

If this was all a ruse, it was a very convincing lie. Because I could feel his emotions in our bond, his sincerity a warm sensation creeping through my veins and going directly to my heart.

There were no words for me to say.

No accusations or rants.

I could fight him forever, hate him for deciding all this on my behalf, or I could choose to recognize how many of his choices had been stolen from him as well. I could choose to admire how he's dealt with all the weight on his shoulders. I could choose to forgive him for his actions. I could choose to trust him. I could choose to embrace him.

I curled my fingers around his arms, feeling his heat and masculinity through the soft silk of his jacket.

And then I went up onto my toes to press my lips to his, making the *choice* to kiss him.

Making the choice to grant him a piece of my heart.

Making the choice to allow this moment between us to grow.

Making the choice to accept our intertwined fate.

It wasn't perfect.

It wasn't a fairy tale.

It wasn't even kind.

But it seemed right.

I choose to believe you, I told him with my lips, kissing him gently. *I choose to accept us.*

He wrapped his arm around my lower back, his opposite hand still against my neck, and he returned my embrace, his tongue sliding into my mouth to find mine.

His essence swirled around me, his power an addictive flavor I wanted to revel in for all of eternity. My soul rejoiced, life thriving inside me as he awakened a dormant part of my spirit.

My long-lost mate.

My Kai.

I clung to him, indulging in the heat and prosperity of our connection. Then sighed as the kiss slowly came to an end.

"I'm sorry," he whispered against my mouth. "But if we continue this, we'll never get to the Blood Gala, and I owe you the truth, Aflora. You have to see everything to understand our destiny."

I nodded, agreeing with his intentions. "Promise me you won't harm anyone."

"I promise I won't harm anyone without provocation," he countered, capturing my chin between his thumb and forefinger. "If anyone means to harm us, I will retaliate."

That seemed fair, so I conceded with another dip of my chin. "I accept that."

He smiled. "Good." He brushed his lips against mine once more. "Now hold on to me. We're going to portal-jump several times to cover our tracks."

CHAPTER TWENTY-ONE

ZEPH

I walked into Kols's bedroom and paused at the sight of him bending over the bench at the foot of his bed.

"Almost ready," he said without looking at me, his focus on tying his shoe.

I leaned against the doorway and folded my arms, more than content to enjoy the view of him in that all-black suit. Our relationship had deepened over the last few weeks, the blood ties to Aflora and each other stirring foreign sensations inside of my soul that left me evaluating life a little differently.

Kols had bitten me, taking charge of our relationship in a way he'd never done before.

Then he'd submitted to me in the next moment, knowing that it was what I needed.

The male I'd known all my life had grown into a man so far beyond my worth. I had no idea why or when he'd chosen me. Fae knew I didn't deserve him. But as he turned to face me now, his golden irises swirling with power, I couldn't claim a single regret.

Except for our missing link.

Aflora.

"I wish she were here, too," Kols said, sauntering up to me.

"Reading my mind?"

"More like your expression," he replied. He slid his palm around the back of my neck and pulled me into a kiss, his boldness flooring me. I grasped his throat, squeezing it a little as I took control of the kiss with my tongue.

He pressed his groin to mine as fire ignited between us.

We hadn't touched each other like this since the other night, our focus on other things. But the bond was alive and hot between us, begging Kols to finish it with a final bite.

Between Kols and Aflora, I felt so utterly complete that I almost didn't recognize myself. They'd breathed new life into my lungs, given my heart a reason to beat, and provoked a sizzling heat inside me that begged to be sated.

I needed her.

I needed him.

I needed *them*.

My teeth skimmed his lip, threatening to bite. I could feel him urging me to do it through our partially formed link. We couldn't hear each other, not quite. But years of experience coupled with the deepened bond had left us with new insight.

"Zeph," he groaned, his grip tightening on the back of my neck. "I—"

The clearing of a throat cut off whatever he'd been about to say, the presence behind me reminding me that I'd left the door wide open.

Fuck.

"Look, I don't care what you two do behind *closed doors*. But please be mindful that others live in this house. And your mother would not appreciate this." Malik Nacht's voice held his usual chastising undertone, but a hint of amusement lurked in his golden irises as I slowly turned to face him.

The Elite Blood King had been in an unusually good mood the last few days, which Kols and I didn't understand. Everything had gone to hell with Aflora. Shade couldn't locate her, at least as far as the Council was concerned, and Kols had technically failed his trial. Yet Malik had proceeded as though everything was normal, going as far as to invite me into their home like he used to do when I served as Kols's primary Guardian.

"Sorry, Dad," Kols said, his shoulder bumping mine as he came to stand beside me. "Everything set for the Blood Gala?"

"Yep. Just a few things we need to go over first. And Zeph's missing a key piece of his attire."

I frowned, looking down over my all-black suit—the exact same style as Kols's suit, only his tie was skinnier than mine. I glanced at him to see my confusion reflected in his expression.

Malik slipped a hand into his jacket to pull out a box. He handed it to me with an expectant look. "I believe this goes on your lapel."

My heart stopped.

It can't be…

He doesn't mean…

I looked at Kols again and caught the same glimmer in his eye as I felt in my chest. *Hope.*

It took all my willpower not to outwardly react. Warrior Bloods were taught to be stoic. Hard. *Tough.* I couldn't afford to show any ounce of emotion, especially if this was what I thought it might be.

I cleared my throat and lifted the lid, the familiar gold-and-red pendant inside blinking up at me beneath the lighting. *My Guardian pin.*

Malik had taken this from me after everything that went down with Dakota. And now… now he was giving it back… "Does this mean I'm reinstated?" I asked, my voice forcibly flat.

"Yes," Malik replied. "I think you have been for a while. This just makes it official." He clapped me on the shoulder, then turned to Kols. "Now we need to talk about tonight. There are some things I haven't told you."

Just like that, the moment was done.

Congratulations, Zeph. Your fuckup is officially forgiven. You can hereby continue risking your life for my son. Moving on…

My eyes nearly rolled, but I forced my features to remain uncaring and instead focused on his commentary concerning the Blood Gala.

He started with the usual bullshit regarding toasts and celebrations of Midnight Fae independence from the Quandary Blood's nefarious interference.

It was all the typical political gnat-crap until he said, "And I've taken the liberty of writing your speech." He slid a paper from his pocket. "Given the complexities of our current position, particularly with your grandfather calling for a delay in the ascension, I thought it best that I prepare this for you. If you deliver it right, then at this time next year, you should be well on your way to taking over my throne."

The words *"If you don't deliver it right"* seemed to hang between us unsaid. A lingering threat that required compliance.

Or perhaps his father just didn't see any alternative.

Kols glanced at the note, his eyes hardening as he read. "Right," he said when he finished. "Thank you, Father."

Father, not *Dad*.

That indicated he wasn't thrilled by whatever speech Malik had drafted for him.

"Brilliant," his father replied, obviously oblivious to his son's displeasure. "Now there's just one more thing I need to make you aware of, as I don't want the announcement to blindside you later." He paused to look at me, considering. "Well, you're reinstated, so it can't hurt to bring you in on the secret. You are protecting the future king, after all."

I blinked, doing my best not to react.

But I really did not like where this was going.

"The efforts to find Aflora have proven difficult, and we've unfortunately not located her yet. But Chern and Shadow were able to identify the whereabouts of someone else that the Elders have been hunting for over a thousand years."

Kols tensed. "Who?"

"Zenaida," Malik replied, his golden irises swirling with triumph. "The Warrior Bloods are on their way to take her into custody now. And we intend to present her for justice as our closing act."

"Zenaida, as in the former Midnight Fae Queen?" I asked, making sure I understood this announcement correctly.

"Exactly. The woman who turned her back on us all for her mates. We've finally found her." Malik had given up trying to contain his excitement. Apparently, the act of hunting down a female fae and making a show of her was what got him off at night.

"I thought she was dead," I replied, doing my best not to lose my shit. Because what the *fuck*?

"So did we all," Malik said. "And soon, she will be." He uttered that last part with the glee of a villain looking forward to his next crime.

Kols forced a smile. "Well done, Father. I'm sure Constantine is thrilled."

"He's off with the Warrior Bloods now, ensuring all goes to plan," Malik replied. "Well. Best to leave you to it. See you in a few. And do try to be kind to Emelyn tonight. She'll be your mate soon."

He left in a swirl of black, disappearing down the hallway with a hitch in his step that indicated his excitement over the coming events.

I shut the door and locked it, then turned just as Tray and Ella burst into the room, clearly having been listening through the adjoining door to Tray's rooms.

"Did I hear that right?" Tray demanded. Shade gave up the location of his grandmother? And the Warrior Bloods are on their way to capture her and bring her to the party to put her on trial?"

"A fancy phrase for torture and kill her," I muttered, knowing exactly what Malik Nacht and the Council intended to do.

"That's my highest concern," Kols said, his focus on the door.

"Aflora?" Tray guessed. "Is she with Zenaida?"

"No, she's with Zakkai. She's fine." Kols turned to me. "Zeph. That man was not my father."

"What?"

"The magic around him was all wrong. And my father would *never* celebrate the trial of a fae in such a public setting. Either he's been bespelled or someone was wearing his skin. And this?" He held up the speech. "*This* is not something my father would *ever* ask me to say."

He handed me the speech as though to prove it to me.

Only three sentences in and I had to agree. "You're right. This has your grandfather written all over it."

"Something's very wrong," Kols said.

I nodded. *Aflora?* I called, opening our link.

Silence.

I frowned and tried again.

More silence.

"Aflora's not answering me," I said, my brow furrowing. "But our link isn't closed. It's… it's almost like all I hear is static."

"Fuck. This isn't good." Kols took the note back and slid it into his pants, then began to pace. "Can we try to locate Shade?"

Normally, I'd laugh at such a ridiculous request. But I was fresh out of amusement at the moment. "I don't know how to find him."

"I don't either," Tray added.

Aflora? I tried for a third time, hoping that maybe I'd just messed up for the first two calls.

Still nothing.

"You don't think she would try to attend the gala, do you?" I asked, thinking out loud.

Kols stopped to glance at me. "Who? Aflora?"

"Yes."

He snorted and resumed his trek around the room. "Why would she attend?"

"Why would Zakkai allow her to dream of us every night?" I countered.

"To make her more agreeable."

"Yes, to what end?" I pressed. "We've known from the beginning that he's wanted something from her. That was his reason for allowing her to talk to us. What if attending the Blood Gala was his request?"

"He'd be insane to come here. The Warrior Bloods are tripled around the border tonight. Not to mention the myriad of wards and spells. He'd die upon arrival."

"He's the Source Architect," I reminded him. "He can undo all that."

"To what purpose? To crash the gala?" Kols started to chuckle at the thought, then slowly came to a halt again. "The Warrior Bloods are looking for Zenaida." He whirled around to face me. "That means there are fewer guards than usual. Because they're distracted."

"Do you think he's planning something?"

"I think if he is, he's going to have hell to pay for it," Kols replied. "And that doesn't explain whatever the hell that just was with my father. Or the fucking speech."

True. I palmed the back of my neck, trying to think and coming up blank. "Maybe Shade will be at the gala."

"Not likely," Tray interjected. "He's never attended before."

"If he's up to something, he'll be there tonight," I countered. And that Death Blood was always up to something.

"Maybe we should go check it out," Ella suggested. "See what's happening."

"It's too early," Kols replied, his shoes wearing a hole in the floor as he paced. "I have to wait for Emelyn to arrive as well." He uttered that phrase through his teeth, his annoyance palpable.

He'd tried several times this week to convince his father to allow him to attend alone, but it was no use. Traditions were important to the Nacht family.

"I could go early," I said. "Actually, I could go now, then meet up with you after you arrive to fill you in with my findings."

It was the best plan I could come up with given everything.

And the look Kols gave me said he agreed.

"I'm not giving that speech," he muttered. "I'd sooner out my mating to you all first."

My lips twitched. "I'd enjoy that speech."

"Yeah, up until the point the Elders call for our deaths, I'm sure," he drawled.

I plucked the pin from the box in my hand, then tossed the container aside and made a show of adorning my Guardian symbol. "I don't care if it was your father or not. I'm keeping this."

"It's where it belongs," Kols replied, walking up to me again and grabbing my face between his palms. "Don't do anything brash."

"I don't do brash."

"Not usually, no," he agreed. "But Aflora has a tendency to encourage us to act out of character."

My lips twitched. He wasn't wrong. "I'll behave."

"Well, now that's not what I said at all," he replied, a hint of teasing in his tone. He pressed his lips to mine, which seemed to only accentuate his commentary regarding us acting out of character. Because he never used to be this bold with me. And never in front of others.

Sure, Tray knew we fucked around.

But we kept it private.

And the way Kols was kissing me now was very much the opposite of private.

It was downright indecent, and I returned the favor by sinking my teeth into his lower lip and drawing blood. His golden irises swirled in response as I laved the wound.

Then I took a step back before he could repeat the action on my lip.

We weren't ready for the final stage yet.

Not without Aflora.

"I'll find you later," I vowed. "Try not to kill Emelyn while I'm gone."

Kols grunted. "I'm not promising anything."

I smirked, then I nodded to a bemused Tray. He seemed speechless after the display of affection between me and Kols. Meanwhile, Ella was just grinning like a loon.

I rolled my eyes and let myself out.

Aflora, I murmured into the void of our connection. *If I find out you're here, I'm going to bend you over a table and spank your ass, then fuck you raw.*

No reply.

My jaw ticked.

I should be able to at least sense her, but I couldn't hear a damn thing. Almost as though she'd been completely sealed off from me… like when she had the collar around her throat.

I paused midstep, my eyebrows lifting. *Oh, fuck…*

CHAPTER TWENTY-TWO

ZAKKAI

Nacht Manor gave me the chills.

The snakelike vines, gargoyles, and other dark wildlife roamed the grounds, all with one goal in mind—protect the Nacht family.

It had taken me thirty minutes to rewire the defensive spells. Aflora had stood silently beside me while I worked, her mind attuned to mine. If anything, it provided us yet another lesson in Quandary magic.

"Did you memorize everything I just did?" I asked her as we entered the grand hall, having just given our invitations to a nearby Warrior Blood.

No one took notice of us, not even the two gargoyles at the Warrior Blood's feet.

"Yes," she whispered. "It was fascinating to watch. Is that how…?" She trailed off, her eyes finding mine as she asked a question I couldn't hear.

I frowned. "Is that how what?"

She held my gaze for another beat, then her lips curled down as well. "Can you not, uh, hear me?"

"I'm hearing you just fine."

"No, I mean…" She made a quick gesture at her head.

Oh. You mean in your mind? I wondered, engaging our link.

She continued to stare at me.

Can you not hear me? I asked.

Nothing.

"Hmm." I released her hand to wrap my arm around her back and steered her into the ballroom, not wanting anyone to notice our hesitation.

She followed my lead, moving effortlessly alongside me through the mass of red-clad and black-clad attendees. It was the same theme every year—women in red, men in black. I would have remarked on how cliché that was for vampire-like fae, but I suspected there was a reason that humans frequently associated the colors with creatures of the night.

Gold and red decor adorned the walls, as well as a variety of torches and candles. All of them held real fire, as did the chandeliers overhead.

Gargoyles walked around with trays, offering drinks.

The tables were finished with black silk.

And the stage at the front contained a throne in the middle of several other ornate chairs, each one representing a Councilman or a progeny.

I forced smiles as we meandered along, not stopping to talk to anyone and instead plucking two blood-infused red wines from a passing tray. I handed one to Aflora and kept the other for myself, then led her to one of the tables near the back. Other couples had behaved similarly, everyone wanting to select an optimal seat for tonight's event.

Because this was no ordinary gala.

It was more of a theater production, all meant to honor the current political regime.

There would be mingling and talking over wine.

Then a grand entrance from the Midnight Fae Council, including all second-in-command reps and any progenies.

And then the real party would begin, led by Malik Nacht.

A tale would be woven through the air, accompanied by magical charades as they acted out the scenes with fiery figments.

Following the inaccurate portrayal of our history would be toasts and charming words from each power player, the last coming from the Elite Blood King.

I suspected Prince Kolstov would be forced to speak tonight.

I couldn't wait to hear what he had to say about all this, particularly as he'd mated a Quandary Blood this year.

Aflora cleared her throat, her eyebrow arching. "Why can't we hear each other?" she asked in a soft voice.

I set my wine down and reached over to stroke her necklace. "This really is lovely, dear," I said, hoping she caught the insinuation in my offhanded comment. I wasn't ignoring her; I was *answering* her. Or at least providing her with my best guess. We were both wearing power-masking jewelry. It was likely the cause of our inability to hear each other.

Her brow came down. "Oh."

Yeah, she received the message. "I didn't realize how impactful it would be against your skin," I added. "It's really stunning."

"Thank you," she replied, fingering the star pendant, her eyes telling me she received the message loud and clear.

The message was twofold. First, I hadn't realized the impact it would have on our link. And second, there were eyes and ears everywhere. So we couldn't exactly hold a candid conversation here.

She went to pick up her drink, but I pressed my hand to her wrist, leaning forward to give the contents a sniff. "Oh, I think they used B negative in this one, darling. I know how much you dislike that. Hopefully, we can find a tray with another flavoring."

Her eyes rounded as she nearly dropped the glass.

Yeah, I'd only picked those up for show. Hence the reason I left mine on the table.

She carefully set hers down beside it, her nose wrinkling as she cleared her throat. "Thank you, *sweetheart*. I would hate to drink something so sour."

My lips twitched. Blood wasn't *sour*, but I'd let her have that jab.

"Oh, I don't know. I hear B negative can be rather flavorful when paired with red wine," a deep voice said as a Warrior Blood sat right beside Aflora. The hairs along her arms rose in response, her nipples beading beneath her gown. "Maybe you should try it, *sweetheart*."

Zephyrus's green eyes narrowed at her before sliding to me, his expression daring me to react.

I merely shrugged, then eyed the pin on his lapel. "Guardian Zephyrus. Shouldn't you be with Prince Kolstov, preparing for tonight's events?"

"You know, I was," he drawled, relaxing into his chair. "But he sent me down early to enjoy the scenery. I think he wants me to pick out a snack for tonight." He dropped his gaze to Aflora's breasts. "I think I found what I want to eat."

She flushed. "That's rather forward of you to say."

"Is it?" he countered, leaning forward to whisper. "I would recognize this body anywhere, pixie flower. But nice dress." He pulled a card out of his pocket, flicked it through his fingers, and set it on the table. "You have thirty seconds to tell me what the fuck you're doing here."

"Neat trick," I said, mentally reviewing the enchantment of his conversation-canceling device. To everyone around us, we were just making typical pleasantries. And any bugs would pick up the same. "We're not here to cause any trouble. I just want Aflora to hear the Nacht family's view on Quandary Bloods."

"That's fascinating," he drawled. "Why can't I hear my mate."

"Her necklace is hiding her essence and power from the room, just like my watch is covering mine." I caught his wrist as he moved to touch her. "Don't remove it. The second you do, she'll light up like a damn beacon." Not my favorite term, but my father was right to use it earlier.

Zephyrus held my gaze for several seconds, then twisted out of my hold and lowered his hand to his lap. "Kolstov thinks his father is under some sort of spell, or perhaps not even him. And the Warrior Bloods are on their way to grab Zenaida. She's supposed to be tonight's culminating act."

My eyebrows flew up at that mouthful of information.

Aflora gasped. "*What?*" She looked at me, her eyes widening. "We need to tell Shade."

"Calm your expression," I said quickly. "The spell Zephyrus ignited only masks our voices, not our appearances." And I'd already drawn some attention by grabbing the Guardian's wrist. Hopefully, they all thought it was just us teasing one another about my date.

Hell, he'd pretty much announced that he wanted to take her back to Kolstov's quarters and fuck her without any sort of introduction or preemptive conversation.

Fortunately, that matched what I knew of his typical behavior around females. He didn't mince words or suggestions.

Aflora schooled her features, impressing me for a brief moment with her ability to feign nonchalance.

Then the Guardian's words came back to me.

"There's no way they've found her," I said.

"According to enchanted Malik, Shade provided the—"

The card on the table sizzled into ash, cutting off Zephyrus's explanation.

But it was enough for me to infer what he intended to say.

Shade gave up his grandmother's location.

That wasn't something he would ever do willingly. Which meant there was another ploy at play here, one I feared Zephyrus had just walked right into.

If the Council knew about their bonds, they'd use those links to try to provoke Aflora out of hiding. And I'd just waltzed her into the heart of Nacht territory.

My senses flared to life, assessing our surroundings and zeroing in on Zephyrus's pin.

Fucking fae.

The Guardian had led them right to us. I should have studied him more closely when he sat down and searched him for signs of enchantments.

Because Aflora wasn't the beacon. Zephyrus was.

"We should go," I said, my words for Aflora.

"Oh, no. I think you should definitely stay," a smooth voice said from behind me.

Zephyrus's gaze widened, and Aflora stiffened.

I just shook my head and sighed. "Hello, Constantine." I'd never had the displeasure of meeting him in person, but I would be able to pick out his voice anywhere.

"Zakkai," he returned, taking the chair beside me as several Warrior Bloods appeared out of an enchanted mist to fill the rest of our table.

Yeah, this wasn't going to end well.

What I couldn't figure out was how they knew we'd attend tonight. I'd been careful with all the wards, and Aflora hadn't breathed a word of it to—

Dakota, I realized, her brown hair flashing in my peripheral vision. *That fucking bitch.*

She gave me a little wave as though she'd heard me and came to stand behind Constantine, her fingers lightly teasing his shoulders. "Will you be needing anything else?" she asked him.

"No, darling. You've been perfect, thank you." He leaned over to kiss her wrist, dismissing her as he did most women.

Zephyrus's jaw clenched, his palm having gone to Aflora's thigh.

Because yeah, Dakota being here meant Constantine knew everything. No wonder she'd been so obsessed with my intentions for the Blood Gala. She was hoping to provoke an incident that the Elite Bloods could squander in some grand display. But all I'd intended to do was show Aflora the truth.

That plan hadn't exactly backfired. She was about to learn some hard truths very quickly. However, this wasn't how I'd intended to show her.

"Where's Kols?" Zephyrus asked calmly.

Constantine shrugged. "Otherwise detained."

Because he knew about Kolstov's ties to Aflora. Brilliant. Honestly, I almost wanted to applaud Dakota for her trickery. "So what was the plan?" I asked, reaching for my wine to swirl it in my glass. "Was Dakota supposed to seduce me like she did with Kolstov and Zephyrus?" Because yeah, I knew all about that incident. "Was she supposed to gain access to the source through me? Then report back to you?"

"Something like that," Constantine admitted. "But your lack of interest made that difficult."

"Yeah, power-hungry cunts aren't really my thing," I drawled, glancing at Zephyrus. "No offense."

He didn't reply or acknowledge the statement, his attention on the new wave of Warrior Bloods who had approached the table. We were up to twenty now. A reasonable number. But Constantine severely underestimated my skill if he thought that would intimidate me.

"So what now, Nacht?" I asked, setting my glass down again without drinking it. Given they knew I was coming, it was probably spiked with something. Even if it wasn't, I would never accept their alcoholic handouts. "Are you hoping for a show? Some grand finale to appease your admirers?"

"Oh, we're all in for quite a show," he said, sounding amused. "And I'll be providing you and your pretty little abomination with front-row seats."

"While I appreciate the intriguing offer, I think we're going to have to pass." I fussed with my tie, then smiled at the ancient asshole beside me. "So unless you want a rather violent prequel to your main event, I suggest you let us leave."

"And I insist you stay," he replied.

A laugh clawed at my throat, his arrogance astounding. As if I—

Aflora released a whimper beside me, her arms beginning to shake. "Kai..." My name left her lips on a tremble of sound. "I... I don't..." She clutched her chest, her body convulsing violently beneath some sort of invisible shock, her eyes rolling back into her head.

Zephyrus reached for her, only a similar quiver worked its way through his limbs, and he grabbed his chest a moment later, his lips parting in shock as he looked at Constantine. "*No.*"

"It had to be done," Constantine replied, rolling his neck. "He's tainted the Nacht name. So I'll do what I do best and restore it." He flexed his fingers as power whirled through the room, the source screaming in agony inside my head.

I dove in to figure out what the fuck was happening, only to be hit with a bolt of energy that knocked me out of my chair.

"Let the show begin," Constantine announced.

CHAPTER TWENTY-THREE

KOLS

Several Minutes Earlier

I f Emelyn Jyn could breathe fire, I imagined she would be doing that right about now. She'd refused to acknowledge me since arriving, her anger palpable and, frankly, exhausting.

I had no patience for it.

If she unleashed WarFire on me again, I'd return the gift in the form of an inferno. I didn't want to be here anymore than she did. And I'd tried all week to convince my father to allow us to go separately. Alas, he'd refused.

I searched for him, wondering if what I felt earlier had been a fluke. But he was nowhere to be found.

Another oddity.

My father was never late. And neither was my mother.

"Have you seen Mum today, Tray?" I asked softly, taking in the modernly decorated space. Our mother had chosen all the fixtures for this meeting room —one that our family rarely used. It was meant for Council business that couldn't take place at the main compound. And once a year, we all gathered here prior to the Blood Gala while we waited for our cue to enter the grand ballroom.

Untouched flutes of blood-infused champagne sat along a serving bench at the back wall. A few were also placed on the oak table, but all sixteen chairs were vacant, everyone choosing to stand instead.

My brother shook his head. "I haven't heard from Mum all day. And it's a bit weird that she's not here yet."

"Indeed," I agreed, stroking my tie. "Perhaps we should go…" I trailed off as Shade entered the room in a proper suit. My eyebrows flew upward. "Well, I'll be damned." He'd never attended the Blood Gala before. As luck would have it, he chose to be here tonight. Good. We needed to talk.

I caught his eye and started toward him, determined to have a word, but his father stepped between us. "Is there something I can help you with, Prince Kolstov?"

"You can help me by stepping out of my way so I can talk to Shadow."

"It's all right, Father," Shade drawled. "This conversation has always been inevitable."

His father sighed. "All right. I'll be over here if you need me."

"Of course." he replied, causing me to frown at their bizarre exchange. They were usually at odds with one another, not operating on the same team.

It left me wondering if the information about Zenaida was true. "Did you really give up your grandmother's location?" I asked him, not bothering for a soft tone.

"The Council has known my grandmother's whereabouts for years," he replied. "So yes, I did, but not recently."

Okay. I'd… missed something. Something vital.

I glanced around again, this time taking in the tension of the room. And the increased presence of Warrior Bloods—something I'd thought was meant for protection but now suspected served an entirely different purpose.

"Oh, what have you done, Shade?" I asked, noting the expressions of all my fellow Councilmen.

Even Lima appeared grim.

But Emelyn stood beside him with an expression of confusion that rivaled the looks worn by Tray and Ella.

"They know everything," Shade drawled, sliding his hands into his pockets and leaning against the wall in the picture of comfort. "They know you've bonded to Aflora. Just as they know she's been with Zakkai this whole time. And right now, your grandfather is using your Guardian to locate them at the party. Because they also know they're here."

"They're here?" I repeated, my eyebrows lifting. The rest was, well, catastrophic, but the thought that Aflora was *here… Oh, fuck.*

Shade nodded, confirming my darkest fear. "You see, I've been reporting to them from the beginning. Because it was what they asked me to do. And it's my duty as the future king of my line to do right by my faction. Just as it was your duty to do right by all of Midnight Fae kind. But you've failed. Rather epically, if I'm being honest."

I narrowed my eyes at him. This wasn't the Shade I knew. It reminded me of that sensation I'd picked up from my father earlier, only it didn't seem to be consuming Shade in the same way.

"Anyway, I tried, Kolstov. But you kept taking every wrong turn. I really was left with no choice. Maybe one day you'll understand. Assuming you survive the descension."

"Descension?" I understood the term, at least on principle. But as far as I knew, it'd never been done. "You can't be serious."

"Oh, he's very serious," my father said as he entered the room, that bizarre energy still wrapped around him. "You've mated an abomination. Hidden key facts about her growing powers. Lied to me and the Council about her whereabouts. Chosen her over all of us and your own kind." He shook his head, his golden gaze holding more censure than sadness.

This is not my father, I thought, searching for the man beneath the shell, the one who would *never* agree to an ambush of this nature.

Yes, I'd fucked up.

But he'd given me life. Created me. *Loved* me.

"Dad, I—"

"Quiet," he snapped, shutting Tray down with a wave of his hand. Power shot from his fingertips, nailing my brother in his chest and knocking him to the floor on a groan I felt to my very soul.

"*What the fuck?*" I demanded, stepping forward, ready to take this imposter down. Our father would never conduct himself in such a manner.

Yet no one seemed to notice.

Everyone just had this vacant acceptance about them, like they were watching some film in the Human Realm, not a father assaulting his son.

"You've been tried and found guilty of conspiring with Quandary Bloods, abusing your position as heir to the Elite Blood throne, and perjury against the Council," my father announced. "The punishment of which is immediate descension and the denouncing of your Elite Blood ties."

My eyebrows shot upward. "When was the trial?"

"Today."

I nearly laughed. "And I wasn't given a chance to speak on my own behalf? To my own damn Council?"

"I spoke for you," Shade said. "As your mate."

My lips parted as realization hit me square in the chest. "You son of a bitch. That's why you bit me!"

The bastard had the audacity to shrug. *To. Shrug.* Like it meant nothing that he'd taken all my rights away with a single damn bite!

And no, the irony of this situation was not lost on me.

Because he'd just done to me what he'd done to Aflora in the beginning.

"This is so fucked up," I said, shaking my head.

"What's *fucked up* is my own son, my *blood*, choosing an abomination over his duty to the crown." My father—or whoever this dick was—shook his head. "The descension begins now."

"Who are you?" I demanded.

"*Your king,*" he replied, power underlining those two words and wrapping around my neck like a noose. "Now *kneel.*"

"Fuck you," I choked out, my own gifts roaring to life, preparing for a fight.

I wasn't going to bend over and take this shit. The source had chosen me for a reason. *I* was the future king. And I let them feel it by unleashing all my power in a rapid wave of fire that engulfed the room in red embers.

"Kols!" Ella shouted, her small frame collapsing over Tray, her defensive shield rapidly melting beneath my fury.

Phoenix fire! I yanked my essence back, sparing her and my brother, only to feel my father's energy flare outward. It struck me directly in the chest.

My knees buckled beneath the impact, the air whooshing from my lungs. *No!* I pushed back, creating a shield to protect myself against the onslaught, but it was too late.

Dark energy rippled along my arms, the source calling upon my spirit to relinquish control. It hit me from inside, spreading a sharp demand through my veins, sucking the life from my very soul.

I cried out, the agony shredding apart the core of my being. It felt as though I was being ripped in half, my purpose in life dying before my eyes.

Don't do this. Please don't do this! I begged as the dark source reneged on every promise it had ever made.

The Council didn't help.

My father continued to pull... pull... *pull.*

"You're killing him!" Ella screamed.

Tears streamed from my eyes, my vision blurring as I attempted to yank some of the power back into my veins, my soul screeching in anguish at having my essence ripped from me without permission.

This can't be happening, I thought, bewildered and dazed. *How is this happening?*

I wasn't given a trial.

I wasn't given a chance to speak.

"*Stop!*" Emelyn demanded at the same time Tray wheezed out, "*Dad...*"

Wind rippled through the room, silencing them all and zeroing in on my chest as another spell pounded into my heart.

The denouncement.

He was *eviscerating* my essence. *Exsanguination.* I'd seen this done. I knew the chances of survival were slim, and after having the source ripped from me? I would never recover from this.

I was going to die.

By my father's own hand.

For falling for an abomination.

For choosing right over wrong.

For not wanting to subject an innocent to the death penalty just because our archaic laws dictated it.

I curled into a ball, my soul weeping as the blood drained from my body, squeezing every bit of life left from my veins.

I'm sorry, I thought to Aflora. *I'm so sorry I failed you.*

And Zeph

Oh, fuck, *Zeph.*

He would die, too. Not because of my death, but because the Council would require it.

All of them would pay the ultimate price.

Because I couldn't protect them. Because I'd failed them. Because I'd missed what was right in front of me this whole time.

Tray, I whispered, my twin, my other half, weeping in the distance. He was inconsolable. His sounds pricks of pain against my ears.

I reached for him, my spirit longing for his familiarity. *He's gone. They're all gone.*

The Council was vile and depraved. So fucking corrupt. So horribly behind the times.

I can't die like this! I thought, searching for the last of my reserves, needing to do something, *anything,* to hold on.

But there was nothing for me to grasp.

Everything had gone dark. *So. Fucking. Dark.*

No source.

No Midnight Fae essence.

No magic.

I was a shell of a fae. Left to wither and die alone. Because I'd never finished the mating bond. I had no one. Except *Night.*

A caw in the distance answered my call, black feathers touching my cheek as my familiar curled against me with the god-awful sound of death leaving his beak. It shattered the last of my reserve, knowing I'd failed him too. My sweet, loyal crow. So beautiful. So full of life. So… so… still…

No, I wept, clutching him to me as tears rolled down my face. *Not you, too.*

The injustice of it all curled in my stomach, my world disappearing in a cloud of torment.

"Nooo!" The scream pierced my ear. *Aflora.* I desperately tried to see her, to tell her to run. But I couldn't move.

Aflora, I thought, trying to picture her beautiful face and failing. Why couldn't I see her? Because we weren't mated. Not fully. She was never mine. And for the life of me, I couldn't remember why. It was a horrid twist of fate.

There would be no coming back from this.

Run, I whispered. *Run, sweetheart. Run.*

Silence fell, and regret threatened to overwhelm me.

We never had our chance. I'd chosen duty for too long. Arrogance had consumed me. An endless life of immortality. But sometimes fate plays tricks on us all.

Aflora…

My story was the punch line of a cruel joke. I took it all for granted. I should have known.

There's so much… I would have done… This can't be the end…

I choked, the last of my breaths escaping. I used it to breathe her name, my apology and regret whispered on the wind.

Leaving me alone with a withering soul and my dying crow.

Staring into the abyss.

Of a starless.

Everlasting.

Night.

CHAPTER TWENTY-FOUR

I couldn't breathe.

I'd *heard* Kols in my head, begging me to forgive him, screaming for another chance. And telling me to run. But my limbs were frozen from the onslaught of his agony.

So much pain.

So much regret.

So much *loneliness*.

Tears dampened my cheeks, and my knees curled into my chest as I struggled to regain control of my lungs. But the severing of his life rendered me immobile.

He's gone, I thought, feeling the last of his breath leave his body. *He's gone and I can't even see him!*

I screamed, not caring who heard, giving up on everyone around me, on life, on the world. The injustice! The incredible, *horrible* decision. And why? Because of a bond? One we'd created?

Earth Fae were all about life.

We valued vitality and sunshine and beautiful creatures. I longed for my leaves. My roots. My beautiful, adoring flowers.

This kingdom resembled death and misery.

They killed Kols.

Why?! I wanted to shout, my heart shattered. *We weren't done!*

He was my mate. My rock. My chosen half.

The earth source shrieked at the loss, one I let loose through my own lungs, my soul in tatters. *How could you?!* I wanted to demand. *What is wrong with you?!*

He was just a man.

A royal.

A good fae.

With a kind heart.

My Kols. My prince. My elemental mate.

It felt as though they'd severed one of my roots, the tree inside me wilting and dying from the loss. It burned. Oh, Elements, it burned!

I forgot how air worked.

Stopped allowing my heart to beat.

It was all gone.

He's gone.

My Kolstov... "How could you?" I breathed out loud, my voice a choked whisper of sound, hoarse from all the screaming. "*How. Could. You?*"

Energy rippled out of me, pouring into the ground as I released all my fury and pain and anguish. I was done. *So done!*

I hated them all.

They would *burn.*

Flames shot from my fingertips, scorching the ground.

Shrieks followed.

Power rippled.

And still, I unleashed, furious at those who had harmed me and mine. *My. Mate.*

They took him from me. They destroyed everything. I hated them! They would *pay* for what they'd done. Voices called my name. I ignored them, my agony too loud, my tears too fierce, my fire too *hot.*

Earth Fae create.

Midnight Fae destroy.

They considered me an abomination—a combination of the two.

All right.

I'd accept that. And now? Now they could feel what happened when I used *both* powers.

The earth source brightened as I ripped the necklace from my neck and released the reins. Create and destroy. Create. And. Destroy.

Brighten it all.

Then burn it down.

Life.

And.

Death.

Welcome to my world. Prepare to bow.

CHAPTER TWENTY-FIVE

ZAKKAI

S tunning.

Aflora resembled a goddess, her power pouring out of her at an impressive rate, turning over tables and eliciting screams in her glorious wake.

Burning thwomps sprouted all over the ballroom, their charred limbs shooting toward the ceiling and releasing flames of monstrous proportions.

She screamed again as she sent their branches searching, spearing all those in their paths.

"Aflora!" Zephyrus shouted, his green eyes wild with concern. He'd ripped off his pin the moment he'd realized how he'd been used, his annoyance palpable. Now he resembled a disheveled guard, his dark hair wild and his eyes layered with unshed tears.

If anyone should understand Aflora's reaction, it was him.

Yet he seemed hell-bent on stopping her show of power.

"Let her be," I said, adoring this passionate display of temper. It was a literal dream to watch her let go, to use all that harnessed energy in vengeful glory.

Hmm, although, those who deserved the brunt of her explosion weren't here. All the Councilmen and Elders were in another room. Except for Constantine.

It would do for now. He deserved this more than anyone.

However, his eyes were gleaming with approval as he met my gaze, his victorious smile giving me pause. Then, like a switch, that look dissolved into one of horror as he shoved away from the table, yelling, "*Abomination!*"

It took me two long seconds to realize his ploy, and to curse myself for not seeing it sooner.

"Everyone, run!" he screamed, his power igniting as he took on a defensive stance, the Warrior Bloods aligning with him. "*Run!*"

Fuck.

He was making an example of Aflora. Using her provoked display of power as a platform to stand on in his war against Quandary Bloods and abominations.

An alarming fact that came to fruition as whispers cascaded around the ballroom, the mounting terror feeding into his performance.

This was the real show.

And Aflora responded to her role in kind as flames engulfed all the exits, her emotions driving her reaction, not logic.

There were too many innocents in this room.

If she exploded now, she would never be fit to lead, even under a new regime. Everyone would fear her, realize Constantine was right to abolish those with too much power, and we would suffer another thousand or more years of this imposed segregation.

Destroying Constantine and the Council was what I'd always desired, and Aflora could absolutely accomplish that in this state.

But it wasn't the right way.

Now wasn't the right time.

It wouldn't be on Constantine Nacht's terms but on ours. I couldn't afford for him to use her as a pawn like this, not after everything else he'd done.

He would not win. Not this round. Not ever.

I ripped my watch off and engaged my mental connection to my mate. *Aflora. You need to calm down. This is what Constantine wants. He's going to use this episode as a platform to stand on in his quest to annihilate us all.*

She didn't reply, her concentration on the destruction growing inside her, that beautiful ball of cerulean energy mingling with green and purple and her earth.

Life and death. She was repeating the words in her head with another phrase. *Create and destroy.*

No, Aflora, I said, crawling over to her on the floor.

She'd fallen off her chair moments after chaos erupted in the source, and I hadn't stood back up after Constantine had hit me with a spell. I'd been too dazed and confused by the descension of power to attempt to fight. My father had drilled strategy into my mind from a young age, a gift I was astutely thankful for right now.

I grabbed her wrist. *Aflora.*

Flames sprang up between us as she tried to shove me away with her cerulean WarFire. I inhaled the spell with my mind, dismantling it before she could burn me. Then I encircled us with an impenetrable bubble. Zephyrus fell inside it, my enchantment tied to those with Aflora's best interests at heart —which apparently included him.

Fine.

He could stay.

"Help me," I demanded, catching his gaze. "We need to ground her."

I flinched as Constantine hit my shield with a spell meant to eat through the fabric of my outer layer. The source energy gave me momentary pause, my gaze sliding to his through the invisible barrier.

Then I caught the inky lines writhing across his skin, the dark source growing in him by the second, confirming his re-ascension. Only, it wasn't the traditional form. No trials. No rituals. Just a call to the dark source to grant him access, to name him the rightful king.

And another piece of the puzzle snapped into place.

He was using this incident as a reason to retake the throne. He would claim Malik wasn't powerful enough to stop Aflora, so he took over the mantle to protect his people.

A fantastic platform for a dictator.

All with Aflora at the heart of it. Then he'd use his newfound rise to power to call for mass extermination again, and this time, he would have the full backing of the people.

Fear was a motivator.

And Constantine was an expert manipulator.

I saw it all play out in my mind, his strategy masterful.

"Zakkai!" Zephyrus shouted as more WarFire poured out of Aflora, heading straight for my shield. I yanked it back with my mind, squandering it and shoving her to the ground.

"Stop!" I commanded, my hands on her shoulders, my legs straddling hers. "It's what he wants!"

"We need to bite her," Zephyrus said. "It's helped before."

"Her other implosions were unintentional," I gritted out through my teeth as she started creating a wall of her own in her mind to block us all out. If she succeeded, my barrier would dissolve beneath her power, and she'd destroy the fucking room.

I leaned down to kiss her, putting the full force of my power on display while I took control of her as the Source Architect. I weaved my energy through hers, dismantling her wall block by block. She growled, creating more, faster and faster, but I countered each one and kissed her harder.

Come on, Aflora. Hear me.

No! she shouted, her agony a blade against my soul. *They killed him! They killed Kolstov!*

I know, I whispered.

You wanted him dead, she accused. *You. This is all because of you!*

I sighed, hearing the pain in those words and realizing how much she would have hated me had I fulfilled my plan to end the entire Nacht line. It was too late now, the deed already done, and no apology would right this wrong for her.

So I tried another avenue. *There's too much innocent life in this room, Aflora. The ones who deserve retribution aren't here. Look at their souls, sweet star. See who they are.*

He's here, she growled. *He's right there!*

And he's surrounded himself by innocents, I tried again. *This isn't the way.*

It's what you wanted.

I know, I agreed. *But not like this.*

Another scream split her lips, more power rushing out of her in tormented fury, her emotions piercing my heart and temporarily muting my senses.

"*Aflora*," Zephyrus breathed as he collapsed beside us, clutching his chest, his eyes wide as fiery energy swathed him like a lethal blanket. His defenses came alive as he tried to fight it, but her power destroyed it in a flash, touching his skin and eliciting a tortured bellow from his mouth.

"You're going to kill him!" I shouted, my hands moving to her throat and giving her a squeeze. "Focus, Aflora. See what you're doing!"

She snarled at me, so I cupped her cheek and tilted her head toward Zephyrus. The flames had engulfed him completely, and I didn't have the energy to dismantle that spell and keep up our barrier—which Constantine had almost gotten through with his growing magic.

A gasp caught in Aflora's throat, the energy dying in an instant as she tried to squirm toward him. I moved, allowing her to reach his now still form.

Constantine threw another deadly spell our way, one I caught this time and volleyed back at him while Aflora's dangerous energy morphed into one of life and vitality.

She pressed her palms to Zephyrus's chest, her new spell warm and comforting as she pulled her negative enchantment from his spirit.

He inhaled sharply in response, then muttered a curse and clutched his chest. Tears poured down Aflora's cheeks, apologies flying from her lips. But we didn't have time for that. We had an irate Elite Blood hammering on my shell with far too much power.

Ascensions took time for a reason. They were about balance and control, neither of which he seemed to possess at the moment.

And he was surrounded by Warrior Bloods and Malefic Bloods, their combined energies forming a lethal weapon that would destroy us all if we didn't find a way out.

"Aflora," I whispered. "I need you to shadow us."

We weren't ready for this battle.

And there were still too many innocents, Aflora's flames having blocked their exits.

"Aflora, I need you to shadow us," I repeated, grimacing as the final layer of my shield began to crumble. "*Right fucking now!*"

She grabbed my wrist, her other palm still touching Zephyrus, and engaged her connection to Shade. It was visceral and real, my mind so connected to hers that I *felt* her growing energy.

She found what she needed from him without much thought, her powers working on instinct alone. Then she whirled the three of us into a cloud of dark magic and took us to a bedroom I didn't recognize.

I collapsed on the floor, my energy reserves depleted and in dire need of restoration.

Aflora fell to the ground beside me, her shoulders shaking as she deteriorated into sobs. Zephyrus pulled her to him, holding her with a ferocity that made me envious. I wanted to do that. I wanted to comfort her. But I couldn't fucking move.

And I knew she didn't want me right now.

You wanted him dead, she'd said, the accusation thick in my thoughts.

Had I known what it would do to her… I… I wasn't sure I would have been able to go through with it. It'd been my goal all along. But seeing her now, hearing her cries, watching her fall apart… I never wanted to be responsible for such agony.

She was my mate.

My other half.

My Flora.

I would never put her through something like this. Fuck, she'd been through so much already. She didn't deserve any of this.

It left me wondering what would have happened had I refused my father's command. No bond. No yanking her into this world of war and destruction. Would she be in a flower bed now? Playing with her earth magic? Smiling at some boy, a *good* mate, who made her trees and other forms of blooming life?

My heart thudded wildly against my ribs, my mind forming the picture perfectly.

Sweet Aflora, growing into her Earth Fae Queen status.

Happy.

Twirling in a circle.

Flowers in her hair.

So fucking beautiful.

But her cries to my left reminded me of her reality, her dark hair spilling across the carpet, as her body trembled beneath violent sobs.

The enchantment had worn off. She was herself again. Except her cerulean irises were blurred with tears, her cheeks red, her shoulders rounded.

This wasn't who she was meant to be. She reminded me of a wilted flower, her final petals falling to the ground as the life disappeared from her features.

I'm sorry, I whispered into her mind, my heart breaking for her, for *us*. *I'm so fucking sorry, Aflora.*

I reached for her, needing to do something, when feet landed to my right, Shade's essence clawing at my senses and drawing my gaze up to him and the body in his arms. "I need you all to listen and do exactly what I say," he declared. "Or we'll lose Kolstov forever."

CHAPTER TWENTY-SIX

SHADE

"*H*is *death will be your burden to bear,*" my grandmother had warned me weeks ago.

"*I think I screwed up,*" I'd told her that night.

"*Come,*" she'd replied. "*We'll discuss it over cookies.*"

I knew then that she had bad news for me. But this… I hadn't expected her to warn me about *this*.

She'd said that Kolstov's life was the price I would pay for all my fucking around with time.

Well, I don't accept that, I thought, repeating the words I'd said to her that night.

There was no way to come back from death. Once a life strand ended, no amount of magic or time manipulation could fix it.

Which was why I couldn't afford for Kolstov's life strand to permanently end.

Come on, Emelyn, I thought. *Do your thing.*

She was my distraction. The ticking time bomb. The one I knew would explode if pushed enough. And I needed her to erupt for me now.

All I need is a few seconds. My teeth clenched a little at the thought, but I quickly schooled my features once more and covered the oversight with a yawn. No one could sense my intentions. And I only had one chance to get this right.

Come on. Come on. Come on.

My pulse kicked up a notch.

Just a little meltdown. I know you have it in you. I've seen it.

"You're killing him!" Ella screamed, lunging forward and being thrown back by one of Malik's spells. Lima winced as Ella hit the wall.

A few other Councilmen exchanged glances.

I looked at Tadmir. He angled his chin just a little, saying, *Not yet.*

He knew what I planned to do.

He'd helped me strategize this entire event.

He also knew what would happen if I got this wrong. *"Only one shot, Shade. And you'll be risking everything to do it,"* he'd warned.

"Kolstov doesn't deserve to die for my choices," I'd told him.

"If he knew the alternative fate, he might disagree."

"We're not having this discussion," I'd snapped. *"Either help me fix this, or fuck off."*

I very rarely lost my temper, but I was at wits' end with all this bullshit. Aflora had detonated seven times under my watch. Nearly destroyed countless lives. Then almost took her own life after realizing the extent of pain she'd caused others.

Never again.

Tonight, we would get this right.

Just as soon as I fixed this problem.

Malik gathered energy into his palm, readying the next phase of Kolstov's punishment. A few Councilmen gaped at his decision to force his own son to serve both sentences back-to-back. This would kill him, and they all knew it.

Yet no one spoke.

My father even grinned.

Could no one see the truth before their eyes? That this wasn't really Malik, but Constantine's doing?

"Stop!" Emelyn shrieked as the power grew.

"Dad," Tray whispered, his eyes rounding in horror.

Emelyn shot forward, WarFire forming on her fingertips.

This was my moment.

Five seconds, I thought, concentrating on Kolstov's soul and whispering an enchantment through my mind. *Alqiama Fi Al Mawt.* Energy hummed along my skin, subtle and disguised by Emelyn's outburst as she nailed Malik with her power.

Several gasps followed, then the Elite Blood King hit Emelyn with a paralyzing enchantment that stunned her into immediate silence. Lima cursed, catching his daughter as she fell.

"This is why females are forbidden in Council matters," Malik seethed, the words ones I'd heard Constantine say almost verbatim. "Too emotional. Get her out of here."

Lima didn't argue, carrying his daughter from the room on quick feet.

Tray gathered Ella close, shielding her with his body, his eyes wide with horror as his father resumed his spell, nailing Kolstov with the exsanguination charm.

A jolt hit my chest as I absorbed the spell with Kolstov, my ties to his soul forcing me to endure the pain with him.

My burden, I thought, gritting my teeth. *I. Accept. This. Burden.*

It burned like a motherfucker, sucking the life from my lungs and weakening my knees. To everyone else, they would see our bond dying and chalk up my reaction to the pain of losing a mate.

I'd planned this moment perfectly.

Previous experience had prepared me with a manipulation plan, one where I informed Constantine of everything as it happened. Including the mate bonds.

Because he already knew everything from Dakota.

She'd been his asset all along, having seduced Zephyrus and Kolstov to teach the future king a valuable lesson. Then she infiltrated the Quandary Bloods under the guise of being ousted from society after the prince ruined her reputation.

So rather than hide, I presented myself as forthcoming and trustworthy. But I only went to Constantine with my information, then he told me what to tell the others.

He thought I was his puppet, that I believed his lies about grooming me as the future king.

I played every game, won every riddle, and volunteered for the tasks he desired, all the while knowing how they would truly benefit me in the end.

Constantine used Aflora's disappearance as a way to discredit Kolstov, stating he'd failed his trials. Then he'd told me to let Chern sense the other bonds, to have him reveal the truth to the Council.

I'd claimed innocence. *"Their bands hid the link from me,"* I'd said. *"But Chern detected them while searching for Aflora. Her essence leads to Zeph and Kols."*

Several Councilmen wanted to bring Kolstov in for questioning.

Constantine quieted them, said to watch him instead, and suggested I be in charge of monitoring the Midnight Fae Prince.

And that was when I'd recommended the bite. *"It'll provide me with a way to really keep tabs on him, just like Aflora."*

The approval in Constantine's irises had been unnerving.

Then Malik had disagreed.

And the two had dismissed themselves to engage in a private conversation, one where Constantine weaved a spell that no one seemed to see except for me. Perhaps because I'd witnessed variations of it in other timelines.

Regardless, permission was given.

The link was formed.

And everyone thought I'd done it out of duty.

My knees buckled now as the last of Kolstov's life began to slip away, his crow appearing from thin air to caw in devastation against his master's chest.

Ella burst into tears.

Tray sat stunned.

And I focused on that thread... the single speck of life that I needed... to bring Kolstov back.

Don't you dare let go, I thought at him, aware that he couldn't hear me, his final breath touching the air. *Work with me here, Kolstov. Don't give up.*

But I felt him slipping away, his heart slowing as the final specks of his blood disappeared.

Fully dry.

Depleted of his essence.

Dead by all definitions of the word.

I hung my head, my heart in tatters. If this was what losing a first-level mate felt like, I couldn't imagine what I'd endure if something happened to Aflora.

Death consumed me, my energy wilting beneath the onslaught of loss. But that flicker of life remained, tugging at my essence, sucking at the needed power to remain alive.

Don't let go of me, I whispered. *I've got you.*

Tears blurred my eyes, the impact of loss overwhelming and terrifying.

Fuck, Kols. Just… hold on.

Because I couldn't bear to truly lose him. And I didn't even really like him. This had to be destroying Aflora.

As though she heard me, a rumble of power went through the ground, her energy flaring to life.

My eyes widened at the impact, then my lips parted as a burning thwomp shot up from the floor, decimating the table.

Oh, shit.

The Councilmen reacted, Malik running to the door and leaving his son's corpse behind without a second thought.

Tray crawled toward his twin, his expression one I never wanted to see on another person again. *Devastation. Loss. Abject terror.*

"Tray," Ella whispered, her voice choked.

But he didn't hear her, his body collapsing over his brother on an anguished cry.

I swallowed, my fractured heart hammering against my ribs.

Tadmir was suddenly at my side, kneeling with his palm on my back. "Now, Shade. You have to take him now." The words were a breath against my ear, lost to everyone else as they all started charging from the room, running toward Aflora's intense destruction.

"He'll be fine," Tadmir said in a louder tone, a smirk in his voice. "But I can't say I'm not enjoying his pain."

"Oh, fuck off," my father snapped.

"Come on, Aswad. It's putting some much-needed hair on his chest," Tadmir taunted.

I knew what he was doing—goading my father into another distraction, to give me time to act.

Once I did this, everyone would know my true allegiance.

The game would be up.

A final decision. Because there would be no coming back after this. Playing with time would no longer apply, not with Kolstov's pending resurrection.

I've got you, I repeated, tugging on his dwindling spirit, his life literally slipping through my fingers with each passing second. *We can do this, Kols. We. Can. Do. This.*

I pushed myself to my feet, my limbs shaking with the effort. But adrenaline pushed me forward.

Tray snarled at me as I approached, his fury a whiplash to my senses. Then he broke again on an agonized cry that had Ella shattering beside him.

"I'm going to fix it," I told them in a hushed whisper, my voice barely carrying. I wasn't even sure if they heard me, and I didn't have time to say it again.

Kolstov's essence was almost gone.

Now, I thought, using a blast of power to push Tray away from his brother. Then I bent and picked up Kolstov.

"Shadow?" My father's confusion was palpable in his tone.

I ignored him, instead shifting my focus to Aflora as she engaged our bond. *Shadowing,* I heard her instincts whisper. I pushed the gift to her and told her where to go without words.

Then I followed her with Kolstov.

And landed shakily on my feet beside Zakkai.

His silver-blue irises flashed as he looked up at me.

"I need you all to listen and do exactly what I say," I said. "Or we'll lose Kolstov forever."

Then I collapsed beside him, my tether to Kolstov snapping like a band inside my soul.

His essence floating... floating... *gone.*

CHAPTER TWENTY-SEVEN

ZAKKAI

I caught Shade's spell in my mind, yanking it back to life and realizing with sharp clarity what he'd done.

Kolstov.

He'd cast a Death Blood necromancy spell meant to hold on to life for as long as possible after death, typically used when wanting to question a spirit in the afterlife.

A clever fucking trick.

One that might just work.

"Aflora," I said, needing her to bolster the spell, my energy waning fast. *Help me*, I demanded into her mind, shoving the enchantment at her and forcing her dark magic to life.

She gasped, her confusion quickly melting to shocked understanding.

"*Kols,*" she breathed, throwing herself at the body on the floor.

His essence, I hissed, yanking her mental focus back to me and the spell I barely had a hold of in my mental grasp. "What do we do with it?" I demanded through my teeth. "*Shade. Tell me what the fuck to do with it.*" Because I was about to lose it.

Aflora joined me, her mind forming a treelike branch that she used to ground the spell, her soul functioning as the root.

She started to shake beneath the power, the afterlife demanding its due.

This was the heart of true dark magic.

And she was using her affinity for life to keep Kolstov's soul in our reality.

Shade began to chant, his voice a rasp of sound.

"What the fuck is going on?" Zephyrus demanded.

"Ground her," Shade growled. "Bite her. Give her *everything.*"

Zephyrus looked at the Death Blood only once, then slid his fangs into Aflora's shoulder. She cried out as his essence swathed her in a cloak of defensive energy. She immediately sighed, her relief palpable as her branch grew, twining around the magical strand inch by inch and disappearing into the ether.

I'd never seen anything like it.

The combination of magic a stunning sight.

"You, too," Shade said through his teeth. "*Now, Zakkai.*"

Aflora trembled again, her lips parting in agony.

I mimicked Zephyrus's position, kneeling on her opposite side with Kolstov's still form on the ground before us, and bit her neck, her blood an aphrodisiac on my tongue that made me moan. *Fuck, it's been too long.* I rarely drank from the vein. And lately, I had only indulged in blood-infused foods.

But Aflora…

Dear Fae, *Aflora…*

She cried out, causing my magic to instinctively react to her pain, cloaking her in my energy and giving her access to whatever she needed.

Puzzles ran through her mind as she sorted through the cacophony of information my essence provided.

Then she shoved all those details into her branch, using it to bolster her hold on Kolstov's life, infusing him with dark magic once more.

Shade joined us next, taking a position across from Kolstov, wrapping his fingers through Aflora's hair, and yanking her mouth to his. Rather than take her blood, he provided his own, feeding her his essence with his tongue before guiding her to his neck and encouraging her to bite down.

She didn't hesitate, absorbing his power directly from the vein and engaging my Quandary side to learn all the Death Blood spells she needed to force Kolstov's soul to heed her call.

Then she moved to Zephyrus, forcing him to release her shoulder so she could sink her teeth into his neck next. She used his Guardian bond to Kolstov to locate the remnants of the Midnight Fae Prince's soul in the source, guiding them back to his being, pulling him back together one piece at a time.

Shade bent over Kolstov, whispering those words, his palms on the other man's chest.

Air whirled around us, the source responding to the call to *restore*.

I closed my eyes, diving into my dark home and granting the required permission to *create*. The powers responded in warm welcome, recognizing their chosen architect and allowing Aflora's enchantment to flourish.

My hair blew back from my face, my teeth leaving Aflora's throat as she yanked me into a demanding kiss, her incisors piercing my tongue.

I allowed it, groaning as she sucked my essence into her mouth, swallowing greedily. Then I guided her to the pulse point of my neck and closed my eyes as she bit down.

Euphoria poured through me, my reserves somehow replenishing as though she'd just gifted me with the bite of life. Then I felt her pull everything she could from my soul and shove it through her link to Kolstov.

I flinched, the redirection of power uncomfortable.

But I felt her doing it from her other bonds as well.

And then from herself.

She poured the mixture into her branch, infusing the strand with intense vitality.

Shade took hold of the mental cord, his hum of Death magic causing all the hairs along my arms to rise as he closed his eyes and unleashed it all through his palms into Kolstov's chest.

Silence followed.

None of us daring to breathe.

Aflora shivered, her cerulean irises on Kolstov, her bloody lip clenched between her teeth.

I swallowed.

Everything had been done on instinct, Aflora taking charge and demonstrating why fate had chosen her for this destiny.

But had she done it right?

Shade's palms remained on Kolstov's chest, his focus on the prince's face. He narrowed his gaze, then lifted his wrist to his mouth and bit down. "Blood," Shade said. "He needs blood." He started to lower his offering to Kolstov, but Aflora caught his arm.

"He needs mine." She bit down on her wrist and pressed it to Kolstov's lips.

Energy pooled around her as she combined all our essences inside her and poured it through her bloodline, directly into the man's mouth.

Seconds passed.

Nothing happened.

I met Shade's gaze, wary.

Zephyrus wore a similar expression of concern as I looked at him.

Then a subtle *thud* met my ears.

A second one ensued.

And a third.

Followed by a gasp from the male below as his eyes flew open, his golden irises dimmed to a burnt bronze. His focus fell entirely on Aflora, his throat working as he swallowed her blood.

Magic swirled around all of us, coating our skin in a unique essence that smelled like flowers in bloom.

Aflora.

She was claiming us all with her elemental soul.

Securing our bonds.

Strengthening us with earth.

Her source welcomed us, admiring our different powers and zeroing in on me as a known architect.

Warmth touched my spirit, power igniting and merging and creating life all around us.

Vines crawled along the walls, flowers budding at the tips, adding a splash of color to the otherwise modern room.

A bed of grass formed along the ground beneath us, overtaking the carpet and creating our own little oasis.

Aflora shifted, drawing my attention back to her and Kolstov. She'd bent to comb the fingers of her free hand through his hair, the auburn locks tinged with ash on the ends.

Kiss of death, I realized, noting his burnt irises again.

He no longer bore the mark of the dark source, but a branding from the afterlife.

I studied his magic with my own, noting the way everything had manifested inside him.

Part Earth.

Part Death Blood.

Part Quandary Blood.

Part Warrior Blood.

And a tiny bit of Elite Blood.

A true abomination. A complete work of art. A miracle.

I stared at Aflora, awed by her power and kindness. I finally understood why fate had instructed us to walk this path together.

She possessed all the qualities that a royal should.

A true monarch.

My queen.

The kind of female worth giving up all my plans for, which I'd done when I helped her revive the prince I was destined to kill.

Or maybe it was never him at all.

But the king who had taken over his ascension.

Constantine Nacht. The Elite Blood who started it all.

"He needs more blood," Aflora whispered, her fingers still combing through Kolstov's hair.

Zephyrus bit his wrist and held it out for the other man, his eyes falling closed as his lover and friend latched onto him for a drink.

Aflora pulled her own arm away, the wound still fresh. I took her hand and pulled her wrist to my mouth, laving the laceration and gently kissing her tender skin.

She leaned into me, seeking strength, which I happily provided.

Shade gave Kolstov blood next, the Elite Blood's eyebrows drawing down at the offering but accepting it when Aflora whispered, "Drink."

I was last.

Leaving me with a choice.

Give him the essence he needed to finish the healing process, or walk away.

A week ago—hell, an *hour ago*—I would have laughed and left him to his fate. But now I understood the destiny carved out before us, the path we were always meant to walk, and the reason Shade had gone to such lengths to coax us into this line.

I held my wrist to Aflora's mouth, allowing her to do the honors with her blunt teeth, then lowered the offering to the bewildered male on the ground.

He jolted as my blood touched his tongue, the power inside me writhing in response to the former heir's essence, bathing him in dark magic and restoring the last of his reserves.

A bond slid into place between us, tying our souls together for eternity and officially squandering my ability to ever kill him.

Because our lives were linked now, and the flare of his nostrils confirmed he felt it, too.

I sensed his finalized bond to Zephyrus and budding one with Shade.

And his nearly complete tie to Aflora.

Thank you, she whispered into my mind, aware of what I'd just sacrificed by allowing him to imbibe my essence. My retribution would need to be redefined.

But I already knew that.

It'd been obvious the moment I felt her pain. I would never allow her to experience such agony again.

I leaned in to kiss her, allowing my mouth to do all the talking without words.

With one arm around her and my opposite hand at Kolstov's mouth, we formed a pretty awkward triangle. Only heightened by the other two men in the circle, their presence an unexpected comfort to the situation at hand.

It allowed me to devour her properly, without having to keep my guard up to protect her.

Because I knew Zephyrus and Shade had that part covered.

Then Kolstov released my wrist, his energy warming the air. Aflora slowly pulled away from my kiss, her cerulean gaze falling to the former royal on the floor.

They stared at each other for a long moment, his expression intense. Then he glanced at Shade, his eyes narrowing.

A humming current floated through the air, the Death Blood engaging a telepathic link with Kolstov that the rest of us could feel but not hear.

They were only mated on the first level, but Shade was no ordinary fae. I wasn't surprised that he could converse mentally at an initial stage of a mating. He probably could have done the same with Aflora.

"Out loud," Zephyrus said, those two words underlined in command.

"I'm telling him how we saved him," Shade replied, his voice soft and reverent. "How *Aflora* saved him."

"We," she corrected. "You were right to say *we.*"

"What happened?" Zephyrus asked. "How did…? Why did…?"

"Constantine knew about the mating," Shade said, holding Kolstov's gaze. "He's known since the beginning. And not initially from me."

"Dakota," I muttered.

"Yes," he confirmed. "But I knew from previous experience that she was feeding him information. So I did as well to win his favor."

"How many times has this happened?" I asked.

But I already knew the answer.

There was no turning back time with death.

We were in the final version of events, Kolstov forever in this state. If we went back, we risked leaving him behind.

"Everything always comes to a head at the Blood Gala," Shade replied, his voice gruff. "Aflora detonates. People die. But this is the first time Kols has ever been stripped of the source."

"What about your grandmother?" Kolstov asked. "They were going to get her?"

Shade snorted. "That was a ploy to make you both react. But it's true that Constantine has known my grandmother's location. Dakota told him, as did I —again, to win his favor. However, he can't use the information because of where she created the paradigm."

I smirked. "Yes, the Hell Fae realm isn't typically fond of visitors. I've always wondered how Zen convinced them to allow her to hide there." She must have engaged in a deal with Lucifer. From what I understood of the old fae, he was fond of those.

Kolstov and Zephyrus looked at me for a moment, then the latter shook his head.

"Okay, so what changed?" Zephyrus demanded. "Why would Constantine choose to act now and not before?"

"The bonds," Shade whispered. "They didn't exist before. Not for you. Not for Kolstov. Not like this."

"She always undid them," Kolstov replied, his voice gruff. "In my suite."

"Yes," Shade confirmed softly, his gaze going to a stunned Aflora. "You carried through with your threat in various ways, sometimes that day, sometimes a few days or weeks later. But it always ended the same way. And it took me seven catastrophic events to realize what you needed. What *we* needed. And it's finally done. We're finally… here."

Silence fell, all of us consuming that information in our own ways.

I already suspected most of this, had dreamt of many different instances that just felt too real to be fantasy. Aflora detonating… then nothing.

"You never let her finish," I realized out loud. "That's why there's no end."

"Not exactly," he replied. "I… I watched her lose herself… and I *saw* what it would do to her in the end. All those lives taken and destroyed, by her hand…"

"She destroyed herself afterward," I said, swallowing thickly. "That's what you foresaw." Or perhaps not him, but Zen.

He dipped his chin once, confirming. "Every time."

"I would never… I could never…" Aflora shook her head, looking between us all. "Don't ever let me do that."

"We stopped you tonight," I reminded her. "Which I'm guessing has never happened before."

"The catalyst for her eruption changed," Shade said. "Constantine has always found a way to provoke her, but he's never used Kols."

"Because Kolstov always sided with Constantine," I translated.

"Yes," Shade replied.

Kolstov shook his head adamantly. "I would *never* side with him."

"You have and did," Shade assured him. "Several times. Zeph, too."

"Bullshit," Zephyrus retorted.

Shade sighed. "She severed the bonds. Which took a great deal of power. And the experience changed us all in varying ways."

"Because severing bonds requires sacrifice," I said, something my father had to know yet never told me. However, it made sense to me now. "It's soul magic. Undoing it…"

"Hurts," Shade finished for me. "It hurts. *A lot*. Which you already know."

"I never unraveled our bond."

"But you built a cage around it and blocked yourselves from feeling it," he replied. "You know what it takes and what it can do."

I stared at him for a long moment, slowly understanding his statement. "It changes you," I said, repeating what he'd already said. "Makes you not recognize who you used to be."

All these years, I thought it was my father's training that had altered me on a fundamental level. But that wasn't it at all.

Closing off our link, ignoring half of my spirit, was what morphed me into a darker person with a desire for vengeance. Experience helped, too, but it went so much deeper than that.

"It's like killing off half of your soul," I breathed.

"Exactly," Shade replied. "And it took me far too long to realize that. But when you alter fate in such a way, you're burdened with a price."

"Kolstov," I said.

"Kolstov," he agreed, gazing down at the male in question. "However, I wasn't willing to pay that price. So I bit you and worked with Tadmir to come up with a plan that would save your life. And it worked."

"Which means we've altered another strand of fate," I murmured, my eyes narrowing. "What path are we on now?"

"One that has yet to be written," Shade replied, his voice thick with emotion. "One we can never go back from."

Because it would jeopardize everything we'd just sacrificed for Kolstov.

Another bout of silence fell, the four of us kneeling on the floor around Kolstov's prone form. I squeezed Aflora's side, my arm still around her lower back.

She glanced up at me and then at each of her mates, her cerulean gaze alight with renewed power. "What now?" she asked.

"We kill Constantine," I said without missing a beat.

"We kill Constantine," Zephyrus and Shade agreed in unison.

All of us looked down at the former Midnight Fae Prince, awaiting his verdict. "We'll need a plan," he finally said. "A good one." Then he glanced around, frowning at the bedroom. "Where the bloody hell are we, anyway?"

Great fucking question, I thought, following his gaze to take in all of Aflora's earthlike decorations.

"A paradigm," she whispered. "Shade created it."

The Death Blood grinned. "That I did, little rose."

"I can feel your energy all over it," she admitted, her eyes closing in content. "I can feel all of our energy here." Her lips curled as more earth sprouted to life around us, her power humming through the air with renewed strength.

Renewed strength underlined in *need*.

She'd expelled a lot of energy.

Had exchanged so much blood.

And now the Earth Fae in her was craving invigoration of a different sort.

My lips curled. *Oh, little star. Do you need something from your mates?*

Her muscles tensed along her back as she clenched her thighs beneath the dress, her pulse a beacon begging to be bitten. Zephyrus noticed it as well, his green eyes roaming over her with the knowledge of a man well versed in reading female anatomy.

I glanced at Shade, noting his smirk.

We all sensed it. Even Kolstov was reacting to it, albeit a little slower than the rest.

This was a safe place. I could feel it in the infrastructure of the paradigm. But I added a touch of my magic to it, bolstering the walls and adding a few trigger warnings, just in case.

Because I had a feeling we were about to be preoccupied for a while.

Well, at least Aflora would be. I might just stand by and watch her work. I didn't want our first time to be with an audience.

That said, if she kept radiating all that sexual energy, I might be inclined to change my mind.

What's wrong, Aflora? I hummed into her mind, well aware of what bothered her. But she hadn't answered my question, which really was more like an offer.

If she wanted to play, we'd all oblige.

It'd been an intense day. We could all use the relief, and sex would provide that.

I... I feel... She trailed off, biting her bottom lip.

Needy? I suggested, leaning in to nibble her neck. *Hot?*

Yes, she moaned into my mind. *But I don't... I...*

I smiled. For someone so incredibly fierce, I found it rather amusing that she could revert so quickly to her shy and delicate side. Or perhaps she didn't yet understand that her body required nourishment to help replenish her reserves. She'd expelled so much today, more than she likely ever had before. And now her spirit required supplemental nutrients from her mates.

Technically, some blood would help.

But I preferred her body's suggestion instead.

"Aflora?" Kolstov breathed, his pupils dilating as her sensual energy rolled over him. He, too, would be craving life after being so close to death.

All of us were.

A hum stirred among us, one simmering with desire and yearning—a yearning only our heart could appease. Our *Aflora*.

Kolstov breathed her name again, reaching for her as she opened her eyes.

"Kols," she whimpered, her instincts taking over as she practically collapsed on top of him. Her body molded to his, her mouth claiming his.

My blood heated in response, her power a seductive pull that left me useless to stop her.

Bow to the queen, her essence whispered.

And so I bowed, my soul hers to command.

CHAPTER TWENTY-EIGHT

AFLORA

Vitality surrounded me, my earth essence humming all around us.

We'd created life.

Renewed a destroyed soul.

Stirred energy into a being who deserved so much more.

Fire flourished through my veins, my powers all mingling together in a culminating moment of rightness, with Kols at the heart of it all.

I kissed him as though my life depended on his, because it did. I'd tied us all together, rooted my soul in each of my mate's beings, ensuring we were forever connected.

A circle of life in its truest form.

We might not have planned for this to happen. We might not even really like each other. But it didn't matter. We belonged to each other now, and would for eternity.

"Bite me again," I whispered, begging Kols to finish our connection. I'd felt his mating bond snap into place with Zeph, and I wanted to experience the same. I *needed* to belong to Kols just as much as he belonged to me. "Please, Kols. Please bite me again."

He lifted his hand, his fingers threading through my hair as he secured his grip. Then he pulled my throat to his mouth, his incisors piercing my skin on a delicious wave of ecstasy I felt all the way to my toes.

Somehow, we were all still dressed.

A miracle, considering the inferno heating my skin.

I wanted to be naked.

To mate my men.

To experience lust in its primal form.

Unzip me, I begged Zeph. *Unzip my dress. Please.*

His amusement touched my thoughts. *I do love it when you beg, pixie flower.*

But rather than force me to repeat myself, his fingers went to my spine, drawing the fabric down to expose my bare back.

The dress had been too tight to wear anything comfortably beneath, a fact I was now very pleased about. Because it meant I had nothing else to remove.

Except the zipper ended near the base of my spine, leaving me far more clothed than I wanted. *Off. Get it off me. Please, Zeph.*

I chose him because I knew he required control.

The others would do whatever I asked.

But Zeph would do what he preferred.

Fortunately, he agreed with me being naked, because he ripped the gown the rest of the way, then tugged on the straps, breaking them with ease.

I breathed a sigh of relief, the cooler air a welcome touch to my senses.

Then Zeph drew a palm up the back of my thigh. I knew it was him by the warmth and measured course of his movements, his hand both a caress and a brand against my overheated skin.

Kols released my throat on a groan. "*Fuck*, it's weird having you in my head."

Zeph chuckled as he bent to kiss my shoulder, his touch drifting higher to the growing dampness between my thighs. I sat astride Kols's hips, placing my center directly over his growing arousal—an arousal Zeph could now feel since he'd slid his hand between us. He knelt behind me, his heat a welcome blanket against my back.

"Kiss him again, pixie flower," he whispered. "I don't think he's had enough of your sweet mouth."

I shivered at the dominance in his tone, my nipples beading against Kols's button-down shirt as I kissed him just like Zeph demanded.

My essence coated his tongue, my blood tying us together on the final level that married our souls.

Four mates, I thought, sighing as all their spirits mingled with mine.

I'd somehow bonded them all on the third level as an Elemental Fae as well, missing only one final culminating act. One that would require another Elemental Fae to administer.

Later.

We would do that later.

For now, I needed them to fulfill another need. One I felt rivaled in each of them. Even Zakkai. Although, he'd chosen to shift a few feet away, content to watch Zeph work.

Don't leave, I said.

I wouldn't even if I could, star, he replied into my mind. *Besides, you'll need me after your "adequate" experience with them.*

I smiled against Kols's mouth, amused by Zakkai's teasing. *They're more than adequate.*

Mmm, we'll see.

"Is there any lube in this paradigm?" Zeph asked, his touch sliding from my damp center to my backside and sending a shiver down my spine. I wasn't sure if he planned to use that on Kols… or on me. It was something we hadn't done yet. Something I'd *never* done.

"Yes," Shade replied. "Nightstand."

"Grab it," Zeph demanded.

If your Warrior Blood tries to command me, he'll quickly learn that the only one I will ever consider kneeling to is you, Zakkai murmured into my mind. *So let's hope he doesn't think I'll acquiesce as easily as the others.*

He likes control, I replied, arching as Zeph inserted a finger into my ass. "Oh," I breathed, my lips leaving Kols's.

"How about we move her to the bed?" Shade suggested. He stood beside it with the bottle in his hand, just like Zeph had requested.

Well, *demanded.*

I like control, too, Zakkai informed me softly. *Think you can handle two alpha males in your life, sweet star?*

Pretty sure I'm surrounded by four, I replied as Zeph lifted me into his arms and carried me to the bed.

"Kols. Strip," he said as he set me on the mattress.

"Make me," Kols replied, a challenge in his tone that had me squeezing my thighs together. He'd stood up, his regal posture a sight to behold after he'd been so near death. Yet somehow he appeared even more royal now with his ash-tipped hair and bronzed irises.

He resembled a conqueror. *Conqueror of Death,* I mused, liking the new title.

"You want me to make you?" Zeph arched a dark brow, turning toward Kols as he removed his own jacket, laying it beside me on the bed. "Yeah, I'll make you," he decided out loud, walking up to him and grabbing him by the throat. He captured Kols's mouth in a kiss meant to bruise, making me moan on the bed at the erotic sight.

I loved watching them together. It was so *hot.* All that battling masculinity and dominance. It had me longing to be in the center, which I sensed was the plan.

But there was also an underlying emotion to Zeph's movements, his touch harsh yet gentle. Demanding yet reverent.

He's alive, Zeph whispered to me.

I know.

You brought him back.

We *brought him back,* I corrected. *Now strip him for me. I want to fuck.*

Zeph released Kols on a laugh and glanced over his shoulder. "Oh, do say that out loud, Aflora. You know how much I love that mouth."

"Strip him for me so we can fuck," I reiterated.

Kols's burnt irises met mine, his pupils flaring at the statement. "I'm biting you again."

"Good," I replied. "I'll bite you again, too." Because imbibing their blood had been oddly invigorating, something I never could have anticipated.

"I'm tasting her first," Shade said, kneeling on the bed. He'd removed his jacket and tie, leaving him in just his dress shirt and pants, his icy blue eyes filled with intent. "Spread your legs for me, little rose."

I shivered but did as he asked.

He pressed a kiss to my lips, then shifted to lie on the bed between my thighs. His tongue licked my seam, drawing all the way up to circle my clit.

I groaned in response, my body on fire from that mere touch alone.

Fuck, you're beautiful, Zakkai whispered into my mind.

I looked for him and found him leaning against the bedpost at the foot of the bed, his arms folded as he admired the view. He still wore his suit jacket—no tie—his silver-blue gaze brimming with lust. I wanted to reach for him, to tug him down to me with a fistful of that long white hair, but Kols's mouth was suddenly on mine, his palm squeezing my breast.

I thought I lost you, I said through our link, speaking into his mind for the first time. *I was broken without you, Kols.*

I'm here, he replied. *I'm here because of you. Because of Shade. Zeph. Even Zakkai. And I've never felt more alive.* He deepened our kiss, his tongue whispering a benediction against mine.

Shade's incisors skimmed my clit, drawing me back to him, and I cried out in response. *You're going to need to learn how to pay attention to all of us, little rose. We're very demanding mates.*

I know, I moaned, reaching down to grab his head while wrapping my other palm around Kols's neck. *You guys are killing me.*

Then I heard the cap on the lube pop open. "Here," Zeph said, handing it to Shade. "Prepare her."

Do you enjoy anal, sweet star? Zakkai asked. *Or is Zeph just fond of it?*

I… I like being in the middle, I admitted, bowing off the bed as Shade slid two fingers into my slick channel. *But I've not… we've not… usually one is in my mouth, and the other, ohhh…*

Shade's lips sealed around my sensitive nub, sucking hard as he drew my wetness backward to my tighter hole. He added lube, working me over with his hands and his mouth as Kols devoured my mouth, his fingers pinching my nipple, then massaging the hurt.

He kissed a path down my neck to my breasts, then took a stiff peak into his mouth while holding my gaze.

It was intensely erotic, especially as I could see Shade behind him with his dark head between my thighs.

Then Zeph was suddenly before me, his lips whispering over mine in the ghost of a smile. He'd lost his shirt, revealing all that sinewy muscle I loved tracing with my tongue. But he had other ideas for my mouth.

I lost myself to his kiss, his dominance all-encompassing and requiring my submission with each sensual stroke of his tongue against mine.

I missed you, pixie flower, he whispered into my mind. *I'm never letting anyone take you from me again.*

I missed you, too, I replied, releasing Kols to palm Zeph's cheek and return the ferocity of his kiss. *I want you to fuck me.*

I intend to, he promised. *But Kols is going first.*

I-I thought you wanted my ass? Crude terms were Zeph's favorite, so I always tried to use them when talking to him. I also really wanted to experience having them both inside me. Like, front and back. Not just mouth and front.

His approval radiated through the bond. "You want me in your ass, Aflora?"

"Yes. I want you to fuck me with Kols," I said out loud, earning me a groan from the man at my breast. "Double penetration," I added, in case I wasn't being clear.

"What about Shadow?" Zeph asked. "He's eating your pussy so well. I think he deserves something in return."

"I want her mouth," Shade replied, his words a hum against my sensitive bud. I tightened my grip in his hair, my body clenching in response to his ministrations and his words.

Because all three of them together?

Oh, yes... The fantasy played through my mind, my body tensing in response.

"I'm close," I moaned, needing Zeph to know. He liked when I asked permission, and it was on the tip of my tongue to do so now. But Zakkai spoke instead.

"We know, star." He still stood by the foot of the bed, his arms crossed just as they were moments ago. "Can you handle all three of them at once?"

It was the kind of thing Zeph would ask, as evidenced by the dark glimmer in his gaze as he looked at Zakkai now.

"I can handle them," I said, my stomach twisting with anticipation. *Yes. Yes, please.*

They were my mates.

I trusted them to take care of me and to ensure my safety. Their essences layered me in protection, their respect and adoration clear through the bonds.

My muscles tightened, my spirit coming to life with the expectation of taking them all at once while Zakkai watched.

Oh, Fae...

"I want this," I whispered, meeting Zeph's gaze. "I *need* this."

He smiled, then softly kissed me, the gentle caress so at odds with the inferno building inside me. "Mmm, do you want to come, pixie flower?"

"Yes," I whispered, my blood humming in anticipation. "Please."

He drew his nose along my cheek, his teeth nipping my earlobe as he murmured, "I love it when you beg, sweet flower." He kissed the sensitive spot below my ear, then skimmed my throat with his teeth. "Bite her," he said, his incisors driving into my neck as Kols followed suit against my breast.

I screamed in response, their collective bites stoking my inner flame to a dangerous level.

And then Shade culminated the act by sinking his teeth into my clit.

Words left my mouth on a wave of sensation unlike any of my existence. It took me under a cloud of incoherence, whirling me around in a catastrophic climax that shook my very *soul*.

I forgot how to breathe, how to speak, how to *move*.

I was drowning in masculinity and virility, a slave to their mouths as they swallowed my essence, leaving me boneless on the bed. Shade released me first, his tongue providing temporary relief against the tender wound. Kols was next, his lips kissing my nipple before taking the other into his mouth in a loving caress.

And finally, Zeph pulled away from my neck, his pupils dilated and filled with insatiable hunger. He kissed me, his own blood touching my tongue as he fed me his essence, replenishing my own.

Then Kols crawled up my body and repeated the action with his own mouth, his blood an intoxicating mix of power that left me groaning as he ended our kiss.

Shade finished the act, his mouth a prayer against mine as his Death Blood energy slickened my throat.

I swallowed every drop, my mind buzzing with electricity as they finished. Only to be suddenly short-circuited upon finding all three of them naked. Even Zeph.

Zakkai, however, still stood beside the bedpost, his gaze roaming over me with abundant interest. *Still adequate?* he asked softly.

Better than adequate, I replied, licking my suddenly dry lips.

Zeph grasped my chin to draw my gaze back to him. He studied my features for a long moment, then his lips curled. "She's ready."

CHAPTER TWENTY-NINE

Kols's eyes gleamed, his irises an alluring shade of bronze. I rather preferred it to the gold. It grounded him somehow, perhaps because the color made me think of earth.

Which reminded me of our mate, like she'd marked him somehow during the transition.

I stroked my finger down her sternum, all the way to the delectable apex between her thighs. *Do you want her pussy, Kols?* I asked, engaging our mental link—something I fully intended to abuse.

I want her, he replied. *Any part of her.*

Hmm, I hummed in agreement. *She said she wants us to fuck her, and Shade desires her mouth. So what'll it be, little prince? Ass or pussy?*

There's nothing little about me, he retorted, amusing me immensely. *I'm also no longer a prince.*

I faced him, cupping his jaw. "You're still a prince to me," I said out loud, dragging him to me for a kiss that had Aflora moaning in approval on the bed. She loved watching us together, and I enjoyed indulging her. I also liked kissing Kols. So it was a winning situation for us all.

He bit my lower lip, drawing blood. "I want to fuck," he said. "Now."

"Resurrection looks good on you," I replied, amused by his impatience. "Go lie on the bed."

His eyes flashed, but rather than challenge me again, he chose to comply.

"Straddle him, Aflora. Put him inside you. Slowly."

Dick, Kols muttered into my mind.

Lie there and take it, I returned.

He more or less flipped me off with his thoughts, then groaned as Aflora did exactly as I demanded, her slick cunt taking him all the way to the hilt. "So beautiful," I praised, admiring their position. "Don't move."

I'm going to kill you, Kols threatened.

"That goes for you, too, *little prince,*" I added out loud. "Shade?"

The Death Blood glanced at me, then went to kneel near Kols and Aflora, his palm wrapping around the back of her neck. "I'll take this part from here," he said, guiding her to his mouth first and kissing her soundly.

She shivered in response, goose bumps pebbling her flesh as she likely tasted her own arousal on his tongue. I grabbed the lube and squeezed some into my hand, then gave my shaft a pump while I watched the two men play with our mate

Kols had cupped her breasts, and Shade had tightened his hold on her neck, content to kiss her for now. I respected that he didn't want to rush her, and decided to follow suit as I climbed onto the bed behind her.

We hadn't done this together before, and I suspected she was new to it as well. *Have you ever been fucked in the ass, pixie flower?* I whispered into her mind.

She groaned, her muscles tightening. *No.*

Then I need you to tell me if this is too much, I replied. *You know how I feel about communication. Make sure you use your words.*

I will, she promised.

I'm trusting you, Aflora, I said, sliding two fingers into her ass to test her preparedness. *Too much?*

No, she replied. *Not enough.*

I added a third in reply, and she moaned. *Better?*

Yes, she hummed, approval radiating through her.

Can you take more?

She nodded, her head falling back against my shoulder as Shade released her. His mouth went to her breasts as Kols dropped his hands to her hips.

We would work on the two of us first, then depending on how she felt, Shade could try for her mouth. He seemed to already know that, the Death Blood more in tune with us than I ever could have anticipated. Perhaps because of his bond to Kols.

Regardless, it worked.

I didn't even mind Zakkai watching, aware that he was acting as protector while we played.

He'd proven himself… mostly. I wasn't sure I'd ever truly trust him, but for tonight, I did.

Aflora groaned as I began moving my fingers inside her, and Kols cursed into my mind. *I need to move, Zeph.*

Not yet.

I fucking hate you.

No, you don't, I replied softly. *You know I'm about to make this so good for you, too.*

He didn't argue with that, fully aware that I would keep that promise. But his need mounted as Aflora began to writhe, her body losing itself to the sensations of being filled from both ends.

I kissed her shoulder, allowing the deviation from my command, and slowly withdrew from her backside. A protest left her lips, only to be morphed into a sound of approval as the head of my cock pushed against her entrance. *The initial thrust is the hardest to take,* I warned her, pressing into her slowly.

Shade sucked her nipple into his mouth, and Kols pressed his thumb to her clit, both of them doing their best to distract her from the initial pain.

Her resulting whimper quickly morphed to a needy little hum, her body trembling between us as I slid the rest of the way home. "Oh," she groaned, tossing her head back against my shoulder again. "Oh, *Fae.*"

"Fuck," I corrected against her ear. "That's the term you're looking for."

"Hmm," she murmured, her hips gyrating in a sensual motion that had me palming her belly to hold her in place.

"Not yet," I said, wanting her to acclimate.

"His two favorite words," Kols muttered.

"Fuck me," Aflora demanded. "Fuck me right now."

Zakkai chuckled in amusement, his position shifting to the bedpost at the front of the bed for a better view. "Yes, Zephyrus. Fuck her."

I ignored him to focus on Aflora, my lips skimming her hammering pulse as I withdrew and slammed back into her. A wanton little gasp left her pretty mouth, followed by a cry of pleasure when I repeated the action.

Now you can move, I told Kols.

Thank fuck for that, he replied, thrusting upward in time with my movements.

Aflora practically melted between us, her sweet arousal scenting the air as we drove into her in tandem, leading her toward an oblivion she would never forget.

Then Shade threaded his fingers through her hair and guided her mouth to his groin. Her palms went to the bed to stabilize her upper body while he cradled her head, his touch far more gentle than the pace Kols and I set between her legs.

I drew my finger down her spine, monitoring the responses of her body to ensure this didn't hurt, concerned slightly by the contortionist position she'd put herself in to suck Shade off. But she swiveled her hips in a manner that suggested her excitement, her body practically purring with pending rapture.

Keep massaging her clit, I demanded.

I know, Kols returned, his voice gruff with pleasure. *Grab her tits.*

The command made my lips twitch, but I reached around her to palm her breasts because I rather liked the idea. Her resulting moan around Shade's cock made it worth agreeing to Kols's not-so-subtle demand.

She's close, Kols said. *She's squeezing the fuck out of my shaft.*

I felt a similar sensation against mine as her ass clenched. *Fuck her harder.*

He pistoned his hips upward at the same time I thrust downward, causing Aflora to scream around Shade's dick. His fingers knotted in her hair, holding her to him as his stomach muscles flexed, his orgasm nearing. "Fuck, Aflora," he groaned. "Those sounds... from your throat... are vibrating... my... *fuck...*" He tipped his head back, another curse leaving his mouth as she swallowed him deep, coaxing him to orgasm with her clever mouth.

Minx, I breathed into her mind. *You made him come early.*

Only doing what I was taught, she replied, her mental tone coy and yet filled with satisfaction as she swallowed his essence with greedy little gulps.

Someone was thirsty, I murmured, slamming into her. *You ready for me?*

Yes, she hissed, arching between us and releasing Shade with a pop. "Oh!"

"Yeah. Oh." I took control of her hair, yanking her back to me as I really drove inside her, making her feel every inch of me and Kolstov below. Then I sank my teeth into her shoulder, holding her there while I fucked her into oblivion.

My bite coupled with our pace below sent her headfirst into another climax, her scream of delight one I wanted to record and replay for years on end.

Or maybe I would just strive to make her repeat that sound over and over and over for eternity.

Yeah, I liked that plan more. *So fucking hot*, I told her. *You're perfect, Aflora.*

She moaned, her hips undulating between us as her orgasm extended with our repetitive penetration. Then Kols tumbled after her, his mouth parting on a rapturous sound filled with life and ecstasy and demanding I join them both in this delirious euphoria.

I groaned against her neck, releasing her from my bite, then tugged her head back to meet my kiss while I emptied myself inside her, claiming her in the most intimate manner known to fae.

She was mine.

No. She was *ours*.

To cherish and to adore.

To protect and to worship.

To admire and to love.

I trembled with the overpowering emotions, my mind incapable of understanding what this all meant to me. To *us*. Not yet.

But I knew she belonged to us, just as we belonged to her.

For forever and eternity.

Our powerful mate.

Our Aflora.

Our queen.

EPILOGUE

AFLORA

My mates washed me, then fed me. And eventually, they tucked me into bed between them.

Zakkai had helped initially but remained in his suit the whole time.

When I tried to drag him into the sheets to play after my earlier two orgasms, he'd merely cupped my face between his hands and kissed me. Then he'd suggested a warm bath to ease my tightening muscles.

Don't you need to…? I'd voiced the question into his mind, unable to complete the full sentence without blushing.

Our first time won't be in a group situation, he'd replied. *And no, the dreams don't count.* He'd kissed me again, the gesture sweetly intimate.

But then he'd disappeared after our meal.

I searched for him now, his mind awake as he wandered the paradigm, reinforcing the boundaries. Zeph, Kols, and Shade were all passed out around me.

Are you coming to bed? I asked Zakkai.

Not today, little star. But perhaps I'll nap when you all are awake later.

I frowned. *You're guarding.*

I am.

Why?

Because the war has just begun, he replied. *And while this paradigm is beautifully built, I can't help but feel a sense of looming dread. Something's coming.*

I considered his words, then stretched my senses to the paradigm and beyond, searching for what he said and finding a similar disturbance in the source. *Constantine.*

Yes, Zakkai replied. *His aura is all over the place. But I haven't figured out what he's done. I'm not sure it's complete yet.*

I shivered. *Do you think he knows we brought back Kols?*

Likely, yes. He'll use it to increase the urgency of hunting us.

They would hunt us either way, I pointed out.

True, he agreed. *But now my people will hunt us, too. I saved a Nacht. They won't take kindly to that.*

He's not Constantine.

I understand that now, Zakkai admitted softly. *But my father... I don't think he'll ever understand.*

What about Zenaida? I wondered.

Zakkai fell silent, considering. *I think we'll need to ask Shade about that. But wait until nightfall. You all need your rest.*

You need to rest, too.

I will. Just later, he promised, his voice a kiss against my mind. *Go to sleep, Aflora.*

Okay, I agreed, snuggling deeper into Kols's chest. I also had my leg draped over his. Shade spooned me from behind, while Zeph rested on the other side of Kols with his arm stretched out and his palm on my thigh.

It was a bit of a pretzel, but it warmed my heart.

Sweet dreams, darling star, Zakkai whispered.

I hummed an incoherent agreement, then my brow furrowed. *Why do you call me that?* I wondered. *Star, I mean.* The nickname always made me smile, but I never understood why he used the endearment.

Don't you remember loving the stars as a child? he asked. *You used to always want to go out at night, lie on the ground, and admire the sky.*

I smiled. *I do remember that.*

Well, that's why you're my star.

My heart warmed. *I like that.*

I know, he replied. *Now go to sleep. Dream of me.*

I thought you said dreams don't count.

Not for our first time, but I didn't say we couldn't play in the dreams. I could hear the smile in his voice, his teasing palpable. *I rather enjoy being your figment.*

My lips curled. *All right. Tanoomeen Ma Ana.*

His chuckle followed me all the way into my dreams.

Only, what waited for me when I opened my eyes wasn't a fantasy at all, but a nightmare.

One covered in blood.

My blood, and that of my mates.

"Hello, Aflora," Constantine greeted, his smile cruel. "I think it's time you and I had a little chat."

∼

The Midnight Fae Academy series concludes with *Midnight Fae Academy: Book Four*

MIDNIGHT FAE
ACADEMY
BOOK FOUR

PROLOGUE

AFLORA

Do you know what it's like to leave a dream and tumble face-first into a nightmare? Because I do. One moment, everything is warm and happy, and the next, it's stark, frigid, and daunting.

Just like Constantine Nacht's golden irises. They remind me of icy, hard metal. Whirling with power. Sucking me deeper into his web. And grounding me in a reality that isn't mine.

He smiles. Callous. Cruel. Cold.

And then he begins to chant.

An ancient rhyme. A hum I don't understand. Magic swirls through the air, calling to my Quandary Blood heart. I memorize the words. I study the patterns. I hold on for dear life. I drown beneath the wave of foreign energy engulfing me from head to toe.

He said he wanted to talk.

He lied.

No shocker there. He's a wicked old Midnight Fae with a black soul, and it's swallowing me whole, dragging me down, down, down…

I shiver.

I scream.

I freeze.

Then I *burn*. So intense. So bright. So insanely *dark*. Earth weeps inside me, my spirit fracturing beneath the onslaught of energy threatening to consume me.

And on he chants.

Chants. Chants. Chants.

My name is a whisper on the wind. An ascension is brewing. *Consuming.* Lighting me on fire from within.

Wrong, I think. *This is wrong.*

My roots are dying.

My flowers cease to bloom.

The sun turns to night.

Darkness. Death. Blood.

It's overwhelming and bleak and ripping me in two. Inky lines crawl up my arms like poisoned ivy, slithering and purring and captivating my focus. They remind me of snake-vines, hissing and daring me to play.

This isn't real, I tell myself. *This is a nightmare. I'll wake up soon. I have to wake up soon!*

"You're ascending," a deep voice says.

Constantine Nacht.

"Soon they'll see you for what you are, Queen Aflora. An abomination in the truest form. A monster. A being consumed by power, both Elemental Fae and Midnight Fae in nature. And I can't wait to watch you burn."

He cackles.

I scream.

Then silence engulfs us both, his final words a threat on the breeze, swathing my being in a kiss of obsidian. "Welcome to your first ascension trial, future dead one. May it forever destroy your soul."

CHAPTER ONE

ZAKKAI

Power rolled through the paradigm, electrifying my senses as the Source Architect.

One moment, I'd been indulging my mate in a flirtatious mental promise. And the next, I took off at a dead sprint toward where Aflora slept.

Constantine was *here*. I felt him in every breath, his Elite Blood aura tainting the paradigm with his malevolent presence.

I dove into the source, searching for his magical core. It throbbed brightly at the center, his powers fully engaged and suffocating everyone and everything around him.

What is he doing? I wondered, stopping cold in my tracks as I watched a volt of magic enter another soul. *Oh, shit! Aflora!*

I took off again, her aura screaming in agony at the unexpected intrusion of the dark enchantment.

Too much power, I thought. *That's too much power.*

I tried to grab hold of it in my mind, to rip it away from my mate, but the source had already anchored itself inside her, pouring wave after wave of energy into the core of her being.

"*Fuck!*" I shouted, bursting into the cabin covered in wilting flowers.

Her earth magic was weeping at the intrusion, her soul fracturing beneath the wrongness of Constantine's actions.

"He's forcing her ascension," I said, talking to no one and everyone at the same time. "He's redirecting the source *into her*." It came out on a growl, my fury palpable and violent.

I fell to my knees beside her, the inky lines spreading from her heart to her limbs decorating her as the source's choice.

"That's impossible," Kolstov breathed. "That's not how this works."

I shook my head. Because he was wrong. "It's entirely possible," I replied, furious at myself for not seeing it before. "She's mated to two royal lines and the Source Architect." That provided Constantine with the access he'd needed to the core of her essence. It had allowed him to breathe the enchantment used to call upon new rulers, and redirect it to the rightful heir.

The fallen Midnight Fae Prince's mate.

The Source Architect's chosen other half.

The Death Blood Prince's soul mate.

An Elemental Fae Royal.

All markers that would note her as a potential candidate.

"*Shit*." I cradled Aflora's face between my hands and attempted to redirect the heart of our power away from her, to rewrite the path and send it back to Constantine, but the source had already chosen.

Worthy, it whispered darkly. *Fresh. Young. Honorable conduit.*

The words weren't real, just sensations that prickled my spirit and told me there wasn't a damn thing I could do to stop this.

Instead, I reached for Aflora and tried to guide her, to ease her pain, to shift her into the ascension with a softness the source lacked.

Her screams echoed in my head, her confusion piercing my heart. She didn't understand what was happening, had lost herself to the fog of the obsidian essence mounting inside her.

"Zakkai!" someone snapped. A deep voice. Harsh. *Furious.*

I lifted my eyelids to meet a pair of fuming green irises. "What?" I demanded, irritated by the interruption.

The Warrior Blood—*Zephyrus*—appeared ready to kill me. "Tell us what you're doing."

"Helping her ascend," I replied shortly.

"Do we need to bite her? That's what we did last time she exploded with power."

I shook my head, gritting my teeth. "No. That was from my ascension." The night I became the Source Architect. There hadn't been an outlet for my power exchange, so everyone had felt it. Including the Nacht family. It had caused Kolstov to unleash his power in a rampage that had destroyed Aflora's room. And then she'd come undone in the LethaForest.

I hadn't witnessed it. But I'd sensed it. And I'd later learned about it from Shade.

"Biting won't help her this time. Constantine is overloading her essence with dark magic and forcing an unwilling royal to ascend." I locked gazes with the Warrior Blood. "I know how to help her, but I need to be able to focus." And I couldn't do that with him interrupting, something I told him with my expression.

"Do it," he demanded.

I didn't acknowledge his *permission*—because I refused to call it a command. Instead, I closed my eyes to return to my task.

Silence followed as I continued down my original path, only this time Zephyrus's protective energy trailed after me. It served as a foreign taunt to my senses. I wasn't used to feeling the warmth of a Warrior Blood. Of course, it wasn't for me but for Aflora. Regardless, it created the aura of safety that I needed to dive further into Aflora's psyche. Because I didn't have to focus on my surroundings. Zephyrus had that part covered.

I dug deep into the core of her, flinching as her agony pierced through my mental shields.

Ascending *hurt.*

Like molten fire flooding the inner spirit. I'd experienced it when I'd accepted the Source Architect position. However, I'd gone into the situation knowing what to expect.

Aflora was neither willing nor expectant.

I should have seen this coming, but I would never have anticipated this from Constantine. He was handing her the source. Only because he intended for it to kill her. Still, she could survive—*would* survive—making it a huge risk, one I never thought he would take.

"I don't understand how this is possible," I heard Kolstov saying. "The ascension trial requires blood."

"Nacht blood," Shade replied.

"Yes," I agreed, my voice slightly strained from trying to maintain a connection to Aflora while also talking to her mates. "Her connection to the Nacht family line—via Kolstov, and I suppose through Zephyrus's Guardian bond—would have granted him initial access to perform the enchantment. Then the source accepted the link because she's mated to a Nacht and a Morte."

Morte being Shade's bloodline. Though he rarely used the surname.

"She's also the Earth Fae Queen," I added, swallowing as a volt of energy slammed into me from the source. It served as an order to mentally step away from Aflora and allow her to fully ascend. I responded by crafting an intangible wall around her and then made myself a proverbial door. The energy pushed against me, forcing its way through and turning me into a siphon of sorts.

It burned.

But I accepted the burden.

Because it was the only way to ease her into this... to give her a fighting chance.

"A royal by nature and blood," Shade said, his voice oddly distant. "So all Constantine needed to do was recite the ritual—"

"And the dark source went right for her," Kolstov finished for him. "Shit."

"Precisely," I tried to say, my lungs squeezing with the effort.

A hand met my shoulder, the palm large and unwelcome. Then Zephyrus's power rolled over me, his protective enchantment providing a foreign balm of sorts.

I shuddered, the tranquility of his touch... unexpected.

It granted me space to breathe and somehow shifted my burden to him temporarily. I studied his charm, curious as to what spell he'd cast. *An absorption spell,* I translated faintly. Not what I'd expected, nor anything I'd ever experienced before.

Zephyrus pushed more into me, forcing me to take it.

I almost shoved it back at him in retaliation. This group dynamic was going to annihilate my patience. I didn't work as a unit. I preferred to lead and be followed, not collaborate.

But for Aflora… I'd try.

And as this helped me relax, I accepted his assistance.

"She needs to pass her first trial," Kolstov said, answering some question I'd missed. Or maybe he was just thinking out loud. "*Trust.*"

I nodded in confirmation. She would have to rely on those closest to her to guide her. "But it hasn't started yet. The source is still settling." I could feel it filling every inch of her soul, blackening out her access to the elements. Or trying to, anyway. Her roots were fighting the intrusion, denying the dark source a proper home.

She gasped, still unconscious and yet fully awake at the same time.

The inky lines writhed in annoyance.

Her roots held.

"Fae," I whispered, awed and terrified by the convoluted mix of magic dancing inside her. It was hypnotic and beautiful and so damn wrong. Cerulean sparks bonded to black lines, green flares, purple smoke, and deep red contours. But at the center of it all was a thriving tree, the branches a swirl of color and magic, as the dark source tried to penetrate her elemental home with a variety of cruel twists. "She's fighting it."

Perhaps not intentionally, but instinctively.

"Her earth source is refusing to release her," I continued, lost to the stunning array of enchantments unfolding inside Aflora.

I'd closed my eyes again, the lightning display absorbing every ounce of my attention.

I was lost to it. To *her*. To the beauty of the sources dueling and marrying and dueling again. Every time the darkness found a new entrance, a strand of cerulean met the ends and untangled them, my darling little star learning and memorizing spells faster than I'd ever seen.

I felt her tugging on my mind, my power, my energy, and using it to craft and mold her reactions appropriately. So quick and nimble and alluring.

"She's *teaching*," I whispered, still utterly engrossed in the sight before me. "She's teaching the sources how to join inside her." That was why it looked like they were fighting, then connecting, and then fighting again. She was finding a way for both powers to exist inside her, to ground herself in earth and hold on to the dark magic as well.

Temporarily, I thought. *This is your temporary solution.*

"She's giving us time," I told the others, then frowned. "But we can't stop the ascension." I voiced that statement out loud and through the bond to Aflora. She didn't comment, her mind lost to the power engulfing her spirit. I wasn't even sure if she could hear me. However, she definitely felt me. Just as I felt her tugging on my essence to help ground her.

"No, we can only ensure she survives it," Kolstov replied. "By passing the initial test." He paused, and I sensed him looking at Zephyrus even though my eyes were still closed. It was a weird sensation, one that confirmed we were truly *bonded*. At least on the first level. Because I'd saved him, using my blood to bring him back to life. Thereby tying our fates together for eternity.

Perhaps that was why Zephyrus could help me as he did—my ties to Aflora and Kolstov, two of his fully bonded mates.

Blood worked in tricky ways, especially for Midnight Fae.

"It'll evaluate her relationships, just like it did to me and mine," he said.

"Which means it'll involve all of us," the Warrior Blood inferred aloud.

I'd undergone a similar trial as the Source Architect. My trials were different from those of a royal ascension—more convoluted and in the form of puzzles and riddles. Aflora's would likely be a mix because of her ties to me.

"You had to rely on Tray's instincts and my sight," Zephyrus continued. "To make it through the blinding light."

Kolstov's responding shiver was palpable—something I again felt more than saw. "Yes." It came out soft, the memory lurking in his voice. "The source will put her in a situation that won't allow her to escape on her own."

That sounded about right.

Except my task had been completed alone. Because there hadn't been anyone for me to rely on—my mating link had been cut off, and my father had insisted I master my source ascension by myself.

It hadn't been easy.

But nothing with the source ever was.

Kolstov blew out a breath and repositioned himself beside me on the bed, causing my eyes to flicker open. He'd pulled on a pair of boxers and nothing else. Zephyrus and Shade remained naked on the other side of Aflora, their concern evident.

"Any second now," Kolstov said after evaluating the obsidian lines crawling down Aflora's arms.

I agreed with a nod, the energy seeming to settle around her, preparing for the next phase. It had all passed through me now, leaving her to battle the remainder on her own.

Silence fell as we all held our breaths.

A scratch at the door disturbed the momentary peace.

All three men took up defensive positions, their wands seeming to appear out of thin air.

"Relax," I said, aware of who had made the sound.

Zimney.

My arctic wolf familiar nudged open the door with his big white muzzle, then shoved it wider to allow Clove to fly through. The falcon's wings nearly clipped Zephyrus and Shade as she soared between them to land right beside Aflora.

It was a familiar's job to protect the fae who had conjured it. And Clove clearly sensed Aflora's unease, just as Zimney had likely sensed mine. Or perhaps he'd followed Clove.

The two were bonded in a unique manner since it'd technically been my magic that Aflora had tapped into to create her familiar. It meant Clove responded to me, too. Which she would have anyway as Aflora's mate.

I eyed the two creatures and frowned. "They sense something." I couldn't quite hear it, but I felt the knowledge of it traversing through my connection to Zimney. "They're here for the first trial."

A bat entered next, settling on Shade's shoulder.

Followed by the hiss of a three-headed snake that magically manifested around Zephyrus's neck. Three sets of creepy eyes went to my wolf, the slithering creature clearly agitated by my much larger familiar. Zephyrus muttered something to the reptile, ending with the name *Raph*.

I glanced at Kolstov, curious to see what animal would appear for him. But none did.

Because Kolstov had died.

Which meant his familiar had perished as well.

Shit.

"That's the test," I realized out loud, my heart skipping a beat. "Something with your familiar." Would Aflora have to bring the being back from the dead? Conjure a new one? Work through a puzzle involving his fallen familiar? There were so many options. *Too many* options.

I ran my fingers through my hair, the ash-blond strands falling into my face for just a moment and hiding my reaction from the males around me. A reaction underlined in momentary uncertainty.

Had we all bonded enough for Aflora to successfully pass this test?

Because I didn't trust any of them. Not really. Only my little star.

However, what if the test wasn't just for her but for all her mates as well?

Would I be forced to rely on the others? To put my faith in those who had mated Aflora? Saving Kolstov from death had been trial enough. Except that I hadn't even hesitated in helping him. Once I'd seen what it would have done to Aflora to lose him, I'd known he'd had to live. Would this be all that different? How much was I prepared to sacrifice to ensure Aflora's survival?

I wasn't given a moment to consider the answer to that because in the next breath, Aflora started to shake.

I pressed my palm to her breastbone in an attempt to hold her down, only to have my skin burned by the power radiating off her.

Zephyrus cursed.

Shade winced.

And Kolstov collapsed beside her on a violent shudder.

Clove released an agonized caw, making Zimney growl. Then magic spilled in through the room, fracturing the paradigm around us. Shade jumped to his feet, spells spewing from his lips as he tried to hold the enchantment in place. I immediately bolstered the edges, giving him the leverage he needed to repair the breaks, and Zephyrus underlined it all with his Warrior magic.

A natural team effort.

One being threatened with every passing second.

The trial had begun. Aflora's first task was to wake up.

And the only one who could help guide her through the test was the fallen royal beside her.

If they failed… she'd die.

Another thunderous hit against the paradigm sent a shiver through my being. "Constantine knows where we are." Because he'd used all of this as a distraction to locate us, knowing we'd be weakened while Aflora attempted to pass her first trial.

Clever bastard, I seethed, sending up a massive wave of power to rewrite all the spells surrounding the exterior of the makeshift dome. It wasn't visible, just an alternate use of space that Constantine had clearly located by using Aflora as a beacon of sorts.

That was what I'd felt last night, why I hadn't been able to rest.

He'd been close by, his power a fiery blade against my senses that had alerted me to his nefarious whims without providing the finite details.

And then he'd distracted me by forcing Aflora's ascension.

Zephyrus cast a defensive spell that captured my awareness, the Warrior Blood proving incredibly capable in the moment. I memorized his enchantment and echoed it throughout the paradigm, bolstering it with a little Quandary Blood twist that would make it a bit more difficult to undo.

Shade added his own flavor of Death magic, allowing the three of us to craft a unique shield that would hopefully buy us a little more time.

"I need to find somewhere for us to jump to," Shade said quickly.

"Go," I replied, power deepening my voice to a rumble.

Zephyrus sent up another enchantment that I immediately copied as Shade disappeared into a cloud of black smoke.

"He'd better come back," Zephyrus said under his breath.

"He will." If there was one thing I could count on Shade for, it was his protection of Aflora. "Keep bolstering the paradigm."

Zephyrus grunted in response but did exactly what I'd told him to.

Although, I doubted it had anything to do with my demand and everything to do with the unconscious pair on the bed.

They were the owners of his heart.

And so he did what a Warrior Blood was trained to do—*guard*.

CHAPTER TWO

AFLORA

A maze.

Everywhere I turned was a dead end, the riddle sprawling out before me in an impossible mess of obsidian vines. Not snakes, but midnight roots intertwining and binding and holding me hostage.

I spun around in a circle, lost to the foreign darkness.

It consumed me, threatening to destroy my earth. But I fought back. I forced it to behave, to blend, to bind with my current existence and allow me the chance to breathe. It'd been a natural response, one grounded in Zakkai's power. His essence had washed over me, followed by a kiss of protection underlined in Zeph's ability. Both of my mates had helped me ascend into this garden of dead roses.

Then the vines began to whirl and build, locking me inside.

And Constantine's final words repeated on the wind. *Welcome to your first ascension trial, future dead one. May it forever destroy your soul.*

I shivered. This was a test of sorts, some type of trial designed for me to fail. I didn't know the rules or what it all meant. I didn't know how to survive. However, I had no choice. Constantine couldn't win. Not like this. He'd forced this power into me, ensuring my abomination status, and I would find a way to undo it.

I'd memorized the chants and the magical creation. I just had to figure out how to unwind those binds and release the source once more.

After I escaped this maze.

Kols? I whispered, trying to connect to the one who I knew could help me most. As an Elite Blood and the true Midnight Fae Prince, he'd know what to do.

But silence met my words.

Shade? I tried next.

Silence.

I bit my lip, uncertain. Was this even real? Or was I still lost in a nightmare within my mind?

The power pulsing inside me felt real. As did the forbidden weave of magic marrying the dark source to my earth source.

Claire, I thought, trembling slightly. *Can the Elemental Fae feel what I've done? Am I hurting them right now?*

Chancellor Elana had darkened the elements with her connection to Midnight Fae magic. But that'd been an active, conscious decision on her part to absorb more power.

I didn't want more; I wanted less.

I tried to push it to my mates, to relieve some of the fiery ache blistering inside me, but the block between us remained.

I don't accept that, I decided, pushing against the barrier and searching for the source of the obstruction. It had to be a spell—one Constantine had woven—and I'd just have to undo it.

Ignoring the maze, I closed my eyes and focused. This was all inside my mind, a mental gymnasium of writhing energy and foreign connections.

A tree had sprouted at the core of my being, the branches all whirling with an array of colors.

Red for the Elite Bloods.

Navy for the Sangré Bloods.

Green for the Warrior Bloods.

Purple for the Death Bloods.

Black for the Malefic Bloods.

And cerulean at the heart, dancing along the veins of the trunk for the Quandary Bloods.

I mentally stroked the beautiful creation, marveling at the multicolored leaves that sprouted along the twigs. So strong and full of life. Yet tipped with ash.

It'd been my compromise—the way I'd coaxed my earth source into coexisting with the dark source.

Such an unnatural formation, and yet, it felt as though it belonged.

I allowed myself a final glimmer of admiration, then focused on my mates and our obstructed bonds. Zakkai had helped me ascend, as had Zeph. I'd sensed Kols as well, his bloodline thriving through my veins. And Shade, my forever dark shadow, had gifted me with his assurance that everything would be fine.

All of them were with me and yet not.

Because of Constantine.

You will not win, I told him. He couldn't hear me. Or maybe he could. Or maybe all of this was just some sort of wicked nightmare.

Regardless, the sentiment remained.

He'd tried to kill my mate. And now he'd forced me into this ascension.

I'll undo it. Then I'll ensure you can never hurt anyone else ever again.

I had no idea how I'd achieve that, but I felt the assurance of my task deep within my roots. He would pay for his sins.

Inhaling slowly, I delved deeper into my bonds, searching for the magic that didn't belong. I sensed it circling Kols, my link to his bloodline seeming to have provided Constantine with the access he'd needed to weave his nefarious enchantments.

Zeph, too, I realized, tugging on that cord and finding an anchor in my Warrior Blood mate as well.

The strands linked back to Shade and Zakkai—from Kols. Because of their initial mate-bonds that were established last night.

Constantine's spell presented itself in intricate waves, the fiery ends fizzling with embers that made touching it dangerous. I peeled apart the layers with my mind, seeking the enchantment's pattern, but he'd woven too many together to undo without risk.

I needed Zakkai.

Which meant I needed to figure out how to pass this trial.

I opened my eyes, the darkness around me having grown while I'd poked at my mate-bonds. It was almost pitch black now, the weaving vines having formed a canopy of sorts over my head.

A chill swept down my spine. This definitely wasn't a nightmare. But it wasn't real either. I could sense the magical binds lining the horizon, the dark source serving as the designer of this course.

I knelt to touch the charcoal blades, my earth magic flickering to life as I absorbed the genetic makeup of the landscape and tried to manipulate it to my will. Flowers sprouted along the vines, dotting the world with color. Then the petals turned to ash in the next instant as the black magic killed my new life.

My heart ached at the loss, my breath catching in my throat.

I tried again, demanding the world shift to accept the core of my being. But it responded by strangling my energy, denying me any form of light.

"Aflora." Constantine's familiar voice floated to me on the wind, causing my teeth to grind together in frustration.

He'd returned to watch my trial. *Tulip-burning willow stump,* I thought, standing to face him. I couldn't see him, just heard him, his shadowed figure about ten feet away.

"Thank fuck," he breathed, his dark form stepping closer. "Are you all right?"

I arched a brow. "Is that your version of a joke? Because you'll have to try harder to provoke a laugh from me."

The being stilled. "A joke? Why the bloody hell would I joke about this?"

"I'm not sure why you do a lot of things," I admitted. "Like forcing an ascension on an Earth Fae Royal, for example."

"You think I did this to you?"

"I know you did," I retorted, placing my hands on my hips. "But I'm going to find a way to undo it. And I'm going to survive this trial, marking you as the *future dead one*." Not that I would kill him. That would make me no better than him.

Earth Fae craved life.

And I would be an Earth Fae until my dying breath.

"Who do you think I am?" Constantine asked slowly.

I ignored him and focused on my surroundings. He was clearly here to distract me from my task, and I'd already wasted enough breath on him.

My flowers had all turned to ash again while talking to him, and the remaining light overhead glimmered like little stars between the dark vines. I tried to tap into their magic to unweave them, but the dark source hissed in response.

"All right," I said to it. "Then how about this?" I took hold of the roots and called on a burning thwomp. It sprouted high and proud, fire billowing from its limbs and blasting right through the roof of my canopy.

I grinned, proud.

And then the thwomp cried out in pain as it incinerated into dust.

My heart skipped a beat, the sudden blow knocking me to my knees.

Constantine rushed forward, his hand grabbing my arm as he shouted my name.

I shoved him back with a bolt of power, Zeph's Warrior Blood thriving inside me and alighting me from within. The spell left my lips on instinct, the enchantment one Zeph had taught me during one of our sparring matches. And it shoved Constantine to the ground.

"What the fuck?" he demanded on a wheeze.

"Touch me again, and I'll paralyze you." Then I cocked my head to the side. "A spell courtesy of your prickly little thorn, Dakota." It would be fitting to use the enchantment on him since he'd sent that lying fae to infiltrate Zakkai's camp.

"What are you talking about?" he asked, sounding shocked and dismayed. "Aflora, who do you think I am?"

"Is this the part where you remind me that you're a former king and demand I bow? Because I don't think I'm in the mood for that. If anyone is going to bow, it'll be you." And I would thoroughly enjoy making him do it. Assuming I could. The fact that he bent beneath Zeph's spell was an interesting development. Constantine should have been powerful enough to block it.

"A prince," he hissed. "And no, *princess*, I'm not going to demand you bow. But hit me with another spell and we're going to exchange some words."

"Sounds like an empty threat since you're already talking," I told him.

And again he'd distracted me from my task.

Sprinkle dust, I need to focus.

He was just a—

A volt of electricity hit me in the side, knocking me to the ground on an "Oomph."

In the next beat, the shadowy figure had me pinned to the ground with a knee between my thighs. "What's wrong with you?" he demanded.

"Get off of me!" I shouted, a spell lining up on my lips.

But his mouth captured mine, silencing me in an instant.

Technically, I could still utter the spell in my thoughts. However, I wasn't as well versed in the art of mental enchantments. And my brain also failed to function properly.

Because Constantine is kissing me.

What in the lily cookie?

Why is he…?

His tongue parted my lips, the familiarity of the taste hitting my taste buds and cascading me beneath a wave of confusion.

Kols.

He tastes like Kols.

How?

Because they're related?

Ugh, gross. Gross, gross, gross! I tried to shove him off me, but the male remained heavy on top of me, his hands on my hips.

Something jolted inside my head, my mate-bonds screaming in fury.

I tried to latch onto them, to unlock the spell, but those blistering ends threatened to singe my mind—and the minds of my mates—in the process.

A tremble worked down my spine, my mouth responding to the familiar kiss while my body rebelled.

Why is he kissing me? I wondered, my brow furrowing. Constantine had no reason to do this. Sure, he could evoke confusion in this manner… but he'd already been succeeding in that before touching me.

He also hadn't fought back when he could have easily blocked my spell. *No.* Constantine *would* have blocked my spell.

So why let me hit him? Why kiss me afterward?

Unless…

Unless this wasn't Constantine at all, but Kols.

I blinked.

No.

He sounds like Constantine.

But I couldn't *see* him.

Who do you think I am? he'd asked twice. And he'd called me *princess.* Constantine referred to me as an *abomination* and *future dead one.*

Kols often called me *princess.*

Which Constantine would know if he'd somehow tapped into the history of our bond. Was that possible? I had no idea. But I didn't know anything about Midnight Fae or how the ascension and bloodlines worked.

However, Kols did.

I bit his tongue, drawing a low rumble from his chest. "Aflora," he growled.

"Stop," I demanded.

"Try to blast me with another spell and I'll kiss you again," he warned. "I know we don't have time for it, but that fucking hurt, Aflora. And I can't exactly hit you back."

Constantine would be able to retaliate. Unless he was playing another trick on me.

I tried to make out the features of his face, but they were masked behind a curtain of black.

"Can you see me?" I wondered out loud.

"Can I see you?" he repeated. "Of course I can fucking see you."

I tried to find his mouth, then his eyes. I knew where they should be but couldn't make out the details. "You're shadowy and dark."

"What?"

"I can't *see* you," I explained, reaching up to touch his face. He still sounded like Constantine. However… he didn't feel like Constantine. Not that I really knew what the Elder felt like, but I didn't sense him in this shadow figure.

It could be a ploy.

Or the ploy could be making me think this was Constantine.

"Kols?" It came out on a whisper, mostly because I felt foolish even asking. But everything was… a mess.

"Yeah, sweetheart?"

"You sound like Constantine," I admitted quietly, biting my lip.

He fell silent for a moment, then cursed. "It's the trial. It's about trust. So you're seeing me as someone you absolutely shouldn't and wouldn't trust at all."

"Trust?" I repeated.

"Yes. There are seven ascension trials, each one designed to test different aspects of royalty and leadership. And the first one is about trusting those who support you." He cupped my cheek. "The dark source is testing your ability to trust your mates, Aflora."

"By making you sound like Constantine," I said, leaning into his palm. Constantine wouldn't waste his breath explaining the trial to me. He'd just wait for it to kill me.

Which confirmed that this wasn't Constantine at all, but my Kols.

My earth bond pulsed in agreement, the link to him a thick root that connected our souls. That wasn't something the Elder Midnight Fae could manipulate. He had no control or manipulative power over my earth magic.

I brushed my lips against Kols's mouth, telling him without words that I knew it was him. Then I drew back to look up at him. "What now?"

"Now we find our way out of this maze and wake up," he replied softly. "And to do that, you need to follow your instincts."

"My instincts say to burn the vines to the ground and allow the light to illuminate my path." I always preferred the light over the night. But Midnight Fae were all about the dark.

He gently went back to his knees, then stood and held a hand out for me to help me up. I accepted, realizing as I stood that I could see his shadow clearly despite the blackness settling around us.

Actually, he was the only figure I could make out now that the twinkling lights above had been fully covered by the vines.

That had to be related to this trial—my ability to see the one I trusted through the obsidian fog.

"Where are the others?" I wondered out loud. "Why can I only sense you?"

"I don't know," Kols replied, a frown in his tone—a tone that still sounded like Constantine. "Zakkai thought your test would have something to do with Night."

"Your familiar?"

"Yes. All the others appeared during your ascension, except for my Night." A hint of sadness tinged his deep voice, further confirming this was Kols and not Constantine.

"Maybe we need to find him?" I suggested.

"I felt him die," Kols whispered. "When... when I died."

I winced, recalling what it had felt like when I'd lost Clove all those months ago. I hadn't known I could bring my familiar back. But Kols had been the one to teach me. "Have you tried calling for him?"

The silence that followed indicated his hesitation.

He hadn't tried.

And I understood why.

"You're afraid he won't reply," I said, reaching for his hand and squeezing it. "You once told me familiars are tied to our lives, that they only die if we do, and you didn't die, Kols. Shade held on to your life strand long enough for me to give it roots."

Which meant Night was still here.

He had to be.

Because Kols was very much alive.

"Try calling for him," I encouraged, my voice low yet underlined in confidence. "Bring Night back to you."

My Elite Blood mate remained quiet for another moment, making me wonder if I'd been wrong, if this had all been a trick, but that pulse inside me throbbed with knowledge. *Earth mate. Midnight Fae mate. My Kolstov. My prince.*

Kols wasn't known for his hesitation. He thought through his options and acted.

But this was a surreal situation.

He'd almost died.

He'd felt his familiar's death.

It was on him to trust his own soul.

My eyes widened. "That's it," I breathed. "Trust."

"What?"

"You need to call for Night." Because it would prove he trusted in himself... because I trusted in him. "You need to *trust* him to find you." I pressed my palm to his chest, my opposite hand still holding his. "He's here. I know he's here. Call for him so he can help us find our way out of here."

I felt the rightness of this path to my very soul.

Kols had said this was about trusting my instincts and trusting my mates.
And now I just needed my Elite Blood mate to trust me.
The full circle.
A complete trial.
With only one path forward.
It was Kols's turn to choose.

CHAPTER THREE

KOLS

The ascension trials were never straightforward. They tested more than just the source heir; they tested everyone *linked* to the heir as well.

Which made Aflora's statement true.

I needed to trust Night to find me. I needed to trust that he'd survived. And I needed to trust that what Aflora and the others had done was enough to bring not only me back from death, but my familiar, too.

Her dark hair framed her beautiful face and fierce expression as she waited for my agreement. She knew this was the right path, and I needed to *trust* her instincts.

These trials were devised to trick us all. Only the strongest were meant to survive. I'd been more than strong enough, but I'd been tricked by the Elders—my own grandfather—and betrayed by my Council.

I would seek vengeance in my own way, starting by helping my mate ascend.

Constantine Nacht wanted Aflora to fail, to make a mockery of her ascension.

I'd ensure the opposite happened.

I'd help her become queen.

"*Ahaminee,*" I breathed, invoking the incantation for calling a familiar. "*Ahaminee, Night.*"

Aflora's fingers curled into my chest, her blue eyes glistening with approval.

She had said I resembled a shadowy creature to her. How very odd. I had no trouble seeing her. But everything else was dark and covered by the power vines. It made me wonder if I'd even be able to see Night.

Assuming he was still alive.

I swallowed, the echo of his dying caw infiltrating my senses and eliciting a wince from deep within. He'd been a part of me, a being of my own creation. And I'd failed him.

Not by choice.

Not even on purpose.

But because of my grandfather's greed for power.

I'd never anticipated him going to the extent of killing me to take back the throne. It had all happened so quickly, so unexpectedly, that I'd never even considered the potential outcome.

And now this—forcing the ascension onto Aflora. It made no sense.

What are you trying to prove? I wondered as a wave of power swirled around us.

An echo of cawing began, the darkness moving in flaps of wings as the vines melted into a series of crows. Aflora gasped, her grip on my hand tightening. I wrapped my arm around her lower back, holding her to me as the feathers beat over our heads.

It reminded me of the transportation yard back at the Academy with all the crows forming a vessel for students to travel to and from within.

But no keypad appeared here.

This whirlwind of energy wasn't meant to help teleport Midnight Fae; it was meant to serve as a test. Another layer of trust. "We have to follow our instincts," I realized out loud.

More than that—I had to follow mine, and Aflora had to trust me to choose. To pick a crow I thought might be Night and follow him to our freedom or our doom.

I explained the realization to Aflora, felt her stiffen against me, and understood how difficult this task would be for us both.

She had to trust me.

And I had to trust myself.

I wasn't in a position to rely on my instincts. I'd nearly died yesterday. All my powers were convoluted and messy, strands of various magic helping to bolster my soul and keep me alive.

I was no longer an Elite Blood, but something significantly other.

An abomination.

Just like my mate.

I could feel Shade, Zakkai, and Zeph inside me. Aflora, too. A collection of strength that shouldn't be possible, yet existed nonetheless.

"Kols?" Aflora whispered, the feathers closing in around us. "What are your instincts telling you? Because mine are saying to run."

"Hold on," I replied, closing my eyes to focus on the beating wings. *Where are you, Night?*

Rather than focus on the sounds around me, I searched for the familiar strand of life—*my* life. Both new and old. Former and current. But the essences swarming through the air all blended together, masking the one I sought.

Minutes passed as I chanted the spell under my breath, demanding my familiar find me.

Yet nothing happened beyond the whirl of feathers, some of them slicing my cheek and arms like charcoal blades. Not feathers, but metallic stone. Dangerous. Lethal. Cruel.

Come on…

Night had to be here somewhere. Aflora's certainty washed over me, giving me the strength I needed to keep searching. She trusted me to find him. Which meant he was here somewhere, cloaked behind the mass of power created by the dark source.

Aflora's palm wrapped around the back of my neck, her lips capturing mine.

It took me so off guard that I didn't immediately return her embrace.

But as her tongue parted my lips, I realized her plan—*blood*. Her essence hit my senses, lighting my veins on fire with her power. I swallowed her heated kiss, her energy swarming inside me and grounding me in a field of existence beyond comprehension.

Mine, I thought. *Aflora's mine.*

Some sort of barrier fizzled into ash between us, our connection smoldering to life. And in the next breath, she released me, my mind suddenly clear and focused on my task.

There! I yanked my mouth away from Aflora's, my gaze locking on a crow just a few feet above my head. "Come here." The bird cawed in response, clearly agitated over being called away from the swarming array of feathers, but as he dove down, I felt the rightness in our connection. *Night.*

Aflora hummed in agreement, a spell warming her breath as she weaved some sort of Quandary magic through the air. An invisible dagger sliced through my heart, stealing the air from my lungs, and on my next inhale, I felt rejuvenated with life.

Finally, she said into my mind. *Constantine did something to our bonds. I figured out how to unfasten his hold on you, but the others are still quiet.*

I frowned, attempting my link to Zeph and finding it closed off. I'd been so focused on Aflora before that I hadn't thought to reach out to him. Having a mental link to him was still new, but so was my link to her. And yet, all my attention had been on finding her.

Odd.

A year ago, my first instinct would have been to reach out to him.

That didn't necessarily mean I loved her more or him less, just that my priorities had changed. I supposed I'd also been consumed with the need to find her because of the ascension and my desire to help her.

Kols, Aflora said, drawing me back to the present. She looked up with her pretty blue eyes, a smile tugging at the edges of her mouth. I followed her gaze to find Night hovering above us, his wings spread wide as he soared in a circle around our heads.

I dropped my arm away from her back and grabbed her hand once more. "Lead the way," I told him, confident in his ability to guide us out.

Night took off through the mess of feathers, creating a path for us to follow, and we sprinted after him into the sea of darkness.

A resounding hiss trailed behind us, the power vines sizzling and reforming into something new and dangerous. But I kept my gaze on Night, my hand firmly holding Aflora's, as we ran… and ran… and ran.

Not once did she glance backward, no matter how much noise and chaos echoed through the air. Aflora was resolute in her choice, her faith in me a tangible kiss to my senses.

I'd known from our first meeting that she was an ideal mate. Royal. Beautiful. Strong. Feisty as hell. And now she was truly mine. For eternity.

She'd brought me back from certain death, claimed me with her power, and rooted herself so deep inside me that I would forever belong to her, and her to me.

I love you, I whispered, the words a stroke against my heart. I hadn't said that to her before. I hadn't really considered it entirely. But I knew with every fiber of my being that Aflora was always meant to be mine.

I love you, too, Aflora replied, her blue eyes momentarily meeting mine. *But we're escaping this place.*

I know we are, I assured her. *And when we do, I'll confess my feelings out loud.* Because I hadn't said the words to her now out of fear; I knew we would make it out of here alive. The moment had just felt right.

I pushed those emotions to her now, the certainty of our fate underlined in the love I felt.

She didn't outwardly smile, but I sensed her responding joy.

Just as I sensed her tingle of uncertainty as Night led us to a bright white light. It blanketed the world in white, chasing away the darkness and leaving nothing behind.

"Kols?" she asked.

"We jump," I told her as Night disappeared into the horizon.

"Okay." She didn't falter. She merely kept running, our hands still linked.

And we leapt into the core of the dark source's power, the light blinding us both. Her palm disappeared from mine, but we woke up in the bed beside one another in the next breath. I inhaled sharply, looking at her and meeting her gaze.

Then the mattress shook beneath us as power ripped through the air.

Zakkai and Zeph were both on their feet, their wands in their hands as they fought an attack from outside. *Fuck,* I thought, trying to sit up and join them. But my body refused the movement. Aflora appeared to be having the same struggle beside me, both of us weakened by her first ascension trial.

You passed, I assured her. *Six more to go.*

She groaned in response. Then she closed her eyes and began murmuring enchantments that had my eyes widening. They were advanced incantations, ones I hadn't taught her.

But a glance at Zakkai told me where she'd learned them—through their mating link. His silver-blue gaze fell to her, pride momentarily lightening his expression before he growled at the incoming attack from the outside.

The foundation rocked around us, knocking me into Aflora. Power blasted out of her, hitting the sides of the paradigm with a fortification charm that had my heart stopping in unadulterated awe.

Energy rippled down her arms, the dark source's mark marring her pale skin with inky lines.

She finished the incantation on an exhale, and the world fell silent.

Zakkai and Zeph immediately fell to the bed, their exhaustion evident.

Then Zakkai bit into his wrist and held it to Aflora's mouth. "Drink," he demanded.

Zeph followed suit, putting his wrist to my lips. "You, too, little prince."

I tried to snort at the nickname, but I could barely form the sound. So I latched onto his vein instead, sinking my incisors deep into his skin and taking my fill of his blood.

It only took a few pulls for life to thrive through my being, reinvigorating my reserves and drawing me firmly back into the present. The dreamlike filter over my eyes dissolved, allowing me to truly see the damage around the room.

Although, I wouldn't exactly call it a room anymore.

Because there was no roof.

And the bed?

It was a mound of dirt overlaid with dead flower petals.

"What the fuck happened?" I asked as I released Zeph's wrist.

"War," Zakkai replied flatly. "A damn war."

CHAPTER FOUR

ZEPH

"Constantine attacked shortly after you fell unconscious," I added. "Shade fucked off to who knows where, leaving Zakkai and me to uphold the paradigm alone for… I'm not actually sure how long."

"Two hours and seventeen minutes," Shade announced as he appeared. "I've been trying to get back inside, but Constantine had a mass of energy blocking all entries and exits." He looked at Aflora. "I have no idea how you did that, little rose, but it's mighty impressive."

I was torn between punching him in the face for leaving and agreeing with him.

Considering he returned, and it probably was Constantine's fault that he hadn't been able to enter, I opted for the latter. "Very impressive," I echoed, brushing my knuckles across her cheek.

Then I frowned. "Now why can't I hear you?" I couldn't hear Kols, either.

"Constantine did something to our bonds," she said, her attention going to Zakkai.

A question formed over her lips, but the Quandary Blood said, "Take what you need," before she had a chance to voice it.

He leaned down to press his forehead to hers, their mouths grazing in a light kiss that had me narrowing my eyes.

Kolstov and Shadow I could accept.

Zakkai was going to take time.

He'd taken my mate. Kept her from me—from *us*. Hidden her. But he'd also protected her. Which was the only reason I allowed him to remain in such an intimate position with Aflora.

She closed her eyes as energy pooled around her. Clove flew in from above to settle beside her in the destroyed remains of the bed, her wing brushing Aflora's shoulder.

Zakkai's wolf lingered in the former doorway while Raph slithered around my neck.

Then Kols's familiar soared in to land beside Clove. I blinked at the crow's ash-tipped black wings, the color rivaling the ends of the Elite Blood's auburn hair. He glanced at Night and noticed the same thing, his fingers reaching out to stroke the discolored feathers.

They'd both been marked by death.

Shade's icy gaze traced over Kols and Night as well, his expression holding a touch of wonderment. Then he flinched as magic swarmed around him. The same happened to me half a second later, my mind suddenly paralyzed by Aflora's enchantment.

Something snapped.

Prickled.

Crumbled.

My heart ached for a solitary beat before emotion and thoughts came rushing through my mind and soul, Aflora's affection and frustration and fear and relief a torrent of sensations that stole my breath.

I reached for her in the next breath, pulling her mouth away from Zakkai and up to mine, my gratitude at having her inside me again an oppressing wave that I couldn't release. She returned my embrace with equal fervor.

"Good thing she was done," Zakkai muttered.

I ignored him, my focus on my beautiful mate and the power rippling through her. *My queen*, I thought reverently.

Not yet, she returned, her fingers threading through my hair. *I… I don't know if…* She trailed off, her uncertainty winning over her other reactions.

"It's all right," I whispered against her mouth. "We're going to figure this out."

"I want to undo it," she admitted just as softly. "There has to be a way to undo it."

Kols's opinions on that graced my psyche, but he didn't voice them out loud. *Not possible*, he said first. *And even if it is, is it the right recourse?* I followed his analytical reveal, reveling in the ability to be so utterly close to him and his beliefs.

"Voice that out loud," I suggested to him. "Tell Aflora."

"Tell me what?" she asked, her focus on me and then the others. "I assume you're talking to Kols?"

"He is," Kols replied, flashing an irritated glance my way. "You being in my head is problematic."

"And very useful," I countered. "Tell her."

He sighed, his fingers combing through his thick reddish-brown hair as he shook his head. "My grandfather forced your ascension in an effort to kill you. However, you passed your first trial. Not only that, but the source also embraced you. I was just thinking through what that means and wondering if fate might have a point. If perhaps you should be the Midnight Fae Queen."

I righted my spine, my palm still around the back of Aflora's nape. Zakkai stood nearby with Shade on his other side. But my pixie flower's eyes were on

Kols, who still rested beside her on the petal-adorned bed. "How could I be the queen? I'm an Earth Fae."

"An Earth Fae who is mated to four Midnight Fae," he said softly. "An Earth Fae who found a way for the two sources to talk to each other. An Earth Fae who should be thrumming with an overabundance of power right now, seeking to destroy—at least according to all the rumors about abominations— and yet I can hear you still putting your people first. You're not thinking about yourself or what it'll mean for you, but for everyone else. And that is the mark of true royalty, Aflora. That is the mindset of a queen."

I released Aflora, aware of Kols's intention.

His palm found her cheek as he rolled into her. "You were always destined for this," he whispered, his mouth brushing hers. "I think Shade's known that all along, too."

The Death Blood merely smiled, but the look certainly confirmed Kols's statement.

"As touching as this is, we need to move," Zakkai interjected, his tone lined with authority, but I caught the flicker of regret in his silvery gaze. He didn't want to interrupt. However, the brush of energy to the exterior of the paradigm told me exactly why he'd felt the need to.

"He's right," I agreed, my defensive energy already flaring to life. "Constantine is still here." Or nearby, anyway.

"Midnight Fae Academy?" Zakkai asked, arching a brow at Shade.

"Yes," the Death Blood agreed. "My grandmother gained the appropriate permissions, but he's demanded a meeting with you."

Zakkai snorted in response. "Of course he has. He's been trying to meet me for years."

Shade just lifted a shoulder. "You know how he feels about making deals."

I frowned at them. "Who are you talking about? And why would we go to the Academy? That's the first place they'll look for us."

"Your Academy, yes. This Academy, no." Zakkai redirected his attention to Shade. "And I accept the deal."

"That's not the only one they made," Shade replied. "He also wants a boon at his point of choosing."

"From me or Zenaida?"

"You know my grandmother prefers to be called Zen." Shade gave him an indecipherable look. "And *he* didn't clarify."

"I see," Zakkai murmured. "Well, I'm prepared to pay whatever price so long as we're hidden. I'll be sure to thank *Zenaida* later for arranging it."

The Death Blood snorted. "It's already done because I agreed to it on your behalf."

"Presumptuous of you."

"I knew you would do anything for Aflora," Shade returned.

"True," Zakkai agreed without missing a beat, looking down at her now. "We need to go, little star."

She nodded. "I can feel him."

"We all can," Kols said. "But what Academy are you talking about? There's only one in existence for Midnight Fae."

"Is there?" Zakkai countered. "Where do you think all the outlawed Midnight Fae go to study? In the Human Realm?" He conjured a flaming dragon in the next breath, sending it up into the sky to attack those beyond the paradigm walls. "Because I doubt they teach this at local universities there."

Shade just shook his head and disappeared again.

I glared after him. "Another damn secret."

Zakkai smirked. "He's full of them."

"As are you," I replied, stepping toward him. His arrogance was starting to grate on my nerves. "If this is going to work, we all need to start communicating."

"If?" His smirk intensified. "You act as though there's a choice in the matter."

"There's a choice if I remove you," I threatened, not at all amused by his tricks and games and riddles. He was just as bad as Shade. No, he was worse. A lone wolf used to doing whatever the hell he wanted, however he wanted. I started to take another step, but Aflora slipped off the bed to stand between us, her palm against my chest.

"Can we all try to focus, please?" she asked, her voice regal in its softness. My gaze immediately dropped to the lines of power writhing over her arms, my heart leaping into my throat.

She was right.

There were more important items to focus on right now.

I cupped her jaw, my Warrior Blood gift flourishing beneath my skin with the dark desire to guard her. "We'll figure this out, pixie flower. I vow it."

She nodded, but her hesitation remained. She wasn't sure she wanted this.

However, I agreed with Kols's statement—she was made for this.

Zakkai moved into her back, his power an irritating wave of warmth that I could feel pulsing around and through Aflora.

Kols slid off the bed then, joining us, our bodies forming a protective circle around our Aflora. Her shoulders relaxed slightly as she breathed in our scents, her resolve somewhat thickening.

I glanced at Kols, his gaze reflecting what I already knew. There would be more trials, all of them equally dangerous and difficult.

While Kols had had his entire life to prepare for them, Aflora had only spent a few months at the Academy. Her knowledge was inferior, her skills rudimentary. Kols had also benefited from his father being the one to outline the trials.

However, Constantine was in charge now.

And there was no telling what he would do or how he would frame Aflora's future.

Preparing her would be the hardest task of our lives. But I silently vowed in that moment to do whatever was necessary to guard her and help her ascend.

I'd die for her.
Kols echoed the sentiment, both of us promising her eternal loyalty.
She would be our royal.
Our future Midnight Fae Queen.

CHAPTER FIVE

KOLS

Shade returned several minutes later with clothes that rivaled our Academy wardrobe—slacks and button-down shirts for the men. Cloaks, too.

And a skirt with a blouse for Aflora. She pulled on the boots with a sigh, her fingers brushing the fine black material. It was a unique leather made from Midnight Fae magic rather than animal product. She seemed to approve, her Earth Fae side preferring enchantment over unnecessary death.

I finished buttoning up my shirt before wrapping my arm around her slender waist and pulling her to me for another kiss. She seemed to have calmed down now, her acceptance of fate growing with each passing second.

Yet I still sensed her trying to find a way to reverse the ascension.

She and Zakkai were having some sort of mental discussion about it. I couldn't hear it, just felt the hum of their discussion brushing my psyche.

What will happen if she undoes the ascension? It had nearly killed me, but that was because of the manner in which my father had done it. My heart ached just thinking about it. But it hadn't been him. My grandfather…

I swallowed.

Phoenix fires.

I couldn't even process it.

And Tray. I pulled away from Aflora on a jolt. *Shit, Tray!*

"Tray will be okay," Zeph rushed to say, his hand reaching for my shoulder to give it a squeeze. "Once we're somewhere safe, we'll reach out to him." His green eyes went to Shade. "Which reminds me, where are we going, Shadow? You never actually said."

I tried to allow his distraction to pull me from my dark thoughts and concerns, but I felt to my soul that something was very wrong. Tray wasn't okay at all. None of us were.

Aflora leaned into me, her head on my chest. She didn't say anything, just offered me her emotional strength and support by cuddling me in a moment of intense need.

Zeph was at my back as well, his intensity a protective cape that billowed around me.

"To a place Constantine can't go," Shade said softly. "To the Academy he knows exists but can't breach."

I frowned. "He knows about this other Academy?" It'd never been mentioned to me. Of course, it seemed the Council and the Elders had hidden several key items from me. So I supposed this wasn't new information.

"Your grandfather knows everything," Zakkai replied before Shade could speak. "I'm guessing your father does, too. But I find it fascinating that they kept you in the dark. Did they do the same for your twin?"

"Kai," Aflora interjected, her tone quiet yet stern. She still had her head against my chest, but her focus was on the Quandary Blood.

His silver-blue eyes went to her, and his features softened marginally. "I know, little star." He looked at Shade. "Does Lucifer want to meet me now or after we arrive?"

"He didn't say," Shade said before I could react to the infamous name of the Hell Fae King. "So I believe we have safe passage to the paradigm, at least until he decides otherwise."

"We're going to the Hell Fae realm?" It came out as a question, but I meant it as more of a statement. Because that was the only explanation for what they were saying. "The other Midnight Fae Academy is hidden… in the Hell Fae realm?"

Zakkai and Shade both looked at me with expressions that said, *Obviously.* But only Zakkai actually said the word out loud.

"How long has this paradigm existed?" I wondered out loud.

"Zenaida arranged it with Lucifer about seven hundred years ago, right?" Zakkai casually asked the question, like this wasn't a big reveal or life-altering information.

"Roughly," Shade replied.

"That's where you disappear to," Zeph said. "You shadow off to the other Academy."

Shade lifted a shoulder. "On occasion. But not for classes."

"And my grandfather knew." The words came out slowly, my mind failing to believe them even as I voiced them.

"Yes. My grandmother lives nearby." His icy eyes went to Aflora. "It's where Aflora's meadow is, too."

"In the Hell Fae realm?" she whispered, her head leaving my chest so she could look at the Death Blood. "That's where the paradigms are for the Quandary Bloods who prefer reformation over retribution?"

Shade dipped his chin. "Yes. Lucifer already gave you entry as a marked abomination. As you're probably aware, he has a soft spot for them." His gaze lifted to mine. "Which is how I negotiated your entry as well. Zeph was the primary issue."

"Well, in that case, I refuse my meeting with Lucifer and Zeph can stay here," Zakkai replied.

Aflora bristled in my arms, her attention shifting from Shade to the Quandary Blood. "*Kai.*"

"I'm joking, little star."

"Hilarious," Zeph deadpanned. "Can we go now? The defenses are beginning to fail again."

Aflora nodded. "Yes, I feel them crumbling."

"Shade?" Zakkai prompted.

"Already working on it." The Death Blood's voice sounded strained, his eyes closing on a grimace.

Frowning, I locked into my link with him and noted his waning energy reserves. *You need more power.*

He grunted in reply, our mental connection firmly intact even at the first-level mate-bonding.

Take some vitality from me, I told him.

You're not the one I need to tap into, he replied, shutting me out with a click of a door.

I scowled. "Don't be a stubborn dolt," I told him out loud since I couldn't voice it in his mind. I didn't know how he'd blocked me out, but it was a trick I wanted to learn.

"Fuck off, Kols," he gritted out.

"Shade," Aflora said, slipping away from me to reach for him. "What do you need?"

"Power," I answered for him. "His reserves are depleted from whatever he's been doing for the paradigm."

"I'm fine," he snapped.

"You're not fucking fine. You're on the verge of passing out." This whole solitary operation needed to stop. We were a unit now—*all of us*—and it was time we all accepted it. "Let us help you, Shade. We're your mates."

"He's right," Zakkai said, surprising me. "You're hurting all of us by saying you're fine when you're not. Do you need Aflora's blood?" He studied the other man. "Yeah, that's what you need. Not much, just enough to push forward." He nodded to Aflora. "Don't let him refuse."

She grabbed Shade before he could even try to argue, her lips finding his on a demanding kiss. A hint of metallic blood tinted the air, suggesting she'd bitten her tongue prior to embracing him. His responding groan confirmed it, his arm circling her waist as he indulged in the essence she fed him. Zeph's arm came around my upper body in a partial hug, his chest meeting my back. I relaxed into his familiar embrace as Zakkai moved forward.

A black cloak whirled around us all half a beat later as Shade engaged his ability to shadow.

My stomach rolled with the sensation of moving through space and time beneath his enchantment.

Then goose bumps prickled my arms as we landed on a dusted path of embers and charcoal fibers.

Hell Fae realm, I thought, wincing at the heat blazing around us. My grandfather certainly wouldn't track us here, not with the blistering magic and underlying cruelty in the air. He also wouldn't be welcome.

However, it was rather fascinating that Lucifer had allowed Zen to build a paradigm here.

Hell Fae weren't known for their kindness. She'd either traded him something extremely valuable, or they had some sort of unique arrangement.

Quandary Bloods were extremely powerful. The Hell Fae King would find that useful.

Shade released Aflora's mouth as we all materialized, a sigh of content coming from his lips. The familiars appeared shortly after, his spell having captured them as well. Or perhaps they'd followed on instinct. Familiar magic was unique in how they could appear and vanish at will.

"The entrance is just over there." Shade gestured with his chin toward an obsidian arch. "A set of gates will exist on the other side. They'll remind you of the other Academy, but once you enter, you'll immediately sense the difference. All the excommunicated Midnight Fae—at least the ones who chose not to follow Laki—and creatures reside in there. It's sacred and deadly and very well protected. So any ill will won't be taken lightly."

"You act as though we plan to burn it down," Zakkai drawled. "I've visited your grandmother before, Shade. Just recently, if you recall."

"My warning wasn't for you," Shade replied, his gaze finding mine and Zeph's. "Don't overreact. With everything going on, we can't afford to be ousted, because there is literally nowhere else for us to go. The Midnight Fae are searching for us in droves right now, furious over Aflora's ascension."

I frowned. "They already know?"

Shade's expression took on a sardonic twist. "Yeah. Constantine told them all that she stole the throne and she's a power-hungry fae who is out of control. He's notified the other fae as well."

"How do you know all that?" Zeph demanded, suspicion underlying his tone. He still had his arm around my upper body, his tension palpable at my back.

"Because my grandmother told me," Shade bit back. "We've entered the proverbial endgame now, so I have no more tricks up my sleeve. I'm telling you everything I learn as I learn it. But I just spent several hours trying to return to you, so forgive me for the delay."

"Thank you for being forthright," I interjected before Zeph could speak. I felt his ire and annoyance boiling through his thoughts, and I didn't want to instigate any more fighting. We needed to work as a unit, and if that meant leading by example, I would. "Do we know how the Elemental Fae are reacting to the news?"

Shade's lips curled down, then he gave a subtle shake of his head.

"They'll excommunicate me," Aflora said softly. "Especially after what Elana did to them."

I hated to agree with that statement, but knowing Exos and Cyrus as well as I did, I found myself nodding. "They'll fear what they don't know."

"Which is why I need to revert the ascension," she pressed. "I can't be an Earth Royal and queen to the Midnight Fae kingdom. All of the fae realms will hunt me and try to kill me."

"They're going to do that anyway," Zakkai inserted. "Which means we need you to be the most powerful being to ever exist so you can protect yourself."

I nodded. "Yes."

"No," Aflora replied. "I don't want all this power."

"Which is why you're the perfect fae to embrace it," I argued. "You won't use it for nefarious purposes. You'll provoke change."

"Much-needed change," Zeph echoed.

"Precisely," I murmured.

Aflora sighed and shook her head. "Let's just… go inside. And then we can keep talking about it. I could really go for a sandwich."

"Shroom loaf?" Zeph offered. "Mustard berries?"

"Mouseberries," she corrected with a smile.

"Mussleberries," he said softly, a grin in his tone. "Of course. Coming right up."

Aflora rolled her eyes, but some of the tension in her stance melted at the playfulness of his words. "Spritemead, too. And a dragon steak."

"Someone's hungry. Did we not feed you properly last night?" He released me with a kiss to my neck, then walked around me to press his lips to her cheek. "Because I seem to recall feeding you quite well."

Her cheeks turned a beautiful pink shade as she tried to glare up at him. "*Zeph.*"

The Warrior Blood brushed his mouth over hers, his palm wrapping around the back of her neck. "Come on, pixie flower. Let's go explore this new Academy. Then I'll ensure you're *properly* fed. Again."

She swallowed. "Then I want a salad patty."

"I'll give you everything and anything you want, Aflora," he replied softly, his forehead resting against hers for a brief moment. "Including *mouseberries.*"

Her expression brightened. "Yes, please."

"I thought he was a Guardian turned headmaster," Zakkai said conversationally. "Is he a chef, too?"

"He's good with a wand," Shade explained.

"Ah. The food spells make up for other weaker areas." Zakkai nodded. "I understand."

Zeph ignored him.

Aflora just shook her head.

Shade smirked.

And I started taking mental bets on how long Zakkai and Zeph would last in a room together before one of them tried to kill the other. Both men were alphas to their cores, neither inclined to bend.

I'd have to keep an eye on them.

Especially when alone with Aflora.

She might not survive a duel between them.

A concern for later, as we had much more pressing items to deal with—such as the issue with my grandfather telling all of fae kind that Aflora had manipulated her own ascension. Given the trial requirements, this would be a problem. Because one of those levels required her to gain approval from Midnight Fae kind.

And that wasn't likely to happen if they all believed her to be a power-hungry abomination with the ability to ascend illegally.

I rubbed a hand over my face, exhausted just thinking about it.

Hopefully, venturing into the Hell Fae realm would give us a little more time to prepare. Or a lot more time. I'd been gifted twenty-plus years to ready myself for the trials.

Aflora… had had all of a few minutes to accept it.

No wonder she wanted to revert the ascension.

Shade stopped by the obsidian arch and pressed his hand to the right side of it to pull up a keypad. Then he demonstrated how to enter by giving us the codes to activate the swirl of power beneath the arch and the subsequent passcode meant to prove our allowance to proceed through the enchantment.

It felt like a show of faith from him—a way of confirming that we'd finally breached his inner circle.

About fucking time, I heard Zeph think.

I snorted in agreement.

While I understood Shade's penchant for secrets all these months, it was nice to finally be on the other side.

However, as we stepped through the gate onto the Academy grounds, I realized there was a myriad of secrets yet to be revealed. Because holy fuck, the exterior resembled Midnight Fae Academy.

The stone walls were all covered in hissing snake-vines. A pair of gargoyles stood by the gates, their swords already drawn.

My brow furrowed. "You said we were welcome."

"We are," Shade replied, confusion evident in his tone as the snake-vines began to writhe angrily.

A series of charcoal crows cawed in fury above.

Burning thwomps shot fire into the sky.

Gargoyles inside all took up arms, rushing the gates.

Stonepeckers snarled.

A phoenix landed a few feet away to expand his feathers in a furious show of color.

Fire gnats began to swarm.

And a sinking sensation churned in my stomach.

"Shit," I breathed, locking gazes with Zeph. His expression told me he'd figured it out as well.

"What?" Aflora demanded. "What's happening?"

"It's your next ascension trial." With Constantine running the show, he hadn't bothered to give her a break. And of course he chose to engage this one next. "You remember how I told you all Midnight Fae creatures were mine to command?" I asked softly, stepping up beside her.

"Yes," she whispered, her fear palpable.

"Well, you're the incoming monarch now. The second ascension is about taming the Midnight Fae creatures to your will. Show them you're their queen and they'll kneel at your feet."

Fail… and they'll eat you alive.

CHAPTER SIX

AFLORA

*Y*ou *and I are going to have a very serious discussion about these trials and what to expect,* I snapped at Kols through our mental link. *Assuming I survive.*

You will, he replied immediately. *I'll ensure it.*

Those snake-vines say otherwise. I'd never been a fan of the hissing, writhing vines that surrounded Midnight Fae Academy. And they'd never been a fan of me.

But Kols had always commanded them before, which meant they'd mostly left me alone.

The way they were circling and acting now told me that would not be the case today.

Tell me what to do, I thought at Kols. *Quickly.*

You need to win them over by proving you're their superior. I recommend picking the biggest and baddest of the creatures to tame first. Some of the smaller, less volatile ones will bow on instinct.

I took in all the beings surrounding us—including the fiery birds soaring above. They were smaller than the phoenix but still deadly in appearance. Mostly because their feathers were flames, not soft bristles.

"Clove," I whispered, calling my falcon to my shoulder.

She landed with a ruffle of wings, her beady black gaze on the sky and the approaching creatures.

A dome of magic appeared from Zeph in the next instant, his defensive skill manifesting just as two of the fiery birds dove toward us.

They hit the green-glowing shield with a sizzling spark that reverberated through the air, their agonizing cries splintering my heart.

Death isn't necessary, I thought to myself. *But death is the Midnight Fae way.*

Did that mean the creatures would only understand if I reacted violently?

There had to be another way, a more peaceful manner to tame them. To prove my worth. To be their queen. It didn't matter that I wanted to undo the ascension later. I needed to master them now, to survive this trial, then find a way to fix everything.

However, I refused to do it through dark methods.

Zeph's shield zapped another approaching creature, making me wince.

That's not the way.

Two more fell from the sky, their beautiful lights fizzling out as the birds perished from whatever enchantment he'd woven. I understood that he was just trying to protect us, that all Midnight Fae had been taught to fight savagery with responding barbarity, but Earth Fae believed in *life*. We desired light and sunshine and fresh air and flourishing flowers and happy animals.

I knelt, my fingers digging into the dark rocks of the path, my eyes falling closed as I sought out the plants and trees around me.

The burning thwomps.

The black flowers.

The charcoal blades.

All the foreign Midnight Fae *life*, and showed them the source inside me. Not the dark one, but the one filled with sunshine and elements—my connection to *earth*. Then I manipulated their strength and bolstered their vitality, renewing their purpose and providing enhanced growth.

Roots settled deeper. The charcoal blades stood a little taller. The flowers bloomed.

Around them, the fire gnats buzzed in curiosity, temporarily distracted by the thriving plant life.

My power stretched and grew to the snake-vines, the organism more plant than reptile. They resisted me at first, displeased by my manipulation. But a few gentle strokes of vivacity had them purring instead of hissing, their vines thickening to a more robust shape that slithered with a strength resembling the rocks behind them.

Which was what I stroked next—the gargoyles.

They were made of stone, beings of the earth, and I surrounded them with my element, marrying the darkness to the light and providing them with a freshness and vigor unlike any they'd ever felt before. I felt their confusion and surprise, two emotions that bled into respect and adoration.

It all happened so fast, so naturally, so *kindly*, that the other creatures began to swarm in curiosity rather than anger. They'd expected retaliation—a fight. But I showed them affection instead. I introduced them to the Elemental Fae way of existence while also proving my dominance by being the one in charge of their restoration.

You're all mine to groom, I was telling them. *Mine to strengthen. Mine to empower.*

What wasn't said—what they all *knew*—was that they were also mine to destroy.

Yet deep down they could sense my unwillingness to hurt them.

Which I proved by pushing life to the fiery birds that had fallen, demanding their wings flap once again.

That came from the dark source, the ability to resurrect and revive life a Death Blood trait that I naturally understood with a spell from Shade's mind. Or maybe it came from Zakkai. All my mates were so much a part of me that I could pick and choose enchantments at will, my Quandary Blood connection allowing me to write and rewrite incantations without much thought.

So perhaps it had been a combination of effort, coming from Shade and Zakkai both.

Regardless, it worked, the firebirds flapping their glowing wings as they took off for the sky once more. Zeph had dropped his shield, ensuring that the beings weren't harmed again. The other creature had been a stonepecker—the rare birdlike rodent known for absorbing and dismantling spells.

He took my enchantment now to bring himself back to full health, then scurried off to hide among the snake-vines.

The phoenix was last, the large bird standing so tall that I looked directly into his multicolored eyes as I slowly returned to my feet. He cocked his head, intrigue flourishing in his intelligent gaze.

We didn't speak so much as communicate with our spirits, mine brushing his in astute praise of his beauty and prestige.

He responded by fluttering his stunning plumes, showing off in a masculine way that reminded me a bit of my mates. *I bet you do that for all the pretty girls, hmm?* I thought at him.

He preened in response, strutting along the ground and showing off his long, elegant stride.

Yeah, you know you're pretty, I told him, lifting my hand. He stepped forward without fear, his assuredness born of being a profound predator known for dismantling his prey.

His feathery head met my palm, his stunning plumes soft and welcoming beneath my fingers. "Very beautiful," I praised.

Clove clicked on my shoulder in agreement.

The phoenix bowed in response, his beak brushing my stomach before he took a step back.

"Cocky fucking bird," I heard Zeph mutter to Kols.

"If you're envious of a phoenix, then I suspect you and I are going to have issues later," Zakkai drawled.

Zeph snorted in response.

Shade smothered a chuckle.

I merely smiled, tilting my head in a bow back to the phoenix to show equal appreciation. He released a loud caw in response, drawing the attention of several creatures as he expanded his wings to take off into the sky.

A series of chitters followed, the charcoal crows following in his breezy wake.

And then an echo of stones moving followed.

I turned to see the gargoyles stepping through the gates with their weapons drawn in a battle stance. I frowned, confused for a moment until they all took a saluted position along the path, their arms rising high to create a wall of stone and sharp swords, all their edges pointed directly up to the sky.

"How long did it take you to pass that trial?" Zeph asked conversationally. "A week?"

"Nine days," Kols replied. "Nine very long fucking days."

"Hmm." Zeph sounded amused.

"She had the earth advantage," Kols said, his tone light and his expression full of pride. "Using life to court life." He nodded in approval. "Very effective, princess."

Shade grinned. "Constantine is going to be pissed." He glanced at Zakkai. "I hope Tadmir records his reaction."

Zakkai didn't seem to share his amusement, his expression serious as he analyzed the gargoyles and surrounding creatures. "We should go inside while we can. If Constantine realizes she passed this quickly, he'll just engage the next trial."

"Which is?" I prompted.

"A topic for once we're through those gates," Zakkai replied, pointing at the entry. "After you, my queen."

CHAPTER SEVEN

SHADE

My grandmother stood just inside the gates with a platter of cookies, her smile welcoming and knowing.

Because she'd probably foreseen that trial outside the gates.

A heads-up would have been appreciated, but that wasn't her way. Fortune Fae never wanted to alter fate, just project potential paths. And I'd made it my life's work to alter my own—hence Kols standing beside me.

My grandmother cast a cursory glance over him, her blue eyes taking on an appreciative gleam as she studied his hair.

I arched a brow, daring her to say something.

She didn't.

Instead, she held out the treats for everyone to enjoy while formally introducing herself to Zeph and Kols. I didn't partake in the cookies, because I knew what they meant—more bad news.

"Take them on a tour," she advised. "Then come see me afterward."

I dipped my chin in agreement, knowing she meant for me to visit her, not the others. But a glance at Zakkai told me he saw right through the act and he would be attending that meeting with me.

I'd hidden a lot from him over the years. However, he always seemed to know, as though he could remember the timelines just like I could. I knew he couldn't actually recall them because that was impossible—his memory had been altered with all the others.

Although, his Quandary Blood ability probably allowed him to sense those alternate timelines. Or perhaps the manipulation of the power was what he felt.

Regardless, he'd suspected my interference and questionable allegiances our entire relationship. Which meant he would either follow me to the meeting or attend at my side.

The latter was preferred, especially as we both were tied to Aflora now.

She walked along beside me as I provided the tour my grandmother suggested. "It's similar to the other Academy, at least in terms of architecture. But this campus doesn't have a Death Blood dorm or building, or an Elite Blood, or anything categorized. All the classes are combined because the majority of the fae are Quandary Bloods. However, there are a few from every type. There are also a handful of other fae, like Hell Fae, who attend. It's part of Lucifer's arrangement with my grandmother."

Among other things.

I didn't understand everything they'd worked out, as their deal predated my existence by several centuries, but I'd gathered educational opportunities had been involved.

"These are the dorms," I said, gesturing to a series of gothic-style buildings. They were reminiscent of the other Academy grounds, framed with darkness and a high moon, but they weren't exclusive to a single Midnight Fae type. And they didn't require spells for entry.

Gargoyles moved around more here, walking or flying to different locations, rather than residing behind doors.

They bowed to Aflora as she passed, their reverence palpable. But she was too busy studying the campus to notice.

"You don't have charcoal blades," she noted, gazing out over an obsidian courtyard of sharp rocks and dangerous grooves.

I caught her elbow as she bent to touch the ground. "Don't."

She frowned at me, then gasped as a swirl of fire erupted from the center into a geyser of furious flames. "Mother Earth…"

A few passing fae tossed sparks into the pit, their cerulean embers dancing with the red and yellow flickers. Then it all whirled together into a tornado of heat and sucked the air around it right back down into the hole, disappearing.

"It's like… like a burning thwomp?" she guessed.

"Only worse," I replied. "There are certain aspects of the Hell Fae realm that couldn't be erased, so my grandmother altered the paradigm to accept the nuances."

"That's fascinating." Kols had gone to his haunches on the cobblestone path, his burnt-gold gaze on the black rocks. "I can feel the merging of magic."

I nodded. "Yeah, certain areas of the paradigm are stronger than others."

"The meadow?" Aflora wondered.

"Is in a neutral area. Not all of the Hell Fae realm is fire and heat. It's… sporadic." And why other fae refused to visit.

Well, that and the Hell Fae didn't take kindly to visitors. They were all shunned abominations, with Constantine Nacht being enemy number one among them.

"Where will we be staying?" Zeph asked, his arms folded over his chest as he analyzed the field with a speculative expression.

"In one of the dorms near the back of the campus grounds," I told him.

Aflora appeared disappointed. "Not in your cabin?"

"Our cabin," I corrected her with a squeeze of her hand. "And no. It's too far from the Academy grounds. We need room to practice and learn, and we can't do that in our meadow. These buildings are meant for training and mastering magic. So it's best for us to stay here."

"Oh." Her lips pinched to the side, then she slowly tilted her head in agreement.

I urged us along, showing them a few of the academic areas and recommended enclosures for practicing offensive and defensive arts. Zakkai and Zeph took interest in those, their calculative natures taking over. Kols just seemed to take it all in stride, observing all the Midnight Fae we passed and studying the general makeup of the paradigm.

It was all very real—as paradigms should be—but the underlying presence of Hell Fae lurked in the area around campus. Mostly because of the protection charms. Since some of Lucifer's most powerful fae attended the Academy, he helped bolster the natural defenses around us.

The village where my grandmother resided didn't have the same feel because it was on neutral ground.

I used a spell to bring up a map for Aflora, explaining where the different sections of the paradigm resided and how each one interacted with the Hell Fae realm. She gaped at it, fascinated.

Zeph appeared to be memorizing it.

Zakkai merely gave an appreciative grin. "Zenaida's clever." He admired the sky and the buildings, his approval evident. "I never considered mingling elements the way she has. It bolsters the structure while helping it blend."

"Going to pass notes to your dad?" I wondered out loud.

Zakkai snorted. "I doubt he'll want to talk to me anytime soon. I saved a Nacht, after all."

True. It didn't matter that Kols was innocent in the war; his grandfather had started it. And the Quandary Blood wanted the Nacht line exterminated.

"Am I still considered a Nacht?" Kols called a cloud of magic to his hand, the colors a swirling mix of purple, red, cerulean, and green. "I don't really feel like an Elite Blood anymore." The flames extinguished in a flip of his palm, his burnt-bronze gaze flickering with curiosity and a hint of something else. Not sadness—I felt his comfort with being part of our mate-circle thriving via our connection. Yet there was a sense of loss in him.

For Tray, I realized.

Yes, Kols replied, our link open and allowing him freedom in my thoughts. I considered pushing him out like I had earlier but didn't. Instinct told me he needed the bonds right now. Because the one he'd established at birth was suffering.

He couldn't exactly feel Tray, but their souls were joined in a unique manner—one that would never truly be severed. "You're still a Nacht," I said. "But a good one. Like Tray."

Kols blinked at me.

However, it was Zeph who spoke. "Was that a compliment?" Shock underlined his words. "Like an honest-to-fae compliment?"

"I think so," Kols replied, humor in his tone.

"How odd." Zeph's green eyes found mine, a grin lurking in their depths. Probably a joke at my own expense. Or maybe I'd pleased him. It was hard to say with the Warrior Blood.

"Shade has many layers," Aflora said, dissolving my map spell as she stepped through it to wrap her arms around me. I kissed the top of her head, her embrace immediately putting me at ease.

Thank you, little rose, I whispered.

She responded with a rumble in her stomach, her hunger evident.

Zeph smirked. "Someone wants some mustard berries."

Aflora shook her head against me, mumbling the appropriate term back to him like she always did.

The Warrior Blood's gaze sparkled with delight, loving their banter.

Zakkai ignored them all, his focus on me, his eyes telling me that he was impatient to meet with my grandmother. He'd wanted a full briefing on security and everything else that went with the paradigm, too.

"The dorm we're staying in is just over there," I said, gesturing with my chin over Aflora's head.

The others followed as I led the way, Aflora's hand in mine once more. A week ago, this would have felt surreal—like a dream. Seven timelines had ended in destruction and near death.

And number eight had led to this.

To a union between five Midnight Fae.

I knew better than to rejoice in the victory. We were nowhere near done. Focusing on unity became all the more imperative with Constantine engaging us in this new dangerous game.

Zakkai and Zeph were the two who posed the biggest threat.

Two alpha males vying for dominance.

Aflora was the key to keeping them in line, and I wasn't entirely convinced she had Zakkai under control.

He moved behind me with silent steps, his presence a threat and a comfort. Power radiated off him, his connection to the source rivaling Aflora's ascension.

I moved up the stone steps to the double doors of the dorm where two gargoyles waited, their eyes cast down in a sign of respect.

A third stood just inside with Kols's crow perched on his stone head. "Sir Kristoff," I greeted with false cheer. The little creature loathed me for all my dates with time. He didn't know all the details but possessed certain memories of Kyros and me twisting fate on numerous occasions.

"Death Blood," he muttered. Then he inclined his head. "Mistress Aflora."

She paused midstep, her blue eyes falling to the short stone being. His head didn't even reach her knees. "Mistress Aflora?" she repeated.

Kols moved to her other side. "You're the ascending royal, sweetheart," he explained against her ear. "And you passed your second trial. The creatures all respond to you now."

"I transferred your box to your new quarters, Master Kolstov," the gargoyle informed him after standing up straight. "Nothing is remiss."

"Good to know your loyalty is unwavering," Kols replied, grinning.

"I've never liked Constantine," Sir Kristoff muttered. His tone displayed a hint of emotion—a rare trait for a gargoyle. "Power-hungry and cruel."

He stomped off toward the stairs, taking over the job of host. My grandmother had only told me we would be staying somewhere in this building, mentioning something about the gardens behind it. Fortunately, it seemed Sir Kristoff knew where to take us.

"Do all Midnight Fae creatures know how to find this paradigm?" Aflora asked as we trailed after the gargoyle.

"They know how to locate Midnight Fae," I replied, my hand releasing hers and going to her lower back as I moved upward beside her.

"Does that mean they're all allowed here?" Her mind added a follow-up inquiry soon after, telling me why she'd voiced the first question. *If Kristoff can enter, is it possible for Constantine to send in a less loyal gargoyle or something worse?* she asked herself.

"No," I answered, addressing both of her queries. "There are numerous protective spells and layers that will prevent anyone and anything with ill intentions from crossing the boundary into the paradigm."

"Can't they just use a stonepecker? Like that day on campus?" she pressed.

"Hell Fae wards are not something stonepeckers can absorb and regurgitate," I assured her. "Which means it wouldn't even be able to reach the paradigm boundary to try to learn the spells."

"Because the ill-intentioned creature would be destroyed upon entering Lucifer's gates," Zakkai added from right behind us. "Extremely useful setup, and also why your grandmother afforded us that meeting the other week. She knew I had good intentions."

I lifted a shoulder. "Caution is what keeps her alive."

"It's more than caution, Shadow. Zenaida's brilliant." The conviction in his tone told me he meant the praise in his words.

I nodded in agreement and continued up until the stairs stopped, indicating our floor. It was nearly impossible to know what level we were on because the steps had just continued up and up and up until they ended on a floor with a single door.

"Concealment charms," Zakkai mused. "As I said, brilliant." He stepped up behind Aflora, his hands finding her hips and trapping my palm between his abdomen and her lower back. "Can you sense the magic, little star? All the secret wires pulsing through the floors and hiding all the rooms except the one intended to be ours?"

She leaned into my side and back into him, allowing us to hold her as she considered the enchantments of the building. "It's… intense."

"It's beautiful," Zakkai whispered. "Like you." He kissed her neck, then relaxed his chin on her shoulder. "But can you see through it? To the electrical energy beneath?"

"I sense it," she admitted. "But I don't understand it."

"Close your eyes," he breathed, his arms slipping around her middle while my palm remained between them. It created an intimate connection between the three of us, Zakkai seeming unbothered by the fact that I stayed close while he engaged their mental link to coach her through the magical lesson.

Her thick black eyelashes splayed across her cheekbones as she did as he'd instructed, her lips parting at whatever he unleashed inside her.

Kols and Zeph shared a look while Sir Kristoff stood stationary in the hallway.

Static hummed through the air as Zakkai and Aflora spoke mentally to one another, and after several minutes of intense silence, Aflora opened her eyes once more.

"What floor are we on, little star?" Zakkai said.

"The fourth one. Room seven."

"Well done," he praised, kissing her neck again. "Very well done." He released her then, his focus falling to the gargoyle. "Continue."

Sir Kristoff gave a subtle bow, acknowledging Zakkai as superior because of his Source Architect role. Or maybe because he was Aflora's mate. Regardless, the gargoyle led us to our room and through the door into a living area surrounded by windows.

My eyebrows lifted at the courtyard beyond it. "Fourth floor?"

"Another impressive illusion," Zakkai said. "That's a roof garden above one of the other rooms."

"Filled with real plants." Aflora practically ran forward, her intrigue clearly replacing her need to eat because she ran right past the kitchen and open dining area to the sliding doors at the side. Zakkai sent a spell ahead of her to open the glass doors, allowing her to dart straight into the garden of flowers and trees.

The four of us chuckled at her excitement, then Zeph wandered after her and leaned against the doorway. "Are you going to strip like last time, pixie flower?"

That piqued Zakkai's interest. "She stripped in a garden?"

"In Central Park." Zeph didn't take his eyes off her while he spoke. "The humans didn't approve."

Aflora muttered something back about only removing her sweater last time before collapsing onto a pile of green grass beneath a tree. "Oh, so pretty!"

My lips twitched at her amusement. Then I glanced up at the high moon. This part of the paradigm never saw the sun, so it was hard to determine the time. However, I suspected my grandmother expected me any minute now.

I glanced around the open living area, spotted a hallway to the side, and wandered down it by four different bedroom doors—all of them open. The biggest bedroom was at the end of the hall, where I found a walk-in closet filled with clothes. Most of them were feminine and appeared to be Aflora's size. There was also a dresser inside with four wands on top.

Because Aflora still didn't have her own.

Odd that the dark source hadn't gifted her one yet.

With a shake of my head, I grabbed my own and turned to find Zakkai behind me, expectant. "Do you want your wand?" I asked him.

"No. Leave it for Aflora."

A good answer, I decided. He followed me back into the living area, where Zeph and Kols were both watching Aflora in her element. She'd completely lost herself to her Earth Fae nature. Roots were dancing along the ground as she renewed the soil with life, causing the trees to elongate and the flowers to blossom.

"I need to go meet with my grandmother before she sends for me," I told them. "Can you make sure Aflora remembers to eat something?" Because I suspected she had forgotten all about her hunger now.

Zeph nodded without looking at me.

Zakkai didn't bother commenting, just turned to lead the way.

Because we both knew he was going with me, and he didn't feel the need to mention it to the others.

Rather than comment, I followed him out and ensured that my connection to Aflora remained wide open. It was my way of telling her there would be no more secrets.

Whatever my grandmother said, I'd share.

Because Aflora and I were finally on a true path—as fully bonded mates.

No more alternate timelines. No more Paradox Fae. Just a single way forward, with all four of us by her side.

Hurry back, she whispered to me, acknowledging that I'd left.

I won't be far, I promised.

I know, she replied. *Just like I know how to find you now.* She breathed a spell into my mind, telling me she'd not only learned how to use my shadowing ability, but she'd also memorized it.

Good, I murmured. *Eat something.*

Mmm, she hummed, her mind purring with life and earth once more.

I laughed under my breath as we exited the building. "When this is all over, we need to find a place with a real garden for Aflora."

"So we can watch her frolic in the nude?" Zakkai asked.

My lips twitched. "Among other things."

Many other things.

CHAPTER EIGHT

AFLORA

Warmth. Beauty. Passion.

I reveled in it, rolling around in the grass and soaking up all the magic. "There are so many types of earth," I marveled out loud, speaking to no one in particular. "So much life!"

There were plants from all the fae realms, including some from my own. And the human world, too.

"These are tulips," I said, encouraging one to blossom. "So very different from the orchid." Which was beautiful and white but required much more attention than the tulip.

I returned to the tree again, leaning against the trunk and sighing happily. "Such a mighty oak you are," I praised. "Strong and big, with a stunning girth."

"Is that a euphemism?" Zeph asked as he approached with a plate in his hand. "Should I be jealous?"

I giggled, high on life and drunk on the earthy vitality surrounding me.

Zeph's lips curled as he sat across from me. Kols trailed behind him with another plate and a large mug.

"Spritemead." The word escaped through my lips on a prayer, my mouth suddenly parched. I reached for the frosty glass, practically panting with need.

"That look is giving me so many ideas," Kols said as he lowered the mug for me.

I grabbed it and took a big sip, my heart rejoicing at the splendid flavor. *Yes, yes.*

"Was she like this in Central Park?" Kols inquired as he sat down beside Zeph.

"Yeah, only topless as well," Zeph replied.

"No wonder you fucked her up against a tree." Kols set the plate down on the grass, the salad patty and dragon steak making me squeal in excitement. I handed him back the spritemead and dove right into the feast.

No silverware required.

Just hands.

And food. Delicious, amazing food.

Zeph's plate cradled a loaf stuffed with mouseberries. A red pudding rested beside it, causing my eyebrow to inch upward. "What's that?" I asked around a mouthful of salad patty. I'd forgotten all about my hunger, and now it returned with a vengeance.

"Sweet paste," he replied.

That certainly wasn't something from the Elemental Fae world. "What's in it?"

"Blood." No hesitation. No mincing words. Just a single statement that had my stomach churning. "You need it, pixie flower."

I shook my head, denying him. Because, no, I did not need blood right now. Particularly, not with my food. *Yuck.* Drinking from my mates was one thing. Imbibing with my meals was entirely another.

"You're ascending as a Midnight Fae," Kols said gently. "Blood is how we connect to the dark source, Aflora."

I gagged, the salad patty suddenly losing all flavor in my mouth.

My head moved back and forth in denial. *No.*

"Hmm, I think she needs a little coaxing, Kols."

"I think so, too," the Elite Blood agreed. "She had no problem with blood last night."

"No, she definitely didn't."

"So maybe we need to engage in something similar to inspire her?" Kols suggested, setting the mug of spritemead down in the grass.

"It's like you can read my mind," Zeph drawled, his finger swiping through the red paste. I half expected him to bring it to my lips, but he lifted his hand to Kols's mouth instead.

And proceeded to paint the texture along his lower lip, his gaze on me the whole time.

Then he slowly leaned sideways, his attention shifting to the other man, and licked the paste from Kols's lip before dipping his tongue inside to kiss him thoroughly.

My Elite Blood mate groaned in approval, his eyes falling closed as he lost himself in Zeph's embrace, the two of them indulging in each other as much as the taste of the food.

Fire licked through my veins at the sight of them, my stomach tightening in expectation.

Then Kols took some of the paste with his own finger and drew a line down Zeph's neck that he followed with his mouth, licking his skin clean in the process.

If you were shirtless, I would do this to your breasts, Kols whispered into my mind. *Then I'd bite your rosy nipple and sink my teeth into your flesh to really taste you.*

My thighs clenched in response.

Zeph created a zigzag pattern along Kols's throat and used his opposite hand to begin unfastening my Elite Blood mate's shirt. His mouth followed the path down, the buttons releasing ahead of his tongue until he reached the other man's navel.

"Fuck," Kols breathed, falling to the grass.

"So easy," Zeph murmured, skimming his teeth along Kols's lower abdomen to his hip. "Do you think Aflora would help me lick your cock clean if I decorated it with sweetness?"

Kols groaned, his eyes falling closed. "Don't make promises you won't keep."

"I would never do that," Zeph replied, his palm going to Kols's groin.

"Liar," Kols growled, arching into his Guardian's hand.

Zeph chuckled. Then he popped open the button of Kols's slacks and drew down the zipper.

No boxers.

Just bare skin.

My lips parted, my pulse skipping several beats.

Zeph bent to press a kiss to the growing arousal, then his smoldering green eyes met mine. "What do you want to do, pixie flower? Torture Kols?" He reached for more paste and traced an inviting line down the other man's thickening length. "Or please him?"

He lowered his mouth to demonstrate, eliciting a sensual moan from Kols. Then he created another alluring red trail and invited me with his eyes to join him.

I promise you'll like it, he whispered in my mind. *And I'll reward you for tasting it, too.*

His gaze lowered to the apex between my thighs, his nostrils flaring with enticement.

He meant to reward me by licking me *there.* With the paste.

Dear Fae, I thought, swallowing thickly. *How…devious. And so very Zeph.*

His irises pulsed in response, his expression expectant. He knew I wouldn't decline. Not with an offer like that.

But if I hated the taste, it would certainly spoil the mood.

Only one way to find out. I shivered, taking in Kols's pulsating shaft and the promising gleam in Zeph's green eyes.

Trust me, he murmured to me. *You'll enjoy every minute. And so will he.*

I slid the plates to the side, leaving them near the discarded mug of spritemead. Then I crawled over to Kols.

His pupils dilated as he watched me, his muscles flexing along his torso as he clenched his fists at his sides. "Thank fuck," he said, his tone thick with need.

I lowered my mouth to his abdomen, kissing him just below his belly button. Then I started downward with my tongue, tasting his skin along the way and reveling in his renewed life.

A hint of sweetness taunted my nose as I inched closer to his groin, the paste boasting a subtle aroma that reminded me of hot cocoa—a decadent drink Elemental Fae enjoyed making with cinnamon and floral berry infusions.

Blood wasn't a staple in my diet.

But I'd tasted it from my mates before.

And it hadn't been horrible.

Actually, it'd been rather erotic.

Swallowing, I moved the final few centimeters to Kols's pulsing erection and tentatively licked the tip.

He cursed in response, his body strung tight from what probably felt like the ultimate tease. "Aflora," he murmured, his fingers brushing my jaw.

Zeph caught his wrist and placed his hand by his side once more. "No touching."

"I fucking hate you." It came out on a growl, Kols's desire a hot sensation against my mouth.

"You'll love me again in a second," Zeph promised.

Rather than torment my mate more, I closed my mouth around his head and started a path downward. His hiss encouraged me to go deeper, the food painting his skin an intriguing flavor that had me groaning in response.

Because it was good.

No, it was *delicious*.

I took as much of him as my throat would allow, then released him to lower my mouth to the base and finish licking him clean.

Zeph added more paste in the next second, having retrieved the plate once more. I indulged in another taste, and then another, treating Kols like some sort of decadent treat.

His hands were fisted at his sides again, his arousal hard and throbbing in my mouth. Zeph switched focus to Kols's mouth, kissing him deeply while I licked him to completion.

It was erotic.

Hot.

Perfection.

Zeph reached for me, his fingers threading through my hair as he helped guide my pace, his opposite palm against Kols's throat. "Don't come yet, Kolstov."

My Elite Blood mate growled in response, causing Zeph to chuckle darkly. "Sadist," Kols accused.

"Mmm, but you already knew that," Zeph replied, kissing him again.

His control was resolute, his grip unyielding as he continued to dictate my movements as well as Kols's pending orgasm.

The display had my thighs straining, my insides burning with an intensity that reminded me of the source.

Heat spilled through my veins, lighting me on fire from within, and I realized I was feeling Kols's growing pleasure. He couldn't contain it, the arousal spilling into his bonds as he pushed his need to me and Zeph.

"Cheater," Zeph stated on a low groan.

"Let me come and I'll share that, too." Kols's tone held a promise and a threat in it, his voice deep with yearning.

Zeph hummed in a considering manner, his grip forcing me to take Kols even deeper. His gaze slowly lowered to mine as he remained beside Kols from above. "Are you ready to swallow, pixie flower?"

Yes.

"Out loud," he encouraged, not allowing me to move upward. "Say it around his cock."

"Yes," I managed, the sound slurred and obstructed by Kols's pulsing heat in my mouth.

"Fuck," Kols panted in reply. "*Fuck.*"

"Is that your preference? Instead of her swallowing?" Zeph asked, his attention returning to the Elite Blood.

Kols made a dark noise, his fingers digging into the ground beside us.

Zeph smirked knowingly, then he slowly lifted my head up to the tip and plunged me back down again. A shocked gasp escaped me, the penetration deep and cutting off my airway.

But the responding growl from Kols made it worth it. He shook beneath me, his abdomen clenching as his release shot into the back of my throat.

I swallowed because there was no other option. Not that I desired one. Tasting Kols was like a reward, his essence one I craved and needed to survive. He lifted one hand from the ground, his knuckles brushing my cheek as he continued to come undone, that solitary beautiful touch a display of gratitude while he came apart beneath me.

My heart warmed in response.

There was so much love and adoration in that graze against my skin.

I love you, he said into my mind. *So fucking much, Aflora.*

I love you, too, I replied, drinking from him both figuratively and literally.

He shot off one more trickle down my throat, then calmed beneath me, his explosion one I felt warming our bond and igniting a fire within me.

But I sensed he gave more to Zeph, using his orgasm as a way to punishingly taunt the other male. The Warrior Blood palmed himself, a growl mingling with a groan as he squeezed his shaft through his trousers. "I'm going to return that favor later," he threatened.

"Good," Kols replied, his tone lazy and sated. "I look forward to it." He went to his elbows, his bronze gaze finding mine. "But first, I believe you owe our mate a reward. Unless you'd like me to do the honors?"

"You can help," Zeph offered, his green irises smoldering with promise. "Lie down, pixie flower. And lift your skirt." He swiped his finger through the paste again, leaving little to the imagination as to what he wanted.

And I wasn't about to refuse.

So I did what he'd asked, lifting my skirt and showing off my lack of underwear.

Both men groaned in response.

Then I spread my legs and they cursed.

Kols moved to my mouth first, his tongue tracing the seam of my lips to demand entry as his palm went to my breast. I moaned against him, arching into his touch while returning his kiss with reckless abandon.

Alive, I thought. *He's alive.*

I knew this, had been part of his resurrection, but the continued reminder of his existence set my soul on fire for him. Because he was mine. In more than one way—*mine*. And I would have been utterly destroyed without him.

I ensured he knew that by opening my mind to his, pushing him my feelings of gratitude and devotion, wordlessly telling him what he meant to me.

He responded with a broadcast of his own emotions, drowning me in his adoration and worship.

Then Zeph parted my folds with his tongue, demanding my focus.

Ohhh…

His finger followed his mouth, then he traced his touch, licking the paste from the intimate heart of me.

Who knew food could be so exciting?

I shivered as he did it again, then Kols's lips trailed down my neck as his fingers deftly unfastened my blouse.

Goose bumps trailed across my skin, my body primed and ready to explode.

But a nibble to my clit told me I didn't have permission yet.

You really are a sadist, I thought at Zeph.

He hummed in agreement, his mouth wicked and skilled and far too knowing against my sex.

Kols added to the fun, painting my breast with the remainder of the paste and doing exactly what he'd vowed to do earlier—decorating my nipple and taking it into his mouth. Then his teeth sank into my flesh as he drew my blood, his tongue licking the wound in his wake.

An inferno blazed through me, knocking out my senses and reducing me to a writhing mess of insane craving.

My two mates reveled in it, drawing me close to climax only to deny me the end result.

Beg, Zeph told me. *Beg for what you need.*

"Please," I whispered. "I… I need to…" I jolted as Kols bit me again, this time on my other breast. "*Oh!*" I was going to die by the touch of my mates. Blow up in a source of madness and sensation. "Please let me come." The words came out in a jumble—or they sounded distant to my ears, anyway—because I was too lost to their mouths and tongues and hands to think through my words.

Zeph made a noise of approval, his teeth sinking into my delicate flesh and eliciting a guttural scream from my throat.

It hurt.

It burned.

It captivated me entirely.

Fae… It was like he'd turned me inside out, drawing the deepest of pleasure from my soul with his teeth, and yanked the blossoming flames from me with a pull of his mouth.

Blood. My blood.

I felt him swallowing in approval, his yearning for me a searing kiss to my senses.

Now, Aflora, he said, giving me the permission I sought and craved. *Come for us.*

I didn't have to think; I just complied, my body trained to his will and listening to him more than me. Stars blinked into my vision, darkness overtaking my senses, as I fell headfirst into a consuming ocean of ecstasy.

Down, down, down, I went.

Drowning.

Blissfully surviving on pleasure alone.

Shaking and combusting and losing myself to my mates.

They owned me. My heart. My soul. My body.

But I owned them in kind, their strength rooted into my spirit and yanking me back to life in my next breath.

Zeph's mouth captured mine. Then Kols. Then Zeph again. Their hands were everywhere, stroking me with undeniable affection and grace.

Water surrounded me in the next second, my mates having taken me to wash off in a shower.

I barely felt the warmth of the droplets, my focus on Zeph and Kols and their exploring fingers and touch.

They did this to me—took away all my worries and concerns and introduced me to a world of sensation and living unlike any other.

Shade's mind brushed mine, his knowing thoughts driving me onward.

Zakkai was there, too, his protective energy allowing me to completely let go and just *be.*

I collapsed into Zeph and Kols, let them bathe me, love me, cherish me, and indulged in everything they had to give.

My mates.

My loves.

My world.

CHAPTER NINE

KOLS

Aflora sat at the table in a robe, her dark hair falling in wet waves around her shoulders. She had a satisfied gleam to her features, her cheeks pink from the exhilaration of the shower.

Zeph had taken her from behind while I knelt and worshipped her clit. Then I'd fucked her up against the wall.

She'd taken it all, her mewls of pleasure a residual sound in my head as I twirled pasta around my fork.

Her blue eyes fell to my plate, her forehead scrunching. *Bloody noodles and brown crap.*

I chuckled, recalling our first meal together. "Spaghetti and meatballs," I corrected her before taking a bite.

She grimaced and picked up her version of a sandwich.

Zeph had one on his plate, too. He seemed to be making a conscious effort to eat Elemental Fae cuisine with her. But I sensed his distaste for the soggy texture when he bit down.

I smirked. Then I took another mouthful of my favored Italian cuisine.

While the foods were similar to those from our first night together, the feelings around the table couldn't be more different. Trust and content floated between us.

And it only strengthened when Shade and Zakkai returned.

Both of them kissed Aflora on top of her head, then rummaged through the fully stocked fridge for something to eat.

They both opted to join me in spaghetti, making Aflora's nose scrunch upward.

Then Zeph distracted her with a plate of dragon steak, and she no longer seemed to care about anything other than the meat in front of her.

I shook my head, amused by her antics.

Food was clearly the way to her heart.

Zeph waved his wand to add a round of mugs to the table, all of them filled with spritemead. Aflora's eyes sparkled with approval. Then she looked at me. "Now would be a good time for that ascension lesson."

My lips twitched. During our first dinner, we'd discussed Midnight Fae order at a high level. And now she wanted to get to the heart of it by reviewing the trials.

"First, I want to know if Shade's grandmother had anything interesting to say," Zeph interjected, his sharp gaze on the Death Blood. "No more secrets, Shadow."

Shade ran his fingers through his thick, dark hair and relaxed into his chair. "I'm not Kols. I don't do orders."

I snorted. "If you think I accept all his demands, then you don't know me at all." In the bedroom, I indulged in a few of Zeph's commands. But only because I regularly enjoyed the reward of appeasing his sadistic side.

"Shade," Aflora interjected, her voice soft yet underlined with authority. "Please."

His expression warmed at her words. "Anything for you, little rose."

Zeph grunted.

I merely grinned and took a sip of the spritemead.

Shade offered a brief rundown of his discussion with his grandmother, focusing on the important bits. Which were mainly surrounding the trials and her urging for all of us to prepare. Advice we didn't really need, but I understood Zen feeling the need to stress the importance of readying ourselves for the trials.

"We have to work as a unit," Shade concluded. "That's the gist of what she was saying." His focus shifted to a silent Zakkai. "Pretty sure that entire lecture was for your benefit."

"I gathered that after the third sentence," Zakkai replied flatly. His silver-blue eyes met mine. "But I think there was an underlying word of caution regarding certain trials, too."

"Respect and unity," I murmured, having inferred that from Shade's summary of what Zen had said.

"Indeed." Zakkai set his fork down. "Those will be the biggest challenges, as Constantine is claiming that the Source Architect redirected the power from you to Aflora. He also has everyone believing that I possessed Malik, which I did not." He looked pointedly at all of us as he uttered that last bit.

"I know you didn't," I said, my instincts telling me that statement was needed. "I've only met my grandfather a handful of times, but it's become quite apparent that he's an excellent strategist." It was a truth I couldn't deny. "But together, we will outmaneuver him." My attention drifted to Aflora beside me. "Which brings us to the ascension trials."

"Yes," she agreed.

"There are seven," I began. "They can come in any order but have historically followed a specific pattern. Although, with my grandfather at the helm, it's possible that pattern will be altered."

I dove into an explanation on how the current monarch typically organized the trials. With the Midnight Fae King being the closest to the dark source, it made sense for him to foster the tests accordingly.

"However, my father has clearly been possessed." A comment that made me grimace. "Which is why I believe my grandfather will lead the trials, particularly as he's the one who forced the ascension onto you."

"Also a fair assessment since he just orchestrated two in one day," Zakkai inserted.

I nodded. "My father would never do that. Nor would he force Aflora to ascend in this manner." My father valued his connection to the dark source and took his mantle seriously. He would never risk it by forcing the power into a non-Midnight Fae. Nor would he ever force another to become an abomination.

No, this had my grandfather written all over it.

And the fact that he was spouting lies about the ascension to all the others only confirmed his orchestration of the events.

"There are seven trials," I continued. "Trust and creatures are the two you've already passed, the first being to test your connections by proving their worth through a trust trial. The second one being to win over all the creatures in the Midnight Fae world."

"And creatures in general," Zakkai interjected. "At least, as Source Architect, I had to win them all over because of the uniqueness of my abilities."

"I only had to win over those who reside in the Midnight Fae realm," I clarified.

"Interesting." Zakkai picked up his fork again to continue eating, telling me with his eyes to keep talking.

"The other trials revolve around acceptance, unity, sacrifice, respect, and the final source ascension. These tests can be delivered through a variety of means. My acceptance trial was the easiest for me because it was about accepting the dark source's power and understanding what it could do. As the son of the current king, I was born understanding and accepting my place. Unity was my fourth trial, which focused on you."

"Because your father wanted you to bring the factions to a unifying decision on her fate," Zakkai translated. "Clever."

"What was yours?" I wondered out loud.

"Uniting the Quandary Bloods for retribution," he replied. "Which, when you consider it, seems like the opposite of unity, given that it divided the Quandary Bloods into two factions."

"You won the respect of both sides through your leadership," Shade said softly. "My grandmother might not agree with the thoughts of retribution, but she's always honored your ascension and rightful place as Source Architect."

Zakkai dipped his chin in acknowledgment. "It's why our two sides have never warred. Something I fear is about to change after what she said regarding my father's displeasure."

Shade's lips pinched to the side. "We'll cross that bridge when it arrives."

"Do you expect him to come here?" I asked, choosing to literally translate Shade's statement rather than allow the cryptic response to hang in the air undefined.

"Yes." Shade's icy eyes met mine. "Yes, I do."

"He'll want to discuss new terms," Zakkai added. "It might serve as Aflora's unity trial."

"My grandfather would never orchestrate that."

"The source may not provide him with a choice," Zakkai pointed out. "Not all trials can be controlled. And I'm also the architect, so I do have some say in how this progresses."

"Fair," I agreed. "Well, I failed my trial by not bringing the fae together." A fact that would forever haunt me, but not nearly as much as almost being killed by my father's hand.

"No, you didn't," Zeph inserted. "You were still in the middle of your trial, but Constantine took over and destroyed your ability to pass."

"He's right." Zakkai twirled his fork around some noodles while Aflora watched in obvious disgust. "Actually, I imagine the dark source would agree with your choice. Particularly as it accepted Aflora's candidacy for queen. You kept her alive so she could ascend. That's a successful outcome, not a failed one."

I hadn't previously considered that point of view, but it was a fair assessment, one I much preferred to my own.

"You may not have unified the Midnight Fae, but when Aflora does, you'll both pass," Zakkai concluded, the assurance in his tone lacking any note of hesitation.

"Okay, but what if I undo the ascension?" Aflora asked.

We all fell silent.

She'd said this a few times, and while it might be possible, I feared the outcome of that decision.

Zakkai broke the silence by returning his fork to his plate again and inquiring, "Why do you want to undo it?"

"Because it's wrong." She uttered the words as though they were obvious. "I'm an Earth Fae, not a Midnight Fae."

"Yes, you've said that, but you're mated to four Midnight Fae. And as you've witnessed, our magic bleeds into our mates when we bond." He lifted his finger and whispered a spell that created a smoky cerulean structure in the middle of the table. As it grew, I realized he'd crafted a tree of sorts, the magical strands flickering bright with multicolored branches.

Aflora admired it with a hint of a smile.

"I see this inside you," Zakkai murmured. "You crafted a joint source of magic, marrying your Earth Fae heritage to the Midnight Fae blood running through your veins." He looked pointedly at the inky black lines writhing beneath her skin.

"I did that to survive the ascension."

"You did that to become queen," he corrected. "Zenaida's right about certain things—we need reformation. And I believe you are the key to that reformation."

"A millennium of male-led authority," Zeph mused. "Driven out by a woman."

"And an *abomination* at that," Zakkai added. "You have the power to prove to all fae kind that abominations can be good, Aflora. That they don't need to be feared."

"Constantine Nacht is the reason fae hunt and kill abominations." Zeph glanced at me and then at Aflora. "It would be entirely fitting for you to dismantle his throne of power by proving him wrong."

"It would," I admitted. Constantine Nacht might be my grandfather and blood, but that hadn't stopped him from trying to destroy me. And I fully intended to repay that favor.

"You all make this sound so easy," Aflora muttered. "But what if I become the abomination they all fear? Elana—"

"Isn't you," Zeph interrupted, not allowing her to even finish that thought.

"All you think about are others and what's right for your kingdom," I said quietly. "It's what makes you a suitable queen, Aflora. It's why my soul called for yours from the very beginning, why I've considered you a worthy mate all along. You're everything a royal should be, and more."

The others nodded in agreement.

"What if I don't want this?" Aflora asked in a low whisper. "What if I don't want to be the Midnight Fae Queen?"

"You don't," I replied, my voice just as soft. "Which is what makes you perfect for the task. You're going to accept the role because it's what's right, not because you desire it. But because you know you're the best one for the job." I reached over to cup her face, my thumb tracing her cheekbone. "You were born to be a queen, Aflora. You're strong. You're smart. You're a survivor. You're going to make history and change us all."

"And we're going to help you every step of the way," Zeph vowed, taking her hand.

The tree on the table began to throb, a heart pulsing at the center of the trunk. "Trust us to guide and teach you," Zakkai said. "We're your heart for a reason, little star."

"And I didn't go through seven lifetimes just to fail now," Shade added. "We're in this for eternity, Aflora. Not just now. Not just yesterday. But forever."

"We won't let you down," I whispered, drawing her in for a kiss. "To us, you're already our queen."

She shivered and melted against me. "You guys are going to kill me."

"Only in the bedroom," Zeph drawled.

Aflora huffed a laugh and shook her head, tears glistening in her blue eyes. "Thanks for believing in me."

"We'll be the belief you need when you doubt yourself," I promised her. "But you're wrong about one thing."

She stilled. "About what?"

"It absolutely won't be easy," I said seriously. "We might make it sound that way, but we know what's coming."

"Which is why we need to begin training immediately," Zeph replied.

"Indeed," Zakkai agreed, meeting my Guardian's gaze. "I already have a course schedule in mind."

"Good," I interjected before Zeph could demand a full itinerary. "Traditionally, Midnight Fae ascend in their twenty-fifth year, giving them ample time to prepare. But with my grandfather absorbing the dark source and forcing it on Aflora, the rules have clearly changed. We'll need all the structure we can get."

Ascensions were powerful.

And Aflora's would be legendary.

We had to begin preparing now.

"What happens if I fully ascend?" Aflora asked after a beat, her expression hesitant.

"*When*," I corrected. "*When* you fully ascend, you'll become one of the most powerful abominations in existence."

CHAPTER TEN

ZAKKAI

I'd chosen the bedroom closest to the living area, preferring to be the first line of defense. It'd seemed to work well for Kolstov and Zephyrus, who had decided to take the largest room at the end of the hall together. Shade had picked the room beside mine. And Aflora… had bypassed the remaining room to join Kolstov and Zephyrus.

However, I felt her awake now.

Restless.

Pacing.

I sat up to find Zimney curled up at the foot of my bed, his eyelids lifting briefly before closing once more. *Not moving*, he was saying.

I snorted and slipped from the covers to pull on a pair of pajama pants. Shade's grandmother had fully stocked our closets and rooms with everything we needed. Whether she'd done it herself or hired someone, I wasn't sure. But I thanked her silently for it nonetheless. It made life easier.

That she knew which rooms we would pick—evidenced by the correct sizing of our wardrobe—served as a show of power. She'd foreseen our choices. Or perhaps she just knew us all well enough to know where we would want to sleep.

I stepped out into the hallway, listening for signs of life, and heard the soft slide of paper against paper. Following it into the living room, I found Shade reading on the smaller of the two couches, his upper body exposed as he wore a pair of pajama pants similar to mine.

His icy eyes remained on his book as he said, "She's outside."

"You should be sleeping," I told him.

He lifted a shoulder. "I wanted to be nearby in case she needed something."

It seemed I wasn't the only one with the protective gene engaged. "I'll keep an eye on her," I said, my voice soft. "Go rest, Shadow. You've done enough these last few days, and we all need your reserves fully restored."

Aflora's training would officially begin tomorrow. I'd developed an intense curriculum—one Zephyrus had fortified and Kolstov and Shade had perfected. It would require all of us to be at our best, not exhausted.

Shade set his book on the table. "She needs rest, too." He stood and stretched his arms over his head. "Perhaps you'll be better suited to convince her."

"I'll do my best."

His lips twitched as he stepped up to my side. "You'll have to do better than that. She's stubborn."

"I know how to handle her stubborn side," I promised.

He huffed out a dry laugh before heading down the hallway toward his room. When the door snicked closed, I wandered over to the table, curious to see what he'd chosen to read. I smirked at the title, familiar with the fictional trilogy from the Human Realm about hobbits.

It seemed just like Shade to indulge in such an epic tale.

Leaving the book alone, I redirected myself outside to the beauty lying on the ground. It seemed she'd ceased her pacing and had chosen to admire the sky instead. "It isn't real," she said to me as I approached. "But it certainly looks real."

"It's real to an extent," I replied, sitting down beside her on the soft bed of green grass.

The firm texture and vibrant life told me she'd bolstered it with her power, ensuring its strength beneath our bodies. I leaned back to join her in the prone position, my knuckles brushing hers as I aligned our arms alongside one another. Her fingers flexed toward mine, curling around the tips to hold me in her own way.

"Does the Hell Fae realm have stars?" she asked.

"I imagine it does in certain areas, but I've not explored it to know for sure." My paradigm was in the Human Realm, in Antarctica, which definitely had stars at night. Not that one could actually venture outside to admire them.

She tilted her head toward me, her blue eyes full of questions. But she didn't voice any of them. Instead, she just studied my features, content to coexist for a moment in silence.

Seconds turned into minutes as we watched each other, thousands of unspoken words and memories floating between us.

Then she leaned in closer to brush her lips against mine.

A token of trust.

A gift of gratitude.

We had been best friends once upon a time, our lives filled with a childish innocence that neither of us had ever fully understood. We'd bonded and loved each other in a way meant for children. And now we were very much adults, our connection shifting and growing into something very different.

It was a tentative link founded in confusion.

Aflora hadn't understood my motives or my purpose, just as I hadn't fully grasped her desires in life. But a few weeks together had opened our eyes to a whole new world of existence, one where our goals learned how to intertwine and grow as a unit rather than as separate strands.

My sweet little star had fused us together, tied our roots in a love-knot at the source of our beings, and ensured we were forever bound.

In essence, she'd captured my heart. I wasn't sure how or when it had happened. Perhaps in our childhood. Perhaps during that first dream when she'd demanded I please her without even asking my name. Perhaps when she'd fought me in my bedroom shortly after waking up.

Perhaps she'd always owned me.

I rolled onto my side to more properly face her, preferring to admire her over the starry night. Tucking my arm beneath my head, I placed my other hand on her abdomen, my pinky sliding beneath the fabric of her tank top to stroke the warm skin below it.

She didn't move, her eyes holding mine while we continued to stare at each other.

No words.

Just the sound of the perpetual night and the slight rustle of leaves and flowers, responding to the queen among them.

Her eyelashes fanned over her cheekbones as she blinked, her gorgeous features captivating my full attention.

I could gaze upon her for hours and never tire of it.

She possessed so much power and strength, the source's mark properly branding her as royalty. Cerulean ribbons glowed in her dark hair, lighting up her features and proclaiming her as my mate. I lifted my hand away from her stomach to draw my fingers through her soft strands, smiling as her energy kissed my skin.

"You're so beautiful that it almost hurts," I marveled, completely consumed by her and the vitality pouring off of her. I drew my thumb along her jaw, my touch instinctively reverent. "I know you're worried about the trials and marrying your power sources, but you were born for this, little star."

Her confidence continued to waver through our bonds.

It wasn't that she didn't believe in herself so much as she questioned whether or not this was the right path.

"You grew up being told that abominations are evil," I continued softly. "I grew up knowing that abominations can do good, too. Look at the Academy around us. This is here because of Zenaida, who, by all rights, is an abomination herself, and she worked with Lucifer, the unequivocal king of abominations, to create it. Does it feel wrong here? Evil? Dark? Nefarious? Or do you sense the life and love in this paradigm like I do?"

Similar sensations existed in my own paradigm, the one I'd created for those who favored retribution. But beneath that life had been a sense of anger and resentment toward other fae.

What I felt here was an underlying promise, a true sense of purpose for the future.

No violence or desire for bloodshed.

Just a desire to learn and work together.

A show of unity—something I hoped would be useful to Aflora later on.

"Peace," she whispered. "They feel at peace here. Protected. Safe. Like they can be themselves without worrying about punishment for doing so."

I nodded. "Because they're allowed to be themselves here. Abominations who just want to live, not fight. And it's not just within this paradigm, Aflora. You're picking up on it from the Hell Fae, too. They're a race of beings who have been shunned for so long that they built their own society to escape the others."

"Some of them are angry," she said softly. "I feel their ire like a weight against my soul. But others are just tired. They want to be accepted."

"And you can help them in that quest," I told her, my thumb tracing her cheekbone on my way to fondling her hair once more. "Being an abomination doesn't make one evil, little star. The soul is corrupt with or without power. Constantine is proof of that. He's a Midnight Fae who will destroy anyone and everything that stands up to his methodology for order. Hell, he took an inclusive council that worked positively together and turned them against their own hearts—the women who are the true figureheads."

It was despicable and wrong and so expertly crafted that I couldn't help developing a smidgen of respect for the bastard.

My father used to tell me that admiring one's enemies was to understand and never underestimate them.

I understood that now.

And I would never underestimate Constantine again.

"Constantine succeeded because he knew what weakness to exploit," I continued. "Emotion. What we need to do is show him how powerful emotion can be, by demonstrating how powerful our bonds are together."

I pressed my palm to the ground on the other side of her head, using it to balance myself as I leaned over to graze my lips across hers.

"We're going to train you, little star. We're going to help you through each trial. We're going to ensure you become the most powerful queen the fae have ever seen." I pressed my mouth to hers once more, my voice lowering to a whisper. "And when you fully ascend, we're going to kneel at your feet and show those Elders what a real council looks like."

She stared up at me for a beat. "Kiss me."

I brushed my mouth against hers, lingering for half a second before pulling back to study her features.

"Again," she whispered.

A variety of comments populated my thoughts, several of them taunts regarding her other mates leaving her needy for more. But rather than voice them, I adhered to her sensual command, this time parting her lips with my tongue to properly taste her.

We'd engaged in dreams, all of which resulted in me wearing something very similar to this while I pleased her with my hands and mouth.

But I wanted to experience the real her. The physical being. My *mate*.

Feeling her beneath me, her hands roaming up my back, was so much better than a fantasy. She knew me now. She accepted me. She trusted me. She could *feel* me, not just on top of her, but inside her.

And she wanted me.

I sensed her yearning, her innate recognition of what we meant to each other, and her subsequent happiness with our connection.

No dread. No doubts. No refusal.

Just pure, unadulterated acceptance.

It was the most amazing realization to learn that my mate desired me as I desired her, to know she considered me hers just as I considered her mine.

"Aflora," I whispered, deepening our kiss with my palms pressed to her cheeks to angle her appropriately.

Her nails drew down my back, her touch impatient yet adoring.

She wanted more.

She wanted me.

She wanted this.

I'd been with a few other women but had never felt connected to any of them. They weren't mine. They weren't Aflora. It was something I hadn't understood at the time, my intent always having been to only bond with Aflora for her protection and as a debt to be repaid to her parents.

Then I saw her again.

Felt her.

Worshipped her with my tongue.

And I'd never experienced such completion as I had in that moment.

Until now.

Until settling between her thighs and feeling her legs wrap around me in warm welcome.

Until tasting the craving on her tongue and feeling her dampening center against my growing arousal. Even through my pants and her shorts, I knew she was ready for me, that she wanted me—her mate—her Kai.

I never knew sex could feel like this, so much passion and heat and desire.

I'd watched her with her other mates, had seen how they'd pleased her, how she'd come undone with them with such devotion and grace.

I wanted to do that to her now, to be the one she cried out for, to finally claim my mate in the most traditional of manners.

"Yes," she whispered against my lips. "Yes."

I hadn't asked her. Hadn't voiced the desire. But she felt it in my mind, our bond, her heart responding to mine on instinct alone.

However, I didn't want to do it here. I wanted to be alone, to cherish her behind closed doors, to make it just us.

I stood and pulled her up into my arms, carrying her inside and to the room I now called my own. Zimney was nowhere to be seen, the wolf probably sensing my intentions and running off to frolic somewhere else.

The door shut quietly behind me, my steps silent against the white carpet.

I set Aflora on the bed, her legs hanging off the edge as she sat up with her hands on my hips. I stood between her thighs, staring down at her in wonder. Then I bent to capture her mouth once more.

Her fingers drifted across my lower abdomen, her quest clear as she unfastened the tie at my waist to push the soft fabric down over my groin to my thighs.

I righted my spine, allowing her to finish the task of removing my pants.

Then I stepped out of them and back between her splayed legs.

Her pretty eyes ran over me in deep appreciation, her pupils dilating as she took in my thick arousal.

She licked her lips and pulled her tank top over her head, presenting me with her beautiful breasts. Then she leaned forward to take my cock into her addictive mouth, her tongue running along the bottom of my shaft in clear and obvious invitation.

I threaded my fingers through her hair, a curse slipping from my mouth as I pushed myself deeper, loving the way she eagerly accepted me into her. Almost as though I'd always belonged. And I likely had.

But this wasn't the claiming I'd had in mind.

I needed to be inside her in another way.

To complete our coupling by fucking her to oblivion.

A very masculine, competitive part of me needed the others to hear it, too. To know she was mine just as much as she belonged to them.

Her blue eyes sparkled knowingly as she released me from her mouth.

She scooted back onto the bed, hooked her thumbs into the fabric of her shorts, and pulled them off her long, athletic legs.

I stood beside the mattress, watching the show.

All of this was done without words, our bodies speaking for us.

An erotic dance of knowledge and passion and intensity.

And just pure need.

I braced one knee on the bed, watching as she found a place in the middle of the comforter. Her dark strands decorated the pillow in a welcoming gesture, her thighs parting to allow me to see her beautiful, sweet, wet pussy, the heart of her aching for me to take her.

My mouth watered, my desire to taste her almost overcoming my need to be inside her.

But the latter won out.

I could taste her later, indulge in her sweet flavor for hours, and ensure everyone heard her screaming my name.

Tonight, I needed to complete us.

I prowled forward, crawling over her and caging her beneath me. "This is about our union," I told her softly, lowering to press my groin to hers as I balanced myself on my forearms on either side of her head. "I'm not usually this gentle, Aflora. But something about the moment requires it."

She reached up to draw her fingers through my hair, the white strands loose around my face and falling around her like a curtain of false purity. "I'm not fragile."

"I know," I whispered, pressing my arousal into hers to feel her welcoming heat. I slipped through her folds, my head nudging her clit before drawing downward to the heart of her. "But I want to make sure you remember this," I told her, lining up with her entrance. "And I want to hear you scream my name."

She began to speak, but her words cut off on a cry as I drove into her, giving her a brief introduction to the power in my hips and my ability to dominate her entirely. Then I slowly withdrew and entered her again, gradually now, softer, ensuring she felt every inch.

Her mind rolled with comments, comparing sizes and strengths and girths, and my lips curled when she admitted I was the largest of her mates.

I already knew that.

However, she hadn't. Because she hadn't properly felt me yet.

Zephyrus certainly rivaled me in some ways, his propensity for being in charge equal to mine, but unlike him, I knew how to be gentle.

Which I showed Aflora now as I set a sensual pace meant for this moment, the one where our bodies declared themselves to one another.

She grabbed my shoulders, a soft moan leaving her lips as I tortured her with my unhurried pace.

Her little growl made me smile.

She responded by digging her nails into my skin, demanding with her body that I do more.

"You can't have it hard every time," I whispered, taking her mouth in a kiss meant to silence. She started to argue in my mind, only to cut off on a groan as my tongue engaged hers in the battle she craved.

All the way in, I said to her. *And almost all the way out.*

I repeated the action over and over, drawing out each thrust and ensuring I nudged that spot deep inside her with every downward stroke.

She scratched a path down my back, her legs wrapping around my hips as she tried futilely to press up into me and dictate a faster pace.

But this wasn't about a quick fuck. This was about unleashing an experience for our *souls*.

I rolled onto my back, bringing her on top, and allowed her to drive. She sat up, eager to comply, her thighs straddling my hips as she began to ride me. Her breasts swayed enticingly with each hurried shift of her hips, her lips parting on a moan of excitement. However, after a few more urgent swivels, she caught her lip between her teeth and stared down at me, her dark hair framing her beautiful face.

Understanding seemed to light her up from within.

I sat up to join her, my lips ghosting over hers as I braced myself on one hand behind me and wrapped my opposite palm around her nape. "Tender can be just as good," I told her, my tongue licking the seam of her mouth before sliding inside.

She shifted, her legs moving to wrap around my back as she more firmly sat astride my thighs. A little mewl caught in the back of her throat as she realized how deeply I penetrated her in this position.

And then we both began to move.

Not hurriedly, but languidly, indulging in the sensations and bringing ourselves closer and closer to the precipice with long, thorough movements.

"Oh, Kai," she breathed, her nipples hard against my chest.

Sweat covered us both, the effort with which we fucked driving us both to a point of near madness. It was just so fierce, so utterly exhaustive in each glide and calculative stroke, that we were overwhelmed and fatigued by the sheer intensity of it all.

I felt her starting to come undone, our magic dancing together as one as cerulean sparks graced the air.

This was the culmination of a mating years in the making. Our paths finally intersecting after wandering off course. Our souls rejoicing in returning home, *together*, in a beautiful moment of bliss and harmony and absolute perfection.

I kissed her, confiding my deepest, darkest histories in the blink of a second, unlocking my mind to her and throwing away the key.

She responded in kind, her faith in me resolute.

And together we fell over the edge into a rapturous beginning that went on for what felt like hours, our bodies locked together in harmonious bliss and refusing to stop.

She cried out, my name a beacon that caused my heart to soar.

I followed her in kind, chanting *Flora* on repeat, my little star finally lighting up the dark, cruel night of my spirit.

Her lips whispered against mine, her body moving, taking, repeating, writhing some more.

And eventually we collapsed onto the bed, only to continue our sensual dance, our groins locked together in a kiss meant to last a lifetime.

She destroyed me.

She completed me.

She ensured we would remain forever together.

I sank my teeth into her neck, desiring that promise in blood.

She responded in kind, taking my essence deep into her mouth and swallowing before slamming her mouth over mine once more.

My Kai, she breathed.

My Flora, I returned. *My gorgeous, bright star.*

Our sensuality followed us into our dreams, the riddles fracturing between us and creating new, complex locks—ones no one would ever be able to break.

When night finally came, the sunset of our new life, I woke her in the same way we'd fallen asleep. Then I finally tasted her, and I confirmed that our dreams had nothing on our reality.

This is the real dream, I told her. *My life with you. That's the dream, Aflora. And I hope I never wake up.*

She smiled, her heart in her eyes. *Neither do I, Kai. Neither do I.*

CHAPTER ELEVEN

ZEPH

"All right, new schedule," I said, standing at a stone board with my wand. I pointed the end at the obsidian marble. "Today is defensive training." The words scrolled across the rock in a fiery scrawl.

The action repeated as I said each new course by day.

Defensive magic.

Death magic.

Offensive magic.

Crash course into royalty affairs, including ascension with historical references, and general strategy.

Quandary magic.

"We'll go day by day, taking turns in the demonstrations. But we'll all be attending and learning together." That final sentence was for Zakkai, who sat beside Aflora with his arm lazily draped over the back of her chair. He cocked a white brow, his arrogance grating on my nerves.

Because I'd just spent the better part of the last twelve hours hearing him pleasure Aflora on repeat, all damn day. Which meant she hadn't slept well.

And neither had I.

Fucking prick.

Our only saving grace was the fact that we had bought ourselves some time by coming here, because I highly doubted Lucifer would strike a deal with Constantine anytime soon.

"This is our training facility." I glanced at Shade for confirmation, and he nodded.

"The gargoyles are ensuring the other students don't bother us," he added out loud. "This area is used for advanced courses, but the headmasters agreed to move them elsewhere for the time being for safety purposes."

"Good." Because we were about to unleash some intense and dangerous spells. Best not to be interrupted, especially should I decide to do a defensive demonstration with Zakkai. "Then let the fun begin."

Aflora didn't hesitate, her willingness to learn evident in the way she responded to our first day of training. She was tired by the end, her body and mind sore from everything I threw at her, but she didn't break or bend or beg me to stop. All she said was "More."

The next day, in our defensive magic course, went much the same way with her memorizing, manipulating, and regurgitating spells. She even put me on my ass a few times—a feat very few could claim. Of course, I was distracted by her mouth because all I wanted to do was kiss her when she managed to replicate an advanced shield using her hands instead of a wand.

The courses continued, Aflora never once wavering or complaining. She was focused and the definition of determination, doing exactly what we told her and adding a few twists of her own.

By night, she was an apt pupil, learning and excelling and perfecting her skill.

And by day, she engaged in a similar routine… in the bedroom.

Constantine remained quiet, the trials lurking somewhere on the horizon. Shade met with his grandmother often, seeking updates. But aside from ensuring that all of Midnight Fae kind hated Aflora, he hadn't given anything away regarding his next trial.

However, we all knew something was coming.

He would be furious that she managed to pass two ascensions with such efficiency, and so quickly, too.

"He's strategic," Kols was saying now as we watched Shade and Aflora practice offensive magic. It was her third course in the topic, as we were well into our third week here at the Academy. "And the longer he takes, the more nervous I get."

Zakkai nodded, his silver-blue eyes on Aflora. He'd tied his white hair back at his nape today, displaying his long, athletic neck. And the bite marks Aflora had left there during her time in his bed today before class.

We'd developed a routine on sharing her, with our mate choosing to sleep in a different room each night. She never slept in her own space. I wasn't even convinced she knew a fourth bedroom existed.

Twice, Shade had chosen to join Kols, me, and Aflora.

Zakkai never did, preferring his solitary time with her.

It was different, but it worked. Because I wasn't sure I could share her with him. He would try to dictate the show, and I refused to submit to him.

Shade didn't exactly roll over for me either, but he seemed content to follow my lead.

Zakkai would sooner bite me than follow my direction, something he proved weekly during the Quandary magic classes. I told him not to push our mate too hard, and he translated that as *Put Aflora in the most dangerous position possible and see if she can survive it.*

Dick, I thought, not for the first time.

At least we agreed on Constantine. "He's definitely planning something big," he said. "Either Zenaida can't see it coming, or she doesn't want to risk the outcome by warning us." He ran his hand over the stubble dotting his jaw, then reached around to roll and pop his neck. "Regardless, we need to be ready."

"Yes," Kols agreed. "We do." He folded his arms and observed Aflora dismantling one of Shade's resurrection spells with a bout of life from her earth magic.

"Impressive," I murmured, grinning as she created a root from the figment and wrapped it around Shade's leg. She yanked on it, dropping him to the ground on an *Oomph*. "Ready to duel with someone stronger?" I asked her.

A shadowy figure flew at me half a second later, the Death magic stealing my breath and taking me to my knees.

I called up a defensive disfiguration spell, dismantling his enchantment and freeing my lungs. Then I shot an offensive charm at him meant to blister his eardrums—that he blasted away with his wand.

"You were saying?" the Death Blood drawled.

"That he wanted me to play with Aflora," Zakkai replied, sending a net of magic over her that sizzled and sparked and drew a surprised yelp from her. "Figure that out, little star."

She growled in response, making the hairs along the back of my neck stand on end. "What did you do?" I demanded.

"We're reminiscing." Zakkai cocked his head. "Stop snarling, little star. You need your oxygen."

I stepped forward. "Take it off her."

"No." Zakkai looked at me, his stance defensive. "And I don't recommend trying to help, or it'll make it much worse for her."

I lifted my wand at him. "Undo it, Zakkai."

He glanced at my hand and snorted. "Try and you'll definitely regret it."

I'm. Fine, Aflora snapped into my mind, drawing my attention to her on the ground, where she appeared to be paralyzed beneath a layer of cerulean magic.

You don't look fine, Aflora.

"Trust her to undo it," Zakkai interjected. "She might not have us all for her trials. She needs to learn how to work on her own without handicaps. Give her a moment to solve the puzzle."

He won't let anything or anyone hurt her, Kols added in my mind. *This isn't just about trusting Aflora to fight her own battles, but also having faith in her mates to keep her safe.*

She doesn't look fucking safe, I snapped back, wincing as she whimpered inside the net. *She looks pained, Kolstov.*

She does, he agreed. *But I have faith that she'll figure it out. And if she doesn't, I know Zakkai will step in.*

What if it's too late when he does? I countered. *What if she gets hurt?*

Then he'll feel like hell afterward, similar to how you did when you killed Clove. His burnt-bronze irises met mine, his auburn brow arching. *What happened to the headmaster who wanted Aflora to blossom and grow?*

He fell in love.

Kols grinned. *Yes. Yes, he did.* His focus returned to Aflora, his amusement disappearing behind a mask of concern as she struggled across the floor.

I took a step forward, only for Shade to step in front of me. "Let her learn," he encouraged, his hand wrapping around my wrist to lower my wand to my side. Then his icy gaze flickered to Zakkai, telling me with a look to check out the Quandary Blood.

When I glanced at him, I found his expression tight with concentration, his silver-blue gaze intense as he watched Aflora work.

His distraction could work to my advantage. I could knock him out and help Aflora.

Or I could fuck this all up by not trusting him and risk hurting her more with him unable to assist due to a magical coma.

My jaw clenched, my irritation over the situation making my heart beat a little faster.

I did not appreciate having my control taken away and a random lesson being inserted into today's plans. This was not what we were meant to do here.

But Zakkai was the wild card, the one I couldn't rely on or trust.

And instances like this only made that lack of faith worse.

Aflora gasped, seizing my entire focus.

Then she uttered a long, wicked enchantment and sent the web flying back at Zakkai.

But it didn't engulf him. He caught it instead and absorbed the magic back into his wand. "Beautiful," he breathed.

Aflora narrowed her gaze and hit him with another strike of blue magic, then spun a ball of WarFire into her palm. It whirled with a multitude of colors, the intoxicating mix clearly deadly.

"Do it," Zakkai dared.

She released it, throwing it right at him.

Where it landed against his chest.

Aflora shrieked, jumping up to her feet and running to him in a daze of concern. Only for the fire to sizzle and disappear, his clothing and chest fine. But he caught her by the back of the neck and drew her in for a kiss, one that ended in her biting his tongue.

He chuckled as she slapped him. "What was that?" she demanded.

"Defensive magic," he drawled, glancing at me. "Just the upgraded variety."

I narrowed my gaze. "Are you trying to piss me off?"

"I don't think I have to try, Zephyrus," he replied. "You're in a constant state of *pissed off* around me."

"Hmm, I wonder why that is?" I pretended to think about it. "Maybe because you don't know how to be a team member and fucking communicate."

"No, I'm rather certain it's because I won't get on my knees and suck your cock like all the others," he returned. "I'm not one of your students or your lover. I'm your *better*. Yet you attempt to dictate to me like I'm one of your pupils, when in reality, I've been playing with your spells since I was five years old. So if anyone is going to kneel for anyone, it'll be you on your knees for me."

"Okay, maybe—"

"That's never going to fucking happen," I snapped, cutting off whatever Shade was about to say. Because fuck this. "Those spells I'm teaching Aflora are ones I learned as a boy, too. But she's a new Midnight Fae. I can't just throw advanced enchantments at her and expect her to learn."

"And yet that's exactly what Constantine is going to do," he countered. "We can't baby her. We can't go easy on her. We have to go hard. Because the dark source sure as fuck isn't going to treat her like a child with training wheels." He stepped up into my space, his silver-blue irises swirling with power. "I'm ensuring she survives. What the fuck are you achieving by coddling her?" He lifted an eyebrow, daring me to argue.

But I didn't know what to say.

Because the bastard was fucking right.

I focused so much on protecting her—because my natural instinct was to *guard*—that I'd forgotten how to truly prepare her. How to *teach* her.

I took a step back, needing my space from him… from them all… to *think*, to process what to do next.

"Zeph," Aflora murmured, moving toward me.

"No, Aflora." I looked at her, a shield of magic immediately encasing me, my desire not to be touched clear, and perhaps not fair to her, but necessary nonetheless. "He's right. The bastard is fucking right." And I hated admitting that. Hated him for pointing it out. Hated him for *existing*.

I shook my head. "I just… I need a minute." I backed away, heading toward the room's exit.

I needed to rethink everything.

To create a new plan.

Three weeks wasted.

Three weeks of elementary training.

Preparing for a war that would destroy my mate if *I* didn't properly prepare her. No, we. If *we* didn't properly prepare her.

This was why Zakkai had created the original training plan; he'd known we would have to be harsh on her. But I'd pushed back.

We couldn't hold back anymore.

We had to drive her harder. Test her limits. All but destroy her.

Because Constantine would certainly try.

Now I just needed to decide if I was strong enough to do this—strong enough… to hurt my mate.

CHAPTER TWELVE

SHADE

I folded my arms and fought the urge to wince as Aflora fell to the floor on a gasp.

"Again," Zeph demanded.

He'd escalated Aflora's training to a whole new level after Zakkai's pep talk the other day. No more coaching. No more words of praise. Just harsh spells and commands to keep going.

Aflora didn't complain.

She merely stood back up and started over.

Again. And again. And again.

I admired her tenacity and drive, but I also wanted to kill Zeph and Zakkai.

Phoenix fires, Kols whispered into my head as Zeph nailed Aflora with a particularly painful spell. *He's taking this a bit far, yes?*

Yeah, he's being an ass. I understood why. I even agreed that it had to be done. But that didn't mean I enjoyed watching it happen.

"*Atlaqi Sarahee.*" Aflora breathed the words and made a circle with her finger.

They were practicing defensive spells without wands today—Zeph's idea to prepare her since she didn't have a magical conduit of her own.

The snakelike enchantment from Zeph dissolved, allowing her a sigh of relief.

Until he followed it up with an even more powerful charm that slammed right into her chest.

Kols stepped forward, but a glare from Zeph kept him from interfering.

He's in quite a mood, Kols muttered.

I'm taking Aflora later, I replied. *I don't trust him to give her what she needs after this. Not in his current mood.*

No. He needs someone who can withstand his aggression and return it. Kols's bronze irises flared. *I will gladly be that partner, as it'll provide an excellent opportunity to kick his ass.*

I smirked. *Good.*

Zakkai leaned against the wall, his hands in the pockets of his black pants. He was shirtless like the rest of us, dressed to spar. Aflora had on another tank top and pants of a similar stretchy fabric. She was barefoot and sweating, her dark hair pulled up into a ponytail at the back of her head.

"*Dayani Adhabat,*" she snapped, her finger drawing a dash across the air to dismantle the strangulation charm Zeph had released. "*Asqati Mayatun.*" Her hand flexed with the words, a dark ball appearing in her palm. She threw it at Zeph, the deadly ball disappearing before it could hit his face.

She followed it up with another sphere right after it, aiming for his abdomen, then added the strangulation charm on top of it all, bringing the Guardian to his knees.

Zakkai grinned in amusement.

Aflora growled and hit Zeph with a fourth spell, one meant to be a punch to the gut.

Zeph deflected most of the power with a few defensive shields.

Then he lashed out with another offensive enchantment that knocked Aflora on her ass again.

She released a frustrated noise but didn't otherwise speak. Cerulean flames engulfed her from head to toe as she fought his new spell.

Then Zeph cursed as a burning thwomp shot up from the ground beside him. "No thwomps," he reminded her.

He dismantled the tree before it could set the room on fire. Given that the floors and walls were all obsidian, I doubted it would do much damage. But better not to tempt fate.

Their lethal dance continued, Aflora's outfit tarnished and nearly destroyed in the process. By the end, all I wanted to do was pull her into my arms and hold her for hours.

Zeph vibrated with irritation. He hated doing this to Aflora, but he and Zakkai were the best suited among us to teach her.

I'll distract him, Kols told me. *Take Aflora.*

The agitation pouring off Zeph suggested he wanted to soothe Aflora, but in a violent way. He needed to console himself as well, to know he hadn't actually hurt her. However, the anger he felt at himself for hurting her would end up translating to aggressive sex.

And that wasn't what she needed right now.

Aflora deserved some tenderness after the last few days of roughness. Yes, this all helped prepare her to face the inevitable, and Constantine wouldn't go easy on her. But having her mates grounded her and gave her an advantage that the Elder would never understand.

Therefore, she needed both harshness and love.

Zeph and Zakkai could focus on the former, as they excelled in combat.

Meanwhile, Kols and I would offer her the emotional support she required to truly flourish.

Zeph stepped toward Aflora, his expression lined with intent. Kols moved between them, and I shadowed to Aflora's side. Zakkai caught my gaze and gave a slight nod, aware of my intention. Then I wrapped her in a cloak of darkness and took her to our meadow.

She trembled against me, her head finding my shoulder as she silently cried in frustration. I held her, my hands roaming over her tattered tank top and offering her my touch and support.

You're magnificent, little rose, I told her.

There's so much violence, she replied, shuddering.

Her tears weren't a sign of weakness or sadness. They were about her difficulty in accepting the darkness of being a Midnight Fae. Her heart was all light and joy and sweet elements. This world that she'd fallen into blackened her soul, and only the strongest of fae could accept such a thing.

But even the strongest of fae needed a soft moment to reflect.

I pulled Aflora with me to the ground, her petite frame curling into my lap on instinct. Then I held her beneath the shade of the tree until the sun began to rise over our meadow. We didn't speak. We just basked in her earth, her life, her desire to create.

As the heat touched her skin, she lifted her head on a sigh and admired the rising sun. She knew it wasn't real, that the paradigm manufactured it, but that didn't stop her contentment from flowing through our bond.

"Can we stay here today?" she asked softly. "To sleep, I mean."

"We can do whatever you want, little rose," I promised her.

Her lips curled a little. Then she began to fashion a bed of flowers, the petals soft and colorful and filled with her strength.

I watched as she worked, content to lean against the trunk.

Sometimes Aflora just needed a day to play. And I gave her that, allowing her to flourish in her earth magic and giving her a chance to reinvigorate her soul.

Floral scents surrounded us, her element in full effect as she gave herself over to her Earth Fae heart.

Then she sprawled out on her bed, lost the tie in her hair, and allowed the strands to flow over the ground in cerulean and black waves.

I smiled, admiring the sight of her all content and warm and happy.

"Join me," she whispered.

I replied by pushing away from my tree and crawling to her. She grinned when I reached her side, then she wrapped her palm around the back of my neck to gently guide me toward her for a kiss.

We remained like that for hours, just letting our mouths do all the talking.

No sex.

No physical need.

Just a moment for our souls to heal, to love, to indulge in each other.

I told her with my mind how much I adored her. How much I respected her. How proud I was of her for embracing this new path.

And she told me how thankful she was to have me as her mate. How she forgave all my secrets. How she wanted to live a lifetime together to heal all the previous ones I'd endured.

It was an intense, beautiful moment, one that left both of us replete in an entirely different way than ever before.

As the sun reached high noon, she snuggled into my chest.

And together we slept on the mound of flowers she'd built, the sky providing a natural blanket of heat that allowed us to dream.

Although, as I closed my eyes, I lost myself to a vision where the darkness of my world threatened to engulf Aflora whole, dismantling her light.

Something's coming, I thought, asleep yet very much awake. *A new trial is brewing. And this one will bring death.*

CHAPTER THIRTEEN

AFLORA

Zeph and Zakkai were being particularly cruel today.

We'd been living in this paradigm for five weeks now, almost six, and they'd decided it was time for me to face them collectively.

Which meant they were attacking me from both sides.

Kols and Shade hadn't been able to watch, their instincts to protect overriding the cause of today's session. But as the hours drew on, I started to wish they'd return and whisk me away from this hell.

I understood the purpose of this test, that Zakkai and Zeph were merely trying to prepare me to handle the ascension on my own, but that didn't make it hurt any less.

They were both lethally serious, their spells ones that would have killed me a year ago.

Fortunately, the dark source leapt to my aid, consistently allowing me to dismantle each enchantment thrown my way.

I tried to engage my earth side as well, but today's exercise required me to use my Midnight Fae powers instead.

Which I suspected was the point.

They wanted me to learn how to rely on the Midnight Fae part of me over the Earth Fae part, as they assumed Constantine would do the same.

I shivered as Zakkai's silver-blue eyes flared with power, his long white strands billowing in a magical breeze off his shoulders. The calculating edge to his cruelly handsome features told me I wasn't going to like whatever he did next.

Zeph attacked from my side, his fiery incantation wrapping around my leg as Zakkai hit me with a strategic web of magic that rendered me speechless.

I fell to the ground beneath their joint assault, wincing when they didn't stop.

Shield, Zeph demanded.

I threw up a mastery of defensive arts, the barrier invisible yet studiously deflecting their spells while I attempted to undo whatever they'd incapacitated me with.

It burned through my veins, stealing my breath and drowning me in a toxic chemical that fractured my ability to think.

Instincts, I thought numbly. *They want me to rely on my instincts.*

Zakkai had warned me that today's lesson would be difficult. I understood now—they'd purposely dismantled my ability to recall spells by verbal memory.

This was about relying on physical reactions.

I hated them.

Loathed that they struck my shield repeatedly while I futilely tried to undo the harsh restraint on my mind.

We were beyond kindness today. Hell, *this week*. They'd been on me repeatedly, barely letting me sleep, forcing me to learn, learn, learn.

There were so many spells, *too many spells*.

I was being given a crash course in five weeks that should have been delivered over twenty-five years. As Kols had pointed out, I wasn't even of age to ascend. At least not according to previous Midnight Fae rituals.

All of this was being thrown at me because of a devious, underhanded, wicked male who wanted to use me to make a point.

I refused to let him win.

But in moments like this, it was easy to see how effortlessly he could best me. Because I couldn't fight this. I didn't know how. They'd handicapped my mind, leaving me defenseless beneath my deteriorating shield.

Stop feeling sorry for yourself and fix it, Zeph berated me. *You're more powerful than you realize.*

I hate you, I seethed.

Good. Then I'm getting through to you. Now fucking dismantle the charms.

I growled at him.

He snarled back.

And I suddenly wanted to cut through his magic just to return the favor.

There'd been this weight of darkness hanging on my shoulders for weeks now. A sense of foreboding. A thick feeling of dread.

I tapped into it now, wrapping myself in the black web of magic and allowing it to flourish through me. Ice drilled through my veins, dismantling my inner warmth yet bolstering my resolve in the process.

It coiled.

Strengthened.

Coiled some more.

Until I couldn't hold on to it for another second, the magic too intense and terrifying to maintain.

It exploded out of me in a cerulean flame, eating through all the enchantments in the room, including my shield, and seeking the two males attacking me.

Zakkai absorbed the tension with a wave of his hand.

Zeph created a shield that deflected the blast.

Then the two of them stared at me on the floor. The power had destroyed my clothes.

Zakkai walked over to a bag on the floor, found a new pair of pants and a tank top, and tossed them to me. "Get dressed. We're doing that again."

I shivered, my body too weak to repeat all that. "No."

"Yes," Zeph interjected. "Now, Aflora."

"*No*," I repeated. "I'm done for today." That power had been too much. Too dark. Too destructive. Too *not me*. It'd overtaken my earth, leaving me without a single glimpse of light. I refused to accept that. Refused to embrace it. Refused to allow it to happen again.

But Zeph wasn't having it. He slammed me with another bolt of power, this one sweeping my legs out from beneath me and pinning me to the ground. "We're not done."

A rumble started in my chest, my irritation mounting. He wasn't hearing me. "I'm. Done. For. Today."

"That's too bad, little star," Zakkai said, tossing my clothes to the side. "Because I agree with Zeph. We're doing that again."

I wanted to scream. To maim. To kill them both. I needed a break. I *deserved* a break. We'd been at this for hours. Days. Weeks. I hadn't complained once, taking everything they'd given me and memorizing their rules.

I'd put up with their treatment, Zeph's volatile behavior and Zakkai's wicked spells, and I wanted to take the rest of the night off. Right now.

I took in Zeph's offensive spell, copied the general structure, and sent it back at him. He deflected with his wand, already preparing another enchantment. "*Enough*," I said through gritted teeth. I was too tired. Too done. Too—

"Do you think Constantine would listen to you right now?" Zakkai asked. "Because I think he'd revel in your show of weakness and drown you in it."

"I'm not weak!"

"Your current situation suggests otherwise," he countered.

Then he slammed me with another of those webs meant to dismantle my thoughts.

And Zeph followed up with another spell.

And another.

And another.

I tried to build a shield, to counter them, to protect myself, but my energy reserves were depleted from the darkness I'd allowed myself to release.

However, it still lingered.

Hovering on my shoulder, waiting for me to embrace it once more.

But I couldn't. It made me feel too cold. Too wrong. Too *powerful*.

I curled into a ball instead, denying that flicker of energy and absorbing the brunt of Zeph's and Zakkai's hits instead.

Aflora? Kols whispered into my mind. *Are you all right?*

No, I replied, trembling beneath the pain and agony of having my own mates attack me when I'd told them to stop. They were trying to make a point. I understood it. But that didn't make me accept it. *They won't stop.*

I sounded so weak. So pitiful. And I could almost hear Zakkai and Zeph taunting me for it, calling me out for giving up.

They wanted me to be strong.

To stand up to them.

To give them a display of power meant to destroy them all.

I hate them, I told Kols. *I hate them.*

I could hear the sadness in my voice, a perpetual moping that I loathed.

I'm stronger than this, I thought in my next inhale. *So much stronger.*

But it required me to block an important part of me. My earth. My tie to the element I loved and adored. Choosing strength meant I had to welcome the darkness.

I shivered, abhorring the choice.

However, the electricity roaming over me, as well as Zeph's shouts to fight, left me no choice.

I tapped into that black hole, pulling it into me once more, and released it on a wave of energy that had tears falling from my eyes.

Everything stopped.

Inky flames engulfed the room.

Then Zakkai cut through it with a blast of cerulean magic that tamed the darkness back into a little ball of spinning power that seemed to seep back into me, inch by inch.

I didn't move, my arms locked around my legs as I remained in the center of the room.

The spells were all gone.

But the aggression remained.

"Aflora?" Zeph asked, his deep voice holding a touch of concern.

I ignored him.

"She's fine," Zakkai said. "Or she would be if she accepted the dark source the way she needs to."

"Does she look fucking fine to you?" Zeph demanded. "Because she looks broken to me."

Zakkai snorted. "You're allowing emotion to cloud your judgment. That's why she's not as prepared as she should be—because you've wasted all her time by coddling her. So now we have to resort to this to ensure she's ready because *you* failed to train her."

"I failed to train her?" Zeph's deep voice reverberated through the room, making my skin crawl with goose bumps. "You're the one who mated her first, Zakkai. Then you left her in the Elemental Fae realm to be raised by a bunch of Earth Fae. And you're blaming me for her lack of preparedness?"

"She wasn't ready then."

"And she wasn't fucking ready when she started at the Academy, either," Zeph retorted. "But I did the best I could with what I had to work with. She couldn't even make a damn sandwich right when we started."

I flinched at the way he said it, like my lack of dark-magic skill made me somehow weak in his eyes.

"Maybe things would have been different had you been the one to take her that day instead of Shade," Zeph continued.

"Oh, they absolutely would have. You'd all be dead right now. Instead, I'm stuck putting up with your arrogance on a daily basis—an arrogance you have not *earned*."

"You say these things like you know what I can do," Zeph replied, a lethal edge in his tone. "But how about you put that *arrogance* of yours to the test, hmm?"

"Happily," Zakkai replied, a bolt of magic singeing the air.

Zeph responded in kind, causing the hairs along my arms to dance on end.

What's happening? Shade demanded in my head.

But I was too consumed by the growing power in the room to reply. *Danger,* my instincts whispered to me. *Protect.*

I lifted my head to see Zakkai and Zeph engaged in an all-out duel, their aggression mounting with each strike.

They refused to yield.

Refused to acknowledge the other as superior.

Because they were the same—both dominant and proud and powerful in their own ways. Zakkai had the edge as the Source Architect, but Zeph had spent his entire life training for a battle like this. He was a Guardian, one assigned to protect the incoming Midnight Fae King. And he demonstrated that now by unleashing all his power into Zakkai.

My eyes widened, realization striking me in the chest.

He *had* been going easy on me. Even when I thought he was giving me his all, he'd never fought me like this.

And for some reason, that angered me.

They were supposed to be training me to fight Constantine. He wouldn't even consider lessening his blows. Yet Zeph had held back, afraid that I couldn't handle him in his full force of power.

Which was precisely what Zakkai had kept arguing, that Zeph needed to remove the emotional filter and test me. *Really* test me.

And I'd reacted like a brat today, telling them to stop. Just when we were on the cusp of unleashing my greatest power.

The chip on my shoulder… that inky spot that weighed me down… was my connection to the dark source.

I understood that on a level but hadn't *accepted* it. That'd been the reason for Zakkai's pushing. He wanted me to allow the darkness out to play so we could realize my true potential.

We'd spent five weeks going through trivial spells and historical potentials and studying scenarios meant to help me pass my trials.

But today was the first time I'd experienced the real power flourishing inside me—the one that would guarantee I excelled.

Zeph snarled as Zakkai hit him with a cerulean spark. Then he volleyed a green one underlined in black back at him.

I sat up, my eyes widening. *They're trying to kill each other.*

There was no going easy here. No submitting. No *acceptance.*

They were part of the problem—the harsh point in my bonds. They didn't trust each other. Nor did they like each other. And it was coming to a head now as they dueled in a way only alpha males could.

I had to stop them. To force them to see reason. If one of them was injured in this aggression, I'd never forgive myself, or them.

"*Stop,*" I told them.

They were too lost in their furious energies to hear me, their duel intensifying with every passing second.

I went to my knees, calling on that power once more and allowing it to consume me entirely, needing it to protect me *and* my mates.

It culminated, curled, and grew inside me.

Zeph cursed as Zakkai struck him with something harmful. It only seemed to enrage both men more, heightening their need to declare victory over the other.

"*Enough!*" I shouted, releasing my energy into both of them and knocking them to the ground.

They weren't prepared for my reaction, too focused on each other to notice me. I used the final vestiges of my strength to stand, my hands on my hips as I glowered at them both.

"No more," I stated, power flickering around me in warning as I replenished my depleted reserves directly from the dark source. It was foreign and cold, but necessary because my earth magic couldn't refuel the blackened part of me.

Zakkai's lips curled faintly, his white hair a tangled mess around his shoulders. "Well done, Aflora."

"That was a fucking test?" Zeph sounded pissed.

Zakkai merely lifted a shoulder. "Does it matter? It worked."

"I'm going to kill you," Zeph threatened.

Zakkai pushed up to his feet and shook his head. "You'll try," he taunted, moving to stand behind me. "You'll fail." He kissed my neck, his lips going to my ear. "You're burning so bright right now, Flora. Just like a star."

I shivered beneath his praise, but a bolt of irritation still lingered in my veins. "You pushed me too far today."

"I pushed you just far enough," he countered against my ear, his tongue licking the shell before pressing another kiss to my thundering pulse. "And you were magnificent."

Zeph left the floor and positioned himself across from us, his fury a palpable spike against my senses. "You need to learn to fucking communicate."

"I've been communicating. You've not been listening," Zakkai murmured, his mouth drawing a path to my shoulder. "You taste like darkness, sweet star."

His touch sent a shiver down my spine, his hard body cradling my back as he more firmly pressed against me. He was shirtless—something all my mates seemed to do daily now for training—which allowed me to feel his heat directly against my skin.

"So decadent," he hummed, licking back up my neck to my ear. "You feel it, right? The power? The intensity?"

"Yes." I swallowed, my gaze on Zeph. "But I'm not sure I forgive you for provoking it."

He chuckled against my neck. "I know. However, you will." He slid his arms around my abdomen, holding me to him. "Would you like me to worship you with my tongue, my queen?"

"I…"

He nibbled my pulse. "We can make the Guardian watch," he suggested.

Zeph narrowed his gaze and took a step forward, his hand finding my hip. "Or maybe I'll make *you* watch."

My heart skipped a beat at the intensity pouring off of them.

Zakkai might have provoked that duel to test my resolve and power, but Zeph had eagerly engaged back with the intent to kill.

A dangerous game.

A lethal provocation.

They were too strong, too dominant, to share. Yet I couldn't pick between them. They were my mates. My future. They owned equal parts of my heart, and I needed them to accept that, to accept each other.

I went to my toes to kiss Zeph before he could speak again, my teeth dragging along his lower lip and demanding he reciprocate. He didn't right away, his grip tightening against me in warning. Then my tongue slipped into his mouth, and some of his tension left his jaw.

Zakkai didn't release me, his arms locked around my abdomen as Zeph stepped closer to press against me, sandwiching me firmly between them.

I reached behind me to grab Zakkai, ensuring he didn't leave.

And used my opposite hand to wrap around Zeph's nape.

You're both mine, I told them through my wide-open links. *I claim you equally.*

Zeph growled in response.

Zakkai matched the sound with a vibration of his own.

I released Zeph's mouth to meet his blazing green eyes. "I will not choose."

CHAPTER FOURTEEN

ZEPH

The intensity in Aflora's features gave me pause. "You think I want you to choose?"

I would never ask for such a thing. It would be akin to asking her to kill a piece of her soul. We were all part of her, whether we liked each other or not. And while I certainly did not care for Zakkai, I acknowledged who he was to her.

I could also admit his use to her as a protector as well.

There wasn't anyone else in this world better suited to guard Aflora than Zakkai.

"I would never want you to choose, pixie flower," I added in a low voice, my hand cupping her cheek while my opposite palm remained against her hip. "We're your mates, even when we hate each other."

"*Hate* is a little strong," Zakkai replied, his lips ghosting along her neck to settle over her pulse. "Dislike, maybe. Hate, no. I just wanted to make a point. *Again.*"

My jaw clenched at his words, mostly because I understood them. Respected them, too. Because his point had been needed.

And admittedly, I hadn't possessed the ability to push her the way he had.

She wasn't the delicate flower I'd first met, but a being of superior magic and strength that I admired to the depths of my soul.

However, it was hard for me to see that part of her. Because it required me to hurt her to ignite the power within her, and I had learned over the last few weeks that harming my mate was not a natural skill of mine. In the bedroom in a fun way? Yes. In reality, where she could seriously be injured by things outside my control? Absolutely not.

Zakkai seemed able to provoke her without regret. Like he was somehow programmed to mete out dangerous training.

I envied that about him. It granted him a measure of control over our situation that I couldn't attain. And I did not handle a lack of control well.

I met his gaze over her shoulder. "I may not agree with your methods," I said slowly. "But I can't deny the outcome of those methods."

His responding nod was short and to the point. Then he returned his focus to Aflora's neck, his lips worshipping her skin. "I don't hate your Guardian lover, little star," he informed her. "I just refuse to kneel to him."

I snorted. "Likewise."

Aflora sighed. "You both are going to be the death of me." She relaxed between us while she spoke, her fingers tracing my nape near the edge of my hairline. "Can I please be done for today?"

Zakkai's eyes met mine once more, a foreign understanding passing between us. "No," he said softly. "We still have another lesson to deliver."

His palm slid up her side to her breast, squeezing her flesh while holding my gaze.

A new activity.

One about unity and understanding.

He was inviting me in his own way to help deliver that lesson. We might fight one another on many things, constantly striving to best the other, but at the end of it all, we were still her mates. And we would never make her choose.

"You did well today," I told her.

"Extremely well," Zakkai added. "But you failed to understand something important, Aflora."

"Yes," I agreed, drawing my thumb along her lip.

"What?" she breathed. "What did I miss?"

"The fact that we will never make you choose," I told her, leaning forward to kiss her.

"But we might make you take us both," Zakkai murmured at her ear.

"B-both?" she stammered against my mouth.

"It's a suitable lesson, isn't it?" I studied her eyes, noting her flared pupils. "You doubted our intentions. Now we'll demonstrate them thoroughly."

"By not letting you choose," Zakkai finished for me. "And neither of us will submit, Aflora. Which means you'll be forced to handle us together."

"At the same time," I said.

"Indeed."

Aflora shivered. "I... I don't..."

"No choosing, remember?" I skimmed my teeth along her lower lip, then bit down gently. "You'll take us and accept us. As one."

She inhaled heavily, her cheeks turning an adorable pink shade.

Zakkai's palm left her breast to explore downward to the sweet apex between her thighs. His growl of approval told me what I already knew.

"You're soaked," he whispered, his finger gliding through her folds to pierce her deep. "You want us inside you, don't you, little star? All that power turned you on just like it did to us. And now you want to expel some of that residual energy by taking us into this sweet pussy and screaming out our names."

Kols and I had done this once before, but not with Aflora.

Her eyes widened at what Zakkai had implied, her mind whirring with impossibilities. I silenced her with a kiss while he stroked her below, his arm brushing my abdomen as he taunted her lower half. She gasped as his teeth pierced her neck, his throat working to draw her essence from her vein.

I speared her mouth with my tongue, distracting her while he lit her internal fuse with his vampiric kiss and clever touch.

She moaned, shivering between us as he drew her closer to a climax. It would take some of the tension out of her body, making her more pliant as we prepared her.

I let go of her hip and drew my touch upward to her protruding nipple. She released a breathy sound as I pinched the hard peak, massaging it in time with Zakkai's ministrations below.

He released her neck, his gaze flashing to mine. I took over his bite, sinking my teeth into the same grooves he'd created, providing Aflora with a demonstration on how we intended to share her as equals.

She belonged to us just as much as we belonged to her.

Zakkai threaded the fingers of his free hand through her thick hair and guided her head to the side and slightly up so he could kiss her. It exposed her neck to me even more, the column of her throat stretched to accommodate us both. Just like we would soon do to her tight little body.

Aflora canted her hips into Zakkai's touch, her skin fevered with arousal as she strove to find her release. *Zeph*, she whispered. *Zeph, please...*

I grinned against her neck, enjoying that it was my permission she sought while Zakkai penetrated her.

Then he pinched her clit, causing her mind to fracture as she came undone beneath his command, not mine.

He didn't look at me while he did it, but I sensed his pride nonetheless.

She was his, too.

And if he wanted her to come, she would. With or without my permission.

I fought the urge to growl in response and instead focused on Aflora's euphoric blood. I could taste her orgasm in her essence, her excitement an aphrodisiac to my senses and drowning me in her heady scent.

Her fingertips remained against the back of my neck, her nails digging into my skin as she writhed in pleasure.

Then Zakkai added more pressure and she stilled.

"You can take it," I said against her neck. "Just relax and let us guide you." It was an act between me and Aflora that I always assumed would be shared with Kols first. But the significance of this with Zakkai wasn't lost on me.

Aflora needed this.

Our circle needed it.

Because it would join him and me in a way we couldn't undo, while also showing Aflora what she meant to us. This wasn't just about sharing but about teaching her what we were prepared to sacrifice for her.

Zakkai wasn't the type to share.

And I wasn't the type to bend.

We would have to rely on each other to control the situation, to read her cues, and to ensure her safety and pleasure throughout.

That wasn't an easy task, but it was a necessary one.

"Take off Zephyrus's pants," Zakkai said against her mouth, releasing her in the next breath. "Now."

I swallowed down the urge to correct him and issue the command myself. Instead, I focused on her gaze as she looked up at me.

Do what he says, I whispered into her mind.

Her throat worked as she licked her lips, then she reached for the drawstring at my waist.

I kissed her forehead, thanking her without words for acquiescing. This had to be an intimidating lesson for her, but she showed her faith in us by doing exactly what we'd told her to do.

She pushed the fabric from my hips, causing them to drop and leaving me naked before her. We never wore shoes while dueling, and I rarely wore a shirt. Zakkai was the same, his pants the only clothing remaining between the three of us. He removed them himself, kicking them off to the side before licking Aflora's essence from his fingers.

Then he did something I would never have anticipated.

He created a bed with a spell and sat down in the middle of the black sheets.

I arched a brow.

He merely said, "Come over here and straddle me, little star."

He was offering to be on the bottom, at least in a mild manner. He was still sitting and very much in charge, but he wouldn't be the one driving into her from behind.

Which meant he expected me to set the pace for her after he finished preparing her for my entry.

I stroked my shaft in anticipation. *Go to him, pixie flower. Take him in that tight cunt so I can hear him tell me how wet you are for us.*

Aflora visibly shivered, then followed our orders without an ounce of hesitation.

Zakkai entered her with ease, her body more than ready to receive his cock. But mine would be another matter entirely. "Not ready yet," he said, reaching between them to stimulate her clit with his thumb as he slid another finger into her alongside his shaft.

She moaned in response, her breasts flushing with color. They were all signs of a needy, expectant woman. Not one fearing what we were about to do, but one looking forward to our intentions.

"Think you can suck my cock while he prepares you?" I asked, stepping up to the side of the bed. "I'm feeling a little *dry.*"

Zakkai chuckled, the sound deep and languid. "You won't be in a few minutes."

"Mmm," I hummed, agreeing. Then I lightly took hold of Aflora's chin and drew her focus to me. She was at the perfect height while sitting astride Zakkai, her lips level with my groin. "Part your lips for me."

The flaring of her nostrils told me she approved.

Then her mouth confirmed it as she took me deep, her tongue a velvety touch against the underside of my shaft. "Fuck," I breathed, loving the way she sucked me.

She knew everything I liked, her actions all ones I'd taught her, with a few moves tossed in that were just pure instinct.

Such an apt pupil.

The perfect student.

She murmured something against my shaft as Zakkai flexed below, her eyes rolling into the back of her head.

I grinned, seeing all the signs I craved in her—appreciation, excitement, arousal.

She wanted us.

We wanted her.

And we were about to embark on something that would change the landscape for all of us.

Zakkai had yet to embrace her other mates, choosing to watch rather than play.

Tonight, he opted to engage in the most intimate way imaginable—all to show Aflora that he could share in his own way.

If she'd said no and meant it, we wouldn't do this to her. That wasn't what we meant by this lesson and her not having a choice.

We were telling her that *we* accepted the dynamic and that we would never allow her to choose between us.

Instead, we would ensure she could always take us both.

Even if that meant a little pain with her pleasure.

Which she seemed to be enjoying now as her hips undulated against Zakkai.

He braced himself on one hand while his other continued to prepare her, his thumb circling her clit and stimulating her the way he should.

It was exactly what I would do.

Although, I'd probably have her take Kols first, then position myself behind her and prepare her that way so I could intimately feel our Elite Blood mate penetrate her with my fingers.

An activity for later.

This lesson was about Aflora indulging the two dominant males in her life.

And about us accepting each other.

Her teeth skimmed my dick in a taunting caress, her blue eyes flickering up to mine.

"Siren," I whispered, brushing my knuckles across her teeth. "But I'm not coming down your throat, pixie flower." I wrapped my palm around the back of her neck to encourage her to take me deeper while I spoke, my hips forcing her to take as much of me as her mouth allowed.

I waited a beat before withdrawing, smiling as her irises glistened with erotic need.

Her tongue licked my tip, kissing me in her own way, just as Zakkai confirmed her readiness with a look.

No words, just a knowing glint.

I released her nape and went to kneel on the bed behind her.

Zakkai didn't lie back the way Kols would have. He chose to remain seated, his gaze holding mine in a war for dominance as I found my position against Aflora.

His hand blocked my entry, his fingers still lodged deep inside her.

Then he slowly withdrew but kept his cock inside her.

This would be undeniably intimate, an act neither of us likely ever intended to share together. Yet it was oddly appropriate given the circumstances.

His damp fingers went to the back of her neck, claiming her as he pulled her in for a kiss meant to distract her.

This would hurt at first.

And this was his way of saying he'd do his best to keep her preoccupied.

I reached around her to resume his ministrations with her sensitive nub, my thumb finding the swollen flesh with ease. She shuddered between us, another orgasm lurking on the horizon of her thoughts.

He'd properly stimulated her.

Now we were going to utterly annihilate her, blacken her senses, and show her an ecstasy few had ever experienced.

I lined myself up with her entrance, my head touching Zakkai's shaft.

Neither of them reacted, Aflora lost to his kiss.

But I knew he felt me.

And I suspected this was unlike anything he'd ever done before.

I kept one hand against her center while I used the opposite to guide myself toward her entrance.

She froze as I started to slide inside, causing Zakkai to growl and bite down on her lower lip.

You can take it, I assured her as I pressed in slowly, my patience and control resolute.

Zakkai remained equally still, his cock pulsing in response to the added pressure but otherwise staying firmly lodged inside her.

Aflora whimpered a little, her body tensing between us. I kissed her shoulder and then her neck before pressing my lips to her ear.

"You feel amazing," I praised her. "So good. So tight. So wet." I rocked into her a little more, easing her into this intensity, knowing how easily we could accidentally hurt her like this.

"Oh," she moaned, arching into me and tilting her head back to find my mouth.

"Perfect," I whispered against her lips. "Fucking perfect." I penetrated her with my tongue, taking full advantage of our kiss as I slid the rest of the way inside her.

Zakkai groaned, his palm skating up her side to capture her breast as he continued to brace himself on his opposite hand.

Aflora whimpered, the sound one of pleasure underlined in torment. I massaged her with my thumb, renewing her ecstasy in hopes of drowning out the pain.

Her tongue sensuously touched mine, then Zakkai did something to her breast that had her gasping.

She whipped around to face him, and he took her mouth in the next breath, demanding her attention as he tweaked her nipple.

We didn't move or thrust, giving her the time she needed to accept our joint size.

Zakkai wasn't small and neither was I.

However, Aflora took us both, her body seeming to expand to accommodate her mates.

Elemental Fae were known for their sexual appetites, something I'd indulged in thoroughly these last few months. And we had a lifetime to explore her true limits.

This certainly wasn't one of them.

Something she demonstrated as she began to tentatively move between us, her soul firing to life at the sensation of being so utterly filled by her men.

I allowed her to dictate the pace at first, wanting her to enjoy the experience as much as we were.

Zakkai clearly felt the same way, his body tense with control, giving her time to explore and feel and indulge.

Her nub pulsed beneath my thumb.

Her breathing escalated.

Her heart beat loudly.

And her moan reverberated off the walls.

"Fuck me," she panted, her words going straight to my groin.

She never cursed unless we were in bed together, and she only did it to provoke my passion. Now was no different, her demand one I happily accepted.

Zakkai clearly agreed because he thrust upward into her, his shaft stroking mine in tandem with her and sending a jolt through my system.

Because fuck, that was intense.

His eyes met mine as he pulled away from Aflora's mouth, his expression telling me he felt the same way.

So he did it again.

Then I repeated the motion.

And we found a rhythm together that had Aflora singing between us, her body breaking beneath a rapturous typhoon of hot sensation.

We all felt it, her exuberance gracing the bonds and spilling into our own pace. I groaned, my blood on fire from her reaction to being filled to the hilt by two of us.

Then Zakkai let me set a pace, my position on my knees giving me greater momentum.

He kissed Aflora again, his hand leaving her breast for her hair as he tugged her into him with a need that was borderline feral. I felt it *through* her, his power a whiplash to my senses that drove me onward, compelling me to take us all over the edge in a ferocity of movement that would either kill us or take us to the brink of death and back.

It no longer mattered.

We were beasts fucking and reveling in the shared energy rolling between the three of us, Aflora a beacon of power we could only worship and praise.

I kissed her neck, her shoulder, her cheek, and eventually her mouth as Zakkai released her lips to feast upon her breasts.

I lost track of time, my control slipping into a vortex of consuming passion.

Aflora's walls began to tighten, her body strung tight as her clit pulsed beneath my thumb.

One more flick, a single circle, and it sent her off into the stars on an explosion that pulled me right along with her. I cursed, my orgasm so intense it sliced through my insides and left me paralyzed against her back. I was only vaguely aware of Zakkai shooting off with us, his growl one that seemed to echo through the room.

And then the three of us collapsed in a pile of limbs with Aflora limp between us.

"Power expulsion," Zakkai said, his voice hoarse.

It took me a moment to understand, then I felt her energy thriving through my veins. Another one of those dark balls of power had erupted from her, but not in a fight this time… in ecstasy.

And she'd released it directly into our bonds.

That was what had taken me over the edge with her, along with her tight cunt squeezing my shaft in that addictive pulsing motion. My balls tightened at the memory, my lower abdomen clenching. We were no longer inside her, my cock against her damp thigh and Zakkai's against her abdomen.

He drew his fingers through her hair, his expression reverent.

"Kols," he said softly.

"What?"

"Kols," he repeated. "She'll need someone to take care of her when she wakes up. Shade and Kols are best for that."

I wanted to argue because I very much excelled at aftercare, but with how destroyed I felt right now, I realized he was right.

Kols, I said, opening my link to him.

I'm already here, he replied, drawing my attention to where he stood leaning against the doorway.

Oh. That was why Zakkai had said his name—he'd been calling for him to join us. I'd been so lost to Aflora that I hadn't even noticed Kols was here, something that should have concerned me, as I was always aware of my surroundings. But that joining with Aflora had removed my ability to focus on anything other than her and the act that had followed.

You all right? Kols asked, clearly sensing the direction of my thoughts.

Zakkai calling to Kols suggested he hadn't lost his awareness at all, not even when we all detonated. I wasn't sure if that impressed me or annoyed me.

Zeph? Kols prompted when I didn't reply to his question.

I'll live.

Will she? he countered.

She's fine, I replied, brushing my lips against her temple. *Just lost in subspace.* She'd been dominated by two men and had erupted on an avalanche of power. I wasn't surprised that she'd passed out afterward. Hell, I felt like I was on the edge of unconsciousness, too.

Kols snorted into my head. *Dangerous game you two just played.*

She loved it.

I know. His words implied he'd witnessed her falling apart.

Are you upset? I'd never shared women with other men, only with Kols. But this situation was unique.

No. I enjoyed the show. He pushed off the door and sauntered toward us. "I'll take her from here." He lifted her into his arms and cradled her against his shoulder. "Try not to kill each other while she's gone."

With those parting words, he left.

And all I could do was laugh.

Because killing Zakkai was absolutely not what I wanted to do at the moment.

He seemed equally against the idea as he sighed in content, his arm falling over his eyes. "I'm taking a nap."

I considered leaving him to it, then rolled my head against the bed beneath us. "Yeah. Me, too."

Right here.

Next to him.

"Class dismissed," I added on a yawn.

Because after that performance, who the hell cared anymore?

He snorted in agreement.

I closed my eyes, forgetting his presence beside me. And let sleep take me under.

CHAPTER FIFTEEN

KOLS

Shade met me outside, his expression giving nothing away as I carried a naked and replete Aflora toward him.

Several Midnight Fae had gathered around the area, the energy radiating from the building behind me an electric spire everyone had sensed. Aflora had detonated four times over the last few hours, the first three during combat and the final one during sex.

I hadn't witnessed the others, only the fourth.

And it'd been a sight to behold.

But she would not approve of everyone looking upon her now in this state, something I whispered into Shade's mind as I approached.

He responded by wrapping us both up in a black cloak and shadowing us to a meadow bathed in moonlight. I frowned, glancing around.

"It's my place, the one I keep taking Aflora to," he explained. "Still within the paradigm, but not on Academy grounds." He cocked his head. "I'll show you." He led the way toward a tree… and stepped through it.

With a raised brow, I followed and found myself in a modest room with a big bed, a living area, and a small kitchen. "Ah, this is where you've lived when not on campus, too." I could tell because it smelled like him. Which meant he stayed here often.

He shrugged. "My grandmother is nearby. I visited enough over the years that she decided I needed my own place." He started toward the bed but passed it on his way to a set of double doors. "I think she also foresaw my desire to share a private space with Aflora, but I really don't want to think about what prompted that vision."

I smirked. "We all know what prompted it."

"Yeah, like I said, that doesn't mean I want to think about it." He disappeared through the doors.

I trailed behind him, pausing on the threshold as he bent over a large bathtub—that was the size of a small pool—rimmed with marble benches for seating and a stone exterior for decoration. He turned on the water, then tested it with his hand before clicking a button that increased the flow of water and stopped it from draining.

Aflora remained unconscious against me while he worked, completely oblivious to the salts and scents he added to perfect the bath.

It took nearly fifteen minutes, his work studious and meticulously planned.

When he finished, he stripped off his clothes.

Then he stepped into the water and sank down into it before turning on the soft purr of the jets. He didn't turn off the faucet, but it changed to a more subtle flow, the drain seeming to work in tandem with the incoming water. It appeared to be cycling somehow, which made it ideal for bathing because the bath would continue to refresh itself.

Give her to me, he whispered into my mind, holding out his arms for her.

I walked over to do as he asked, mostly because it was clear he intended for me to join them. The tub could have fit Aflora and all her mates, making it ideal for whatever he had in mind.

I removed my button-down shirt, slacks, and shoes in the closet beside the bathroom. Then I returned to join Aflora and Shade in the tub.

He had her head on his shoulder, his arms around her to ensure she stayed above the water.

"There's a comb over there," he said softly, gesturing with his chin to some of the supplies he'd set beside the tub. I hadn't caught all the items he'd grabbed, but noted now that they were all things meant to help cleanse and care for Aflora.

I picked up the item he'd mentioned and used it to brush through her knotted strands.

The jets kept the water warm and moving, the scents all relaxing and obviously meant for healing.

Aflora slowly came to while I drew the comb through her dark hair, her eyes going to Shade and then to me. She stretched her legs a little, then lifted her head to give me better access to her strands.

No words were spoken, just emotion as she let us take care of her.

We all knew what had happened, how Zakkai and Zeph had joined inside her. I'd detailed it to Shade while I'd watched, wanting him to know what they were doing to Aflora and how she was taking it.

He'd been concerned at first—as had I—but I'd trusted Zakkai and Zeph not to truly hurt her. And they hadn't. If anything, they'd taken her to new heights.

It'd been strange to see Zeph with another man, but I'd felt his emotions the whole time. He hadn't been with Zakkai out of love or desire, but out of a need to prove to Aflora that he accepted all her mates.

It'd been their way of ensuring trust within our circle.

I'd accepted that. As had Shade.

"How are you feeling?" he asked Aflora after several minutes of soft silence.

She didn't answer for a moment, her focus on stretching her legs and arms once more as she languidly lounged against him. "Relaxed," she said. "Used, in a good way. Sore."

I set the comb down and picked up some bodywash that Shade had procured. It would dissolve into the bath, but with the way the jets seemed to work, it'd cycle through and replenish with clean water.

Aflora allowed me to run the soap over her arms and along her torso, down to her legs. It wasn't as precise as a shower, but it worked, and it gave me an excuse to check her thoroughly for bruising and any pain points.

She didn't flinch at all, her body seeming to be utterly relaxed between us.

I sensed her reaching out to check on Zeph and Zakkai, her lips curling slightly at finding them passed out.

Well, I assumed they were both asleep, anyway, because I could sense Zeph resting contentedly. He and Zakkai had been in charge of most of Aflora's physical training, leaving both males more exhausted than me and Shade.

I'd led more of the open dialogue on what Constantine might plan, providing as much background and detail of my own trials as possible. I'd also instructed her on how to listen to the source, something she seemed to be doing more and more.

Today's episode was certainly proof of that—or at least, it'd been the first time I'd seen her accept power directly from the source itself.

Shade had assisted her in other ways, mostly teaching her escape mechanisms and helping her to master shadowing.

He kissed her cheek as she moved off his lap to sit between us. Then she sighed as her head fell back. "This bathtub is better than spritemead."

I chuckled at her drunk-like comment.

Shade merely smiled. "Glad you approve, little rose."

"Definitely approve," she murmured, her legs lifting to kick slightly. "This has to be a Water Fae's wet dream." She snorted a laugh at her own joke, then covered her mouth as she giggled.

"I'll have to send Cyrus notes," I drawled. The Water Fae King would certainly enjoy playing in a tub like this. Although, I suspected he already had one.

Aflora giggled again, then slipped off her bench with a true laugh.

Shade grabbed her arm to pull her back up onto the seat between us, and she shook out her wet hair with a happy sound that made my lips curl.

"You're quite fun while drunk on sex," I informed her, my palm going to her thigh to hold her in place beside me.

She stilled.

Then her hand went to mine to draw it higher.

I glanced sideways at her, grinning when I found her peeking at me through a curtain of dark, damp strands. Her pupils were blown wide, her plump lips begging to be kissed.

Even after all that she'd been through with Zakkai and Zeph, she still craved more.

That was what the dark source could do—it revitalized and recharged, providing ample energy to the one wielding the direct link. And she had the earth source inside her, too.

I cupped her tenderly between her legs, watching her expression as I drew my finger through her slit. She rested against me in response, her eyes closing.

Is she swollen? Shade asked, his icy gaze locked on her face.

I dipped a finger inside her and shook my head. *No, she feels like she always does. Wet and ready.* I leaned in to kiss her mouth, wanting to taste her. She opened for me, her tongue dancing with mine as I stroked her beneath the water.

Her hand rested on my wrist, her nails digging into my skin to encourage my movements. Then she released me and reached for Shade, pulling him to her and kissing him thoroughly.

He languidly indulged her, his palm on her thigh in a similar location to mine moments ago.

I nibbled her neck, my tongue skimming her pulse. It was steady and slow, her movements relaxed.

After her fevered experience with Zakkai and Zeph, it was clear she wanted something a little less hectic. Something more tender and sensual, and Shade and I were more than willing to give her that.

Whatever she wanted or needed, we'd provide.

Even if it was just holding her while she slept.

She shifted away from me to straddle Shade, her arms circling his neck as she continued to engage him in a tender kiss. Not hot or intense, just filled with emotion and love. I felt the emotions thriving through our bond, her contentment to just exist and hold him, her gratitude over everything he'd sacrificed, and her desire to worship him the way he always worshipped her.

She angled her hips to take him inside her, a soft moan parting her full lips as he filled her to the hilt. Then she pulled her mouth from his and focused on me.

"Kols," she whispered, begging me to come closer with her passion-filled gaze. She held out her hand for me as well, ensuring I understood what she wanted.

I drifted toward them in the water, my lips finding hers on impulse as I pressed my palm to her lower back to push her back into Shade. She gasped against me, his hips sliding up at the same time, filling her once more. The water made us all buoyant, creating a languorous rhythm between them.

Her lips left mine to travel down my neck, where she nibbled my pulse.

Then I locked gazes with Shade, his irises smoldering as she rocked against him. His arousal touched our bond, his need an icy kiss to my senses.

I'd never really felt his desire.

He'd always hidden it from me before.

But I sensed it now, our bond wide open and accepting.

Aflora's teeth sank into my neck, drawing a surprised hiss from my chest. Then she swallowed my essence on a groan, her body seemingly possessed by dark magic.

She's learning to embrace her Midnight Fae inclinations, I thought at Shade.

Yes, he agreed, his palm lifting to cup the back of her head. *She's finally realizing who she is.*

Our queen.

Our queen, he echoed on a groan as she righted herself, my blood painting her lips.

He stared up at her through hooded eyes, his hunger spiking through our bond.

Then he pulled her down to lick my essence from her mouth, strengthening our connection to the next level.

It was impulsive.

Yet right.

And it sent a shock wave through my system.

"Take me to bed," Aflora whispered against his mouth. "I want you both to take me to bed."

CHAPTER SIXTEEN

AFLORA

I was drunk on my mates.

Kols kept kissing me, his touch soft and knowing.

Shade licked me, nibbled me, explored me with his hands.

One of them was between my legs, feasting on my needy flesh. The other was in my mouth, his cock hard but not demanding.

We kept switching positions.

Our limbs everywhere. Our mouths dueling. Our bodies gliding, roaming, owning each other.

I lost myself to the sensations, drowned in their combined passion, and gasped when I found them kissing each other. They were just as lost to the connections as I was, their tongues mastering one another before sinking their teeth into each other's necks.

I groaned, the image so erotic and beautiful and intoxicating.

Then Shade took my mouth again, Kols's blood lingering in our kiss. My Elite Blood mate kissed a path down the center of my body to lick me to completion again. I moaned their names, lost to the oblivion they created.

I watched as Kols went down on Shade, his mouth wicked and perfect and bringing the other man to climax after a few knowing pulls.

It all felt like a dream, a fantasy come to life, but the bite marks and bonds confirmed the reality of our intimacy. I felt Zeph and Zakkai in my head, their contentment palpable.

All my mates had bonded in some way, respecting our dynamic and completing our circle in a manner I hadn't realized we'd needed.

Kols slid inside me, his cock thick and pulsing with need. He hadn't come yet. But Shade had orgasmed twice. The first time had been in my mouth. The second time between Kols's lips. And now the Elite Blood—who tasted like my Shade—wanted to come.

I wrapped my legs around his waist, encouraging him to drive into me.

But he kept his pace slow. Loving. Tender.

I groaned, lifting my hips into him, demanding more.

However, his pace never wavered. He kissed me lazily while Shade nibbled at his shoulder. Then Kols guided Shade to my mouth, forcing our tongues to dance while he continued to slide in and out of me. *Slow. Purposeful. Strokes.*

It was the antidote I needed after a long few weeks of training.

The tenderness I hadn't realized I craved.

One of their thumbs—I thought it might be Shade's—found my center, drawing out more pleasure from me. I clamped down around Kols, my ecstasy too great to hold back, and forced him to join me.

He never increased his pace, maintaining those thorough thrusts.

And after he finished, Shade licked me clean.

The two men had never indulged in each other this way, and I could feel their increasing interest through every intimate move. Shade kissed Kols once more, sharing the taste from our lovemaking, and groaned when Kols sucked his tongue clean.

Then they both looked down at me and kissed me at the same time.

It was erotic.

Hot.

Beautiful.

A fantasy I never anticipated.

And I lost myself to them all over again, allowing them to worship me and each other for hours. They kissed away my bruises, renewed me with fresh blood, and ensured I was physically perfect before finally lulling me into a dreamland.

I relaxed, more replete than I'd felt in a very long time.

Only to feel a prickle of heat in my mind, the dark source calling for my attention. *Something isn't right,* I realized, following the strand of discomfort.

No, it wasn't the source... but Midnight Fae.

I could sense them, the disruption, the agony rippling through the kingdom. *What is it?* I wondered, searching for the cause.

So much anger. So much hatred. So much *pain.*

The village.

I could picture it, the tavern up in flames, Anrika's body floating in the sky with a spell inscribed beside her. *Risaleea.*

I searched my memories and those of my mates for the translation, then recognized the spell from Shade's psyche. It was a Death Blood charm cast by a dying Midnight Fae when someone wished to leave behind a message for a loved one.

Is this real? I returned to the village, noting the fires and billowing smoke from the buildings nearby. Everyone was silent, their focus on the stage.

Constantine stood at the center with a scroll in his hand, speaking.

I couldn't hear him, my vision not quite realized.

But all the onlookers appeared distraught.

What's happening? I longed to ask them. I whirled around, sensing the heat and embers of the attack.

Anrika's body looked so alive, her long white hair floating around her like an angelic cape. Her green irises flared with life, but her marbleized skin suggested death.

She didn't blink.

She didn't speak.

Her lips were parted, perhaps from voicing the spell.

And her clothes were singed with ash.

Two more Midnight Fae were on the ground, their skin holding a similar texture. But their eyes were closed, their hands clasped together in peaceful death.

I could sense through the source that they were dead. All of them. That this was real. That what I witnessed now was happening in real time.

Somehow, I was seeing this through the eyes of the crowd, like my link to the dark source had granted me access to all their minds.

I refocused on the stage, my lips parting as Emelyn appeared beside a stoic, dark-haired man. Tears tracked down her cheeks as she tried to plead with him, the word *father* seeming to fall from her lips. But I couldn't hear her, only see.

And then I gasped as Constantine struck her with a spell, yanking her soul from her body and turning her to marble like the others.

No, I thought. *No!* This couldn't be happening. This couldn't be real!

Before I even realized what I was doing, I'd engaged Shade's shadowing ability and I was flying through space to land in the crowd of silence. No one noticed my arrival, the onlookers too busy applauding Emelyn's death.

The sound reverberated through my ears, my arrival allowing me to hear.

But the cheers weren't what I wanted to experience. They were applauding Emelyn's death.

Her dark eyes looked out upon them, frozen in time, agony etched into her features.

He killed her.

Constantine killed *Emelyn.*

My heart stopped, my world crashing to a halt. I couldn't stop staring into her eyes, the lifeless orbs echoing a pain I felt to my very soul.

I was too late.

I couldn't save her.

She was already gone, taken from me, from this realm, by the Elder standing stoically on the platform.

My fingers curled into fists at my sides, my ire mounting by the second.

Only for my blood to freeze in the next minute as a familiar voice screamed, "Tray!"

My neck refused to work, my eyes locked on the stage. A fae approached to remove Emelyn... by smashing her body with a large hammer, shattering her marbled form into a thousand pieces.

I covered my lips, my gasp drowned out by the booming approval around me. *They're celebrating her destruction.* Tears smothered my vision, my soul screaming at the unfairness and wrongness of it all.

Then Dakota appeared, her dark hair styled in an elegant bun that somehow matched her too-perfect face. I nearly growled at the sight of her, the traitorous bitch having hurt more than one of my mates.

Except the wiggling blonde fae beside her captivated all my attention in the next breath.

Ella.

I stopped breathing, my heart no longer functioning, and I barely heard Constantine speaking above the roar in my ears.

"This Halfling traitor knowingly helped an abomination to escape our kingdom, her antics nearly taking the life of her mate, Trayton Nacht. Based on the testimonies of her male mate, the Midnight Fae Council finds her guilty on all counts and has hereby sentenced her to immediate exsanguination."

"He's lying!" she screamed, tears streaming down her cheeks. "Tray, tell them he's lying!"

But Tray did nothing.

He merely stood with the Council off to the side with an expression of indifference. A foreign energy wafted around him, rippling in hypnotic waves as though lulling him into a bizarre state of comfort. *This is just a nightmare. This isn't real.*

However, it felt real.

The dark source pulsed inside me, protesting these antics. It wanted me to act, to do something to stop this madness.

"Please!" Ella cried out.

Dakota laughed, the sound cruel and cold and grating my ears.

Constantine handed her his scroll and pulled a wand from his cloak. Then he began to murmur a spell, the chords of the enchantment underlined with death.

"*Tawaqweej!*" I shouted, blasting his incantation to literal pieces. Shard of rocks splayed across the stage, hitting Ella in the face, but keeping her very much alive.

Constantine didn't hesitate, his lack of surprise telling as he pointed to me in the crowd. "Seize her!"

I'd unknowingly shadowed in with a cloak around my shoulders and hiding my head, which was why no one had noticed me.

But they did now.

A horde of Warrior Bloods appeared from the shadows, the trap evident in the way they moved directly into sight, their focus on me.

Yes, this was definitely real.

Which meant Anrika and Emelyn were dead. Because of this monster. This *thing* that the Midnight Fae chose to follow. Several fae from the crowd pulled their wands and directed them at me, their propensity for violence a dark mark against my psyche.

Midnight Fae kill, I thought, looking around at these lethal beings and their love for drawing blood. *What is wrong with you?*

They all craved death.

They all wanted *my* death.

They all were okay with standing by to watch innocents die.

Unworthy, I thought. *You're all so unworthy.*

Midnight Fae in general weren't kind. They were bad. Evil. Vile. They didn't value life or joy or brightness. They craved the darkness inside their hearts.

I blocked all their incoming spells, the shield Zeph had taught me how to make nearly impenetrable.

And behind it, I growled.

I hated all of them. I hated Midnight Fae. I hated their desire for gruesome displays of torture.

They'd all been enraptured by Constantine's demonstration. Some of them had even *applauded*. Despicable. Wrong. Cruel beings.

I don't want to be like any of you. I don't want to be your queen or represent your kind. You're evil, all of you! I knelt to the ground, a spell lining my lips. I would destroy them all just the way they liked. Teach them all—

Aflora! Shade yelled into my mind, stopping me mid-spell and breaking through some sort of block I'd created in my mind. In the next breath, all my mates entered my thoughts, but Zakkai was the loudest among them.

It's a trial, Zakkai said, his urgency in my mind granting me a brief moment of clarity.

It's not real? I asked, hopeful.

It's real, he replied sadly. *But it's still a trial.*

Anrika… Emelyn…

I know, he replied.

He killed them.

I know, he repeated. *He must have felt you embracing the dark source during training, and he chose to act accordingly. He did all this to trap you.*

I'd already guessed that with the Warrior Bloods.

But I hadn't considered the trial.

Kols had told me the acting monarch could arrange the trials for the successor. This must have been Constantine's idea of an ideal test. *Sick bastard,* I thought, glaring at his smug face through my shield.

Spells continued to bounce off of it, the edges beginning to fray.

Shadow back, Zakkai urged.

I met Ella's frightened blue eyes on the stage and noted Tray's lack of a reaction again. *I can't.*

She'd become one of my closest friends. She'd accepted me before everyone else had. I couldn't leave her. I'd already failed Emelyn. I wouldn't do the same to Ella.

Because there are good Midnight Fae, I realized. I was staring into the eyes of one of them and had four more yelling in my head.

Constantine had enchanted these fae. Or at least some of them, like Tray. Now that I'd removed my fog of fury, I could see that Tray wasn't relaxed at all but was fighting the essence surrounding him, trying like hell to save his mate.

However, whatever incantation Constantine had woven over him was too powerful for him to counteract.

I longed to help him, to dismantle the spell for him, but I didn't have time. The others were almost through my protective barrier. Taking him back to the Hell Fae realm wasn't an option. That spell around him would trigger all sorts of alarms within Lucifer's borders. They'd either kill Tray or deny him entry.

Either way, he'd suffer.

We'll return for you, I promised him, then winced as the final vestiges of my shield began to crumble.

There was only one option left for me now.

I tapped into the dark source, allowing it to consume me like I had several times already, and this time, I granted it access to stay. I didn't expel it. I didn't push it out of me. I *accepted* it as part of my being.

Something clicked inside, a proverbial crown circling my mind, as I stood up tall and stared Constantine right in the eye. "You will bow," I promised him.

Then I shadowed to Ella's side and yanked her away from Dakota before the dark-haired female had a chance to react.

And disappeared back to the paradigm within the Hell Fae realm.

CHAPTER SEVENTEEN

SHADE

Aflora appeared in our meadow, her cloak billowing in the smoke around her. Ella collapsed beside her on a scream that had Kols running right for her.

I grabbed Aflora, checking her for signs of injury beneath the dark fabric surrounding her smaller frame. "Where did you find this?" I asked, stroking my palm down the cloak along her arm. The foreign material contained an electric current, the magic running through it unlike any I'd ever felt.

"I don't know," she whispered, her blue eyes peering up at me from beneath the hood. "He killed Anrika, Shade. And Emelyn."

I flinched, having heard those details from her mind.

"There were others, too," she continued. "And they were *cheering*. Happy. Reveling in the deaths of fellow fae." Her anger lashed at my senses, but her expression radiated pain. "How can they be so cruel and disrespectful with life?"

"Because they've been led to believe it's the only way," my grandmother replied from the tree line, her voice soft and carrying through the meadow on a subtle breeze. She stepped into view beneath the rising sun, her dark hair glittering with the light.

No cookies.

A good sign.

But my grandfathers were behind her, which meant they felt the need to protect her.

Not a good sign.

But as Zeph and Zakkai burst into the meadow, I realized why. While my grandmother admired and respected Zakkai, my grandfathers interpreted his abilities as a potential threat.

An apt reaction. Zakkai was fucking powerful. However, I trusted him with Aflora because I felt her faith in him through the bonds.

"Aflora," he said, his palm finding her face beneath the hood and pulling her to him.

Zeph studied her expression for a beat beside him, pacifying himself with her safety, before switching focus to the shrieking female on the ground.

Ella hadn't stopped crying.

She was telling Kols everything that had happened to Tray, how the Council had taken him and changed him into a dark figure of who he should be. She told him about his father as well, saying Malik was acting just like Tray. And she no idea what had happened to Kols's mother, either. She hadn't seen her in weeks.

"But they're not themselves, Kols. It's not Tray. And your dad isn't your dad," she was repeating again now. "I… I don't know what the Elders or the Council did… but he… Tray told them to kill me. He gave them permission to… to…" She trailed off on a broken sound, and Zeph knelt beside her, his protective energy pouring over her.

"He was surrounded by dark magic." Aflora swallowed. "I could see it, the ropes binding him, but I didn't know how to free him. There wasn't time. And I wasn't sure if… if the Hell Fae realm would accept him like that."

"It would have triggered the wards," my grandmother confirmed.

"With Ella, I somehow knew the wards would accept her. It was instinctual," Aflora continued as though she hadn't heard anyone else. "But Tray… we need to go back—"

"Constantine will be waiting," Zakkai interjected, his thumb hooking beneath her chin to pull her attention to him. "He won't hurt Tray. He already has him on a leash. And if anything, he'll use him as bait. Which means he needs him alive."

Kols growled, not liking the sound of that at all.

He's right, I whispered to his mind. *Constantine won't hurt him any more than he already has. And we need time to formulate a plan. Reacting rashly is what your grandfather wants.*

You think I don't know that? the Elite Blood snapped back at me.

I met his burning irises.

He glared back.

I'm making sure you don't run off and do something that will hurt us all, I told him softly. *He's your twin, Kolstov. We don't always think rationally when it comes to those we love.*

My words and concern came from a tender place inside me that had only ever existed for Aflora. But my relationship with Kols had evolved over the last two months, becoming something I could never have anticipated.

I cared about him.

And last night, we'd shared something… different.

We'd also solidified our mating, having bitten each other several times during our sexual moments with Aflora. He was firmly inside me, just as much as I was inside him.

Which meant he could feel all my emotions, hear my concern, and understood the reasoning behind my words.

While the statements irritated him—his mind quickly telling me that he would never react without thinking through his actions first—he also appreciated my concern.

We'll work together to bring him back, I promised him. *We'll help your dad, too. And I'm sure your mom is okay, just locked up somewhere.*

He grimaced.

We're going to save them, I reiterated, ensuring he heard me.

I know, he replied after a beat, his glare softening to display a measure of understanding before his focus shifted to Aflora. His mind fought for a change of subject, his need for a distraction clear as he whispered, *That cloak is radiating dark energy.*

Yes. I could feel it beneath my fingertips.

Zakkai seemed equally enthralled by it, his palms roaming over the fabric in a similar way to mine moments ago. "This is a gift from the source," he marveled.

"Yes," my grandmother agreed, reminding us all of her presence. "And I have the matching staff."

We all looked at her. "Matching staff?" I repeated.

She merely smiled, then cocked her head. "Come. Breakfast is almost ready."

"Cookies?" I asked warily.

"Eggs," she replied. "And blood shakes. Aflora will need one soon. As will Ella."

"Will Lucifer be okay with her presence here?" Zakkai wondered out loud, voicing a concern I hadn't considered.

My grandmother's blue eyes sparkled knowingly as she glanced at him. "Yes, Kai. I cleared it with him already."

"Have you cleared anything else with him?" he pressed.

She blinked. "Why? Do you sense something?"

He didn't reply, just stared at her.

She studied him for a long moment, then turned toward the trees without another word.

His jaw ticked in reply. "She's not telling us something."

"Welcome to my world," I muttered.

"You mean other people keep secrets from you?" Zeph asked, feigning a note of shock. "How horrible for you. I have no idea how that feels." The sarcasm in his tone made me snort.

"Where are we?" Ella's soft tones drew our focus to her. She hadn't moved away from the ground, her pale features marred by tears. But she seemed to have stopped crying for now, her attention distracted by the meadow around us and the rising sun.

"A paradigm within the Hell Fae realm," Aflora replied. She pulled away from me and Zakkai to look at Ella. "And I'll get Tray back for you. Soon."

She sounded so regal and confident, the dark source swarming around her with free abandon.

I glanced at Zakkai and then at Kols. Both of them were studying her cloak again.

Zakkai spoke first. "You accepted the dark source, passing your third trial."

"Yes," she confirmed. "But I'm still the Earth Fae Queen, too."

"Because you taught the sources how to play nicely together," Zakkai said, appreciation evident in his tone and features. "It's beautiful, Aflora." He stepped toward her again, his palm returning to her face as he tipped her head back for a kiss. "You're stunning."

She returned his embrace, her power flowing openly through all our bonds.

"Breakfast will get cold." My grandmother's voice carried to us on the breeze once more, her energy brushing my skin. "Aflora needs blood."

"I do," my mate confirmed, her voice suddenly tired. "The source… requires it."

"Yes," Kols agreed, his tone soft. "It's taxing and will need to be fed daily."

Aflora nodded, her hand reaching for mine. "Lead the way, Shade." Energy sizzled along her palm, crawling up my arm as I laced our fingers together. She'd definitely grown in power, her acceptance of the source subtly altering her.

She no longer doubts herself, Kols said to me. *That's what you're sensing. She finally sees herself as the rightful queen.*

I think it's more than that, I replied. *It's not that she sees herself as the rightful queen so much as she wants to help those who need her, to be the queen they deserve, and to remove the ones tainting the Midnight Fae realm.*

When I'd crashed through her walls earlier, I'd felt her uncertainty and her displeasure over the pain lurking inside the dark source. She wanted to fix it, to become the entity that righted the wrongs of others, that set the Midnight Fae on the correct path.

It was what made her the perfect queen—she always put others before herself. She understood the value of leading by example. And she would never allow the power to consume her.

Her blue eyes slid to mine from beneath her cloak, her expression warm and welcoming. *I love you, Shadow. I love that you see me.*

We all see you, little rose, I told her. *And we all love you.*

Her lips curled.

I stopped walking to pull her in for a kiss, my lips whispering over hers as I said, "And I more than love you, Aflora. You're my reason for everything."

They were publicly said words meant for her ears alone. But all her mates heard them.

No one commented.

No one interrupted.

They just allowed the moment to prosper for one beautiful second, then I resumed our path toward my grandmother's home. It came into view beyond the trees, the door open in invitation.

All six of us entered, the room expanding to accommodate us all as we stepped inside. "Clever," Zakkai murmured, impressed by the magic.

The table elongated as well, then several chairs appeared out of thin air. I led Aflora to one and took a seat beside her. Zakkai settled on her opposite side. Zeph, Kols, and Ella all sat across from us. Then my grandfathers took the heads of the table, leaving the chair across from Aflora available for my grandmother.

"I don't believe we've met," Kols said, looking at my grandfather Vadim. "But I can see the resemblance." He glanced at me and then back at my grandfather.

We both had dark hair, ice-blue eyes, and sharp cheekbones. He also somewhat resembled my mother, but Kols wouldn't know that, as my mother was rarely seen in public.

Grandfather Kodiak resembled a Fortune Fae with his bulkier build and alpha fangs. Although, his blue eyes weren't slitted like a true alpha, his transition having been paused in a unique way when he'd mated with my grandmother.

"King Vadim, yes?" Kols continued.

"I prefer Vadim, no 'King,'" my grandfather replied, his lips twitching as he glanced at his Fortune Fae Alpha mate.

"Not happening," Grandfather Kodiak murmured.

"Pity," Grandfather Vadim replied.

My grandmother snorted as she set a glass of blood in front of my grandfather Vadim, then she passed an orange juice to Grandfather Kodiak. "Behave."

"Never," they said at the same time.

"I feel like this is my future," Aflora murmured, blinking at the two men. "Only multiplied by two."

My grandmother smiled at her. "A beautiful path, yes?" She reached for the blender to pour Aflora a shake, then brought it over to the table. Her blue irises landed on the rest of us, her gaze calculating. Then she went back to the blender to create more.

I magicked a straw for Aflora, sliding it into her drink before she could take a sip. *Thank you,* she whispered into my mind.

You're welcome. I kissed her temple and waited for my grandmother to finish serving everything. I would have offered to help, but I knew she'd scold me for trying. She liked to entertain. This house was her domain, something both my grandfathers knew and respected, so they didn't try to assist either.

Omegas were particular about their space.

Especially with a nest nearby.

She adorned the table with a platter of eggs, a dish of bacon, a basket of breakfast pastries, and more red-tinted shakes. Then she placed a floral fruit salad adorned with leaves in front of Aflora.

"Oh, look, mustard berries," Zeph said conversationally.

"I believe they're called mouseberries," my grandmother corrected.

"See?" Aflora arched a brow. "*Mouseberries.*"

"Hmm," he hummed, reaching across the table to steal one from her plate. "Delicious."

"Liar," she replied, grinning. "Thank you, Zen."

"Of course, dear. I didn't think you would enjoy the bacon." She sat down with a flourish as my grandfather Kodiak began to assemble her plate. She might have served us all, but he would ensure she had the first helping.

We all waited as the Fortune Fae Alpha worked. He assembled a dish for Grandfather Vadim as well, then started on his own before handing the serving utensils to Zakkai.

It was a symbolic gesture, one that said he felt Zakkai was the unequivocal alpha of our circle.

Kols met my gaze with a smirk, having heard my thoughts. *Don't tell Zeph.*

Not today, anyway, I agreed, momentarily entertained. *But when this is all said and done? No promises.*

Deal, Kols agreed.

Zakkai, who was very well versed in Fortune Fae formalities, assembled a plate for me first, suggesting he saw me as the group Omega. I rolled my eyes at him. "Hilarious."

He just grinned and went about creating a dish for Kols, who was equally unamused by his antics.

Then he started assembling a dish for Zeph, only for the Guardian to say, "I'll get my own."

Whether he understood the significance of that or not, I wasn't sure.

Zakkai replied by finishing the plate and handing it to Ella.

"Thank you," she whispered, clearly overwhelmed by the table politics.

Zakkai didn't acknowledge her gratitude, instead looking at Aflora. "Do you want anything else, little star?"

She shook her head, already halfway through her fruit plate. "No, thank you."

He kissed her temple, slowly fixed himself a plate, and eventually passed the utensils to a quietly simmering Zeph. "Here," he said.

Kols bit his lip to keep from smiling.

I just shook my head at their dominance war. Apparently, the little fuck fest yesterday hadn't solved their alpha duel problem.

But it was a little less tense, like the two of them knew how to see eye to eye and work together now. At least where Aflora was concerned.

She sipped her shake through the straw, then watched as I took a bite of eggs with bacon. Her nose crinkled as she leaned forward to sniff my plate. "Troll fat?" she asked, making me choke.

"What?"

"Cooked troll fat," she replied, grimacing. "You call it bacon?"

My grandmother released a small laugh. "It's from a pig in the Human Realm."

Aflora blanched. "A *pig*?"

"You remember that brown crap on the bloody noodles?" Kols asked conversationally, causing Aflora's eyes to round.

"Ugh, yes. Don't remind me."

He chuckled, then shoveled a forkful of egg and bacon into his mouth with an "Mmm" sound.

She gagged and focused on her fruit salad again—a fruit salad that magically grew as Zeph discreetly hummed a spell. Some of her disgust seemed to melt at the sight of her colorful berries, her gaze flicking up to him in clear gratitude.

He winked in response.

Then the rest of us ate in silence.

Ella was the only one who didn't seem to share in any of our amusement, her expression melancholy as she forced herself to sip her shake.

My heart ached for her. "Have you seen or heard from Ajax?" I asked her softly.

Her blue eyes lifted to mine, the sadness in them making my stomach clench.

I swallowed. "What happened to Ajax?"

She shook her head, a tear falling down her cheek. "They… they separated all of us. He was in line behind me. In line to be…"

"Executed," Aflora finished for her, magic seeming to swirl around her being. "I have to—"

"He's safe," my grandmother said, reaching for her hand. "Trust me."

"Safe like Aflora's parents were safe?" Zakkai asked. "Or safe like Aflora is now, safe?"

"Careful," Grandfather Kodiak warned in a low growl.

Zakkai looked at him without an ounce of fear. "It's a fair question, Kodiak."

"Your uncle has him," my grandmother said. "With Kyros."

My shoulders sagged in relief. If Tadmir and Kyros had Ajax, then he was fine. Unless… "Does he know about Emelyn?"

"Yes." My grandmother's expression was sad. "That's why Tadmir has him. He's trying to calm him down."

"Does he know about his parents yet?" Zakkai asked.

"His parents?" I repeated.

Aflora gasped, dropping her fork. "The two bodies under Anrika…"

Zakkai cast her an apologetic look. "Yes, little star."

"Oh, Fae…"

My appetite dissolved, the food in my stomach beginning to turn restlessly inside me. *Fuck.* "I need a minute," I said, pushing away from the table to step outside. *Fuck. Fuck. Fuck!*

Ajax's parents had already been attacked once. Now they were dead? And Emelyn, too?

I felt Kols join me, his warmth a presence at my back. *Why would Ajax care about Emelyn?* he asked softly, his mind searching mine. I didn't reply, but he found the answer he wanted lurking inside my mind. *Ah. I see.*

He leaned against the house, blowing out a breath. "Shit."

"An adequate summary," I muttered, pacing and running my fingers through my hair. Ajax was strong. He could withstand a lot. But this… "I need to find him."

"No," he replied.

"What do you mean, *no?*" He had to know me well enough by now to realize that I didn't adhere to authority. I managed my own life, made my own choices, and I wasn't about to bend to his will in the process.

"I mean, *no,*" he reiterated, his tone all regal elegance. "You can't go to him."

"Fuck off," I said, no longer interested in whatever he had to say. "Just because we're bonded doesn't mean you have a say in what I do and don't do now." Only Aflora had that right. No one else.

"Yet you felt the need to remind me of my purpose here when you felt my yearning to go to Tray, and that was all of, what, thirty minutes ago?" His bronze irises narrowed. "Is this truly so different, Shadow?"

His words hit me in the heart, the rightness of them drawing a curse from my lips. Because fucking Fae, he was right.

I gripped my hair by the roots and closed my eyes.

He pressed a palm to my lower back half a beat later.

Then he pulled me into his arms, offering me a hug that I hadn't realized I needed. Part of me wanted to punch him for touching me, for correcting my path before I could even walk down it. And a weaker part of me just wanted to collapse.

I'd played with time, nearly costing Kols his life.

And now Emelyn, Anrika, and Ajax's parents were gone.

Never to return.

Dead.

Because of me? I wondered. *Because of my altering of fate?*

Because of my grandfather, Kols corrected, his opposite arm wrapping around my shoulders to squeeze me tight. *Not you, Shadow. Never you.*

I released a shuddering breath, my heart in my throat.

Then I buried my face in his neck and inhaled his spicy aftershave. It was underlined with roses, reminding me of Aflora. *You smell like our mate,* I mused.

So do you, he murmured. *But not roses. I smell power and mint.*

That could just be me, I drawled.

He chuckled and let me go with a shake of his head. "You wish." Then he clapped me on the shoulder. "You good?"

"No," I admitted. "But I will be."

He nodded. "When we kill my grandfather."

"When we kill your grandfather," I agreed.

"Sounds like the perfect date," Zeph said from the doorway, his shoulder propped up against the door frame. "Will there be chocolates and flowers afterward?"

"Depends on our mate," Kols replied, turning toward him with a grin. "Or maybe just some paste."

"Mmm, now you're speaking my language." Zeph pulled Kols in for a searing kiss before meeting my gaze in challenge. *Mine,* he was saying.

I rolled my eyes. "He's all yours, Headmaster." Except for when Aflora wanted to play with us again. Then I'd indulge her desires because they were secretly becoming mine, too.

I heard that, Kols murmured.

I wasn't exactly hiding it, I told him.

No. His auburn hair flickered like fire from the sunlight spilling in through the trees, the ash-tipped strands particularly bright. *No, you're no longer hiding at all.* A hint of emotion touched his bronze irises. *I can feel what you've sacrificed for us, Shadow.*

My first instinct was to shove him out of my head, but I was too tired to try. If he wanted to play in my memories, I'd allow it.

They don't understand what you've given up for us, but I do. As does Aflora.

I didn't reply.

Because there really wasn't much left to say.

We're on the right path now, he whispered. *Now come back inside.*

He turned to lead the way with Zeph beside him.

Zakkai glanced up as I walked inside. He had his arm around Aflora's chair, his thumb brushing her back through the cloak. She'd dropped her hood but remained otherwise wrapped up in it.

Which reminded me of why we'd come here in the first place. "Tell us about this staff," I told my grandmother. "Please."

CHAPTER EIGHTEEN

ZAKKAI

The power radiating off of Aflora seduced my senses, taunting my Quandary Blood abilities. I kept losing myself in her cloak, the tendrils whirling around her filled with delicious energy.

She leaned into my side, her strength waning despite the blood in Zenaida's shake. Aflora would need to properly feed soon. Yesterday's training and today's trial had left her replete and in need of more sustenance. I would ensure she received those nutrients just as soon as we finished up with whatever game Zenaida wanted to play.

She'd made a show of cleaning up the dining table, but Kodiak had insisted on helping her with the dishes, saying she needed to focus on the guests. I gathered from her pinched brow that she would be having a word with him on that later, her desire as an Omega to manage her space evident in the way she kept glancing over to inspect his work in the kitchen.

Her eyes took on a silvery gleam for a moment as the future presented itself to her. After a beat, her features relaxed and she led us to the living area —which expanded like the dining room to accommodate everyone.

I took a seat on a couch with Aflora. Zephyrus settled into the cushion on her opposite side, his arm stretching out behind her while I clasped her hand in my lap.

Shadow and Kolstov took over the love seat.

Ella, short for Isabella, sat in a solitary chair, her shoulders hunched. However, her eyes were vivid and very much alive. I'd never met the girl, but I knew of her through Aflora.

A Halfling.

Mate to Trayton Nacht.

Not all that powerful, but an Elite Blood with mortal qualities after being raised in the Human Realm.

Aflora liked her. They were friends. Therefore, I would protect her by default. Even if I didn't approve of her mating a Nacht.

Kolstov's twin, I thought, pinching my lips a little.

Well, if Trayton ended up like Kolstov, I would forgive it.

Maybe.

Aflora laid her head on my shoulder. *Tray's a good Midnight Fae*, she told me softly, showing me a strand in her mind that blinked brightly within the dark source. *We will save him.*

As you wish, little star, I whispered, awed by how easily she pulled up the life strands of Midnight Fae within the dark source. She didn't seem to realize how advanced that was in terms of power. The dark source was already treating her like a queen, despite the four trials ahead.

"This is the staff," Zenaida said, pointing at the table.

I arched a brow at the flat, empty surface.

But Aflora gasped as something revealed itself to her exclusively. "May I?" she asked.

Zephyrus met my gaze over her head, his bemused expression rivaling my own feelings. *What do you see, little star?*

Magic, she whispered. *Beautiful magic.*

"Yes," Zenaida replied as she settled onto Vadim's lap. The chair he'd taken over was wide enough for them to share it side by side, but the Omega seemed to be craving the touch of her mate. Perhaps because her Alpha was still cleaning the kitchen and she needed someone to hold her back from taking over the task.

Or maybe she just wanted to be held.

He wrapped his arms around her, the adoration in his face reminding me of the way Shade often looked at Aflora.

Aflora leaned forward, her fingers curling around air—air that manifested in a vine as she lifted it from the table.

My eyes widened.

Not a vine. A staff.

But the obsidian rock curled around the long, dark pole like a snake-vine up to the impressive sphere at the top. Color glittered from the orb, flashes of cerulean, purple, red, and green, with the underlying core being as black as a starless night.

Magic hummed through the air, reminding me of a wand, the staff immediately taking to Aflora and alighting with powerful approval.

I pulled out the wand Aflora had been using to compare, noting how the magical conduit no longer acknowledged her as the owner.

Because she'd just inherited her true source—the staff. "Where did you find this, Zen?" I asked, using her preferred name only because I wanted her to give me a real answer, not a riddle.

"It's the royal staff," Kolstov whispered, awe in his tone.

I glanced at him, having never heard of such a thing. "Royal staff?"

"A relic." He admired the electricity swirling around the circle at the top. "It was rumored to have been stolen and destroyed by the Quandary Bloods."

Zenaida snorted. "Not stolen or destroyed, but rightfully mine as the Midnight Fae Queen. However, that cloak around Aflora's shoulders is a sign from the dark source. The staff has chosen a new owner. Which is why she could see it when the rest of you couldn't. Set it back down, Aflora, and show them."

Aflora bent to lay it on the table, and sure enough, the magical conduit disappeared.

However, the energy lingered behind it, my Source Architect power allowing me to identify the general makeup of the staff without actually seeing it. Sort of like looking into an electrical field and sensing the magnetic pulses but being unable to identify the unique layers themselves.

"That's fascinating," I said, impressed. "Who created it?"

"Who creates wands?" she countered.

A fair retort to a stupid question on my part. "The source." Of course. Just like the dark source had created the cloak around Aflora's shoulders and the choker at her throat holding it on her.

The clothes beneath the cloak were magical as well, but I suspected those were born of necessity for propriety more than the dark source gifting her magic. She would have been naked when she'd shadowed to the village. Just as I'd been naked when I'd started running toward the meadow earlier to find her.

A quick spell had gifted me a button-down shirt, pants, and proper shoes.

Zephyrus wore a matching outfit.

Kolstov and Shade were just in their sleep bottoms and T-shirts.

What an interesting pack we made, our magic all unevenly matched and yet complementary to each other.

I lifted my ankle to rest it on my opposite knee, my focus on Zenaida. "What else did you and Lucifer negotiate?" I asked her, changing the topic away from the staff because I knew that wasn't the only reason she wanted us here.

Zenaida adored her word games.

And I was a master at solving riddles.

Her blue eyes gleamed with amusement, pleased to have had her game spoiled. Of course, we both knew I'd been aware from the beginning that she was hiding something from us.

I'd just given her time to play hostess, had indulged in breakfast—which, thankfully, had not been poisoned, something I'd verified with magic before taking a bite—and had allowed her to give Aflora the staff because I'd assumed it would be beneficial for her next trial.

"Your father has requested entry," Zenaida said softly. "I negotiated it, and the request has been granted."

"Unity trial," I replied, looking at Kolstov and then at Aflora before refocusing on Zenaida. "How long do we have to prepare?"

The Fortune Fae Omega blinked. "Not long."

Meaning he was already on his way here. "Is he at the gates yet?" I asked casually, already mentally considering our options.

"Yes," Aflora replied, reaching for the staff, power rippling around her. "I can feel them." Her blue eyes met mine. "He's brought several Quandary Bloods with him."

"That's quite the negotiation, Zenaida," I muttered, glancing at the seer. "I assume you failed to give us notice for a reason?"

"There are no other paths, Zakkai. We were always destined to meet again. And Aflora deserved the break, regardless of how fleeting it could be." She clasped her hands in her lap. "So now the sides will either join forces or…"

"Destroy each other," I finished for her. "Thank you for the meal." That'd been her version of helping us rejuvenate before Aflora's next trial. My poor mate wasn't even being given days to recover, just hours. But now that the source had marked her with the cloak, it would want to accelerate her ascension—something Constantine had assured would happen with his antics today.

The Elder had out-strategized me again.

My jaw ticked at the knowledge, my veins flooding with anticipation. "Time to go."

"There's more blood in the fridge," Zenaida murmured. "Take it with you. Aflora will need it."

Rather than take the offer, I bit into my wrist and held it to Aflora's mouth.

My mate didn't hesitate, taking what she needed before Zephyrus followed suit.

Zenaida merely smiled, her gaze knowing. "We'll keep Ella here while you negotiate," she said softly. Then she looked at the woman, her expression brightening. "I'll make you cookies, dear. You'll love them."

Shade glanced sharply at his grandmother, but she was already on her way back to shoo Kodiak out of her kitchen.

His icy eyes met mine, his concern palpable.

"We approach them as a unit," I said as Aflora finished drinking from Kolstov's vein. Shade was last.

Then the five of us left with Aflora carrying her new staff and leading the way, her confident strides a novel behavior that I hadn't seen from her before.

It was a definite improvement.

And befitted a queen.

My lips curled at the sight, and I realized all the others wore similar expressions.

Because they were all thinking the same thing as me.

She's ready.

CHAPTER NINETEEN

AFLORA

The staff reminded me of a wand in weight, the magical conduit fitting in my hand and moving with me like an extension of my arm.

Magical swirls danced around it, tickling my skin as the source embraced me with fiery little kisses that disappeared into my cloak.

It all felt so natural, like my connection to earth, the life and darkness swirling through me with renewed vigor after having taken blood from all four of my mates.

The act of drinking from them didn't bother me.

But I would absolutely not be indulging in their cuisine choices.

Pig Yuck.

I'll make you all the shroom loaves you can eat, pixie flower, Zeph vowed, having caught my thought. *I'll even add your favorite mouseberries.*

Dragon steak loaf could be fun, I replied. *Topped with potato frites?*

Are those like french fries?

What are french fries? I asked, frowning at him.

Fried potatoes.

I blinked. *Purple ones? Or green ones?*

He glanced at me, his green eyes sparkling. *We are definitely not talking about the same food.*

Probably not, I decided. I almost opened my mouth to detail the flaming mush, but a disturbance within the paradigm had my focus shifting to the Academy.

Shade had shadowed us most of the way back, saving us time and energy from having to walk. We were near the main gates now, and I could see the group of Quandary Bloods lurking beyond it.

The gargoyles were all agitated, as were the snake-vines, but a breath of calmness from me settled them all as we approached.

Other Midnight Fae watched from the sidelines, their expressions grim. "Go back to your dorms," I said to them, my tone holding a command to it. It was the middle of the day. They should all be asleep despite the ever-present moon on this side of the paradigm.

Several bowed and scampered back into their buildings, giving me slight pause.

Hot, Zeph praised. *So fucking hot.*

All I did was tell them to go inside.

In a regal-as-fuck queenly tone, he said. *I want you to use that on Kols later.*

I almost rolled my eyes. *Do you ever not think about sex?*

A chorus of *"No"* sounded in my head, all my mates apparently having heard my question. Probably because it had the word *sex* involved.

Zakkai's fingers locked with mine, his palm heating my senses as his power rolled through me to flirt with the embers created by the staff in my other hand.

Zeph stood on my opposite side with Kols and Shade behind us.

A united front, just like Zakkai had said.

The gates opened for me as I approached, Laki standing on the other side. He had his hands tucked into the pockets of his charcoal-colored dress pants, his white button-down shirt unclamped at the top with the sleeves rolled to the elbows on each arm.

He looked a lot like Zakkai—same color eyes, similar shade of hair, tall, lean, muscular. Their Midnight Fae genetics gave them a brotherly appearance more than a father-son one, similar to how Zen resembled Shade's older sister, not his grandmother.

But ages for fae were in the eyes.

And I could tell as I met Laki's gaze that he had at least a millennium on Zakkai.

Which made sense with Midnight Fae royalty ascending once every one thousand years.

"Father," Zakkai greeted.

"Son," Laki returned. "I see you're still mated and that you've acquired some new bonds."

"Only one," he replied, glancing back at Kols before redirecting his focus back to his dad. The challenge in his stance dared his father to comment or issue a command, but rather than acknowledge whom Zakkai had bonded to, Laki's attention shifted to me.

"Aflora." He uttered my name with a softness that surprised me. "You've certainly blossomed into something unexpected." His silver-blue irises admired the staff and then my cloak. "Midnight Fae royalty looks good on you."

"She does wear it rather nicely," Zakkai agreed, squeezing my hand.

I smiled and stepped deliberately to the side. "Let's do this inside the gates. While the exterior of the paradigm is well protected, the creatures would feel more comfortable with us inside the walls." My words were instinctual and caused by the agitated hissing of the snake-vines. They weren't upset by the arrival of the Quandary Bloods so much as their location.

Laki's ash-blond eyebrow cocked upward in surprise, then he nodded in agreement and led the others with him inside.

There were fifteen Midnight Fae in total, including Laki, making up only a fraction of the ones I'd seen back at Zakkai's paradigm. "Where are the others?"

"Waiting for the outcome of this discussion," he said.

"I see." I considered where to take them. We needed a place big enough for everyone to speak.

The history library, Shade suggested softly. *It has a big table at the center that will seat us all, and it'll be abandoned at this time of day.*

Where is it? I asked.

Rather than reply, he stepped up to Zakkai's side and gave him a look. The Quandary Blood nodded, releasing my hand.

Laki watched the exchange with a curious expression, his surprise palpable as Zakkai stepped behind me to walk beside Kols.

This way, Shade said to me, taking over the group and leading us to a building toward the center of the Academy.

"I miss this place," Laki said conversationally as we walked. He'd taken up a position beside Zakkai, placing him near Shade's back.

But the lack of aggression in the air told me no one was in the mood to fight. Laki and his followers had arrived to talk, just like he'd said.

That probably had a little bit to do with Lucifer as well. No one would want to tempt the Hell Fae King into coming down to dole out justice for breaking whatever rules he'd set for this paradigm.

I'd heard whispers and stories about Lucifer, enough to know that, depending on his mood, he might actually enjoy watching a battle unfold here.

Fortunately, no one seemed to be in the mood to tempt fate and invite him out to play.

Shade guided us toward a set of large double doors outside a particularly beautiful building with stone walls and tinted glass windows.

Inside, the ceiling appeared to be at least twelve stories over our heads despite the exterior being no more than two floors tall, and all the interior walls were covered in books and windows. *Oh*, I thought, admiring the beauty of the shelves and the winding staircases leading up to each area individually. *Why haven't you shown me this place?*

We've been a little busy mastering physical arts, he replied. *And no, that's not a euphemism for sex.*

Any other time, I would have laughed.

But we had a horde of very serious fae behind us.

Shade squeezed my hand, then started toward the center of the space where a table with four chairs sat conspicuously in the middle of an ornate blue-and-white rug fringed with gold.

He placed his foot on loose strings, then stepped back as the table and chairs began to rattle.

"Oh, hello, hello!" a feminine voice called from above. "Well, well, what do we have here?"

"A party of twenty, please," Shade said.

"Yes, yes, of course!" Wind whipped through the air as an invisible figure began pulling the table apart.

A figment? I guessed. *Like at Acaward?*

Figments, Shade replied. *And yes.*

I almost asked why it was plural, when another female called, "No, no, over here."

"Yes, just like that," added a third.

"Drinks? Snacks? Blood?" a fourth offered.

"Blood coffees," Zakkai said. "And scones."

"Oh, he's fancy. Fancy, fancy, fancy. I like fancy." His white strands blew around his face as the figment did something to his cheek.

Did she just kiss you?

Unfortunately, he muttered, glaring at the space.

"Grumpy, too!" The figment giggled and repeated the action against his face.

"Careful," Zeph drawled. "He belongs to the Midnight Fae Queen."

"Oh, I don't mind," I said, absolutely amused by Zakkai's expression right now.

His silver-blue eyes slid toward me. *You're going to regret that later, little star.*

Am I? I gave him an innocent look. *How terrible for me.*

Brat, he accused, grunting as the figment placed a third kiss against his face with a loud smack before tittering off into the distance. *Pretty sure she just grabbed my groin.*

I'm sure it impressed her, I replied. *She'll probably kiss you again now.*

Laki cleared his throat, I thought perhaps to grab my attention, until I realized it was to smother a chuckle. "Figments are always attracted to power," he said, his tone not matching the humor in his gaze.

"Then, by that account, it's Aflora they should be hitting on," Zeph drawled.

The figments all giggled again, chairs and table pieces appearing out of thin air as they reassembled the center of the room. I stepped back as the rug began to grow to accommodate us, the area transforming in a wild show of moving furniture and chittering figments.

When they finished, one of them kissed me on the forehead, and another whispered, "Lucky, lucky queen," in my ear. I suspected that comment was from the figment who had fondled Zakkai.

After a whirlwind of activity, the air began to calm, coffee cups and carafes manifested along a white cloth down the center of the table, and plates of scones appeared at every place setting in front of twenty chairs.

"Enjoy!" the figments cheered, disappearing up into the rafters above, likely to watch and wait for further desires.

Well, that… I swallowed. *That was something else entirely.*

Welcome to the library, Shade replied, then pulled out a chair at the center of the table. Somehow he knew I wouldn't want to sit at the head position, but among the others to better hear them all.

He took the position on the other side of me, then Zakkai held out a chair next to me and looked pointedly at Kols.

The Elite Blood stared at him for a beat before taking the offering.

Zakkai settled in the seat beside him, stretching out his arm along the back in a show of clear protection of Kols, and placed his palm on my shoulder.

The Quandary Bloods in attendance watched the interaction with rapt attention.

Laki might be their leader, but Zakkai was their king.

And he'd just demonstrated through action that he considered Kols to be under his protection. More than that, he'd treated him as royalty by pulling out his chair like one would for a better.

Zeph sat down next to Shade, his expression giving nothing away. But I heard the wonder in his mind, his surprise over Zakkai's actions evident. I think we were all feeling that way.

Having a link to my Quandary Blood mate allowed me to understand why he'd done it. He was demonstrating his affiliation with our circle, claiming us as his.

Which meant his people should treat us with respect.

"Be seated," he told them.

Laki smirked but did as his son had demanded, taking the position across from us. Then the others began to find their locations as well.

I turned to lean my staff against my chair, not wanting to hold it through the meal, and rotated back around to find the entire table staring at my magical conduit. Frowning, I glanced back at it, then at them, and then back at my staff again. *What?* I asked my mates. *What's wrong?*

It disappeared again, Zakkai explained, his focus on the others. *And going by the expression on my father's face, he knows why.*

"Zen gave you the staff," Laki said, admiration in his tone. "Which, I gather, means that you now speak for her and those under this dome. I suppose we should begin, then."

CHAPTER TWENTY

ZAKKAI

Symbolism, I realized. That was the meaning for Zenaida giving Aflora the staff today.

Oh, I had no doubt it was also because of the cape and the source showing its favor by kissing Aflora with magic, but Zenaida had strategically chosen that moment to present the staff, knowing my father would see it for what it meant—*Aflora is our queen.*

Clever, Zenaida, I mused, relaying my knowledge to Aflora in a brief synopsis of the thoughts in my head.

Does that mean she agrees with my path forward? Aflora wondered.

Undoubtedly, I said. But I could have told her that without the staff. Hell, I hadn't even known the thing existed until today, but clearly, my father had recognized it.

"You never mentioned the staff to me before," I said to him. "Why?"

"Because it was never relevant. Zen was the Midnight Fae Queen, the staff a gift presented to her by the source over a thousand years ago. She rarely used it, and I never expected her to give it to another fae." His focus went to Aflora. "But I'll admit, it suits you."

"Yes," I agreed. "It does."

A few others murmured positive remarks as well, the respect at the table seeming to increase with each passing second.

Finally, the other Quandary Bloods sat, their gazes reverently downcast rather than staring at Aflora head-on.

Zephyrus broke the silence by reaching for one of the carafes first, filling Shade's mug and then his own. My lips twitched in memory of the breakfast where I'd done the same to Shade, treating him as the Omega of our circle.

His icy gaze slid to mine now, his lack of humor evident.

I made a show of distributing coffee on my side as well. First to Aflora, then to Kolstov, and eventually to myself before passing the ceramic carafe to my father.

Everyone else began pouring their own, some of them taking eager sips after tasting the blood lacing the warm liquid.

Aflora only gingerly tasted hers before focusing on my father once more.

He relaxed into his chair, eyeing her with a mixture of admiration and wariness.

"So I assume you've chosen the side of reformation, then?" he guessed.

It wasn't a question for me, or he would have spoken in a harsher tone.

This one was for Aflora, and I was genuinely curious to hear how she would reply.

"No." She leaned forward, clasping her hands on the table beside her untouched pastry plate. "I've not chosen reformation or retribution. Because you're both wrong."

A few of the Quandary Bloods glanced at each other. My father merely lifted an eyebrow. "I see." He studied her for a moment. "Then tell me what you believe is right. Detail your plan."

She shook her head. "No," she repeated. "First, I need you to understand why retribution isn't the correct path." Her gaze flickered to Kolstov apologetically, causing my brow to furrow.

Then I felt the energy shifting in the room as she brought up a memory spell to showcase what she'd observed in the village earlier.

I wasn't even aware she knew this charm, but before I could ask how she'd learned it, the memory began to play before my eyes like a vivid picture.

I could not only see everything, but I could also feel the warmth of the crowd, hear their laughs and cheers, and sense the urgency coming from the dark source, just as Aflora had earlier.

Emelyn was already dead.

Then Dakota appeared, dragging an unwilling Ella onto the stage.

Constantine read out her conviction.

Ella screamed.

And Aflora focused on Trayton.

Which was where she froze the memory, her voice entering all our minds as she said, *Do you see it? The compulsion wrapping around him like a thick rope, strangling the male beneath?*

She increased the clarity, ensuring we all could see and feel the malevolent energy.

Then she slowly pulled the memory from our minds, returning us all to the room on a shiver of cold air.

She picked up her coffee to take a sip, her stance perfectly composed, but I felt her aching for Trayton as well as for Kolstov.

A hum of static opened between them as he spoke to her, and her to him.

Then he reached beneath the table to press his palm to her thigh, squeezing it gently.

She set down the ceramic mug, the sound echoing in the stillness of the room.

"Well," she prompted, meeting my father's impassive gaze. "Did you see it?"

"Yes."

"You're aware of what it means?"

"Yes," he repeated.

She nodded. "For the others, in case you couldn't sense the compulsion charm around him, Tray is a prisoner in his own body. The spell isn't visible to others. He acts and appears completely normal to them. But the dark source showed me the truth. And it showed me that truth because it aches for those who are being manipulated by this magic, which tells me Tray is not the only one compromised by this spell."

A fair deduction.

And a reasonable explanation.

"Constantine is clearly the orchestrator of this magic," she continued. "So he needs to be removed."

My eyes narrowed slightly at her word choice—a word that reverberated through her mind, telling me she'd chosen it with purpose. But she didn't allow me to follow it to completion, her strategy already moving ahead to the next phase of her decision.

"Once he's removed, we will need to try those who have been involved in the extermination of Midnight Fae and test them for this spell." She clasped her hands once more on the table, leaning forward ever so slightly. "Those found to be complicit by choice will be dealt with accordingly. Others will be freed from their confinement."

I took a sip of my coffee, considering her words along with the others.

Not once did she mention death. Just *removed*, which was a very carefully selected word.

Because my mate was all about life.

And that told me whatever she truly intended to do would be about creation, not destruction.

"It's not a fully contrived plan, but it's a fair one," she concluded. "It marries retribution to reformation. Because we will punish those who have wronged the Midnight Fae, and we will reform this realm."

"And you expect us to just join you in this effort? To trust you to see it through?" my father asked, a hint of censure in his tone.

"Yes," she replied.

Both his eyebrows shot up. "Just like that?"

Now it was her turn to repeat the word. "Yes."

He huffed a laugh. "I had no idea you were so naïve, Aflora."

She responded with a laugh of her own, but it lacked humor.

"Why do all Midnight Fae mistake my sincerity for naïveté?" She voiced it as a rhetorical question, her expression sobering after a beat. "I'm not naïve, Laki. I'm the Earth Fae Queen, a mantle I took on at the young age of seven after the Midnight Fae Elders killed my parents for consorting with Quandary Bloods."

She pressed her palm on the table, a tree beginning to take root over her fingers, growing while she pressed on.

"I'm not naïve. I'm a survivor. A survivor who stood up to a crazy abomination not once but twice, and lived. A survivor who was bitten against her will and taken to a kingdom starkly different from her own, yet learned how to not only use their magic but embrace it as well."

The tree sprouted upward, igniting in a flurry of branches as she stood, her hand functioning as a root beneath the creation as she continued to speak.

"A survivor who nearly destroyed a roomful of Elite Bloods in fury after the Midnight Fae Council killed her mate. A survivor who then helped bring that mate back from the dead, only to be rewarded with an ascension she never wanted, thereby marking her as an abomination for life."

Magic swirled through the limbs, the tree itself only about a foot tall but boasting a hell of a lot of power.

"A survivor who has mated *four* different Midnight Fae lines," she said, the smoky tendrils of energy taking on the various hues of all her mates. *Cerulean. Red. Purple. Green.* "A survivor who has passed three ascension trials in less than two months, earning favor with the dark source and finding a way to successfully combine it with the earth source."

The tree began to grow upward, the movements measured and controlled by Aflora's power.

"I'm not *naïve*. I'm energy redefined. A queen of two worlds. An abomination. And a royal who craves creation and life over death. Midnight Fae have been taught to adore violence for too long. It's time for an outsider to show them how to *live* again. I'm that outsider, the survivor who knows how to fight without bloodshed. The survivor who knows how to *win* without killing those she's up against."

Multicolored leaves sprouted from the branches as she sent the tree sprawling across the table like vines, the organism morphing before our eyes.

"The Midnight Fae have forgotten how to love and respect one another," she concluded softly, her focus falling to her invention as the roots and branches began to twine together to form beautiful arrays of color as their pieces blended and matured as one. "Together, we can unite the Midnight Fae." The branches went up in flames in her next breath, her stunning tree disintegrating to ash. "Or together, we can watch them all burn."

She took her seat once more, clasped her hands before her, and said, "The choice is yours."

CHAPTER TWENTY-ONE

KOLS

weet Fae.

Aflora's display of power, coupled with her words, had me wanting to push back from the table and bow at her feet.

She'd burned down her tree. Destroyed it. And then she'd accompanied it with a statement that had floored me.

I had no idea what to say to her. Hell, I'd forgotten how to fucking breathe.

From the expressions of others at the table, I wasn't the only one wanting to worship the goddess among them.

But it was Laki everyone waited for.

He studied the ash on the table, his expression giving nothing away. Then he stood, causing Zakkai to straighten in his chair beside me, immediately on guard.

Aflora didn't move, her eyes holding the former Source Architect's gaze.

He walked around the table, all of us observing his every move.

"Stand," he told Aflora as he moved into position behind her.

Zakkai appeared ready to tell his father what he thought of that demand, but Aflora shadowed to a standing position beside him, her show of power not lost on the others in the room or the male now standing before her.

They locked gazes for another long moment.

And he knelt at her feet. "I choose to unite the fae." A softly spoken, powerful announcement that sent a rush of energy through the room.

It's done, I realized. *She just bloody passed her fourth trial.*

This amazing, beautiful female had achieved what I had not.

She'd just united the fae in her own way, proving her worthiness to the dark source and ascending to the fifth level.

Rather than rejoice or celebrate, she went to her knees in front of Laki as well and drew his gaze to hers. "Then we unite as equals," she told him. "I don't want a constituency that bows. I want one that stands proudly together, rejoicing in life and our prolonged existences. I desire equality among the Midnight Fae factions. No more superiority."

Laki gave her a soft smile. "Then you truly are our queen," he told her. "Because only a queen could deny her obvious superiority in favor of unity." He leaned in to kiss her forehead. "Your parents would be proud. Just as I'm proud of my son, too." He looked at Zakkai. "He's a survivor, too. And with all he's endured, he never truly lost his heart."

He stood then and held out his hand for Aflora. She accepted the offering, more as a symbolic gesture than anything, and allowed him to pull her to her feet.

The Quandary Bloods at the table all seemed to relax, their stances suddenly tired, and I realized how on edge they had been for this meeting.

They want revenge for what happened to them, Aflora whispered. *But that doesn't necessarily mean they crave death.*

Only she would be able to see that. In a realm riddled with darkness, it was hard to find the light. Especially when everyone was drowning in the need for blood.

She took her place beside me once more, the figments reappearing to fill our mugs and plates again.

The conversation flowed from Aflora's plans to a discussion on what the future world might look like. Laki offered some suggestions for council development, as did Zeph and Zakkai. Aflora listened without commenting, taking in all the ideas and hearing from several of the Quandary Bloods as well.

Shade and I remained quiet as former members of the Midnight Fae Council. While we had our own suggestions and opinions to share, we were more interested in listening to the others.

Aflora must have known this because she didn't ask us to speak. Instead, she sat between us, holding both our hands in each of hers while absorbing the comments from the others.

When they concluded their discussions, Zen arrived in a flourish, saying she'd finished preparing their accommodations. They might not be staying indefinitely—something Laki made clear when he said they would be leaving after they rested—but at least they would be comfortable.

"You're welcome back anytime," Zen informed Laki. "Or at least until Lucifer says otherwise."

Laki snorted. "I will never understand this arrangement you have with him."

She merely smiled.

I would like to understand it, too, I thought at Shade.

Understanding my grandmother is an impossible task, he replied dryly. *But I know their arrangement involves him being allowed to send a set number of Hell Fae to study here annually. They're too powerful for his Hellhounds to guard and train, so he lets her do it.*

Intriguing, I admitted. *Have you met him?*

Yes, Shade replied, his tone telling me he didn't want to elaborate on it.

As our mate appeared ready to pass out, I decided not to press him and caught her by the waist instead. She'd just finished saying goodbye to the last of the Quandary Bloods and looked ready to sleep on her feet.

Zakkai was in front of us in an instant, his mouth finding Aflora's as I held her steady with her back to my chest. The metallic scent of blood taunted my senses, telling me he was feeding her his essence to help bolster her strength again.

I frowned and engaged my link with Zeph. *She just fed from us earlier.*

Yes, he replied, watching the exchange. *The dark source seems to be taking a lot from her. Is that normal?*

I don't think so, I replied. *My father never required this much blood.*

Is it because she's mostly taking from other Midnight Fae and not the human vein?

Perhaps, I replied. *But the blood coffee contained more than enough mortal essence to replenish her today.*

I considered her as she moaned against Zakkai's mouth, her body hungry for more of his blood. He didn't hesitate in offering more, but my lips curled further downward at the display.

I think the source is preparing her for the next trial, I said slowly to Zeph. *It must sense something big coming.*

Sacrifice, he replied. *Yes?*

It doesn't necessarily have to come in that order, but yes, that would be the typical path. And it could require so many things of her.

With my grandfather leading the way, who knew what he would do?

Then let's take her back to the suite and properly nourish her, Zeph suggested.

Yes, I agreed.

We'd bathe her in blood if that was what she needed.

And then we'd hold our breaths and hope that we'd given her enough.

CHAPTER TWENTY-TWO

My stomach cramped, stirring me from my sleep.

Hungry, I thought. *So hungry*.

But I'd fed from all my mates before falling into bed. Then Zeph and Kols had invited me to play sex gymnastics with them… and they'd fed me again before I'd passed out.

Yet I was *starved*, and it wasn't food that I desired, but blood. *Ugh*, I groaned to myself. Zeph slept soundly beside me, his palm on my hip.

Kols was at my back with his arm wrapped around my waist, holding me to him.

Both of them were sound asleep, content, and well sated.

Disturbing them felt wrong. *I'll just, uh, shadow to the kitchen, and pop back after I have a bag of blood.*

I'd never actually indulged straight from the plastic before because Zeph had been adding it creatively to my meals. But I knew there were bags in the fridge for that purpose.

Twisting my lips to the side, I engaged in Shade's ability to teleport by shadow and magicked myself a pair of pajama pants with a tank top as I materialized in the kitchen.

Zakkai stood next to the fridge with his shoulder braced against the wall and a bag of blood already in his hand. "It's warm," he said softly.

"How did you…?"

"You were dreaming of blood," Shade murmured from behind me.

I looked over my shoulder to find him sitting at the table with a book and a glass of red juice beside him.

"Made this in case you prefer it over the bag," he said, gesturing to the drink. "Or in case you need both."

I swallowed, my mouth watering.

Zakkai handed me the bag, the top uncapped and releasing a metallic aroma.

I wrapped my lips around it and sucked, groaning as the liquid hit my tongue. Zakkai remained against the wall as he watched, his irises flaring with power. He was dressed in a pair of sleep pants and nothing else. Just like Shade.

When I finished the bag—in what had to only be a minute—Shade stood and handed me the juice.

I put the straw between my lips and began to suck while Zakkai disposed of the bag and pulled another from some sort of warming unit next to the refrigerator. It appeared to be uniquely crafted for the purpose of heating blood.

It wasn't until I finished the juice and the second bag that I finally felt like I could breathe again, the ache in my stomach subsiding.

But somehow I knew it would only be a temporary reprieve.

"Is this normal?" I asked. Because Kols had never needed blood like this. Or, if he had, I hadn't noticed.

"No," Zakkai replied, not bothering to sugarcoat it. "We suspect the dark source is preparing you for the next trial."

"Or that perhaps it's already started." Shade resumed his seat at the table, sliding his book to the side. "Constantine won't like that you not only circumvented his trap but also passed another trial soon after. So it's likely he's already initiated the next one in hopes of catching you off guard while you're exhausted."

Zakkai dipped his chin in agreement. "Yes, and if that's the case, then the dark source is aware of what's coming and wants you prepared, which is why you're craving an abundance of blood."

"I see." I shivered, both explanations unnerving. "And you didn't crave blood like this before any of your trials?"

He shook his head. "No. Just the normal amount."

"Oh." I bit my cheek. I'd have to ask Kols about this as well, but I suspected his answer would be the same as Zakkai's. "Um..." I trailed off to clear my throat, my mouth suddenly dry despite all the blood I'd just imbibed. "What...? What was your fifth trial?"

"My sacrifice trial?" he clarified.

I nodded. Kols had told me all about his own trials in an effort to prepare me for mine, but he'd never moved beyond the unity test.

"Yours will be different from mine," he warned.

"I know. I'm just curious about what you had to sacrifice." Maybe it would give me an idea of what I'd have to sacrifice in mine.

He fell quiet for a moment, his gaze flicking to Shade before returning to me. "I had to sacrifice memories of my mom," he admitted. "But in doing so, the source strengthened me by helping me to heal wounds I hadn't realized were left open from her passing."

I considered that for a moment, my lips tugging downward. "But how do you know that if you can't remember those moments?"

"Because the source returned my memories upon my ascension," he explained. "After I'd healed."

"So the source… helped you?"

"In a way," he replied. "The trials are about preparing a leader—testing their boundaries and helping to strengthen their weaknesses. In forgetting my mother… I was able to better focus. And then I was able to better appreciate her memory when I ascended, too."

That made sense in a way. "Do you think the source will take the memories of my parents?"

He studied me for a moment, his expression giving nothing away.

"Tell her," Shade said. "Tell her your theory."

I glanced at him and then back at Zakkai. "You have a theory?"

He threw a glare at Shade. "I do."

"She needs to know," my Death Blood mate insisted. "It'll help her prepare."

"Or freak her the fuck out for no reason."

"You're the one who keeps lecturing Zeph about her training," Shade retorted. "Go eat your own words, *Kai*."

Zakkai clenched his teeth together, his irritation and discomfort palpable.

"He's right," I told him softly, my palm lifting to rest over his heart. "Tell me your theory."

He remained silent for a moment, breathing expertly even as he released some of the tension in his shoulders and jaw.

His lashes fell as he blinked.

Then his expression mellowed.

"Given your increasing thirst, I think the dark source might require you to make a choice—between Midnight Fae and Elemental Fae. It might make you sacrifice your connection to the earth."

My heart dropped to my stomach.

Oh.

Now I understood his hesitation.

"That's an impossible choice," I whispered.

"Which makes it a likely trial," he replied. "Especially with Constantine holding the reins."

I reached for the counter, needing to steady myself. "I really hope you're wrong," I admitted.

"I hope I am, too."

Silence fell between us.

Then my stomach growled again.

Zakkai said nothing, just went to the fridge and began warming another packet of blood.

It only took a few minutes. By the time he handed it to me, I was already salivating again, confirming his theory that this was somehow related to my pending trial.

I sucked it down while considering everything he'd said.

It was an intelligent prediction on his part, one I really hoped didn't come true.

He took the bag from me as I finished, and tossed it away. Then he returned and tucked a strand of my hair behind my ear before tracing the pointed tip. His ears were rounded like those of the other Midnight Fae. The touch almost made me want to jokingly ask if my points would disappear as a result of choosing his kind over my own.

But I wasn't ready to joke yet.

Instead, I focused on his eyes and the tenderness radiating from their depths.

"Thank you," I said, expressing my gratitude to him for telling me about his suspicion. Then I met Shade's pretty eyes and repeated the words, making sure they knew I was thankful to both of them for taking care of me.

We'd all come quite a long way in our relationships. It was night and day compared to my first days at Midnight Fae Academy.

The forbidden bite.

My enrollment.

Being trapped in a suite with Kols.

The rivalries.

Looking between Shade and Zakkai now, I couldn't help my smile. They appeared so relaxed and content in the kitchen, something I doubted would have happened two months ago.

"What put that grin on your face?" Zakkai asked, his silver-blue eyes gleaming in the moonlight streaming in through the glass doors of the dining area.

"Just thinking about how much I love you all."

His eyebrow lifted. "Even me?"

"Even you," I replied, going to my toes to brush a kiss against his lips.

"Shade?" he said against my mouth. "Be sure to take notes. Blood is how we provoke emotion from Aflora."

"That's definitely not the only way," my Death Blood mate drawled as he slid up behind me to gently nibble the back of my neck.

I shivered, their touch doing things to me that it probably shouldn't after spending so many hours playing with Kols and Zeph.

But these men made me insatiable.

For both sex and blood.

Zakkai hummed in approval against my mouth, his tongue tracing the seam before sliding inside to engage me in a deep, sensual embrace underlined in passion and adoration. I moaned, curling into him and losing myself to his touch as Shade drew his teeth to my pulse. Rather than bite down, he sucked on my skin until my knees threatened to give out beneath me.

My palms went to Zakkai's shoulders, my nails digging into his muscles as I fought to remain standing.

He growled, the sound hypnotic and taking away my breath.

I expected him to grab me, hoist me up onto the counter, and rip the clothes off me.

But he pulled his mouth away from me instead and stared down at the wolf standing just inside the door. "What?" he demanded.

I realized then that his growl hadn't been meant for me... but for Zimney.

Zakkai studied the creature, then released me to walk over and kneel before him. "What's wrong?" he asked, his voice gentler as he reached for the arctic-white beast. "What's in your mouth, Zimney?"

The wolf grumbled in reply.

Then it whined as its black eyes met mine.

Zakkai glanced back over his broad shoulder, my nail prints still embedded in his skin. "He's saying it's for you."

I swallowed. "Do I want to know what it is?" Because the blood pooling from the beast's mouth suggested I didn't.

He made a noncommittal noise before studying his familiar's jaw again, the low lighting of the moon painting dark shadows on the wolf's muzzle. "Looks like..." He tilted his head, glancing at the other side. "A stonepecker." He frowned. "Why are you bringing Aflora a stonepecker?"

"Didn't Clove bring you a stonepecker after the attack on the Academy?" Shade asked.

"Yeah," I whispered. "Right before the Warrior Bloods showed up to search Kols's quarters."

Was Zimney trying to give us a warning? To tell us that Midnight Fae were coming?

"We never did find out who sent that stonepecker," Zakkai said slowly. He reached for Zimney's mouth, only for the wolf to back away, his eyes still on me. "He really wants you to take it, Aflora."

"What's going on?" Zeph's low voice came from the kitchen entryway, his dark hair mussed with sleep as he walked in wearing a pair of pajama bottoms like the others. Kols followed close behind, his palm hiding his yawn.

"Zimney brought us a dead stonepecker." Zakkai straightened, his brow furrowed. "You're the one who disposed of the last one, right?"

"Want me to do it again?" Zeph guessed.

"No, I was wondering if you'd noticed any magic on the other one. I was just saying to Aflora that we never found out who'd sent it. I thought it might have been Zimney playing with Clove, but after she told me the purpose of it, I know it wasn't him. He would never put her in danger like that." He folded his arms over his bare chest, his legs bracing like he expected an argument.

But Zeph just shook his head. "I destroyed it in a hurry because Shade showed up to say the Warrior Bloods were coming."

Zakkai glanced at Shade.

"Don't look at me," my Death Blood mate replied. "I was just trying to protect Kols. And I definitely wouldn't give Aflora a dead stonepecker as a gift."

"Tadmir?" Zakkai guessed.

"Why would Tadmir give her a stonepecker?" Kols interjected.

"Because he's Zakkai's uncle and he's the one who left me the rock," I replied, trying to avoid a snarky reply from the Quandary Blood.

The twitch of his lips told me he knew exactly why I'd been the one to respond.

"We never found out why he'd done that, either," I added, thinking back to the day I'd cast that object history enchantment. "You were talking to me…" I frowned. "Except, no, it wasn't your voice." It was deeper. Different. "Was it Tadmir talking to me? He said he was coming for me. That I knew him. That I would become him. Why would he say that?"

"To move fate along," Shade replied. "He was probably pretending to be Zakkai in order to prepare you." He shook his head. "It's hard to say exactly what he intended, but I know it wasn't nefarious."

Zakkai nodded. "I agree. He's been working through time for too long to be trying to hurt you or any of us."

"Hold on." Kols held up his hand, his expression one of stark confusion. "*Tadmir.* As in, Malefic Councilman *Tadmir?* He's your uncle?"

"Half uncle," Zakkai explained. "He's a Paradox Fae Quandary Blood masquerading as a Malefic Blood."

Kols just gaped at him.

Zeph, too.

"And he's been on our side the whole time," Shade finished for him. "He helped create a diversion after your, uh, excommunication."

I cleared my throat. "He also left the rock, so I'm wondering if the stonepecker is from him. Like a message, maybe? Or a warning? Did he send me the stonepecker and rock before as a warning?"

No, that didn't seem right either.

I'd never met Tadmir, so I had no way of knowing if it'd been his voice in my head or not.

My nose scrunched.

Then I shook my head.

"There's really only one way to find out," I continued. "We'll just take the stonepecker and, uh, run some spells to find out who sent it." I grimaced with the words, not liking the idea of playing with a dead animal. But I didn't see another option, and the looks coming from my mates said they didn't either.

"You're the commander of the creatures now," Kols said. "That makes you closest to them."

"And you can use my magic to see if there are any messages left within its death," Shade added.

I nodded. "Great. Okay. I just need to get it from Zimney."

Take the dead stonepecker out of the beast's mouth. Right. Easy. Everyday task. Yep.

I shivered as I stepped toward him, the metallic scent all wrong. It made my nose scrunch, unlike the pouches I'd drunk from a bit ago. Probably because this blood came from a corpse.

"Aflora?" Zeph said. "Do you want…?" Zimney growled as he took a step toward the wolf. "Or maybe not."

"He won't give it to me, either," Zakkai muttered. "And he's *my* familiar."

"It's fine," I said, stealing a deep breath and kneeling before the beast. I held out my hand. "I'll do"—Zimney dropped the stonepecker into my palm—"it."

Energy hummed through the air, causing the hairs along my arms to dance.

My forehead crinkled, the sensation leaving me queasy.

"Uh, guys?" I asked. "Do you all feel that, or...?" I started to turn as I spoke, only to realize the room no longer existed around me.

My mates were gone.

Zimney had disappeared, too.

Just the stonepecker remained.

Aflora! Zakkai's voice echoed through my mind, his presence oddly distant.

Kai?

The stonepecker began to writhe on my palm, causing me to drop it in alarm. Roots shot up out of it as it spun across the dark space at my feet.

"I'd grab those if I were you," a deep voice said from the shadows.

"What?" I spun around, searching for the source.

Then the stonepecker began to whine, and my mates all yelled in my head.

I looked down to see the creature twisting into smoke, the roots the only part left behind.

Except, no... those weren't roots. *They're souls,* I realized, recognizing the essence from Shade's Death Blood magic courses.

The beings twisted in agony, their hums of magic familiar.

I reached for them on instinct—all four strands—then jolted as they shot out in all different directions, their ends securing themselves to the inky walls around me.

What...?

The beings began to stretch, causing me to cry out as they dug their opposite ends into my palms, their roots deep and solid and joining with my being. *Again.* Like they had always been a part of me and it was the atmosphere around us that had forced me to release them.

What's happening?

"Poor Aflora," the deep voice murmured, Constantine's tones familiar and recognizable. "Always choosing her mates over herself."

I couldn't see him, but I felt him all around me, his power pulsing against mine, demanding I stay put until he finished toying with his prey. My mind stroked through his spell, trying to learn the nuances of it and how to counteract it, but the yanking on my strands had me focusing on the here and now and my innate need to *hold on.* They rooted deeper, securing themselves to my soul... their voices beginning to return...

"Did you know that stonepecker is how I first confirmed your connection to my grandson?" Constantine asked conversationally, like I wasn't being ripped apart by the vines digging into my hands. "I originally sent it with the expectation of it being found among his things during the search. But a falcon disrupted my spell. A familiar. *Your* familiar. Which I found deeply fascinating at the time. Until I realized *why* that familiar had interfered."

Aflora? Kols's voice trickled through my mind in a whisper, the soul in my palm vibrating.

I'm here, I told him. *I'm—*

"You mated my grandson, the heir to the Midnight Fae kingdom. No doubt because you bewitched him with your abomination magic. I'd hoped he'd be stronger. I had also hoped the Death Blood had been lying. Alas, here we are. And it seems Shadow was attempting to outmaneuver me, too. But I'm the one holding the final play in this game." He paused. "Actually, no, that's not quite right. *You* are holding it."

The souls writhed against my palms, their agony touching my soul as the space began to move, stretching them… taking them from my *heart*.

"Who will you sacrifice?" Constantine asked, his voice low and menacing. "Which soul will you release to survive?" His energy kissed my skin. "Let the trial begin."

CHAPTER TWENTY-THREE

ZEPH

Aflora's agony shredded my heart into a thousand pieces. I hit her with another defensive spell, trying in vain to pull her from this magical coma.

She didn't move. Didn't respond. Barely breathed.

Zakkai had caught her when she'd fainted, the stonepecker disappearing into black mist. His familiar had howled and cowered in a corner, his tail firmly between his legs. He was still there now, shaking with fright as Zakkai ran a spell over him.

Kols and I had moved Aflora to the couch, where Shade paced frantically back and forth. He kept fisting his hair and cursing himself for not seeing this sooner. "Your grandfather did this," he said, looking at Kols. "He used to send me messages via Draco all the time, always in the form of dead crows. He thought it was symbolic."

"Of Night," Kols inferred darkly. "That piece of information would have been useful ten minutes ago."

"He's never used Zimney for that purpose before," Zakkai interjected. "*I* should have sensed what was wrong. He tried to tell me by disobeying my word and looking to Aflora for direction. But I deduced incorrectly that he was deferring to her as the queen." He ran his hand over his face, his frustration palpable. "That fucking grandfather of yours needs to die."

"Indeed," Kols agreed.

Aflora's shriek inside my head sent me to my knees beside her, along with the others. "What is he doing?" I demanded, my chest aching as though I'd just finished an intense battle session with a fellow Warrior Blood.

I felt drained.

Ruined.

Exhausted.

"Is she pulling energy from us to survive?" I wondered out loud as I massaged my agonized ribs.

"It's all the blood." Zakkai's voice was as strained as mine. "The source was preparing her... to hold it together."

"What?" I didn't understand what that meant.

"I can feel it fracturing. The trial Constantine has set is requiring too much. The dark source is in agony. That's what we're feeling—Aflora's reaction to the source being split into pieces."

"How is that even possible?" Kols demanded. "Constantine isn't stronger than the source."

"No. He's just the acting conduit. And he's commanding a hell of a lot of power right now—more than any monarch should. Which means *all Midnight Fae* can feel this right now. Just as they can sense Aflora's anguish over having to keep it all together."

"Do you think he realizes that?" Shade asked.

"I think he's too arrogant to see beyond this trial," Zakkai gritted out. "I'm trying to help her, but it's too... too chaotic. And it's draining too much."

Kols collapsed against Aflora's abdomen, his breath leaving on a wheeze. "It... it's like...' A subtle hum came from his mind, causing Shade's eyes to widen.

"Oh, fuck," the Death Blood whispered. "No."

"Yes," Kols hissed.

"What?" I demanded. "What is it like?"

"When I died," Kols breathed, his forehead touching Aflora's flat abdomen.

A burst of energy sent me forward, my hands roaming over her, checking her vitals and evaluating her still form. She felt okay, like she was sleeping.

Then Kols released a wheezing cough, and my gaze went to Zakkai. "You said it's like the source is breaking and protesting the trial. Because it doesn't agree with the sacrifice?" It came out as a question, but as I voiced it, I could sense the answer. "She's being forced to choose." Something I vowed only this week would never happen. "Fuck."

"She's holding our life strands," Shade said, his pupils flaring. "Just like I did with Kols."

My Elite Blood mate nodded wobbly, his skin exceptionally pale. "Feels... like... that."

"And Kolstov is slipping fastest because he's the clear choice for death," Zakkai said solemnly. "He cheated it once already. The source is demanding its due... by forcing Aflora's choice. That's why it's breaking."

"It feels the wrongness of the trial," I realized in a breath. "We have to do something to help her. There has to be a way."

But Zakkai's expression said otherwise.

As did the grim line of Shade's mouth. "There's nothing we can do. This is her path to walk... and her path alone."

CHAPTER TWENTY-FOUR

I screamed, my arms stretched impossibly wide as I refused to release any of my mates.

Constantine's cruel laughter circled me in an invisible rope of sound, slithering across my skin and taunting my ears.

I hated him.

Hated *this*.

"I refuse to choose!" I yelled.

Which only made him laugh harder.

"Oh, Aflora. You act as though that's an option." His voice came from right in front of me, his body encased in shadows, leaving me in the perpetual dark with the ropes of magic tearing from my palms. "You must sacrifice one."

"No." I wouldn't do it. I could never sacrifice any of my mates. I'd rather die. I'd rather lose. I'd rather not ascend. "Take it all back. Take the power. Take the source. Take it all back!"

His amusement blackened my soul, telling me there was no reasoning with him.

He's insane. Mad. Completely lost to this idea of genocide.

I could feel his hatred whipping around me, his need to destroy all those he considered to be *other*. Abominations. Vile beings with too much power.

Except *he* was the one abusing the dark source now, forcing me into a wicked web of death and despair.

This isn't the way, I thought. *This isn't how the dark source wishes for someone to ascend.*

I could feel it weeping, begging the ruler—*Constantine*—to stop. To take it all back. To redirect the trial to something of growth and potential, to have me prove my worth in a more appropriate manner.

But Constantine ignored the plea, his mind made up.

This was the path he'd chosen, this cruel game of "sacrifice a mate."

I shivered, my heart fracturing into a million pieces. I could feel Kols's strand weakening, his ties to death too tender and fresh. The dark source was absorbing him, the lesser of all evils.

He'd almost died once.

It made logical sense to take him again and finish his path.

No, I thought, shooting energy down that strand and emboldening it with my earth source. I was a being of life and creation, and I used that gift to root Kols to me now.

Aflora? he whispered, his voice a beautiful caress to my mind.

Kols, I breathed, sending more vitality to him and renewing his strength.

What are you doing?

Holding on to you, I replied, strained as the source rippled around me in a demand for me to release a mate.

I cried out as it pulsed, stretching me wider, thinning the souls of those I loved most. *No!* I screamed, slamming the vines with another bout of inner strength, drawing my own version of vines around them to reduce their strain.

But to the detriment of my own soul.

It burned.

Ached.

Left me breathless in this mass of black magic.

You can let me go, Kols said, his voice soft and understanding. *It's okay, sweetheart. I've already been gifted with more time, a chance to say goodbye to you all. To love you, even in my short weeks left. It's enough for me to dream of you for eternity while I rest, Aflora. It's enough for me to have lived a full life.*

No! I snapped. *Stop telling me this.*

I wouldn't let him go.

I wouldn't choose.

I wouldn't allow him to be the sacrifice Constantine demanded.

There had to be another way.

There had to be—

"This is pathetic," Constantine said. "And it's exactly why a female can never rule. You're thinking with emotion and not practicality. Kolstov is the obvious sacrifice as the closest to death. But rather than choose the weak link, you're making them all suffer. What a pitiful queen you would be."

I growled. "You know nothing of the queen I will be."

Because he underestimated the powers of the bonds, the strength of mating, the bolstering of the heart. This Midnight Fae Elder only thought in terms of practical recourse, making decisions about life and death on a whim.

No ounce of remorse.

No concern for others.

Just a need to be in charge, to lead by his own example, and to never accept anyone outside his skewed view of superiority.

He was the reason abominations were shunned, the reason Lucifer had had to reopen the gates to the Hell Fae realm a thousand years ago, and why Zen had had to craft the paradigm to protect the exiled Midnight Fae.

That wasn't the mark of a worthy king, but of a dictator who led the people by his own instincts alone. Never listening to his fellow fae for guidance or requesting their opinions. He merely told them what to do and expected them to bow.

He'd tricked the Quandary Bloods into his ascension, rewriting the power away from the Morte line to bolster his own, because he had a vision for his people.

A vision that cast out women.

Cast out those he believed were stronger.

Cast out those with the ability to stop him.

Then he'd forced the ascension onto me as some sort of trick of fate, to paint me as a monster to his people. When, in fact, he was the evildoer in this scenario, the villain who craved a worthy opponent.

And he'd chosen *me*.

The dark source had accepted *me*.

My mates had claimed *me*.

"I won't choose," I said again, my voice stronger now. "They're my *mates*. My heart. My soul. Without them, I'm not worthy enough to be queen. They're my rocks, my foundation, my roots. I won't destroy them. I won't release them. I won't sacrifice those who make me who I am, because otherwise I'll lose myself."

"Then they'll all die," Constantine whispered, his words cruel. He kissed me with his power once more, the pulsing walls yanking on me with a vengeance, the dark source bellowing in agony at being forced to abuse the one it had chosen to ascend.

I screamed with it, my soul in tatters, my mates yelling inside my mind and heart to stop this madness, to embrace the choice.

They all told me to pick them, to sever them, to live, to survive.

But this world wouldn't work without all four of them together.

My mates represented four branches of Midnight Fae kind, their bloodlines invaluable, their power insurmountable.

Yet I felt them all dwindling, their energy waning, their lights blinking in and out as the trial raged around me, Constantine demanding my sacrifice.

I couldn't just forfeit or walk away.

He'd ensured that I either picked one mate… or I lost them all.

Either way, I'd lose my heart in the process.

Aflora! Kols called to me again. *Please, sweetheart. Listen to me. I can't let you do this. Pick me. Sacrifice me. I can't live in a world where Shade and Zeph are gone. They're dying, love. They're… we're all… I'm ready… I swear to you that I'm ready, that I can do this. Just let me go, sweetheart. I'll be with you always. You know that. I'll be part of the source for—*

Don't you dare listen to him, Zeph interrupted. *I can feel his energy waning, Aflora. Don't listen to him. Don't let Kols do this!*

Aflora, Shade whispered. *Just take me… I've already lived seven lives with you. Eight including this one. It's enough… it's enough for me to know… that you've chosen this path, that you're—*

Zakkai's growl infiltrated my mind as I released a pained gasp, the darkness roaring around me. *I'm trying, but I can't… I can't hold on much longer… Aflora… Aflora, you have to…*

No! I shouted to them all. *I won't choose!*

This wicked game had to end.

I wouldn't sacrifice them.

I couldn't.

And I told them that with a blast of power that left me breathless… yet bolstered their strands. Similar to what I'd done to Kols, my vines thriving around him, solidifying my grip.

I did it again.

They all pulsed back to life, their voices clearing more in my head.

Aflora, Zakkai warned.

I ignored him, shoving more vitality and power into their cords as the darkness around me began to shiver and retreat.

When I stopped, it crept forward again, yanking on my mates and weakening their bonds.

But when I pulsed outward once more… it stilled.

Constantine's presence seemed to pause around me, his confusion a tangible brush to my senses.

And I smiled.

"I will not choose," I said for a third time.

Then I released all my power and vitality into my mates, blasting them with every ounce of my strength and life, giving them my entire heart… and soul.

They shouted in my mind, demanding I stop.

But I couldn't. I wouldn't.

This was my sacrifice.

Wind whipped around me, the dark source accepting my path.

My veins began to throb, the energy spilling from me through four strands, invigorating my mates as my own soul began to weep.

They begged me to stop.

Kols demanded I listen.

Zakkai's power wrapped around me as he tried to control my efforts, but I snapped his spell with one of my own, my heart breaking a little in the process at his resounding agony. *I love you,* I breathed to him.

I love you all, I said, whispering through their minds with my final words as I fell to my knees on an exhausted wheeze.

I was wrong before. Constantine wanted me to choose. I refused. Until now.

"I choose to sacrifice myself."

My palms met the black floor.

And I unleashed every last drop of my being into their vines, their cries of pain at my loss… following me down… down… down…

CHAPTER TWENTY-FIVE

SHADE

This isn't happening.

Eight lifetimes.

Seven of which I'd watched her nearly die. I'd always changed time. I'd always brought her back. I'd always started over. I'd always *fixed* her.

But there was no coming back this time.

I had no Paradox Fae. I had no sword. I had no power to stop this.

"Aflora," I whispered, looking down at her bluing skin. The obsidian power lining her veins was gone. No more dark source. No more ascension. No more… *life.* Just like Kols. Only worse.

Because it matched a fate I thought I'd altered.

I'd done everything right this time, had finally taken us down the path meant for eternity.

And now… My heart cracked. *Little rose…*

"Please don't do this." It came out in a whisper, my voice failing me.

So many lifetimes. So much sacrifice. So much pain.

But nothing amounted to this, to watching her skin change… hearing her breath rattle… seeing her soul wither…

My pulse refused to beat. "No." It left my lips on a choked sound. "No, Aflora. *No.*" I whispered a spell, my mind latching onto her final strands, my soul refusing to release her. "*No!*"

I yanked her back, my magical hold slipping as she fought me, her spirit moving on without my permission.

"No!" I shouted again, desperate now.

Too many lifetimes.

This couldn't be the end.

This couldn't be it.

I'd loved her for what felt like eons of an existence, our souls tied in a way few others would ever understand. I'd bitten her. She was mine. I would keep her. She couldn't leave me. That wasn't how this worked.

"This isn't supposed to happen!" I raged at her. "I gave up everything for you! Why wouldn't you let me give you this?" I would have been her sacrifice. I would have died at her feet if it meant hearing her breathe once more.

My grasp on her soul slipped again, and I grabbed at the air, my fingers going through her. My spell was waning. Dying. Just like her. Just like my heart. Just like my own fucking soul.

Zakkai whispered some sort of incantation next to me, his attempt to bring her back bolstering my hope for a split second of time.

Until her final gasp graced my ears.

A sound I would never forget.

A sound that would follow me to my grave.

A sound that told me I'd failed.

"Eight lifetimes," I whispered, my head falling to her chest as her pulse slowed to a silent beat.

I love you. Her words blew across my mind, her soul kissing my cheek as she escaped my last attempt to hold on to her.

I'll always be with you, Shade. Watching from above. I will forever love you. Something soft and feathery fell across my hand.

A rose petal.

Graced by her magic, her Earth Fae touch… her final goodbye.

My little rose. My sweet, beautiful Aflora. Taken by this world. This unfair, cruel, wretched existence.

There was no coming back from this.

No more tricks of time.

No more plays up my sleeve.

This was it.

Just me… my Aflora… and her final kiss of a rose petal on my wrist.

He's won, I realized. *Constantine… has won.*

I was always meant to love her and lose her. *Because death will always find a way.*

CHAPTER TWENTY-SIX

ZAKKAI

Aflora's life strands circled my wrists, the invisible power one I could feel more than see. "She's here," I said, talking to no one and everyone.

But no one replied.

Shade had his forehead pressed to her chest, his shoulders hunched in agony at her loss.

Kolstov and Zephyrus were behind him, watching with expressions of horror mingled with pain.

They were in shock.

"She's here!" I repeated, my voice strained as I tried futilely to grab their focus. But they were lost to their grief, seeing her body frozen and not breathing, her heart no longer beating.

I growled in annoyance, not ready to give up.

But I felt Aflora pulsing through the dark source web, the last vestiges of her strength urging me to release it.

It's my choice, she seemed to be saying. *Let me go, Zakkai. Please… let me go.*

My chest ached, my mind unwilling to comprehend what had just happened, how quickly I'd lost my mate.

Sacrifice wasn't supposed to be like this.

Sacrifice was about growth, perseverance, *power*.

It wasn't about death. It wasn't about giving up the cords of life to the dark source. But Constantine had forced that trial upon her, making her choose.

And she'd chosen herself.

Like a true queen, putting everyone else before herself.

All of the Midnight Fae knew. They'd all felt her decision, her sacrifice, her putting our love and lives over her own.

I felt them weeping, sensed the dark source breaking from the loss of a powerful royal, an ideal candidate to rule.

And I sensed Constantine's victory over it all, his malicious laughter as he watched her perish inside that dark void… alone… without her mates.

Aflora, I breathed, her soul slipping through my fingers, the spell Shade had uttered disappearing into the wind.

She'd kissed his hand with a rose petal.

Just as she whispered her love into my mind.

I'm okay, she told me. *It's okay… to let me go… to let me be free, to lead the fae to life. I'll watch you all from above. I'll see you from the stars.*

My knees gave out, tears blurring my vision as a bright light blinked above her, twinkling like a little sun.

My star.

My little star.

My sweet, beautiful star.

Aflora… She'd been my other half for so long that I wasn't sure how I'd survive without her.

This was so much worse than cutting off our bond all those years ago. So much worse than all the pain Constantine and the Elders had inflicted on my life and being. So much worse than my own ascension and the pain of taking on the Source Architect role.

This was like having a million stars combust inside me, leaving only one above to guide me and watch over me for an eternity of solitude.

Because there would be no other Aflora.

No other queen.

No other star.

She was my one and only… and I'd failed her.

I'd failed… my sweet… beautiful… star…

My head fell to my hands, my world breaking as the dark source wept with me, the pain echoing through all vestiges of my being and spirit.

The Midnight Fae knew.

Their queen had just died… because she'd sacrificed for them all. Not just for her mates, but for all of Midnight Fae kind.

A demonstration of what power should be, how it should be used, how a true queen should lead.

The dark source blinked with the rightness of her choice, praising her for her leadership and grace. It was a beautiful goodbye.

And a stunning… *hello.*

I blinked, feeling the paths and magic whirling and shifting and embracing the sacrifice she'd given… by regenerating with life.

My hands fell from my face as I stared up at that blinking light, the star in the room that only I seemed able to see.

Her light in the dark.

Her life at the center of the dark source.

A royal… ascending to her desired throne.

Sacrifice and respect, I realized. *She just passed two trials at once.*

Because she'd sacrificed herself for those she loved, and all of the Midnight Fae had felt it… and respected her choice.

Which left only one trial for her to pass—her ascension.

Energy shot through me, the dark source calling for my focus once more as it revitalized our bonds, reigniting Aflora's veins, and shoving power back into her heart.

I felt her moving, her soul venturing *through* the dark source and back into the light.

Her light.

Her radiant star.

Her earth.

Her life.

Her vitality.

Soaring through the Midnight Fae web of power with a finality befitting a queen.

And landing in the still-warm body before me.

Her eyes opened, stars painting her pupils in blinding lights. And she took a renewed breath.

Our queen has officially risen.

CHAPTER TWENTY-SEVEN

KOLS

She's alive.

I could feel it in my bones, in my soul, in my every breath. The dark source had accepted her sacrifice. And allowed her soul to pass through the heart of Midnight Fae power before returning to her corporeal state.

She passed her trial.

Not just the sacrifice test, but the respect one as well. The knowledge echoed around us, the whole of Midnight Fae kind bowing to their chosen queen. It was the sort of respect that didn't need to be seen, but felt. And it sent me to my knees.

"My queen," I breathed, tears pooling in my eyes, battling the moisture that already existed from my earlier sadness. These new tears were ones of profound happiness and pride. "You did it."

Zeph stilled beside me, so lost in his grief that he hadn't noticed her return. Then he fell to his knees beside me for an entirely different reason, emotion ripping from his chest on an anguished cry he'd held within himself for too long, his pain overwhelming our bond.

I reached for him, steadying him and allowing him his moment. He'd been so shocked, and then stricken, that he hadn't been able to react. And now that Aflora was awake, he'd released a wave of anguish he could no longer contain.

Anguish that quickly turned to exuberance as he crawled toward her, his hand seeking hers.

It was probably the one and only time I would ever see him bend in such a way.

Shade? I whispered, noting his hunched shoulders and broken form. His forehead rested against Aflora's chest, his body unmoving.

He didn't reply.

Zeph kissed Aflora, a possessive growl going through him. "Don't you ever do that again."

Shade? I repeated, trying to find his mind in our connection. But all I heard was silence.

"Are you all right, little star?" Zakkai asked, kneeling beside the arm of the couch, close to her head and near Zeph.

Shade still didn't move, even as Zeph's body nudged him from the side.

Aflora nodded slowly, her blue eyes blinking up at Zakkai and Zeph. She glanced at me next, then down to Shade's bowed head.

She lifted her hand to run her fingers through his hair, saying nothing out loud. But I felt the hum of energy that suggested she spoke into his mind.

He didn't react.

I frowned.

"Shade." Aflora's voice was soft with sleep, like this had all been a strange nightmare, not a heartbreaking experience. "You've given us everything, Shade. It was my turn to sacrifice something for you."

Her fingers continued to comb through his hair, her motions tender and rhythmic.

"It's still the right path," she continued. "And you're the reason we're here." She looked at each of us. "You all are my purpose for being here." Her attention returned to the broken man against her chest. "And you made that possible, Shade."

She drew her touch down to his nape, his dark hair a stunning contrast to her pale skin.

"Life cannot exist without death," she whispered. "I understand that now. Because of you, Shade. Because of all of you."

She smiled, her expression breathtakingly real, and yet she glimmered like an intangible goddess.

You wear power beautifully, I said into her mind. *You're stunning.*

Electricity kissed my skin as she responded with magic instead of words, her control over the dark source nearly resolute.

"You're mine to protect now, too," she murmured to Shade. "We will all make sacrifices for each other. It's what makes us stronger. And we all know we have you to thank for paving the way for us. You gave us a gift that will never be repaid. But I will spend my eternity with you, trying to repay it."

"I don't want to be repaid," he muttered against her chest. "I just want you."

"You have me," she vowed. "You have me entirely."

His head slowly rose from her chest, his shoulders still rounded in pain. "It's my path in life to take risks for you. Not the other way around."

I had never heard him speak so gravely. He always boasted a worry-free air about him, like nothing ever disturbed him. But he acted with the utmost seriousness now.

"And it's my path in life to love you all," she whispered. "To never have to choose."

She pulled him to her, his body moving beneath her physical command.

"I would give anything and everything for all of you. Including myself. Because you demonstrated the importance of sacrifice, Shade. You showed me how to live. You taught me how to hate and how to love. You helped me learn how to fly free without restraints. And you're the reason I'm here today. Right now. Right here. With all of you."

She kissed him, her devotion branding our bonds as she committed herself to us all on a level that defied existence.

We were hers.

She was ours.

And together, we would persevere.

Together… we would fly.

We surrounded her, each taking turns to worship our goddess with our mouths, to express our gratitude and love and absolute reverence.

I was last, my lips tasting hers and all her other mates. A perfect union. A joyous occasion. A tender embrace.

She whispered my name, her fingers in my hair as I indulged in another kiss. Languid strokes. Heat. Beauty. Love.

I pressed my forehead to hers, sensing the budding urgency inside her.

It wasn't sexual, but arduous. Our embrace one underlined in the future, and a destiny calling her name.

Queen Aflora.

"It's time," she breathed, her power wrapping around all of us as she engaged Shade's shadow and took us to the LethaForest outside the main Academy, to the place where Midnight Fae life originally began.

It was a sacred platform surrounded by creatures and night and the hum of approval in the air. *Pure magic.*

Midnight Fae only congregated here once every one thousand years, the grounds a known place for dark source ascension.

That was what made the LethaForest so dangerous—the plant life, animals, and air were haunted by ancient magic. It made events unpredictable.

But today, the LethaForest was quiet. Hopeful. Waiting.

Aflora stood in the middle of it all with her enchanted cloak and staff, her blue-black hair blowing in an intangible breeze created by power and not the elements around her.

A circle of ancient trees surrounded us, their black branches flickering to life with fire to illuminate the night.

Magic brushed my skin as my cloak appeared at my shoulders, my bare chest suddenly covered by a button-down shirt, and my pajama pants replaced by black trousers.

Zeph, Zakkai, and Shade were all adorned in similar attire.

But the clasps of our cloaks were ruby roses with glistening stars at the center. The edges flared with defensive energy borrowed from Zeph, and the clasps connected themselves to the fabric with a series of multicolored roots.

One for each mate.

My heart warmed at the clear claim, our queen having gifted us all with her own token of favor.

And they shimmered in the moonlight, the red petals bleeding with renewed colors to match the roots.

A truly magical series of charms.

I stroked it with my thumb, sensing Aflora's touch, and smiled. *Thank you, love.*

She blew a kiss into my mind, then finished her own wardrobe with a flowing black dress that glimmered like a diamond, showcasing all the colors of the Midnight Fae.

Her gaze went to the tree line, her stance powerful as the branches began to rustle.

Then a wave of spells flew at her from the forest's edge—each one bouncing off a shield I hadn't felt her create.

Magnificent.

Our cloaks were the shield, her clasp the bearer of the protective spell. That was why I'd sensed Zeph within the magic. He'd taken up a guarded stance next to her with Zakkai on her opposite side, their positions ready for a fight.

But Aflora was clearly done with this battle.

She didn't cast any enchantments back at the approaching Warrior Bloods. She merely absorbed their charms and turned them to rose petals on the ground.

Shade took up a position behind her, so I stepped in front of her, the four of us creating a clear mate-circle around her.

That didn't stop the Warrior Bloods or the Elders behind them.

However, every offensive spell disintegrated into flowers, Aflora's power resolute.

Her hand settled on my shoulder, her petite frame hidden by my much taller one. I shifted as she stepped to my side, Zeph coming up next to me, with Zakkai and Shade completing the line on Aflora's left.

My grandfather appeared with my father and brother beside him, their collective fury stealing the breath from my lungs.

"Abomination!" they shouted.

"This cannot stand," my grandfather concluded.

"Yet you ensured my ascension yourself," Aflora replied calmly, a memory charm appearing as she blasted the event to all Midnight Fae.

"Soon they'll see you for what you are, Queen Aflora," my grandfather's voice reverberated through the LethaForest and all our minds. *"An abomination in the truest form. A monster. A being consumed by power, both Elemental Fae and Midnight Fae in nature. And I can't wait to watch you burn."*

"An abomination, yes," she agreed. "But I'm not the monster, Constantine. I'm not the being consumed by power. However, they all witnessed me burn, just like you'd said. And now they know my true nature, too."

Aflora's pity poured through our bond, her heart breaking for the man before her.

Not my father.

Not my brother.

But my grandfather.

"You want to control them all," she whispered. "Because you fear what you do not understand. You refuse to listen, to observe, to *learn*. You crave power as a protection, and it's consumed you entirely. Because you never learned balance."

Energy flowed through our connections as Aflora grounded herself by pushing the dark source to her mates, demonstrating her version of balance.

"You never learned how to love," she continued sadly. "And for that, I'm sorry for you. Emotions are what root us to life. Without them, we soar too high and forget how to feel. My mates—the ones you tried to force me to choose between—are my rocks. My foundation. The reasons I'm able to absorb and maintain connections to two sources."

She reached for my hand and Zakkai's, squeezing our palms.

"These Midnight Fae represent my balance. They're my kings. My equals. My own personal council. They're the reasons for my ascension today. Because they taught me how to live and love."

Silence fell, my grandfather's eyes narrowing.

However, all around the tree line... the Midnight Fae began to kneel.

Not to the Nacht line.

But to Aflora, Queen of the Midnight Fae.

A sliver of power slipped from beneath our shields, Aflora's energy wrapping around my father and brother as she untangled some invisible web from their auras. I couldn't see it, but I felt it.

Zakkai reached out as well, emboldening her work.

"What are you doing?" Constantine asked, sensing it as well. His eyes began to widen. "Don't you feel this witchery?" He looked to the Elders and the kneeling Warrior Bloods. "She's enchanted you all. Don't you sense it?"

"I'm not the one weaving enchantments, Elder Constantine," she replied. "I'm merely... undoing them."

My father gasped as he collapsed to one knee, his hand at his neck.

His golden irises found mine, abject horror radiating in his depths. "Kols..." Then he looked down at his own hands in shame as memories of what he'd done rolled through his features. "Dear Fae..." His attention turned upward to the man beside him. "My own son. You made me kill *my own son.*"

"For the betterment of Midnight Fae kind," my grandfather growled. "Which, clearly, you've all forgotten because *that thing* has bewitched you." He pointed to Aflora, his ire mounting by the second.

Zakkai's stance straightened, his gaze narrowing, his reaction telling me that my grandfather had accessed the dark source.

But a wave from Aflora's hand dismantled it all and caused flower petals to rain down from the clear sky.

My grandfather cursed.

And Tray clocked him with a fist to the side of the face. "Where the fuck is

Ella?" he demanded, taking the old man by the collar and strangling him with his grip. "Where is she?"

"She's coming." Aflora's reply was carried on the wind, her power so resolute that even I wanted to kneel. I'd never felt anything like it. My father had always boasted an energy that took my breath away, but Aflora… she was like holding on to the source itself. "She's safe, Tray."

My brother crumpled then, his agony shattering my heart.

I wanted to go to him, to hold him, to promise him that Ella would forgive him.

But a stroke from Shade's mind kept me steady.

Because my mate needed me more right now, my position beside her symbolic in so many ways. And she'd meant what she'd said—we were her anchors, the ones who kept her grounded.

If I left our cocoon of protection, my grandfather would use me against her. I couldn't allow that to happen.

My grandfather blasted Tray with a spell that put him on his ass, then lifted his hand with a lethal ball of WarFire meant to destroy. "You're all useless," he hissed, taking aim.

A jolt hit my heart, the fear on my twin's face causing me to take a step forward.

Don't, Shade demanded, his word freezing me in place.

The WarFire left my grandfather's palm, angling downward toward my brother's chest.

Tray! I tried to move, to go to him, to save him from his fate, but Zeph caught my shoulder, holding me in place.

My brother cried out as the spell hit him, only to freeze half a breath later as stone engulfed his form. I blinked, shocked by the instant marbleized state of death.

My father bellowed in fury, the dark source responding to his call and wrapping my grandfather in a sea of darkness.

But the man just laughed, dissolving the spell with a flick of his wand and shooting a volt into my father's abdomen, sending him to his knees beside Tray's still form.

"Magic is fascinating," a new voice said, deep and carrying and familiar. "It can be manipulated in so many ways." Tadmir stepped through the trees with several Councilmen at his back.

Gone were his usual black robes, replaced by a cloak edged in cerulean, his long white hair flickering with bluish-green flames.

"Sorry I'm late," he said. "I had some spells to unwind." He directed his wand at my brother, the stones fracturing around Tray's skin to reveal my irate twin beneath.

I blinked, confused by the sight of him squirming out from the marble encasement.

My grandfather appeared equally as enthralled and partially dumbfounded. He gaped at the approaching Councilmen, his gaze settling on the white-haired one at the front.

"Oh, yes, you don't recall this from our history together," Tadmir drawled. "Well, in a previous timeline, you knew my true nature. You killed my Quandary Blood mate. Tried to take my son, too."

A dark-haired male with tattoos swirling up his arm appeared in the next instant to lean against a tree. My eyebrows lifted in recognition. *Kyros. Paradox Fae.* He'd been the one helping Shade manipulate time.

The male winked at me as though he'd heard my thoughts, then kicked up his foot behind him to rest against the trunk of the tree.

"Unfortunately, time did not allow me to save my mate. But it did allow me to properly prepare for you and your destructive plans for the Midnight Fae." He waved a hand over himself. "You wanted an all-male council, so I became a Malefic Blood and took a new mate—a female who was best friends with my previous one. It's a long, drawn-out story that ends in a myriad of timelines, this one being the preferred avenue, of course."

His eyes lifted to Aflora.

"The timeline where she becomes queen," he concluded with a smile. "I told you that you knew me. And now you see why. We're alike, you and I. Abominations who use our power for the betterment of the world, not to destroy it."

"The message on the rock," she breathed, her lips curling faintly. "I remember, and now I see."

"You do," he agreed, bowing his head in subtle reverence. "My queen."

"This is what I've warned everyone about," my grandfather said, his fear palpable. "That abominations live among us and will take our kingdoms. You're proof. This is proof. The fae kingdoms need to see!" He sent up a spark of power that blew in a sudden gust of wind, dissolving in fire a beat later.

He gaped at it, then his gaze flew to the tree line as an abundance of power rocked the earth.

A familiar presence touched my senses as the trees parted in reverence, allowing the Elemental Fae Queen to enter with her Spirit Fae King and Water Fae King mates on either side of her.

And a very irritated-looking Earth Fae behind them.

I swallowed.

The last time I saw that giant rock of a man, he'd introduced his fist to my face. And I really wasn't in the mood for a repeat performance.

A Fire Fae and an Air Fae appeared next, the queen's entire circle surrounding her in obvious protection.

Then her gaze locked on Aflora.

Everyone stilled.

Until my grandfather smiled. "I told you she was an abomination. Just like Elana. I think you know what has to be done."

Oh, fuck.

CHAPTER TWENTY-EIGHT

AFLORA

I squeezed Kols's hand, sensing his tension.

We both knew what Constantine's words implied and how they might be perceived, but I felt the earth source shining down upon me. Which meant Sol could sense it, too.

His green-brown irises met mine over Claire's head, his concern evident in his features. But one look and his lips curled at the edges.

He knew I was still me. Just a new and improved version.

An enhanced one.

More powerful.

But still an Earth Fae at heart.

I curtsied to my Elemental Fae Queen, showing my respect. "Queen Claire," I greeted softly. A few months ago, I would have run up and begged her to take me home. But seeing her now, surrounded by her mates, I realized that they no longer represented my preferred haven.

The Midnight Fae realm was my home now, my roots having grown deep into the soil of this world and claimed it as my own.

Because of my mates.

And the dark source.

These fae needed me more, too. They required my light and life to guide them into a phase of regrowth and prosperity.

Which required me to do something destructive first.

Something I would never have considered doing just weeks ago.

But I'd learned through my trials that sometimes we must destroy to pave the way for re-creation. For life could not exist without death.

Constantine was a bad seed, his mentality so warped by wrongness that he could no longer see the light. Being a queen required tough choices, and this would be my burden to bear.

My final ascension trial.

Returning the bad seed to the earth, where it could eventually be reborn and blossom into something good.

Claire studied me, her blue irises intense and guarded as memories flashed through her eyes. I recognized the haunted gleam in her features because I often felt it myself when I thought about Elana. She'd destroyed nearly all the Spirit Fae with a plague that she'd later turned on the Earth Fae.

I'd felt that dark magic, had absorbed and dismantled it before it could reach the heart of my source. I hadn't understood it at the time, my mind working on protective instinct alone, but now I knew that gift had come from Zakkai.

As his Quandary Blood mate, I'd been able to save my fellow Earth Fae by reconfiguring Elana's spell and pushing it away from my kingdom.

Which meant I'd been an abomination all along, since the young age of seven.

Yet I lived in peace with my fellow Elemental Fae. And now I would share that peace with the Midnight Fae.

"I'm not a threat," I told her softly. "It's not how much power we have that matters; it's how we use it." And if anyone would understand that, it would be Claire. As an Elemental Fae with access to all five elements, she knew better than anyone what power could do to a fae.

"Being connected to two sources makes you beyond powerful," Constantine seethed. "It makes you wicked and deceitful, and I'll ensure that everyone sees through this charade you've created." Inky wisps of energy seeped from his fingertips while he spoke, but no one else seemed to notice.

The dark source protested in my heart, telling me this wasn't the way, begging me to fix it.

This was the magic he'd used to manipulate and control others, the wicked spell that had consumed two Elite Bloods and likely several others.

Tadmir's obsidian gaze met mine, knowledge sprouting from his depths.

He can't see it, but he can feel it, Zakkai explained. *Just like me. Although, I can sense it more clearly through your mind.*

It's like black tendrils of smoke, I told him. *Pouring out of him in waves.*

This is his final stand, Zakkai whispered as the power strengthened, sending electric sparks across my psyche.

Yes.

But I wasn't going to fight Constantine.

Enough fae had been injured and hurt by his games and antics. I wanted to blossom on a platform of regrowth and life. Not stand on the skulls of those who had wronged fae kind.

This kingdom had been ruled by death for far too long.

It was time to demonstrate what vitality and light could do.

Constantine sent his power outward on a rush of air, touching the souls of everyone nearby, even Claire. But I caught the roots before they could connect to the cores of their beings.

And I gently pulled it back, refusing to allow their spirits to be tarnished by his darkness anymore.

"Constantine Nacht," I said, my voice carrying through the LethaForest and beyond. "You rule from a throne of destruction and hate. It's time for a new era of re-creation and love."

I pulled his spell into my staff while I spoke, the black ribbons easily responding to my call.

"Abominations are not who should be feared. They're beings of love, created by fae who choose to mate outside their kingdoms to other beings of similar but different heritages. That's something to be celebrated, not destroyed." I looked at the Elemental Fae Monarch. "Wouldn't you agree, Queen Claire?"

She was a Halfling, a being born of an Elemental Fae and a human. But because of her mortal half, no one seriously referred to her as an abomination —just a few used it as an insult when feeling cruel. However, was it really so different?

"I would," she replied, her tone regal, her head high. "Love is the most powerful element of all."

"Emotions are powerful tools," I agreed, returning my attention to Constantine. He'd created more of that smoke, his expression impassive in his attempt not to give anything away. Because he had no idea I could see him for who he really was—a broken soul trapped in the body of a powerful Elite Blood Elder.

Destroying his shell wouldn't fix the darkness inside him.

He needed to live. To see. To *witness*.

His fate appeared to me in the blink of an eye, the dark source agreeing with my decision in my next breath as I began to spin those obsidian fibers into vine-like roots near his feet.

He didn't notice, too focused on creating more… and more… his desire to manipulate and control consuming him from the inside out and blackening his ability to decipher his destiny.

He was a being of his own creation.

Dark ire.

Obsidian flames.

Obsessive soul.

Tadmir gave a brief nod, having either seen my intent or felt it, I didn't know. But Zakkai's palm squeezing mine suggested the latter. Because he could see the enchantment forming now, weaving around and through Constantine's legs as the Elder continued to exude power.

He didn't seem to understand why it wasn't working, his frustration beginning to mar his brow as he issued a demand through the dark source.

But the dark source no longer responded to him.

It was mine to command.

I couldn't say when I'd ascended, but I felt it thriving through my veins, the energy calling me queen as I stood upon the ancient breeding ground of Midnight Fae power.

I'd had no idea why I'd run here all those months ago to expel the abundance of vitality swimming through my being. But I understood now. The LethaForest had called to me for a purpose, demanding I revitalize the land here in preparation for my eventual ascension.

I'd been the chosen queen all along.

Kols had been the Midnight Fae Prince meant to guide me through his trial… and then sacrifice his throne to me, the rightful royal.

An Earth Fae Queen connected to two regal Midnight Fae bloodlines, the mate of the Source Architect, and the chosen ward of a strong Warrior Blood.

This is the path we were always meant to walk, I whispered to Shade.

Yes, he agreed. *It just took eight tries to get it right.*

I merely smiled. *I have some stubborn mates.*

He snorted. *Understatement.*

I heard that, Zeph replied dryly.

I think we all did, Kols replied.

Our minds were connecting in a strange way, almost as though I'd crossed all our wires to ensure we could have one open link. I still had my links to each of them as well, but this new open forum… was the result of my Earth Fae magic.

I glanced at Claire in surprise, noting her smile.

Earth Fae bonds, I realized. *The fourth level.*

It always required a ceremony, a ritual of magic and words, but somehow Claire had urged us all along, creating a divine mating unlike any I'd ever heard of existing.

Her access to the elements had grown. I could feel that now as she lurked on the edge of the earth source, her roots stroking the energy without anchoring.

Because she respected me as the Earth Fae Queen.

And this gift of intensifying my mating to Kols, Zeph, Shade, and Zakkai was her way of demonstrating that it was indeed not about how much power we possessed, but how we used it.

Thank you, I thought, conveying the message with my eyes.

She smiled slightly and curtsied, her head bowing in deference, just as I'd done when she'd arrived.

Two queens acknowledging the rule of the other.

Respecting boundaries.

And celebrating each other's monarchy.

Which meant she knew I wasn't Elana, that despite my abomination status, she trusted me in a way. And from the looks of her mates, they did, too.

Constantine growled then, drawing my focus back to him, his fury a sharp spike in the air as he tried one last time to issue an enchantment. But it was already too late for him. The roots were well dug into the soil below him, the smoky embers of his earlier spells solidifying to obsidian rock around him as the trunk of a new tree sprouted upward in a series of lethal vines.

His eyes widened. "Don't just stand there!" His shout was directed at the still-kneeling Warrior Bloods. Or maybe at the other Elders and Councilmen. "Do something!"

"We are," Tadmir replied flatly. "We're watching and admiring our Midnight Fae Queen's choice of punishment." His black orbs sparkled at me, his lips curling in faint amusement. "Which I must say is quite fitting."

Indeed, Zakkai agreed in my mind. *You're trapping him in a tree.*

I'm creating a symbol of our future, I corrected. *By… wrapping a tree around him.* Which would trap him for eternity, but that wasn't the point.

His hand squeezed mine, his entertainment palpable.

I ignored the urge to smile and focused on the life growing against the earth below. "Destruction is sometimes required to renew life. But it's how we administer that destruction, and the lessons that are born with it, that matters most," I told Constantine softly. "You'll forever serve as a reminder of that, as your soul will reside within the tree of your own magical creation… for eternity."

He opened his mouth to reply, his gold irises flaring with magic, but the trunk of the tree silenced him as the dark, tendril-like vines slid over his mouth and wrapped around the back of his head.

Blissful silence fell as the life continued to sprout upward, the trunk sturdy and wide and wrapped in all the dark sins of the man beneath. I'd taken his dark magic and made it corporeal, each pulsing vein a spell I'd retracted from the Midnight Fae of this realm.

Because now that I knew what enchantment he favored for his manipulation, I could sense them all over the kingdom.

I pulled them back through my connection to the dark source.

And wrapped the power around the base, watching as it curled higher and higher until the tree was several stories in the air, its branches dusted with burning flames that would always burn as a reminder to the Midnight Fae of how far we'd come.

"A show of rebirth," I sighed, content with the design. "A tree of retribution, meant to inspire reformation."

A show of light came from the forest, little dots flickering in the air as hundreds of Midnight Fae approached, their wands held like torches.

Zenaida led one side.

Laki led the other.

Midnight Fae of all types followed behind them, entering the clearing of the trees, filling up as much space as the ground would allow.

They lifted the wands toward the sky.

And bowed their heads.

"Our queen has ascended," Zen proclaimed.

"Our queen has ascended," several repeated.

And then they began to chant an ancient hymn, the words lyrical to my ears.

It's a song of the Midnight Fae, praising the dark source for its choice, Kols explained softly, his lips ghosting over my temple. *They're singing about you, Aflora. About our new Queen of the Midnight Fae.*

CHAPTER TWENTY-NINE

KOLS

"Your ascensions are a lot more exciting than ours," Cyrus murmured as he sipped from a glass of fiery lemonade. His water magic kept cooling the liquid before it reached his tongue, thereby defeating the entire purpose of the spell. But I wasn't about to correct the Water Fae King.

"You turn former kings into trees, nearly burn down a forest with a bunch of flickering wands, and then throw one hell of a party," he continued. "I mean, seriously, I'm impressed, and a little miffed that this only happens once every thousand years."

I snorted. "I assure you, they are not all like this." At least, none that I knew about, which was arguably only one.

And actually, that'd been a rather deadly ascension considering the Quandary Blood extermination that had followed.

I frowned.

Maybe Cyrus had a point.

"I know a way to make this all even more exciting," a deep voice said behind me, the tone reminding me of grating rocks.

I shivered as the giant boulder of an Earth Fae placed his palm on my shoulder and gave it a good, not-so-tender squeeze.

"Kolstov," he said.

"Sol," I replied. *Shade? I might need you to shadow me in a moment.*

His amusement came back through the bond. *And miss watching that Earth Fae knock you in the face with his fist? Nah, I'm good right here.*

I narrowed my gaze at him. *Shall I tell him how you bit Aflora against her will? Then insist upon an introduction afterward?*

"Cyrus," Zeph's voice interjected, his presence at my side reassuring and protective as he looked at the hand on my shoulder and followed it up to the owner. "Sol."

"Zephyrus," the Earth Fae replied coolly.

"Well, this ought to be fun," someone said from behind us, causing Cyrus to roll his eyes.

"You just want to watch them fight," the Water Fae King said.

"Correction"—Titus, who I assumed was the one to speak previously, joined our little circle and bumped shoulders with Zeph—"I want to see this one fight."

My Guardian snorted. "You couldn't handle me in a fight."

"Is that a threat?" Sol demanded.

I sighed. *Aflora?*

She shadowed over to us in a blink, her blue eyes blazing with power. The second she appeared, Sol released me and engulfed her much smaller frame in a hug that had Zeph growling beside me. She squealed as the larger Earth Fae picked her up and whirled her around, then she laughed as he set her down, their friendship clearly born of brotherly and sisterly love.

But I also knew she used to harbor a crush on the brute.

So that soured some of my amusement.

As did the look he gave me as he put his arm around her.

Protective didn't even begin to describe that look. It was more of an expression that said, *If you hurt her again, I will rip you apart and enjoy it.*

Claire joined us then, her indulgent gaze going to Cyrus and Titus before Sol. "No, you can't turn them into rocks. Aflora wouldn't approve."

He grunted. "Soiling my fun."

Soil, I thought, snorting. *Earth Fae puns?*

I suddenly see where Aflora's vocabulary comes from, Zeph returned.

"Stop being such a boulder, Sol," Aflora murmured, kissing him on the cheek and earning another low growl from Zeph.

"I think you need more lemonade," I suggested lightly, glancing up at my Guardian.

He didn't move.

"Right," I murmured. "Well. Thank you all for coming."

I wasn't sure what else to say, so I kept to the formalities of thanking the royals for attending the ascension. I'd learned from Cyrus that Constantine had reached out to the other realms to tell them about Aflora and had requested assistance. Claire had been the only one to respond, the other fae kingdoms telling him to handle his own mess.

I suspected the Hell Fae King had something to do with those refusals. I couldn't say why; it was more of an instinct that I'd inherited from Shade.

Keep rummaging in my head and you'll lose yourself, he warned now, picking up on my thoughts.

Shouldn't have mated me, then, I tossed back.

Wouldn't change it for the world, he admitted, flashing me a quick grin before refocusing on Tadmir. He'd been in the middle of providing an update on Ajax, something about him taking a new position with Zen. I hadn't quite followed but intended to ask about it after the ceremony.

Especially since whatever Tadmir was saying about Ajax seemed to have

Kyros's full interest as well, something I gathered might not be common for the Paradox Fae.

Aflora stepped out of Sol's embrace and squeezed in between me and Zeph, her arm going around his waist as her head rested on my shoulder.

Where's Zakkai? I asked her.

With Zen and Laki, she replied on a sigh. *They're talking with your dad about how to move forward.*

Is that where you were? I wondered, feeling bad for interrupting such an important discussion.

Yes.

Do you need to go back?

No, I'm tired of discussing politics, she replied. *I would much rather act as a barrier between you and Sol's fist.*

I snorted. *I can handle myself.*

You can. But I want to be the only one who draws blood from you. She shifted to kiss my jaw while the Earth Fae watched.

He clearly didn't approve, but a nudge from his queen had him relaxing marginally.

Titus had taken Cyrus's drink from him, his fascination over the flames evident as he created several of his own to dance with the embers. Meanwhile, Cyrus had lowered his focus to the neckline of Claire's dress, which he clearly found more intriguing than the lemonade in Titus's hand.

What an odd little circle we all made.

Exos and Vox were off talking philosophy with Chern, who Aflora stated wasn't under a spell at all. The Sangré Blood Councilman had never outwardly displayed emotion or preference, marking him as a Midnight Fae to watch. However, I suspected he approved of Aflora's ascension because he'd told her sincerely that it was a logical choice.

Tray and Ella were nowhere to be seen, having run into each other's arms shortly after the wand ceremony. I had a pretty good idea of what they were up to, but didn't want to go searching to find out. I would share a private moment with my twin later. For now, I was satisfied knowing my twin was healthy and alive.

Everyone else seemed to be tentatively conversing, several fae having not seen old friends for over a thousand years, and younger Midnight Fae softly asking Quandary Bloods questions about their paradigms and how they'd been hiding.

The sky above was bleeding with color, the sun rising to overtake the moon.

Our evening ascension was slowly coming to an end, the LethaForest preparing itself to return to its usual protective antics.

With Constantine's tree lingering at the center of it all, the twisted black branches littered with flames.

It was a sight to behold, one I could never have imagined.

So many lives had been lost. Friends, family, innocent fae.

But as Aflora had said, where there was life, there was death.

Fortunately, my mother was not among those souls. She'd been locked up by my grandfather and now stood in the clearing near Shade's mom.

Aswad lurked nearby, his expression one of confusion and loss. He'd been a victim of my grandfather, as had several other Councilmen, including Emelyn's father, Lima, who had broken down into hysterics shortly after being freed from the spell. At least, that had been Tadmir's report and explanation as to why Lima had not attended the ceremony.

I felt for the Elite Blood on some levels but blamed him on others. Lima had always craved power, hence his arranging a marriage between me and his daughter. So while he might have been more recently under my grandfather's spell, he hadn't always been that way.

As far as Aswad was concerned, I wasn't sure how I felt. I could sense Shade's disbelief surrounding his father's sincerity and his questions around whether or not he had truly been under a spell. However, Tadmir did confirm that he'd unwound the manipulation charm himself prior to the ceremony. And he also sensed that it had been there for quite some time.

Exos had overheard our brief conversation and mentioned something about a Spirit Fae named Mortus undergoing a similar experience with Elana. Shade had asked if he trusted the Spirit Fae, and Exos had frowned, saying, "Not quite."

A sentiment Shade and I shared not just about Aswad but about the other Councilmen and Elders as well.

We'd be watching and ready to deal with those threats as they arose, because no one would be touching our queen.

Zeph hummed in agreement in my head, our connections wide open, thanks to the Earth Fae bonds that had settled between us all.

Although, Aflora mentioned it wasn't normal for the link to be so vast, saying that she was fairly certain Claire and her mates couldn't speak this way. Of course, she'd never sought definitive proof of that belief because it really wasn't anyone's business whether or not Claire's mates could speak to one another.

Regardless, I suspected our ability to converse was due to the mingling of dark source and earth source together, and perhaps the result of several of us sharing our own bonds with each other, too.

Aflora sighed contentedly against me, her body seeming to sway.

I think our star is ready to go home, Zakkai said to us all. *The question is, which home?*

I know a place, Shade replied.

Of course you do, Zeph drawled. *Another paradigm?*

A final secret feels like a right of passage, Shade said, ignoring the question. *Shall we?*

Aflora hummed, saying she needed to wish a few fae goodbye, which included Claire and all her mates. They were heading back to their kingdom rather than staying, Exos stating that the Death magic was irritating his ties to the Spirit Kingdom—a fact Shade found amusing.

Eventually, the formalities were done. I didn't hug my father but told him we would talk. His expression said he understood, our last meeting not having been a favorable one. And if I was honest, his inability to stand up to my grandfather bothered me a bit. As the Midnight Fae King, he should have been stronger.

But that was a conversation and concern for another day.

Shade didn't approach his own father but did hug his mother.

When I couldn't find Tray or Ella, I decided to give them their peace and returned to my mate. *They're okay,* she whispered to me, taking my hand. *I can sense their content.*

Thank you, I replied, reaching for Shade as he wrapped us all up in a cloak of shadows.

He grabbed my hip, pulling me toward him and stirring a growl from Zeph.

I just shook my head and smiled. Because possessive Zeph was my favorite kind.

Which meant we were in for a whole day of wicked fun.

CHAPTER THIRTY

SHADE

My heart skipped a beat as we materialized in the middle of a rose garden—one I had created a month before I'd bitten Aflora.

I'd promised myself then that I wouldn't come back here until she was ready.

And I hoped now that I'd made the right choice. Because I couldn't imagine a better time.

Zakkai frowned as he wandered to the edge of the garden to look over the cliff into the ocean, his white brow arching upward as he glanced back at me. "California?" he guessed.

I nodded.

"Why California?" Kols asked, his eyes on the bright blue sky overhead. "This isn't Death Blood territory."

"No. But the future Fortune Fae Alpha of this region is a friend." Assuming he got his shit in order and followed his right path. Unfortunately, his mother's death might alter it. In addition to a dozen other obstacles. But I had faith he'd work it out. In time.

"Seif?" Kols guessed, aware of my friendship with the Death Blood who had recently turned into a Fortune Fae Alpha.

"Yes."

He stared at me for a moment, a question lingering in his mind about how I knew this would eventually be Seif's territory. But rather than voice it, he just went back to admiring the sky. *Does he know about Anrika yet?* he asked softly.

Grandfather Kodiak said he was handling it. I would have done it myself, but with everything else going on, there hadn't been time. *He's making sure Seif receives Anrika's death message, too.* Because she'd cast a charm above her body, the message of it meant for Seif. I didn't know what it said, nor did I want to know. Some things weren't my story to tell.

"This is beautiful," Aflora whispered, her fingers traveling over the rosebushes and causing the flowers to bloom. She knelt to touch the soil, excitement radiating off her as she began studying all the life around her.

This was why I'd chosen this home.

It went on for acres along the cliffs, the expensive property front private and stunning and perfect for a little garden nymph to run around and play.

She seemed to sense that purpose now as she giggled and began to frolic through the garden to the copse of trees beyond. There was a pool somewhere, too. But I doubted that was her intended destination.

Zeph followed her with a predatory grin, something I felt Kols responding physically to through our bond.

Zakkai seemed content to admire the sea, his nostrils flaring as the ocean breeze tousled his thick white hair.

"My mother used to love the ocean," he told me as Kols followed Zeph in pursuit of Aflora. "I remember her always wanting to make sandcastles with me as a child." His lips curled with the memories. "Aflora and I used to make them, too. But out of dirt in the Elemental Fae realm. I wonder if she remembers."

"I'm sure she does," I said quietly.

He dipped his chin, then sighed. "This is a beautiful home, Shadow. I suppose all those trips through time allowed you to gamble a little with human currency?"

I merely stared at him, not inclined to give anything away.

"Don't suppose you stopped by a casino in the region? Perhaps one in the Vegas area?"

"Why would I do that?" I countered, neither confirming nor denying the obvious guess.

"Why indeed?" He slid his hands into his black slacks and looked out at the ocean again. "How many times do you think Tadmir has taken all of us back in total?"

"Too many to count," I answered honestly.

He nodded. "My thoughts exactly." Then he smiled, the sight a rare expression of enjoyment in his features. Because it lacked mockery. This was just Zakkai... grinning in content. "We owe you both a great deal of gratitude."

"You more than them," I half joked.

"Yes, I imagine I was quite difficult."

"Because you knew." Not a question, but a statement.

"Because I knew," he admitted. "Just not the extent or particulars of what you were doing, but I could feel it as a result of my ascension."

Yeah, I suspected as much. "Why did you go along with it this time?" In previous timelines, he'd always fought me or found a loophole. But in this one... he was almost acquiescent.

"Maybe I was tired."

"Or maybe you fell in love," I suggested.

"I absolutely fell in love," he agreed, his irises flaring as he looked in the direction Kols and Zeph had gone. "We should go after them before they have all the fun."

"Yes, I imagine Aflora is already naked." Because I could feel Kols's amusement and intrigue in the bond.

"She is," Zakkai replied, grinning. "She's gone full garden nymph, just like you desired."

"Poking around in my head?"

"Always." He glanced at me with an unrepentant look. "Your mind is fascinating, Shadow. So many secrets and hidden agendas. Which reminds me, that meeting with Lucifer that you scheduled on my behalf for next week? You're coming with me."

I sighed. "Of course I am."

Wickedness darkened his features. "It'll be fun, Shadow."

"Deals always are," I muttered, walking with him to find our Aflora.

She was indeed naked.

And dancing through a bed of flowers that definitely hadn't been there when we'd arrived.

Zeph had taken up a position by a tree, his shoulder braced against the bark. Kols stood with him, both of them aroused and entertained by the sight of our mate spinning with glee.

"Don't we need to fuck to finish the Earth Fae mating?" Zakkai called to her, his direct manner causing her to stumble and nearly fall.

I shadowed to her side, catching her on instinct. And she giggled against my chest. Her blue eyes met mine, the little nymph drunk on her earth source. "Sex sounds nice," she said on a sigh. "Shade goes first."

Then she pulled me down to the flowers and covered us in a canopy of petals.

Zeph and Zakkai both protested, while Kols merely laughed.

My clothes disappeared beneath her power, leaving me as naked as her and on my back in the soil. I arched a brow. "No foreplay?" I teased, already rock hard from her show of strength alone.

"Mmm." She straddled my hips, her expression radiating pure, unadulterated joy. "We've been playing for months." She seated herself to the hilt, her body moving sensuously against mine. "Now I just want you, Shadow. My Death Blood Prince. And your very impressive *cock*."

I chuckled, grabbing her hips to flip her to her back. I settled between her thighs and drove into her again, my lips going to her ear. "You've been talking to Zeph too much. He's dirtied your mouth."

"Do you prefer *willow stump*?" she asked on a breath as her hips rose eagerly to meet mine.

"Do I feel like a *willow stump* to you?"

"I don't know," she moaned. "Fuck me harder and I'll report back later."

I chuckled against her neck. "You really are a nymph, little rose."

"Yes," she agreed. "Now stop talking and take me to oblivion."

"Anything for you," I whispered, loving her with my body, my mouth, and my hands. Our Earth Fae bond was very much alive and fully in place, but sex was how Elemental Fae culminated the act.

And I felt it now, that warm energy of her sunbathing me in rightness, claiming me as Aflora's mate, and ensuring my roots forever twined with hers.

"I love you," she told me softly, her arms around my neck as our bodies joined together as one.

"I love you, too, little rose." I kissed her then, unleashing all my gratitude and longing and appreciation into her mouth. All those years of dancing with fate. All those timelines. All those mistakes. All those near ends. I'd almost lost her so many times. But here she was, my sweet, beautiful Aflora, in a bed of her own creation, blossoming with life and happiness.

Finally, I thought, reveling in the dream of the moment. *It's finally… done.*

She cupped my cheek, her legs encircling my waist as I slid deeper into her. *You can rest now, Shade,* she murmured. *You can finally enjoy the moment without worrying about what comes next. You can finally… exist.*

With you, I replied, my pace increasing. *I can finally exist… with you.*

Yes. Her teeth skimmed my lower lip. "Bite me," she breathed. "Bite me like it's the first time. Claim me as yours the right way."

I shivered, then did exactly as she'd asked, my teeth sinking into her throat as I pulled her powerful blood into my mouth on a groan that traveled miles and miles.

She moaned in response, her tight sheath squeezing me as she came undone, her orgasm yanking me down with her, our shared pleasure burning through my veins and touching my very soul.

Her blunt teeth caught my pulse and she bit down, drinking from me as I'd done from her.

Our connection only strengthened, our souls already married as one.

But some part of me felt even more complete, even more owned, even more accepted. I pressed my head to her shoulder, panting from the exertion of our connection.

Then I closed my eyes and did exactly what she'd said.

I existed and didn't worry about the next moment.

Because, for the first time in my life, I didn't have to.

I could just… be.

CHAPTER THIRTY-ONE

ZEPH

I watched Aflora take Kols deep into her mouth, my little garden siren coming alive as she drank down his climax and urged him to give her more with her tongue.

She was stunning.

Perfect.

Alluring as fuck.

I was so damn hard, my balls aching in protest at wanting to be inside her. But this was about bonding. She'd already taken Shade… *twice*. Now she'd finished with Kols, leaving me and Zakkai naked on either side of her.

We'd never all played at once, but something about the uniting of earth had required it.

Aflora had beckoned us into her garden, her canopy of flowers growing to create a pretty little shelter to hide our afternoon fuck fest.

Shade was off to the side, watching from beneath heavy lids.

Kols crawled over to him, and they started making out, which only seemed to make my cock harder and Aflora needier.

She was three orgasms in, two from Shade and one from my mouth.

But the Earth Fae bonds required more.

Elemental Fae were famous for their insatiable need, particularly with their mates. And we were all fourth-level bonded now, which explained her growing desire for *more*.

She wrapped her palm around my neck, pulling me to her as she went to her knees, and forced me to accept her kiss. Gone was my obedient little Earth Fae, and in her place, a hungry vixen who took what she wanted. I knelt with her, aligning our thighs and pressing my cock into her lower abdomen.

Zakkai moved in behind her, his tongue traveling down her spine as his hand disappeared between her spread legs.

I knew what he intended because I felt it through the roots in my mind—he wanted to take her from behind while I went in the front.

I hadn't planned to make sharing Aflora with him a regular occurrence, but I wasn't going to complain.

The man packed a hell of a lot of power.

If he wanted to fuck her with me, then I'd be a fool to say no.

She moaned against my tongue, liking what he did below.

I reached up to palm her breast, her nipple tight and needy against my skin. She threaded her fingers through my hair to guide me down, needing my lips against her tender skin.

Fuck, Kols whispered in my head, drawing my attention to him.

Shade had kissed a path down the other man's body to suck him in the same way Aflora had only moments ago, and from the pleasure in her features now, she very much approved of the show.

I distracted her by skimming my teeth against her tit and capturing her rosy peak.

She shuddered, then moaned as Zakkai entered her pussy, filling her to the hilt without warning.

Then she groaned in annoyance when he pulled out.

I met his gaze, saw the certainty in his features that she was ready for us both, and watched as he slid into her ass.

She grabbed my shoulders to steady herself for his intrusion, her eyes flaring wide with lust and excitement.

It was the look of a woman ready to be shared.

I caught her mouth and grinned as Kols cursed again, Shade proving to be quite skilled with his tongue.

Something I might have to indulge in someday.

But for now, I wanted Aflora's slick heat and tight channel.

I moved into her, securing her between me and Zakkai. Then I lifted her leg up to wrap around my hips, leaving her to balance on one knee.

She didn't protest, her body already angling toward me in preparation for my entry.

Rather than deny her, I slid home in a single thrust, filling her to completion and feeling Zakkai's throbbing shaft through the thin wall inside her.

So hot, I thought, groaning into her mind. *You're so fucking hot.*

Fuck me, she replied, using my favorite command. *Fuck me hard. Don't hold back. Please don't hold back.*

I don't think I could if I tried, I admitted, setting a pace that Zakkai met in equal measure.

He had one palm on her hip, his other around her throat as he guided her back to kiss him. I held on to her leg, my other hand sliding between us to better access her clit.

She moaned, her nipples sharp little points against my chest as we drove into her.

Kols and Shade had stopped their playing to enjoy the show, their intrigue only heightening the moment.

Then they both moved forward to worship Aflora with their mouths, kissing her shoulders, her arms, licking her fingers, and ensuring she felt them with her as Zakkai and I took her body.

It was sinful decadence and depraved indulgence, and I loved every fucking second of it.

My teeth sank into Kols's throat, needing his essence.

He groaned in response, then pulled Aflora's mouth away from Zakkai to kiss her.

Zakkai went to her throat, biting her deep and eliciting a tender sound from her lips.

Our fucking turned animalistic, blood-sharing happening between all of us as Aflora bit our tongues while kissing and we bit each other to fulfill our darker cravings.

Aflora's hands left my shoulders, her palms wrapping around Shade and Kols on either side of her as she strove to provide them with as much pleasure as we were giving her.

Her power pulsed around us, her inner vixen demanding we unwind and come as one.

"Fuck," I breathed. "*Fuck*, Aflora."

Zakkai echoed my sentiment, his muscles strained as he teetered on the edge of climax.

"*Now*," Aflora screamed, energy shooting out of her through our bonds and taking us beneath a cloud of ecstasy that blanketed my mind in dizzying passion.

My stomach clenched, my cock throbbing as I unloaded inside her, filling her with my seed as Kols and Shade came undone on either side of us, their cum painting Aflora's skin.

Zakkai was last, his orgasm whipping through us all, his power making me explode again, right on the heels of my first climax.

So damn intense.

So fucking amazing.

So incredibly *us*.

I caught Aflora's mouth, feeling her tight sheath pulse around me with the residuals of her own pleasure, and told her how much I loved her, how perfect she was, and praised her for accepting us all.

She kissed me back, then Shade, then Kols, and finally Zakkai, her heart wide open and ours.

And we gave our love and adoration back to her in kind.

Then I scooped her up and carried her inside the large home Shade clearly owned, and asked, "Where's the bedroom?"

CHAPTER THIRTY-TWO

AFLORA

A Month Later

I sat at the counter, watching as Zeph cooked an orc steak on the grill pan. Zakkai stood near him, his brow furrowed. "Is it supposed to be purple like that?"

"Sometimes," I replied. "It can be blue, too."

His nose crinkled. "How appetizing."

"It is," I insisted, my stomach growling in anticipation as Zeph flipped the steak over.

Kols and Shade were at the table sharing some pasta dish they'd just picked up in Rome. Because my Elite Blood mate was obsessed with Italian food, something I'd learned over the last month in this realm.

We'd spent most of our weeks here in Shade's home on the cliffs, indulging in our bonds and enjoying a much-needed break from Midnight Fae life.

However, Shade and Zakkai had left a few times to "tie up loose ends." Which I translated to mean meeting with Lucifer, meeting with Zen, and generally supervising the former Councilmen.

They'd also tracked down Dakota, as she'd been missing from the ascension ritual. I wasn't sure what they'd done to her, but I'd felt her life strand sever from the source. Which told me she was dead. I just didn't ask how, because I preferred not to know.

And Kols had gone back home twice to see Tray and his parents. He and his father were still on uncomfortable terms, but at least they were talking. Tray had also moved out with Ella, and they were residing in Massachusetts right now at the Nacht Estates.

I intended to go visit them next week, as I missed them.

But for now, I was content to just be here. Relaxing. Living. And preparing for our next steps.

Which was pretty straightforward—we needed a new Midnight Fae Council.

While most of the Councilmen had been under Constantine's control, it remained to be seen how long they'd been suffering from his power trip. They'd also lost the faith of Midnight Fae kind. As had the Elders. Even those like Kols's great-grandfather, who had been put into a magically induced coma by Constantine, were no longer trusted.

Therefore, we were proposing a new Council and allocating advisory positions to take over for the former Elders.

"Have you spoken to Tadmir about Stiggis and Cordelia?" I asked Shade.

He finished swallowing his bite of food and nodded. "Yeah, he's still talking to them about the Council. I think he wants them to shadow him for a bit first since neither of them was ever really prepared to take over. Well, Stiggis was to an extent, but not Cordelia. And I think she might be the better option."

"She's certainly more even-keeled than her brother," Zeph agreed. "Minus losing her shit over your infidelity."

Shade snorted. "It was an arranged marriage front that gave me access to Tadmir."

"I don't think the poor girl saw it that way," Zeph drawled. "Hence my questioning her ability to be on the Council. Anyone who loses their mind over you is clearly not stable."

"Don't mind him," Kols said, setting down his fork and reaching for his beer. "He's just sour that you won't suck his cock."

"And he wonders why I won't," Shade muttered.

My Warrior Blood mate glowered while Zakkai grinned, entertained by their bickering. "Well, I think Cordelia has potential," Zeph said. "But I'm disappointed that Tray won't join."

"He doesn't want to have anything to do with Midnight Fae politics right now after they almost killed his mate," Kols replied, glancing at me. "I can't say I blame him."

"We'll give him time." Which was what I'd said earlier this week when Kols had delivered the news about his twin turning down the Council position. "Change doesn't happen overnight, which is why we have a mix of ages and expertise on the Council."

Shade's mom had agreed to join, so long as Shade sat with her. She was a timid woman after being kept in the dark for a thousand years. But we would be patient and work with her on reform.

Zen had also turned down a position, stating she had other obligations to the Hell Fae King to fulfill first. But she'd agreed to act as an advisor so long as we ventured to the Hell Fae realm to visit her.

Kols's father would serve as an Elder, but a well-watched one.

And Vadim had agreed to an Elder position as well.

"What are we going to do about Svart and Chern?" I asked, referring to the Warrior Blood and Sangré Blood Councilmen.

Zakkai was the clear choice for the Quandary Blood position, with Laki as his Second. Kols had taken the Elite Blood leadership role—where he would wait until Tray either agreed to take over or perhaps join as his Second-in-Command. And Shade had agreed to the Death Blood mantle, with his mother serving as his Second.

All of us looked expectantly at Zeph.

Who proceeded to say, "No," for the thousandth time.

I sighed. "You're a clear choice for the Warrior Blood Councilman position, and you know it."

"I have a duty to guard my queen, not play politician. So no."

My lips pinched to the side as I glanced at Kols. *So stubborn.*

Tell me about it, he replied. *We might need Shade to suck his cock after all.*

I laughed out loud, causing them all to look at me.

Kols merely smirked.

I cleared my throat and acted as though I hadn't just snorted a laugh in front of all of them, and refocused on the Councilmen discussion.

But Zeph was adamantly against joining.

So we started going through other names and making a list of whom to visit. Chern was on our *potentially trust* list. He hadn't been consumed by Constantine's power, but he also hadn't been for his plans at all. He'd apparently voted down several of the Council decisions but had been ignored in favor of the majority.

What concerned me was that they claimed those decisions had been unanimous.

So either he was lying—huge possibility—or Constantine had lied—also a huge possibility.

Regardless, we were watching him. And he couldn't remain on the Council.

"We don't have to figure it out today," Zeph said, sliding a plate of orc steak with a side of berries my way. "That's the beauty of time."

"At least in this path," Shade interjected.

A few of us smiled at him, then silence filled the dining area as we all ate our respective meals. Zeph had apparently made beef steaks for himself and Zakkai, which, gross. Their penchant for eating animals in this realm was seriously unnerving.

I'd sooner try a stonepecker.

Shuddering, I cut off a piece of orc and brought it to my lips as a commotion sounded outside near the in-ground pool.

Zakkai groaned as Zimney howled. "Your fucking snake is going to drown one of these days," he said, looking at Zeph.

"He sees your beast as an equal and just wants to play," Zeph returned. "I'm not going to stop him."

More splashing sounded, followed by Clove chittering as she chastised the animals for roughhousing.

Draco swooped in through a window to huddle on Shade's shoulder, his bat wings vibrating with irritation.

Then Kols's crow landed on the windowsill with an expectant look.

I studied them all and shook my head.

This was my life now, filled with crazy familiars, stubborn alpha mates, and a future with no end date.

Zeph's irises smoldered as he caught my gaze, his mind prodding mine and hearing my thoughts.

Which meant I could hear his and the plans he had for me later in the garden.

He kept making all these jokes about seeds and growth.

Each time, I rolled my eyes, but inside, his puns spoke to my Earth Fae heart.

Yeah, this wasn't a bad life at all.

Actually, it was a pretty amazing one. Surrounded by beautiful men. Protective familiars. Magical spells. And bonds built to withstand eternity.

My heart blossomed with joy as my thighs clenched with anticipation.

Earth Fae were all about creating and joy.

And I couldn't think of anything or anyone who brought me more joy than my four handsome mates.

You have five minutes to finish that, Zeph told me. *Then I want to play a game of "hide the snake in the garden."*

I looked at him. *Well, good. Because I could use a little seed.*

He smiled. *I'll give you more than a little, pixie flower.*

I can't wait, I whispered back to him.

And I meant it willingly.

Who needed orc steak when I had four ready and willing mates to fill me up?

I stood up and waved a spell that disintegrated my clothes. "Come and get me," I said, taking off for the garden with a chorus of growls in my wake.

Definitely an amazing life, I thought, grinning when the first of them caught me just as I reached the flower bed. *One I wouldn't trade for anything in the world.*

Now I knew what it was like to wake from a nightmare and be fully immersed in a dream.

A dream built to last for an eternity.

With four sexy Midnight Fae mates.

And a future that was entirely our own.

No more meddling. No more games. Just me and my mates. For the rest of time.

EPILOGUE

SHADE

SEVERAL YEARS LATER

"You realize you don't have to accompany me every time I go to visit my grandmother, right?" I asked as a presence materialized behind me—an action that made me strongly regret bonding Zakkai because now he could shadow anywhere he wanted at will.

Which was great for protecting Aflora.

And horrible for my privacy.

"I'm aware," he replied. "Just as I'm also aware that Lucifer will be there today, and I'm eager to check in on my pet project. You know, the one from that meeting? The power exchange that I didn't want to do but had no choice to do because you had already agreed to it on my behalf?"

I snorted, this incident one he loved to bring up despite it being several years old. "You would agree to anything where Aflora is concerned."

"Yes, but that's not the point, is it?"

I sighed. "I'll never apologize."

"I know."

"And you'll forever bring it up anyway."

"I will."

"Excellent," I deadpanned, shadowing to my grandmother's front door.

Zakkai appeared beside me, humored by my annoyance. Because he was a dick who enjoyed provoking me.

Pretty sure that was why we'd bonded, too—just so he could have more thorough access to my thoughts and ample opportunity to piss me the fuck off.

Aflora also likes watching us together, he added via our link. *And I like making her happy.*

Couldn't fault him for that logic.

I lifted my hand to knock, only for the door to open. My grandmother stood on the other side with cookies, which elicited another sigh from me. *More bad news.*

What food does she make when it's good news? Zakkai wondered.

Not cookies.

Ah. He stepped inside and took a chocolate chip cookie, then proceeded to inspect it for magic with his mind.

If she wanted to poison you, she wouldn't use cookies.

You say that, he drawled. *But Zenaida is quite clever.*

Which means she knows you're inspecting her cookies and would ensure you couldn't feel or find whatever she's hidden, I pointed out, ignoring the platter of treats and hugging her instead. "Hi, G'ma," I whispered against her ear before kissing her cheek. "I've missed you."

"I know. I've missed you, too," she replied, leading us to the table. "But Ajax keeps me on my toes."

"It's true," the male in question agreed as he appeared in the middle of the living room. He'd been living in the Hell Fae realm with my grandmother, helping her maintain the paradigm. My grandfathers were here, too. But my old friend had become her pupil of sorts, training to become whatever it was Lucifer had in mind.

Ajax wandered over to the table and sat down, his tall, muscular form flexing with the movement. Zakkai studied him, his calculative nature taking over.

"Hmm," he hummed. "Your magic is finally settling."

Ajax grunted. "Just in time, too."

"For what?" Zakkai pressed.

Ajax merely smiled. "You would like to know, wouldn't you?"

"Yes, I would," Zakkai admitted. "Particularly as it's my ability that has morphed your power."

That had been his part of the deal with Lucifer—the Hell Fae King had asked him to rewrite Ajax's magic and align him to the Hell Fae source.

Zakkai had refused at first.

However, then he'd realized Ajax wasn't just a willing subject but an eager one as well, and he'd complied, after penning a whole bunch of loopholes into the agreement with Lucifer, of course.

It'd been a fascinating debate to observe between Zakkai and Lucifer, both of them evenly matched in power, and neither afraid of the other.

Zakkai had essentially made it so Lucifer could never ask Aflora for a single favor or demand anything from her or her mates.

In exchange, he'd help him as required with Ajax's development only.

And anything with my grandmother was up for negotiation, meaning Zakkai would step in to help her if he wanted to. And I knew he would under the right circumstances.

"It's the opening ceremony of the bride trials." The deep tone belonged to a dark presence lurking in the shadows of the room.

Zakkai didn't react, clearly having sensed Lucifer's arrival before me. "That sounds vile," Zakkai murmured. "Tell me more."

Lucifer chuckled as he stepped into the room through some sort of invisible door. My grandmother didn't react, just set a cup of coffee at the head of the table and took a seat beside me.

The Hell Fae King took the chair like one would a throne. The white streaks in his black hair glimmered beneath the low lighting, his piercing blue eyes flashing with amusement as he nudged the mug aside. "Nice try," he told my grandmother.

She shrugged.

And Zakkai snorted. *See?*

So maybe she did attempt to bespell drinks or whatever.

She wasn't a typical Fortune Fae Omega by any stretch of the imagination, her magic having been altered by Grandfather Kodiak a thousand years ago.

"I'm organizing a bride trial to satisfy the Hell Fae males of my world," Lucifer said conversationally. "As you know, the source rarely accepts females. Which means I'm governing a bunch of bloodthirsty men. The best way to tame them is to mate them. So. Bride trials." He spread his hands like that explained everything.

"And where are you acquiring these females?" Zakkai asked, his tone just as casual and calm.

Lucifer's lips twisted into a feral grin. "From other fae realms, of course."

"Through deals." Zakkai didn't voice it as a question but as a statement.

Lucifer merely waved his hand again as though to say, *Obviously.*

Zakkai studied him for a long moment before focusing on my grandmother. "And you knew this was going to happen. That's been your agreement all along, hasn't it? That you could protect the Quandary Bloods in this paradigm and build a magical school to train them. All the while preparing for the inevitability of Lucifer turning this into a training camp for potential Hell Fae brides."

My blood ran cold at his suggestion.

But the look in my grandmother's eyes told me he was right.

"There's always a price for leadership, Zakkai. I did the best I could with what I had on offer. And now I'm fulfilling my part of the obligation."

"By acting as Headmaster to these brides," he completed for her.

"Not entirely accurate." She looked at Ajax. "He's the chosen Warden. I'm merely here to keep the paradigm safe and alive while Lucifer organizes his trial."

Zakkai whistled. "That's one hell of a price." Then he looked at Lucifer. "Aflora has no part in this."

"We've already negotiated our deal, Source Architect. I'm merely here for amusement purposes today." He smiled and cocked his head. "But how is your beautiful mate? Pregnant yet?"

"Is this the part where you demand our firstborn?" Zakkai tossed back.

He looked affronted. "I would never do such a thing."

Zakkai grunted, his disbelief palpable.

"You're right. I absolutely would and have, but your pretty mate is free from my negotiations."

"Good," Zakkai and I said at the same time.

Lucifer met my gaze, his amusement carrying a lethal edge that made me uneasy. "I've always liked you, time meddler. You're… exceedingly resourceful." He smiled before focusing on Ajax. "Are you ready to begin welcoming the bridal candidates?"

"I am, sir," Ajax replied, his serious tone nothing like my easygoing friend from our Academy days. This new version was hard around the edges, strong, and held a sorrow in his dark gaze that never seemed to abate.

He'd taken Emelyn's death hard, having wanted to lash out with revenge.

But with Aflora taking over and reforming the full Council, there hadn't been anyone for Ajax to hurt.

So Tadmir had brought him here… where Lucifer had recruited him.

He'd seen a broken soul, and he'd offered him something he couldn't refuse—a chance for retribution.

Which was the whole point of this project.

Lucifer would take female fae from all the realms and force them to fight. Those who won would be rewarded with a forced marriage to a group of his men. Those who lost would die.

Either way, it served as a wicked form of justice against those who had ostracized abominations for over a thousand years.

It made me wonder what trick my grandmother had up her sleeve. She would never agree to such a ploy without some sort of secret path.

As I glanced at her now, I caught the knowing twinkle in her gaze.

It was similar to the one she'd given me years ago when I'd told her about Aflora.

A plot was unfolding.

And it seemed Ajax and Lucifer were at the heart of it.

I would have laughed, but something told me this would be a dark tale lacking in humor.

Fae were going to die.

But in the end, perhaps the deadly Hell Fae King would find something he never knew he needed. *Love.*

USA Today Bestselling Author Lexi C. Foss loves to play in dark worlds, especially the ones that bite. She lives in Chapel Hill, North Carolina with her husband and their furry children. When not writing, she's busy crossing items off her travel bucket list, or chasing eclipses around the globe. She's quirky, consumes way too much coffee, and loves to swim.

Want access to the most up-to-date information for all of Lexi's books? Sign-up for her newsletter here.

Lexi also likes to hang out with readers on Facebook in her exclusive readers group - Join Here.

Where To Find Lexi:
www.LexiCFoss.com